I0818057

The INTO the MISTS TRILOGY

THE INTO THE MISTS TRILOGY – HARDCOVER EDITION

Conneeley, Serene
The Into the Mists Trilogy by Serene Conneeley
ISBN: 978-0-9925316-8-3 (hardback)

Website: www.SereneConneeley.com
Email: serene@sereneconneeley.com

Published by Blessed Bee Books
PO Box 449, Newtown, NSW 2042
Australia

Cover artwork: *Lost Soul*, *Storykeeper v2* and *Dreamlike*
by Selina Fenech, www.SelinaFenech.com
Illustrations: Daniella Spinetti and Justin Sayers

The Into the Mists Trilogy

Serene Conneeley

Blessed Bee Books

Contents

INTO the MISTS

"Death leaves a heartache no one can heal,
Love leaves a memory no one can steal."

From a headstone in Ireland

Contents

Chapter 1

A Life Shattered

The mists rose up around her again, clouding her vision. Sparkling lights surrounded her, and the pain in her temples left her gasping and clutching her head. She took a deep breath, exhaled slowly, and tried to calm the rapid beating of her heart.

She gazed downward, but the swirling mists obscured her view of the ground beneath her, of the path ahead of her. Hesitantly she took a step forward, but it seemed as though she was walking through the shimmering heat of an oven or the liquid warmth of a tropical sea, struggling to get anywhere against an invisible force. Her body felt heavy, languid, and everything was in slow motion. Sound and light were distorted, and she had the strangest sensation that she was no longer in her body. For a moment it was as though she was looking down at herself from a great distance. She stifled a swell of panic and tried to breathe herself back into her physical self.

As she peered ahead, she thought she saw a tiny light through the mists, a warm glow like a candle flame illuminating the darkness. She stumbled forward, drawn towards the glimmer of light and the sense of comfort it gave her. She knew if she could just get there she would be safe – although what she'd be safe from she had no idea. Her brain hurt, a stabbing pain, and she couldn't focus on anything, or work out where she was, or why. She took another tentative step forward…

Suddenly a blinding brightness shone in her face, and something grabbed her arm. She snapped her eyes open, adrenaline flooding her body as she stared around her, scared and disorientated. She felt herself sucked upwards as a clattering of metal assaulted her senses.

Wincing, she clutched at her head again, as consciousness slowly returned. That loud throbbing noise was the engines of the plane, the first plane she'd ever been on. The searing searchlight was the man next to her turning on her overhead light instead of his. And the clattering of metal was the sound of cutlery smashing together as he knocked the untouched platter of food on her tray table into her lap.

"Sorry," he mumbled, sounding mortified. "Let me help you."

She shook her head and turned away, oblivious to the dripping noodles splattered across her shirt or the man's deep embarrassment. As sleep finally released her from its icy clutches, awareness returned with a crash. Curling in on herself in the cramped seat, she gave in to the tears that had been threatening for so long.

Her parents were dead, and it was all her fault. And now she was being sent to live with the grandmother she'd never met, never even heard of. A woman who had turned her back on her own daughter more than twenty years ago, cast her out into the big bad world and never spoken to her again. Not for the first time, she wished she'd died with her mum and dad that night...

Thirty-five hours after setting out from her now former home on the east coast of Australia, the plane finally approached London, which was sprawled out below her under a desolate grey sky, too big to even comprehend. She still couldn't quite process the idea that she would never see her home near the beach in Sydney again. She would never fall asleep in her old bedroom under the pale green glow-in-the-dark stars sprinkled across her ceiling. Never sit beneath the leafy old tree in their backyard reading her favourite book. Never wander along the shoreline or go for a surf on a bright summer morning before school. Never squeeze through the gap in the back fence on her way to visit her best friend. Hell, she'd probably never see her best friend again. Tears filled her eyes once more, but she brushed them impatiently away.

As she'd stood in line at the airport check-in counter two days ago, her eyes had rested on the departures board. Paris. Prague. Venice. Vienna. New York. New Orleans. Romania. Rio de Janeiro. Exotic destinations that fired up the imagination, inspired poetry and literature, and promised magic and adventure.

But that was not for her. Instead she was going to live with a stranger she was dreading meeting, in a small, boring village in the countryside of England. She'd wished that she could board one of those other planes, run away to a place where no one knew her, where she could escape within the cracks of a city of colour and light and reinvent herself. Hide from herself. *Become* someone else, someone with a bright future, and things to look forward to.

All the emotions swirling within the airport had filled her with desperate longing. There was so much humanity there, so much passion, as people set off on their dream holidays, went to see family or friends, began their honeymoons, cried their goodbyes, laughed and kissed their hellos. So much love and loss. Hearts breaking and healing. Being bereft or fulfilled. Even the goodbyes seemed nice to her, for those people still knew that their loved ones were in the world somewhere, alive, living every moment with joy, and with the knowledge that they would eventually be reunited.

Not her. All her family members were dead. There was no going back, no happy reunion. Just like that, her life was over.

Of course her flight had been delayed, which hadn't helped her head space – she was going to collapse into a shivering wreck if she spent much more time alone with her thoughts. Later, a day after they'd finally departed, she'd sat for hours in a cramped, hot room on an interminable stopover, second-hand cigarette smoke curling around her throat, adding to the pressure of the fear and the pain that was slowly strangling her. Her head ached, her eyes were sore from crying, and she was drowning in an ever-increasing despair, resigned to trying to survive through an endless existence that stretched out before her filled with nothing but loneliness, misery, guilt and self-recrimination.

Now her plane was finally touching down at the end of this long journey, and the beginning of her awful new life loomed large and close, filling her with dread. The heavy, threatening storm clouds of the metropolis matched her mood. She grabbed her backpack from the overhead locker, cursed as she banged her knee against someone's metal case, and shuffled out into the stream of tired, grumpy people impatient to get through customs and get on with their lives. Jealousy flared up within her as she thought of her fellow travellers happily reuniting with their loved ones.

The impending sense of doom that had followed her for the last two weeks tightened around her, and she wondered if she'd ever feel normal again. If she'd ever feel joy again. Then she groaned. She had to shake off all this miserable self-pity – she was annoying herself now, and was thoroughly sick of her gloomy goth-horror mood.

Dragging her feet through the customs hall, she suddenly wished that the trip was still in progress, that she could remain in the strange in-between realm of journeying, where you were no longer where you had set out from, but still not at your destination. Where the sense of possibility was so much greater than the harsh reality she now faced, of somehow picking up the pieces of her shattered life.

The customs officer beckoned her forward, and she slowly approached, handing over her ticket, her passport and the letter her mother's friend Sandy had written for her. After a few moments the officer's expression turned sympathetic, and he stamped her passport and ushered her quickly through. The pity in his eyes made her angry, but she was grateful for that small mercy. She still wasn't up to explaining to a stranger just how black her life had turned.

After a few false starts, a stale sandwich, her umpteenth cup of coffee and more painkillers to try to dull her aching head, she was finally on a bus heading out of the city, migraine still throbbing but headphones in. When Paul Kelly's song *Sydney From a 727* came on she thought she'd never stop crying. His music was uniquely Australian, so poignantly of the great south land she'd always loved but taken for granted, and so closely linked to countless memories of her teenage years. Already they seemed a lifetime ago. How could she feel so ancient when she'd only just turned seventeen?

She gazed out the grimy window through tear-stained eyes, not seeing the landscape as it passed by, but dreaming instead of her old home. Of walking along the beach at Cronulla with her best friend Emily. Running a marathon with her mum down to the golden sands of Bondi, then having coffee and cake together in a cafe on the promenade when it was over.

Catching the train over the bridge and across the sparkling waters of Sydney Harbour with her dad on their way to the zoo, and spending a whole day walking and talking with him, climbing the steep paths, returning again and again to see the adorable Tasmanian devils, to coo at the baby tiger cubs, to giggle at the penguins. Boarding the ferry back to the city at sunset, and watching the breathtaking silhouettes of the iconic bridge and the sails of the Opera House contrasting with the lights of Centrepoint Tower and the sweeping skyscrapers, all ablaze with life and energy and immense presence.

Going to concerts and movies and amazing art exhibitions, seeing her favourite bands, and knowing she would spend her whole life in this beautiful vibrant city where she'd been born, which was so much a part of her, its energy coursing through her blood and her heart.

Her grief swelled – grief at losing her parents, losing her best friend, losing her home and her life and her future – and she thought she would drown in it if it didn't stop soon. Now she knew why people drank alcohol to dull the pain, to stop feeling, to forget. She longed with all her heart for some kind of oblivion.

Chapter 2

Meeting the Monster

She woke up as the bus lurched around a corner and then came to a screeching stop in a narrow street. The driver motioned to her, so she rose, still disorientated and not quite in her body, and gathered her backpack and her small suitcase. Slowly she stepped outside into the hazy late afternoon gloom.

Her heart beat a little faster as she stood on the dirty pavement and looked around the small village. Across the road were the tumbled grey ruins of an old church, huge gnarled trees providing shade, and little creeping vines twining over the old stonework. Behind her the lights of a greasy spoon cafe switched on, blinking boldly as the light faded from the sky.

Nervously she looked around. Wasn't her grandmother supposed to be meeting her off the bus? As much as she was terrified at the thought of having to live with the old woman whose cruelty had destroyed her mother's life, she felt vulnerable and uneasy at being so alone in a new town, a new country.

She tried to remember what Sandy had told her before she got on the plane, but the past two weeks were a blur of pain, confusion and vivid anger, and she hadn't been especially polite or open to listening to her mother's best friend. For the first time, a sliver of fear crept into her heart. What if she was here all on her own? What would she do?

Where would she go? Shivering from a cold breeze as well as her nerves, she pulled her coat more tightly around herself.

From along the street she heard the cheerful tinkle of a bell and the slam of a door, then she saw a woman walking towards her, long purple dress swishing around her feet, long silvery hair falling around her like a cloak, and a black cat weaving around her ankles. She looked just like a stereotypical witch from one of those faerytales, but there was no sense of menace.

"Carlie?" the woman asked softly, hesitantly.

She stared at her, unprepared for how, well, *grandmotherly* she looked. She'd expected a monster, someone whose meanness showed on her face, in her manner. This woman looked completely unthreatening, and seemed... *kind*?

For a moment she forgot to be angry, and for the first time wondered what this stranger thought of having a teenager she'd never met suddenly foisted upon her. Had she even known she had a grandchild before last week? And how would she feel when she discovered that said grandchild had killed her daughter? No matter what had happened between them, that was certainly a conversation she was dreading.

"Um..."

"Rose," the older woman offered gently. "And this is Luther," she added, gazing fondly down at the cat.

"Hello Rose," Carlie said, trying to smile but failing miserably. Kneeling down, she let her long dark hair fall over her face like a curtain as she stretched her hand slowly towards the cat. When he inclined his silky head for a pat, Carlie felt a glimmer of warmth, and nearly broke down again.

"He likes you," her grandmother said, a touch of surprise in her voice. "He won't go near most people." She smiled for a moment, then grew serious again. "But you must be tired after your journey. Come, it's not far from here. I'll have the kettle on in no time."

Carlie slung her backpack over her shoulder and picked up her suitcase. With a deep breath to try to steady herself, she followed the silver-haired woman, trailing a few steps behind her as she attempted to gather her thoughts and compose herself. And, if she was really honest, tried to avoid being engaged in conversation.

They walked up a slight hill, past a lush green park with swings in it, and more enormous old trees, then turned left into a street at the top. At the end of that street they took a right, then halfway down the block Rose stopped abruptly and swung open a wrought iron gate. A honeysuckle vine twined around it on one side, while a blackberry vine climbed the other side, small pale flowers seeming to smile in the gathering gloom.

As her grandmother opened the door to the neat little cottage, Carlie paused, then reluctantly walked in after her. The hallway was dark and narrow, and there was a chill in the air. She shivered, and her heart quailed at the thought of living in this gloomy old village, in this gloomy old cottage, with this gloomy old woman. Luther brushed past her, startling her back to the present, and raced down the passageway before skidding to a halt then turning and miaowing as he looked longingly up at them.

Rose laughed affectionately. "Just a minute Luther," she scolded lovingly, before turning to face Carlie. "Your bedroom is at the top of the stairs," she said, pointing. "My room is this one here. The main bathroom is the next door along, just there, and there's a small ensuite next to your room. We'll be in the kitchen out the back whenever you want to join us."

And she was gone, the black cat close on her heels. Carlie was grateful that the older woman was giving her some space, and grudgingly admitted how considerate that was. Then, with a sigh, she heaved her suitcase up again and dragged it with her as she clumsily climbed the narrow stairway, suddenly tired beyond measure.

There was an open door at the top, and she walked through it into a sweet little room. A lamp was on, illuminating the small desk where it sat, and showing the narrow wrought iron bed along the opposite wall. But while the bed looked inviting, and part of her wanted to curl up on it right away, pull the blanket over her head and never get up again, it was the window with the billowing curtains that drew her.

She dropped her luggage on the floor and tiptoed across to it. One of the tall glass panes was open, and a cool breeze was making the curtains dance. She gazed outside through the flickering gloom. There was a small neat garden directly below her, but her eyes lingered on the huge, hulking hill topped with a crumbling stone tower that stood behind the garden.

All of a sudden she couldn't catch her breath. It was like the hill was looking deep into her heart, reaching out to her, welcoming her perhaps, but challenging her too, stripping away the layers of protection she'd walled up around herself since the night of the crash. Full of wonder she stared, shivering a little in the crisp air, but unable to move away from the window.

She didn't know how long she'd been standing there – it could have been moments, minutes or hours. It could have been a whole day. But slowly she became aware of a presence behind her, and she swung around to the doorway, shy again. Her grandmother stood there, still and silent, a steaming mug in her hands. Cautiously she held it out to her, but she didn't move into the room, into her space.

"Thank you," Carlie said, stepping across to the door and taking the cup. She took a sip, startled that it was exactly the way she liked her tea – strongly brewed earl grey, with just the right amount of soy milk and honey. No one else had ever made her a cup of tea the same way as she made it herself.

Her grandmother smiled tentatively. "Summer Hill," she said, motioning to the slope outside the window, faintly outlined by the last streaks of daylight. "It will twist its way into your dreams, and into your heart."

Carlie stared at her quizzically, but her grandmother said no more about it, abruptly changing the subject.

"Anyway, you've been travelling for days. If you want to go straight to bed I understand," she said quietly, gently. "I've got some chickpea and vegie soup on the stove, if you want to join me for dinner. I'll just be going over the books for the shop though, so you don't need to come down on my account."

She paused, and the two women stared at each other warily, one young, one old, the distance and the caution and the sense of loss they both felt swimming in the air between them. "I'm glad you're here," Rose finally said, voice soft.

Carlie felt tears starting to well again, and sniffed loudly, trying to hold them back. She didn't want to start feeling grateful to, or grow to like, this woman who had deserted her own child when she'd been the same age that she was now.

"Thank you," she muttered, then winced at how rude she sounded. But her grandmother just nodded, before turning and walking slowly back down the stairs.

Carlie took another big slurp of tea, then closed the door firmly and lay down on the bed, staring up at the ceiling. Shadows from the lamp danced on the walls, and there was a rose pattern around the edges that made her smile dreamily. Roses in Rose's house. *How apt…*

It was her last thought before sleep claimed her.

Chapter 3

The Beings Within the Hill

She was stumbling through a dark tunnel that ran deep within the earth. She could see the warm flicker of a blazing torch up ahead, but it never seemed to get any closer. She felt a slight panic, yet she wasn't sure what she was afraid of – was there something behind her, that had chased her into the hillside, or was she moving forward to an uncertain fate? Out of the corner of her eye she saw shimmery presences hovering, and the flutter of wings, and she felt the goodness of these beings radiating out towards her. Part of her knew that they would help her, if she could just work out what they were, work out what was after her, work out where she was, and why. She felt as though she'd been running for days – her limbs were heavy, and she was exhausted beyond endurance, mentally as well as physically.

Suddenly she tripped over and sprawled headlong onto the hard ground, hitting her forehead on a rocky outcrop as she fell. She lay there for a minute, stretched out on the earth, feeling a steady hum vibrating through her body. It was comforting, nurturing. She wanted to stay there and sleep forever, but she also felt the weight of the hill above her pressing downwards, not just a physical sensation but also an oppressive heaviness she could feel within her soul.

When she heard footsteps approaching, she somehow knew that she had to get up and move, get away from them. But she could also hear the sound of many voices raised together, singing a sweet and airy song that was so soothing. She tried to cling to the melody, to wrap the sound around her like a blanket that would keep her safe.

Her sense of peace was interrupted by a bright light shining in her face. Terrified, she staggered to her feet… And found herself sitting up in a strange narrow bed, moonlight streaming in the window and across her face. Her heart raced as she stared wildly around her, scared of the unfamiliar surroundings and the shadows that danced grotesquely as the curtains billowed.

Tears ran down her face as reality crashed over her. Her mum and dad were dead. She was in a room on the other side of the world, sent to live with a stranger. She'd never see her friends again. She was alone, helpless, with the blood of her parents on her hands. God, how she wished she'd died with them. The nightmare, as perilous as it had felt, seemed infinitely preferable to her waking life.

Suddenly there was a thump at the end of her bed, and she almost cried out. Then she heard a small miaow, and her grandmother's cat walked daintily up her legs until he was sitting in her lap. As she stroked his head, a deep purr rumbled out of the fuzzy black warmth, providing comfort and reassurance, and she finally drifted back to sleep curled up around her only friend in the world.

When she woke again, there was sunlight streaming through the window. Luther was sitting on the chair opposite her, leisurely washing himself. There was a dull throbbing at her temple – when she touched it, she felt a bump that hurt, and there was a trace of blood on her fingers as she took them away. She remembered hitting her head in the dream, but that was a ridiculous thought, and she rolled her eyes at her silliness. She must have bumped it when she was putting her bag in the overhead locker on the plane or something, and just not noticed.

She lay in bed, listening carefully, but couldn't hear any sound from downstairs. When her tummy rumbled for the third time, she accepted that she had to get up and face the day, and face her grandmother. Dread flooded her. She was always uncomfortable around strangers, and this was even worse – she had to *live* with this stranger.

Sighing, she realised that she couldn't hide out in her bedroom for the rest of her life, no matter how much she wanted to. So she psyched herself up and reluctantly climbed out of bed, still wearing the jeans, t-shirt and jacket she'd left Sydney in a few days ago, but deciding that finding food had to be her first priority. After that she could soak in a hot bath and wash away what felt like the grime of the ages, then finally put some clean clothes on.

Nervously she walked down the stairs, shy about seeing her grandmother again. Luther threaded himself between her ankles, a soothing presence. And the house sounded empty.

At the bottom of the stairs she turned towards the back of the house, walking through a cosy, comfy-looking lounge room and out to the kitchen. Sunlight filtered into the small but tidy room, and off to the side there was a glass-walled breakfast nook, with a round wooden table in the centre. A vase of yellow roses stood in the middle, and there was a note propped up against it.

Good morning Carlie,
I hope you managed to sleep, and Luther didn't keep you up all night demanding pats...

Hearing a noise behind her, she quickly spun around, panicked, but it was just Luther, who had leaped up onto the kitchen bench and pushed two cups up against each other. She turned back to the note.

I'm working at the healing centre today, but I should be home by 5pm to start making dinner. There's food in the fridge in the meantime, so please make yourself at home.
Lots of love, Rose xx

A key sat next to the note. She glanced at the clock. It was midday.

After tea, toast and a hot shower – because running a bath seemed way too hard right now – she picked up the key, grabbed an apple off the bench, slung her backpack over her shoulder and headed out the front door. She hadn't seen Luther again, but she figured he could take care of himself.

She retraced her steps from the previous night, walking back past the sun-dappled park and the stone ruins. Just past there the shops began – the cafe, just opening for the day, a newsagent, a small supermarket, a healing centre attached to a shop that sold crystals, books and herbs, which had a sign for psychic readings and healing sessions in the window. Her grandmother's shop? She walked on, not quite ready to face her, to have to make conversation, to admit to her that not only was her daughter dead, but she had killed her.

Turning right up the High Street, she went past a tourist office, a pub, a book store, another cafe, a fabric emporium, a post office and a dark, sweet-smelling retail space that sold incense and hippie clothes from India. She only saw one person as she walked, an older man leading a small dog, who raised his hand as if to greet her, then gave her a strange look and scurried on past her. She shrugged. She was too tired, too dislocated from her life and her self, to ponder the meaning of that.

At the top of the road, near a church, she turned right and headed back along the street towards her grandmother's house. Eventually she saw it just ahead of her on the left, all neat and cheerful in the sunshine, but she didn't want to go back inside just yet, so she kept walking. Soon she saw a narrow dirt pathway that ran between two houses. A small sign was emblazoned with the words Summer Tor, and they had an arrow beside them, pointing down the laneway. She frowned in concentration.

Tor. Hill? Shrugging, she turned onto the path. It was cool, dark and shady, with old trees leaning in towards each other and making a canopy overhead. It looked like the kind of place faeries would live, although that thought had her rolling her eyes at herself. She was seventeen, a little too old for faerytales, no matter how much she wished they were real. *God, if only a handsome prince would sweep her off her feet and rescue her from this awful new life.*

Up ahead the track widened, then opened out onto a grassy meadow. A rock-lined path wound its way up the hill, and she shaded her eyes with her hand and gazed upwards. The tiredness she'd felt a moment ago lifted, and she decided to climb to the top. It was steeper and much higher than it had looked from her bedroom window, but after three days spent sitting on her butt in a succession of cramped planes, departure lounges and buses, and her recent week in a hospital bed, she was grateful for the chance to stretch her legs, her body, her stiff, sore muscles. To feel the blood pumping through her veins, and the cool wind on her cheeks. The sensation of life running through her, even as part of her yearned for death.

The exertion of the climb made her breath ragged and her cheeks red, but it felt so good to be anchored in her body again, alive and present. For the past fortnight she'd felt insubstantial, like a ghost. She'd longed to *be* a ghost. But now, for the first time since that awful night, she felt alive, and filled with the possibility of wanting to stay that way. *How strange.*

Halfway up the hill she stopped, pausing for breath. When she saw something out of the corner of her eye, she slowly and silently turned towards it. There was a small brown rabbit sitting there, ears alert, stance wary, eyes never leaving hers. Then suddenly a huge black raven swooped down towards them, and the rabbit raced off, quickly disappearing into a small tunnel in the hill. She stared after it. The sensation of the previous night's frightening dream, of being trapped inside this hill, pursued by monsters, crept up her spine and around her heart, but she determinedly shook it off. The sun was out, and there was no space for darkness and shadow today.

Finally, breathless and red-cheeked, she reached the top of the tor. She spun around, arms out, long skirt flaring around her, awestruck by the views stretching out in every direction below her. Green fields, a sea of fluffy white sheep and rolling hills. The stone ruin in the centre of town, and a body of water way off to the west, sparkling in the sunlight. She felt anchored to the earth, part of the ancient hill, at one with the humming that reached up through her feet and sent a strange sensation of longing washing over her. She shivered. Despite the sunshine, the wind was chilly, restless, and she pulled her jacket more tightly around herself as her gaze continued to sweep across the beautiful landscape.

Sitting down on the grass, she tried to breathe a sense of peace back into herself, so she could try to make sense of the sudden tragedy of her life. Two and a half weeks ago she'd been studying for exams, thinking about which university to apply to, hanging out with her friends, borrowing one of her dad's wetsuits so she could surf in the chilly winter sea.

She'd had her whole life ahead of her – she was excited about her future, happy at the way it was mapped out, and had a trip to Uluru with her best friend Emily planned for the upcoming school holidays. Yet now she didn't know what was going to happen tomorrow, let alone next week or next year. The only certainty was that nothing she had planned, nothing she had looked forward to, would ever come to pass.

When a few drops of rain fell on her, she ventured inside the ruined tower on the crown of the hill and sat on the bench there, knees drawn up and arms wrapped around them. Her eyelids kept fluttering closed, and she drifted off into a daydream. A daydream where her parents were still alive, where her best friend still lived around the corner, and where her biggest worry was whether to change her elective from history to geography.

She must have fallen asleep, because the next thing she knew she was abruptly woken up, head jerking from her chest, startled by the sound of a cawing raven. Noticing how much the light in the tower had changed direction and intensity, she suddenly panicked about how long she'd been up there. As much as she hated her situation, and hated her grandmother, she didn't want to worry her on her first day of staying with her. A shiver raced up her spine.

"Staying." Horror engulfed her as she acknowledged the permanence of the word. This was no short-term plan, no nice-nice, on-your-best-behaviour, going-home-soon kind of visit. This was her life – but this was certainly not the way she'd planned to spend it.

Chapter 4

The Key To the Mystery

By the time she got back down the hill she was out of breath and angry again, furious at the injustice of everything, and terrified that she wasn't going to be able to cope with living in this tiny grey town in this depressing country, with a woman she barely knew and couldn't bring herself to even want to like.

She'd had no idea that she *had* a grandmother until her mum's best friend Sandy had told her just over a week ago. And Sandy hadn't known much more than that, just that her mother Fiona had been born and had grown up in a small English village, but was forced to leave in a hurry for some undisclosed reason when she was seventeen. Sandy was as much in the dark as Carlie about the reasons for this, or any other details. Her mum had never really spoken about her childhood – to her best friend or to her daughter – and she'd always got the impression that her parents were dead.

Carlie couldn't even begin to imagine what a mother would have to do to make her child run away, to the other side of the world no less. To cut all contact with her, and refuse to speak about her to her own daughter. She and her mum had been so close. Sure, they'd had the odd argument, but nothing like what her school friends went through. And now her mum was gone, and she had to live with the monster. *It wasn't fair*, she thought bitterly.

When she got back to the cottage she took out her key and walked inside, slamming the door behind her. "Hi Sweetheart, I'm out in the kitchen," her grandmother called out. Carlie winced at the endearment, then took a deep breath and nervously walked through to join her. She realised how hungry she was when she smelled the frying garlic and felt her mouth water.

"I've made a vegetable and lentil casserole, but I can fix you something else if you'd prefer," her grandmother said, tentative again.

Maybe she was just as scared of Carlie as Carlie was of her. She was certainly disarmed somewhat by her grandmother's consideration. And maybe she'd mellowed in the last twenty years? When Carlie's tummy rumbled, she blushed and sat down at the table. "That sounds fine, thank you," she muttered.

Her grandmother served up two bowls of the casserole on a bed of brown rice, and put a plate of poppadoms on the table between them. Then she sat down opposite Carlie. Picked up her fork, put it back down. Forced a smile, then tried to look natural. They were both shy around each other, wary of hitting a raw nerve by accidentally saying the wrong thing or offending the other.

Her grandmother tried to make conversation though, she had to give her credit for that. She spoke a little bit about her healing centre, the crystal courses she taught, some of the regular customers. She seemed relieved when Carlie said she was a vegetarian too, then raised her eyebrows in surprise when she told her that her mum had been as well. A shadow flickered across her grandmother's face then, and she shivered, but it was fleeting. When Carlie glanced back up from her plate a moment later, Rose's face was still again. Watchful.

It was all so awkward. Neither of them knew what to say, because there was so much that lurked beneath. Why did you abandon your daughter? How could you refuse to speak to her or even write to her? What do you have planned for me? *And how can you ever forgive me for killing her?*

In desperation, her grandmother started to talk about books, and Carlie gave half-hearted replies. It seemed they both loved Juliet Marillier's Sevenwaters Series.

And Carlie had recently finished reading author Felicity Pulman's Janna Chronicles, about the daughter of a twelfth century English herbwife, which led them to a discussion about herbal healing. Rose said she had a large herb garden in the backyard, which Carlie was welcome to tend, to pick from, to plant more in, and that she taught a herbal healing course at her centre if she ever wanted to learn more.

Carlie nodded politely, and tried to seem interested, but their conversation gradually became more stilted, the silences longer. Finally she excused herself, totally exhausted and so uncomfortable in the presence of this mysterious stranger she'd suddenly discovered she was related to. Ignoring the dishes, barely able to mutter a civil goodnight, she stomped up to her room, slammed the door shut, threw herself onto the narrow bed, and was asleep within minutes.

They were the same dark tunnels, but this time there was a door ahead of her. It was locked, but she felt such a compulsion to open it, to go inside, as if all the mysteries of the universe would be solved if she could just see what was in there. She stood there for ages, trying to get in, using her own key, a hair pin, a credit card that she inexplicably found in her pocket, and finally trying to bust it open with her shoulder, a painful attempt that left her bruised and sore but no closer to getting inside. Nothing worked, and finally she collapsed in a tired and aching heap at its base, wondering if someone would come along soon who could open it for her, and determined to wait until they did.

But before anyone approached her, the piercing glare of the bright moonlight streaming through her window woke her up. This time she only freaked out for a moment, then she breathed in the silvery light of the lunar orb, feeling herself drawn back into her body and aware again of where she was, and why – which was reassuring after the panic of the previous night, if not particularly comforting.

She winced as she felt a throbbing pain in her shoulder – the same one she'd been trying to bash the door open with in her dream. She tried to shrug it off, but she felt a quiver of fear in the pit of her stomach at the thought that her dream injuries were carrying over into real life. But that was ridiculous, beyond impossible, and she had to stop these crazy thoughts before she really went off the deep end. Obviously she'd just slept on it funny. *Hadn't she?*

When her eyes had adjusted to the gloom, she slipped out of bed to tiptoe to the ensuite. But as she opened her door, the moonlight spilled in through her window, over her shoulder and across the landing, illuminating a door opposite hers, which must open into a room at the front of the house. She blinked a few times, then rubbed her eyes, yet it wasn't a trick of the light. There was a door there that she hadn't noticed that morning. How could she not have seen it?

As quietly as she could, she crept over to it and cautiously turned the handle. It was locked. The frustration she'd felt in her dream washed over her, and suddenly she was desperate to know what was inside. But the door wouldn't budge, and she didn't want to make any noise, afraid that she'd wake her grandmother. How would she explain such trespassing?

When she heard a floorboard creak behind her, she spun around, heart in her throat. Luckily it was only Luther, gazing up at her with big green eyes, but she felt so guilty that she quickly dropped her hand and tiptoed back to her own room. What was she doing? It was the middle of the night, and her grandmother was asleep. If she wanted to keep a room locked, that was her business. Climbing into bed, she lay back down and tried to sleep, but she couldn't shake the feeling that there was something important in there, some clue to her mother's life, to her own.

She started shivering, although she wasn't sure if it was a physical or an emotional chill she was feeling. Turning on the lamp next to her bed, she walked over and opened the cupboard, relieved when she saw a thick patchwork quilt pushed into the back corner. Clumsily pulling it down, she wrapped it around her shoulders then huddled back under the covers. Her mind continued to whir for ages, tying itself in knots, until she finally fell back into a restless sleep.

The next morning Carlie waited until she heard Rose leave for work, then hurried downstairs to find something to eat. Maybe she'd have to buy some muesli bars to keep in her room, if she was going to keep avoiding her grandmother and not starve to death.

When she entered the kitchen she saw that there was a fresh vase of flowers, with a nicely worded note for her, so polite and considerate. She felt a pang of remorse, that she wasn't even trying to get on with her grandmother, or get to know her, that she was so lacking in gratitude, but she quickly pushed it away. She was pretty sure that her grandmother wanted her here as much as she wanted to stay – not at all. If she'd driven her own daughter away, why would she want a granddaughter to live with her, to remind her of the past?

After breakfast she tried to read for a while, then she attempted to write a thank-you note to Sandy, but she couldn't concentrate. Finally she stood up, too restless to remain seated. Luther padded across the kitchen floor and lifted a little paw, pushing it against the back door, ignoring the cat flap and gazing imploringly up at her.

Giggling, she walked over and opened it for him, then followed him outside. The scent of lavender wafted up from the bushes on either side of the kitchen door, and she could hear the buzzing of bees as they darted from blossom to blossom. Rose's garden was beautiful, small but well tended, with a huge old apple tree in the far corner, ivy weaving around its lower trunk, and a wooden swing hanging from one of its branches. Had her mother once swung on that swing? Had she sat beneath the tree and daydreamed as she crunched into a just-picked apple? Had she helped her mum plant the neatly laid out herb beds, and looked after them as they'd grown?

A narrow gate in the back fence caught her eye, and she wandered over towards it, lifted the latch and pushed against it. Behind the yard was a dirt laneway, not quite wide enough for a car, and on the other side was a murky, shaded meadow that must lead up to the tor. A pretty butterfly floated past her, and she turned to watch as it flew along the path, heading away from the village. On a whim she decided to follow it, not sure she wanted to climb the hill again just yet, but needing to walk, to clear her head, to try to make sense of her dreams, her new life, her abruptly changed future.

She stepped onto the path, turned to the left to see where that went – it seemed to head back to the village – then she turned to the right, the path the butterfly had taken. Her eyes welled as her favourite Green Day song flitted into her head. It was all about turning points and forks in the road, and her choice of which direction to take had brought it to mind. It was also about making the best of every moment before it's too late, and photographs and memories, all of which had a new, sadder resonance for her now.

It was the song she'd always wanted to have played at her funeral, many years from now. She'd loved the bitter-sweet nature of it, the raw vocals, the longing and the sense of potential and choice woven into the lyrics.

But now it just made her cry. Now that death had come so close to her, shattered her life and taken away her future, she didn't want to think about funerals, or remember the day that her parents had been buried, side by side, in the local cemetery, with all their friends there, trying to comfort her but failing so miserably. It broke her heart that she couldn't even visit their graves. Would anyone tend them, now that she'd left the country?

Shaking her head, she tried to get a happier song lodged in her brain to chase that one away. She walked on, and after a while the lane widened, and the backyards seemed to get bigger. When she reached the path that had led her to the hill yesterday – another fork in the road – she didn't turn onto it, but crossed right over it and kept on walking.

Chapter 5

The Mists Descend

Slowly she became aware of the mist just ahead of her, covering the lane, shrouding the grass and weaving around the base of each tree. She felt a slight chill as she walked into it, and then noticed that there was a gentle haze to everything around her. The sound of bird song had receded, the light through the trees seemed distorted somehow, and when she looked around her, everything was a little blurred around the edges. She frowned.

Her surroundings were suddenly dreamy, and she felt slowed down, as though she was in a different dimension – physically she was walking along the laneway, but some part of her seemed far away. The same sense of dislocation that she'd experienced on the plane, and the same pain in her head, enveloped her.

Breathing deeply, she tried to slow her panic and steady her thoughts. The butterfly swooped in front of her again, and she smiled and reached out for it. She saw a low hedge of orange jessamine ahead of her on the right, and leaned over to inhale the beautiful scent.

A blackberry vine was twining through the leaves, and a few deep purple berries poked through. She picked one and popped it into her mouth, then stood admiring the adorable wooden cottage on the other side of the hedge. The gate that led onto the path to the back door was open, inviting, and she could see the flickering golden glow of candlelight from one of the windows. It looked so warm, so welcoming. She felt a push at her back, as though someone or something was guiding her towards the house, but she shook her head, knowing she should resist the feeling. She didn't know who lived there. She couldn't just walk up to a stranger's door. What on earth was she thinking?

Suddenly lightning split the sky, there was a clap of thunder overhead, and the heavens opened. As rain poured down she hovered at the gate, indecisive, but when she felt hailstones slamming into her head, and the ferocity of the rising wind, she raced up to the verandah, praying this weather would soon pass, and that whoever lived there wouldn't mind her sheltering from the storm until it eased.

Looking around, she was surprised to see the amount of cobwebs on the windows, the layers of dust over the glass. She peered through one of the panes, and saw that the house was dusty and deserted inside as well. A small wooden coffee table seemed to be the only furniture left, but it too was covered in dust.

Hearing a floorboard creak, she spun around guiltily – to see a black cat stalking over to her. It looked just like Luther, but surely it couldn't be him walking across the verandah towards her. No cat would follow someone so far, or be outside in this weather, surely. She laughed at herself, and her vivid imagination. Besides, this one was a female cat, black as night and looking up at her through Luther's green eyes, but with a little white star on her forehead. Maybe it was Luther's sister? Then she rolled her eyes. No doubt there were plenty of black cats in the world!

This one wound itself around her ankles, purring in a friendly manner, then pushed her towards the doorway. As she approached, the door swung open, just as an extra thick gust of rain and hail blew in against her. Shivering, she debated for a moment, then quickly hurried inside before she lost her nerve. The door slammed shut behind her, and while it creeped her out a bit, she felt instantly warmer. Shaking off some of the raindrops, she took off her jacket and hung it to dry on a hook behind the door, then looked around curiously, puzzled that there was no candle. She was sure she'd seen one in the window, its golden light drawing her forward.

A memory suddenly hit her of her dream on the plane, when she'd been wandering through a mist exactly like the one she'd just walked through, heading towards the candlelight she could see in the distance, which had been beckoning her on through the fog. How creepy, that a dream had turned into reality. Was that what deja vu was? But how did it work? How could she have dreamed about something that would happen in the future?

That train of thought was lost as she sneezed. The cottage was dusty, and virtually empty. Clearly no one had lived there for years. Along one wall were the remains of a kitchen, similar to her grandmother's in layout. One of the windows was broken though, and leaves had come in through it, forming a red and brown pile on the wooden floor that smelled richly of the earth. In one corner was a pile of broken beams, as though someone had considered doing the place up, then thought better of it. And there was a rickety staircase leading to an upper floor, but it looked dark and a little too spooky up there to explore. Besides, who knew who owned this place, and whether anyone else came here for shelter, or for any other reason. Shivering at the thought, she turned away from the stairs.

There was a clay pot on the kitchen windowsill that still had rosemary growing in it. Rosemary for remembrance. She'd planted some on her parents' grave, and the memory of that day, of that pain, brought her to her knees. The sharp scent was making her dizzy too. Crouching on the floor, she forced herself to take several long, deep, steadying breaths, before she could finally climb back to her feet and continue looking around.

Curious about the coffee table she'd seen through the window, she walked over and sat down cross-legged in front of it. There was a huge book sitting on it, leather-bound and dusty, with beautiful ironwork around the corners and along the spine, and a writhing pattern of spirals and symbols carved into the front cover. She noticed a candle stub and some matches on the floor, so she lit the wick, taking comfort from the warmth of the flame and the soothing golden light. Shadows danced across the walls, and she almost jumped out of her skin when the black cat wandered over to her and put its paw on her leg. It sat down next to her, facing the book, and seemed to be waiting for her to do something with it.

Tentatively she reached out towards it. It looked so ancient. The cat leaned closer to her, purring quietly, and seemed to be sending energy, strength and confidence to her. Finally she summoned up her courage and placed her hand on the front cover – and instantly felt a surge of heat, and of power, rush through her body. Moments ago she'd been shivering from the cold, from her wet hair and damp shoes, but now she was warm and toasty, and felt oddly dry, enveloped in some kind of etheric blanket. Slowly she opened the book to the first page, and felt a shock of electricity zap through her. *Violet's Book of Shadows* was written across the page in her mum's large and distinctive curly writing. What? How?

Her hand shook. It couldn't be, surely. There was no way on earth that a book her mother had written could be in a cottage on the other side of the world from where she had lived. And her name wasn't Violet anyway, it was Fiona, Fee for short.

Carlie laughed at her silliness, at her longing for connection, but when she turned the page and saw the same looping script scrawled across it, saw the symbol of a star in a circle that her mum had always signed her letters off with, the tears started flowing. And although she fought desperately against it, she began to re-experience the horror of that fateful, fatal night all over again, playing out across the inside of her closed eyelids.

The rain, the slippery roads, and her at the wheel, only her third time driving at night, and the car skidding out of control, spinning around at ferocious speeds until it crashed into a tree. Flashing lights, screaming sirens, agonised whimpering, white-hot pain searing through her head. Then darkness. There had been a few days of blissful dark, blissful ignorance, until she'd finally woken up in that hospital bed, white light blinding her again, and the slow drowsy surfacing to consciousness unfolding within her.

As soon as she'd learned the truth of what she'd done she had wanted to dive right back into that realm where she'd been, where she hadn't felt any pain – not the searing red-hot physical pain of her head and her ribs, or the agonising emotional pain of knowing she had caused the death of her parents. She'd killed them. She might as well have shot them herself.

Her mother's friend Sandy had been there when she woke, unable to hide her distress, voice choked with tears, face white with shock. She'd been kind, pretending it wasn't Carlie's fault, even though her eyes revealed that she knew it was.

Whatever her personal feelings, Sandy had organised her mum and dad's funeral for her, dealt with the lawyers, and packed up their family home, put it on the market and sold their car, depositing the money in Carlie's bank account to get her by until settlement on the house concluded. And she'd managed to track down her grandmother on the other side of the world, with only the flimsiest of information to go on. She hadn't complained once.

Carlie had been so grateful to her – she couldn't function at all, even though she knew all that stuff had to be done. But while Sandy did it all without fuss, Carlie could sense that she couldn't bear to be around the girl who'd caused the death of her best friend, that she was doing these things to honour the memory of the person she was closest to, not for the horrible daughter who had killed that friend. And she didn't blame her one bit.

An image of the funeral came next, Sandy so strong, so kind, giving voice to everyone's disbelief, everyone's shock, everyone's love. Carlie had sat there silently, head near exploding with the pain of a migraine – a side effect, apparently, of the crash – and glad of it. She should be punished. She was the girl who'd killed her parents. She welcomed the pain. She wanted to suffer.

Within two weeks of that fatal night she'd been packed up and put on a plane to her hitherto unknown grandmother, her bruises slowly healing but the emotional wounds gaping wide open and aching. Rose was the only relative Sandy could find for Carlie, her paternal grandparents having died when she was a toddler, and her parents both being only children, with not even a cousin between them.

But she and her mum and dad had never needed more family, they were complete as they were. It was the three of them against the world, her mother always said. And her parents were both still young

– it was the eve of her mum's fortieth birthday that night. They'd been out celebrating with friends at their favourite restaurant, and Carlie had been driving home because she was the only sober person after the lengthy dinner and all the bottles of wine, which had been followed by rounds of cake, coffee and liqueurs.

Eventually she became aware that the rain outside had stopped, the sky had darkened, and the cat was curled up on her lap, asleep, a comforting paw still on her arm. But she didn't deserve comfort. And she had to get home before her grandmother started worrying about her. She might not like her, or want to be around her, but letting her know she was okay – well, as okay as she was ever going to be – was the least she could do.

With some regret she closed the book and stood. She'd come back again soon and read more, try to work out what it was and what it meant, but right now she had to go. After giving the cat a farewell pat, she hurried back to her grandmother's cottage – and was relieved to find another note from her on the kitchen bench.

Hi Carlie,
I'm sorry I missed you, but I'm teaching a meditation class tonight, so I won't be back until 10pm. There's a chilli bean bake in the oven for your dinner... Hopefully I'll see you when I get back, but I'll understand if you need an early night...
Lots of love, Rose xx

Breathing a sigh of relief that she had the house to herself for a few hours, she ate a leisurely dinner, then tried to read a book for a while, but she kept getting distracted. Finally, at nine o'clock, she jumped in the shower, then went upstairs and threw herself down on her narrow bed. She wasn't tired, but she didn't want to have to talk to her grandmother – she didn't have the energy for *that.*

And her emotions were starting to blur, which was confusing her deeply. Now she didn't know whether she was angry about being sent here by Sandy, angry at her grandmother for failing her mum all those years ago, angry at her parents for leaving her all alone in the world, or perhaps just guilt-ridden over her own actions, and terrified that her grandmother would find out what she'd done and send her away. Surely neglecting or rejecting your child paled into insignificance next to killing your parents?

Reaching for her headphones, she hit play and sang along for a while, the music soothing her, and her spirits lifting a little as she remembered dancing to some of the tracks at the recent school social with Emily. Which seemed like a lifetime ago now.

When the haunting opening chords of *In Your Memory* by Weddings Parties Anything began, she broke down again. The lyrics had always torn at her heart, but now it was even worse. Now it was real. Now she really was boring people with her crying, just as they sang, and clutching desperately at every memory she had of her parents. She pictured herself in the kitchen at home as her mum baked her favourite treats for her birthday. Visualised her dad coming in to join them, cracking jokes, turning up the stereo, twirling her mum around the dining room as they all laughed together. And now that she knew a little more about her mother's childhood in England, the words to the song were even more bitter-sweet.

Curling up in bed, she let the tears fall as she hit play and rewind over and over again. But as soon as she heard the key in the front door and her grandmother quietly coming inside, she quickly turned off the music and switched out her light. And huddling under the colourful quilt, she finally drifted off to sleep.

Chapter 6

The Day the World Stood Still

She was in a cold white room, lying on a narrow, sterile bed under bright white lights, strapped to machines. She could sense something terrible moving towards her, getting closer and closer, but she was pinned down, unable to move. Finally there was a dark shape in the doorway, and she felt fear shoot through her as it turned to face her, then stepped into the room. She was frantic now, rolling from side to side on the bed, desperate to get away. She shrank in on herself, trying to disappear, as it walked towards her. She screamed…

The scream woke her, and she sat bolt upright, gasping for air. Panicking, she looked around, trying to work out where she was. It was dark, not bright white, and there was nothing walking towards her. Slowly she got her breathing back under control, but it was a long time before she could lie back down again without trembling all over.

She'd had this nightmare before, and each time it brought the memories of her hospital stay, and the reasons for it, flooding back, drowning her again in the horror that had become her life.

Her eyelids had fluttered a little, eyes not opening fully, but some movement evident for the first time in days. Slowly she began to surface from the icy black depths of the place she'd been hiding, awareness growing, crawling back, along with the physical pain and the mental anguish. The tall blonde woman leaned forward in the cold white plastic chair next to the hospital bed, anxiety creasing her forehead. She pressed the button for the nurse, who hurried in to see what was wrong.

"I think she's about to wake up," Sandy said, her voice equal parts relief and fear.

The nurse checked the machines and looked at the chart, then smiled reassuringly. "She'll wake in her own time, don't worry. She's a bit battered and bruised, but she'll be herself again very soon. Her body's just healing itself now, so all we can do is wait. All her vitals are positive though – she'll be fine." And she bustled back out again.

Sandy shook her head. Fine? She wasn't sure Carlie would ever be fine. And while her body would no doubt mend, there was no quick fix for her heart or her emotions, for her life itself. She looked at her watch. She really should be at home with her husband and daughter, looking after them, but her heart was breaking for the girl in the bed, the daughter of her best friend, who she'd watched being born, who she was godmother to, who she had babysat on countless occasions, and who she had spent so much time with on joint family holidays. The girl who still had no idea that she'd suddenly become an orphan.

Standing up, she rearranged the flowers in the vase, then went over to look out the window. She debated going down to the nurse's station to call her husband, but decided against it. She sat back down, picked up her book and tried to read a few pages, but couldn't concentrate.

Slowly her eyes began to flutter closed, but she was brought abruptly back to the present by a soft sigh from the bed. She reached out her hand to the girl in the hospital gown and smiled at her as reassuringly as she could, watching as Carlie's eyes opened, blinked, closed for a few moments, then finally opened again.

"Carlie, honey, you're okay," she whispered.

The pale-faced girl gazed up at her from the white pillows, confusion etched on her face.

"Hey Sandy, what are you doing here?" she asked, her voice laboured and cracked, her throat swollen and dry. "Where am I? Ouch!" she yelped as she reached a hand to her temple, and felt the thick bandage around her head. "What happened to me?"

Sandy was stricken with a mixture of fear, pain and sorrow, each emotion crossing her face one after the other. Agonised, she gazed down at Carlie. How did you tell someone that their whole world had suddenly ceased to exist?

"There was an accident Carlie, a car accident. But you're going to be fine – just a few cuts and scratches, a few bumps and bruises, a light concussion. Your ribs might hurt for a while," she explained, as Carlie winced again in pain. "But you'll be okay. You should be able to leave here in a few days, they just want to keep you in for observation for a little bit longer."

"But what's wrong Sandy? Why do you look so sad, and so scared? Where are Mum and Dad?"

The nurse came back in then, letting Sandy off the hook for the moment. Coolly efficient, she checked Carlie's vital signs, scribbled something down in her chart, then left the room again. Sandy sat on the edge of the narrow hospital bed and held one of Carlie's hands.

"Honey, your parents didn't make it. They both fought valiantly to hang on, to be here for you, but your dad was pronounced dead in the ambulance on the way to the hospital, and your mum never regained consciousness, and died the next day," she said, pain raw in her voice.

"When was this? What's wrong with me? Why can't I remember anything?" Carlie was frantic, panicked.

"It was three nights ago. You've been unconscious, but you'll be totally fine," Sandy insisted, her voice gentle, imploring, as she echoed the nurse's ridiculous word.

"Fine? How can I be fine?" Carlie screamed, horror on her face. "You just told me my parents are both dead."

Sandy sighed, and felt herself drowning in her own grief as well as in her supreme inadequacy to deal with this situation. When she'd agreed to be Carlie's godmother all those years ago, she'd imagined supplying great birthday presents, encouraging her to listen to a wider array of music than her parents did, offering a shoulder to cry on if necessary, perhaps taking her to a few church services if she wanted to explore different religions. She'd never in her wildest dreams imagined this situation. But when she heard Carlie's agonised voice and desperate sobs, she shook herself and forced her attention back to the girl in the bed.

"What happened?" Carlie begged.

Sandy took a deep breath. "You were driving back from your mum's birthday dinner. It was raining, and there was a car..."

"Wait! I was driving?" Carlie demanded.

"Honey, it wasn't your fault..."

"Stop, just stop!" Carlie choked out, before a wave of anger, guilt and tears engulfed her. "I killed my parents," she sobbed.

Sandy tried to calm her down, to insist that she really wasn't to blame, but that only made things worse. Carlie sat up in bed and attempted to get out, to flee, but she was so distraught that she fell onto the floor with a crash.

"I should be dead!" she wailed. "Or in jail. Sandy, let me go," she yelled, struggling to escape the woman's arms. She wasn't sure if she wanted to jump out the window to her death or find a police station so she could turn herself in, but she couldn't stay still. Sandy tried to hug her, to restrain her, to save her from herself, but the young girl was getting more and more worked up.

Summoned by all the noise, a nurse finally came in. She ushered Sandy out, then lifted Carlie back into bed and gave her an injection to calm her down. But it was a long time before she drifted off into unconsciousness and an uneasy kind of peace, and even longer before the tears stopped pouring down her face.

When she woke up the next morning there was a brief moment before she plunged back to awareness, a short respite from the knowledge that would define her life. It took her a little while to remember what had happened, but then it crashed back over her and the sobbing began again. When she saw a police officer walk past her doorway, she became hysterical. A nurse came in again to calm her down, and so it went, Carlie occasionally surfacing to awareness, then plunging back into the darkness, welcoming the temporary amnesia of the sedative, the thought that she'd killed her parents much too awful to cope with.

Sandy came in twice a day, but the nurses shook their heads. A counsellor had been in to talk to the patient, and said that for Carlie to see her right now would be too painful for her, the link to her mother a repeated blow. Finally, four days later, when Carlie had been in the hospital for a week, Sandy was allowed back in to see her, and Carlie lay there quietly as she gently explained what had happened, and what would happen next.

Two months ago her mother had made Sandy accompany her to several meetings with lawyers, where she'd made sure that everything she and her husband owned was transferred into Carlie's name as well as theirs, with Sandy as the executor of the estate, such as it was. She'd opened an international bank account for Carlie too, and insisted that Sandy have access to it.

Last of all, she'd written down the name and the possible street address of a woman in a small village in England. Sandy had asked questions, but Carlie's mum had been vague. "Just in case something happens to us," she'd said. "You're all she has here, so you'd have to help her organise everything. But that is the name and address of her grandmother in the UK."

Sandy had gasped, jaw dropping in shock. In more than twenty years of knowing each other, her friend had never once mentioned that her mother was alive, or mentioned her at all. Sandy had assumed that both of her friend's parents had died before she'd moved to Australia.

"Only if she really needs her," she'd insisted to Sandy, and then the subject was firmly closed.

Now Sandy took Carlie's hand, sympathy flooding her as she gazed at her best friend's daughter while she too tried to come to terms with such a huge secret. "I don't know why your grandmother's existence was a secret, I can't explain that at all," she admitted, shades of hurt and confusion in her voice still. She'd been lied to by the person she'd trusted the most too. "But I've spoken to her a few times over the last few days, and she sounds really lovely. She didn't know that she had a granddaughter, but she's really excited to meet you."

"She's coming here?" Carlie asked, aghast. She really didn't want to have to meet a stranger right now, or see anyone. She wanted to be alone with her misery.

"No, um, you're going there," Sandy said to her goddaughter, watching her anxiously, worried that she'd feel rejected. "It's all organised – you leave for England a week from tomorrow."

Carlie paled even further, eyes wide. "I have to leave my home to go and live with a total stranger?" she demanded.

"Not a stranger honey, she's your grandmother. She's family. It's what your mum wanted."

Carlie started sobbing again, and wouldn't listen to anything else Sandy said. The doctor came in then, and informed her that she would be discharged in the morning with a clean bill of health. Physically at least, if not emotionally. So the next day she showered then dressed in the jeans and sweatshirt that Sandy had brought in for her, and went home with her mum's best friend, to stay with her and her family for the week before her exile began.

One afternoon she went over to her former house to pack up what she wanted to take with her, to sort through her parents' things, and to let Sandy know what she could keep, throw out or give to charity. She didn't keep much for herself – everything reminded her of happier times, so she couldn't bear to look at it, and she just couldn't picture herself or her future any more, so she really had no idea what she might need.

These days were even worse than the hospital – she felt like she was sleepwalking through her life, a ghost of her former self. She was plagued with awful migraines that left her crying into the night, and wherever she was or whoever she was with, she felt that she was intruding, bringing everyone around her down with the grief that she was drowning in.

Her best friend Emily came to see her, but Carlie was too angry and grief-stricken to be nice to her, or even polite. She'd climbed the stairs to the guest room where Carlie was hiding out, and tried to cheer her up. She told her all the news from school, and handed her a get well card that everyone had signed for her with sweet messages of love and support.

"The maths test today was awful," Emily said, rambling from subject to subject in the face of Carlie's stony silence. "A few of us think we're going to fail – you're lucky that you missed it."

Carlie pushed back her greasy hair and glared at her friend. "Lucky? Lucky to have no parents? Lucky to be staying somewhere I'm obviously not wanted? Lucky to be on my way to live with a monster?"

Emily blushed. "Of course not Carlie, you know I didn't mean that. I'm so sorry," she said, voice catching on the tears she was trying to choke back. "My god, I don't know how you're coping, none of us do – I'd be a complete wreck."

She trailed off as Carlie's face flushed red with new anger.

"Coping? I'm not coping! How does anyone cope with this?" she shouted. "Why don't you just go back to your perfect house with your perfect parents and leave me alone," she spat.

She broke off when Sandy walked in with milk and cookies, and stared out the window, ignoring them both. Emily was on the verge of tears, but she forced a smile and nodded slightly when Sandy asked if she was okay. She stayed for another half hour, biting her tongue, speaking carefully, trying to find safe topics to talk about. Trying not to let her best friend's pointed barbs hurt her. When she finally left, the relief she felt at being away from there was tempered by the sadness and horror of seeing her best friend so crushed.

And while Carlie knew she wasn't being fair to her friend, that she deserved better, right now she didn't care. All she had was her anger, her pain, her guilt, her sense of injustice. She put her headphones in and flipped through until she found her favourite album, then turned it up as loud as it would go. Platinum Brunette always provided the perfect soundtrack to her anger, her pain, her bitterness. It was like they were the only people on earth who understood how she felt, the only ones who had been left, lost and betrayed by those closest to them, just like she had...

Sandy also struggled to stay calm in the face of Carlie's anger. She understood, and so she forgave her, but it was hard for her to see her best friend's daughter lashing out at those who loved her, and being so self-destructive. She kept her own family out of her way, and prayed that Emily would try again to reach Carlie, to let her know that so many people cared about her.

And she did. The next day Emily walked hesitantly to the front door and knocked quietly, her body language screaming that she didn't want to be there, but her desire to make peace with her dearest friend keeping her on the doorstep until Sandy ushered her in and pointed her up the stairs. She knocked on Carlie's door, walked in without an invitation, and went over to her and hugged her.

"I love you Carlie, you're my best friend in the world, and I'm devastated that I'm losing you," she said. "And I know you feel that you're the only one grieving, but it breaks my heart that you're going away, and I know Sandy is distraught at the loss of her best friend too."

Carlie raised an eyebrow.

"Your mum was her closest friend, so she's grieving her loss as well, and feeling terrible that she can't help you more."

Carlie started to snap something back, some scathing retort, some blast of vitriol, but Emily held up her hand. "No, just listen. We understand that you're angry, and you have every right to be. But don't push us away, don't think it will be easier for you to leave if you've alienated everyone who cares about you," she said, a sob catching in her throat as she tried to keep her voice steady.

"We love you, and we always will. And we'll always be here for you, even if it's only by phone and letter for the next little while. But we'll both be eighteen soon, we'll have finished school and we can go to university wherever we want to. So this isn't really goodbye, it's just farewell for now," she finished.

Carlie was silent, tears streaming down her cheeks. A flicker of remorse for her anger crossed her face, then just as quickly disappeared. Emily kissed her on the cheek, hugged her briefly then walked out. It was killing her to see her friend like this. She wanted them both to remember each other as they had been, best friends since they were five years old, each other's only comfort through school problems, family fights, romantic fiascos and teenage angst. She was ashamed of herself for not wanting to spend more time with Carlie, but it was pretty clear that she wasn't welcome. And she understood, she really did. It was just breaking her heart to see her like that.

Carlie's mood didn't improve as the days passed. She was belligerent with Sandy's husband and daughter, when she spoke to them at all, and she lashed out at Sandy whenever she had to speak to her. Part of her knew that she was being unforgivably rude to her mum's best friend, and that she didn't deserve it, but she couldn't help it. She was wracked with guilt that she'd killed her parents, as well as irrationally furious with them that they'd left her all alone in the world.

And she felt betrayed by Sandy, for sending her to live with a total stranger, and angry at her mother too. Why had she told everyone that her own mother was dead, that Carlie had no grandmother? Who was this mysterious woman? And what had she done to her own daughter that had made her pretend to everyone in her life that she was dead? She must be truly awful, this stranger woman, to have been cut out of her daughter's life so completely.

And now she was on her way to live with her.

Chapter 7

Lashing Out

When she woke up the next morning, Carlie's head was still filled with images of her nightmare – of the hospital, of Sandy and Emily, and of her fear of her grandmother. She lay in bed for a while, listening carefully. When she heard the front door close she sighed with relief and padded downstairs in her pyjamas, feet bare. Her grandmother was in the kitchen when she walked in.

"Oh, I heard the door, and thought you'd left for work already," Carlie said, then bit her tongue and blushed. *Wow, that was subtle.*

Her grandmother looked over at her calmly and smiled a wry hello. "I just got back from the newsagent," she said, indicating the newspaper on the table.

"Oh, sorry," Carlie replied, cursing herself for coming down so early – and for not shutting her mouth.

"Carlie, I know you're upset, and that this is all very strange for you, but I want you to know I'm happy that you're here. You don't have to avoid me on my account."

Carlie stared at her, surprise momentarily silencing her. Then she laughed. "Avoid you for your sake? I never even thought of that. I just... I don't want to be here. I don't want to be with you. I don't want to talk to you. I want to go home, be with the people who care about me, who I care about."

Fighting back tears, she grabbed an apple and raced back upstairs, slamming her door behind her and throwing herself down on the bed. She cried until she was exhausted, then lay there, shaking slightly and staring vacantly up at the ceiling. She couldn't believe what had happened to her life, and she was so angry, and so helpless, that she felt totally numb. She wanted to physically hurt herself just so she'd know she could still feel. Looking wildly around the room, her eyes alighted for a moment on the scissors poking out of her little sewing kit. Then she sighed dispiritedly. She didn't have the courage for that.

Trying to calm herself down, she picked up the glass of water on her bedside table and took a sip, but part of her wanted to squeeze the glass until it shattered in her hand, break it into tiny pieces and watch the blood pour out of her palm. She wanted to blot out the mental pain with physical pain, pain she could understand, that she could soothe. Shakily she returned the glass to the table, and tried to take a deep, steadying breath.

She was so mad, but she felt a little bit bad too. She'd seen the look on her grandmother's face just before she'd turned away. She'd seen it on her best friend Emily's face too, the last time they'd been together. Although she'd been so mean to Emily each time she'd come to visit her in the days after the crash, her friend had still persevered. And she'd tried one last time, coming over to Sandy's the morning that Carlie was flying to England. They'd sat outside together on the back verandah, drinking hot chocolate, both feeling awkward. It was a cold and stormy day, which suited Carlie's grey mood perfectly.

"How are you feeling?" Emily had asked, her heart breaking in the face of her friend's deep and obvious anguish.

"How do you think?" Carlie had snapped. She saw the look on her friend's face and cringed inwardly. "I'm sorry Em, I just... I don't want to hurt you, but I don't know how to act around other people. Maybe it's best that I'm being sent away, to the other side of the world no less," she said, anger building in her voice.

"It's not a punishment Carlie! She's your grandmother, she's family. Your mum wanted you to go and live with her if... if anything happened to her," she trailed off.

"So how come she never told me about her? How come she didn't stay in touch with her? She must be awful, for Mum to have cut off all contact with her. How is this not a punishment? Why isn't Sandy my guardian? Why can't I stay with you?" she wailed.

Emily sighed. She didn't know either, and she felt terrible for her friend, but she didn't think they should be dwelling on the negatives. It went without saying that Carlie's life sucked at the moment, but at least she did have family she could go to.

"It's only until you're eighteen, then you can come back home, and we can get our share house in the city and go to university together, study law, just like we've always planned. Besides Carlie, I'm just so glad you survived," Emily said, tears in her eyes and catching in her throat as she tried to speak.

"Me?" Carlie snapped. "I should be the one who died! It was all my fault. I killed my parents. How can I be a lawyer, be anything? I'm a criminal – I can't practise law. At the very least I should be in jail." Abruptly she broke off. Stood up, paced. Sat down again. "I have to go upstairs and lie down," she said, holding her head as if it was hurting. Which wasn't exactly a lie. She'd had terrible migraines ever since the accident, and no doubt one would return soon.

Emily stood up and tried to hug her. "I'll miss you so much Carlie. You're my best friend in the world," she sighed, her voice dripping with pain and sorrow. She handed her a card, and a little box wrapped in soft gold material and tied up with a red ribbon.

Carlie shrugged. "You're better off without me," she growled, tossing the card and the gift on the table, sighing theatrically, then turning her back on her friend and stomping upstairs to the guest room. Slamming the door, she threw herself down on the bed and cried and cried. She'd done a lot of that in the last two weeks. Sometimes it seemed that was all she was capable of now.

She hated herself for hurting Emily, but she couldn't seem to stop herself doing it. She didn't deserve to have friends, and it would be better for Emily if she found new people to hang out with, found someone else to share her university dream with, share a house with, plan a future with. As much as she hated the idea of going to live with her evil grandmother on the other side of the world, she knew she couldn't come back home to Sydney when she was eighteen. There were too many awful memories, too much pain, too much pity. She didn't want to face anyone she knew ever again, she just wanted to drown herself in the alienation of a foreign land, of strangers who didn't know her, or know what she'd done. She didn't have the strength to end her life, but she wished desperately that she'd died in the crash. That would have been easier for everyone.

And now here she was, far away from everyone she'd ever known. This was what she'd wanted, right? She sighed, then cried again, then rolled her eyes at herself, bored with her own self-indulgent misery. She tried to read for a while, but she couldn't focus, and then she dozed off. Later she woke abruptly, and stared out at the hill that still seemed to be calling to her, before eventually falling asleep again. At one point she heard her grandmother outside her door, asking if she needed anything before she left for work, but she ignored her, and eventually she went away. Then she felt a stab of guilt and loneliness, and slumped back on her bed, filled with despair.

For a while she played some music, then she slipped off into another nightmare, jerking back awake after an hour or two, heart thumping and sweat pouring off her. Clearly jetlag on top of everything else wasn't helping her frame of mind, so she decided that if she wanted to stay in bed all day, who would care? She knew she couldn't go on like this for much longer, but she had no idea what to do about it, or how to get out of her constant black mood.

After another short and fitful sleep she jerked awake, and sighed that so little time had passed. She picked up her book again, and when Luther came in and jumped up on the bed beside her she patted him, grateful for his uncomplicated company. With him curled up in her lap she managed to read for a while, the weight of his warm body and the vibration of his purring strangely soothing. When she heard her grandmother come home, she stayed where she was, breath held, and felt happier than she'd imagined she could that Luther remained with her instead of running downstairs for his dinner.

Finally, as it grew dark outside, her grandmother knocked tentatively on the door, to let her know that dinner was ready. She wanted to refuse, to stay hidden in the cosy gloom of her small room, but she was too hungry. She cursed her traitor body. If only she could just hole up in here and never have to leave, never have to eat, never have to talk to anyone. Sullenly she opened her door and followed her grandmother down the stairs, book in hand. Maybe she could just read, and ignore her altogether?

"How was your day Sweetheart?" Rose asked her, as she served out two generous portions of vegetarian lasagne.

Carlie shrugged, not wanting to engage in conversation, but the food smelled so good that it was hard to stay angry. "It was okay. Yours?" she muttered.

Her grandmother smiled at her as she handed her a plate. "It was pretty good. I did a few healing sessions at the centre, then came home and pottered in the garden for a while. There were so many ripe tomatoes, and the basil smelled so good, that I decided to make lasagne. It was your mother's favourite."

Carlie stared fiercely at her. Picked up her glass of juice, then put it down again because her hands were shaking so badly.

"I'm sorry," her grandmother said quickly, remorse in her eyes. Carlie wanted to flee, to escape this awkward moment in this awkward new life she'd found herself lumbering through. She took a deep breath, had a sip of juice, then nodded curtly.

"It's delicious, thank you Grandmother," she finally said, forcing herself to be polite before lapsing into silence. She didn't open her book – she'd decided that was just too rude, even for her – but she didn't speak again either. She ate as quickly as she could, then asked if she could be excused. Her grandmother nodded sadly, and Carlie dragged herself up to her room and crawled back into bed.

Chapter 8

The Woman In Blue

When Carlie woke up the next morning, she felt as though there was a black cloud hovering over her head. Her mood was glum and brooding, and she couldn't shake off the oppressiveness that surrounded her. She heard Luther poke his head in the door – she had no idea how he managed to open her firmly closed door, yet somehow he'd figured out a way – but he took one look at her and walked back down the stairs. Which didn't help her mood. She was in trouble if even the cat didn't want to be around her.

Finally she got out of bed, threw the quilt back in some semblance of neatness, and stamped her way down the stairs to the kitchen. Her grandmother had already left for work, which filled her with relief. She got out a bowl and slammed it on the bench, then poured in some muesli, cursing as it spilled out onto the floor, then sighing with frustration when the milk slopped over the side of the bowl. Her efforts with the kettle and teapot annoyed her just as much, and she vowed to buy some teabags for times like this. She wasn't sure exactly why she was in such a foul mood – fouler than usual, she should say – but she couldn't shake it.

When she saw the note addressed to her leaning up against the vase on the table she felt her annoyance grow even higher, but it wasn't her grandmother's fault that she'd gotten up on the wrong side of the bed, so she picked it up, read its contents – and slammed her mug of tea down.

Rose wanted her to go to the big town an hour's drive from them to pick up an order of herbs for her – and the bus was leaving in ten minutes. She ran up the stairs, tripping over and banging her knee quite hard, which caused a further outbreak of swearing, and pulled on her jeans and grabbed a jacket. Quickly she brushed her teeth then raced back downstairs, ignoring her half eaten breakfast and dirty dishes and grabbing her bag, a banana and the list on the way. She sprinted along the street towards town, turning her ankle on a rock along the way. Tears sprang to her eyes at the pain, but she shook her head resolutely and kept going.

The bus was already there when she arrived, and just about to pull out. She jumped on, clumsily pulling out a five-pound note and smiling a polite hello as she handed it to the bus driver. He printed off her ticket and picked out her change. "Such a pretty smile," he said. "Have a beautiful day."

She grimaced inwardly, but as she hobbled down the aisle to find a seat she felt the black cloud start to lift from her shoulders a little. How strange, that such a small thing – a simple kind word – could pierce her stubborn bad mood, and if not actually change her frame of mind, at least snap her out of her wallowing self-pity for a moment. Sitting down, she gazed thoughtfully out the window, finally seeing her surroundings. It was really beautiful here, if you liked the green-fields-and-old-trees kinda vibe.

She spent a few hours wandering around the town – which was tiny compared to Sydney, but considered almost a city here. It was pretty, she conceded, and so ancient, such a change from her home country, where the oldest building was only two hundred years old. Here many of the streets were cobbled. Old stone houses covered with twisting vines overlooked small, neat green gardens, and there was a gorgeous university on the bank of the river that reminded her of Sydney's, with its ivy-clad walls and pretty courtyards.

It made her long to speak to Emily – and then to start panicking about her future. She knew she didn't want to be a lawyer any more, couldn't be one, but she didn't know what else she would be capable of doing, let alone even want to do. But maybe she could find out what courses they had at this one, and see if anything appealed to her. She still had another twelve months of school to finish, since a new school year was about to start here, despite it being more than halfway through in Australia, but she figured that she had to start sorting out what she wanted to do with her life at some point, and seeing what they offered might inspire her. But not today. The future terrified her, and she knew she wasn't up to handling any extra disappointments or stresses today, feeling as fragile as she did.

After picking up her grandmother's herbs, she wandered into a grocery store to grab a sandwich and some juice, so she could sit in one of the leafy green parks for lunch. As she walked down the aisle she saw a little old lady trying to reach something on one of the higher shelves. She hurried over and asked if she could get anything for her. "Bless you lass, I've been standing here for ages now trying to get it down, hoping someone would come over and help me." She turned to her with tear-filled eyes. "Thank you, truly," she said softly.

Carlie helped her get down what she needed, then smiled a farewell. She was amazed, again, just how much the tiniest gesture could touch someone, and how doing it offered a moment's respite from her own darkness. It was no skin off her nose to help, barely any effort at all, but feeling how much the woman appreciated it made her feel warm inside. Who knew that being kind could make you feel good too?

But her better mood soon faded, and by the time she got back home late that afternoon she was grumpy and annoyed again. There was another note – her grandmother had already been home from work, and had left again for the meditation class she taught. Carlie took the herbs out to the kitchen and left them on the bench, then made some toast and stomped upstairs to her room. She threw herself onto her bed, restless still, and not knowing what to do. Had she ever been bored like this back home? There she'd always had friends to go visit, the beach one street over if she wanted to swim or surf, a cinema down the road, netball on weekends, concerts to see – and her mum to cook dinner with and her dad to go to the gym with.

There had been no time to feel bored. But here, she didn't know anyone, and there was nothing to do. How could anyone bear to grow up in a tiny town like this? What did they do with themselves? Were they all just waiting to graduate from high school so they could leave the village and go to the city, where their real lives could begin? She thought she'd die of boredom before school ever started – and what on earth would school be like in a place like this anyway?

Groaning, she finally stood back up, deciding that she had to keep moving or her thoughts would drive her crazy. She raced downstairs, out the back door and through the garden, stepping through the gate and turning right into the laneway, heading towards the tor. After a brisk climb she reached the top, and sat down on the grassy edge, gazing off into the pretty sunset-drenched clouds on the horizon and feeling the swirling mists start to coalesce around her.

It reminded her of the sunrises she used to watch with her dad when they went to the beach together before school to check out the waves. Her eyes welled up, and a huge sob wracked her body. She tried to hold it in, but the grief was overwhelming, and she gave herself over to the tears that flooded through her. She cried for what seemed like hours, her body shaking with the violence of her anguish.

After a while she felt a presence near her, and she tried to stifle her sobs. Then an arm went around her and she froze, fear slicing through her body. Within moments she felt inexplicably calmer though, and not as shocked as she would normally be that someone had come so close to her, was physically touching her. It was as though a spell was weaving its tranquil power over her, calming her, wiping away her fears, silently letting her know that everything would be okay.

She struggled against the sensation, every part of her wanting to flee, wanting to get away from whoever it was who dared to touch her, dared to offer her comfort. And yet, it felt really nice to not be angry for a moment, so almost against her will she could feel herself relaxing into it.

Glancing sideways, she saw a woman sitting beside her, with long wavy red hair, and eyes that were filled with such compassion and empathy. She tried to get her sobs under control, to try to figure out what was going on, but the warmth and security emanating from the mysterious woman made her feel that she could cry, that she *should* cry, that in this moment all she had was her tears, and it was perfectly acceptable to give in to them, to let all the grief she'd been bottling up spill out into the world and away from her.

"There there," the stranger crooned, her voice as soothing as honey. "It's okay, let it all out." The woman was stroking Carlie's hair as she held her close, and she felt a sense of peace float over her and settle around her like a blanket. She hadn't felt so safe, so loved, since... well, since before her parents had died. She cried even harder at that thought, her whole body shaking, yet somehow being held safe in the arms of this blue-clad woman.

Eventually a sound wound around her mind and settled in her heart – it seemed that the woman was singing, some kind of lullaby, each word so soothing and soul-nurturing. And eventually she felt her tears easing and the violence of her sobs abating, the occasional hiccup now the only evidence of her long and desperate crying fit.

Then the woman spoke again, her voice there but not there, somehow inside her head and her heart. "Oh Carlie, no one blames you for being angry, for railing at the world."

Carlie glanced up at her sharply, alarmed. How did this stranger know her name? Who was she?

The woman continued speaking: "You have to know that your grandmother loves you, and how happy she's been since you arrived. She has something to live for again, because you've given her a new purpose in life. And maybe she can do the same for you," she offered.

Carlie sat in silence for a long time, thinking. Slowly she shrugged off the woman's arms and sat upright, feeling the steadiness of the earth beneath her, the coolness of the grass against her feet, the warmth of the setting sun on her face. She couldn't work out what was happening. Was the woman really there, or just a figment of her imagination? Was this another dream, or was her grief unhinging her, opening her mind and her heart to those things on the outer edges of reality and beyond? Is that what madness was?

Finally she couldn't bear the uncertainty any more. "Are you real?" she demanded, turning to face her, and not caring how rude she sounded. But the woman just smiled at her, tenderly touched her tear-stained cheek, then faded back into the mists. Carlie sighed. What was happening to her? Did the woman even exist? This place was so strange, but she had to admit that it was slowly growing on her. She'd never be able to tell Emily about what had just happened – not that she'd have any idea how to explain it even if she wanted to – because her friend would totally think she was losing her mind. Hell, *she* totally thought she was losing her mind.

A thought hit her, and she wondered if Rose had ever seen the blue-clad woman. Did you have to have been through something tragic in order to see her? Or perhaps she was one of their ancestors, watching over them, comforting and nurturing them on their journey through life? Suddenly she laughed. More likely she was just starting to lose her mind, her brain snapped by grief, which was making her hallucinate. Or perhaps it was even more mundane than that – she was simply talking to herself, and giving a face and personality to the part of her that was replying.

As the sun began to set, she thought about pain and loss, and the fine line between sanity and that state beyond. In that moment it seemed to Carlie to be a very fine line indeed.

Tears blurred her eyes, and she sat for a long time on the side of the tor, staring into the sunset. Breathing in the colours and the sense of serenity that she felt up there on the hill, on her own, connecting to the earth. Maybe nature really was healing.

When she got home it was almost dark, and the house was quiet. She went straight upstairs to her room and collapsed into bed. She was too emotional to want to eat, too upset to stay awake, and too raw and confused to face her grandmother.

It was nice to know that she was welcome, she supposed, but in a way that was just bewildering her even more. All she had was her anger, her pain, her sense of injustice. But in order to accept that the blue-clad woman's words were true – that her grandmother really was happy to have her here, and that there was hope for a happier future for both of them – she would have to let Rose in, and she wasn't ready for that. She needed the barrier she'd walled up around her heart, otherwise she feared she'd just crumble apart, would cease to exist as she shattered into a million tiny pieces.

Chapter 9

Weaving the Quilt of Life

All night she tossed and turned, her dreams filled with blood and violence, darkness and dripping redness. Fear, guilt, pain and anger. At one point she sensed someone in the room with her, stroking her forehead, comforting her. She cried and cried, held safe in strong arms, but when she woke again hours later she wasn't sure if that had been real or just part of the dream. She hoped it was the latter. She didn't want to imagine that she'd woken her grandmother with her crying, and that she'd come upstairs to comfort her. That was too weird.

Now it was just before the dawn, too early to get up, but she was too scared to go back to sleep and plunge into her red-tinged nightmares again. So she lay awake, shivering with a bone-deep chill, and pulled the quilt up over herself, the weight of it a welcome sensation, and a distraction from her flickering nightmare flashbacks. Gazing up at the ceiling, she prayed for an end to the fear and the pain, and wondered if she'd be able to avoid her grandmother again today.

A little while later there was a hesitant knock, and she reluctantly answered. Her grandmother opened the door slowly, but didn't come into the room. "I'm just going down to the fruit market, if you want to come, or I could pick something up, if there's anything in particular you'd like?" she asked. Then she stopped abruptly and stared hard at the quilt Carlie had wrapped around herself so tightly.

Carlie looked down at the patchwork squares, puzzled at her reaction. "I found it in the cupboard, I hope that's okay. I got really cold," she said, defensiveness making her voice harsh.

Rose nodded, and smiled sadly. "I made that quilt for your mother for her seventeenth birthday," she said, coming into the room for the first time and sitting on the edge of Carlie's bed. "It took months, finding all the pieces, stitching them together." Her hand reached out to stroke a small black cat embroidered on one square.

"Luther's mother, Shadow," she smiled. "Your mum loved that cat, she let her sleep on her bed every night. She had green eyes and was jet black, just like Luther, except for the tiny white star on her forehead."

Carlie froze. Surely it couldn't be the cat she'd seen the other day at the cottage. *Could it?* Her mother had left more than twenty years ago, and that cat didn't look very old.

Her grandmother's sad eyes were still taking in the rest of the quilt, drinking it in like she hadn't seen it for years. Perhaps she hadn't. "That green piece was from her first school uniform. The pale pink tulle was from her first ballet recital. And the embroidered bees were part of a piece we worked on together, trying to learn how to do tapestry. We weren't very good at it, but we always loved spending time together," she said, a rueful smile drifting across her face.

Carlie tried to picture her mum as a teenager, staying in and sewing with her own mother, but all she could envisage was anger and screaming fights. If they'd gotten on so well, as her grandmother was implying, why on earth did her mum leave this village, this country even, and never go back? Why did she never even mention her childhood or her parents to anyone? She shook her head, trying to clear the images, trying to concentrate on what her grandmother was saying. She watched numbly as Rose reached out to touch another section, a rainbow of eight coloured strips stitched neatly together.

"From our altar cloths. We'd dress a little altar to the goddess every sabbat – the seasonal festivals of the magical year," she explained, as Carlie looked at her blankly. "We'd bring in flowers and herbs from the garden, light candles, then climb the tor to watch the sun rise."

Her eyes gazed off, dreamy and distant, focusing on the grassy mound of the hill outside the window. Then she blinked quickly and brought her attention back into the room. Unshed tears glittered on her lower lashes, but didn't fall. She reached out to stroke a bright violet-purple square.

"And that was a piece of fabric left over from the dress I made for her to wear at her seventeenth birthday party. The morning of the party she opened the package with the quilt in it first, and loved the colour of this piece so much – so you should have seen the joy on her face when she opened the next parcel, which had the dress in it. Ah, my sweet little Violet..." she whispered, voice breaking with pain.

A trail of violets had been worked into the border, and her grandmother traced them slowly with her finger.

Violet? That was the name in the book she'd found in the derelict cottage. Why would her grandmother call her own daughter by the wrong name? Or was that her mother's real name, she wondered suddenly, as a shudder of anger ripped through her again. Everyone called her Fee, for Fiona, and she'd just called her Mum. But was it actually Vee, for Violet? Had her mother changed her name when she left home, in a further attempt to erase her past?

Carlie's mind was a jumble of questions, of accusations, of confusion. This woman had clearly loved her daughter. The quilt she'd laboured over for months and the story of each carefully considered square was testament to that. And she seemed to be mourning her lost daughter still. But that didn't make any sense. Her mother had run away to the other side of the world to get away from this woman, and had never so much as mentioned her existence to her daughter or her best friend. Well, not until just before she died. God, had her mum known she was about to die? Is that why she'd finally revealed her secret to Sandy?

"Why did you drive her away then?" Carlie demanded, her rudeness forcing Rose to look up abruptly, shocked at her tone and at the question. A single tear was slowly running down her cheek. "It sounds like you did love her," Carlie continued, voice starting to falter.

"Love her? Of course we loved her! She was our whole world!" Rose croaked.

"And we didn't send her away, she left us. One morning she just disappeared. I didn't even know she was alive until her friend rang me two weeks ago, to tell me… what happened. To tell me about you."

Her grandmother's tears began to fall at last, pouring down her face. Her shoulders shook as sobs wracked her body, and for the first time Carlie saw how frail she was, how fragile. She stared at her, trying to reconcile this distraught elderly woman with the monster in her head. A mother who'd hated her daughter so much that she'd driven her away – driven her to the other side of the world. Who'd never written, or sent a card, who'd never called. Who didn't seem to care that she had a granddaughter. But what if she'd never actually known that she had a grandchild? Never even known her daughter was still alive? Could that be true? And if it was, what did that mean to everything she'd ever believed about her mother, or herself?

Before Carlie could untwist her tangled thoughts enough to ask another question, to challenge Rose's statement, the doorbell rang. Her grandmother jumped, startled, then shakily stood up and backed out of the room. Carlie heard her feet, heavy on the stairs as she slowly walked down them, the creak as she opened the front door, the muted chatter of voices. Finally the door closed, and she heard her grandmother's hesitant steps at the bottom of the staircase, before she changed her mind and hid herself in her own room.

Carlie sat on her bed, mind racing but not yet able to move, poring over the quilt in her lap, searching desperately for clues. If what she'd just heard was true, then her grandmother had spent more than twenty years not knowing whether her only child was dead or alive, imagining all kinds of ghastly scenarios – and had only found out that she *had* been alive all these years when she got a phone call from Sandy notifying her that her daughter had just died. It felt so cruel.

Could this be the truth? Or was it all an elaborate web of lies, told now to rewrite a past the old woman was ashamed of? It certainly appeared to be real – her grandmother's grief felt genuine, tangible, and the pain in her eyes when Carlie had demanded to know why she'd sent her daughter away was naked and deep.

Her heart felt like it was breaking, not only for this sad, broken person who had taken her in – a total stranger, dumped on her doorstep without notice – but also for the pain that she had obviously lived with for so long. She'd lost her daughter, but never known what had happened to her. Feared her dead, but had no body to bury, no answers, no closure. And what had happened to her husband?

Head spinning, she wondered what else of her mother's life had been a lie. And how much of her own story was real?

Carlie's finger traced gently over the sun pattern embroidered on a sky-blue square, which conjured an image of the beach near her Sydney home. A printed bunny on what looked like the material of a toddler's bib caught her eye next – the exact replica of one she'd been wearing in a photo of herself when she was a baby. Surely that was no accident, that her mum had bought her the same bib she'd had as a child? And if that was the case, didn't that mean that her mother must have had some fond memories of her early life?

When her tummy rumbled for the second time, she reluctantly pulled on some clothes and headed downstairs to the kitchen. She was eating a bowl of home-made muesli with fresh strawberries when her grandmother came in and put the kettle on.

"Tea?" she asked quietly, her voice trembling only a tiny bit.

Carlie nodded. "Thank you." Rose smiled a little.

"Um, Grandmother? Your husband? What happened to him? Mum never mentioned him either. I thought he must have died when she was a baby or something?" she asked softly.

Rose looked like she'd been stabbed in the heart. Her body shuddered, and she clung tightly to the kitchen bench. She took a slow, deep breath, then another one. Lifted down the teapot and two mugs, then carefully selected a jar of dried herbs from the cupboard.

"Louis died a month after Violet... left us. He couldn't handle her loss, couldn't see any way forward without her. The not knowing what had happened, or why, tortured both of us. You can't imagine the things that crossed our minds, the nightmares we had about what might have happened to her. He started drinking, a lot. Cried every night. Then he became angry, argumentative, just plain mean. He got into a fight with his boss, and was eventually fired. I couldn't reach him. I tried, though I was dying inside myself." She paused, trying to calm her tears, and concentrated hard on getting the next words out.

"Finally it was too much for him. I found a note when I got home from work one night, saying goodbye. When he still hadn't returned home the next morning I rang the police, but a part of me already knew. They found his body later that day – he'd driven off the bridge and crashed into the water below. He'd taken some sedatives the doctor had given him to help him sleep, and drunk a bottle of whisky. If he hadn't already died from the impact, he would have drowned. They ruled it an accident, but everyone knew he'd taken his own life. And all of a sudden I had no daughter and no husband."

Carlie's heart ached with sympathy, and her eyes welled with tears. "But you stayed..." she whispered.

"I could never leave, just in case she came back. What if she just hadn't been able to reach us? Had had an accident and lost her memory? Or maybe she'd reconsider one day, and try to find us, or let us know she was okay at least. Even years later, when I knew the chance of her ever returning, let alone being alive, was so slim, I couldn't bring myself to leave this village, or this house. If there was even the tiniest chance, I had to be here."

She gazed across at Carlie, pain radiating from her. She tried to smile, but failed miserably. Instead she concentrated on pouring boiling water into the teapot. "I'm glad I did stay," she said finally, voice soaked with distress as she tried to keep it even.

"Your mum's friend, Sandy? She rang the minister at the local church, asked if there was anyone who might have had a daughter once, a daughter who went away. He's new, I've never been to his church, but he asked the ladies at the St Vinnie's shop, and they knew it must have been me. It's a small town..." She shrugged, then poured some soy milk into a jug and took it and the teapot over to the table, before returning for the mugs and setting them down.

Carlie poured some tea into her cup then clumsily stirred in the soy milk and honey. Her mind was reeling from her grandmother's words. "I'm so sorry, I had no idea. I can't even begin to understand why she left you, or why she never told me about you or her life here," she whispered. "What did she say?"

"Only that she had to leave home when she was very young, that she met my dad when he was working in one of those Aussie backpacker pubs in London, and that they went back to Australia not long afterwards, because his mother was sick and they had to care for her…

"Oh god, I'm sorry!" Carlie broke off, mortified at what she'd just said. Could she have been any more heartless?

Rose shook her head, trying again to smile, to seem okay, but Carlie felt like she'd just plunged another knife into her heart. Her mum hadn't cared enough to let her own mother know that she was alive, but she'd packed up and left the country to nurse a stranger through a long illness?

"I just… I don't know what to say," Carlie whispered. "I don't understand. She was always so kind. My… other nanna… lived with us when I was little, and it was Mum who looked after her while Dad worked. I just… I don't get it. She was a saint, everyone said so, yet… she must have been a monster too."

Her grandmother smiled sadly. "I guess we'll never know. She must have had her reasons, I just…" she sighed. "I just don't know what they could be. We were always so close. We worked together at the healing centre – she was going to take over eventually, that's the reason I opened it in the first place, so I had something to leave her." She started sobbing, and Carlie moved nervously around to her side of the table, awkwardly patting her shoulder, but feeling shy and a little uncomfortable too.

When the clock chimed the hour, Rose looked up at it and sighed. "I have to go in to the centre, just for a few hours. Will you be okay here on your own?" she asked.

Carlie nodded. She should write her best friend a letter, let her know she was okay. After hearing her grandmother's story, she never wanted to leave anyone wondering again. Hurrying up the stairs, she grabbed a notebook and pen from her room, then came back down to the kitchen table and opened it to a blank page.

"Dear Emily," she began, then stopped. She got up to make more tea. Sat back down again. Walked over to the pantry to look for cookies, or chocolate, or something. After a fruitless search she sat back down and picked up her pen again, determined to write something…

But finally she threw it down in frustration. She didn't know what to say to her friend. How could she explain that her grandma was lovely, not the ogre they'd both pictured, and that it was her mum who had been cruel? Her mum who was dead. Who would never be able to hug her again, never be able to explain what she had done and why, never be able to justify leaving her mother in this twilight of grief. And who would never see her own daughter grow up and have a family of her own, never be a grandmother herself.

Carlie felt restless, unsettled. She needed to walk in order to think. And she needed to go back to the cottage and read that book. She knew now that her mum's name was Violet, or it had been. Maybe she'd find some answers in those hand-written pages. She tied a jacket around her waist, slipped the key into her pocket and walked out through the back garden and into the sunshine.

Chapter 10

Pictures of You

It was such a beautiful day, despite her whirring mind and the deep sadness she felt. She wandered down the laneway, crossed over the path that led to the tor and kept walking. The flowers on either side sparkled in the sun, the hedges on her right that screened backyards from passersby threw their heady fragrance into the air, and she smiled as she inhaled their sweet scent.

But after walking for a while, she stopped, puzzled. She was sure she'd gone far enough to have passed the cottage by now, but she still hadn't reached it. She walked a little further just to be certain, then shook her head and turned to retrace her steps. Eventually she found herself back at her grandma's gate. Disappointment welled in her heart, and without thinking she kept on walking, back towards town.

This time she did go into Rose's healing centre, although she couldn't see her behind the counter or in the shop. One of the girls working there greeted her with a basket of crystals, each with a little note attached, and offered it to her as a lucky dip.

Closing her eyes, she reached in and pulled out a pretty pink crystal. She peered at the neatly written tag. *The crystal of love and inner peace, rose quartz emits a calming, cooling and loving energy that works on all of the chakras. It gently removes negativity and amplifies the calm, gentle force of self-love. It restores tranquillity, soothes heartache, and aids clarity of vision after a time of chaos or crisis. It soothes the crown and third eye chakras, producing a gentleness that comes from within and around the user. And it can restore understanding to a strained relationship or friendship, and wrap the wearer up in a cocoon of love and peace.*

The girl smiled at her. "Does that make sense to you?"

Carlie nodded shyly, then tried to hand the crystal back.

"Oh no, that's for you," the girl said. "You might like to keep it in your pocket, or place it under your pillow at night. A rose quartz pendant that sits over your heart chakra would be very helpful for you, but no hard sell. This little piece will start working for you now, and will bring you some peace and comfort."

Carlie felt her eyes well up. "Thank you," she whispered.

The girl frowned when she heard her accent, and peered more closely at her. "Oh! You must be Carlie! You're Rose's granddaughter. She said you'd arrived."

Carlie nodded.

"You look so much like your mum," she continued. "I've seen her photo in Rose's office, she's beautiful. *Was* beautiful," she added, then trailed off, embarrassed. "Sorry, look at me, prattling on. Little Miss Chatterbox, that's me."

Carlie smiled, and tried to shrug off her annoyance at the bubbly, blundering girl. She was just trying to be friendly.

"Rose is with a client at the moment, doing a healing, but she'll be finished in an hour or so. Do you want to wait for her, or can I give her a message for you?"

Carlie shook her head quickly. "No, it's okay, no message. I'll just see her at home later on. Thank you for the crystal, and it was lovely to meet you, um..."

"Oh, sorry, I'm Sharne," the girl said, and swooped in and hugged her. Carlie flinched, still unused to physical contact, especially from strangers, and Sharne slowly released her, smiling and waving as she walked out of the store.

Next she wandered up the High Street, stopping at the newsagency to buy a magazine and some postcards, then making her way back to the little park. She lay down on the grass under a huge old oak tree and started reading. It felt strange to be alone, to have nothing in particular to do, no one to visit or talk to. At home one of her parents had always been there, or she'd been at Emily's or vice versa, or she was at school or a netball game, surrounded by shrieking teenagers, or at a shopping centre or a crowded Sydney beach. Not the quietest places to be. Not the most conducive to peaceful thoughts.

No wonder she felt so bored, she mused. But maybe she should try to embrace the quiet and the solitude here – try to welcome it. She sure as hell didn't want to make conversation with anyone, or have to tell her story to them, or listen to any more stilted, awkward attempts by people trying to talk to her.

When she finished the magazine she rolled over and gazed up at the sky peeking through the leafy branches of the oak, smiling as she saw sunbeams dancing in the light that streamed through the tree's leaves. She let her mind wander, and was surprised to discover that the nightmare images that usually chased her into her waking mind were absent, and the sheer terror she felt in each moment was slowly easing. Not gone, not by a long shot, but not quite so omnipresent.

When she finally got back home to the cottage, Rose was in the kitchen, and the scent of onions, garlic and basil was a warm and soothing balm to her soul.

"Hi Sweetheart. Sit down, it will be ready in a few minutes," she said, pouring a bowl of freshly cut tomatoes from her garden into the saucepan and gently stirring. "I found something too. Here, it's a photo album of your mum when she was young."

Her grandma handed her the album, and Carlie opened it slowly, reverently – and totally unprepared for the pain that hit her. It was like looking in a mirror, down to the same hair colour, the same hairstyle and the same green eyes. She'd never seen any photos of her mum as a child – no doubt when she'd left the country she'd been travelling light – so she'd only ever known her as a short-haired blonde. But in this album, in these memories, she had dark hair still, and it was much longer than she'd ever had it as an adult.

"You look like sisters," Rose whispered hoarsely. "You're both so beautiful."

Carlie tried to smile through her bitter tears. It was so bizarre to see her mum looking like this, almost a stranger to her. And it saddened her, that she was learning how little she'd actually known her mother, or her younger self anyway. It was so eerie, seeing her mum as a child, looking so much like she herself had at the same age. She'd always felt that they were really different, almost opposites – her dark haired to her mum's blonde, her pale skinned to her mum's permanent mahogany tan – but apparently they weren't.

It was only now that she realised how much her mum had lightened her hair, how deeply she tanned her skin from a bottle, sometimes, or from hours spent sunbaking at the beach. Carlie had always surfed early in the morning or late in the afternoon, before or after the sun was too high and too hot, and if she did have to be out during the day she slathered herself in sunscreen, so she wouldn't burn her delicate pale skin. Pale skin that she now realised was a testament to her newly discovered Celtic genes.

The young Violet had pale skin and dark hair too, and there was one photo that made her heart skip a beat. She had an almost identical picture of herself on her first day of high school, with the same expression on her face. She glanced up at her grandma, whose eyes were wet with tears.

"You look just like her Carlie. It's as though the goddess has returned her to me. Not that I think you are her, don't get me wrong, I don't think you're here to be a replacement daughter. But I just feel so blessed that we were able to find each other, and share our grief. So don't ever feel like you're an imposition or a bother Sweetheart – I can't think of a single thing that would mean more to me than having you here."

She pointed to one of the pictures on the last page. Violet was wearing a lushly deep and dark purple dress – the one made from the same fabric as the violet-coloured square in the quilt upstairs.

"That's the last picture I took of her before she... went away," her grandmother said. "She left a month after her seventeenth birthday, so to me she will always be that age."

Carlie froze. She was the exact same age now. She felt a shimmer at the edge of the room, and she rubbed her eyes, suddenly dizzy. In some bizarre way it felt like she'd dropped back into her mother's childhood home, and life. That it wasn't her sitting at this table, but a rebooted version of her mum, as if the last twenty-odd years didn't exist. Violet had disappeared a month after her seventeenth birthday, and now Carlie had arrived a month after she'd turned seventeen.

"It's okay Carlie," Rose whispered gently. "I'll never replace your mother, and I don't want to, I promise. But I'm here for you, okay?"

Carlie nodded, and tried to force a smile. This was too weird. Because perhaps it wasn't that her grandma was replacing her mother for her, but rather the reverse, that she herself was standing in for her mother, becoming a replacement daughter for the woman who had lost hers. But that was a bit creepy. Her mind whirred, and her brain felt like it was being squeezed from the inside.

Her grandmother sensed her mood. "Do you mind if we watch some television while we eat, just this once?" she asked. "There's a documentary on about our area, and all the prehistoric finds they've been making lately."

Without waiting for an answer, Rose ladled out their dinner, then, balancing the plates, led the way into the lounge room. She opened a cupboard door, then lifted out a small television set and plugged it into the wall. She smiled when Carlie looked questioningly at her.

"I don't usually watch TV, but one of my friends from our circle was interviewed for the show, so I thought it would be fun to see it. And if you ever want to watch it you can," she added with a grin. "I'm not morally opposed, there's just rarely anything worth watching."

Carlie smiled back. She realised that her grandmother had a way of putting people at ease, of knowing when to talk and when to leave a subject alone for a while. Even that first night, when she'd just arrived from Sydney, all angry and broken, her grandma had been careful to give her some space. Now she took her bowl of pasta and sat down on the couch next to her and watched the show, which was far more interesting than she'd expected.

Later, when she asked, Rose took her over to one of her many bookshelves and pointed out various books that had been written about their small town, everything from travel guides and stories of myths and legends, to tomes on how the goddess manifests herself in the landscape, biographies on spiritualists who'd lived in the area, guides to witchcraft and magic, and one on what could happen to you when you walked into the mists.

She giggled. Some were clearly far-fetched, and based more on wishful thinking and a yearning for magic and faerytales on the author's part, than any actual facts. She passed over those ones, and finally picked up one of the travel guides and took it up to her room. But even this one touched on the enchantment of the area and its mystical hill, and the spiritual experiences people claimed to have had when they visited.

It seemed that this village, and this countryside, so rich with magical lore and people seeking other dimensions of spirit, was the perfect place for someone who had been cast adrift from all she knew, and who desperately needed to recover and recreate her life plan and her dreams.

Chapter 11

Finding the Way

That night Carlie's dreams were full of witches in black hats with black cats, and ghosts that chased her back into the dark tunnels of previous nightmares. She felt something on her arm which jolted her awake, and was more relieved than annoyed that Luther had woken her up again, as he'd saved her from her dreaming. She patted his head and drifted back to sleep.

Now she was in a car, being chased down a late-night cobblestone street in the rain, with black cats watching from every doorway, and the full moon illuminating the beauty of the night even as it amplified her fears. Her heart was thumping as she turned the wheel and heard tyres squealing, then felt everything start to spin. In the dream she closed her eyes and waited for the inevitable crash, and the blackness she knew would follow.

But again Luther pulled her out just in time. She sat up, gratefully patting the warm body beside her, but no matter how hard she tried, she couldn't keep her eyes open for long, and her lids soon fluttered closed again.

This time though, Carlie smiled. She was holding her mother's hand as they walked through a grassy meadow, scattered through with yellow buttercups. The sun was shining, catching her mother's golden hair. Her bleached blonde hair, as it turned out. Her own longer, darker hair flowed around her, lifting in the breeze as she spun around. They were waiting for her dad to get home from work so they could set out on their journey up the coast, heading to Byron Bay and a month-long holiday full of beach swimming, forest hiking and healthy food.

"I'm worried about your dad," her mother said.

Carlie stopped twirling. "What do you mean?" she asked.

"I keep thinking I'll get a phone call, saying he's gone off the bridge, or crashed into a tree. I know he's a great driver, careful, but I just can't shake the feeling."

Carlie put her arms around her mother, and murmured comforting words. But when the phone rang they both froze, until Carlie felt herself being pulled away from her mum. Desperately her hands reached out for her, trying to catch her, but she was swept further and further away. The ringing went on, then stopped abruptly as she surfaced back to wakefulness. Her eyes snapped open as she heard a door open, then click closed.

She let out a breath she didn't know she'd been holding, as she realised that she was in her grandmother's house, on the other side of the world from Sydney or Byron Bay, the other side of the world from her life up to this point. But the dreams had elements of truth – not only had her father died in a car crash, but her mother had too, killed when the car Carlie was driving smashed into a tree. And her grandfather had driven off a bridge, as a result, ironically, of her mother's flight from her home.

Tears poured down her cheeks as she tried to hold on to the image of her mother from her dream, when they were in the meadow together, happy. She patted Luther where he purred on the bed next to her, then slowly got up. Her mother still felt close, and she had a sudden urge to try again to get back to that cottage and read more of her book. She wanted to feel connected to her again.

Quickly dressing, she crept quietly down the stairs, careful not to wake her grandma in this pre-dawn hour. As she tiptoed into the kitchen she marvelled at the tiny streaks of pink trying to pierce the misty, grey-cloud morning. Silently she stepped outside into the back garden, shivering a little from the cold. She pulled her coat more tightly around herself, and wondered if she'd be able to find the cottage again – or if it even really existed. Again she felt the stabbing disappointment of yesterday's failed quest, and was apprehensive about it happening again.

At the gate she hesitated, staring down the laneway in each direction. A cold mist was starting to form, and she saw a butterfly hovering. Deciding that was a good sign, she set out after it, heading away from the village. Then she wondered if she really had lost her mind. Signs? Animal guides? She'd always mocked such things. She shrugged and held the rose quartz crystal she'd been given more tightly in her hand, eyes on the butterfly.

The air was chilly but invigorating, and the scent of roses was strong, which made her think of her grandma. Ah, how funny that she now thought of her as grandma, not grandmother. When had that happened? Her heart must be thawing a little. Continuing along the lane, she crossed over the path to the tor and kept going, the mist getting thicker the further she walked. She was a bit nervous. Had she just imagined the derelict cottage?

But finally there it was, a warm glow of candlelight spilling out of the window and through the mist, and the outline of a cat sitting on the ledge. She climbed the three steps to the back verandah, and wasn't particularly surprised when the door swung open again for her. She walked in, looking around for the candle whose flame she had seen from outside, but once more there was nothing lit. Shrugging, she pulled one of the candles she'd brought with her out of her pocket, lit it and placed it on the low table the book was still sitting on. Then she sat cross-legged on the floor and opened the dusty tome.

Seeing her mother's name – her real name – and her so-familiar handwriting nearly made her collapse in tears, but she took a few deep breaths, until she was steady again, then turned over to the next page. There was a sweet message from Rose, who'd given her the book as a sixteenth birthday present, which she hadn't noticed the first time, and a dedication from Violet to her Craft. Craft? Did that mean Witchcraft, Carlie wondered with a flicker of fear. She skimmed lightly through the book, more interested at this stage in the overall feeling contained within the pages than specific entries.

There was a spell for joy and a spell for health, as well as a spell for love, which had a hastily scrawled note below it that made Carlie smile.

Oops! I've read a little bit more about spellcrafting, so I've reversed this magical working. Seems it's very important not to compromise anyone's free will... And also, I didn't want to always wonder if he liked me for me, or because of the spell. I've been learning lots this week about the consequences of magic!

Her mum had also written out a dream she'd had about her animal companion, who she called her familiar, Shadow. As Carlie read that entry she sensed movement behind her, and suddenly the mysterious black cat was sitting next to her again, a soft paw on her knee. She smiled shakily, patted her head, then continued on through the book.

There were tarot readings her mother had performed, some of them the answer to a specific question she'd had, others general card readings, practise it seemed, as she worked to master the art of divination. There were sections on herbs, on crystals, on the sabbats, whatever they were. She'd also written at great length about the rituals she'd done with her mother – and the tone was loving, respectful. There was no clue, not a single hint, as to why she'd fled just a year after she began chronicling her magical journey within this book. It was all so strange.

As she continued flipping slowly through the pages, she saw the details from a reading her mum had had at Rose's healing centre, with one of the psychics who worked there. It said she had an amazing life ahead of her. That she would work at her mum's shop, help many people to heal through both reiki and herbalism, and would one day have a daughter who she and Rose could share everything with. The Power of Three, she'd written, then underlined it several times.

Carlie stopped, brow furrowed. Her mother's life seemed wonderful. She lived in a beautiful, spiritual town, where her obvious interest in magic and the esoteric was being nurtured. She had a great job waiting for her when she left school, a purpose in life – to help and heal – and a loving relationship with her parents.

What on earth had gone wrong?

She kept thumbing through the book, impressed by her mum's knowledge of herbs, crystals and divination, and sad that she'd so clearly hidden that part of herself in Australia. And she was struck with the realisation that the girl writing the book – her mother – was the same age she was now when she was mapping out her magical rituals and path of learning. Not the woman she'd become, the mother Carlie had known, but a girl just like her – a girl who had loving parents, but would soon, inexplicably, lose them. Be an orphan of sorts, just like she was.

A wave of grief overwhelmed her, and she cried – cried for the parents her mother had lost, the daughter she'd been, and the young magical self that she'd abandoned. She cried for Rose and her husband, and their terrible loss. And she cried for herself, orphaned and alone. Before, her sadness had always been intertwined with the guilt she felt for her part in the accident. This was the first time she allowed herself to feel only the loss, the awful pain of losing her anchor in the world. She felt like a small child, desperate for love, support, parental care – just at the same moment she was realising that she was now all grown up. She wasn't totally self-sufficient, and she was grateful for her grandmother, but she was alone now.

After a while the intensity of her sobbing started to ease, and she felt the mysterious cat put a gentle paw on her arm. She glanced up, and saw how much lighter it was outside. Quickly she closed the book, snuffed out her candle and hurried back to her grandma's, where she let herself quietly in the back door and put the kettle on. Rose appeared from her bedroom a moment later, and nodded gratefully to Carlie when she asked her if she wanted a cup of tea, before jumping in the shower then getting ready for work.

Over breakfast, her grandmother nervously told her that she had an idea, if Carlie was feeling bored and wanted something to do to fill the time. "There's a three-day reiki healing course happening at the centre, which starts this morning... If you'd like to come?" she offered, trailing off hesitantly, clearly worried that Carlie would snap at her again.

But Carlie felt that strange shimmer again, and thought of the psychic reading her mum had described in the book, which said that she'd help people through her healing work by using reiki and herbalism. It seemed like a wonderful coincidence, a great way to feel closer to her mother, to try to understand her better and get to know her. She nodded to her grandma and ran upstairs to brush her teeth and grab a notebook and pen.

She wasn't sure how she felt about coincidences, but she certainly didn't have anything better to do. At the very least she'd learn a new skill, and best-case scenario? She shivered as she thought again about stepping into her mother's old life. Was that possible? Would she like it? Was her presence here somehow redeeming her mother's absence all these years?

Luther weaved around her ankles, purring, and when she looked down at him he seemed to nod. Argh, perhaps she was just going crazy, thinking that cats could talk to her. But she ran down the stairs and headed out the door with her grandma to walk into the village.

The course was held in a pretty, light-filled room above the shop, and the other participants seemed really lovely, friendly without being overbearing. Carlie was surprised by how much she enjoyed it – it was fun, and it was a relief to have something else to focus on other than herself and her sadness for a change. When they stopped briefly for a lunch break, she went downstairs to find her grandmother, who was deep in conversation with a tall man with dark hair, who looked like he was close to her mum's age. He turned as she approached, and his face went white, like he'd seen a ghost.

"Carlie, this is Mike. He was your mum's, um, friend," her grandma said hesitantly.

She shook his hand, smiling politely.

"You look just like her," he whispered, clearly shocked.

This was still weird to her. Her mum had always been blonde, since Carlie was born at least, but apparently that didn't happen until she left home. Before then she'd had the same long dark hair that Carlie had now. She felt a moment of sadness, that she'd always looked so different to her mum, while longing to be just like her. To find out now that they had been so similar just added to her loneliness and feelings of loss, and the sense of isolation she was drowning in. After a lengthy silence, she looked back up and realised that Mike was speaking again.

"My daughter Rhiannon is your age, and we live close by, if you want a friend. I'm guessing you'll be in the same class at school too. No pressure though," he added quickly. "It's a small school, so I'm sure you'll get to know everyone pretty quickly. And you might want some time alone anyway. Just know we're here if you need us. We all loved your mum..."

He turned away, but not before she'd seen the pain etched so deeply across his face. She wondered what he wasn't telling her. And *really* wondered what her mother had been like when she was her age. What had it been like growing up here, so loved? With people so open to the alternative stuff her mum had obviously liked back then? She remembered her mum complaining to her friend Sandy that no one where they lived had any imagination, no one wanted to look beneath the surface, to explore anything remotely magical.

And yet, if she'd stayed here in her hometown, she would have been surrounded by all the stuff her dad used to refer to as oogeldy-boogeldy. She would have worked at the local metaphysical store, done reiki healing, treated people with herbs and read fortunes with oracle cards. Instead she lived on the other side of the world, estranged from her family and friends, working as a high-flying lawyer and limiting her exposure to the "alternative" side of life and healing to something that she and Sandy only did every now and then, just for fun, like going to the Mind Body Spirit Festival for an afternoon or having a girlie lunch followed by a fortune teller they saw for a laugh. Had it secretly meant much more to her mum?

Shaking her head, she tried to clear her thoughts. She had to grab some lunch before the afternoon session began, so she waved goodbye to her grandma and shook Mike's hand again, then headed back upstairs to the reiki room. There were salad sandwiches and jugs of fruit juice on a side table, and she gratefully grabbed a plate and a glass of juice and sat down on the floor, thumbing through her notes as she ate. After a while a few class members came and sat with her, and she was surprised to find that she liked talking to them, liked meeting some of the locals. If they were shocked that she was Rose's granddaughter they didn't say, they just welcomed her, introduced themselves, then involved her in their conversations.

Carlie loved learning the healing method her mum had once used, and proudly practised on her grandma each night for homework. When Rose promised that she'd be able to do it in the shop on weekends, if she wanted to, Carlie was shocked by how happy that idea made her feel.

She'd been so sure she would hate this town, the place and the people who she assumed had hurt her mother so badly that she'd run away, but already she felt at home. And while she was still shy around her grandmother, the excruciating awkwardness she'd feared would be between them forever was definitely decreasing a little.

Chapter 12

The Journey Within

The clock chimed four, and Carlie looked up at it with a sigh. She'd promised to meet her grandmother at half past so they could get some groceries and make dinner together, but leaving the house was the last thing she felt like doing. Everything seemed so hard, so much effort, today. She'd been in and out of nightmares for all of the previous night, and felt like she could sleep for days. Reluctantly she put down the book she was reading and tidied away her lunch dishes. Luther looked up at her and miaowed, and she crouched down to pat him.

"You hungry, boy?" He gazed up at her with his big green eyes, so like the cat at the cottage, and she laughed. "All right, you know I can't resist your sweet little face. C'mon, I'll get your dinner, but then I have to go. I can't be late for Grandma."

When she arrived at the healing centre though, a little out of breath but right on time, Rose was helping a customer, and gave her an apologetic smile and a little wave. Relieved, Carlie browsed through the shop as she waited, poring over the pretty crystal jewellery, casting her eye over the well-stocked bookshelves, flicking through the rack of hippie-style clothes and flowing robes, then lazily shuffling through an open pack of oracle cards. Without much thought, or serious interest, she pulled out three cards.

Acknowledge Anger. Anger itself isn't a bad thing, it's what you do with it that can be damaging. Expressed well it can help you change your life, release things that no longer serve you and create a fresh start.

Spiritual Rebirth. Let your old self die and be reborn, by performing a ritual to release your attachment to your past. Once you let go you can move forward fearlessly – transformed, renewed and re-inspired.

The Moon. Connect to the cycles of the moon, which represent life, death and rebirth. The energy of this silvery orb activates your intuition and will imbue you with the power to manifest your dreams.

Gazing at the cards she'd chosen, she had to admit that the three she'd picked seemed quite relevant for where her somewhat tragic life was at right now. But then she flicked through the rest of the deck and rolled her eyes. *Nice coincidence.* Any of them could be applied to her life if she thought about it hard enough. She looked up as her grandmother came over.

"I'm so sorry Sweetheart, I'll still be here for another hour, then I've got to take the meditation class because Sharne isn't well, so I won't be home until late. Will you be okay on your own?" she asked.

Carlie nodded, part of her quite glad that she wouldn't have to spend time with her grandmother that night.

"Take that card deck with you," Rose added. "Have a play, read the meanings, write in your journal if you want to."

Grudgingly Carlie thanked her, then slowly walked back to the cottage. She was mildly curious about the cards, especially after reading her mum's Book of Shadows, so once she got home she hurried upstairs to her room and flopped down on her bed. Stretching out, she flicked through the deck until she found the three cards she'd chosen in the store, and laid them out in order. Then she opened the guidebook. It explained that in a three-card reading, the first card represented the past, the second the present, and the third the future. Intrigued, she delved further to discover their individual meanings.

Past: Acknowledge Anger.

Anger itself isn't a bad thing, it's what you do with it that can be damaging. Expressed well it can help you change your life, release things that no longer serve you and create a fresh start.

Anger has for so long been portrayed as negative, but it is neither "good" nor "bad", it just is. It is an emotional response to an event, circumstance or person, and you should always be honest with your emotions, acknowledging how you feel, working out why you feel that way, learning what you need to know from the situation, then releasing it and moving on.

This card is asking you to examine what is making you angry, and to honour your feelings. Don't try to deny your anger, sweep it under the carpet or repress it, as repressed anger can lead to illness and fiery, damaging outbursts. Equally however, don't wallow in it or use it as an excuse to lash out at others or as a reason for your bad behaviour. While there is often a valid cause of your anger, it is not an excuse to treat people badly.

A familiar rush of anger coloured Carlie's cheeks, but she also felt recognition, as well as a tiny kernel of hope unfurling within her heart. She couldn't let her overwhelming anger at the injustice of her parents being dead, and her being sent away from all she knew, turn her into a bitter, mean-spirited person. That's not who she was, or who she wanted to be.

Besides, being angry certainly wasn't helping her, it was just making everything harder, and making her hate herself more. Being so angry all the time and lashing out at people just made her feel bad about herself. Seeing the hurt she'd caused Emily so clearly emblazoned across her friend's face had mortified her, but at the time she just couldn't stop herself. It was as though she thought that the more everyone else hurt, the less she would. That if she could inflict enough pain on others, hers would be lessened. Which was ridiculous. It didn't work like that.

She was embarrassed when she thought about how she'd treated Sandy too, and especially mortified by how she'd acted towards her grandmother. But while she knew they would all tell her that it was okay, it was understandable, that she shouldn't beat herself up for the way she'd lashed out at them in her anger and grief, enough was enough.

Their patience wouldn't last forever. She knew she couldn't change how she'd already acted, what she'd already done, but she could take responsibility for her behaviour, starting now. She could acknowledge that she was angry, and had every right to be, then get over herself. Stop being a spoiled brat. She wasn't the only person who'd lost someone – Sandy and Emily had lost their best friends too, and her grandmother had lost her daughter all over again.

Expressing your anger gently and positively – blah blah blah... Be honest, compassionate and respectful, truthful about your own part in the situation, and ready to apologise if you have contributed to the problem in any way – yada yada yada... Once you've identified... ponder the situation, etc etc etc...

She skimmed the meaning, rolling her eyes here and there, dismissing much of it, and hearing her dad's words of scepticism in her mind, which made her smile. But then another bit caught her attention.

Sometimes however a situation is beyond your ability to change or control, and you must learn to deal with it in a constructive rather than destructive way. It can be hard to accept some situations – the death of a loved one, failing at something you really wanted to achieve, a terrible injustice in the community or the world – and being angry is perfectly reasonable. For a while.

Eventually though you must move on, come to some kind of acceptance of the situation, and let its power over you go. This doesn't mean you forget what happened, but simply that you work to reduce its power over you, and stop using it as fuel for negativity or as an excuse to become self-destructive or cruel. The only real loser in that scenario is you, because living in anger, bitterness and eventual regret is no kind of life.

As reluctant as Carlie was to face it, she knew this was true. And it was time for her to start working out how to go on. She was here now, living with her grandmother, and she should be grateful for that, rather than petty, selfish and cruel. Yes, her life now would be much different to how she'd planned it, but that didn't have to mean it would be terrible. Mourning her lost future wouldn't give it back to her, and she still had some choices left to her.

And maybe she owed it to her parents to make the best of this situation. She was lucky to be alive, as Emily had reminded her, and she should start acting like it, rather than making the people around her suffer – and making herself suffer too. What was that expression? Cutting off your nose to spite your face?

As she made the decision to accept her new circumstances, she felt a sense of loss, as though it meant she was turning her back on her parents. But stubbornly clinging to the idea that she should sacrifice her own life to keep them close didn't serve her, or them. And she knew they would expect her to continue on, not give up her future in some stupid act of self-sacrifice – and a pointless sacrifice at that, which would only negate her own happiness, because nothing she could do would ever bring them back.

Perhaps just as importantly, she had to forgive herself for her anger too. Her response was quite normal, she imagined – anyone would feel angry and bitter, feel the injustice of losing both parents so young. But she had wallowed for long enough. The people who cared about her might forgive her for a short-term outburst, but that would soon wear thin. Already she felt embarrassed by her behaviour, by the self-indulgence of her "poor little me" act. It was time for her to stop all that and take control of her actions. She was responsible for herself, and for how she made other people feel. Pleased with her conclusions, she flicked through to the meaning of the next card.

Present: Spiritual Rebirth.

Let your old self die and be reborn, by performing a ritual to release your attachment to your past. Once you let go you can move forward fearlessly – transformed, renewed and re-inspired.

When you draw this card it is calling you to let go of an event or a belief that has been holding you back, in order for you to step forward lightly and fearlessly into a more positive, more authentic future, one where you can achieve your potential and become all that you can be, free from the shackles of whatever weighty issue you are dragging around with you.

Performing a ritual of release is a powerful way to let go of the emotions you've been carrying around for so long and lay down the baggage from your past, opening the way for healing and allowing you to move forward with more energy, strength and power. There are many ways to do this, and the best one for you will depend very much on what you want to let go of, and on which actions are meaningful for you.

A ritual? What did that even mean, she wondered, picturing chanting monks in orange robes and stony-faced priests waving huge brass containers of incense. But her scepticism was quickly interrupted – an impatient miaow was all the warning she got before Luther leaped up onto her bed and gazed at her sternly, then settled down comfortably on her pillow, face serene but tail still twitching with annoyance at her. Fine, she'd try to take this more seriously, she vowed. Certainly she would like to let go of some of her baggage.

You may wish to write down what the issue is, or draw a picture that represents it. Then burn the paper in a small cauldron, in a candle flame or in a fire, releasing your attachment to the past and cleansing yourself through the element of fire as you do so.

Or you could work with the element of earth, transferring the emotions weighing you down into a pebble, stone or crystal. To do this you can hold the stone and use the power of intention to transfer your emotions into it, employ a shamanic technique and physically blow your pain into the stone, sleep with the pebble or crystal under your pillow, or have it in your pocket as you go for a walk, allowing it to absorb everything you want to let go of. Then bury it in the ground, so all the negativity is transmuted and transformed by the earth.

You could do a similar ceremony by pouring the emotions you want to release into a leaf or feather, then letting the wind take it away, clearing your pain and suffering with the power of air.

The element of water can also be a powerful part of your releasement ritual, as it is associated with emotions, cleansing and letting go. You could throw your pebble or leaf into a flowing river, a well or the ocean, knowing the effect of the past is being washed away as the object is purified by the water.

It went on and on, with more suggestions, about ritual baths and sacred springs amongst many other things, but she got the picture. Sort of. She skipped ahead to the end of the page.

It's important to remember that every day the world is born anew – and this applies to you too. You can let go of anything that has angered you, saddened you or limited you, and begin again with a clean slate. Create a ritual to shrug off your grief, your fear, your anger, your regret, and become your authentic self. Who you are now, and who you want to become going forward. It all starts in this moment, if you let it.

Carlie grimaced. It was certainly true that recent events had made her less considerate than she normally was, or wanted to be. Sighing, she realised that she had to face it – she'd been cruel to people, and that was not what her "authentic self", whatever that was, should be. And she liked the sentiment. Every day is a new day...

A new day, a new start. That sounded nice. As cynical as she was, she figured there was no harm in doing what was suggested, some kind of ritual to let go of her mean and nasty self, or, she corrected herself, in a moment of self-forgiveness, the pain that was making her vent at those around her.

She didn't really know what would be the most meaningful way to release the impact of the last few weeks from her heart, her mind and her psyche. And she didn't want to lose everything – she didn't want to let go of her love for her parents, and she would never stop missing them, or wishing they were with her. But she knew that she had to somehow let go of her anger and guilt, and the way it was influencing her actions and personality.

It was making her lash out at those who didn't deserve it, and making her bitter, and unsure of herself and her future. Somehow she had to accept what had happened and move forward. *Easier said than done though*. Sighing, she looked up the meaning of the last card.

Future: The Moon.

Connect to the cycles of the moon, which represent life, death and rebirth. The energy of this silvery orb activates your intuition and will imbue you with the power to manifest your dreams.

This card asks you to trust your own inner power, and remember your own inner strength. Consider how you can start to integrate the lunar energies into your life, to bring more magic into your everyday existence, and to honour and develop your intuition. It can also mean that you must look deeper than you have been, because something is being hidden from you, or there is a very important truth that you are refusing to see.

The moon is linked to the subconscious, and can help you connect to your shadow self, to the hidden aspects of your psyche, and to the mystical realms of divination and the inner worlds. It enhances intuition and sensitivity, increases psychic visions, and boosts dream awareness and spiritual awakening.

She started skimming again when it turned to ancient lunar goddesses and the phases of the moon reflecting the stages of a human life. *Huh?* Yet despite her scepticism, she was intrigued.

Historically, these periods of lunar waxing, waning and completion were used to influence the outcome of rituals, spells and ceremonies, and today they are still used to empower any project you want to complete or dream you want to manifest, and to help you connect to your inner magic.

The moon is also symbolic of the feminine energy and power that runs through the universe and within every person. It is a sense of gentleness and intuition you can tap in to, a source of energy that is calm, receptive, centred and spiritual, with a quiet yet intense power. This feminine vibration encourages you to embrace qualities such as nurturing, contemplation, receptivity, emotional intelligence and peace. If this card has come up in your reading, take some time to examine some of the ways in which you either need to nurture others or be nurtured yourself, and how you can access the quiet place within and connect with your inner wisdom.

The energy of the moon, and of feminine power, is present in the moon itself, in the healing power of sacred springs, in gentle rain and the ebbing and flowing of the tides, and in the rainbow-depths of a moonstone crystal, which will help awaken your inner eye, your inner heart and your inner self.

For the first time, Carlie realised just how strong she'd had to be recently, leaving her home, her friends, everything that was safe and familiar to her, and having to start over again on the other side of the world with a total stranger. Perhaps it was time she acknowledged that she might need a little nurturing, and to treat herself a little more gently, rather than the constant self-loathing. Continuing to read, she skimmed over the lunar meditation, but made a mental note to go in and buy a piece of moonstone from her grandma's shop, so she could connect with the nurturing lunar energy in that way.

At the very least, spend time outside in the moonlight and become aware of its phases as it waxes and wanes, which will activate your intuition, connect you to your feminine energy, and imbue you with the power to manifest your dreams.

Part of Carlie was rolling her eyes at these comforting new-age words, but another part of her was wondering. She hurried down the stairs to the kitchen, where she'd noticed that her grandmother's calendar had the moon phases included for each day. Tonight was apparently the dark moon, which sounded significant, so after making a cup of tea, she went to Rose's bookshelf and flicked through some of the many books on magic.

It seemed that the dark moon was the time just before the new moon, when it was totally invisible – and supposedly it was the perfect time to release emotions and banish negativity so that you could move forward at the new moon into a new way of seeing, feeling and being. Whether it was just a coincidence or something else, the fact that tonight was the dark moon did fit in well with her card reading's instructions to release something from her past.

After making herself some dinner, Carlie ran a bath, adding some jasmine and chamomile essential oils, then relaxed into it and read another one of her grandma's magical books, trying to get her head around the kind of ritual that might work for her. Once she'd dried off and thrown on some clothes, she went back upstairs to her room and sat down at the small desk with some pretty stationery. She lit a candle, then picked up her favourite purple pen and started to write down all that was in her heart. She poured out all of her anger, her guilt, her pain, and her sense of betrayal and loss.

When she was finally done she felt drained and totally exhausted, yet strangely calm. Carefully she got her things ready for the morning, then curled up in her bed, the quilt pulled tight around her, comforting her with its link to her mother. She smiled when she heard Luther come in and settle on her feet, a watcher through the darkest phase of the moon, the darkest part of the night, the darkest night of her soul. Later she heard her grandmother come home and go quietly to bed, and for once her presence in the cottage soothed her.

It was still dark when her alarm went off early the next morning. As silently as she could, she crept from her bed, pulled some clothes on, picked up her bag and tiptoed down the stairs and out through the kitchen then the backyard. She walked carefully, placing each foot tentatively so as not to fall, or make too much noise, her eyes slowly adjusting to the dark, and her mind recalling the way she had already walked several times.

She turned in to the laneway to Summer Tor, and breathed in with awe when she emerged into the lower meadow, the bulk of the hill making the faintest silhouette in the darkness, the sky around it sprinkled with stars, the sense of immensity and beauty touching her soul and wrapping around her heart. She began climbing, her heart rate speeding up, the chill in the air cooling her reddening cheeks.

When she reached the top she sat down on the grass, facing east, where the sun would soon rise on a new day. Pulling out the small candle in its glass container, she lit it with a match. The flame flickered for a moment then grew strong. She gazed into its centre, her focus reduced to the small wavering light – according to the oracle deck, an aspect of the power of the element of fire. Then she took out the words she'd written last night and burned the paper slowly, imagining that she saw the ghosts of her pain being released into the darkness just before the dawn.

She felt a little strange and spaced out, yet she was hyper-aware of everything around her – the cold air on her face, the wind in her hair, the deep, throbbing vibration of the earth aligning with her breath, so that it was as though she and the planet inhaled and exhaled as one. And she realised that she felt anchored and protected, like she was being held safe by the very earth of this ancient land that had become her new home.

Watching carefully, she waited until the mists rose around her, reaching out to her with their sense of mystery and magic. As they came closer she breathed in the watery molecules, felt them on her skin, cleansing her, soothing her, washing her clean. Washing away the painful parts of her recent past, and leaving her feeling somewhat reborn, just like the oracle card had said. She inhaled deeply, calmly, then exhaled slowly, still feeling as though she was in another dimension, a gentler, more nurturing place.

Then she gazed at the sky to the east, distinguishing each of the many shades of colour that washed across it as the sun prepared to rise. The faintest outline of the moon was visible for a moment as it rose with the sun, just the barest hint of silver in the pale sky, but when the sun peeked over the horizon a few moments later, the outline disappeared altogether in the radiant solar glow.

As the sun inched its way above the horizon, millimetre by millimetre, she felt the air of the new day blowing towards her, and breathed it in, feeling it brush away any last vestige of the torturous emotions she'd been casting off this morning. In awe she sat there, watching the sun rise, watching the sky turn every shade of pink-orange-gold-lavender, and feeling a weight lift from her heart. Carefully she blew out her tiny candle flame, bidding farewell to the element of fire that had burned away her pain.

Rising slowly, she whispered her thanks to the earth that had held her safe during this morning's ritual. She smiled at the last wisps of mist curling around the summit of the tor, and honoured them, and the element of water, for cleansing her so she could move forward with peace and confidence.

Still facing east, she breathed deeply and thanked the element of air and the power of a new day for giving her the clarity she needed to begin again, to make a fresh start with her grandmother, and with her life and attitude, and to transform her grief into something more productive. Then she turned and made her way slowly back down the slope, slipping in the back door and back into her bed before anyone but Luther knew she'd been out.

Suddenly she laughed. What on earth had she been doing up on a windy hill in the dark, while everyone else was still in bed, sensibly sleeping? Talking to herself, to the planets, to the very air and earth itself? Being in this place was doing her head in, encouraging her to believe in all this new-age claptrap. How was lighting a candle or whispering to the mists going to help her get over her anger, her grief? Help her be kinder, help her heal?

Yet in the days that followed Carlie did feel calmer and a little less sad, and more patient and respectful of her grandma. *Go figure.*

Chapter 13

A Circle of Magic

A few mornings later Carlie pushed upwards through sleep, her hand still in the woman's, the gentle voice still echoing in her head. And the ringing of the phone continued. She tried to pull the threads of the dream back around her, but they were floating away with the faery woman. *Faery?* Shaking her head, she rolled her eyes at herself. Then she heard her name being called, and somehow knew that it was not from this realm – which made her laugh. Now she was hearing things too!

As she wiped the sleep from her eyes, she remembered that her grandma was taking her away for the weekend. They were driving north, to a quaint little village where Elsie, Rose's oldest, closest friend, lived. It sounded pretty boring to her, but she was trying to be gracious, to treat her grandmother with more respect and appreciation. Plus, it might be interesting to meet this Elsie.

And there was a stone circle nearby, which Rose thought Carlie might like to see, and a mountain with an ancient tomb on the top, reputed to be the resting place of a long-ago faery queen. She smiled. No wonder she'd been dreaming about faeries. Not that she was complaining – it was a welcome respite from the nightmares.

Dragging herself out of bed, she had a quick shower, then picked up her backpack and went downstairs. Her grandma was packing a hamper of food in the kitchen. “Morning Sweetheart. I hope you slept well. Do you want to eat now, or shall we get on the road?”

Carlie shrugged. “We can go now, if you want. I don’t care.” Then she smiled, trying to soften her words. Hadn’t she just decided to be kinder to her grandma, more patient?

They drove for half the day, watching the sun rise over golden fields, passing through beautiful woodland areas and old-fashioned villages. Her grandmother was quiet, content to watch the countryside go by, lost in her own thoughts, and Carlie was grateful that neither felt obliged to fill the silence with meaningless chatter, that Rose never pushed her to talk when she didn’t want to.

Halfway there they stopped for a pot of tea and scones with jam and cream in a cute garden centre, and Carlie laughed at how typically British it all was, or her idea of British anyway.

Opening up a little, she told her grandma a bit more about her life in Australia, about straw hats, sunscreen and sunshine, milkshakes and meat pies, coffee shops on every corner, and the expectation that everyone would be fit, healthy and sun-kissed, not to mention talkative and outgoing. She had to admit that she was really enjoying the reticence to intrude that the English seemed to have, their appreciation for quiet and solitude, and their ability to let people open up in their own time, without being pressured.

After stretching their legs, they got back on the motorway, and Rose told Carlie about the woman they were going to visit. They’d been friends since their college days, when they’d trained to be nurses, and had studied herbalism, naturopathy, crystal healing and art therapy together once they’d graduated.

When Violet had run away and her father had taken his own life, it was this friend, Elsie, who had helped keep the darkness at bay for Rose. She’d moved in with her for a few months, made sure she remembered to eat, looked after her healing centre, and let Rose cry all her tears on a supportive shoulder. And when Elsie was nursing her husband through a lengthy cancer battle a few years later, Rose had happily returned the favour. Carlie was touched by the women’s obvious love for one another, and the depth of a friendship that had endured for more than forty years. Would she ever find a friend like that? She'd always thought that Emily would be that person, but now she didn't even know if she'd ever see her again.

As they got closer to the village, the looming mountain got bigger and bigger, and Rose pointed out the small bump on the top, the reputed resting place of Maeve, known variously as a goddess, a faery and a mythical ancient queen. Carlie was looking forward to climbing the hill – stretching her legs, working her muscles, challenging herself, and letting physical pain replace the mental and emotional for a while.

They arrived in time for a late lunch, and Elsie was as lovely and welcoming as Rose had described her. Carlie still felt she was in the way though, so when Elsie suggested that her grandson could drop her at the stone circle on his way back to London, she accepted gratefully, relieved that she could leave the two women to catch up in peace. Brett drove her down one of the small winding roads that were so prevalent, and so pretty, in this area, then pulled over and pointed to a small gap in the hedge, explaining that it was a ten-minute walk before she'd see the stone circle, which was across a field or two and to the left. Then he waved goodbye and drove off.

Carlie wandered slowly down the narrow, sun-dappled dirt path, a faery path, smiling at the sweet scent of wild roses, meditating on the beauty and the energy and the lush greenness of this place. It was so beautiful, so silent of man-made noise, yet so full of the joyous sounds of nature – bees humming, birds singing overhead, sheep crying out to each other, the wind moving gently through the leaves.

Curiously, she could feel the energy of the stone circle before she saw it. A small sign pointed the way through a field, so she climbed over the wooden stile and walked nervously through a flock of sheep and up a small hill to where the circle lay in the shade of several oak trees. After climbing through another fence, she finally stood before the stones, awed by their majesty and power.

The isolation of the place touched her, and made her feel strong, and connected to a sense of wildness she'd somehow lost. Reverently she entered the circle, her hand brushing the entrance stone as she passed through, and absorbing a tingle of electricity that raced through her body to her heart. She felt tiny, totally inconsequential, yet at the same time a part of the whole web of life. Standing there in the centre, the pain of her loss seemed slightly less – it stopped seeming quite so personal, so cruel and senseless, and became part of the great tapestry of the world.

She felt tears well up – tears of joy, of belonging, of being in touch with some greater mystery. She felt connected to the wisdom of the stones, these eternal guardians, and to the patterns of the earth. And suddenly she felt that she understood the insignificance of a single life compared to the enormity of humanity – as well as the massive importance, in their own little sphere, of each precious life. Totally important, yet without significance – the paradox of life.

Elsie had shared with her some of the myths surrounding this formation. There were tales of battle, of armies meeting and clashing, and the conquered being turned to stone. Of giants who gathered to plot against a wizard, who froze them where they stood. She liked the last one best though, of priestesses transformed by a disapproving priest into statues, trapped within the rocks as they celebrated the full moon, dancing outside in its golden light, transfixed forever in a moment of joy and wonder.

It felt like a magical realm here, a space between the worlds, and a place totally outside of time. Tentatively at first, she stood in the centre of the circle and whispered a prayer of love and thanks to the universe. Then, as she started to feel more comfortable, more confident, she raised her arms to the sky, closed her eyes and threw her head back, asking aloud for the wisdom and strength to discover how to move on with her life when everything she had ever known had been shattered. How to be more patient with herself, and with her grandmother too, and more grateful for Rose and the love she clearly felt for her.

Sinking to the ground, she stared up at the branches of the oak trees surrounding the circle. There was said to be an oakman living within every tree, and according to legend, if you embraced an oak and asked it a question, the spirit of the oak would send you the answer in a dream that night.

So, swallowing down her fear that she would look silly, she slowly walked over and stretched her arms as far as she could around the trunk of the largest one, resting her heart and her forehead against its ancient girth. She whispered her wish and felt it taken away by the wind, whisked off to another dimension. Then she sat down with her back against the trunk, enjoying the sun on her face and the warmth of the earth. She composed epic poems to the beauty of the world, imagined faeries in the undergrowth, watched the sunlight filtering through the trees. And suddenly she was so glad to be there, so happy to be alone for a while in this magical place where she felt her mother so close.

As the ghost of a song flitted into her mind, she remembered a day last year when she'd been so upset about a boy at school, a boy she could barely recall now. Her mum had been trying to cheer her up, to comfort her, to let her know that she'd always be there for her, no matter what. But her eyes welled with tears as she realised that her mum would not be able to be there for her now – or ever. Clearly that had been a promise too hard to keep. She would have to look after herself, solve her own problems.

Yet as she sat under the oak tree, with the sunshine on her face and the earth solid beneath her, she felt connected to her mother in a special way, as though she wasn't really gone, as though she would always be a part of her. And she felt strangely at peace with herself for once, at one with the world.

Submerging herself in nature seemed to bring her closer to her mum somehow, and also make her more able to hear the sound of her own heart, and the longing of it too. What did she want from life now? Where did she wish to be? Who did she aspire to be? How could she overcome her pain and bitterness? When would she stop being so impatient with her grandmother? What kind of person did she want to become?

When Rose and Elsie turned up just before dusk to pick her up, Carlie was sitting under her tree, weaving a daisy chain and murmuring stories to a little lamb that had come over and sat down next to her, the only one of the flock brave enough to approach anywhere near her.

Chapter 14

The Life of Meaning

That night she dreamed of her mother. They were making daisy chains together in a green meadow, with butterflies dancing around them and bluebirds swooping overhead. Her mother looked younger, so carefree and sun-kissed, and she was laughing with more joy than she'd ever displayed in life. As she finished a longer daisy chain and placed it on her head like a crown, she put a hand on Carlie's arm and stared into her eyes.

"Darling, I'm not lost to you," she said gently.

Carlie felt her eyes filling with hot tears, and she brushed at them angrily. "How could you just leave me like this?" her dream self demanded, lips quivering into a pout.

Her mother sighed. "Please don't despair my love. I'm still a part of you, and I'm still alive in your heart and your mind, in your memories. I'm still a part of your soul. My body has returned to the earth, to nature, but you can feel me close to you whenever you're outside, breathing in the beauty of the world."

"But it's not the same! You're not here! I want you back."

"You don't need me any more Carlie, it's time for you to live your life," her mother said. "I'd always planned to take you back to England to meet your grandma – I knew you'd get on so well with her, and you'd be perfect to work with her in the healing centre.

Don't you see, it's all worked out for the best! You can bring the joy to the woman that I never could. You're the daughter she always wanted, that I could never be."

Carlie felt frightened as her mother started to fade away, but then she saw her grandmother approaching her, and she was bathed in the most beautiful feeling of love and contentment.

The feeling clung to her as she woke up early the next morning, snuggled up on the couch with Elsie's dog on her feet. Slowly she became aware of the sound of the kettle boiling, butter frying, and two women laughing together. Carlie began to see her grandma in a new light – not as a demanding parent, a grieving mother, a reluctant caregiver, a business person or a healer, but as a best friend, and as a woman who had worked hard to still find goodness and laughter in a world that had dealt her such savage blows.

Both of these women had endured incredible tragedy and loss, but instead of falling into bitterness and despair, they had become even more caring, even more selfless, even more keen to help others on their journey through life. It seemed strange now that she'd been so afraid of her grandmother. She was so full of love, and Carlie was impressed by her strength too, and hoped that one day she would develop some herself. As she thought this, she felt her mother around her, smiling and nodding.

"Yes darling, you were always my strong and loving daughter," her mum whispered. She felt a hand on her head, but when she lifted hers to try to touch it, there was nothing there.

But the two women had noticed she was awake, and beckoned her over, fingers on lips to indicate quiet. She tiptoed across to the kitchen, feet cold on the slate floor, and gazed out the window to where they were pointing. Two rabbits, looking like mother and baby, were sitting out in the garden, nibbling on grass, noses twitching. The sun was just starting to rise, turning the last wisps of mist into a swirl of pale pink and gold. And in the distance, still surrounded by mist at the summit, was the mountain they'd seen on their approach yesterday.

"That's Winter Hill," Elsie said. "Your grandma thought you might like to climb it. There's a beautiful view from the top, and the grave of an ancient faery queen, or so they say."

Carlie looked over at her gran, who laughed.

"My climbing days are over Sweetheart, but there's a lovely old tea room at the bottom, so we thought we'd drink tea and eat scones while you hike to the top."

Carlie smiled, and raced off to have a quick shower and get dressed. "You'll be wanting something to eat first," Elsie called out after her. "It's a long way up. Come on, we're making pancakes. Then we've got a few errands to run, but the hill's not going anywhere."

A few hours later, Carlie found herself alone in the car park, about halfway up the mountain. She waved goodbye to Elsie and her grandmother, who said they'd be back in four hours to pick her up, then she gazed skyward. A bank of heavy grey clouds was moving in on her, but she hoped they'd continue on their way, and let the sun come back out to illuminate her mini pilgrimage. Instead they got darker and more threatening, and she paused for a moment, hesitant.

Over breakfast she'd flicked through the guidebook, which warned that the weather on the mountain was incredibly changeable, and the climb to the top was not for the faint of heart. She'd dismissed the idea that it could be dangerous as simply a writer seeking drama, but now that she was here, she was starting to believe it.

Yet she had several hours to kill, so, deciding to cross her fingers and hope for the best, she hoisted her little backpack onto her shoulders, took a deep breath and set out along the hedgerow-lined laneway, in the pale light of a completely grey sky. While it wasn't raining yet, thank god, the atmosphere was thick and slightly wet, with a kind of misty, swirling fog surrounding her and making her vision a little blurry around the edges.

Gazing down at her closed fist, she rolled her eyes at herself. She was armed with a pebble that she'd picked up yesterday at the stone circle. According to legend, you were supposed to find a small stone and pour into it all your emotional baggage – the pain you wanted to release, the regret you wanted to forget, the grief you wanted to transmute – and carry it with you on your journey up the mountain, before leaving it on the cairn of rocks at the top to symbolically leave your problems up there to be cleansed by the clear mountain air. She wasn't sure how true it was or if it would work –

this was a strange and shadowy land, of myth and legend and magical tales – but she figured it was worth a shot. And it so closely matched one of the rituals the oracle deck had suggested in her reading, that she decided there was no harm in trying. No one knew she was doing it, so what did she have to lose, beyond her anger and her grief?

The small rocky path, lined with larger stones and blackthorn hedges, soon became narrower, and a tiny stream rushed down over the crevices. Water seeped into her heavy boots, and she wrinkled her nose as the cold hit her feet. It quickly became warm and squishy though, and she could feel the flush in her cheeks from the exertion of climbing the steep mountainside. A rock slid out from under her and she faltered momentarily, but she quickly steadied herself, determined to pay more attention to where each foot was going. Tread gently on the earth, they said, both literally and metaphorically.

When the laneway ended she walked through a wooden turnstile and started climbing straight upwards through the paddock. A few sheep were watching her, and calling out, their voices piercing. But were they encouraging her to keep going, or warning her to go back?

Soon she had to stop to get her bearings. She had absolutely no idea where she was going or how much further it should be, because suddenly the mists had descended, or she'd moved into them, and she could only see a few inches in front of her. It was the strangest sensation, walking into this swirling thickness – so Otherworldly. Smiling, she imagined the mists clearing and finding herself in the land of the faeries. Of course she didn't believe in them, but it really felt like a space between the worlds had opened up, much like it had at the stone circle. It was all so mystical and mysterious.

Giggling, she wondered if she should be hoping for an Otherworldly guide. Then she shrugged. She could sense that she was climbing upwards, and the only way was up, right? She did feel vaguely curious about the danger element though – these were obviously the conditions they advised people *not* to climb the mountain in, being surrounded by heavy mists that so obscured the vision. Would she get to the top without knowing it and fall off the mountain? And where was the top? Shaking herself mentally, she reminded herself that Elsie had lived here for years, and wouldn't have suggested that she do anything dangerous.

It was really steep though, much steeper than Summer Hill, and so much higher. She felt so out of shape – her breath was coming fast, her heart was pounding and her legs were burning – and she didn't know how much further it could be to the top. For a moment she thought about stopping, of giving up and turning back around, but she kept scrambling up the slope, determined to reach the summit.

And finally a shape loomed out of the mists, and she stumbled upon the mysterious cairn, made up of thousands of tonnes of rocks perched atop this lonely mountain like a pyramid. Clumsily she climbed it too, and found a flat, grassy surface at its peak, with a tiny stone pile in the middle, like a model-sized cairn.

Feeling a bit silly, she held her pebble in her hands, clutched to her chest. She tried to think of the right words to say, something to remember this moment by, but eventually she realised that the words weren't important right now, it was the emotions she was trying to release – the overwhelming pain that had no spoken word equivalent, the grief that still crippled her and left her speechless, the guilt she tried to hide and could never put into words. And so she gently laid her pebble on the top of the pile, then hesitantly backed away.

Gazing around herself, she became aware of her surroundings again. As the mists thickened she felt a flicker of fear, and for a moment she wished that it was blue-skied and sunny, so she could see the amazing views and get the landscape into perspective – and figure out where she was and where she needed to go. But the swirling mists suited her mood, and they had their own special, albeit slightly spooky, charm. All she could see around her in any direction was white, like she was walking through the centre of a cloud. So strange. So magical. So Otherworldly.

A momentary flashback to yesterday's dream of the faery woman hit her, the one she'd had just before she and Rose had set out on their journey here, but the images floated away in the mists before she could pinpoint what it had been about, what had happened, and what she needed to know. Shrugging, she breathed in the clean, wet, thick air. She felt proud that she'd made it to the top of the mountain, but also a little nervous about how well she would make her way back to the bottom, as she plunged down the rocky slope then slipped and slid her way through the paddocks.

Slowly she climbed down the cairn, feet shaky and her entire focus on each next step, until she was back on the level top of the mountain. She sighed with relief as she finally touched firm ground, then gasped as she stared ahead. A woman was walking towards her, mist shrouding her face and form, and there was something not quite right about her. She was gliding through the mist, silently, hand outstretched, and almost close enough to touch.

Carlie felt her face drain of what little colour it had as she realised it was the woman from her dream – the same blue-clad woman she'd encountered on Summer Tor. Maeve? A ghost? Some faery queen from another realm? She looked wildly around herself, hoping for an escape, some way out and off, but she was trapped on top of the mountain, stranded by the very mist that seemed to be breathing life into the apparition before her.

"Who are you?" Carlie whispered. "Are you real?"

The woman smiled, and seemed to gather all of the mists into her long blue robes, into her very being. "Do not be scared Carlie, I am not going to hurt you… And I am not a symptom of the loss of your sanity," she added. While her mouth didn't move, Carlie could hear the laughter in her voice. She blushed. Was this woman reading her thoughts too? How could she know that she'd just questioned her own state of mind – and not for the first time? Surely either this country was bordering on crazy, or she was. And she wasn't sure which option scared her more.

"You have to let it go Carlie," the woman said softly, her honey-voiced tone as comforting as the words themselves. "You are not responsible for what happened."

Carlie felt as though a warm cocoon was enveloping her, soothing her heart, easing her pain, erasing her guilt. Was this another spell being woven over her? She tried to focus, to concentrate, to remember what she needed to know about herself and that night, but it was all melting away.

"No," she gasped, desperately trying to hold on to the threads of her life that made sense, awful though they were. "It *was* my fault. I caused the crash. And I can never let that go, never forget that it was me who killed my parents."

The woman glided even closer to Carlie, and wrapped her arms and her cloak around her. The warmth felt so good that she wanted to just stay there forever, but she fought against it. She couldn't surrender to this sweet comfort, couldn't let herself dissolve in this sense of peace, beautiful though it was, and act as though the events of that night had never happened.

"Carlie, it was not your fault," she insisted.

"Well, we'll have to agree to disagree on that one," Carlie said, voice surly. "What I don't understand is why it happened."

"Not everything has a reason," the woman replied calmly.

"But Mum always said everything happens for a reason, that there's a divine plan to the world. That our mission in life is to work out what our purpose is and fulfil our destiny. And..." she paused, voice a whisper. "In my dream she said that she and Dad died so that I would end up living with my grandmother."

The mist-shrouded woman gazed into her eyes, and Carlie felt the swirling sensation of peace and contentment envelop her again. But she shook her head resolutely. She wouldn't be placated by a spell, or whatever magic this being was wielding.

"There is no 'meaning of life', no pre-ordained plan, no grand reason for tragic things to occur," the woman said matter-of-factly. "Sometimes bad things just happen, with no rhyme or reason, no great purpose. It is a very human thing to assume that something would happen just to teach you a lesson, or change your life, but it is also incredibly arrogant. Did the other people involved in the accident experience such a shocking event just to help you out?"

Carlie looked at the ground. "Of course not," she muttered.

"Did your parents sacrifice their own lives to bring you here? Rather than just putting you on a plane and coming with you?"

Carlie blushed. "Um, no. That sounds crazy."

"Did Sandy and Emily have to lose their best friends just so your grandmother could have someone to care for again?"

Carlie shook her head.

"Thinking that it is all about you – that the whole world and all its events are somehow taking place just to conspire to teach you a lesson, or make you a better person, or allow you to meet someone, or whatever it is that people believe – is looking at things the wrong way around. Things just happen, then it is up to you to create meaning from it, through what you learn from the experience and what you do in response. What you want to make happen."

Now she was really embarrassed. She didn't think everything revolved around her. *Did she?*

"Life is not always fair," the woman continued. "Bad things happen to so-called good people, and good things happen to so-called bad people. Stuff just happens – the universe is not meting out punishment or giving rewards or keeping score, it does not care whether you meet the love of your life or redeem your mother's running away or stay miserable your whole life.

"You cannot control what happens Carlie, you can only control your response to it. You can write your own outcome, and create your own meaning. And you can use a tragedy as an excuse to give up and be depressed and angry all your life, or as the impetus to make your own life more meaningful. To help others, to live well, and to be a force for good," the blue-clad figure said.

She took Carlie's hands, her voice and manner gentler now. "Only you can make sense of the death of your parents, and choose to live a life that honours their memory – not because they died to teach you something, but just because they died. Any event can make a person or break a person, depending on them, on how they see life, how they want the consequences to play out. You can see their death as an injustice and use it as an excuse to give up on yourself and waste your life away, or you can see it as a tragic event that spurs you on to make the most of your own life, because that is all you have," she explained.

"This is your life Carlie, and you need to take responsibility for it. You need to create its meaning. Let go of all your excuses about why you deserve to just collapse in a heap and cry 'poor me' at every opportunity, and make the most of what you do have," she said.

Carlie blinked, surprised by her brutal words.

"Your parents are dead," the mist-wreathed being continued, voice a little softer. "And that is terribly sad, no one denies that. But you are not alone here, and you have the chance to not only make your own life wonderful, but also to bring joy to your grandmother. She loves you very much, and she has been so happy since you arrived.

"She did the best she could over the last twenty years, but losing her daughter and then her husband nearly broke her. She was too stubborn to just give up and give in though, so she used her pain to help others. And she has done a lot for the people of her village, while never allowing herself to be happy. But since you arrived she has transformed. She has something to live for again, so instead of preparing herself for miserable old age and impending death, now she wants to go on. You have given her a new purpose in life."

Carlie smiled. She was grateful to her grandmother for taking her in – even though it was the last place on earth she wanted to be – but she'd never thought that her arrival could have helped Rose in some way. She felt terrible that she'd been so awful to her, so impatient with her, but she could change that, she vowed.

"This is the only meaning or purpose in life," the woman said. "The one that we give ourselves and each other."

Carlie gazed off into the distance, trying to take in all that she was being told. Was it true? Was there really no great plan, no reason for everything that happened in the world? The possibility was kind of scary, but it was also wildly empowering. It meant the death of her parents wasn't a punishment, of them or of her. She didn't have to define herself by it, and nor did she have to forget them in order to move on. She didn't have to wait around for things to happen to her, for decisions to be made by other people – she could choose what she wanted to make of her life.

And she didn't have to feel bad that she no longer wanted to be a lawyer, because whatever she chose to do, she could make a difference and help others – not because she should, but because she *could.* Because she wanted to. Because she wanted to be like her grandmother

– strong, inspiring, kind – and not like the bitter, selfish person she'd been for the last month. She could decide, right now, to change her life. And she would.

She looked up to thank the woman, but she was already wandering away, back into the mists.

"Wait..." she whispered.

But the woman had gone. And the sky was darkening. The mist swirled around her, against her, a thing alive. She breathed deeply, becoming aware of her location on the top of the mountain, and in her body. Suddenly she realised that her boots were soaking wet and her toes were freezing. Shivering, she cast her eyes in the direction she hoped was the right way, and started slipping and sliding back down the steep slope. The sheep sounded even more eerie in the gathering twilight, but they gave her a direction to aim for.

She stumbled once, hard, and braced herself for a fall, but she managed to right herself without causing too much pain, and kept sliding slowly and cautiously down the hillside. Then, after what felt like hours, she found herself back at the gate, through it to the pathway, then finally at the car park. And there was her grandma, standing with Elsie, a steaming mug of tea held out towards her, which she took gratefully.

"Are you okay Sweetheart?" her gran asked. "You look like you've seen a ghost."

Carlie smiled. "My head's just hurting a bit," she replied, figuring a little white lie was better than any strange and rambling attempt at explanation. "But I'm glad I climbed to the top. And I'm glad I have you Grandma. Thank you."

As the two women led Carlie back to the car, Elsie smiled over at her oldest friend and winked, and Rose discreetly wiped a tear from her eye. Maybe the cynical, bitter teenager was ready to let go of her crap and start her life again, become the wonderful person they knew she could be. They hoped so.

Chapter 15

Playing the Blame Game

When they got back home to their own village the next day, Rose went down to the healing centre to catch up on anything she'd missed, and Carlie put some washing on then flopped down on her bed. There was so much to think about, but her mind was awhir. Each time she tried to focus on her strange encounter atop Winter Hill, she got a little freaked out. She didn't know what was worse – going a little crazy from her grief, which could probably be fixed with counselling and medication, or the possibility that strange beings could manifest themselves out of the mists not just here, on Summer Tor, but also several hours away on Winter Hill.

Needing a distraction, she went downstairs, made a cup of tea, then walked through into the lounge room. Going over to the bookshelf, she picked up a pretty art book and snuggled into one of her grandma's big comfy chairs. The book was full of beautiful paintings of faeries and other mythical creatures that the author claimed to have seen as she travelled through the tunnels in the nearby tor. It made Carlie smile – until she flashed back to one of her earlier nightmares, where she'd been inside those same tunnels, being chased by some unknown threat, and praying for a being of goodness and light to come and save her. Shaking her head, she tried to dislodge the awful memories with the beauty of the paintings in the book.

And as she turned the pages, she was soothed by the sweetness of all the pretty faeries, and the gorgeous illustrations of flowers and their spirits, which the artist had captured so well. But halfway through, she was shocked to see a painting of the blue-clad woman who had entered her dreams, and who she'd encountered twice now in physical form. According to the author, she was a messenger faery, who brought wisdom and guidance from the spirit realm to those still living, and who could shapeshift into a blue butterfly. Carlie giggled at the thought of that, then decided she needed to get outside and go for a walk before her brain exploded.

This time she went out the front door and turned left, walking in the opposite direction to town, along a part of the road she hadn't been down yet. She'd barely gone two blocks before the houses on the other side of the road gave way to paddocks with horses in them. It really was a small village.

She kept an eye out on her side for the front of "her" cottage, but she didn't see any deserted houses – each one looked very much lived in, brightened up with colourful window boxes overflowing with vividly coloured flowering plants or racks of herb pots with bees buzzing happily amongst the blooms. Small white butterflies danced around her, and the air was so fresh and clean, so invigorating. When she thought of her home in Sydney she thought of the smog on the horizon and the refinery not that far away, which sent plumes of noxious gases through her suburb when the wind blew a certain way.

It was possibly because of the beauty of nature here that she was coming to love walking so much. It always brought her back into her body, and at the same time allowed her mind to open, to wander, to wonder, to explore possibilities. She thought about the blue butterfly faery from the book, and remembered it had been a butterfly that led her through the mists to the cottage each time she'd actually found it. A butterfly – symbol of transformation, and of enduring tragedy and emerging through the other side stronger than before.

And although she knew she would never get over losing her parents, and she didn't want to, as the sun caressed her cheeks and the butterflies flitted ahead of her, dancing from one patch of light to the next, she felt for the first time that she would eventually be okay.

No matter what had happened between her mum and her grandma so long ago, right now she felt blessed to have her, to have been taken in by her. Who knows, maybe she was awful twenty years ago, but if so, the loss of her daughter and her husband so close together had transformed her into the warm and caring person she was today. Probably she would never know how it all went down, and ultimately it didn't matter. Rose was who she was now, and Carlie was grateful for that. What would have happened to her if her mum's friend hadn't somehow become aware of her faraway grandmother?

She wondered if Sandy had known anything about her mother's early life. From memory Sandy had been as lost and confused as she was, but she'd been too shell-shocked to think of what to ask after her parents died. Sighing, she made a mental note to write to Sandy, to thank her for all she'd done, and to commiserate with her. The poor woman had lost her best friend, and she'd been too wrapped up in her own grief and guilt to pay attention to her, or to anyone else.

Continuing onwards, she marvelled as the pavement gave way to a gravel path alongside the tarred road, and the trees started growing closer together, making a canopy overhead that the sunlight danced through. When a car sped past, making her jump, she was suddenly brought back to herself, and realised that she'd been walking for ages. Clearly she wasn't going to find the derelict cottage today.

Turning around and heading back, she decided to make dinner for her grandma for once, to show her appreciation. With great sadness, she wondered how long it had been before her parents had died that she'd told them that she loved them, had thanked them for being so great? And now she had no chance. She'd never be able to tell them anything, to talk about her day, ask what they'd been doing, plan a family holiday. She sighed. Best make the most of every moment, and express how she felt as she felt it. Life was too short, and it was more than time that she let her grandma know how grateful she was to her.

When she got back to Rose's cottage, she searched through the pantry cupboards, then walked out to the garden to pick some lettuce, cucumbers, capsicum and tomatoes for the salad, along with coriander, basil and chilli. Maybe she would start studying herbs with her grandma – it felt so wonderful to be outside in her garden, hands in the earth, the scent of the herbs and the flowers swirling through the air, the warmth of the sun on her arms, and the peaceful quiet of nature enveloping her. No low-flying planes here, as there were in Sydney, and few cars. Instead it was just the sound of the birds and the bees and the wind in the trees.

Giggling at her pathetic rhyme, she headed back inside with her arms full of fresh produce and started frying onions and garlic, before adding chillies and the other vegetables to make a pot of Mexican beans. She'd just put the tacos in the oven to warm when her grandma came in the front door and through to the kitchen. She smiled when she saw the spotless benches and the little table set for two, with a vase of fresh roses in the centre.

"It smells amazing Carlie, thank you. No one's cooked me dinner for almost twenty years," she said, and there was sadness and longing in her voice. As she grated the cheese and finished the salad while her grandma had a quick shower, Carlie cursed herself for being so oblivious to Rose's grief all this time. She really had to make amends for her rudeness and self-absorption since she'd arrived here.

As her grandma came back out to the kitchen, Carlie poured the beans into a serving bowl and took it over to the table with the salad, then grabbed the tacos out of the oven and sat down opposite her. They talked some more about Elsie, and her college days with Rose, then wandered on to the people of this town, and what a beautiful and caring community it was. Carlie asked more about the healing centre, the different modalities it offered and some of the other courses they ran, and about the tarot readers and psychics who offered their services through Rose's shop. When she asked her grandma if she read tarot cards too, like her mum had, a look of pain crossed her face, and she shook her head.

"I used to," she finally admitted. "After Violet left I read them every morning, and again before bed, trying to discover why she'd gone, what I'd done wrong, when she'd be back. It was doing my head in. I had to stop."

Tears filled her eyes. "And now I'll never see her again. It's funny, all those years when I tried to accept that something terrible must have happened and I'd never see her again, part of me must have secretly held on to hope, otherwise learning that she was in fact dead now, that my worst fears had been realised, wouldn't have hit me so hard and crushed me so deeply."

Carlie felt awful. Her grandma blamed herself for Violet running away, and she knew how bad the blame game felt. "And I killed her, and ruined everything," she admitted quietly. Tears welled in her eyes, a small warning before a storm of crying would engulf her.

Rose looked at her sharply. "Why would you say that? It wasn't your fault!" she said sternly.

Carlie hiccupped. "Yes, it was. I was driving the car, and I crashed it and killed my parents. Mum always used to tell me I didn't pay enough attention, and she was right. I wish I'd died with them, so I didn't have to live with knowing I'd murdered Mum and Dad. That I'd killed your daughter. And now you're stuck with me, a constant reminder of the loss of your hope."

Her grandma stood up and came around the table, then put her arms around Carlie and held her tight. "Sweetheart, it wasn't your fault. A drunk driver ran a red light and hit you."

"You're just saying that to make me feel better," she sobbed.

Rose shook her head. "It's true. He'd already lost his licence, so he shouldn't have been driving in the first place, let alone drunk. When he crashed into you, over the limit and on a suspended licence, he was arrested very quickly. And when your dad died, and your mum passed away the next morning in hospital, he pleaded no contest to vehicular manslaughter, and has been in jail ever since awaiting sentencing. It *really* wasn't your fault."

Carlie stared at her grandma, angry now. "Of course it was. And everyone knew that. Sandy couldn't bear to look at me, my best friend Emily couldn't face me. I'm a monster. A murderer. I shouldn't even be here, it's not fair on you. I should be in jail."

"Oh Carlie, Sweetheart, you must believe me. It would have been the same outcome if your mum or your dad were driving too – the man who caused the accident drove right through a red light and slammed into your car, sending it crashing into the tree. You'd done nothing wrong, I promise you."

Carlie shook her head stubbornly. She'd been trying to avoid this subject, not yet ready to admit to her part in it, or her awful guilt, but it had been torturing her, and part of her was glad she'd finally told her grandma, no matter what happened now.

She figured she should go and pack, because surely Rose wouldn't want to live with her now. She had enough money to get by for a while, and Sandy would put the proceeds from the sale of the Sydney house into her account once it was settled. She could go to London, start a new life there. Or perhaps another village, somewhere secluded and out in nature, but far from here. Mind made up, she stood.

Her grandmother rose too, and opened a drawer in the cabinet. She took out a large envelope, then pulled out several newspaper clippings. "Carlie, wait. You need to see these. Sandy sent them to me," she said, handing the articles across the table. "She wanted you to know the truth, when you were ready to bring it up, to talk about it. You'll be angry, and that's perfectly understandable. But the driver has admitted he was in the wrong, and has taken responsibility for his actions. You need to stop torturing yourself over this.

"And I'm sorry," her grandma added, voice deep with compassion. "I didn't realise that you blamed yourself. I should have shown these to you before. I was just worried it would hurt too much, to read all this, to re-live that night."

Carlie skimmed through the newspaper stories, the confusion and disbelief etched on her face finally turning to relief. So it *was* true. It really *hadn't* been her fault. She felt dizzy, and a little overwhelmed, but so much lighter now that this guilt was lifting.

There were a few lines in the story that quoted the driver, imploring Carlie to forgive him. She stared, aghast, and her head spun as she tried to adjust her thinking to take in the remorse of this man who had foolishly, accidentally, caused the deaths of her mother and father. But it was way too early for that.

The main thing was, she hadn't killed her parents. She felt a huge weight drop away from her, and managed to smile at her grandma. It was so strange though, seeing the story in a newspaper. Her story. Taking a few deep breaths to steady herself, she got up, put the kettle on and started clearing the dishes away, in auto pilot mode.

When she climbed into bed later that night, the lamp shone on the butterfly on her mother's quilt, and she had a sudden memory of the last present her mum had given her. Opening the drawer of the bedside table, she felt around for the little midnight blue velvet pouch she'd thrown in there when she arrived, when she was still too raw to be able to look at it.

For her seventeenth birthday, a week before the fatal accident, her mum had taken her to a metaphysical store in the city – one, funnily enough, much like her grandma's – so she could select a gift. They'd spent a good hour in there, poring over the books, the card decks, the jewellery, the crystals, the beautiful velvet and lace clothes. Carlie had teased her mum about it, but secretly she'd loved being there with her, loved holding the crystals and smelling the beautifully scented candles, oils and potions.

"Maybe I need a love potion," she'd joked, as she pointed out a shelf full of them to her mum. "Then again, what if I made someone fall in love with me, then I went off them and wanted to break up? I could be stuck with them forever."

She was kidding, and they'd both laughed, but then her mum had become strangely and uncharacteristically serious. "You're right darling, you should never cast a spell on another person, or bind them to you with magic. Instead you should send your intention out to the universe – state the *qualities* you want, not *who* you want. And make sure you cultivate those qualities in yourself too. You want to work on yourself first, because if you're happy and passionate about life, you'll attract someone with similar traits.

"But if I'm honest, I did cast a spell to bring you into my life," her mum had continued. "I asked the goddess to send you – my brave, passionate, intelligent and wonderful daughter. And here you are, all I could ever have hoped for."

Carlie had rolled her eyes at that. "Good one Mum," she'd said, laughing at the thought of her mother in a black witch's hat dancing around a cauldron. "I'll remind you of that next time it's my turn to clean the bathroom."

Back in her new bedroom on the other side of the world, Carlie smiled as she remembered that day with her mum. And realised that this was the first time she'd thought of her parents with joy rather than sadness and anger. Turning the velvet pouch over in her hands, she gently untied the bow and lifted out what was inside. It was a beautiful blue aqua aura crystal set in an intricate swirling pattern, with a moonstone embedded in the clay, and a small silver butterfly attached in the middle.

She held it for a while, staring at it, picturing the butterflies she'd seen on the hill and out in the laneway, which had led her to the abandoned cottage and her mother's magical book. Slowly she slipped the pendant around her neck. The weight of it was somehow comforting, and she was happy that she'd finally found the courage to put it on and wear it.

As she leaned over to close the drawer, she saw the edge of the gold-wrapped box that Emily had given her before she left Sydney, the one she'd so callously thrown on the bench without opening. Curious, she pulled it out, untied the ribbon and lifted the lid. Inside was a pretty silver locket, engraved with their names and a love-heart pattern, which held a tiny picture of the two of them, arms around each other and laughter in their eyes as they'd learned to surf. Unclasping the silver chain she'd just put on, she strung the locket onto it too, so it sat next to the crystal pendant from her mum.

Then she pulled out the second object. It was a tiny glass vial of sand collected from their local beach, with a note attached, which said that, according to legend, having the sand in her possession ensured she would return to that beach again one day. She smiled at the sentiment, then went over to the desk to get a notepad.

Dear Emily,

I hope you are well and happy.

Thank you so much for the beautiful present, I'm wearing the locket on the same chain as the pendant Mum bought me for my birthday. And the sand made me smile. I really do hope I can come back one day. I miss home, and I miss you even more.

More than anything, I'm really sorry that I was so awful to be around in the days before I left, and I'm very sorry I was so cruel to you. I won't try to justify my behaviour, because there was no excuse for it. You deserve much better than that, and I really hope you'll make new friends who are nicer than me.

How's school going for you? I start in a few weeks – right now it's the big summer holiday over here, which has been nice as I try to get my bearings and get my head around the new town, the new people, the new food, the new accent. It means we only get two weeks off at Christmas though, which will be weird, especially as it will be winter here – it might even snow, which would be kind of cool. How strange though, not to spend it with you at the beach...

I'm still not sure what my subjects will be, and I'm nervous – will school be different here? Will the subjects and curriculum be different to ours? What if I go from the top of the class to the bottom? Guess I'll find out soon enough...

Oh, and it turns out you were right – my grandma is really great. She's very kind, and has been so welcoming. I wasn't especially nice to her when I got here, as I'm sure you can imagine, but I'm trying to make amends.

Pausing, she tapped her pen on the paper impatiently. Did she want to tell Emily about the rituals she'd done yet? The releasement ceremony and the card reading? They both used to laugh when their mums went to fortune tellers and stuff, and she couldn't imagine in a million years Emily ever believing that she'd encountered a woman from the mists. She didn't believe it. Maybe in the next letter...

She has a really nice little cottage – my room is upstairs and looks out over the garden, which has a big old apple tree against the back fence, and herbs and stuff. And there's a massive hill just over the back lane – it's pretty steep, so at least I can stay fit, ha ha.

I miss the ocean though. It's weird not to hear the waves crashing at night, or be able to go for a swim. I even miss the smell of the salt air! It is pretty here, but the village is so small – it's lucky that I'll be able to concentrate on school, otherwise I might have been really bored...

She paused again. That wasn't actually true – she had more to do here than she'd ever done at home – but she didn't feel ready to reveal all of that just yet, even if Emily was her closest friend.

Gran said I can work in her shop on weekends if I want to earn a bit of extra money. I think she'd planned that Mum would take over when she retired, so I imagine that if I like it I could work there as much as I wanted to.

It's always good to have options I guess, and it will be something to do to avoid the boredom. It's a shop and healing centre – reiki, herbalism, tarot readings. Apparently Mum was really into tarot cards and energy healing when she was young, although I never saw her use them... There's so much I didn't know about her, which makes me so sad.

But it's 1am and I really have to go to bed – but I promise I'll write more often from now on.

Much love, Carlie xx

Chapter 16

A Kindred Spirit

The next morning there was a knock at the door as Carlie and her grandma were finishing breakfast. Rose rushed out of the room to open it, and came back with a girl around Carlie's age, who looked slightly nervous, behind her.

"Sweetheart, this is Rhiannon, Mike's daughter," she said sweetly. "We were wondering if you could help her today – it's her little brother's birthday tomorrow, and she needs a hand with all the cakes and party food. I have to go to the centre, but I said she could do the cooking here, so as not to ruin the surprise for Brodie."

Carlie rolled her eyes. Her grandma was being none too subtle. She'd been wanting her to meet Rhiannon since she'd first arrived, but she had kept putting it off, not ready for the stress of meeting new people or making new friends. She was fine on her own, and she wished people could respect that.

But Rose was looking at her so hopefully that she couldn't bear to disappoint her – and after last night's revelations, she was certainly prepared to do this small favour for her. Besides, the poor girl she'd dragged in with her was looking so embarrassed that she couldn't help but want to put her out of her misery. So finally she shrugged her shoulders and held out her hand to Rhiannon, who shook it gratefully despite Carlie's surliness.

"So, everything you need should be in here," her grandmother said, opening the pantry door to reveal a lot more baking ingredients than had been there yesterday morning. Carlie sighed theatrically, while trying not to giggle.

"Ever feel as though you're part of a conspiracy?" she asked Rhiannon, who nodded and offered a wry smile in Rose's direction.

"They have our best interests at heart, I'm sure," the girl replied, with a touch of sarcasm in her tone that Carlie appreciated. "But I can do this back at my place, if you have other things to do. I don't want to put you out."

Carlie sighed again, but she shook her head. "It's okay, I didn't have anything planned for today," she said. "I haven't cooked for a while though, so I'm not sure how much help I'll be."

Her grandma waved goodbye and left them to it.

"Maybe we can start with the pastry for the spinach pies and vegie quiches, and work our way up to the cookies and cakes?" Rhiannon offered hesitantly. She was obviously still nervous, so Carlie tried to look a bit more welcoming.

"You're vegetarian too?" she asked.

Rhiannon nodded. "All my life!" she said, as she started getting the ingredients out. She found two aprons in a drawer, and handed one to Carlie. Unfolding it, she saw that it was emblazoned with "World's Best Mum", and she felt tears threatening as she wondered if her mother had given it to Rose when she was her age, living in this house, and if they used to bake together like they apparently used to sew together. Taking a deep breath, she focused on the ingredients for the dough she was supposed to be mixing, and turned back to Rhiannon, face stiff with trying not to let her sadness show.

"I'm so sorry about your parents," the stranger said, her voice kind. "Rose told me. I know how hard it was to lose my mum, so to lose both must be twice as bad, at least. I didn't leave my room for three months," she added. "Dad was really worried about me, and I feel bad now that I wasn't more helpful to him, because he was hurting just as much as I was, if not more."

"You lost your mum?" Carlie asked, shocked. "I'm so sorry."

"Last year," she said softly. "It happened on her fortieth birthday.

Dad kept rambling on about some curse, that everyone he loved would die when they turned forty. I don't know what he was going on about, but I guess grief does drive you crazy for a while, and who am I to judge him on how it affected him?" she asked.

"It was weird though, when we got home from the hospital that last time, I started cleaning up, washing dishes, cooking dinner – for some reason I had to do stuff. My little brother went outside and started skateboarding on the ramp behind our house, trying to keep active, to move, to not let the news sink in I guess. And Dad just sat on the couch and stared blankly into space – I couldn't even get his attention when I asked if he needed to eat."

Carlie nodded in sympathy. They all seemed far more mature responses than her own furious lashing out.

"He's okay now," Rhiannon added. "I mean, he still cries himself to sleep some nights, but he's coping better. Functioning properly, going to work every day, socialising a little bit, although I don't think he'll ever have another relationship." She smiled sadly. "It's so hard being the ones left behind... But I should stop rambling, I don't want to bore you with my story."

Rhiannon found some more bowls and measuring cups, then went to the fridge for butter and milk for the next recipe.

"So how are you settling in here? Dad said you lived in the middle of a big city. I hope it's not too boring for you here."

Carlie shook her head. "It hasn't been boring, that's for sure. Some really strange things have happened…" She trailed off. Laughed mockingly at herself. "Ah, what would I know? I think grief and wishful thinking is making me hallucinate."

Suddenly she saw an image of her mother and Mike together, and wondered what that was about, and where it had come from. What had her grandma said that day at the healing centre? "He was your mum's, um, friend." Why did she think of that right now? Feeling guilty, she tried to dislodge the vision from her mind. Mike had loved someone else, not her mother. *What on earth was she thinking?*

Rhiannon touched her hand gently. "I know that my dad was in love with your mother, when they were still teenagers. He told me he'd wanted to marry her."

Carlie raised her eyebrows in disbelief then shook her head, trying to deny such a hurtful idea. Mike had only just lost his wife, and Rhiannon her mum. They didn't need to be thinking about something from way back in the past, when they had been so young.

"It's okay, it was a long time ago," Rhiannon said calmly. "And apparently your mother had fallen in love with some spiritual guru guy or something, and broken up with Dad. I don't think it ended well for her though – Dad said the guy was very possessive, very jealous, very quick to anger, kind of crazy. And your mum eventually figured that out for herself. She wrote to Dad, saying she wanted to leave the guy, to come back here, but apparently all he had to do was remind her of some terrible prophecy or something, and she'd stay with him. Or so Dad said. I don't really understand it all."

"I'm sorry," Carlie said, feeling helpless, somehow responsible and confused all at once.

Rhiannon smiled at her. "Don't be sorry, Dad never was. He loved your mother deeply back then, and I think he always did, but it didn't take away from his love for my mum when they started dating. They were so wonderful together, and so in love. Although they could be a bit *too* soppy," she grinned. "I don't know, I think sometimes first love is so intense that it wouldn't actually work out long term. It's a kind of idealised thing that can't ever live up to expectations."

"But why on earth did Mum think she couldn't come home?" Carlie pressed. "Surely that's a little too dramatic, thinking anything could stop her? Gran would have loved her to come home."

Rhiannon laughed. "Being a teenager is all about drama! You know: 'I'll *die* if he doesn't love me,' or: 'I love you, best friend, no wait, I hate you and I'll never speak to you again!' We feel everything much more intensely than adults."

Carlie stared at her. "How old are you?" she asked, eyebrows raised as she took in Rhiannon's amazingly mature attitude.

"Seventeen. But I spent a lot of time walking and thinking after Mum died – well, once I finally got out of bed and left my room – and a lot of time reading. Lots of self-help books – how to survive loss, how to cope when love dies, getting over grief, blah blah blah…" Rhiannon rolled her eyes, laughing at herself.

And for the first time, Carlie thought maybe she *could* make a friend here, that she might be able to create a new life. But she still longed for what she'd lost. Longed to walk into her old house and hug her mum and dad. To stay up all night talking to Emily about boys and school and their plans for the future. It was all mapped out. They were going to get an inner-city share house and go to the University of Sydney to study law, then get a job in the same firm. Now she didn't know what she wanted to do with her life.

How could a single event change her so much? How could it suddenly leave her unable to talk to her best friend? How could your oldest relationship fracture just like that? And how could your childhood dream shatter in a single moment? Now she couldn't even imagine studying all those years to be a lawyer, or standing up in a courtroom trying to convince a judge and jury. Dispirited all of a sudden, she changed the subject.

"What's the school here like?" she asked, voice wistful. Rhiannon took the hint, and they spent the next few hours discussing elective subjects, teachers, whether or not it was too late to start learning guitar, and the antics of Rhiannon's little brother.

Their cooking went well too, and they soon had three different kinds of cupcakes, lots of animal-shaped cookies, a variety of quiches, filos and mini pies, and a beautiful birthday cake, all ready for delivery. Halfway through the day, an accidentally over-zealous stirring turned into a flour fight, and Carlie couldn't remember the last time she'd laughed like that. She was surprised by how healing it felt, and although it didn't last long, she was grateful for the brief moment of levity.

They'd just cleaned up the kitchen and put the last tray of cookies in the oven when Rose got home from work. "It smells amazing girls. I don't suppose you baked any extra for dinner tonight?" she asked them hopefully.

"Not yet Mrs Tyler," Rhiannon replied. "But we could whip up another spinach pie really quickly. You've got some more in your garden haven't you?"

Rose nodded, and the girls traipsed out to the backyard to pick a bunch of the green leaves, then put their aprons on again and started making more pastry while Rose went to have a shower.

Rhiannon finally broke the silence that had fallen between them. "So, do you want to tell me about any of the strange things that have happened to you here?" she asked.

Carlie blushed. "You'll think I'm crazy," she said, suddenly shy again, and aware that this girl was still a stranger. "Maybe when we've known each other for, I don't know, at least a week."

"At least that means you see a future for us," Rhiannon laughed. "But I know it can be really hard to be around people when something so awful has happened, so I'll understand if you don't want to hang out again. Just know the offer is there."

Carlie smiled gratefully. "I know what you mean, but I've really enjoyed spending time with you today. It's so nice that you understand. Not nice that you've lost someone too, I don't mean that, but that you get me. My best friend came to see me a few times before I left, and it was so awful. So awkward. I didn't want to be mean to her, but I couldn't seem to help myself. It was like we were in this strange dark world, but she could only see sunshine and pretty birds and flowers, while I was aware of all the monsters that lurked behind the trees, the cruel beasts in the depths of the black lakes, the poisonous snakes poised to attack. I was trying to show her what I saw, how I felt, but she refused to see."

Rhiannon gave her a quick, slightly clumsy, hug. "It's not that she refused to see, she just couldn't see. I'm sure she wanted desperately to be able to reach you, to see the things you feared and protect you from them, but it's hard, unless you've lost someone close to you as well, to know how to act and to be," she said gently.

"Some of my closest friends totally abandoned me, because they were scared of saying the wrong thing, of accidentally upsetting me. But it hurt so much more to be avoided. I didn't mind what clumsy things people said, it was better that they saw me, and included me. I would have been so happy just to be hugged, to sit in silence with them, to listen to them babble on about school and TV shows and normal teenage stuff."

Carlie blushed. "Emily did try that, but I bit her head off," she admitted, ashamed all over again of her behaviour in the weeks after the accident. "She said I was lucky to have missed the maths test that day, and I shouted at her and told her to leave."

Rhiannon smiled. "She'll forgive you Carlie. I'm sure she was mortified as soon as the words came out of her mouth. She wouldn't have hurt you on purpose, she was just trying to connect with you. Better that she tried and failed than not trying at all, surely?"

Carlie's mind raced. She had to make it up to Emily, and to Sandy. The poor woman had lost her best friend, but had to put up with her brat daughter instead of being able to grieve in peace.

"Don't beat yourself up over it Carlie," Rhiannon said. "They'll understand. I reckon you're allowed to lash out and act up for a few weeks after such a tragic loss, to cry and scream and curse the gods, and to think that you're the only person on earth who's ever suffered this badly, this deeply. But then you have to take a deep breath, get over yourself and make amends."

Carlie nodded. "I have to apologise to Grandma too. I wasn't exactly nice to her when I got here – and she suffered more than me, lost more than me. God, I really did mess up."

Hearing a sound at the kitchen door, she looked up in panic. Rose was standing there, a smile on her face, tears in her eyes, and arms open wide. "Sweetheart, you don't have to apologise to me. And there is no 'more than' or 'less than', no competition or measurement of grief. We've both lost so much, but we have each other now, so we've gained something too."

Carlie flew across the kitchen into the hug, tears of gratitude in her eyes, and the pain in her heart a little lighter.

"Now Rhiannon, that pie smells wonderful," Rose said. "Do you want to join us for dinner, or do you need to get home?"

"I should go Mrs Tyler, and smuggle some of these party things into the house and hide them for the night. But will we see you both tomorrow? It starts at eleven, but any time is fine."

After promising to bring the rest of the cookies and cakes over before then, Carlie farewelled her potential new friend and sat down to dinner with her grandma. She was distracted though. What had

Rhiannon meant, about her mum and a spiritual guru guy, and a prophecy that kept her bound to him, and away from her family? Was this man part of the mystery of her leaving home? Had she been unable to return for some reason that no one knew, forced into an unwanted separation from her parents?

She wanted to ask Rose about it, but she didn't want to upset her needlessly. Maybe it would be best to find out a bit more before she broached the subject, from her mum's book in the old cottage perhaps, or even from Mike, before she blundered in with some half-baked theory. Rhiannon had admitted that she didn't understand her dad's words, and she hadn't even been born when Violet was living here, so Carlie resolved to go slowly.

Her grandma broke into her thoughts. "Did you have a nice day with Rhiannon?" she asked, trying to sound casual. Suddenly irritated again about the set-up, Carlie shrugged. "She seems quite nice," she said grudgingly, then lapsed back into silence.

Finally she went upstairs to write to Sandy. She began with an apology for her behaviour before she flew away, and left out the excuses she was going to follow it with. Obviously she was lashing out because of her grief, and Sandy would understand that without her insulting her intelligence by spelling it out.

Then she offered heartfelt condolences for her own loss. She knew how hard it was to lose your best friend, and at least Emily was still alive, if not able to be visited. She told Sandy about her new life too, glossing over the bumpy beginning with her grandma and focusing instead on their gradual journey towards friendship and respect. She didn't talk about the mists, but she did mention Rhiannon, so that Sandy wouldn't continue to worry about her.

Then she climbed into bed, feeling happier and lighter than she had in the last month. And in the morning she couldn't remember whether she'd dreamed or not, except for a flash of an image of Rhiannon and Emily climbing the hill with her, the three of them twirling in the meadow, laughing and chatting. It was the best sleep she'd had since her world had come crashing down.

Chapter 17

Yearning For Grace

The next morning Rhiannon came by bright and early to help them carry the rest of the party food they'd baked back to her place for her little brother's birthday.

"I'm so glad you'll be with me today Carlie – you can't begin to imagine how boring it is being stuck entertaining fifteen six-year-old kids," she said, grimacing in mock horror as she put her food platters down in the kitchen. Taking Carlie's hand, she led her upstairs to her room. "And because we're so mature – although more likely because we made all the food – Dad said we can skip most of the party."

Carlie loved Rhiannon's bedroom as soon as she walked in. It was big and light and airy, with sunshine streaming through the windows, and a purple patterned quilt covering the double bed. There was a window seat too, filled with lots of soft cushions, which looked perfect for curling up in and reading books for hours on end. The whole room just seemed so happy, as though you couldn't not feel good while you were in it.

"It used to be all dark and gloomy, with thick blood-red velvet curtains blocking out the light, and black wallpaper and, well, pretty much black everything," Rhiannon admitted, as though she'd read her mind. "But after Mum died I couldn't bear how it looked. It did reflect my mood perfectly, but I soon discovered that wasn't a good thing. Dad helped me make it over, and even Brodie painted one wall for me. It was that crappily painted one over there of course," she said, pointing. "But the thought was there!"

Tears pricked Carlie's eyes, and she felt a pang of longing as her new friend talked about her father and her brother. She certainly didn't begrudge her still having most of her family, but it hurt her at such a deep level that she didn't want to examine her feelings and reveal the pettiness that must be at her core.

"You're always welcome to stay here if you want to," Rhiannon said, lifting her quilt to reveal a trundle bed underneath. "And don't ever feel that you have to make conversation. If you just want us to sit here together in silence, that's fine. Or we can stay up here and read," she said, gesturing to the window seat. "And if you want to cry and shout and punch the cushions, that's fine too," she grinned.

"I'll never tell you what to do, or to get over it, or to just smile and choose to be happy – that comment has always been my pet hate, even before Mum died. I can sit here with you and your pain and not say a word, if that's what you want, or fill the silence if you'd rather that, or give you a shoulder to cry on."

Carlie was moved beyond words by this girl, still pretty much a stranger, and her empathy and understanding.

"Or if you need a distraction we can get some DVDs and have a silly movie marathon, or go bowling or something," Rhiannon continued, laughing a little to lighten the mood.

"Just know that you never have to put on a brave face with me. It's been almost a year since Mum died, and there are still days when it hurts too much to get out of bed. I imagine there always will be, and I reckon there should be, really, to honour the depth of our loss. So don't ever feel that you have to put on an act around me, or entertain me. I know how much it hurts."

They were interrupted by a knock on the door – Mike was hoping they'd both come down to sing Happy Birthday and cut the cake they'd made. Rhiannon looked at Carlie and lifted one eyebrow in question. She nodded, glad for a brief respite from the intensity, but more grateful than she could ever express for Rhiannon's compassion and consideration, and her generosity in checking whether she would rather not go downstairs amongst strangers.

If only every grieving person could have someone like her to help navigate the murky depths of their loss, to just be there with them, not requiring anything from them, no pretence or brave face, just a place of honesty to sit with their grief and know they were not alone.

Watching Brodie thoughtfully as all his friends gathered around him and sang Happy Birthday, she saw his delight as he unwrapped his huge pile of presents, and his joy as his big sister brought out the cake that she'd so lovingly made for him, shaped and iced to make the head of a lion, his favourite animal.

She saw the fierce love for him, and the need to protect him, in Rhiannon's eyes, and the pride in Mike's as he watched his two brave, resilient children. Saddened, she wiped away another tear, but she felt happy too, to have been welcomed into this family, to share in their obvious love for each other.

Taking a sip of her lemonade, she gazed over at her grandma, who was deep in conversation with Mike. She knew he'd been a pillar of strength to her since Violet had left home more than twenty years ago, and no doubt her gran had supported him through his loss too – first of her daughter, the woman he had wanted to marry when he was just a teenager, and more recently of his beloved, the woman he had wed, and made a family and a life with.

People here seemed to be so much closer to each other than they had been back home. Or maybe it was just these people, who had known so much powerful loss alongside their intense love and joy. Was it necessary to lose someone before you could really live? Or love? Or was she just noticing things more deeply now that she'd lost so much too? Noticing how amazing her grandma was, to everyone. Rose was the embodiment of grace, the embodiment of goodness. Suddenly Carlie felt alienated from all the people gathered in the lounge room, all so smiley and joyful, and wondered if this was her destiny, to always be the downer, to always feel alone.

After a while Rhiannon noticed her brooding against the wall and came to rescue her, plates of cake in hand. They headed out into the back garden, which was bigger than her grandma's, with several apple trees down the back and a few vegie beds running along the sides. In the middle was an old swing set, and they sat there together, backs to the house, swinging a little, their feet trailing along the ground as they listened to the bees and stared up at the tor that shadowed the town.

Rhiannon and Brodie's house was a bit further away from it than Rose's cottage was, and they could see more of it from here. It was strange how the hill seemed to change shape when you viewed it from different angles – from where they were sitting, the tower on the summit looked like it was only halfway up the slope.

"It's strange how it seems to move around isn't it?" Rhiannon asked, and again it was as though she could read her friend's thoughts. "The tower is definitely at the top of the hill, but from here you'd swear it was built at that first resting place, just halfway up."

Carlie nodded, her eyes focused on the hill.

"I've been stuck up there a few times when the mists have come in, and it's so strange, like being in another world," Rhiannon continued. "And I've met people up there who couldn't really exist…" she whispered, then paused, suddenly looking worried that Carlie would think she was crazy.

But Carlie just nodded, and gave her a reassuring smile. Who was she to judge, given that she'd seen the same thing?

"I saw a woman up there too, all dressed in blue," she finally admitted shyly. "She sat down right next to me, and hugged me, and spoke to me – but I'm still not totally sure that she was actually there…" Trailing off, she shrugged her shoulders, trying not to show how terrified she felt now that she'd revealed this. Would Rhiannon think she was mad?

In unison, they both stopped swinging, and lowered their voices, even though there was no one around to hear them. "I've seen her too," Rhiannon said, voice hushed. "Not long after Mum died, I'd climbed the tor to get away from the noise and crush down here, the turmoil and energy of people. And this figure came up out of the mists to me, and just held me. She didn't say anything that first time, just gave me a big hug and held me close. I felt so protected, so loved, so understood. It was probably only for fifteen minutes, although it felt like much longer, but even after she'd left, and the mists had dispersed so I could walk back down, I kind of felt like I had a layer of protection – or her cloak of mist, or something – around me," Rhiannon said, then laughed self-deprecatingly.

"I know that sounds totally crazy, doesn't it? But whatever it was, the little things that had been hurting me so deeply stopped hurting quite as much after that, and I found it a bit easier to cope with life. I was more patient with my brother, and more sympathetic towards Dad. I guess it kind of felt as though Mum was still with me somehow, you know?" she asked softly.

Carlie nodded again. It had been the same for her that first time, the woman in blue coming and sitting next to her on the grass as the mists rolled in, holding her close while she sobbed her heart out. She had felt really nurtured too, and so much closer to her parents in that moment. She'd thought she was just dreaming it, but maybe she hadn't been. Or maybe they'd both had grief-stricken hallucinations, she thought wryly.

"She came again, a few weeks later, when I was alone up there in the mists," Rhiannon continued. "She held my hands and told me I should rethink my career plans." Laughing at Carlie's expression, all taken aback, she raised one eyebrow. "I know, it sounds weird, hey? I still wasn't sure what I wanted to do anyway – sometimes I think I want to be a journalist, other times a children's author, another day I want to be a teacher like my mum. I kind of wish she'd been a bit more specific. Ungrateful of me, I know," she giggled.

Carlie was relieved that Rhiannon seemed to have just as big a streak of cynicism as she did, and a sense of humour that hadn't been dimmed by the tragedy so central to her life. Summoning her courage, she decided she could be brave enough to put her heart on the line too, make her new friend feel a little less alone.

"I always thought that I'd be a lawyer when I grew up, ever since I was a little girl," Carlie said carefully. "Just like Mum. And Emily and I had it all planned out – we were going to go to university together, get a share house nearby, eventually get jobs at the same firm. I wanted to specialise in criminal law, and Emily was going to focus on family law. We had it all worked out, but ever since the accident, I can't imagine doing that any more. It just doesn't feel like me.

"And I know this sounds a bit strange," she added quickly, before she started feeling too silly to go on. "But ever since yesterday, spending time with you, and you sharing your experiences and being so compassionate and so empathetic, I've been thinking that I want to somehow help people who are grieving, who have lost someone. Everything you've said to me has been so helpful, so caring, and I want to be able to help other people the same way, to support them and help them heal, without pushing them to go too fast. A social worker, or a grief counsellor, or something... But I don't know, is that stupid?" she asked. "Is that even a job?"

Rhiannon stared at her, eyes shining. "It's perfect. And my god, that's totally what the woman in blue meant, I'm sure of it. If you don't mind me doing it too?"

"Of course not, you'll be amazing," Carlie said. "I was thinking about it for you before it ever occurred to me that I could maybe do it too. And it would be nice to have someone to share the journey with, to compare notes with." Pausing, she thought of the blue-clad woman on Winter Hill, who'd told her she had to create her own meaning in life, her own way of honouring her loss. Maybe this was it.

"I just... I want to do something with my life that might make some kind of sense of the loss. Something meaningful, that will help people. And I guess in studying for it, it might help me heal too. Of course I have no idea what to do or where to go or even what subjects I should do at school this year in preparation, but it feels right somehow, to work towards that."

Rhiannon nodded, eyes alight. "There's a university that's only a forty-five minute drive from here. I'll check out their courses tonight, and ask them to send us some information."

Just then Rose came outside to get Carlie, as the party was winding down. After hugging her new friend goodbye, she walked home with her grandma in the late afternoon sunshine, smiling to herself when she realised that she had just referred to the cottage as home. This afternoon the whole world had turned golden, and she could sense potential vibrating in the air. The world really was full of possibilities, if you looked.

As they wandered back around the base of the tor, Carlie saw something out of the corner of her eye, and quickly turned towards it. The woman dressed in blue was standing there, smiling at her, seeming to hold the mists within her and around her like a cloak. When she caught Carlie's eye she nodded, then faded into the darkness of the woodland.

"Ah, Brauna has come to you too," Rose said, more statement than question, but there was a twinkle in her eye. "So you made the right decision about something today?"

Carlie stared at her. Her grandma could see the woman too? "I thought I was hallucinating," she admitted sheepishly.

Rose smiled. "She only shows herself to those who have suffered a great loss, but several people from around here have seen her. First she just holds them, lets them cry on her shoulder, gives them a safe space to grieve, and lends them a protective, nurturing strength to dull the impact of their loss a little. The next time she comes, if she does reappear, she gives a message of some kind. And if she appears a third time it seems to be to validate a life-changing decision, a new path that you've just chosen."

Although overwhelmed with shyness again, Carlie nodded, then hesitantly told her grandmother about her plan to study psychology and social work, and become a grief counsellor. She still wanted to do reiki in the shop on weekends, if her grandma wanted her to, but this was what she wanted to do with her life. To help people the way Rose and Rhiannon were helping her. And to somehow honour her parents and all they had done for her, the love they had for her.

Rose wiped a tear from her eye. "I'm so proud of you Sweetheart," she said. "And that's what your mum wanted to do when she was your age, be a social worker."

Carlie felt a shiver run down her spine. "Really? Wow, that's kind of cool. She never mentioned that – it seemed like she'd always wanted to be a lawyer, and she loved her work so much."

Her grandmother smiled. "Maybe our destiny really is laid out for us before we're born," she said gently, then trailed off as one of her neighbours poked his head over his back fence for a chat. Carlie said hello then continued on her own, looking forward to a long soak in the tub and a chance to process all that had happened that day.

Turning on the tap, she poured in some chamomile bath salts then lowered herself into the deliciously hot water. An hour later, she was woken by an urgent knock on the door. Jerking awake, she found cold water swirling around her, and realised she must have drifted off. "I'm fine Grandma," she shouted, as she climbed out of the bath and rubbed herself dry as fast as she could.

They had a quiet night together, eating leftover spinach pies and vegie quiches for dinner and talking about the party, and how proud Mike was of his two children. Then Rose asked Carlie more about her life in Sydney, and about Violet's work, and about her son-in-law, Carlie's dad Oliver. They both felt sad that Rose had never met him, and Carlie talked about him for ages, reminiscing about days they'd spent together, special moments they'd shared. It felt so nice to be able to rave about him. To remember him, and honour him.

Of course it made sense that people here asked about her mother, since they'd known her, or knew of her, and they all knew Rose. But she missed her dad just as much as she missed her mum. It was strange too, the more she learned about her mum the more her idea of her shifted, but her dad would always remain the man she knew and loved. There were no dark secrets she could uncover about him, no way to discover more about his past. This made her sad in some ways, but it was also nicely reassuring. And when she fell asleep that night, all her dreams were peaceful and full of joy.

Chapter 18

Through the Past Darkly

Carlie woke up early the next morning and peered out the window. It was grey and misty, a perfect day to curl up under her quilt and sleep in a little, or read a good book. Then she felt the chain holding her blue crystal and its butterfly at her throat, and opened her eyes. Maybe she'd be able to find the cottage again today, since the other times she'd managed to get there had been grey and misty too. The more she learned about her mother, the more she wanted to know about her and her old life, and she was desperate to find a clue to the identity and importance of the so-called spiritual guru guy Rhiannon had mentioned. Would there be something in her mum's magical book?

Quietly she let herself out the back door and hurried along the laneway, happy that the mystical, mysterious mists seemed to be coalescing around her even more substantially the further she walked. When she got to the derelict block and saw the abandoned cottage with the candle in the window, she rushed up the steps, full of excitement, and pushed the door open. Her earlier qualms and hesitations about trespassing or being discovered had been forgotten. And she was happy, and relieved, to see that Violet's Book of Shadows was still on the table where she'd left it, looking as dusty as it had been the first time she'd come across it.

She sat down cross-legged in front of it, pleased when the little black cat reappeared and climbed into her lap, curling up and purring like there was nowhere she'd rather be. With a trembling hand, Carlie reached out and flipped the book open. It seemed as though there were more entries than the last time she'd looked at it, but that made no sense. Maybe she just hadn't been paying attention before? She thumbed through it, and when two pages seemed to stick together, she paused and read that entry.

A Talisman for a Safe Journey

This is a spell, and a creation, that I can take with me when I leave home. A spell not just for protection, but also for guidance on what I'll need to learn and do. I'm making this talisman on a Wednesday, ruled by Mercury and dedicated to travel.

Within it will be a piece of the shed skin of Lulu, Paulette's snake familiar, because I want to shed my own metaphorical skin, and all the pain and guilt I feel. It represents letting go of the things I can't change and trying to find a way forward, a way to survive on my own, to get through the days, the weeks, the months, the years. It also adds a sense of moving beyond time, between the worlds, creating a journey that will take me back and forward, within and without, to a place without boundaries.

There's a rose quartz for protection and self-love, dried lavender from Mum's garden for peace and calm, comfrey for safety while travelling, and two seeds from Peru, that Andre gave me, a masculine and a feminine one, for balance. After I cast circle and ask the goddess for wisdom and strength, I'll gently wrap all the parts in midnight blue velvet and tie it up with a red ribbon for protection and a yellow one for joy. And I will keep it with me always, to remind me of home, of my witchy friends, and of the magic that Mum has surrounded me with, and connected me to. Even though I'll be far away, she will always be with me, and I hope she'll always hold me in her heart too...

Within this sacred boundary between the worlds, in this circle of salt and golden light,
Goddess and god, please bless my journey, bless my loved ones, and bless this rite.
Spirit of the west, of water, please guide and protect me, and help me to go with the flow on this beautiful new adventure, as I venture away. Help wash away the pain of these fractured relationships and soothe my aching soul.
Spirit of the north, of earth, please guide and protect me, and give me strength and grounding to understand everything that I see and learn so I can integrate it into my life.
Spirit of the east, of air, please guide and protect me, and give me strength and wisdom, and the ability to reach for the stars. Help me find my courage as I travel this world alone.
Spirit of the south, of fire and flame, please guide and protect me, and give me strength and passion to learn and grow. Help burn away the anger and the fear that I am running from.
Please give me the strength and energy to make the most of all my opportunities and experiences, and let the challenges and tiring encounters wash over me.
Please keep my mind and my heart open, and send love and healing, and the strength to move on, to my parents. I want only the very best for them, no matter what it costs me.
Thank you god and goddess, and spirits of the elements, for blessing and protecting my rite.
The circle is open but eternal. So mote it be.

And now to sleep and dream…

Carlie traced over the words with her fingers, trying to picture her mother sitting in her bedroom as a teenager, blending herbs, burning candles, casting spells. *Spells.* It was so different to the person she'd known, the practical mother, the big-city lawyer, the woman who seemed so logical and rational and pragmatic, so devoid of mystery or mysticism, or even imagination – *so unmagical.* She turned the page, and found another spell.

A Dark Moon Ritual

Despite this beautiful soft golden afternoon light, today is the dark moon, which is such a potent time for magic, and ritual, and Otherworldly things. Some witches take the night off, but as it's the most potent time to banish and end things, I'm going to use the energy to cast a spell to release the pain and sadness I feel about Mike. We've been best friends forever, and he was my first love too, but now that we're not together, now that I'm moving on and have found love with Andre, he's being really weird to me, making up stories, trying to convince me that Andre's not good enough for me, not worthy. Which is crazy, because I'm the one who's not worthy of him.

I still can't believe that Andre could like me – I mean, he's a spiritual guru, everyone admires him, and he's just so amazing. I don't know why Mike hates him so much, I guess he must just be jealous, but I'm terrified that he'll say something silly to Andre, something that will make him break up with me.

Yet despite all these misgivings, I still really care about Mike. We've supported each other and been there for one another so many times, so I feel really sad that it has turned into this. I want us to be able to be friends again, for him to let go of his crazy thoughts and be happy for me.

And so I've burned sandalwood incense, to cleanse and purify the room and to bring love, protection and healing. I've set up my altar with a black velvet altar cloth, with a glass of water for the chalice, a tealight candle for fire, a feather I found today and some patchouli incense for air, and my rose quartz for earth, and love. My goddess statue is near the centre, next to the statue of an Inkan god made of pyrite that Andre gave me.

And I've cast circle and ignited my flame to burn away my disappointment, blessed the water to wash away the pain, kissed the rose quartz to ground me in love, and lit the patchouli incense to invoke the spirit of Hekate, goddess of the dark moon, goddess of the crossroads, goddess of endings and thus new beginnings.

I've also lit four black candles for banishing, but I don't want to banish Mike from my life, just banish the negativity I feel from him, and the sadness I feel for him. And so I meditate on my love and happiness for him, trying to let go of the pain and see only our friendship stretching out into the future.

> Goddess and god, please bless and protect this rite.
> Element of fire, please guide and protect me,
> and lend me your strength and your passion.
> Element of air, please guide and protect me,
> and lend me your strength and your wisdom.
> Element of earth, please guide and protect me,
> and lend me your strength and your grounding.
> Element of water, please guide and protect me,
> and lend me your strength, and help me to wash away
> my resentment, my bitterness and my disappointment.
> Flame and fire of my black candles, please help me banish these feelings. Please let Mike's jealousy and anger stop being directed at me, and stop it affecting me, and him.
>
> I want him to find real love, like Andre and I have, and I want our friendship to be as strong as it's always been. I remember when we were thirteen, we cut our wrists a little and mingled the blood, and swore that nothing would ever come between us.
> Hekate, I beg you, remind him of his solemn vow,
> remind him of our history and of our love for each other,
> so that we can retain this friendship.
> Let him know that change is okay, and that loss is okay too, if it comes to that, because through losing one thing you gain something else. Through losing your illusions you gain insight and a clearer understanding of yourself and others.
> Ah, burn away my disappointment, spirits of fire and black candle flame.
> Wash away my bitterness, spirits of water.
> Ground me in reality and peace, spirits of earth.
> And let my anger fly away, spirits of air.
> With so much love I release Mike's impact on me.
> So mote it be…

Carlie had tears in her eyes. How heartbreaking, that Mike had tried to warn Violet about this guy, whoever he was, tried to help her, but she'd dismissed it as jealousy and pettiness on his part. How different everyone's lives would have been if she'd listened. There was no point wishing for what could never be, she knew that, but it made her so sad. Why couldn't she turn back time?

She turned the page instead, but it seemed as though that was the last entry. Disappointed that she hadn't found a definitive answer, she closed the book with a snap, then awkwardly grabbed it as it almost toppled over onto the floor. And as she righted it, something fell out and fluttered to the floor. Tentatively she picked it up.

It was a postcard from London, and her breath caught as she turned it over. It was from her mother to Mike, but while it had been addressed and had a stamp on it, there was no postmark, and no indication it had ever been sent.

Dear Mike,

I'm so sorry, I should have trusted you. You were right about him. He was cruel and violent and so possessive, so angry, and it's been a living hell to be with him. I was going to come home a little while ago – I'd packed up my stuff, what little I had, and booked a train ticket. But when I finally managed to sneak out to ring Mum, someone else answered, and said she was at Dad's funeral. So somehow it did all come to pass, everything Andre said, and it was all my fault, so I can never go home.

I can't stay here though, I have to get away from him. I've made a friend from Australia, so I'm going to go there for a while, to backpack around the Outback or something, stay out of people's way, try not to cause more harm. Start over, with a clean slate.

I can't believe that I left home, breaking Mum's heart, and my own, so that I could save Dad's life – and that it was all a lie. I feel so stupid. I wanted to call you, but I'm too embarrassed. And I imagine you must hate me as much as Mum does, and I'm so sorry about that. I'll always be sorry for that.

All my love, Violet xx

Carlie felt her heart breaking as she read the faded writing, overcome with sadness and futility and a rush of frustration. How could this be the heart of the mystery of her mother? Bad timing and misunderstandings. A lie told to control someone, an embarrassed flight to a foreign land. How could her mother have thought that Rose would blame her for her father's death? And that even if she did, that she would have wished her away forever, to never see her again?

She just couldn't get her head around it. Her mother was so loved – by her family, by her friends, by Mike – and she had such a beautiful life ahead of her. How could she have just turned her back on that? How could she throw away her life because she was too embarrassed to show up and make amends? If only she'd called Mike, he would have talked her into coming home. If only Rose had answered the phone instead of her friend that day, she would have convinced Violet not to flee. And if only she'd thought through what her actions would do to her mother.

How could she have ever thought that running away and never contacting her again would be preferable? She knew Violet had only been seventeen at the time, and maybe she'd convinced herself it was all her fault that her dad died – god knows that she'd wanted to curl up and die when she thought that she'd killed her parents – but surely at some point in the years that followed she could have got in touch with her mum?

Didn't she miss her? Didn't she think Rose deserved even a postcard to let her know that her daughter was alive, let alone offering some comfort over the loss of her husband, Violet's own father? And what about when she'd had her own child – wouldn't that have been a good time to get in touch with her mum?

Then she sighed. She could obsess about this all day, all week, but she'd never come up with an acceptable answer. What could ever explain away the devastating consequences of her mother's actions?

When she felt a paw on her leg she jumped, then came back to awareness of the dusty room, and the growing light outside. It was time to head home. But when she got there her grandma had already left for the healing centre for the day, so Carlie spent an hour going over her reiki notes, then did practice readings with the oracle deck Rose had given her. She'd hoped that using the cards would make her feel closer to her mum, but all she could think as she shuffled the deck was how easily some guy had used the cards against her, how he'd manipulated her into destroying her life, and her mother's.

That night she slipped into a strange dreamscape. She was arguing with a guy who looked like a much younger Mike, which didn't make any sense, until she realised that she wasn't seeing things through her own eyes, but through her mother's, back when she was a teenager and they'd looked so much more alike. Then just as she got her head around that, the dream shifted. She was with teenage Mike again, watching him, and he was pounding on a door. An older man she'd never seen before opened it.

"You lied in that reading you did for Violet!" Mike yelled at him. "You told her she had to leave town or else her father would die, but you just wanted her for yourself. You couldn't handle that the death card probably meant the death of your relationship with her, so you lied to her. You abused your trust, as a teacher and as a healer."

The man laughed. "Now who would ever believe that, Mike?" he asked, with the smuggest look on his face.

"But it's not right. You can't ruin her life like this, ruin her whole family. Do you know what it will do to her mother if Violet runs away without any explanation?" Mike begged. "And her father will be devastated too. He's not strong enough to cope with that."

The man shrugged. Clearly he didn't care either way.

So Mike changed tack. "Are you scared she won't want to be with you if she knows the truth?" he sneered.

The man stared him down, and Carlie was impressed with Mike's courage in standing his ground.

"I'm going to tell her," Mike finally said, voice wavering only a little. "She has to know that you're no spiritual leader, that you're just an insecure and over-possessive creep who wants everything your own way, and will stop at nothing to get it."

The man laughed again. "She'll never believe you – she'll just think you're jealous and vindictive, and making things up to try to win her back. I've already mentioned that to her once or twice, or more, so the groundwork has been laid."

Mike's face turned red, and he started to protest. "I bet you're not even divorced, are you?" he demanded. "You'll just keep Violet stashed away somewhere, waiting on your every whim, cut off from her friends and family but fed lies so she never realises just how lonely she is, how dependent on you she's become, how awful you are. Why can't you just leave her alone?"

"This is none of your business Mike, and I'd advise you not to say a word of any of this to her, or to anyone. You try it, and I'll make sure she never speaks to you again. Do I make myself clear? Don't you value her friendship at all Mike?" he asked, voice dripping with sarcastic sweetness.

Both men turned as Violet climbed the stairs behind them. "Oh, hello," she said warily as she saw them both together. "What's going on? Why are you here Mike?"

The man smiled. Carlie thought he looked sleazy, but her mother was oblivious. "He was just asking about the next healing course, whether there were still any places available."

Violet looked at Mike, surprised. "Really?"

"Sure," he said softly, as he slowly turned away, shoulders hunched and face downcast. But Violet didn't even notice – she was too busy hugging the man at the door, and being swept inside. He leaned out the door and hissed Mike's name.

"Remember what I said Mike. You turn her against me and I'll curse you, I swear it. Every woman you ever love will die on their fortieth birthday," he spat, malice and spite dripping from every word. "Now leave us. We want to be *alone* together."

The man's self-satisfied smirk turned Carlie's stomach, and the bleakness on Mike's face as he sadly walked back down the street, totally shattered, made her cry. Her heart broke for him – and for her grandmother, and the grandfather she'd never met as a result, and for her poor, young, misguided mother too.

Chapter 19

Secrets of the Moon

Beep. Beep. Beep. Startled, Carlie leaped out of bed and hit the alarm. It was 3am, and for a moment she wondered why on earth she'd set the clock for this ungodly hour. But then it all came crashing back. Tonight was the full moon. And it would become exactly full at 4am, so she wanted to be up on the tor when it did. As quietly as she could, she pulled a jacket on over her yoga pants and sweatshirt, tied up her boots and slipped out the kitchen door and through the garden to the back laneway.

When she and her grandma had visited Elsie, they'd stayed up late into the night talking together, the two women plying her with herbal tea and sharing with her their love of the earth and their path as nature-loving witches, attuned to the rhythms of the seasons and the cycles of the planet and the moon. They'd spoken lovingly of working with the lunar phases for connection to nature and their own bodies, and how much more centred they felt when they lived in harmony with them, so Carlie had decided she should start doing that too.

Hence her desire to be up on the tor at the moment the moon became full, so she could take her first step towards harmonising her energies with earth and moon. And of course she hoped that by following in her mum's footsteps, echoing her rituals all these years later, she'd somehow feel closer to her, and understand her better.

The sky was cloudy, and she wasn't even sure she'd be able to see the moon, but she knew she needed to be outside, drinking in the beauty and magic of the night. After a brisk climb, and only a few stumbles, she made it to the summit of the hill by half past three, and sank down onto the cool grass, staring up at the racing clouds, at the peek here and there of the shining moon.

Her mind was a tumult of emotions as she went over all the things she'd learned in the last week alone, from the articles about the drunk driver and the car accident to Rhiannon's revelations about her mum being involved with another man – an apparently controlling and violent older man – and her own discovery of the unsent postcard to Mike that seemed to back this up.

Anger had replaced her feelings of guilt over the situation, and now the loss of her parents seemed even harder, if that was possible. Even more pointless. A drunk driver. A totally random act, just a wrong-place, wrong-time, humans-are-stupid kind of thing. She'd been to parties with her friends when they drank, and watched them become stupid and annoying, saying dumb things, repeating themselves over and over, becoming hostile when she wouldn't join them, kissing people they didn't even like then shrugging the next day: "Oh well, I was drunk." How could you do something you didn't want to do just because you'd had a few drinks?

She knew she'd never touch alcohol again. If an apparently nice and normal man – a father of two, a respected businessman, a guy who'd never committed a crime or wanted to kill anyone – suddenly caused the death of two people, two strangers, because he was dumb enough to drink and drive, then there was something seriously wrong with this freely available, legal drug.

Sighing, she flopped down onto her back. It was all so senseless. Two kind, compassionate people had been wiped off the face of the earth, and it wasn't fair. There was no reason, no purpose. The words of the blue-clad woman on the hill came back to her abruptly, and she realised she was right. It made her suddenly angry at her mum's new-age attitude that everything happens for a reason. Sometimes bad things did just happen, and trying to work out a great mystery to explain them was stupid and dangerous. People needed to take responsibility for their actions, not accept some sanctimonious crap about it being part of the plan, punishment for something they apparently did in a past life, or some grand lesson.

What was the lesson here? Drinking and driving is dangerous? Not a secret. People are stupid? Again, no surprise there. Being a good person resulted in a painful, lingering death? Not the best message to be imparting, surely. Imagine if her grandma didn't have those articles from Sandy, and she'd gone on blaming herself for the rest of her life for killing her parents. Reluctantly she acknowledged that she did have some idea of the panic and self-loathing that would have been going through her mother's mind when she thought she would ultimately be responsible for the death of her own father.

The tears started to flow, and for a while she gave herself over to her rage, her grief and her sense of powerlessness. But finally her tears began to subside, and she scrubbed at her face with her hands and took a few deep breaths. Then her watch beeped 4am, and she looked up into the sky, just as the full moon came out from behind the clouds and poured its gentle golden light down on her.

A wave of energy and power swept over her, and she stood up and spun around, arms outstretched and face turned to the heavens. "Oh moon goddess, please give me the strength to get through this," she whispered. "Let me know what I need to know to carry on, and to help my grandma through her own journey of grief."

She smiled as she thought of Rose. She had been so nice to her, so kind, even when she'd been a total bitch in return. And she was sure it was *just* what she'd needed, a petulant teenager turning up on her doorstep (not!). She'd probably had her fill of angsty teens when Violet was growing up. Or maybe not. It seemed that her mum had been pretty much the perfect daughter, loving and kind, considerate, always wanting to help people – at least until the moment she'd disappeared so mysteriously, without explanation or closure. When she'd run away with some wannabe spiritual leader, if her new friend, and the words in her mum's book, were to be believed.

The cawing of a black raven suddenly brought her back to herself. She didn't know how long she'd been up there, but the first hint of morning light was beginning to glow in the east, while the huge golden moon prepared to set in the west. She should probably head home before her grandma started worrying about her.

But when she looked for the path back down she gasped. An immense, thick mist had rolled in around the summit of the hill, thicker than anything she'd ever seen before – thicker even than on top of Winter Hill. It was like being on top of a mountain, with the clouds stretched out below you. She thought of the book on her grandmother's bookshelf that outlined what happened when the mists came in. Perhaps she should have read that one, she thought wryly, instead of the travel guide she'd chosen.

She looked around carefully, but she couldn't see where she'd climbed the hill earlier, or where the main path down was. Gingerly she took a few steps towards where she thought it should be. Then, steeling herself, she took a deep breath and stepped into the mists.

Chapter 20

Into the Heart of the Mystery

The mists swirled around her, a living presence, parts of it lit up with a golden glow or streaked pink from the rising sun. It was so thick, but kind of peaceful too, like floating in a cloud or journeying through an underwater realm, her way much slower than usual, all languid and dreamy, as though she was being gently held and nurtured as she moved forward.

She still couldn't see more than a few centimetres in front of her, and with each step she took she placed her foot very tentatively onto the earth, nervous that at any moment she might take a step out and into nothing, and fall straight off the mountain. But she felt the mist thinning slightly as she got closer to the ground, and eventually she noticed that she was on a flat pathway. Looking around, she tried to get her bearings, and was surprised to realise that she was at the back gate to her old, deserted cottage.

Except that now it didn't look deserted. The garden was beautiful – full of lush green herbs as well as flowers, much like her grandma's backyard. There was light spilling out of the windows, and she could hear music and movement from inside. Squatters? Faeries? The latter wouldn't really need a house, surely.

Then the back door opened, and her mother walked outside and beckoned her closer. "Darling! We were wondering where you were.

Did you go up to the tor to charge up your crystals and perform a full moon ritual?"

Carlie stared, open-mouthed. What was going on? How could her mother be here? Then she looked down, and noticed that she was wearing clothes she'd never seen before, and her hair was shorter and wavier than usual. She glanced at her mother again. Her hair was the same dark colour as her own, not blonde, and her skin was paler, but other than that she looked pretty much the same as she had the last time she'd seen her, the night before her fortieth birthday.

"Come in darling," she grinned. "Why are you staring at me like that?" Carlie blinked nervously, mind whirring.

"Honey!" her mum called, turning back inside. "Carlie's back, we can go now."

She ran up the back steps, excited yet scared at the same time. Was her dad here too? Then she stopped, shocked, as the man turned around. It was Mike, Rhiannon's dad, who she'd met for the first time when her grandma had introduced them at the shop during the reiki course, and again at Brodie's birthday party.

"Hi love," he said, and picked up his keys from the table.

"Dad?" she whispered.

"Yes?" he asked, frowning. "Come on, are you ready to go?"

She froze. Mike was her dad? And what had happened to her voice? It was different to usual, and so was her mum's. She felt dizzy, and totally confused. What was going on?

"Um, Mum, where are we going?" she asked, and she definitely had an English accent. Her mum laughed.

"Ah, silly, the full moon always makes you a bit ditzy," she said with a smile – the slight British accent she'd had in real life far more pronounced here.

"Come on, we're going out for breakfast together, as a treat, then you're going to do your first day at your grandma's shop. She's had a few bookings already – people are looking forward to there being a regular reiki practitioner in town. Now hurry up, we've got to run if you don't want to be late for your first day."

Carlie picked up her bag from the bench and followed her "parents" out of the house. If this was a dream, it was the weirdest and most realistic one she'd ever had. The three of them went to what was apparently her favourite cafe, and ordered their usual. *Their usual?* This would be interesting. They talked a lot, about their plans for the upcoming holidays, plans for a birthday party for her grandma. Finally the food came, and she laughed. Her "parents" looked at her questioningly. It seemed that in this strange parallel dimension, she ate bacon and eggs.

"I thought we were vegetarian," she ventured, and her mum laughed.

"Well, your gran would love it if we were, but you could never give up bacon!" she replied, biting into a crisp piece of the charred meat with obvious relish.

Carlie shrugged, and pushed her bacon to the side of her plate. She couldn't bring herself to eat it, dream or not.

"Are you guys happy?" she finally asked them, as she politely ate the eggs and drank her coffee. She didn't even like coffee.

Her mum gave her another funny look. "Of course sweetie. Especially since your dad got promoted. And you're still looking forward to our trip to Spain aren't you?"

Spain? Wow. She'd never even considered going there for a holiday. "Yeah, sure," she muttered.

"How's work?" she asked her mum next.

"Well, much the same," she replied. "I'm so glad Mum found someone to help her in the shop, so I could cut back my hours and have time to study. Only one more year to go now."

Carlie raised her eyebrows quizzically. "Darling, social work. Honestly, what's gotten into you today?"

Shrugging, she turned to look at her "dad". He smiled.

"Well, I suppose I can tell you both now," he confided. "We're expanding again, but Laneth has agreed to go to the new store, so I'll only have to be away one day a week now."

"Oh Mike, that's so wonderful," her mum said, throwing her arms around him and leaning in to kiss him passionately on the mouth. Carlie tried not to look too shocked.

When they finished breakfast, and Carlie had somehow blundered her way through the crazy situation without totally giving away that she was an imposter, they dropped her off at her grandma's healing centre, then headed off together. Was this some weird parallel universe where she was living out an alternate life? If her mum hadn't left home when she did, and met her dad – her real dad – and gone to live in Australia with him, would she have ended up marrying Mike?

Rose had implied that they were far more than just friends, and Rhiannon had admitted that her dad had been in love with Carlie's mum when they were teenagers. Violet's Book of Shadows described Mike as her first love too. But she couldn't get her head around it. If that had happened, did Mike's daughter Rhiannon still exist? Would she have ended up in Australia instead of Carlie? And maybe Rhiannon's parents would have died instead of her own?

Strangely enough though, it seemed that her life would have ended up the same either way – about to start working in her grandma's shop, and going to the local high school for her final year. Surely that *Sliding Doors* stuff wasn't really true? Or was there some destiny everyone had that would play out no matter what the circumstances, or who their parents were, or where they were born?

She sighed, then took a deep, calming breath. She had to pull herself together. Apparently she was about to do her first day of work. Nervously she walked into her grandma's shop – the only thing that was familiar to her in this dreamscape.

And it looked exactly as it had when she'd first seen it, her first morning in this town. Even the window display was the same, filled with crystals, a black cauldron, some velvet cloaks and brightly coloured dresses, pots of ivy winding around the pillars, and a selection of books on healing, spirituality and divination.

Her grandma looked up and smiled as she walked in. "Sweetheart, I'm so glad you're here. One of my regulars just popped in, and was hoping she could get a reiki treatment before she goes to work. Is it too early for you to start?" she asked.

Carlie's mouth hung open, and she stared at her grandma in wonder. She looked years younger than the real Rose, the Rose she knew, but it was obviously her. The stress of losing her daughter and her husband within weeks of each other had clearly taken its toll on her, and aged her at least a decade. But in this realm, Rose's daughter was alive and happy, settled down in a cute cottage with her childhood sweetheart and a daughter of her own, and the tragedy of her alternate life had left no mark on her.

"Hi Grandma," she replied, smiling as she walked over to hug her. "How's Grandpa?" she asked, praying that in this reality he was still alive and kicking.

"He's on the mend – he'll be back in his garden in no time," Rose answered, her relief evident. "He doesn't want to neglect his herb patch, or his tomatoes. You know what he's like!"

Carlie nodded, although she had no idea what he was like, since he didn't exist in her real life. If her real life still existed. The longer she stayed here, the further away it all seemed.

"Now, did you want to come through and start on Cynthia?"

She nodded again, and followed her grandma through the curtained partition to the back room. There was a woman already there, seated on a chair and flicking through a magazine.

"Oh Carlie, hi! It's so lovely to see you again – it's been ages. Are you sure it's no trouble to fit me in?"

Mind whirring, she shook her head. "Of course Cynthia, it's fine. Now just take your boots off, then lie down here. I'll light a few candles and grab a few crystals, and we'll start in just a moment."

And she went around the room, preparing, then put a bolster under her first-ever patient's knees and made sure her head was comfortable. Lucky she'd done that reiki course a couple of weeks ago! As she worked her way around all the points of the body, she let her mind wander, trying to puzzle everything out.

The first and most obvious possibility was that this was all just a dream, and soon she would wake up in her little room at her grandma's house. But it had been going for way too long now, and felt so real. And she could still taste the coffee she'd had at breakfast with her mum and Mike.

What else could it be? Was this her real life, and she'd just forgotten, reinventing a past in Australia that didn't exist? Had she fallen on the way back down from Summer Tor and hit her head? Was she feverish, or deluded? Or – and she knew this sounded totally nuts – was there something magical about the mists? Had she stumbled into a parallel universe where not only had her mum not died, she'd also never left home, broken her own mother's heart, or gone to live on the other side of the world with an Aussie backpacker?

If so, what had happened to her real dad? And how did all these people here know her? Cynthia had greeted her like an old friend. But if that was the case, what did that mean for her friends back home? Was her whole existence just erased, and they all went on as normal, just without her in their life? Would Emily have a different best friend? Had her dad married someone else?

What seemed like mere moments later her grandma poked her head around the door, tapped her watch then held up her hand. Five more minutes? Carlie glanced at the clock on the wall above the desk, and was surprised to see that fifty-five minutes had passed since she'd started working on Cynthia. It was time to finish up and bring her gently back to awareness, and time for her to focus again on the here and now. Shaking her head, she tried to clear it of all the confusion and the strange theories racing around inside. This was all too weird, and tying herself in knots trying to figure it out wasn't helping.

She spent the rest of the day doing reiki healings on those who wanted one, and helping her grandma in the shop in between. Curious, she managed to get her talking about the grandfather she'd never met, and realised that she'd inherited a few of his character traits. That made her smile. Perhaps this was what being immortal was – parts of you living on in those who came afterwards. Finally she steered the conversation around to her mother.

"What was she like when she was my age?" Carlie asked.

"She was just like you, sweet and caring," Rose said, smiling wistfully. "But you know, I nearly lost her once, just after her seventeenth birthday." A shiver ran up Carlie's spine.

"She'd been learning to read the tarot, because she'd decided she wanted to work in the shop with me on weekends while she studied to be a social worker. People were always asking me if I could get a psychic reader in, so it was a great idea. She did an introductory course one weekend, then she went along every Monday night after that to study with a quite famous reader and spiritual teacher a few towns over.

"She was still dating Mike – they'd been inseparable all through high school – but she was also enjoying meeting new people and learning new things, and being acknowledged in her own right rather than just as Mike's girlfriend. His parents weren't especially welcoming – they were set on him marrying their business partner's daughter," Rose said with a frown.

"Can you believe it? In this day and age? Of course they came around, and they still think you and your mum are the best thing that ever happened to their family, as you well know," she laughed.

Carlie smiled vaguely, and tried to look like she knew what her grandma was talking about. More relatives she apparently knew well? She'd have to start writing down notes soon.

"Anyway, Violet used her birthday money for a tarot reading from this teacher. And when she came home she was distraught. She refused to tell us what he'd said, no matter how much we begged, but she was really shaken by it, and for two weeks she was quite strange. Vague, teary, depressed – and she snapped at us if we even tried to ask if we could help her. The next weekend we were running an equinox ritual together at the shop. She was doing readings in the morning, then we were going to head home and get our festival clothes and all the candles, ribbons, statues, altar cloths and tools we'd need, and pick the fresh herbs, so we could come back here and set up before everyone arrived, then get dressed together.

"But then three backpackers came in, and they all wanted readings. Normally Violet would have said no, because getting ready together was part of our ritual, and sacred to both of us, but she said she really needed the money, which wasn't like her, and asked if I'd pick everything up from home on my own so she could stay and do their readings," Rose remembered.

"So I left her to it and went home to gather everything we needed, and pick the herbs and flowers for the altar. She'd said that her dress was hanging in the bathroom, but it wasn't there, so I went into her room to grab it – I figured it was probably still lying on her bed. When I walked in, I tripped on something that was poking out from under her bed. I went to push it back under, and saw that it was her Book of Shadows. It was beautiful – leather bound, with gorgeous ironwork around the corners and along the spine, and a pattern of spirals and symbols carved into the front cover. I'd never read it before – I thought it was important that she have her privacy, even though we did all our rituals together – but I was so worried about her. I hoped that maybe it would have some notes from her tarot reading, or some clue to the obvious distress she'd been suffering.

"It did – and I was horrified. This so-called guru, who charged a fortune to study with him and was consulted by politicians and celebrities, had told her that her father was going to die, and she would be responsible. And the only way to save him was to leave home.

"I couldn't believe anyone would say that to a client, especially one so young. Everyone knows that when the death card comes up, it's not about a literal death – it can indicate the death of a project or the end of a relationship or the changing of a plan. But to be so specific, and to blame her for killing her father, not only was it irresponsible and wrong, it violated every single teacher-student bond. And you can't just say that to someone then send them on their way. How did he think she was going to cope with that news?" Rose's face showed her pain, but her voice remained steady.

"I was absolutely furious, but mostly I just felt so bad for Violet. I couldn't even begin to imagine what she'd been going through for the past two weeks. I hoped that maybe something would become clear during the ritual that night, and I couldn't wait to get back to the shop and give her a hug, and impress upon her again that psychic readings are only ever of possible futures, that you can change your life in a moment, by one tiny decision, one missed train, one new opportunity, one chance meeting, one secret shared...

"Anyway, I opened her wardrobe to grab her ritual dress, and the big bag she took for school camps fell out. I picked it up to put it back inside, and was surprised by how heavy it was. Then I saw a piece of paper peeking out of one of the side pockets. It was a confirmation for two weeks accommodation – starting the following night – in London, and folded up with it was a train ticket for the morning. I opened the bag, and it was neatly packed, with the jumper her grandma had knitted for her recent birthday on top, so obviously it wasn't just waiting to be unpacked from her last trip."

Rose paused for a moment and wiped her eyes. More than twenty years later, she was still deeply affected by how close she'd come to losing her daughter. Carlie led her grandma into the little alcove behind the changing room and sat her down, then put the kettle on, reached up for the glass jar of dried chamomile flowers, spooned some into the teapot and sat down opposite her. She held her grandma's hand as she continued her story.

"I went back to the shop with all our stuff, and she was still doing the last reading, so I started setting up on my own. And by the time she finished, the first guests had arrived, so we had to quickly get changed, and we didn't get a chance to talk until we got home. She said she was exhausted and just wanted to go to sleep, but I insisted that we have a cup of tea before bed.

"We talked about the ritual for a while, then I asked her if she had any plans for the morning. She said she'd probably just lie in, and we should too, but she looked so sad. Finally I just came right out with it – said her bag had fallen out when I opened the cupboard, and I'd seen the ticket. At first she tried to explain it away, that she was going up to London for the day to buy my birthday present, and now I'd ruined the surprise. If I hadn't seen the tarot reading I would have left it at that, thought she'd just thrown the new jumper in the bag until she had time to tidy away properly. But I pressed on, and finally she broke down and told me about the reading, and that she had to leave home and go far away, so she couldn't cause her father's death."

The kettle boiled, and Carlie poured the water into the teapot, burning her hand in her haste. She added a spoonful of honey then poured a mug for her gran and one for herself and sat back down, holding her grandma's hand again.

For a moment it struck her as odd, that it felt so normal, so right, to be so intimate with a woman she'd only known for a few weeks, but some part of her felt as though she'd known Rose forever. And maybe she had. Who was to say what was real life anyway? Perhaps this was a dream – or maybe it was the real existence, and the one where her parents had died was the dream. Shaking her head, and feeling dizzy again from all her whirling thoughts, she turned her attention back to her grandmother.

"Eventually I convinced Violet that there was no way she could be responsible for her father's death, that he was fit and healthy, and would be alive for many years to come. And he's still fine," Rose said with a smile. "It taught her a very valuable lesson about psychic readings though, and made her very careful about what she told people, and how she interpreted the cards. I think that's why she's always been so sought after for readings – she helps people see the signs the cards are indicating, and what that could mean for them, then works through it with them so that they're best prepared to meet any challenges or take advantage of any opportunities. She sees the tarot as a great tool to help you create the life you want, not as a final and unbending pronouncement on your future.

"We create the life we want to live in each moment Sweetheart. And any kind of divination or healing or spiritual practice can assist you to make the most of things, to avoid the pitfalls, and to uncover the skills you need to work on or learn in order to achieve what you want to achieve, but it's not the complete truth or final word, it's simply a strand of possibilities," Rose said thoughtfully.

She smiled as she looked at her granddaughter. "I know you've been learning to work with oracle cards too, and I think you'll be great, just like your mum. Just remember, with any person you read for, that it's their life, and they are in control. Only they can create the life they want – the cards will just help illuminate the path a little. And always trust your gut Sweetheart. I still have nightmares about that day, where I did the readings, so it was Violet who went home and picked up our ritual gear – and disappeared from our lives the next morning. I don't think I could have survived if we'd lost her," she said, her voice cracking with the thought of that pain.

Carlie hugged her tight. "Oh Grandma, you could survive anything," she insisted. And she would. Her husband couldn't, unfortunately, and Rose would look a decade older from enduring such a tragedy, but there was no point mentioning that to her. She wanted to break down and cry though. God, what a terrible irony, that it was actually in her mother leaving home, not staying, that were sown the seeds of her dad's demise.

"You're very kind Carlie," her grandma said, patting her on the arm and bringing her attention back to the room. "Now, I'd better let you finish up for the day – your parents will be here to pick you up soon, and they won't want to wait too long. Let me get you your pay for today," she said, standing up. "And a gorgeous new oracle deck came in this morning, which I think you'll love playing with. Just remember, you are in control, not the cards."

Her mum and Mike walked in a few minutes later, and Carlie raced over to tell them all about her first day on the job. "Bye Grandma," she yelled across the room. "See you on Tuesday."

"Thanks Mum," Violet called out. "Love you!"

The three of them walked outside into the cold early evening air. The first hint of snow flickered past, and Carlie laughed and tried to grab at it. She'd never seen snow – or at least, the Australian version of her never had. She followed her parents over to their car, and they set off for the drive to a friend's place for dinner.

As she listened to them both telling her about their day, she turned to look in her bag, to see what kind of card deck her grandma had given her. Opening it up and starting to shuffle the cards, she admired the beautiful artwork.

"Hey Mum, ask me a question," she said.

Her mum laughed, and turned around to face her. As Carlie looked up from the cards, waiting for the question, she saw bright lights speeding towards them, head on, and heard Mike curse. There was a terrible crunching sound, a sensation of flying, then a cold darkness descending on her and wrapping around her in an effort to dull the pain.

Chapter 21

The End of the Faerytale

As she swam back to conscious awareness, Carlie began to feel a throbbing pain in her head. Opening her eyes, she saw her grandmother sitting on the side of her bed, gazing out the window at the tor. She was back in her bedroom, and Rose was looking the same as she had when she'd arrived here from Australia – this was the her-parents-were-dead reality, and her heart ached to be back with her mum, selecting an oracle card for her, reading out the meaning. Tears welled in her eyes, and she sniffled a little.

Hearing her move, her grandma gazed at her sharply. "Oh thank goddess! Sweetheart, you're okay," she cried, and leaned down to kiss her on the forehead.

"What happened?" Carlie whispered.

Rose shrugged helplessly. "We're not really sure. Mike found you lying at the bottom of the tor, and brought you here. The doctor came around, and said there are some tests he can run when you're up again, if you need them, but he thinks you may have just fainted, either from the stress of the last few weeks or from a migraine attack, or maybe you slipped over on the pathway down and hit your head. Is your head hurting now?"

Carlie nodded, then closed her eyes again. "Mum was there," she said quietly. "Mum and Mike. And I grew up here, and worked with you, and we lived just down the street, and Grandpa was there…" She broke off as tears choked her.

Rose paled. "What do you mean?" she asked, apprehension in her voice, but Carlie was too distraught to speak. Then the doorbell rang, and Rose reluctantly went downstairs to answer it. A moment later, she returned with Mike in tow.

He smiled a hello at Carlie, then stood awkwardly, his tall frame hulking in the small room. Tentatively he handed her a small box, and she reached up to take it – but when she saw what it was she gasped, and dropped it like it was burning her hands.

It was the same card deck her grandmother had given her in that dream life, the one she'd been shuffling when she was in the car with her mum and Mike. Clutching her head, she moaned at the pain, and her grandma ushered their guest out. Carlie heard the sound of conversation drifting up the stairs as they walked, but couldn't make out what was being said. Then she heard the front door close, and her grandma came back into the room.

"Do you need anything Sweetheart?" she asked, the worry evident on her face. "Tea? Painkillers?"

"Just some water," she whispered. She needed to think clearly, not dull her mind even more. Rose handed her a glass from the bedside table and helped her sit up a little further. Idly she glanced at her left hand, trying to remember when she'd burned it, then her face drained of colour as she recalled that it was when she was making tea for her grandma in that other reality that she'd poured boiling water on it.

"It was the strangest thing Gran," she began nervously. "This morning, really early, I went up on the tor for the full moon, to do a ritual, but when I was coming back down the mist had covered everything, and I had to kind of wade into it. I wasn't sure where I was, but I ended up at that derelict old house along the laneway – except this time it wasn't derelict. And Mum was inside, and so was Mike, and he was my father…" Part of her knew she was babbling, that she wasn't making sense, but she couldn't stop herself.

"I was so confused. And I had an English accent. And I'd grown up here, and my hair was shorter. And we all went to see you at the shop, and it was you, but you looked different. Kind of, um, younger."

She broke off, scared that she'd offended her grandmother, but Rose motioned for her to go on. So she continued, telling her about the healing centre she'd been in – the things that were different, and those that were the same. She told her about the reiki clients she'd seen, and how good it felt to be able to help them a little. And then she shared the story that other-reality Rose had told her while she was there, about Violet learning tarot, and doing readings at the shop on the day of the ritual, then her getting extra customers so that it was Rose who had to race home and pick up their things for that night.

Then, very hesitantly, she outlined the reading her mum had received from the spiritual teacher and tarot expert, which Rose had read in her daughter's Book of Shadows. She told her about Violet's conviction that she would cause her father's death, and then revealed her plan to run away from home in order to prevent it.

Her grandmother's face was white, and frozen into a mask of distress. She half fell onto the edge of Carlie's bed.

"I remember that day," she whispered. "I remember that ritual. Violet was doing tarot sessions, and a few tourists came in for late readings. Violet was going to do them, but one of the other girls asked if she could instead, so we went home together to get ready as planned. And the next morning she was gone.

"There was no trace of her, no clue. We searched desperately, rang everyone we knew, everyone she knew. I even called the tarot guy, her teacher, but he said he had no idea that she'd been planning to leave, why would he? We spoke to the police too, but there wasn't much they could do – legally she was old enough to leave home, and we did get a postcard a few weeks later, saying she was fine, and would call soon. But she never did."

"But she did," Carlie said.

Her grandma stared at her. "She did what?"

"She did call," she said. "Miscommunication. That was the card I pulled from this deck when I was in the car, and it's on the cover of the box Mike just gave me. She called on the day of Grandpa's funeral, wanting to come home, but the person who answered the phone said you were at his funeral, and she was so wracked with guilt that she couldn't come home, and finally left the country. She couldn't face you, couldn't bear to see the pain she'd caused."

A single tear trickled down Rose's pale cheek. "Someone did ring that day, but I was in the kitchen sorting out the food for the wake, so Carla from down the road picked it up. She said it was just someone sending their condolences, saying how sorry they were for my loss. She didn't get a name…"

Rose looked at her granddaughter sharply. "But how could you know that?" she demanded.

"I read a lot about Mum's life and her rituals in a book like the one you described, a big leather-bound book that had her name in the front, and there was a postcard in it that she'd written to Mike but never sent, about the phone call."

"She took her Book of Shadows with her to Australia?" her grandma asked hopefully. "Do you still have it?"

Carlie shook her head. "No, it was in an old house here, the house that I was living in with Mum and Mike in my dream." Sadly she realised that she'd already relegated that day to her dreamscape, although it still felt far too real for that. Her throbbing hand alone was a strange reminder, let alone this new knowledge about her mother that she had accessed from somewhere.

As her mind raced, trying to make sense of it all, she told her grandmother about the three times she'd visited the derelict cottage, how she'd walked into the mists each time, and a candle that was burning in the window had led her there, although she never could find it once she'd gone inside. That she'd read through the book, and each time she'd opened it there had been more in it, as though it was waiting for her to catch up and learn enough to understand the next bit. And she told her about the little black cat with the white star on its forehead, who had helped her turn the pages, and brought her out of a trance one time by putting her little paw on her leg.

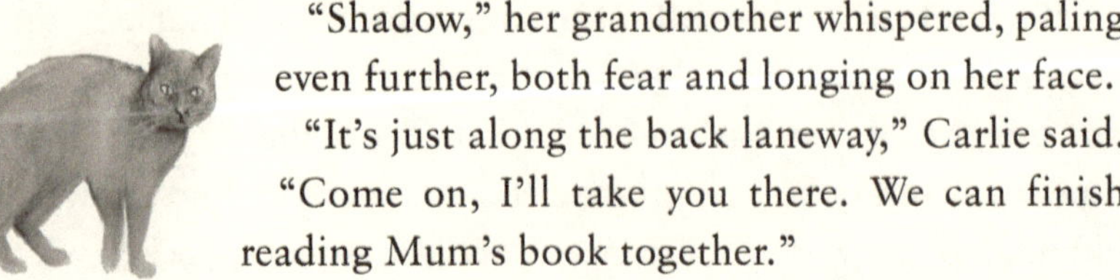

"Shadow," her grandmother whispered, paling even further, both fear and longing on her face.

"It's just along the back laneway," Carlie said. "Come on, I'll take you there. We can finish reading Mum's book together."

Her grandma frowned. "I'm pretty sure there isn't an empty cottage along the laneway," she replied. "Mike's dad used to have one just up the road, but it burned down around the same time that Violet left. For a terrible few days we thought that she'd died in the fire, but they never found any bodies."

Carlie shook her head. "I've been in there, I've read Mum's book," she insisted. "Come on, I'll show you."

Shakily she got up out of bed, holding on to her grandmother's shoulder, then pulled on a pair of jeans from the floor and some sneakers. Rose shook her head, worried, but she followed her granddaughter down the stairs and out through the back garden into the laneway that ran behind their house.

As they walked, she took Carlie's hand, and murmured to go slow, since she'd just gotten up after two days in bed. Two days? Carlie felt like she'd climbed the tor just a few hours ago, and she was as alarmed by the strange lapse of time as she was by the visions. Was her mind going? Had her grief finally pushed her towards a nervous breakdown?

Taking a deep breath, she tried to focus on the here and now – the feel of her grandma's thin hand in hers, the warmth of the pale sunlight through the trees, the sensation of the gravel crunching under her feet. It wasn't a cold day, but they both hugged their jackets more closely around themselves, chilled by this strange mystery, and by the thought of Violet – their mother, their daughter – and her suffering that sat so heavily around their shoulders. They walked past several backyards in silence, until the path finally widened.

"It's just up here," Carlie said confidently – but when they got there they were gazing at an empty block, scorch marks still evident on the massive old oak tree, and the remaining plant life struggling to grow in the blackened earth. Carlie felt dizzy again, and was grateful for the arm her grandma offered her.

"I… I don't understand," she whispered.

"This was Mike's father's place," Rose explained. "He'd inherited it but never lived in it, so Mike had decided that he was going to live here after he left school. He had it all planned out, but the cottage burned down the night Violet went missing. The fire chief said there was nothing suspicious about it, no foul play, and it was ruled accidental. Perhaps the wiring shorted and a spark caught, or maybe a candle had been left alight and it ignited the curtains and spread quickly. The timbers were really old."

Carlie gasped at the thought of a ghost candle guiding her to the cottage each time, through the mists, through time itself.

"Mike's father had been meaning to fix the cottage up, do some repairs and fire-proof it properly before Mike moved in, but he didn't, and neither of them had the heart to do anything with it after the destruction. His dad used the insurance money to build a second house out on Apple Tree Lane, on the other side of the tor, and the land has just stayed like this ever since, blackened and unable to sustain any growth," Rose continued.

"Mike had hoped to marry your mother and live in the cottage with her, so even after his father died, and it became clear that Violet was never coming back, he refused to build anything on the land."

Carlie felt faint. In her parallel universe Mike and Violet *had* been married, and they *had* lived in the house, and they'd been very happy there, with her. She'd even seen the lush garden they'd cultivated together, although all that remained now was the big old oak tree.

She started shaking, and her grandmother put an arm around her and led her back to their cottage to rest, her frail physicality belying her strength. Rose put the kettle on and pulled down a jar of dried chamomile flowers, then spooned them into the teapot on autopilot.

Suddenly the phone rang though, and it was with some relief that Rose told her she had to go in to the healing centre and fill in, because one of the therapists had called in sick. They both needed some time to digest everything they'd discovered, and Carlie's head was still throbbing, from a migraine as well as the mind blowing and totally confusing events of the past couple of days.

Chapter 22

A Daughter's Gift

The next morning Carlie felt a bit better, although she still couldn't get her head around all that had happened. She tiptoed downstairs and boiled the kettle to brew a pot of strong tea – real stuff this time, not herbal – then went to the pantry and looked through the ingredients. By the time Rose emerged, ready for work, Carlie was pulling a tray out of the oven and pouring her a mug of tea.

"Good morning Grandma," she said brightly. "I made some raspberry muffins, and here's your tea, just the way you like it."

"Thank you Sweetheart – and what a perfect breakfast this is for the beginning of autumn," Rose replied, as she gratefully accepted the mug of tea and a warm muffin. "And you look really well, like you slept through the night for the first time in a month."

Carlie smiled. She'd only slept for a couple of hours at most, as she'd lain there all night, awake and desperately puzzling over the events of the last few days, but she didn't want to worry her grandma any more than she already had. And while she was still no closer to understanding most of it, she had come to realise just how much she owed Rose, and how fortunate she was that this woman had taken her – a total stranger, and an angry, grumpy one at that – in without questions or conditions. Who had cared for her and loved her so deeply, even while her own heart bled over the loss of her daughter.

"Thank you Grandma, really," she whispered. "For taking me in. For being so kind. For putting up with my moods and my anger since I first got here. I'm really so very sorry – I know you didn't deserve to be treated the way I treated you. And I'm going to be different from now on, I promise."

Her grandma walked across the room and hugged her. "Oh Sweetheart," she said, voice thick with tears. "It's okay, I understand. Such a loss is terrible, and heartbreaking, and you're so young. But I love you Carlie, and I'm here for you, always."

Sitting down opposite her granddaughter at the table in the glass-walled breakfast nook, Rose took a bite of the muffin. "Mmmm, it's delicious. Thank you so much for this, it's just what I needed," she smiled. "Did you use the raspberries especially for today?"

Carlie shook her head, puzzled.

"It's Lughnasadh, the beginning of autumn, which is one of the seasonal festivals of the year," she explained. "We have a ritual planned at the healing centre tomorrow night, if you'd like to come?"

Carlie looked hesitant. "Maybe. What would I have to do?"

Her grandma smiled. "You don't have to do anything, you can just watch if you'd prefer, or you can be part of the circle – you don't have to say or do anything though, just soak it all up. I've got to get down to the centre now to open up, but maybe we can talk about it more tonight? How about we go out for dinner, do something special? There's a really nice vegetarian cafe, which has great desserts too. Shall we meet at the shop at 6pm?"

Carlie nodded, waved goodbye to her grandma, then got out the bag that held her textbooks and some information for the coming school year. Now was as good a time as any to try to figure out what she wanted to do with her life...

Later, as the sun was beginning to set, she met Rose at the healing centre just as it was closing. Her grandma ushered her inside and insisted that she find something she liked that she could wear to the ritual, her treat. Carlie had never been one for long billowing gowns or pretty fabrics, she was a jeans and t-shirt kind of girl, but she had to admit that she had a lot of fun trying on the different outfits, in colours and styles she'd never even considered wearing before.

When she finally stepped out of the changing room in her favourite one, she heard her grandma's gasp of pleasure, which mingled with the quickly hidden pain in her eyes.

With her long dark hair loose around her shoulders, and a deep red Renaissance-style dress flowing to the floor, Carlie was a vision – she could have been Violet, stepping out of a time machine from two decades ago, the same age, preparing for the same ritual. But Carlie had a depth of expression that Violet hadn't had, at least until she left home, an aura of strength and wisdom mixed with vulnerability.

And Rose knew finally that Carlie would be okay. She was hurting, badly, but she had grown immensely in the month she'd been here, and while she was still filled with anger right now, her kind heart hadn't been damaged by the tragedy of recent events – deep down she'd become more compassionate, more keen to help others.

For a moment Rose savoured the sense of pride she felt for her own daughter, because Violet and her husband had raised a beautiful soul, someone who would bring warmth and love to those around her. And she felt immense gratitude too, that even though her daughter hadn't had the courage to contact her in all these years, she'd given her a gift regardless. She had broken her silence and told her friend Sandy about her mother back in England, so that out of the horror of her own death, she still managed to send Carlie to her, and gift the young girl with a grandmother.

Snapping herself out of her reverie, Rose gave her granddaughter a hug, then sorted out the till as Carlie changed back into her normal clothes so they could head next door for dinner. Over chilli-bean nachos and avocado salad followed by warm berry pie, Rose talked about the upcoming Lughnasadh rite. Carlie had never been to a sabbat ritual, had never even heard of them before, and only knew the tiny bit she'd managed to glean from Rose's bookshelves that day. Her grandma outlined the traditions of the harvest festival, then explained how important these celebrations had always been to her.

When she was young, Rose had been forced to attend church services with her parents, but they sat strangely with her because of the hypocrisy she felt between what her mother preached and the cruelty she inflicted on her daughter, and she realised she was more connected to "god" when she was outside in nature. When she finally escaped her parents and went to college, her friend Elsie introduced her to paganism, although it was all very secretive, since so many people back then thought goddess worship was related to the devil.

After they graduated, she and Elsie marked the festivals together whenever they could, and over the next few years Rose found other like-minded people in her village, and became a part of their circle. Later she'd allowed her daughter to join her, the two of them weaving the magic of the seasons into the fabric of their relationship.

But when Violet disappeared and her husband died, Rose felt as though all the enchantment had been ripped from her world. For a time she turned her back on the goddess, determined to suffer alone, until finally Elsie helped her see that she needed support and shared energy at these special times. So she'd been leading a public ceremony for each festival for almost twenty years, at first in her home with just a few friends, sometimes up on the tor, and for the past decade in the large open hall above her healing centre, which had a wonderful energy, and was big enough for many participants.

There was a core group of women who had celebrated every one of the sabbats with Rose, their friendship getting her through the worst of her grief, and over the many years they'd worked magic together, their love for each other had created a bond that became a vital part of each of their lives, a web of support that had seen them through job losses, illnesses, deaths, weddings, births and everything in between – the tragedies and triumphs of any human life.

There was also a shifting group of other people who had attended throughout the years, teenagers just embarking on their magical journey, partners who came when they could, friends from the city who made it to one or two a year, and visitors to the town who came once on their holiday and were never seen again. And although Rose led the rituals and was the chief organiser, and everyone expressed their gratitude to her for the hard work she put in, she'd always felt indebted to the circle, for she didn't know what she would have done without their loyal and loving support through the years.

Chapter 23

A Festival of Thanksgiving

Carlie woke up early the next morning, but she stayed in bed for a long time, sitting with her mother's old quilt in her hands, tracing over the patterns of the bees and the ladybirds, the silhouette of Luther's mum Shadow, and gently touching the eight coloured strips from the altar cloths her mother and her grandmother had used, long ago, to celebrate these seasonal turning points. Tonight was the autumn ritual of Lughnasadh at the healing centre, and after feeling anxious about it all night, she was now looking forward to it. She was nervous, yes, but she was excited too. She had sensed before that the people of Summer Hill looked up to Rose, and seeing her in her role of priestess of the goddess would be amazing.

But until then, she had a busy day ahead of her. Her grandma had left her with several tasks to complete for the ritual. For the first, she'd given her a pretty woven basket that she wanted her to take on a walk around the base of the tor and through the small woodland, filling it with ripe blackberries. She'd also left the recipes and all the ingredients with which to prepare individual serves of apple and blackberry crumble, candied ginger slices, lemon balm bread, scones, gingersnap cookies and blackcurrant punch for the feast. And there were fresh raspberries for her to make into jam for the scones, since berries of all kinds were part of the Lughnasadh celebrations.

She'd felt sad as Rose had explained that Violet had always baked their sabbat treats, and many of the recipes she'd be using today were hers, but now it felt nice, albeit kind of strange, to be following in her mum's magical footsteps.

So finally she'd gone downstairs to the kitchen and tied on an apron, and spent much of the day kneading dough, crushing herbs, sprinkling in exotic spices, simmering berries, tasting the crumble mix, stirring in more cinnamon and lemon juice, and giggling as an image of the three witches from *Macbeth*, dancing around their cauldron with huge ladles, came to mind.

Now, as she arrived at the healing centre as night gently fell, wearing the pretty, flowing red dress that her grandma had insisted she pick out from the shop, she left her platters of food on the counter with the other covered trays, and walked up the stairs to the room where she'd learned reiki.

She gasped as she stood in the doorway. Tonight it had been transformed into a magical faeryland, illuminated by hundreds of little tealight candles, and with beautiful silky drapes dancing in the breeze from the huge floor to ceiling windows. There was a central altar, lit up with a huge pillar candle that gave off a warm glow and the most beautiful spiced scent. There were statues of the god and goddess, a basket of red and black berries, nuts, ivy, gorgeously coloured autumn leaves, and little dolls made from corn husks and sheaves of wheat. Around the room were four smaller altars, one in each corner, which her grandma had explained represented water, earth, air and fire, the four elements of nature.

A tall woman dressed in red velvet smudged her with a heady mix of sage and lavender incense, and ushered her into the room. There were about twenty people there already, mostly women, all wearing beautiful dresses the colour of autumn leaves, some red, some orange, some golden brown. Their hair was loose around their shoulders, and most of them had ribbons tied into their flowing locks or wreaths of ivy wound around their heads.

Watching them, and painfully shy and unsure of what to do, she marvelled at their easy friendship and the bonds between them. And she'd swear she could see thin gold lines connecting them, like a sparkling web that held them all safe, all nourished, fed by their magic and their bond. But that was crazy, that couldn't be real, surely. She blinked a few times, thinking it would disappear, yet the glow remained, and she smiled as she soaked up the rich atmosphere, standing on her own but feeling perfectly content.

After a while she noticed a hush gradually fall over the group. The sparkles of the web started buzzing, thickening, and she looked around expectantly.

Her grandmother rose from behind the central altar, long silver hair flowing out around her, rich magenta velvet robes spilling down to the floor and catching the candlelight. She looked beautiful, wild and powerful and nurturing all at once. Carlie stared, awestruck at the force of will and sheer power emanating from her.

"Welcome to our Lughnasadh ritual," Rose said, in a voice that seemed to have been drawn up from the very earth itself. "Tonight, as the wheel turns from the abundant ripeness of summer towards the cold barrenness of winter, we celebrate the first harvest, in the fields and in our lives. This cross-quarter day that marks the end of summer and the beginning of autumn is a time of feasting, celebration and thanksgiving, for the life-giving properties of the grain, and also for the things in our own lives that we are grateful for..."

As she listened, Carlie felt hope igniting within her. She had worried that she would never have anything to feel grateful for again, but was surprised to recognise the growing sense of gratitude she felt towards her grandma, and even to this village and its people. She was still terrified that she'd do something wrong tonight, embarrassing herself and her grandmother, but then she gazed around the circle, and noticed Rhiannon standing opposite her, dressed in a faery-like orange gown. She gave her a big smile, and Carlie returned it wholeheartedly, happy that the possibility of friendship still remained to her, and finally more relaxed within the circle.

Her attention returned to her grandmother when Rose picked up a beautiful crystal-tipped wand from the altar, and stepped outside of the circle of people. With the wand held high, she walked slowly around the perimeter in a clockwise direction, and began to speak again in the deep voice that added to the trance-inducing atmosphere of the night, the sweet aroma of the incense, and the magic Carlie could feel deep within her.

By my will a circle formed,
Between the worlds where magic's born.
Contain the energy raised within,
As the veils between these worlds do thin.
Hold us safe throughout this rite,
As we create magic together on this night.
The circle is cast, so mote it be.

As she returned to the starting point, Rose closed the circle by gently linking the hands of the two women at the portal, then she walked back to the central altar. The four women calling the directions and the elements raised their own wands, then took it in turns to speak.

Water: *I call forth the guardians of the west to cleanse, consecrate and protect this space during our rite, and I ask the waters of the oceans and rivers and sacred springs to wash away anything that no longer serves us. Element of water, welcome.*

Earth: *I call forth the guardians of the north to cleanse, consecrate and protect this space during our rite, and I ask the stones, the crystals and the very earth that we walk upon to ground and strengthen us. Element of earth, welcome.*

Air: *I call forth the guardians of the east to cleanse, consecrate and protect this space during our rite, and I ask the winds of the planet, both stormy gales and gentle breezes, and the very air itself, to inspire and uplift us. Element of air, welcome.*

Fire: *I call forth the guardians of the south to cleanse, consecrate and protect this space during our rite, and I ask the flames of light and heat, and fire itself, to burn away anything that no longer serves us. Element of fire, welcome.*

As each direction caller finished speaking her invocation, there was a gentle murmur from the rest of the circle: "Hail and welcome." Carlie was too shy to add her voice to the refrain, but she silently mouthed the words. Then her grandmother raised the central altar candle high, and gazed upwards.

Great Mother, divine goddess of wisdom and light,
Shine your blessings on us tonight.
Lord of the woods, of nature and might,
Shine your blessings on our sacred rite.

Carlie felt each word tingling within her, felt her mind opening to accept the magic she could feel, and her heart opening to accept the immense love she could sense swirling around them.

Following the welcoming of the god and the goddess, Rose led a meditation on gratitude, and for the first time Carlie really did feel grateful, deep in her heart. Before, she had tried to talk herself into it, knowing intellectually that she should feel it, but it had all been theoretical. She hadn't been able to grasp it, or feel it. Now it was a part of her. And at last she knew that feeling this way did not take away from the love she felt for her parents. She would always have that. It was just that now their loss wouldn't be a constant weight dragging her down – now their memory would be a warm glow within her that made her feel stronger, not weaker.

As her grandmother gently grounded them back into the room, and into their bodies, she felt Rhiannon at her side. "It's time for the spiral dance," she giggled, and took Carlie's hand in hers. Someone else grabbed her other hand, and she suddenly found herself being pushed and pulled around the room, the long line spiralling in and out and through itself, laughter rising with each circle, cheeks flushing with the exertion, and the energy in the room palpable. At the end they all collapsed in a heap on the floor, and Carlie smiled as she finally located her grandmother.

Her long silver hair was a wild and tangled mess and her robes were slightly askew, but her eyes were shining with joy, and Carlie finally saw her as the truly strong woman she was – not just as a grieving mother or lonely widow or guardian grandmother, but as the centre of this community, the strength of all the people here. Her eyes welled with tears as she realised how fortunate she was.

Then she sighed. Emily had been right – she was lucky. Not that her parents were dead, obviously, but that she did still have family who loved her, and that her life, though sad now, remained full of possibility and the potential for happiness.

As heart beats returned to normal and people began to refocus, her grandmother got to her feet, straightened her robes and stood again at the central altar. With a voice full of love and gratitude, she thanked and farewelled the god and goddess, then the women who had spoken earlier thanked and farewelled the elements and the directions. Finally Rose walked back over to the portal where it had all begun, and the two women on either side unlinked their hands and took hers. "By my will this circle is closed. Blessed be!" Rose announced.

Everyone raised their linked hands, then spoke as one. "May the circle be open but unbroken. Merry meet, merry part, and merry meet again. Blessed be!" Carlie smiled as everyone enthusiastically echoed the phrase, then let go of each other's hands with an exuberant whoosh of laughter.

Soon a dim globe in the centre of the room was turned on, casting a golden glow over everything, and a trestle table materialised along the back wall, just as the direction callers appeared in the doorway with the platters of food from downstairs. A large container was placed at the end of the bench, on the floor, and Carlie saw everyone approach it, one by one, and place canned foods, packets of rice and lentils, cartons of soy milk and boxes of tea and coffee in it.

"It's part of the ritual, that we all bring non-perishable goods for the homeless charity in town," explained Rhiannon, who was at her side again. "Lughnasadh is a festival of thanksgiving, and it's not enough for us just to speak words of gratitude, it's important for us all to pay our blessings forward."

Carlie smiled. What a wonderful thought. Rose and Elsie had mentioned to her that the way of the witch was a path of service, she just hadn't realised how literally they took that.

Her grandmother came over to hug her, and Rhiannon greeted the older woman, then wandered away to talk to someone else. Carlie was suddenly shy, still a little awestruck by her gran, and the remnants of the priestess glamour still clinging to her shoulders.

"How did you enjoy your first ritual Sweetheart?" Rose asked.

Carlie beamed at her. "It was amazing. You were amazing. But I couldn't..." Before she could say anything further, the four women who had called the directions came over and stood at Rose's side.

"You must be Carlie," East said. "We've all been dying to meet you. And wow, you look so much like your mother, you could be twins. I still miss her so much."

Carlie smiled shakily, but the familiar knife-through-the-heart sensation she always felt when people mentioned her mother didn't slice through her tonight. She was sad, of course, but for the first time the mention of her mum didn't physically hurt her. She also felt incredibly happy and proud that they'd apparently been so alike, even though she hadn't known this while Violet was still alive.

"This is Laura," her grandma explained. "She's the history teacher at your new school, so you'll have one of her classes."

Carlie smiled and held out her hand.

"Oh, so formal," Laura scolded, leaning in and wrapping her in a big hug. Carlie felt the kindness emanating from her, and it soothed her heart to know that her mother had had such great friends, and that her grandmother had been so loved and so supported in the years since she'd lost her daughter and her husband.

Then she felt an impatient tap on her shoulder, and turned to see West smiling at her, eyes dancing with joy.

"I'm Paulette," she said, and Carlie was pulled into her arms too. She laughed as she was then passed to someone else for a hug – and was surprised to realise that she didn't find all of this intimacy frightening, as she normally would have.

"This is Miri," her grandma added warmly, introducing Carlie to the woman who had called South during the ritual. "And this is Joanna, who called North. They are my magical sisters, and my dearest friends."

As Carlie said hello to them, she felt the emotion building, just as it had during the ceremony – then she suddenly felt dizzy. Rose took her by the hand and led her to the food table. "Eat something," she ordered, voice firm with her priestess authority. "You always need to ground yourself after you've done any magical work."

As she picked up a small pumpkin pie and bit into it, her grandmother called her friends over. "Laura, come and try some of Carlie's raspberry muffins, and her blackberry crumble," Rose said proudly. "She made the jam for the scones too, and the ginger snap cookies, which were from Violet's recipe."

Leaning against the wall, Carlie nibbled on the pie as she watched everyone swarm around her grandmother, who was offering a kind word here, asking a question there, hugging everyone she encountered, and spreading so much love and joy with her very presence. After a few curious glances at Carlie early on, everyone had left her alone, and she was relieved. She had so much to process, from that evening's ritual as well as her recent experiences.

More than anything, she couldn't even begin to understand why her mother had left the village. She was the daughter of a priestess, had so many friends who still missed her, and was adored by a whole community. It didn't make sense. She longed to go back to the cottage and read more of her mum's Book of Shadows.

Rhiannon came over to say goodbye, and told her she'd received some information from the university they'd been discussing, so they promised to catch up in the next few days. Her new friend hugged her as she left, and Carlie noticed with renewed surprise that she no longer feared physical intimacy as she once had. Who'd have thought?

Later Laura came over to speak to her again. "I hope you're not too overwhelmed by all of this," she said, voice kind. "I imagine it's a lot to take in all at once, but if you have any questions about it – or about anything – feel free to ask me, or any of the girls. And maybe you'd like to call one of the Quarters at the next rite?"

Carlie froze, then shyly shook her head. She certainly wasn't ready to speak in public, but she assured Laura that she felt honoured to have been asked. And she did have a few things she wanted to know. Laura was a patient and knowledgeable practitioner of the Craft, explaining a little about the next sabbat – Mabon, the autumn equinox – which would fall a few weeks after school started, then setting Carlie's mind at rest about that topic too.

It was a small high school, Laura revealed, but all of the students were very friendly, and all the different year levels did activities together, such as drama club plays, musicals, the school newspaper, even sports. "Your gran tells me you were top of your classes back home, and we won't let you down," she added. "Academically our students do very well, and they also have a really wide variety of electives and extra curricular activities to choose from."

Then she asked Carlie about her career ambitions, but feeling suddenly shy again, she just said she was no longer sure.

"Don't stress about it, I'm sure it will come to you when you're ready," Laura said reassuringly. "You've been through so much, so give yourself some time to make sense of your new home, your new school, your new friends, your new life. And if you ever want to chat, about anything at all, just give me a call. Rose has my number."

As if summoned by her name, her grandmother materialised beside them. Laura gave Carlie a hug goodbye, then kissed Rose on the cheek and promised she'd speak to them the next day. Slowly the others packed up their belongings and headed out too, warm words of welcome and of farewell settling around Carlie like a protective cloak. Her grandma quickly tidied away the ritual tools and gathered up the herbs and flowers they'd used, then locked up so they could head home, wandering through the quiet night-time streets together.

"Thank you so much for letting me be part of it all tonight Gran, it was wonderful," Carlie said, still buzzing from all the energy they'd raised in the circle. "And it was amazing to see you like that, as the priestess – so powerful, so imposing, even a tiny bit scary," she teased.

Rose laughed, then took Carlie's hand. "I've certainly felt a lot stronger since you've been here Sweetheart. Quite a few people commented on that tonight, saying that I look so much younger and happier now. I'm very grateful that you're here Carlie, really. You've given me something to live for again."

Carlie shivered as she recalled the words of the woman in blue who she'd met on Summer Hill that day, then hugged her grandmother as she was overwhelmed by just how grateful she was feeling too.

"You're welcome to call one of the Quarters at the next ritual," Rose said, and this time it was the older woman who had a note of teasing in her voice.

"Thank you for the offer," Carlie said, trying to sound gracious. "Laura mentioned that too, but I might have to work up to that. It was lovely to be part of it though, and to meet your friends. They're all so wonderful and welcoming, and they all seem to care so much about each other. I don't know how Mum could have left all that. No matter what she did – or didn't – do, I'm sure they would have loved her still. *You* would have loved her still."

Her grandma smiled, but there was sadness in her eyes. "Of course we would have. *I* would have. And I feel as though I failed her, that she didn't know that my love was unconditional."

"You can't blame yourself Gran. We're each responsible for ourselves, surely. And I'm certain that you would have let Mum know how loved she was," Carlie insisted.

Rose stopped to hug her granddaughter as they turned into their street. "Thank you Sweetheart, that means a lot to me. I know we didn't get off to a great start, but I hope you know how much I care about you, and how wonderful it is for me to have you here," she said.

Then, unlocking their front door, she headed for the kitchen to pat Luther and put the kettle on. "Would you like a cup of tea?" she called. "I'd love to hear more about what you thought of tonight, and about your full moon ritual up on the hill. The magic is strong in you, I can feel it, and I can't wait to see how your life unfolds."

Chapter 24

The Key To Her Heart

When Carlie walked downstairs the next morning, her grandma was making blueberry pancakes, and there was a pot of freshly brewed earl grey tea on the table. Next to it was a package wrapped in purple velvet, tied up with a silver ribbon.

"Sit down Sweetheart," her grandma said, as she walked over to Carlie and poured her a strong and fragrant mug of tea, then handed her the parcel. "This is for you."

Carlie loosened the silver ribbon and opened the pretty fabric wrapping. It was an antique-looking book, a lot like the one she'd found of her mother's, with swirling patterns of ivy, along with flowers and bees, carved into the leather cover. "It's beautiful," she whispered. "Thank you so much!"

"You're very welcome. I thought you might like to record your rituals in it, starting with last night's, and adding your full moon one too, and all your magical experiences... or anything you like," she added hastily. "No pressure, it's totally up to you." And she went back to the stove and brought over a stack of pancakes, piled high with luscious blueberries, and maple syrup cascading down the sides.

"These look amazing," Carlie said, mouth watering at the beautiful aroma. "The food last night was awesome too – and everyone made their dishes themselves, didn't they?"

"Well, cooking is definitely a witchy skill," her grandma said with a smile. "A recipe is a kind of spell. Not only with the ingredients you choose to use, but also with the intent that you stir into it. You can bake with love, just generally, so everyone who eats your food feels it, or you can stir a specific spell into it, such as one for good fortune or healing or joy. Cooking for the sabbats is an important part of each ritual, and is based primarily on seasonal ingredients – foods of the harvest for Lughnasadh last night, for example, such as loaves of fresh bread, and berries," she added, as she speared one on her fork.

"And herbs of course play a big part – they have magical qualities as well as medicinal. I've got a lot of books about herbs and herbal healing, if you're interested, although the best way to learn is through getting out into the garden and interacting with them – planting them, caring for them, observing them, touching them, smelling them, tasting them."

Carlie looked out the window at the garden, really seeing it for the first time. There were so many neat rows of greenery, some with small white flowers, some with pink, some with spiky grey leaves, others all soft and gentle looking. Grabbing a pen from the bench, she put her hand on the cover of her new book, about to open it. "This is just like Mum's book," she mused, voice quiet. "The one I was reading in the abandoned cottage."

Rose looked up sharply.

"I know you think I'm crazy, or that I'm making this up, but I swear, I'm not! I really was there, in the cottage. Once as it was, with Mum and Mike, all pretty and lived in, and the other times as it may have once been, dusty and derelict, but definitely there. I was sitting on the floor, reading Mum's magical book, the one she'd been writing in since you gave it to her on her sixteenth birthday."

Rose paled at the specifics of her description.

"It had a leather cover, a bit darker than this one, with pretty ironwork on it, and ancient symbols carved into it. And there was a message from you at the beginning, wishing her a magical birthday and an enchanted life," Carlie said.

"She wrote about the sabbat rituals you did together, the green dresses you made for Ostara, the flower wreaths you wove for Beltane, and the love spell she cast, then reversed. Her dark moon spell, and a working for letting go. Her tarot readings were in there too – practice spreads she did for herself, and one she had from a psychic at your shop, a beautiful one telling of a wonderful future. And there was a step-by-step of her ritual as she made a talisman to keep her safe when she left home in order to prevent her father's death."

Rose's hands were shaking now. She dropped her mug of tea, which smashed to the ground in three large pieces, then sank into the chair opposite her granddaughter. Tears rolled down Carlie's cheeks, in response to her own grief as well as the visceral pain her grandmother was experiencing, which she could feel radiating off her. She reached out a hand for her little shoulder bag, which was in the middle of the table, to get a tissue.

Her fingers touched something cold and hard at the bottom of the bag, at the same moment she realised that the bag wasn't actually hers. Well, it wasn't hers in *this* reality. But she remembered picking it up off the kitchen bench at her mum and Mike's cottage – the cottage Rose said had burned down more than twenty years ago. She looked up at her grandmother, fear etched on her face. "Where did this bag come from?" she asked her, as calmly as she could.

Her grandma gazed back at her, puzzled. "You had it with you when Mike found you at the bottom of the tor," she said. "Why, what's wrong? Is something missing?"

"This isn't my bag," Carlie said. "But I had it when I was with Mum and Mike in the cottage, when I'd lived in this town all my life. But… that was just a dream, right?" she asked, tone imploring and slightly desperate. Rose just stared at her, too shocked to speak.

Equal parts scared and curious, she pulled the object from the bag. It was a silver key, old looking, on a key ring that also had a small pewter faery and a vesica piscis symbol on it. Her grandma paled.

"That's Violet's key, the key to her room," Rose gasped. She glanced at the ceiling as she said this, and reached out her hand tentatively to touch the metallic symbols, a look of fear mixed with wonder on her face. "Her room upstairs."

Carlie suddenly remembered the locked door she'd discovered the second night she was here, which she hadn't thought of since. How could she have forgotten *that*? They both stood up, and Rose reached out for her granddaughter's hand. Slowly they climbed the stairs together, until they were standing on the landing outside the other upstairs room. Rose tried to put the key in the lock, but she was shaking too much, and it fell to the floor with a soft clatter.

Carlie picked up the key from the wooden floor, and fitted it into the keyhole. It was stiff, and she had to force it, but she finally managed to turn it. There was a click, and the door swung open. Grandmother and granddaughter stood together on the threshold, breath held. Inside it was dim and musty, as you'd expect from a room that hadn't been opened in almost two decades. There was dust covering everything, and cobwebs across the windows. A little of the warm morning sun streamed into the room in between the silvery webs. Dust danced amongst the sunbeams, and Carlie could have sworn she saw a small black shadow, like a cat, out of the corner of her eye, over beneath the wardrobe.

Her eyes narrowed as she glanced down at the floor beside the bed. Just visible was the corner of a leather-bound book. "Grandma," she said, her voice strangled with emotion. She knelt down and reverently picked it up. It was the same one she'd been reading in the cottage, with the swirling symbols carved deeply into the cover. Sneezing as the dust danced around her, she held the book out to her grandmother. Rose looked terrified, and suddenly several years older than she had the night before. She collapsed onto the bed, but so much dust rose up around her that she quickly stood.

"Bring it downstairs, will you Sweetheart?" she asked softly. "I think we need some better light, and some tea."

Carlie's gaze swept around the room before she headed out. Her mind was racing, trying to reconcile the dark and dust-shrouded museum feel of this space with her fun-loving, fresh-air-and-sunshine-worshipping mum. She wanted to throw open all the windows and let the cool breeze in to clear the air, to scrape off the cobwebs and shake out the dust. But that was up to her grandma. She obviously hadn't been in the room for many years, but perhaps soon, in her own time, she might get around to it, be able to process her grief and let go of some of the pain of the past.

When Carlie got back downstairs, Rose was brewing a fresh pot of tea. Gently she wiped the dust off the book and placed it on the small table, facing towards where her grandmother always sat. Rose came over with their mugs of tea and sank down into the chair, while Carlie stood just behind her, desperate for the book to be opened, scared of what was inside it, and dizzy with confusion over everything that had happened to her since she'd arrived in this small English village a month ago, to live with the grandmother she hadn't even known existed. Had it really only been a month?

Taking a deep breath, she placed a comforting hand on Rose's shoulder. Her heart was full of love for this woman who had lost so much, but who had still opened her heart and her home to her, a complete stranger. It had been a huge surprise for Carlie to discover that she had a grandmother – and it was a total shock for Rose to learn that she had a granddaughter, given that she'd had no idea her own daughter had lived past seventeen years old.

Rose put down her tea and opened the book to the first page. Carlie gasped, clearly not really believing until this moment that it could be the same book she'd been reading in the cottage down the road. But it was – her mother's name was written in her large, curly script on the first page, and the sixteenth birthday message from Rose was written on the next one. Rose's body shuddered as she read her long-lost daughter's name and recognised the handwriting and the little heart she drew instead of the dot on the letter I, and Carlie realised again just how fragile her grandmother was.

"Bring your chair over here Sweetheart, and sit beside me," the older woman said, voice a little shaky, and Carlie dragged her seat around the table and sat down next to her grandma. Picking up her tea and taking a sip, she was aware of the taste of the rosemary, lemon balm and mint of her gran's reviving herbal blend on her tongue, as well as their scent in the air around her. Calming, soothing, strengthening. She felt the herbs unknot a little of the tension in her body, and she smiled at her grandma and squeezed her hand.

Together they turned the pages, and for the next hour they were both lost in a fog of memories – Carlie of the mother she had so recently lost, and Rose of the sweet seventeen-year-old daughter who had disappeared in mysterious circumstances twenty years ago. She'd had no word from her in all that time, no word of her, and had slowly come to acknowledge that the police must be right, that there was very little chance she hadn't died all those years ago. Sadly she'd only discovered that Violet had been alive all that time when she was given the news of her death six weeks ago.

They both smiled as they read through the magical notes of the teenaged Violet, who was so full of joy, of optimism, of her plans to help people and work with her mum in her new age shop and healing centre. When they got to the place where she'd written out the transcript of that final fateful tarot card reading, they were both distraught, and had to stop for a while.

This was the psychic reading that had convinced Violet that she must run away, and leave her family and her home, in order to prevent her father's death. In Carlie's dream, or that parallel dimension, this was the part of the book Rose had read, that had enabled her to stop her daughter catching the train to the city the next morning and disappearing forever. Stopped her enduring an awful, soul-destroying relationship with the so-called spiritual guru then meeting an Aussie backpacker and leaving the country, never to contact her family again.

The devastating irony of all this was that it was Violet's leaving home, not her staying, that had contributed to the untimely death of her father – a tragedy that had left poor Rose both widowed and childless within a month, and aged terribly, as Carlie had seen in the alternate world. And she had remained alone ever since, living in the same house, too scared to move location, or move on with her life, in case her daughter ever decided to come back. It was lucky for Carlie that she *had* stayed, since she'd become an orphan just a few short weeks ago, and had no other relatives.

After a rocky start, they were both so grateful to have found each other, to be able to help one another pick up the pieces of their shattered lives. For Rose it was a chance to have a family again, someone to love and nurture, to care for, and someone to leave her beloved home and healing centre to. For Carlie it was a chance to be cared for, to learn and grow, to have a new future to grow into, rather than the bleak outcome she'd been facing so recently.

They held each other and cried for a long time. Then finally Rose turned back to the book, and went to turn the page.

"That's it," Carlie said, sorrow and yearning plain in her voice. "The rest of it is blank." She remembered flicking through the rest of the book in the cottage and seeing only empty pages.

But it wasn't. The next few pages were also covered in Violet's big curly letters, not her neatest entry, but it was tightly spaced and dense, a huge free-flowing explosion of words.

Reflections on Leaving Home

I don't know what to think. Andre's tarot reading the other day still has me freaked out, and I know I have to leave home to save Dad's life. But when I saw Andre yesterday, for the first time I had the tiniest little doubt. Which is crazy, I know. He's a spiritual guru, a leader, a teacher – people come from all over the country to have readings done by him, and to take his classes. He counsels celebrities, has written books, and runs his spiritual workshops internationally. How could I be so arrogant as to think that I know more than him, or to question his reading or his motives?

Maybe it's just that I still can't believe he's in love with me – it doesn't make any sense, because he could have anyone he wanted. I'm nobody. Why would he want to be with me? I wish I could talk to Mum about it, but I just can't – she'll only say that he's too old for me, that I'm moving too fast, that his soon-to-be-ex-wife will cause problems. And I know she wants me to marry Mike. Who I love dearly, but not like that. He's my best friend, and always will be (I hope!), but being with him just doesn't compare to being with Andre.

I tried to talk to Mike about why I have to go, but he said the tarot reading wasn't true, that a reading would never say you'll cause someone's death, and that Andre had only said those things so I'd go and live with him. Mike's just jealous though, just as Andre said, which makes me sad. But once I've settled in with him in the city,

I'll try to mend those bridges with Mike, and once he sees how happy I am, he'll have to agree that it was all for the best. Andre's booked a gorgeous B&B for me for the first few weeks, just while he finalises his house and stuff, and his wife moves out, then I'll move in with him and we can start our life together. I can't wait!

But I must admit that yesterday was a bit odd – I could have sworn there was someone else with him when I went to his hotel room before work, another woman, but he told me not to be so silly, that he'd just been on the phone organising his house – soon to be our house! And of course it was a ridiculous idea. I guess I'm just nervous about leaving home, and not being able to tell Mum and Dad why I'm going. I know they'll be worried, but I have no choice – I can't stay here and be the reason that Dad dies. I'd rather never see my parents again, but know that they are well and happy and alive, than selfishly stay here and basically kill my dad.

I'll miss them so much though. I'm not sure I'll be able to cope without them, but I must stay strong. And I've worked out the perfect spell to cast… I feel terrible about leaving Mum and Dad, especially Mum, because we love working together, and I know her dream was to leave her healing centre to me. But I'm not strong enough. I can't challenge the gods and ignore what the reading said, even if it's not true. I'd spend my whole life waiting for some catastrophe to happen, wondering each morning if this was the day I'd do something stupid – or not do something – and cause my father's death.

So the best thing I can do is leave here and go away, far away, and live a good life. And have a daughter who can be everything that Mum wanted in her own child. I'll bring her up far from here, so she can escape this curse I feel on me. And when she's eighteen I'll bring her back – or send her on her own, if I can't face it – so she can stay with Mum and Dad, and see how she feels about the legacy, of being heir to the great Rose Tyler's healing work, and her centre and shop. Mum can't see it yet, it's just a bit of fun for her now, started when I went to school so she could fill in her days, but she's going to help so many people, and bring healing and hope and inspiration.

So my last act before I must leave everything I know, love and cherish is a spellworking to attract a soul mate to me. Not a lover but a daughter, one who will be brave and strong and loving, and all the support that Mum needs. I'll call her Kali, because she will be powerful and magical, and will transform the chaos of her family into something incredible, something love-filled, something so much better than I can offer.

And so, on this full moon night, after weaving the strands of Mabon together with Mum and the other women during our ritual, I channel that energy in my spellcrafting, calling on the unbreakable bond between the goddess Demeter and her wayward daughter Persephone. Calling on the loving strength of rose quartz, and the powerful transformative blaze of fire and flame.

I send out my call across the universe. Bring me a daughter ablaze with courage, compassion, strength and generosity of spirit. Kali, I implore you to bless me with this daughter, your namesake. I will nurture her and love her, and help her grow into a woman worthy of you, worthy of my mother, worthy of this world she'll be born into. Full of magic and wonder, imbued with wisdom and grace.

Rose looked over at her granddaughter and squeezed her hand. "Oh Carlie, did you ever know you were so loved? Know how much you were longed for?"

Carlie shook her head, tears in her eyes. "Never. And did you know how much you were loved, how much she wanted to protect you and Grandpa?" she asked.

"No Sweetheart," Rose sighed, tears pouring down her cheeks. "I thought that I'd done something wrong, that she hated me. But I can't bear knowing how much she sacrificed for what she thought was right. She's the most selfless person I've ever known."

Together they gazed back at the book, and carefully turned to the last page.

And I call to the man with the wisdom to help me raise this child. Not today, for I have to get my life in order first, and work out what on earth I'm going to do with myself, but when I am ready, when this child is ready, in the perfect time and place... I think it's Andre, of course, but just in case it's not, I ask for that too, for the best person to help me raise this child for Mum, raise this child to be a better daughter than I ever was or could be.

Goddess, as I set out on this next phase of my life, this grand adventure, I ask not for blessings for myself, because I don't deserve them, but blessings for my parents, for my wonderful, magical priestess mother and my loving, hard-working father. Give them strength to grieve me quickly, and patience until I can send my daughter to them in my place. Please watch over them and keep them safe.

So mote it be...

Rose was sobbing openly now, and had collapsed into Carlie's arms. The strong priestess from the night before had been replaced by a fragile and broken-hearted mother, still mourning her lost daughter twenty years after she disappeared.

Carlie held her grandmother tight, hand gently stroking her back, soothing her as much as she could.

"Oh Gran, I'm so sorry that you lost her. And I'm sorry for how I behaved before. I know I'll never replace your daughter – and I don't want to – but I'm here for you, okay? And I love you so much."

Rose cried even harder at that, hearing the echo of her own words to Carlie when she'd just arrived from Australia. So much had happened in the last month, she couldn't even begin to process it. To have found her daughter only to lose her all over again had broken her heart, but it made her soul sing to have been entrusted with her gorgeous young granddaughter. She tried to calm herself down so she could focus on the latter.

"Sweetheart, thank you. You have no idea how much it means to me that you're here. And I'm sorry I'm being so selfish – you lost her too," she managed to gasp out between hiccups.

"And really, this makes me happy. All these years I've been trying to work out what I did wrong, why she left me, what I could have done differently. This is such a gift, to know that I didn't drive her away, that she *did* love me, and that she left us in the mistaken belief that she was protecting me and her father."

Rose straightened up, kissed Carlie on the cheek, then went to put the kettle on again. Carlie grinned. "It's so English," she giggled, when her grandma raised an eyebrow at her in query. "The idea that a cup of tea will solve everything."

They both laughed – not a huge or happy laugh, but it was the beginning of a healing and a grieving process that suddenly didn't seem quite so impossible.

After their third cup of tea, real tea this time, Rose apologised for having to go in to the shop, and Carlie hugged her goodbye. Then, reaching for her new Book of Shadows, she opened it to the first page, then paused. This had to be done properly.

Carrying it upstairs to her little bedroom, she pulled open the curtains that overlooked the tor, lit a candle and some incense, and found her purple pen. Luther pushed the door open and came and sat next to her on the floor. Stroking his head, she smiled as he began to purr. Now she was ready. She opened the book and began to write.

I am Carlie, also named Kali,
Daughter of Violet and Oliver.
Granddaughter of Rose and Louis,
and Sarah and Christopher.
Today I dedicate myself as a witch,
As a seeker and student, a person who lives their life in harmony with nature and the universe.
As a healer, an intuitive, dedicated to helping people heal from grief, from illness, from the pain of their past.
Someone who takes responsibility for their own life and their own actions, who is aware of the impact of word, thought, deed. Who walks lightly on the earth and strives to be kind and compassionate, and to embody grace in all their interactions.
I vow to help Gran, and get to know the sweet and magical women in her life. I vow to make it up to Emily, and to open my heart to Rhiannon, kindred friend perhaps, who can teach me so much, and who I can perhaps help in some way in turn.
And I vow to honour my mum and my dad, and all they gave me, and the person they made me.

And so I open my heart to the magic,
I open my soul to the mystery,
And step forward into my new life with love, joy, passion, gratitude and hope.

She stopped. That was enough for now. She had to get outside, be in nature, feel the sunshine on her face, the wind in her hair, the earth beneath her feet, and her mother all around her. Closing the book, she patted Luther goodbye and tied a jacket around her waist, laughing as the cat leaped up on her bed and snuggled up on her pillow. Cute creature. He clearly thought he'd done enough work for one day.

Slowly, thoughtfully, she walked around the base of the hill, through the meadow of buttercups then along the edge of the apple orchard and the shadowy green woodland. She was filled with gratitude for being alive, for being here, and for having her grandma. What an incredible woman she was. And to think that just a few short weeks ago she'd pictured her as a scary monster!

She was so happy to have met Rhiannon too, to know that there was someone in this place who understood her, who had seen and felt the same awful things that she had. A pang of guilt flashed through her, that she felt so close to a new friend so quickly, for leaving Emily behind, but it wasn't like she had much choice.

She would always adore her childhood friend, and she was determined to stay in touch with her and include her in her new life. But there were some things she just couldn't share with her. She knew that the depth of her pain made Emily uncomfortable, and while she didn't blame her for that, it still hurt. It felt as though she had to pretend she was okay – which she could do by letter, she hoped, but right now she needed a shoulder to cry on, someone who would allow her to be silent when she needed to be, but could join in the non-stop talk when she wanted to chat, or take her mind off things.

Admittedly she did feel bad, and a little guilty – what kind of friend was she, demanding that Emily cater to her moods and whims, put her needs first? She hoped that Em would find a new friend now that she was gone, would find someone else to live in the city with, live out her dream of being a lawyer with.

And she promised herself that she wouldn't forget Emily. She wanted to stay a part of her life, and who knew where they might both be a few years from now? Emily might want to see the world, and come and spend some time with her and her grandma. And maybe a few years from now she would finally feel able to visit Australia again, to catch up with old friends and explore her old haunts.

She wondered how she would feel to walk down her old street, to see her childhood home, see people she'd known her whole life. Right now she couldn't even contemplate it, but who knew what would happen in the future? She felt like an entirely new person in a lot of ways, yet in others she was still the same. *Wasn't she?*

Acknowledging that part of her was really sad that she was giving up the life she'd always wanted and had long planned, she realised that a far bigger part of her was excited about the prospect of her new life. Helping people, doing healing work, exploring the idea of a new university course and career with Rhiannon, learning to cook and perform rituals with her grandma, making magic with new friends and opening her heart to life, and maybe even love. She knew who she was now, knew who she wanted to be, and while she still hadn't quite become that person yet, she could feel it getting closer.

Until then, her days were jam-packed with rituals and magic and people and places that made her happy. Turning around, she headed for home. *Home.* The place where she was staying, and the place where she was finally happy to be. Her mind flew back to that moment on the tor – *was it just a month ago?* – when she'd cursed the fact that she was staying. Cursed the fact that she was stuck with her monster of a grandmother. Cursed the fact that this was her life. But while this was definitely *not* the way she'd planned to spend her life, she was slowly becoming happy, and increasingly at peace, with where she was now.

Smiling as she heard one of her favourite Everclear songs blaring from someone's back window, she sang along at the top of her voice as she made her way home. Everything *would* be wonderful one day...

Epilogue

She was dreaming of home, her old home, but this time the women from the ritual she'd done were there with her, hands linked in a circle with her in the centre, all of them spinning around and around, long hair flying in the wind. Her arms were outstretched as she twirled, feeling secure and loved in this most basic of magic rites, this most powerful of enchanted circles. As they all turned their faces up to the sun and laughed, she felt her heart soar. Her mother was there too, gazing down on them from the sky, hand reaching outwards to bestow a blessing on them all.

She awoke gently this time, a smile on her face and Luther purring on the pillow beside her head. More than ten thousand miles from her childhood home, had she finally found her real home? Is that what her mum had wanted all along? What she'd cast that desperate spell for as she'd planned to leave home? For her mother and her daughter to meet at last, to be reconciled, to share the love that she'd felt driven to give up?

Her grandma knocked on her door, and Carlie called out a greeting as she jumped out of bed. Today was the first day at her new school, the first step towards her new career dream, and her new life. She was determined to face it bravely and with an open heart and mind.

"When you are sorrowful look again in your heart,
and you shall see that in truth you are weeping
for that which has been your delight."

Kahlil Gibran, Lebanese artist, poet and writer

INTO the DARK

"It's so much darker when a light goes out than it would have been if it had never shone."

John Steinbeck, American writer

Contents

Prologue

Rain poured from the sky, thunder rumbled across the village and lightning split the heavens apart. Shaking with anguish, Carlie ran up the stairs, threw herself through her bedroom door and slammed it closed behind her. Crawling into the far corner, she crouched there, knees pulled up to her chin, arms wrapped tightly around them, trying to make herself smaller, trying to diminish herself in an effort to diminish the pain. She rocked, slowly at first, then less gently, as wrenching sobs shook her body.

Through the mist of her tears, her gaze flickered wildly around the room, coming to rest on the altar she'd so carefully constructed with Rhiannon. The huge chunk of rose quartz sat in the north, mocking her with its promise of forgiveness, compassion and unconditional love. Fat lot of good that had done her.

Close to it was her athame, the ceremonial dagger she'd been gifted by a woman more mist than substance. She snatched it up and held it in her hand, its weight a welcome distraction, grounding her in her body, in her pain. Holding the point of the blade to her wrist, she tried desperately to find one single reason not to draw it across the delicate skin, draw out a river of blood, and draw this painful existence to a close.

He'd promised her that he would slit his wrists before he ever hurt her, but that had clearly been a lie. Fury raged through her, red hot, and suddenly the thought of oblivion, of letting herself drown in this swirling crush of despair and never come up for air, seemed the most welcome idea in the world…

Chapter 1

The Promise

A cold, heavy mist snaked around their ankles as the two girls walked silently through the ivy-wreathed tunnel of oaks to the bottom of the hill. Clad in richly coloured velvet dresses, their long wavy hair fell around them like a cloak, and images of wicked witches danced through their minds. Each clutched a small posie of flowers in one hand and a candle in a glass holder in the other. Their mood was solemn. Tonight they were going to consecrate their newly formed coven with a dedication ritual, and excitement and joy warred with nervousness and a shiver of fear within their hearts.

As the path opened out before them they paused, lifting their eyes skyward. In the soft lavender-gold light of the approaching sunset, the silhouette of Summer Hill rose tall and imposing above them. It was a full moon tonight, the perfect lunar phase for their ceremony, and they wanted to be at the summit in time to watch the moon rise in the east as the sun set in the west. This was a potent moment of magic, and of energy and balance in nature.

The girls smiled at each other in the gathering gloom, then turned away. They'd decided to each take a different path to the top of the sacred tor, to symbolise the individual journeys they'd been on until this point, and the varied experiences they'd had before they met. Then they would join together at the summit, representing the deepening of their friendship and the beginning of their magical partnership.

"Wait," Carlie said. Her friend turned back, her eyes shining with a light that seemed to come from within.

"Maybe we should swap our flowers, so we have something of each other's to bring with us on our climb, to lend each other a bit of strength and support?" she suggested hesitantly.

Rhiannon smiled and nodded, pleased with the suggestion, and Carlie realised that the light in her eyes was just a reflection of her candle flame. And there she'd been, romanticising it all, adding magic where there was none. Reaching out to take her friend's bouquet, she mentally rolled her eyes at herself. Awkwardly they swapped, juggling flaming candles with delicate blooms and trying not to spill wax on themselves. Then they whispered a blessing and turned away from each other again. This was it.

Silky dark hair falling protectively around her, Carlie drew up her shoulders, straightened her back, and took her first step along the path up the hill, the first step on her new magical journey. There were butterflies in her tummy, mostly because she was nervous, but she was excited too. She smiled as she walked – until suddenly she pictured her old friend Emily's reaction to all this, and the look of ridicule that would have been etched across her face if she could have seen her now, draped in purple velvet and climbing an ancient hill to worship the moon. She faltered for a moment, then shook off the thought, lifted her chin and took another step.

A thick swirling fog materialised in front of her, and she drew in a sharp breath, remembering the strangeness of the mists she'd walked into the first time she'd wandered around this place. Perhaps this one was here to comfort her. To shield her and encourage her. Smiling at the thought, she stepped slowly into it, beginning her procession around the base of the tor. Rhiannon had taken the shorter, steeper trail up the back of the hill, leaving Carlie to weave her way along the more gentle, winding pathway.

But as the mists thickened around her, catching in her throat and making her face and neck feel wet, a chill settled around her shoulders. Had something moved up ahead of her?

Focusing on her breathing again, she told herself to calm down. It was probably just one of the rabbits that burrowed its way into the soft ground on the sides of the hill, or maybe it was a raven or a bat. They liked the full moon too.

She took another tentative step, then froze. Something was coming out of the mists ahead of her. A shiver snaked up her spine as she peered into the damp, swirling air ahead of her.

Slowly a form started to emerge from the whiteness, seeming to be half in the hill and half out of it, a natural part of the earth. It was the figure of a woman in a green gown, her eyes gentle yet strong, and the very air that she breathed out, nurturing and comforting as Carlie breathed it in. But how could a creature materialising out of the mists be comforting?

"Just breathe," the figure seemed to whisper, although Carlie would have sworn her lips hadn't moved. "There is no need to worry. I know you have met my sister of the heart, the one you called the woman in blue, and that she gave you a message that you know in your heart to be true," she continued.

Carlie nodded, sensing as she did so the familiar wash of peace and contentment coming over her, the spell that made it hard to think straight or concentrate properly. "Who are you?" she asked, her voice barely a whisper.

"I am the beating heart of this hill, and of the nature and landscape of this country," the woman replied. "I have no name, and no need of one, yet some have called me Brianna. To others I am simply the Keeper of the Hill. I am older than humanity, as old as the land itself, and you can call on me when you need to ground yourself and connect back to the earth, or to feel my nurturing and protection."

Carlie looked at her quizzically. "But I'm okay now," she said, confusion in her eyes and her heart.

The woman stared back at her, head tilted a little to the side, eyes thoughtful, as though weighing up what she should and shouldn't say. "I have been sent to give you a message. Whether you are capable of heeding it or not is of no concern to me," she finally replied, and her voice held a thread of steel and menace. "I am just doing a favour for my friend."

Carlie giggled at the thought of the lady in blue requesting that this stern figure carry out her bidding. She just couldn't picture it. But the look on the green-clad woman's face quickly stifled any sense of merriment she felt.

"I am here to tell you that soon you will have a choice. An important choice. And when you make the decision, you will need to remember how important your friendship is, how much value it has to you, and how good she has been to you."

Carlie stared at the woman. "Of course I know how important Rhiannon is to me," she snapped, bristling at the suggestion that she was not grateful every moment of every day that she had met her friend when she did. "Am I not acting grateful enough?"

"So quick still to anger Carlie?" the woman asked.

"Sorry," she muttered. "Go on."

"Things can change, and people can get in the way," the woman continued, her voice quiet but imposing. "You will be tested. Your loyalties will be divided, and it is within you to betray the people closest to you." Carlie felt a flash of anger bubbling in her stomach, but the protest she wanted to make died on her lips as the woman stared at her, into her, then reached beneath the folds of her gown.

"It is within every person Carlie," she said impatiently. "Now, this is a gift for your friend," she added, offering her a small silver ring. Her eyes flickered to the young girl's pocket as she handed it over, and without consciously thinking about what she was doing, Carlie slipped it inside without even looking at it.

"And this is for you," the green-clad woman said softly, handing over a small package wrapped in deep green velvet. Curious, Carlie unwrapped it, to reveal a small double-edged silver blade with a carved wooden handle. "An athame, a coven gift for you, to cast a circle, to focus and direct energy within that circle, and to remind you to focus on the positive in your life when you are away from the circle, away from your friend. Keep it – and your friend – close to you."

Carlie traced the strange symbols carved in the handle with her finger, feeling the magic that was imbued within this ancient looking ritual tool. Finally she tore her eyes away and looked up, to thank the woman for the strange gift, but there was no one there. She shivered, suddenly aware of the fading light, the cold breeze, and the long walk she still had to make to the top of the hill. Carefully she wrapped the athame back up in the length of velvet and stowed it in the bag that was slung across her shoulder, then she continued up the path.

On the other side of the tor, the steep side, Rhiannon was climbing slowly but steadily. She'd tucked her flowers into the bodice of her dress, so she had one hand free to hold the candle that was lighting her way, and the other free to cling to the earth of the hillside, sometimes pulling herself up a little, other times leaning on it to give herself a boost to continue her upward journey. When the mists started to close in around her, she smiled. They'd always felt magical to her, Otherworldly, and as they swirled around her she felt comforted by their presence, the cool dampness soothing her reddened cheeks and invigorating her just as the climb had started to feel difficult.

She sent a short blessing of gratitude outwards towards the milky wisps, then halted in surprise, her heart suddenly beating a mile a minute as a face appeared to form from the whiteness ahead of her. Nervously she lifted the flowers from her dress and clutched them tight, like a talisman.

A body began to materialise under the head, until a woman finally stood before her. She smiled at Rhiannon, with a look of such love and comfort that her fear slowly faded away.

"Ah Rhiannon, my brave and shining one. You bring hope to me and my kind," she said as she moved forward, without having seemed to move at all, and enfolded her in a hug.

Rhiannon felt a sense of joy and peace come over her at the woman's touch, as though she didn't, and never would, have a problem in the world. She smiled uncertainly at the figure standing before her, dressed in blue, with her long red hair flowing down her back. Was this who she'd met once before, after her mother died, who had held her close while she cried? The one who had shown herself one more time, a few months later, who had taken her hands and encouraged her to reconsider her career plans?

The figure before her inclined her head regally in acknowledgement. "Yes, I am the blue-clad woman, as Carlie calls me, and to Rose I am

Brauna. Others have dubbed me the Keeper of the Well. But my name is of no consequence. I come here tonight to give you a message."

Rhiannon bit her lip. There was so much she wanted to say to her, to ask her, but clearly that wouldn't be welcome right now.

"We are so happy that you are taking this step with your friend, committing to your magic, and to your own growth and inner peace," the woman said, although her lips didn't appear to move, and Rhiannon wasn't sure whether the sound she was hearing was coming from within her own head or outside of it. Could she be making this up, thinking something magical was happening because she wanted so badly for it to be true? Still, she may as well enjoy the moment either way, even if this was just a figment of her imagination. What was she going to tell herself next?

"Rhiannon, I come tonight to remind you of what lies within you. You will need strength for the coming battle," Brauna said.

Battle? She almost giggled. She was going to be involved in a war? "I think you have the wrong person," she whispered. "I'm not strong. I have no weapons, and no will to fight anyone."

"Ah, young shining one. You have the strength of the whole world within you, and then some. And you will need it, because you will be sorely tested in the months ahead. You will need to hold fast to what you believe, and what you know to be true. To trust, even when it seems as though that trust is not warranted."

Rhiannon stared at her. "I have no problem with trusting – some people say I'm far *too* trusting," she insisted.

The woman took her hands and held them tight. "Then remember that. Hold that to you, even when you feel as though betrayal surrounds you. There are things you cannot see, things you cannot know, that will make you doubt the ones closest to you. Remember your faith in them, even when it seems no longer deserved. This will test you as much as them, believe me. And you will pass, if you stay true to you."

Rhiannon shook her head. "I don't know what you're talking about. Tests? Doubt and betrayal? What is this, some kind of quest for the holy grail?"

Brauna's eyes became sad, and Rhiannon felt her heart squeeze at the pain radiating from them. A pain it seemed she was causing.

"The holy grail is symbolic, not real," the blue-clad figure told her. "It is a state of searching that culminates in enlightenment, a state of bliss that results when you can overcome your fears and look into the heart of the world, into the hearts of those close to you – and into your own heart."

Rhiannon tried to understand, to really hear the words and the emotions behind them, and commit them to memory so she could puzzle over them later. Then she saw that Brauna was holding a silver chalice in her hands, and holding it out to her.

"For you, when things get hard," she said, and placed it in the bag slung over Rhiannon's shoulder. "And for your friend," she added, slipping a small object into the hand that held her flowers.

Rhiannon gazed down at it. Even squashed in on itself in her half-closed fist, she could see that it sparkled. "It's beautiful," she breathed, enchanted by the way the candle flame glittered on the crystals. She looked back up at the woman to thank her, but there was no one there. The mists continued to swirl around her, and in front of her. Reaching out her hand, she called out, but there was no reply, no evidence that anyone had ever stood before her whispering messages and prophecy. She shook her head. People said this hill could get into your mind and your heart, play tricks on you, and it seemed as though she had fallen prey to it too.

Yet she felt the weight of something in her hand, a sharp sensation around the stems of the flowers she was still clutching tight. And when she glanced down, her heart skipped a beat. Nestled in her palm was a silver ring, with a delicate silver butterfly on it. This was real, even if the mist-wreathed woman wasn't. The wings were made from sparkling aquamarines, and from the light of her candle she could see the delicate blue crystals reflecting and refracting light. Aquamarines symbolised truth and trust, which seemed to match the message she'd been given.

Wishing that she had a pen and paper, and the time to write down everything that had just happened, she tried to hold on to the words at least, commit them to memory so she could ponder their meaning later. She took a deep breath, then, feeling the ring in her hand, she slipped it into the pocket of her robe and continued her climb.

Carlie was already standing on the summit when Rhiannon arrived, looking as shaken as she felt.

"I have something for you," Carlie said, and put her hand in the pocket of her robe, pulling something small from the folds. "It's from a… I don't even know where to begin. Try it on!" she urged as she handed it over. Rhiannon drew in a breath, part surprise, part awe.

It was a delicate silver ring with a silver dragonfly on it, and tiny pink rose quartz crystals forming its wings. Rose quartz for compassion and love and healing. She held it up to the candle flame, marvelling at the colours and the way it sparkled so brightly. Slipping it on the ring finger of her right hand, where it fit perfectly, she suddenly reached into the pocket of her own dress. Her fingers closed around the matching ring that she'd been given for Carlie, and she pulled it out and handed it to her friend, who looked equally enchanted by it.

"Thank you so much, it's gorgeous. And it matches the butterfly on the aqua aura pendant Mum gave me for my last birthday, so I can wear them together, have you both with me," Carlie said. Then, looking at the butterfly, she sighed. She knew it was a symbol of transformation, of enduring tragedy and emerging through the other side stronger than before – she just wished that stronger side was a bit closer, because right now it seemed as though she was just as broken as she'd been the night her parents died. But she had to stop thinking like this, thinking of loss, because tonight was special, and she had to be in a much better, much more positive, head space for their ritual.

"It's not from me, it's from a mutual friend of ours," Rhiannon offered, voice small and unsure, and Carlie looked up from her hand, where she'd been tracing the pattern of the butterfly.

"A mutual friend? Wait, you met the woman in blue?"

Rhiannon nodded, eyes shining. "And you did too?"

"Well, I met Brianna, the green-clad woman, who said she's a friend of Brauna's. And that she's the Keeper of the Hill, as distinct from the Keeper of the Well. Maybe this means they're happy for us to be here, to be making magic in this sacred place?" Carlie asked.

"Brauna told me that she's glad we're doing this, which was a nice confirmation," Rhiannon agreed. Her smile faded as she remembered her other words. Would her friend betray her? And had the green-clad woman given Carlie a similar message about her? With an effort, she shook that thought off. She needed to think clearly, to put aside any doubts or wondering and focus on the ritual to come.

Deciding to push the unsettling conversations they'd had with women who surely couldn't really exist to the back of her mind, for now at least, Carlie began taking things out of her bag. She and Rhiannon had been talking about starting a group of some kind – she still shied away from the word coven – since the ritual her grandmother Rose had facilitated a few weeks ago. They'd both been spellbound by the magic of the night and of the seasons, and been moved to tears by the camaraderie and nurturing support that Rose, as the high priestess, so obviously shared with the women she wove magic with.

It was the Lughnasadh rite, the festival that marked the beginning of autumn, and the harvest, both metaphorically and in nature. For Carlie, it had been her first experience of group ritual and magic, and it still hurt her brain if she tried too hard to think about it with her usual logic – and her hitherto fairly strong scepticism.

And for Rhiannon, Carlie's new friend and confidante, it had been the first ceremony she'd taken part in since the death of her mother, who she used to attend the sabbats with, so it had been bitter-sweet at times, but had also made her surprisingly happy.

The morning after that ritual, Carlie had started reading the books on Rose's bookshelf, searching for mentions of group work and, although she'd been a little scared of using the word, covens. Rhiannon had begun searching online too, and they'd spent lots of time drinking tea together and making plans.

If she was honest, at first Carlie hadn't believed they would actually form a group, she'd just liked the idea of making a commitment to spend time with Rhiannon. But the more they'd researched and read, and the more she'd thought about the beauty of the Lughnasadh ceremony, the more she'd wanted to do it. And so they'd decided that tonight would be the night to perform their ritual of dedication. Rose was staying with her friend Elsie at her home near Winter Hill, and she'd suggested that Rhiannon might want to sleep over to keep Carlie company. So the two girls had put on their velvet dresses, gathered up their herbs and incense, and made their way up the sacred tor.

Now they knelt together on the lush grass at the summit, looking through their bags by candlelight and the last rays of the setting sun. Rhiannon pulled out the blend of lunar herbs she'd mixed that morning, a piece of charcoal and a clay dish in which to burn them, as well as two large candles in pretty glass jars and a small glass bottle of lavender-infused spring water.

Carlie placed a large piece of clear quartz she'd borrowed from her grandma alongside them, as well as a few different sized candles and a box of matches, then they reverently set up their altar. They placed the quartz in the north to represent earth, the herbal incense blend in the east to represent air, a gold candle in the south to represent fire, and a small cup of the lavender water in the west to represent water. In the centre were the two large pillar candles, a silver one to represent the goddess, and another gold one for the god.

Rhiannon ignited the incense in its dish, then picked up a bundle of dried lavender and lit one end. She gently wafted the smoke around Carlie and then herself, then walked around the circle marked out by their candlelight, cleansing and purifying the space within it with the sweet smelling smoke.

Slowly, reverently, Carlie unwrapped the athame from its velvet pouch. Rhiannon's eyebrows rose in surprise at the unfamiliar object, and she wondered if it had been a present from Brianna, twin to her gifted chalice. She watched in awe as her once-shy friend lifted it confidently to her heart, blade pointing outwards and upwards, carved handle fitting perfectly in her clasped hands.

Carlie raised her eyes to the darkening sky, inhaled a deep, centring breath, then took a step backwards, away from Rhiannon. She began to slowly pace out a circle, moving deosil – with the sun, or clockwise – her athame tracing the lines of its border. She smiled, because she'd discovered today while studying her grandma's magical books that if she'd been doing this back home in Australia, she would be stepping out her circle the other way, since energy was raised by moving with the sun, which in the southern hemisphere went in the opposite direction.

Focusing back on the present, she took another deep breath and began to speak, her voice shaking only a little.

Within this circle, that our intent will form,
Between the worlds, a safe place born.
Ancient beings of this sacred hill,
We call to you with our deepest will.
Please hold us close throughout this rite,
Reveal the magic on this full moon night.

The air seemed to shimmer as she came back to the place where she had started, and Rhiannon gasped as golden sparks danced around Carlie's head, just as the moon began to slowly rise above the horizon, leaving her awestruck as she felt a sensation of warmth and power slide over her shoulders and warm her.

As Carlie stepped inside their circle and moved towards the centre, Rhiannon picked up her chalice, which she'd filled with the spring water, and raised it above her head as she turned to face the north.

Guardians of the north, and element of earth,
Please ground us with your strength and nurturing,
and watch over our sacred rite.

Guardians of the east, and element of air,
Please grant us your intuition and clarity,
and share your wisdom with us this night.

Guardians of the south, and element of fire,
Please burn away our fears and doubts,
and flood us with your power and might.

Guardians of the west, and element of water,
Please wash away all we no longer need,
and allow us to soak in this magical moonlight.

They both walked slowly to the altar at the centre of the circle, and stood opposite each other, one on each side of the two large pillar candles. Gazing skyward again, Carlie raised her arms.

Goddess of love and compassion, magic and moonlight,
Please bless us with your presence through our sacred rite.

She lowered her arms and closed her eyes for a moment, before lighting the silver candle. To Rhiannon she looked as though she was gathering all the energy of the universe within her. Smiling at her friend, she too raised her hands and eyes to the sky.

God of strength and sunshine, love and might,
Please shine your blessings on us tonight.

She bent over and lit the golden candle, then they sat down on the cool grass, the altar between them. Rhiannon inclined her head slightly in Carlie's direction, signalling for her to go first. Carlie nodded, and lifted a small thin gold candle, bending forward to light it from the central flame. She held it to her heart, then looked towards the horizon as the huge glowing ball of the full moon slipped free of it and began to rise slowly into the darkening sky.

"I light this flame to symbolise the growing flame in my heart, as it awakens to the magic that flows within me, and the sense of ancestry that runs through my blood and connects me to this land. I come before you, goddess and spirits of place, humble in your presence, to commit to learning more, understanding more, sharing more. I am grateful to Rhiannon for allowing me to share this with her, and I promise I will work hard, research well and often, remain open minded, be supportive, and commit wholeheartedly to our Tuesday night study circle."

Placing her candle in the small glass holder in front of her, she looked over at Rhiannon with a smile. Her friend nodded, then took her own small thin gold candle and lit it from the central pillar.

"I light this flame to be a beacon of hope and love, to illuminate the darkness so that Mum can see me from wherever she is," she whispered. A tear rolled down her cheek, and Carlie yearned to lean over the altar and wipe it away, to comfort her friend with a hug. But she stayed where she was, too intimidated by the sense of the sacred that they'd created to break it by moving. Rhiannon smiled at her, as though she'd read her mind, then continued her declaration.

"Tonight under the silvery beauty of the full moon, I promise to honour the Old Ways, to step where my mother once walked, on the path of the goddess, and to pledge my support, my time and my heart to the coven that Carlie and I are consecrating tonight. Blessed be."

"Blessed be," Carlie echoed, as her friend set her candle down in front of her. "I wish I had your gift with words," she added, voice tinged with regret.

Rhiannon shook her head. "It's all about your intent, what you say doesn't really matter," she said, her tone confident and assured. "The goddess reads what's written in your heart. Besides, your dedication was beautiful. I'm so glad we decided to commit to this, and to consecrate it in this way. It makes it feel more real."

A cool breeze set their candles fluttering, and the girls collapsed back onto the grass, suddenly feeling a little light headed. Rhiannon pulled a bottle of fruit juice out of her bag and poured it out between three small glasses. Each girl lifted one up and took a sip, then together they raised the third glass and poured it out on the ground, an offering and libation to the spirits of place, and to the goddess and earth mother they revered so much.

Then Carlie lifted a small container from her bag and offered it to Rhiannon, who took two of the spicy moon cookies they'd baked that day, popping one in her mouth and crumbling the other onto the grass. Carlie did the same, smiling as she pictured the black ravens feasting on the crumbs once they'd gone. They were an important part of nature and of life, and if the goddess wasn't hungry, some of her creatures would surely enjoy their offering.

The girls sat in companionable silence for a long time, lost in the magic of the moment, the beauty of the night, the cleansing light of the luminous lunar orb as it sailed across the dark sky, and the sacred promise held within their vows. The scurrying of a creature down the hillside brought them back to the present, and they smiled as they realised that they'd lost all sense of time and place – it really was like another world within the borders of their circle, a place where time didn't exist. They could have been sitting atop the hill for hours tonight, or just minutes. After another few golden moments, something unspoken passed between them, and they decided they'd achieved what they'd gone up there to do.

Rhiannon slowly got to her feet and took up the chalice, walking back around the circle, farewelling the guardians of the four directions and thanking the elements for their presence. Then they held hands across the altar as they farewelled the goddess and the god, before Carlie lifted the athame and walked around the edge of their circle again, widdershins this time, against the sun. Using her words, her intent and the energy she was directing with the ceremonial knife, she dissolved the energetic bonds that had held them safe and nurtured, closing the space they'd forged between the worlds.

They stood for a moment, suspended in that liminal place between the sacred circle and the real world, heads filled with magic and whirling with promise and potential. Carlie's eyes shone, and her heart felt wide open. She gazed at Rhiannon, gratitude filling her as she pondered the kindness and friendship she had so freely offered to her. She shuddered at how empty and grief stricken she would still be feeling right now if not for her new friend. Rhiannon smiled back. She knew it would surprise Carlie to realise just how grateful she too felt for this growing friendship, this finding of a like-minded soul who understood her grief and was also as open to magic as she was.

Finally the moon headed behind a huge cloud bank, and they knew they wouldn't see it again that night. So the two girls gathered up their belongings, lit another small candle each to guide them, and set off home, walking together down the gentle slope to signify their joined purpose and promise. Once home, Carlie unlocked the back door of the cottage and switched on the kitchen lights. They'd set out dinner before they left, and now they both sat down, suddenly ravenous.

Carlie passed the salad bowl to Rhiannon and bit into a carrot stick. "Did you feel the magic up there?" she asked nervously.

"Of course, it was palpable," her friend said, her face alight with passion. "From the moment you stepped out the circle, I felt a shiver of energy go through me, and it stayed with me throughout our ritual."

"It wasn't just the cold air that made you shiver?"

Rhiannon looked at her friend, her left eyebrow raised. "Really? You didn't feel a sense of magic up there?"

Carlie blushed. "I did, of course, I just… sometimes it's hard for me to believe this is real. You grew up around it, you and your mum went to the rituals that Rose runs, and had energy healings and psychic readings. I didn't know any of this existed until I got here eight weeks ago. And it turns out that I didn't know my mother at all, because she grew up here, grew up like you, surrounded by all of this – then she ran away across the world and denied it all," she sighed, voice sad.

Pausing for a moment, she tried to gather her thoughts. "If I think about it too hard, it doesn't make sense. How can magic be real? How can we feel the breath of the goddess or hear the words that she says? How can we talk to the moon and feel the air around us shift?"

Rhiannon smiled. "Don't try to over analyse it or think it away, just try to feel it. Because really, does it have to make sense? If you hear the answer to your question, does it matter if it was the words of the goddess or your own inner voice?"

Carlie shrugged. "I guess not."

"And if Brauna and Brianna are just figments of our imagination, does that change their wisdom?" she asked. "Although given that we've both seen them, and they've given us gifts that we can physically hold in our hands, perhaps they are real," she mused.

They both looked down at the silver rings on their fingers as she said that, and carefully tried not to think of the messages they'd been given. Carlie didn't want her friend to know she had the potential to betray her, especially as nothing on earth could make her do that. And Rhiannon didn't want anyone to know how damaging her doubts could be, how little faith it seemed she really had.

They jumped as Luther knocked on the window, and broke out of the nightmarish daydream they'd both wandered into. Rhiannon smiled as Carlie stood up to let the little black cat in. "If it's real to you, then it must be real, right?" she said, and her friend nodded. "Now pass me the hommus and let me tell you about the boys who'll be in our class. Can you believe we start school on Monday?"

They chatted about that for a while, but although they'd imagined they'd stay up all night talking, they were soon fast asleep, crashed out on the fold-out couch in the lounge room long before midnight, dreaming of moonlit forests and boys in school uniforms…

Chapter 2

Moon Magic

It was mid-morning by the time they woke up, and Rhiannon had to rush back home to help her little brother get ready for school. Carlie folded up the couch and put the blankets back in the closet, then went out to the kitchen to make a cup of tea. As she stared out the window, she suddenly felt terribly alone, and so far from home. A wash of sadness rolled over her, and tears welled. Blinking rapidly in an attempt to stop them, she wiped impatiently at her eyes – then jumped when she heard a sound behind her. Spinning around, she saw Luther striding across the floor towards her.

He jumped up into her arms, miaowing affectionately, and she laughed as she had a vision of the opening credits for the old TV show *Bewitched*, where Samantha turned herself into a cat before jumping up into her husband's arms. "You're not going to turn into a person are you?" she asked Luther, then shook her head. Yep, she was still talking to the cat, and still expecting an answer…

When she heard the front door open she bent down and gently let Luther go. He looked up at her, haughty for a moment, then seemed to smile, before he trotted back through the house to greet Rose. "Hello Gran! Welcome home. Would you like a cup of tea?" she called out after him, and her grandmother poked her head into the kitchen and smiled. "Thank you Sweetheart, that would be great. I've just got to pop these out in the garden, then I'll be right in."

Carlie watched through the window as her grandmother picked up a small trowel, then bent down with the punnets of young herb seedlings and gently planted them out. Her herb garden was so beautiful, so lush and green, and so powerfully aromatic. Carlie had been learning about herbs from Rose since that first ritual, when she became fascinated by all things magical. What they looked like, and how to identify them by sight, smell and taste. How to care for them too, and what they were used for, both magically and medicinally.

Rose had shown her the amazing book that she'd started writing in while she was at college, with perfect hand-drawn illustrations of the leaves, the flowers, and even the roots in many cases, of countless herbs. There were instructions on how to grow them, how much water they liked, and whether they preferred sunshine or shade. Not that they always had much choice in the matter – England didn't come close to the levels of sun that her home in Australia enjoyed.

Sydney was where she'd been born, and where she'd lived her whole life – until that tragic winter's night a week after her seventeenth birthday, when her parents had died in a car accident. A car accident in which she had been the driver.

Eventually, thank god, she'd learned from Rose that it hadn't been her fault – a drunk driver had run a red light and slammed into their car. He was currently serving time for vehicular manslaughter, and while she was relieved that it hadn't been her actions that had led to the crash, she also felt a little sorry for the driver. He hadn't meant to kill anyone, hadn't woken up one day and decided to take someone's life, or planned out how to commit a murder.

It had just been a tragic accident, and she had no doubt that it had destroyed that man's life, as well as his young family's, as much as it had destroyed hers. And he had to live with the guilt. He'd written to her, via a newspaper, from jail, filled with self-recrimination and remorse. There had been a time when she'd raged at the very idea of him, had wanted him dead, or to have suffered the death of one of his family members so he'd know what she was going through. But her grandmother had helped her find a way forward, find a way to live with the loss – not to accept it, never that, but to survive it, to make it a part of her life that strengthened rather than weakened her.

Her grandmother was an amazing woman. She shook her head as she thought back to how rude and angry she'd been when she'd arrived on her gran's doorstep, sent across the world to live with a stranger. Cursed, she'd believed, to a life more miserable than she could even imagine. Now she just felt terrible that she'd never even known she had a grandmother. She still didn't understand why she hadn't known – she'd learned since the death of her mother that she'd been a woman of mystery and deep, dark secrets. She'd run away from home when she was seventeen, and never spoken to her mother again – never even let her know that she was okay.

And Rose, grieving the loss of her husband, who'd descended into an alcohol-drenched haze following their daughter's disappearance, before driving off a bridge to end his pain, also had to deal with never knowing if her only child was even alive. Carlie cringed as she remembered how unsympathetic she'd been to her grandmother when she'd arrived here. It had seemed justified at the time – surely she must have been a monster if her daughter had run away, to the other side of the world no less, and never written, never told her she was married and had a daughter, and never spoken of her to her best friend, her husband or said daughter.

Yet she couldn't have been further from the truth. She smiled warmly as Rose walked back into the kitchen, her long silvery hair pulled into two loose braids, with tiny chamomile flowers woven into their lengths. She was wearing a pale lavender dress that swished around her as she moved, and while there were deep lines of grief etched into her face, she also radiated a sense of peace and compassion, which she shone on everyone in the close-knit community she'd forged in this small village in England's south west.

Rose was the centre of the community, a kind of wise woman and beloved aunt rolled into one, and Carlie figured that while many who lost their husband and only child would have become bitter and resentful, Rose had turned all the love in her heart, and every mothering instinct she possessed, onto the people around her. She'd created a wonderful healing centre in the town, where she offered crystals, spiritual books, ritual tools, spell ingredients and colourful dresses and witchy robes, along with various methods of alternative healing and energy work, and many fascinating courses. And she was always available with a shoulder to cry on for those in pain, and ears and heart to listen when people needed that. She also ran the beautiful seasonal rituals that seemed to be a big part of the glue that held this community together, and was a high priestess of wisdom, strength and power.

Rose had been stunned when Carlie revealed that she had no idea about the kind of pagan magic she practised, and no familiarity with the reiki or the herbs she used to help the people who came to her healing centre. In her turn Carlie had been shocked to learn that her no-nonsense lawyer mum, who seemed to lean towards atheism if she even gave it any thought, had once been a flowers-in-the-hair, crystal-loving, red-velvet-wearing witch with a gemstone-encrusted willow wand and a love of oracle cards and the psychic arts, who'd worked in her mum's shop on weekends, performing reiki on those who needed healing, doing card readings and divination, and taking a central role in the magical sabbat ceremonies that Rose led.

In Australia, Carlie's mum had seemed to have no interest in mind body spirit topics. She'd occasionally gone to a fortune teller with her friend Sandy, but it appeared they did it as a joke more than anything else, and they never seemed to put any credence in what they were told. Her life there was devoid of crystal jewellery, oracle card decks and purple dresses – she lived in suits during the week and jeans on the weekends, and was strict and conventional. Almost boring.

Even her mum's name had been a shock and a secret. In Australia she was known as Fiona, but it turned out her name was Violet, or it had been. Why had she changed her name? Even more importantly, why had she fled the country of her birth and disappeared forever? The only reason Carlie had discovered she had a living grandmother was that just a few weeks before her mum had died, she'd taken her best friend Sandy to a lawyer and made her the executor of her will, leaving everything to Carlie, with instructions on how best to do this.

And she'd given her the name and home village of a woman in England who she said was her mother, who, in the event of her own death, should be contacted so Carlie could go and live with her.

Sandy had been shocked, and more than a little hurt, that her best friend had kept such a secret from her – had in fact lied and said that her parents were dead. But after the accident left Carlie an orphan, Sandy had tracked down the mysterious stranger, and reluctantly sent the troubled teen to live with her, as requested.

Carlie and Rose had discussed this mystery until they had no more words, turning over every single possibility they could dream up, but nothing made sense. If Rose had been a monster then fair enough – that's what had made Carlie imagine she was a hateful old woman who'd done something terrible to her daughter. But she'd discovered her mum's Book of Shadows, in a cottage in the mists that didn't actually exist, and it left way more questions than answers.

Violet had loved her life in the village, had adored her mother, and been so eager to follow in her footsteps. She took part in Rose's seasonal rituals, and was learning divination, herbalism, crystal healing and more, so that she could work alongside her mum and eventually become her business partner. She loved her father too, and had been dating her childhood sweetheart – a man Carlie had met, who'd looked like he'd seen a ghost when he first laid eyes on her, and who turned out to be Rhiannon's dad. *Yep, slightly awkward!*

As Rose came in and washed her hands at the sink, then took the lid off a jar of fresh cookies she must have baked with Elsie that morning, Carlie shrugged off her circling thoughts. Taking a biscuit when the plate was offered, she smiled as the rich buttery taste, complemented by the subtle mix of cinnamon, ginger and nutmeg, exploded in her mouth.

"Are these for tonight's full moon ritual?" she asked, and Rose nodded, smiling, before putting a question to her.

"Do you still want to come along tonight? You don't have to speak, I promise. You can stay on the edges if you'd prefer."

Carlie nodded too, grateful for how welcoming her grandma was, and how much empathy she had. She'd done so much to make her feel secure and included, despite her shock at suddenly acquiring a granddaughter she hadn't known existed, and had opened her magical circle – and her heart – to her with grace and generosity. Carlie had never believed in gods and goddesses, or thought that magic could be real, but since she'd started living with her grandma, she'd become more open to the possibility. So many strange things had happened since her arrival, which her logical mind couldn't quite rationalise. She couldn't even begin to comprehend the how or the why, but for now she was just going with it. Maybe it didn't have to make sense, or be able to be explained in a few short sentences. Maybe some things just had to be felt and experienced.

Giggling, she pictured her best friend Emily, and what she would say about all this if she told her. She would deny outright any possibility that the magic Rose wove could be real, and Carlie would have too, not that long ago. They'd both been sensible, rational and evidence-based, and had planned to go to university together to become sensible, rational lawyers. But now she had a new friend, Rhiannon, and although they weren't proclaiming each other best buddies just yet, she felt like she'd known her forever. Rhiannon had lost her mum a year ago, so they had a bond there, which made them feel close to each other in a way they couldn't with anyone else.

She was still in touch with Emily back in Sydney, but there was a distance between them now that had nothing to do with the oceans that separated them. Emily just couldn't grasp the depths of grief, anger and regret that were so much a part of her now, and Carlie wanted to protect her from that anyway. But she also needed to talk about it, and Rhiannon was a wonderful listener, and had so much empathy for people, so much compassion and insight. It was those qualities, and how supportive Rhiannon had been of her, that had inspired her idea to become a grief counsellor or social worker when she left school, rather than a lawyer as she'd always dreamed. And while this shared passion drew her closer to Rhiannon, it made her feel even more isolated from Emily, who she'd always planned to live with as they completed their legal studies together.

When Carlie sighed, Rose looked up from the bench where she was grinding herbs in a marble mortar and pestle, the heady scent filling the kitchen. "You okay Sweetheart?" she asked.

Carlie nodded.

"Worried about school tomorrow?"

She made a face. "A little."

"I'm sorry Sweetheart, I can't really help you with that one. But I know you'll be fine, and Rhiannon will be there, and Laura too. And I think you'll be happy there, if you give it a chance," Rose said, smiling reassuringly across at her. "Now, will you be ready to leave in half an hour to help me set up?"

"Of course. I'll just go up and get changed," Carlie replied, and clattered up the stairs to her tiny room at the back of the house.

As she started plaiting golden ribbons into her long dark hair, her thoughts turned back to Rhiannon. She was the daughter of Mike – her mum's childhood sweetheart – which had been a little strange for them all at first. But the strange seemed to become ordinary fairly quickly around here…

Faery lights illuminated the room above Rose's healing centre, and the large east-facing windows were open to track the path of the still-full moon when it rose. Carlie smiled across at Rhiannon, who was standing in the circle holding her brother Brodie's hand on one side and her dad's on the other, then focused on Rose as she paced out the boundary of the circle, much like she'd done herself the night before, albeit on a *much* smaller scale. Then four regal gold-robed women welcomed the directions and the elements, and Rose stood again in the centre, the imposing high priestess invoking the god and the goddess, then drawing down the moon.

It gave Carlie chills, to see her grandmother so transformed. It was as though the goddess really had come into her body, and was speaking through her, imbuing everyone in the circle with a sense of peace and power. Rose led a beautiful meditation after that, then they all broke into an energetic spiral dance, before most of the participants leaped into the middle of the circle for the group howl. Carlie was still too shy to take part, but she giggled when she saw Brodie with his head thrown back and eyes closed, his high-pitched yet wolf-like howls rising above everyone else's.

"Real magic is the magic of the everyday," Rose whispered in her ear as they watched Brodie. "The magic of family and friends, of the strength found in community. There's no need for smoke and mirrors, or grand fireworks. You don't even need prophetic messages from

Otherworldly visitors, although that can be nice. But that's magic right there," she said, pointing to where Mike stood with his arms around his children, all of them smiling widely, content to be together. "The magic of family – that's healing magic," Rose added softly, pulling Carlie into an embrace.

She swallowed over the lump in her throat, and felt the gratitude that she had Rose to anchor her after she'd lost her parents envelop her. As her grandma gently pulled away, Carlie thought her eyes were glittering with tears, but a moment later her face composed itself back into the confident, inscrutable visage of the high priestess, and her voice became powerful as she brought the gathered people back to awareness and calm in the softly lit room.

It was late by the time they'd packed up and gotten back to the cottage, and after a tired hug goodnight, Carlie made her way back upstairs, crawled into bed and pulled her mum's old quilt up over her. She was a little anxious about school tomorrow, but at least Rhiannon would be there. Then her mood shifted, and she smiled to herself as she heard Luther push open the door and jump up onto her feet, curling into a big purring ball of fluff that kept her warm as she drifted off to sleep. The huge golden moon shone into her room and cast beams of light across the floor as it rose higher in the sky, but she was fast asleep by the time it started creeping across her bed.

Chapter 3

Welcome To My Nightmare

The scream woke her up.

Carlie sat bolt upright in bed, heart pounding. Her head was still spinning, and she gasped for breath.

She'd had that dream again, and she shuddered as she realised it was her own scream that had torn her from sleep.

Luther was gazing at her calmly from where he lay curled up on the end of her bed. When she smiled at him, he walked up her legs and made himself comfortable in her lap. She patted his head. He was a patient creature, that was for sure. She'd cried herself to sleep many a night, and woken up screaming a few times too, but he was always there, snuggled up on her bed, watching over her.

The little black cat felt like a guardian of sorts, guiding her gently through her grief, and she was grateful for his warm body on her feet as the nights grew colder, and the sense of calm and companionship he exuded. She was also glad that her grandmother didn't seem to mind too much that her long-time feline friend had deserted her.

Settling back into bed, she allowed her mind to wander. She couldn't believe she'd been in this village with her grandma for two months now, and that tomorrow she would start at a new school, half a world away from her old one. Already her life in Sydney seemed like a lifetime ago, her old friends like people from a dream. She still missed Emily, but everyone else was fading from her mind.

Not her grief for her parents though. Their death in a car accident was still a raw and gaping wound, and there were times when she wondered if she'd ever survive through the day, so real was the ache in her heart, so tangible was its sensation of brokenness. Sometimes she would catch a glimpse of herself in a mirror or a shop window, and be surprised that her outer appearance didn't reflect the twisted pain she felt inside.

If it wasn't for her grandmother and Rhiannon, she didn't think she'd still be here. But the moments when she wished she had died with her parents were getting a little less frequent. And while she knew she'd never feel fully whole again, maybe that was okay. She wanted to keep them in her heart, keep them close, and if that meant she never let go of the pain, that was all right. Part of her still felt that she deserved to suffer anyway, since she'd been driving their car that night, chauffeuring them home after her mum's somewhat raucous but friendship-filled fortieth birthday dinner.

Sighing, she tried to recall what she'd been dreaming about, but already it was hazy. Something, or someone, had been pursuing her deep within the earth, in a tunnel under the hill, but every time she got close to seeing it, it curled away into mist. There was something not quite right about it though, because although she was afraid, and was running from it in terror, there was a small part of her that wanted it to catch her, wanted to feel it holding her close, stroking her cheek, leaning down to kiss her gently on the lips.

Wait, what? She gazed down at Luther. If only he could talk. Sometimes she was convinced that he knew all the answers to the universe – and to her small and petty problems – but he just couldn't tell her. If only she could study cat as a language instead of French...

At last she drifted off to sleep again. She was dreaming of home, her old home, but this time the women from the ritual she'd done were there with her, hands linked in a circle with her in the centre, all of them spinning around and around, long hair flying in the wind. Her arms were outstretched as she twirled, feeling secure and loved in this most basic of magic rites, this most powerful of enchanted circles. As they all turned their faces up to the sun and laughed, she felt her heart soar. Her mother was there too, gazing down on them from the sky, hand reaching outwards to bestow a blessing on them all.

She awoke gently this time, a smile on her face and Luther purring on the pillow beside her head. More than ten thousand miles from her childhood home, had she finally found her real home? Is that what her mum had wanted all along? What she'd cast that desperate spell for as she'd planned to leave home? For her mother and her daughter to meet at last, to be reconciled, to share the love that she'd felt driven to give up?

Her grandma knocked on her door, and Carlie called out a greeting as she jumped out of bed. Today was the first day at her new school, the first step towards her new career dream, and her new life. She was determined to face it bravely and with an open heart and mind.

Chapter 4

Meeting the Goddess

As she opened the front door and walked into the old school building though, she had to admit she was terrified. It did help that Rhiannon would be there too, and that she had met one of the teachers at her grandma's rituals, but the last thing she wanted was to be the new girl, to have to explain herself, and why she was here, living with her grandmother. To have to explain what had happened to her parents. She was sure everyone would be kind, but she just didn't want to be the centre of attention, to be stared at and wondered about. She sighed. There was nothing she could do about it, so she pulled her backpack up onto her shoulders and slowly walked inside.

The school was small, insanely small compared to her last one, and it didn't take her long to find the office and scribble down her timetable, and directions to each of the rooms she'd be in. When the first bell rang she took a deep breath and made her way to the classroom, and by the time the second one rang she was inside, introducing herself to the teacher and being directed to a spare desk. Quickly, quietly, she sat down and pulled out her books, trying to shrink in on herself, to avoid notice. She caught a few curious glances directed at her, but she kept her head down, madly scrawling notes and avoiding eye contact as much as she could.

Her fourth class was with Rhiannon, and she breathed a sigh of relief as she walked into the room and saw her friend's smiling face.

Rhiannon waved her over to the desk next to hers, and Carlie crumpled into the seat, thankful for even a slight reprieve from the pressure. The morning had been even harder than she'd expected, and she was tired of feeling so strange, so other. Everyone here knew each other, knew the teachers, knew where they were up to in each subject. She was tired of feeling so out of her depth. So when the teacher walked in and she saw that it was Laura – or Ms Henderson as she was known here, who she'd met at her first sabbat ritual – relief flooded her. She was even happier when Laura simply said hello and welcome, and got on with the lesson. She'd already had a few "introduce yourself to the class" moments today, and she was all talked out.

Carlie sat up straighter when she explained that this term they were going to study pre-Christian gods and goddesses, and would each choose one to do a project on. "No prizes for guessing who you two will do," Laura said, glancing at the girls as she handed the list of deities she'd compiled around the room. They stared at her in confusion. Carlie had recently discovered that her mum had named her for Kali, the goddess of life, death and destruction, but Rhiannon? They ran their eyes down the list, then raised their eyebrows as they saw her name there too.

"Rhiannon is the Celtic goddess of healing, inspiration and the moon. And she's especially associated with this area," Ms Henderson said. "Your mother named you well."

Carlie grimaced as she felt Rhiannon stiffen beside her. It was a year since her friend had lost her mother, and the pain was still raw and deep. Their teacher touched her hand.

"You'll be honouring her memory as you research this project, and you may come to know her even better too. It was no accident that she gave you a goddess's name. I remember her talking about it at your baby shower, just before she went into labour." She broke off, suddenly aware of all the students staring at her, and the unwanted attention focused on Rhiannon.

"Later then," she whispered, then turned to the rest of the class. "Now, are there any on this list that people know about already? And who will you study, and why? Let's go around the room."

Her voice shaking with nerves, Carlie said she would be looking into the myths and meaning of Kali, as her mother had named her for this deity, hoping to instil in her the qualities of the goddess. "I'm not sure how that worked out though," she offered, and her classmates laughed kindly at her joke.

By the end of the lesson, Carlie had realised this was going to be an interesting term. They would be able to spend some of their class time researching, then do the rest at home, and they would all have to do a presentation on their chosen deity before they broke for the Christmas holidays.

Dropping her bag in the lounge room when she got home from school that afternoon, Carlie walked over to her grandma's bookshelves, deciding to start on her research, since the due date would no doubt creep up on her quickly. After making a mug of tea, she grabbed a notebook and pen, and curled up in one of the comfy armchairs with a pile of books, and began to scrawl down some of the key attributes of her chosen goddess.

According to ancient Hindu tradition, Kali was the mother of all, the giver – and the taker – of life. Carlie was a little confronted by the images she came across of this goddess, so often depicted as a harbinger of destruction who was violent and bloodthirsty, although she smiled at some of the tales of her, and the metaphorical descriptions of her helping people, through death, to experience the joy of rebirth. She wondered how this related to her. She was starting to realise that death didn't always mean literal death, in the magical world at least, but could there be some relationship between the death of her parents and the resulting rebirth of herself and her grandma?

Of course she would still swap anything good in her life to have her parents back, but some of the descriptions were reminding her of what her mum had written in her Book of Shadows all those years ago, long before she'd ever known her, when she'd implored the goddess Kali to bring her a daughter who would somehow take her place, and redeem her actions in deserting her own mother.

... And so, my last act before I must leave everything I know, love and cherish, is a spellcrafting to attract a soul mate to me. Not a lover but a daughter, one who will be brave and strong and loving, and all the support Mum needs. I'll call her Kali, because she will be powerful and magical, and will transform the chaos of her family into something incredible, something love-filled, something better than I can offer...

I send out my call across the universe. Bring me a daughter ablaze with courage, compassion, strength and generosity of spirit. Kali, I implore you to bless me with this daughter, your namesake. I will nurture her and love her, and help her grow into a woman worthy of you, worthy of my mother, worthy of this world she'll be born into. Full of magic and wonder, imbued with wisdom and grace...

For the first time, Carlie realised the emphasis her mum had placed on a daughter to somehow solve her problems. She hadn't asked for a boyfriend or a husband or a knight in shining armour to rush in and save her and make her life all right, she'd cast a spell to bring forth a daughter, a family member, a woman. Although she had been madly in love at the time, and thought that man was her whole life, part of her hadn't trusted him enough, or depended on him enough, to be the one to help her mother, to give back what, in removing herself from her family, she was taking from her parents and their life together.

She felt her heart breaking wide open, and a rush of love and pride for her young, scared mother, a seventeen-year-old girl in the thrall of a much-older man, trusting in the goddess and the feminine over anything else. Rose would be so proud too, and so touched to realise that she'd managed, through her actions and the way she lived her life, to instil that in her daughter, no matter what else of her parents she had rejected.

Once again, Carlie felt so desperately sad that she'd never known this side of her mother. She wished with all her heart that she could have stood by her side in a sacred circle and taken part in a ritual with her. God, imagine if all three of them could have participated in a magical ceremony together. High priestess and matriarch Rose, her loving, compassionate daughter Violet, and herself, Carlie, starting to realise that she was descended from two beautiful, powerful witches, two women she admired and respected and was so inspired by. It made losing her mother when she did, before she'd ever got the chance to know this part of her, even more difficult.

And so she vowed to live up to her mum's expectations for her, to live a life of beauty, magic and grace, and to be there for Rose and surround her with all the love she'd been denied since her daughter had run away more than twenty years ago. Her heart broke for her grandmother. She was so strong, such a warrior woman, but she couldn't even begin to imagine how hard it must have been for her, for all those years, to think that your only daughter had rejected everything you stood for, everything you were.

Turning back to the books, she sought the deeper meaning behind what scholars had written about this goddess, the things described as negatives that she could see were in fact strengths.

◊ Kali has unwavering judgement, strong willpower and penetrative insight, which you can call on her to help you invoke within yourself...
◊ She assists by shedding light on those who seek to undermine you, saving you from hurt...
◊ While her methods may seem drastic and dramatic, Kali will force you onto a new and better path...
◊ This goddess represents awakening, throwing off the shackles binding you to the past so you can move forward...
◊ She brings passion, sexuality, sensuality and feminine strength into your life...

Carlie smiled as she scribbled, noticing a pattern. Yes, Kali brought upheaval and pain, but it was transformative. Each experience, no matter how tough, was to help you – or force you – to break through old patterns and conditioning, or to leave stagnant situations, dead-end jobs or people who were bad for you, and to open you up to a new and better existence.

Making a note of the crystals associated with this goddess – ruby, bloodstone, garnet, tourmaline and smoky quartz – she decided that she'd check them out and maybe buy one next time she was at her grandmother's shop. Then she copied out some of the affirmations people suggested for working with this deity.

"I am indestructible."
"I am strong."
"I am powerful."
"I am a warrior woman."
"I can conquer darkness, sadness and loss."

The last one touched her deeply, and she hurried up the stairs to her room to find some coloured cardboard and a gold pen, and wrote them all out again on neat little squares that she stuck to her mirror and slipped into her school books as bookmarks. When she had just one left she gazed around her room for a moment, then gently placed it under her pillow. Then she went back downstairs and made a start on her essay notes.

Kali has a reputation as a dangerous, cruel force, wielding destruction as Cupid wields his arrows of love, but she is far more complex than that. When she lays waste to your dreams, to your patterns, to your life, it is to make you take a new and better path, to leave behind the things you no longer need, the things you hold on to out of insecurity and fear, so you can recreate your life in brilliant new ways.

Some people say that if your life is spinning out of control, it's Kali telling you that you have chosen the wrong path. Through her strength, her courage, and yes, even her harshness, she helps you – forcefully! – find the right path for yourself, and thus find purpose and meaning in your life. She encourages you to purge your life of people and situations that are no good for you, to get rid of excess baggage and emotions that no longer serve you. So while she may be destructive, it's destruction of the negative in your life in order to create a new and more fulfilling existence – so in a way she's actually a positive force ☺

Carlie paused. How much could she write of herself, given that it was for a school assignment? Pondering the meaning of the goddess though, she felt inspired to be brave, to reveal to herself the truth of her life. She trusted Laura – Ms Henderson – and felt it was important for her own growth as well as the success of her essay, to seek the heart of the goddess and her own connection to her, in order to find a deeper connection with her mother as well. And she had to trust herself enough and be brave enough to be honest. Taking a deep breath and screwing up her courage, she began writing again.

I was not only named for Kali, but my mum did a spellworking in honour of this goddess and implored her to bring me to her, so I definitely feel like I have a lot to live up to!

I only discovered this a few days ago, so it's still a bit strange to me (okay, a lot strange!), and I must confess that until I arrived in this town, I had never even considered that all these gods and goddesses could be real. My mum, who worked the spell two decades ago, gave no inkling that she believed in any of this stuff when I knew her, so this assignment will not only be a journey of discovery for me, but a way to connect on a new level with my mum, even though she's gone.

I have to be honest, I'm still not sure I believe that these deities exist, but I'm looking forward to learning more about them – through this essay as well as through my coven research with Rhiannon and my magical workings with my grandmother – and learning more about my mother too…

Chapter 5

Tuesday Night Magic Club

School was a little easier the next day, her fellow students already including her in their discussions, and she was relieved that it hadn't been as difficult as she'd imagined. But she had to admit that she wasn't paying much attention in class – all she could think about was her first coven meeting with Rhiannon that night. She was filled with anticipation, and a little thrill of fear.

When the final bell rang she raced out the door and hurried home, so she could change into something a little more magical and pick up her reference books and her notes to take to Rhiannon's place. On Sunday she'd looked up athames in her grandma's books, as homework for their meeting, while Rhiannon had been looking up chalices, so they could report back to each other and widen their knowledge about the magical objects they'd been gifted at their dedication ritual – both of them crucial ingredients in a witch's tool box.

Skipping up the front steps at her friend's house, she knocked quickly, and was a little thrown when Brodie opened the door. "Where's your pointy hat?" he asked her with a smirk.

Blushing, she was saved from replying when Rhiannon appeared behind him in the doorway and ushered her in. Her friend ruffled her brother's hair as she passed. "You little terror," she said, but the love in her voice made Carlie's heart ache for the bonds of family. "Just for that, you get none of our treats tonight," she teased.

Sticking his tongue out at his sister, Brodie went back inside to "help" his dad with dinner, and the two girls made their way upstairs to Rhiannon's gorgeous room. Looking around her at the neatly cleaned space, Carlie smiled happily and felt herself relax. The pretty window drapes were tied back to let in the late afternoon breeze, and Rhiannon had already created a magical circle with tiny tea light candles, which flickered in the apple-scented air sweeping down from the tor. Within the border was a small altar, and soft, brightly coloured cushions were scattered around it so they could be comfortable while they worked. They took off their shoes at the door then tiptoed within the golden circle of light, mood instantly reverent as they felt themselves transported to that liminal space between the worlds.

"It's beautiful Rhi," Carlie said, taking a deep breath of the cleansing and clearing oil blend her friend had used. She recognised sandalwood, lemon and lavender, and felt their soothing, purifying qualities washing over her, shaking off the stresses of the day and focusing her on the present, right here in this moment of magic and mysticism.

Sinking down onto a huge purple pillow, she pulled out her notebook. She'd decided that she would scribble everything down as it happened tonight, before transcribing it into her Book of Shadows later, when she could worry about being neat and put her jumbled thoughts in order. For now she just wanted to feel everything, rather than worry about her messy scrawl. To be swept away and caught up in the atmosphere of wonder she was feeling.

Rhiannon settled down opposite her and pulled out a pad of paper too. "So, we were planning to dedicate tonight to our studies, is that still cool with you?" she asked.

Carlie nodded. "I researched athames and their use in magical rituals, and I wrote it all out for you too, so you can glue it into your Book of Shadows, or transcribe it more neatly than my scrawl later on, and write it directly onto a page."

Rhiannon laughed. "What are you worried about? That's perfectly neat," she said, then she started reading through the notes.

An athame is a ceremonial ritual knife used by witches and other magical practitioners to store, channel and direct energy, and to cut an enchanted space between the worlds. Casting a protective circle before a ritual or spellworking is often performed with this sacred tool, although a sword or a wand may be substituted if you prefer. An athame can also be used to draw pentacles or other magical symbols in the air, in order to welcome the elements, as well as to cut etheric cords and cast protective spells. This ceremonial dagger is also utilised to symbolise the masculine – to the chalice's feminine – in representations of the Great Rite.

The athame is one of the four elemental tools in magical practice. In many traditions it represents the element of fire, whereas the chalice corresponds to water, the wand corresponds to air and the pentacle represents earth. In Celtic history and myth, these four objects also correspond to the four symbolic weapons – the sword, the cauldron and/or grail, the spear and the shield – and they're also intimately linked to the four suits of the tarot deck – swords, cups, wands and pentacles.

Traditionally an athame consisted of a double-edged steel blade with a black handle, although today there are many variations. There are beautiful ones with sculpted silver handles, some depicting a deity or a magical creature, and others have a wooden handle. Often times magical symbols, deities, crystals or lunar depictions are worked into, attached to or engraved on the handle.

An athame is generally not used to cut physical matter; it is retained for energy workings only. Instead, many witches will use a white-handled ritual knife called a boline to cut their herbs and other spell ingredients. An athame or a boline can also be used for exorcising, banishing and enchanting in magical herbalism rituals. An athame, and indeed all magical tools, should be regularly cleansed if you work with them often. Purifying them by passing them through the smoke of a protective incense blend is a simple yet powerful way to do this.

"This is fantastic Carlie, thank you. I was worried you'd think I was a swot for writing you an essay, but it seems we're as bad – or as good – as each other. I'm really glad you're taking our magic circle as seriously as I am," she said with a smile. Then she paused, blushing. "To be honest, I wasn't sure you really wanted to do this, and I sensed some hesitation when we were talking about it, even at school today."

Carlie laughed. "Don't feel bad, I did have some hesitations," she admitted. "But don't ever think I'm not taking it seriously."

Rhiannon promised not to, then she handed Carlie a sheet of paper covered in her colourful scrawl. "I wrote you out a copy of my chalice research too, so you wouldn't have to focus on note taking tonight," she said, and they both laughed, happy at their many similarities.

The chalice is one of the four major tools used in magical rituals, alongside the pentacle, the wand and the athame. It symbolises the element of water, and may be included on your altar for this purpose. It can be used in the clearing and setting up of a magical circle too, by placing water in it, blessing it, then walking around the circle aspersing the water. It may also be used to hold a libation to the god and the goddess, and to nature and the spirits of place, with a little of its contents poured out onto the ground in outdoor rituals, to give thanks for the magic performed that night. If you're working inside, you could place your offering in a pot plant, or save it to return to the earth later.

In some rites the chalice is filled with water, juice or wine, which is blessed by the group doing the working then passed around the circle, each person taking a sip before passing it on, a ritual which symbolically unites the individual members and helps them slip into ritual consciousness.

As Carlie read this, she looked up, to see Rhiannon offering the chalice to her. She took a sip, then passed it back to her friend, who drank her fill before returning it to the centre of their altar.

The chalice also symbolises the womb of the goddess, and fertility both literal and metaphorical. It's a representation of feminine energies, which is why many are made of silver, since that is the metal associated with the goddess and the moon. Many incorporate magical symbols carved or engraved into their side, and some are encrusted with gems. Our coven chalice has small moonstones around the base, adding to its lunar power, and is engraved with the symbol of the triple moon and triple goddess.

The chalice represents the feminine and the subconscious, whereas the athame represents the masculine and the intellect. Together the two play a central role in the Great Rite, which is performed to symbolise creation and birth, and represents the principle from which all life springs. The athame is placed in the chalice to represent the union of male and female, god and goddess. Like the yin in the yin-yang symbol, it represents the feminine energies of the earth, with the athame as the masculine yang.

This ritual tool also symbolises the Holy Grail in some traditions. Today it's thought by many to be a Christian symbol, representing the cup Jesus used at the Last Supper, and it's often filled with wine to symbolise his blood. But it had been used in magical rituals for thousands of years before Christ, when it was believed to represent the womb of the goddess, and in modern witchcraft and goddess spirituality it still does.

A cup or a cauldron can be substituted for it if you don't have a chalice on hand, and all three can symbolise inspiration and be used for scrying, by filling it with water or another liquid and gazing into the surface seeking symbols and images.

"Thank you," Carlie said, smiling at her friend. "It's all so fascinating." She paused, and Rhiannon urged her to continue.

"Well, I thought it was really interesting that I was given an athame from Brianna, which represents the masculine, and Brauna gave you a chalice, which represents the feminine. It's like they were trying to make our magic balanced and complete, helping us so that together we can make up the whole."

Rhiannon nodded. "Totally! The Great Rite is also known as the Great Marriage, and uses the chalice and athame to represent the marriage of the god and the goddess, the joining of the high priest and high priestess, and the combination of masculine and feminine energy that is at the core of the earth, of people, of all of life."

"Perhaps that's why we were given these two gifts, rather than anything else, so that our dedication incorporated the god and the goddess in a really deep way?" Carlie mused. "I also found a reference, in a very old book, that talked about the Lady of the Lake gifting a chalice and a sword to someone worthy of those gifts. Perhaps that's who you met, the one who gave you the chalice. Lady of water, of blue, of lakes."

Rhiannon's face lit up. "It's such an awesome mystery, isn't it? I mean, who are they? Are they even real? The things they gave us are certainly real, but I can't work out how a person could materialise like that, or have such knowledge about us."

They went back and forth for a while, discussing the gifts they'd received and debating who the beings that they'd met could be, but eventually they both paused, acknowledging that they might never understand, but content for now to leave it as a mystery. Just before they closed circle, Rhiannon held out a piece of paper to her friend.

"I sensed that you're still a bit anxious about this, about us forming a coven. So we can call it something else if you'd rather, Tuesday Night Magic Club perhaps, or you can work through your fear of the word, and realise the only meaning it has is the meaning we give it. And I don't know, maybe you'd like to include this in your Book of Shadows," she offered, voice suddenly shy. "Only if you want to of course..."

A coven is a group of witches who work together to perform ritual and learn and grow together. And while the word itself is not an old one – it was first recorded as being applied to witches in the seventeenth century – the concept of witches working together is. Some simply celebrate the sabbats and esbats (full moons) together, but others are very serious in their dedication to learning more about witchcraft, healing and self-development, and work deep magic together. They meet regularly, and a sense of trust develops between the members which allows them to delve more deeply into witchcraft and magic, developing spells and rituals, exploring magical herbalism and other elements of magic, and supporting each other in rituals and ceremonies.

American eco witch Starhawk described covens this way: "The coven is a witch's support group, consciousness-raising group, psychic study centre, clergy-training program, College of Mysteries, surrogate clan and religious congregation all rolled into one," which is very apt.

Some covens require that all members are initiated into a particular tradition, such as Alexandrian or Gardnerian Wicca, but others form more eclectic groups, with each member following their own spiritual path. Traditionally covens were enshrouded in secrecy and met in private, as there were times when people were executed if it was known that they practised witchcraft. Today, while there is still some prejudice against witches, it is no longer a matter of life or death to maintain the vows of secrecy and silence, and many covens hold open rituals for friends and newcomers, like the sabbat celebrations Rose conducts, along with deeper, more private magical workings for members only.

Carlie smiled at her friend, then reached over and hugged her. "Thank you for this, for taking my nervousness seriously rather than simply telling me to get over it. And I will get over it – I mean, I know from our rituals, both together and with Rose, that there's nothing scary about it, I've just never used the word witch for myself or anyone else – I thought they only existed in faerytales. I've just got to get my head around this whole secret life my mum was part of. I really wish she'd told me about it, shared it with me. It must have been so beautiful when you worked magic with your mum."

Rhiannon nodded sadly, and seemed reluctant to speak about it at first, but finally she shared some of the magical rituals she'd done and some of the experiences she'd had with her mum, some serious, some more light-hearted, and by the end she was smiling a little.

"It actually feels really nice to talk about Mum, to remember the beautiful moments we shared. Thank you for letting me bring her here, giving her a place in our circle."

Carlie leaned over and hugged her again. "Any time."

"And we'll learn more about your mum, and her beliefs and practices, and we can welcome her too," Rhiannon added, and Carlie was grateful all over again that the stars had aligned to bring the two girls into each other's lives. She couldn't think of a better person to be grieving with, or to be picking up the pieces and moving forward with, and she felt excited at the possibility that they could weave together a magical new life for themselves. They had both lost so much, but she was slowly learning to appreciate the things she'd gained too.

They closed their circle, then grounded their energy with chocolate chip cookies and mugs of strong tea that Rhiannon's dad Mike brought up for them at the perfect time. Afterwards Carlie wandered slowly back home, feeling peaceful as the just-past-full moon shone down on her. She was really looking forward to all the things she and her new friend would discover together, about themselves, about each other, about their mums, about the world.

Her grandma had already gone to bed when she reached the cottage, so she was careful to unlock the door quietly and tiptoe up the stairs to her room, laughing silently as Luther greeted her with a miaow and jumped lightly up onto her pillow.

She slid into bed, and when she woke the next morning she had a smile on her face. Drawing the blankets more tightly around herself, she tried to slip back into the dream she'd been having. This was the fourth time she'd had it, and each time it became a little clearer. There was a guy in it, with long black hair that swept down his back in a jumble of loose curls, although she still hadn't seen his face properly. But he was holding her tight, keeping her safe from the thing that was pursuing her, and she was desperate to learn more about him.

As much as she wanted to though, she couldn't get back to sleep, so she lay awake, trying to recall more about him. But it was too hard – a mist seemed to fall over them where they stood together, his arms locked tight around her. A mist that swirled up, thick, white and impenetrable, a mist she'd seen before. Had walked into, and emerged back from, with new knowledge and new wisdom. Perhaps her dreams were a sign she'd eventually feel ready to open her heart to a boyfriend.

Patience, she scolded herself. She was still a grieving wreck, so it was best to guard her heart until it healed.

The following Tuesday night, Rhiannon went to Carlie's house for their coven meeting, and Rose sat with them and shared stories about Mabon, the next sabbat in the Wheel of the Year, which was the celebration of the autumn equinox. She told them the history of the festival and the literal and metaphorical meanings attributed to it, then helped them delve into the herbal correspondences and foods associated with the sacred day, which they scribbled down in their Book of Shadows, eager to catch and capture every piece of wisdom their much-admired high priestess was prepared to offer.

"Now, how about a more practical lesson?" Rose finally asked the girls. "Because surely you've taken enough notes for one night?"

Carlie put her pen down, suddenly feeling guilty. "Is that a bad thing?" she asked nervously.

"No Sweetheart. Knowledge is very important, and traditions are very important, but so is living your Craft. Don't forget to really *experience* the lessons, so you can discover how they relate to you, rather than just taking notes and blindly accepting what someone else tells you – even me. Truth is different for everyone, so be sure to really *feel* the magic within you, and the wisdom within your own heart."

Rhiannon put her pen down too, gazing at Rose with awe as she continued. "All the festivals have a traditional meaning, rituals that have been celebrated for hundreds of years, but the meaning *you* attribute to it is just as important, and just as valid, as anything someone came up with last year, or last century, or wrote in a book. Whatever you feel is right, is right for you, so don't ever let anyone tell you that you're wrong. The magic you create and send out into the world, that comes from you. That's why a spell you dream up will be far more powerful than any you find in a book, because it's imbued with your energy, your intent, your power," she explained.

"In any kind of magic, the physical tools are far less important than your own intent and your own power of manifestation and creation. Ritual tools, herbs, crystals, candles, essential oils, colours – they all have their own innate power to heal and bring about change, and will work on their own in a magical sense too, but it's the magical practitioner themself that really gives a spell or a ritual its power and the added boost to increase the effectiveness of the magic.

"Your visualisation of the outcome you want to achieve, your intent in casting the spell, your charging of the herbs or tools with your own energy, that's what makes the magic happen, that's what gives the spell or the ritual its power. So don't ever give your power away to another person," Rose finished fiercely, looking far more the stern high priestess than the loving grandmother in that moment.

Both girls stared at her, and she laughed at their puzzled faces.

"I'm sorry, it's just one of my pet peeves, people setting themselves up as experts, encouraging others to give away their own power and accept their will, to do their bidding without question. You have as much magic within you as anyone else does, and only you can ever know what is right for you.

"But that's probably enough about that for one night. Follow me," Rose said, mischief in her voice. She stood up and led the way to the kitchen, Luther miaowing at her heels, and started pulling out ingredients from the pantry and the fridge and stacking them on the bench. Switching on the oven, she then took out a mixing bowl, utensils and a silver baking tray.

"Are we going to start making things for the Mabon ritual already?" Carlie asked, surprised given that the sabbat was still two weeks away. But Rose just laughed.

"Sweetheart, you don't have to be so serious all the time! Studying magic takes a great deal of time, dedication and commitment, but it also requires a light heart and a sense of joyous fun. So I thought we'd done enough study for one night, and it was time to bake some shortbread bikkies, brew up a big pot of tea and sit down together and chat about everything and nothing. Life, love and the meaning of the universe... or we could share some jokes, if you have any," she grinned. "Magic needs levity too."

Rhiannon smiled. "I don't know any jokes, but I'm happy to talk about love. Not that I have much experience with it myself – just as I met someone I really liked, well, let's just say I wasn't in the mood to explore that, with Mum being so sick, and then..." she trailed off, misery colouring her voice as she thought of her mum's battle with cancer and her eventual defeat.

Rose poured water from the kettle into the teapot and left it to steep, then walked over to Rhiannon and hugged her. "Sweet girl, there's plenty of time for love. You'll find someone deserving of your time and your heart very soon, you have no need to worry. And he will be a very lucky guy."

Carlie smiled. Her grandmother was amazing – she always knew the right thing to say. Not for the first time, she counted her blessings that she had these two incredible women in her life.

Chapter 6

A Spell For Love

A no-warning maths test a few days later had Carlie feeling a little out of sorts by the time she met up with Rhiannon at lunchtime, but soon they were laughing and joking, and she felt the stress slipping away as their giggles increased. Rhiannon had brought a book of spells to school, and they were flicking through it, wrinkling up their noses at some of the ingredients in the more ancient ones.

"It's the new moon this Sunday – which is the perfect time for casting love spells," Rhiannon said, sneaking what she hoped looked like a casual sideways glance at her friend.

"We could give it a go," Carlie replied with a nervous smile. "I've never done a love spell, or been in love for that matter. But I remember reading in Mum's Book of Shadows that you shouldn't ever cast one on someone specific, otherwise they might fall head over heels in love with you – and then if you ever want to break up with them, they'll just stalk you for the rest of your days, because they can't break free of your spell and will love you regardless of what you say."

"Plus there's no one we actually like here," Rhiannon reminded her. "So it will have to be a general one anyway." She thumbed through the book. "Do you want to cast a spell for love or lust?"

Carlie blushed. "Can't we have both? Or does it have to be one or the other? I mean, obviously love is more important, right? But do you think true love has to be without passion?"

Rhiannon shook her head. "Of course not, I just wondered if you had anything specific in mind. Now, we'll have to work out what kind of qualities we want in a boyfriend..."

"Like that Alanis Morissette song? With the list of twenty-one things she wants in a lover?" Carlie asked. "Although mine would be a lot different to hers," she added, cheeks flaming again. "I'm not so worried about the 'experimental' and 'uninhibited in bed' bit."

Her friend wiggled her eyebrows suggestively. "Really? But you don't want them to be boring in that department do you?"

"Rhiannon!" Carlie exclaimed, face as red as a tomato. "I'm not interested in any of that."

"Okay okay, don't freak out!" her friend laughed. "So we'll switch our coven night to Sunday for this week, and cast a love spell on the new moon, yeah? Do you want to come to my place? I think I have all the ingredients we'll need."

Carlie nodded, then they groaned as the bell for classes rang. "Don't forget to work on your list of things that you do want!" Rhiannon said, as she waved goodbye and rushed off to chemistry class. Carlie giggled as she realised that it would be a very different kind of chemistry they dabbled with on Sunday.

When she got home from school that afternoon, she grabbed some of Rose's magic books then ran straight up to her bedroom, since she didn't want her grandma to know about this particular spellworking. She planned to do some research before their casting, so she didn't come across as too naive or silly. Rhiannon seemed far more worldly than her, and clearly more experienced in matters of the heart. Opening up the closest book, she began to read.

In love magic, and indeed any magic, it is important to never compromise the "harm none" principle, or to influence another person's free will. Love spells are the most popular and widespread magic of all, and in some ways also the most dangerous, because so many people ignore the ethics and cast a spell on a specific person. This is bad news on several fronts.

First, and most importantly, it violates the free will of the other person, causing them to fall for you regardless of their feelings – which would eventually be a hollow victory, for you would always wonder whether they really loved you or it was just the spell. Additionally, such a spell has the potential to backfire on you and cause you great harm. There are many stories about women, and men, who bewitched the object of their affection into loving them, then realised as they got to know them better that they didn't like them after all. But unfortunately they found it hard to escape from the relationship, because they had bound the person to them, so now they didn't want it to end, and would not go quietly.

Instead, you should cast a more general spell to attract love. You could cast it for a type of person – "I want a man who will treat me this way, who does this, believes in that etc" – because a spell is a list of your desires and intent sent out to the universe. Or you can simply ask for your soul mate or true love to appear, for the highest good of all concerned (including yourself!). You can also cast a love spell on yourself, to open yourself up to the possibility of love and let the universe know you are ready, and to allow people to see you at your best and most attractive.

Lust spells and aphrodisiacs can also infringe on someone's free will and violate the "harm none" ethos if that person is not interested in being with you or is unaware they are being fed a potion. Even within a relationship it is not fair to use such spells if your partner doesn't know about it. If lust is your aim, you can cast a spell on yourself to appear more desirable, which will attract someone who wants the same thing. And while if you find infidelity unacceptable it might seem okay to use magic to keep your partner faithful, it is still not right to use magic on anyone without their knowledge, and with the aim of curtailing their free will. If they are cheating, and want to cheat, that is their choice. All you can do is choose to deal with their actions or end the relationship – and make sure you remember to include fidelity on your list next time you cast a spell to attract a partner.

That was true, Carlie thought. She did want someone who was faithful to her, who loved her for who she was, and didn't flirt with other people behind her back or try to make her jealous. Pulling out a pen and a notebook, she started writing. She'd copy it into her Book of Shadows more neatly later, when her thoughts were in order, but for now she just wanted to focus on what was important to her, in a friendship or a relationship, and scribble down everything that crossed her mind.

Finally she narrowed it down – she wanted someone kind, caring, compassionate and open-minded, as in, someone who wouldn't freak out that she and Rhiannon had formed a coven! And she hoped they would be intelligent, interesting, encouraging and motivated, not to mention understanding and patient too. The death of her parents was still so raw and wounding, and she imagined that she wouldn't cope well with anyone who tried to rush her into something before she was ready. *Hmm, how many traits could she request?*

Once that was done, she started flipping through some of the other books so she could figure out spell ingredients. Jasmine would be a good beginning, so she started writing out a page on its properties in the plants and herbs section of her Book of Shadows.

This pretty flower had long been considered one of the most potent ingredients for love spells – Egyptian queen Cleopatra was said to have seduced Roman general Mark Antony with it, and in addition to using it medicinally, Eastern cultures have used it in love spells and as an aphrodisiac for thousands of years, claiming that it penetrates the deepest layers of the soul and opens a person up emotionally, and that it can attract both romantic and spiritual love. As well as increasing love, happiness and relaxation, it is also thought to be helpful in working to heal sexual issues such as impotence and frigidity.

In the Philippines, the name of the jasmine flower, sampaguita, comes from the words for "I promise you", and it represents a pledge of mutual love – young couples traditionally exchanged jasmine necklaces instead of wedding rings. And in India, jasmine flowers represent divine love as well as romantic love, and there the flower is called "moonshine in the garden", with ancient paintings depicting moonlit lovers embracing near jasmine plants.

The scent is extracted from the tiny white star-shaped flowers of the jasmine vine, which are picked at night when the aroma is the strongest, a property that links it to the moon and lunar spells. Not only can you anoint your body with jasmine oil or use it to dress pink candles which are then burned for love rituals, but dried jasmine petals can be added to sachets to attract love, jasmine tea may be served to increase love, and the fresh flowers can be worn in your hair or placed in a vase during ritual.

Hmm, perhaps she and Rhiannon could anoint each other's foreheads with the oil before they began their new moon ritual?

When Carlie walked into Rhiannon's room on Sunday evening, a sweet incense blend was burning on the altar, and the scent took her breath away. Pink and red candles were positioned around the room, flickering warmly against the fading sky outside, and on the altar a large piece of rose quartz sat in the centre, surrounded by pink and white rose petals. The whole scene was so uplifting, and she felt lighter and happier all of a sudden, then sensed the familiar state of ritual consciousness beginning to descend.

"It's beautiful Rhi," she breathed. "And it smells divine."

"I have some jasmine oil too, so we can anoint each other before we begin," her friend said, and Carlie felt a thrill of pleasure that she'd been on the right track with that. Maybe she would get the hang of this witch thing eventually.

"I figured that a simple ritual would be best," Rhiannon continued, as she pressed a few drops of the oil onto Carlie's forehead then handed her the small bottle so she could do the same to her. "If you cast the circle, then we can welcome the elements and the directions, and invoke the goddess – I thought tonight we could invite her in a few of her love goddess guises. Branwen, the Celtic goddess of love and beauty; Aine, Irish goddess of love and fertility; Freya, Norse goddess of love and magic; Hathor, Egyptian goddess of love and beauty; Aphrodite, Greek goddess of love and fertility; Venus, Roman goddess of love and beauty; Ishtar, Babylonian goddess of love and procreation; and Inanna, the Sumerian goddess of love."

Carlie stepped out the boundary of their circle, directing the energy with her athame, then listened, spellbound, as her friend welcomed the deities of love. Then they sat down in the middle of the circle, one on either side of the altar. Each had a red and a white candle, which they anointed with jasmine oil – ah, the beautiful scent – then carved love hearts into with a white-handled boline. Rhiannon handed Carlie a piece of parchment and a pink pen, and they wrote down all the qualities they'd like in the person they were welcoming into their life. They smiled as they envisioned what type of person would make them happy, how they would spend their time together, and what they had to offer to the relationship in turn.

Then at the exact same moment they both put their pens down and looked up at each other, the candlelight sparkling and dancing in their eyes, and together they began to chant:

As a new lunar cycle starts with this magical new moon,
We ask that you send new love to us soon.
Someone whose heart and soul we can fill,
Someone who comes of their own free will...

As they said it for a second time, they gently held a corner of their parchment into a candle flame, and watched as their lists curled up and started to smoke, their wishes released into the cool night-time air and sent skyward to meet the tiny crescent moon.

Just before the paper burned down to their fingertips, they dropped the remains into the small cauldron on the altar, which had a thin layer of sand in the base to absorb the heat. Then they held hands and chanted their verse for a third time, ending with the witchy equivalent of Amen, "So mote it be."

Carlie didn't know if it was the smoke from the incense, the scent of the jasmine oil, or the presence of some of the deities or beings Rhiannon had invoked, who she wasn't sure actually existed, but she felt a tangible shift in the atmosphere of the room, and a strange altering of her perception. She saw a vision of the guy from her dreams, with his long black hair and deep brown eyes, and for the first time she became aware of his delicate cheekbones and the gentle smile that curved across his features. When he seemed to see her too, she gasped and sat frozen, as he looked deep into her eyes, into the very depths of her soul.

His smile widened as he realised that she'd recognised him, and he seemed to be beckoning to her across time and space, hand out to her in welcome, in invitation. She felt such compassion exuding from him, and a level of understanding and patience that touched her heart. Then a cheeky grin lit up his face, and he winked at her then turned away, fading back into the mists sweeping through her mind.

Feeling Rhiannon's gaze on her, she smiled across at her friend, impatient now to close the circle so they could talk about what had happened during their spellcasting. Imagine if the person she'd been seeing in her dreams and visions was actually real, and imagine if he was aware of her. Could that even be possible? The thought excited her, but it also scared her. The idea that a person could enter her mind of their own accord didn't thrill her, even if he did seem kind and gentle. And, well, really cute.

But the mysterious stranger was all she could think about that night when she climbed into bed, and her heart was full of love as she fell into sleep, and into his arms. Waking up the next morning with a smile on her face, she felt like she'd made a real friend, and she couldn't wait to get to school to tell Rhiannon about her dreams and visions, and the melding of the two.

Chapter 7

A Brave New World

The bright lights hit Carlie first, but they were quickly followed by the sound of tinkling bells being swallowed up by the incredible noise, then the double whammy of bright swirling colours and intense heat. It all rose up around her as people pushed against her, and she swayed for a moment, not sure if she would be able to remain standing upright. Looking around the big hall crowded with colourful stalls and streams of people, she widened her eyes at Rhiannon in panic. It was a lot to take in.

Her friend giggled, but took her hand. "Come on, I'll protect you," she said, pulling her into the middle of the first rows of stands.

Carlie hadn't been sure about coming to London for the new age Body Mind Spirit Festival, but Rhiannon had convinced her it would be fun to get up in the dark and catch the early train to the city for it. Her misgivings were returning with a vengeance though, as she battled her way through the crowds, overwhelmed by sensation. But it was nice to be having an adventure with Rhiannon, and she had to admit that their train journey had been fun, chatting about school, about tomorrow night's Mabon ritual, and about when and how they might meet the objects of the love spells they'd cast a week before.

"Do you want to book a psychic reading first, so we can plan our day around that, and then we can go and check out the seminars and see what's on?" Rhiannon asked.

"Sure, whatever you want, I'm in your hands. Just don't lose me," Carlie pleaded, only half joking. It was a much bigger festival than she'd pictured, with four halls at the exhibition centre overflowing with stalls – everything from books, clothes and crystal jewellery to aura photos, wax readings, massage, reiki and spirit guide drawings. Leaving Carlie in the safety of a book stand, Rhiannon made her way through the crowd to the reading room and booked them in.

"Two o'clock. I managed to get us both one at the same time," she said proudly when she'd made her way safely back. Then her eyes lit up as her gaze rested on the stand opposite them. "Oh, it's Rowan! Do you want your spirit guide drawn while we wait?" she asked, dragging Carlie over to a stand whose walls were covered with beautiful paintings of various animals, druids, shamans and what looked like faery people.

The man behind the counter looked up as they approached, his face paling as he caught sight of Carlie. He stared at her, his deep brown eyes feeling as though they were burning into her soul, searching out her mind and heart. She felt flustered under his scrutiny, and a little unsettled. Why did he seem so familiar? Had she met him somewhere? Surely she'd remember that though? Yet Rhiannon seemed oblivious to any undercurrent between them, and he swung his attention to her as she spoke.

"Hi Rowan! We'd love to have a spirit guide drawing done today – both of us if you can fit us in?" she asked, voice a little breathless. "You can do my friend Carlie first," she offered.

He glanced at Carlie again. "Okay," he said to Rhiannon. "You first though. Your friend can come back in half an hour."

Rhiannon turned to Carlie, a question in her eyes. Carlie shrugged. "Sure, I'll see you soon – I'll go for a wander."

As Rhiannon took a seat within the booth, the strange man's eyes followed Carlie until she turned into the next aisle. Shaking off the weirdness, she spent the next half hour taking in the more colourful sights, trying a sample of goji berry juice, gazing at the beautiful crystal pendants at one stand, buying a copy of a spiritual magazine to read on the train home that night at another, grinning at the strangeness of some of the products available for sale and the breadth of healing modalities on offer, and wondering wistfully what it would have been like to come to something like this with her mother – the mother who might have been, but who she'd never met.

Once again, she found herself trying to puzzle out whether the lawyer or the healer was the true Violet, and what the young and idealistic, and very spiritual, version of her mum would have thought of the grown-up corporate Australian version. Her mum had definitely been happy in Sydney, she reflected – still deeply in love with her husband, a caring friend to Sandy, proud of her career achievements, and a really supportive mother too, involved with Carlie's school and encouraging in whatever she wanted to do with her life.

Glancing at her watch, she was shocked that so much time had passed, and quickly headed back. Rhiannon was thanking Rowan profusely as she reached them, and excitedly showed her the painting as she stepped into the booth. Carlie smiled. It was impressively done, what looked like a vision of Rhiannon merging with a proud white swan, the details of the feathering so intricate. In the top right corner a small white horse was depicted, with a trail of golden stars travelling from the centre of its brow to the centre of Rhiannon's forehead.

"It's beautiful," Carlie said, surprised at the incredible skill and the depth of emotion expressed in the painting. Obviously the symbols were personal to Rhiannon, but the image still touched her deeply, seeming to draw her into the painting like a scene from *Doctor Who*. Desperately she tore her eyes away, scared that she really would be pulled into it. The man was staring at her again, a question in his eyes.

"I know, it's amazing," Rhiannon was saying excitedly. "Thank you so much Rowan, I really love it!"

The man reluctantly turned back to her as she handed him some money, then she hugged Carlie. "So, I'll go walk around while you have yours done, and I'll meet you back here in half an hour. Bye!" Rhiannon sang, and headed off in the same direction Carlie had gone before. She watched her friend go, then nervously faced Rowan, offering her hand in greeting.

"I'm Carlie," she muttered. "Um, where should I sit? I'm sorry, I'm new to all this, so I'm not sure what I have to do." He was still staring at her intently, and she was beginning to feel a little uncomfortable. "Is anything wrong?" she asked nervously.

He shook his head, his face clearing as he did so. "Sorry, you just remind me so much of someone…" he trailed off, then smiled and indicated the chair to his left. "Take a seat, just here's fine, and try to relax. I'll meditate for a few minutes, connect with my own guides, then start painting what they show me, and passing on any messages if they have some for you, or if yours want to speak to you."

"Sure," she said, and stared curiously at him as soon as he closed his eyes. She couldn't tell how old he was – he could have been twenty or forty. His face was smooth and free of lines as he gazed inward, yet he exuded a sense of wisdom and strength that made him seem far older and more experienced than he perhaps was. She was amused to realise that she found him attractive – she hadn't even looked at a guy in the last three months, since the accident.

His brown eyes opened again and burned into hers, seeming to see things about her that she wasn't even aware of. Then he picked up a paintbrush and started working silently, as though still meditating. Perhaps he was. When he finally spoke, she jumped.

"You've been suffering from migraines for the last few months," he said. It wasn't a question, and so she just nodded, surprised that he could know that about her. "I've got some herbs that will help with the pain, but the migraines will ease as you heal emotionally, and move forward from the accident."

She stared at him, shocked for a moment, then smiled wryly. No doubt Rhiannon had mentioned a bit of her history to him. That's how it worked with these psychics wasn't it, they were observant, picking up on clues, spinning things out from there?

He raised his eyes from the canvas and stared right at her. "No, your friend didn't tell me anything. She was too busy pondering her own messages." Carlie blushed, but Rowan smiled at her, amused, and the warmth finally reached his eyes.

"There are bees around you," he continued, and she thought of the sweet droning sound that calmed her as she worked in her grandma's herb garden. "They're a good sign – they represent the potential within you, and the possibility of transforming the bad aspects of your life into something good. They're all about sweetness, and letting that into your life, even if you don't think you deserve it."

Taken aback by how close to the bone his words were, she stared at him in shock. She certainly didn't feel that she deserved joy, despite her grandma and her friend trying to convince her otherwise.

"The message of the bees is to celebrate life, even though there are dark times," he continued, and even his voice seemed familiar now. "To focus on the sunshine, and appreciate all the things you do have. This is a good time to manifest your ideas and dreams into reality, to get organised, get busy, get committed, and take practical steps to achieve the life you want.

"And they want you to know that it is safe to trust, and that you can call on their energy to increase your confidence, grow your social skills, and start to allow people into your life. Bees are all about creating community and finding joy in the company of others, so they're advising you to stop shutting people out and saying no to new experiences," he said softly.

Pausing for a moment, he gazed at her thoughtfully. "Just be aware of your sting Carlie. Don't push people away, or lash out at them because of your pain."

She nodded, then looked away, embarrassed by the intensity of his gaze. She didn't want him to see everything about her, or know that she hadn't treated her grandmother well when she'd arrived in England, not to mention her friend Emily before she even left Australia. Sensing her discomfort, he changed the subject. "You're just starting to comprehend the magic within you, and within the world," he said gently. "Sometimes it takes a tragedy to split your heart wide open."

Tears gathered behind her eyes as she thought of her parents, thought of them dead. Looking around wildly, she tried to focus on something, anything, that would distract her from her most painful memories. There were beautiful strings of lights on a stand opposite her, which looked like strands of glowing butterflies in flight.

She smiled as she thought of the butterflies that had led her into the mists, into the strange cottage that had revealed to her the Book of Shadows her mother had written when she was seventeen, not long before she'd left home then fled to Australia and made a new life there. Back when she'd loved the spiritual side of life, and had been immersed in this world. Maybe she'd even come to this festival as a teenager, and been enthralled by all the colour, all the fascinating people, and by the wide variety of alternative healing methods being demonstrated.

"Hey, I'm sorry, I didn't mean to upset you," Rowan said, bringing her attention back to where she was right now.

She shook her head. "It's fine, it's not your fault. Just things I don't like focusing on, but which are always there. Apparently it will hurt a little less as time goes on, or so they say."

"Grief is a strange thing, and it affects everyone differently," he said. "Don't beat yourself up about it, or think you have to stick to some schedule, to be over it by the end of the month or whatever. You have to honour your grief, acknowledge it and accept it, and that can take years to do. Or it can happen much sooner, and that's okay too. You can only be who you are, react in the way that feels most natural to you. Don't let anyone judge you on that – and don't judge yourself either," he added, his voice a little stern.

She nodded slowly, half convinced he was right. It didn't actually change how she felt, but it was nice that he'd tried to make her feel better. That was his job though, wasn't it, to provide comfort in the individual way each person could relate to and accept? He was smooth, she'd give him that. And he cared about people. And, well, he was kind of cute. She shook her head, disappointed at where this was going. She couldn't even think of guys, of dating, of really living.

Shock sent a trickle of ice down her spine. What did she mean, she couldn't think of living? She was happy about living now, *wasn't she?* She'd gone through all of this before, and moved past the half-thought of not wanting to stay alive, which she'd never really meant, *right?*

Focusing back on him, she was unsettled to find him staring at her again, eyes frighteningly intense. "Oh Carlie, it's okay. I know how you feel. Like no one on earth could ever understand what you feel, how horrific it really was to go through all that you did." She nodded, feeling the numbness start to descend. "You can talk to me about it if you want to.

I know what you're going through. No one else will ever understand you like I do," he said, voice low, urgent, and strangely intimate.

While part of her found that thought strange, suddenly she was pouring out her story to him, all her pain, her rage, her guilt, her fear. She surprised herself as she spoke, because surely she'd reconciled all of this in the last few weeks? She didn't still feel guilty, did she? Or as angry as she sounded right now? She jumped as he moved closer, kneeling down at her feet and holding her hands as she felt the tears spilling down her face. As he put his arms gently around her shoulders, she felt the sobs welling up inside her, and her body shook as she finally let them out.

Eventually her crying eased, but his arms remained around her, and she realised that it felt good. Soothing and comforting all at once. A flash of her dream came to her, of being held safe by the man with the long black hair and deep brown eyes, eyes she could drown in. Oh god, was this him? Inhaling the scent of herbs in his hair, she knew that it was. How did that work? How could she have dreamed of him before she'd ever met him? What did it mean?

Suddenly aware of where they were, she felt mortified. What would people think, to see this man holding her so intimately? She leaned back, away from him, and looked around in panic. But no one was even glancing at them, they were just walking down the aisle between the festival stands, wrapped up in their own little worlds. It was as though she and Rowan no longer existed, that they'd turned into ghosts. He dropped his arms from her and smiled at her confusion. "Protective charm," he grinned, then waved his hand through the air. All of a sudden the noise increased around them, and people looked at them as they walked past the stand.

"Wow," she said, impressed. "That was awesome."

"Well, there are times I don't want to be seen," he replied, and although he smiled as he said it, Carlie felt a shiver of fear. Why did what he'd said suddenly sound so sinister? Surely for someone in the public eye, it made sense to not always want to be on display. So why had it set off alarm bells? As though he sensed her thoughts, he moved away from her, turning back to the canvas and continuing to paint, and a sense of peace descended over her once more.

Part of her was suspicious that he was doing that too, enspelling her, but even as the thought hovered on the edge of her consciousness, accusatory, it flitted way, leaving her unsure of what she'd been about to ask him. It mustn't have been important, she figured.

He continued painting, and she was aware that people glanced at them occasionally, but no one stopped to ask him anything, and she wondered if he'd only dispersed half of his charm. She didn't know if she thought that was a good thing or a bad thing though, because she had to reluctantly admit that she liked being with him, liked him focusing all his attention on her, liked the sense of mystery he exuded. Concentrating on his brush strokes, she suddenly worried about what she would look like in his painting. Not that that should matter, she reprimanded herself. This was about showing her inner self, not her outer, and the guides she apparently had around her.

"You're beautiful Carlie," he said, breaking into her thoughts and making her blush. "And you have so much within you, so much power that you will grow into."

"I don't want power," she replied, her voice quavering a little as the uncomfortable feeling she'd had before returned.

"You will. You're destined for greatness Carlie," he insisted.

"Am not!" she said, giggling. "I'll just be happy to graduate from high school, get through university so I can become a counsellor, and work a little in Gran's healing centre. I don't need to be great."

He came back over and leaned down, taking her hands again. "Oh Carlie, I can see it," he whispered, voice thick with passion. "We've been together in past lives, and they've been incredible."

Stubbornly she shook her head. She wasn't sure about all that past life stuff, it had always seemed a little far-fetched to her. Everyone was always someone great, someone famous – no one was ever the maid or the butler or the criminal, they were always the lord or lady of the house, or of the whole country. No one ever claimed they were a slave during the era of the pyramids, they were always Cleopatra or a pharaoh. What did that say about people, she wondered, that they had to imagine themselves being so grand in a past life?

But he was talking again, and she tried hard not to laugh. They had been King Arthur and Morgaine, he claimed, twin flames and soul mates, separated by jealous people trying to shape the nation, who had no idea of true love. "We had such amazing vision, but we were ahead of our time. But now..." he broke off, sensing her scepticism, and smiled at her.

"Another time," he said, and turned back to the canvas in front of him. She wondered what he'd been going to say, then shook off the thought. It wasn't true anyway, so it didn't matter.

Finally he turned the painting to face her, and she gasped. She'd never looked as beautiful as she did in this portrait. She was about to reprimand him for the artistic license he'd taken in portraying her, but he took a step towards her, grasped her wrist, and whispered that she really was that beautiful. She rolled her eyes, but smiled a little as she turned back to the canvas. Her likeness was surrounded by bees and butterflies, and peeking over her left shoulder was her mother, short blonde hair giving her a pixie-like look. She was smiling, but in her eyes was a definite warning. As she gazed back at Rowan, she shivered. He was staring at her again with that intensity he'd had when they first locked eyes, part question, part fear, part...?

"She looks like she's trying to warn me about something," she said, turning to him. The fear spread across his whole face for a moment, then he quickly masked it.

"She's just saying to trust your intuition," he insisted, but she wasn't sure she believed him. Her intuition was telling her to get away from him, pronto, but that was silly, surely. What harm could he do? She'd never see him again after today, and she'd felt so safe in his arms before. She blushed as she imagined being back in the warmth of his embrace, and turned back to the painting again, emotions a wild mess of contradiction.

With a stab of shock, she saw that he'd painted a male figure over her right shoulder, which looked just like him, but older and even wiser looking. Sneaking another quick glance at him, she saw that he was cleaning off his paint brushes, oblivious to her scrutiny, so she peered at the painting again, and realised that it wasn't him at all. What had she been thinking, that he wanted to be part of her life?

She shook her head, embarrassed that she'd imagined such a thing, and willing her cheeks to stop blushing.

When Rhiannon returned for her she was relieved, and stood up quickly, if a little awkwardly. Her friend looked flustered, and when she glanced at the clock at the end of the aisle she realised why – an hour had passed. She was shocked. It had felt like way less time than that. And wasn't Rhiannon coming back for her after thirty minutes?

"I'm so sorry Carlie, I don't know what happened," she said, panic and confusion in her voice. "I started heading back here after twenty-five minutes, but I just couldn't get here – it was like this whole aisle had disappeared. I know that sounds crazy, but I promise, I wouldn't just leave you here."

Carlie smiled at her friend, trying to reassure her. "It's okay Rhi, I think time went crazy everywhere – and Rowan only just finished my picture, so you're not late at all."

Rhiannon didn't look totally convinced, but her eyes widened as she caught sight of Carlie's painting. "Oh, it's beautiful," she gasped, awe in her voice. "You get better every year," she gushed, turning to Rowan in astonishment.

He smiled, thanking her, but his eyes were on Carlie. She reached into her purse for the money to pay him, just as he reached under the table and drew out a small packet of herbs. "Make a tea from them and drink it once a day, just before bed," he instructed. "It will help your migraines, I promise."

Taking them with a grateful smile, she held out her money in return, but he shook his head. "No charge. My guides told me this one was free, friend to friend," he said. She blushed again, mortified that she had doubted his motives. Clearly her intuition wasn't working that well, if she'd thought he was creepy when he was just being nice to her. Selfless.

Once more she tried to push the money into his hands, but when he refused a second time she gave up, instead holding out her hand to shake his, and thanking him profusely. He took her hand, drew it to him, pressed his lips to it and kissed it, then turned away. Confused, she turned to Rhiannon, whose eyes were wide with surprise and... jealousy? She followed her away from the stand, mind buzzing, until they'd found a seat in the crowded cafe. A harried waitress took their order, then left them alone.

"What was all that about?" Rhiannon asked, eyebrows raised, and Carlie squirmed in her seat.

"I don't know, it was really weird..." She paused, trying to gather her thoughts. "I think he was just trying to be nice – he knew I'd lost both my parents, you must have mentioned it to him, so that makes sense. And I kind of broke down about it when he talked about them. He must think I'm an over-emotional fool. Which is fine of course," she added quickly.

Rhiannon was still looking at her strangely, a question in her eyes. "I didn't tell him anything about you," she insisted. "But he is psychic, so I guess it makes sense that he would have picked that up. The weirder thing is that I'd planned to come back at eleven o'clock to get you, because that's when your session was supposed to be over, but I seemed to be pushed away by something – it was like I was lost in a maze, and the way back to you kept changing."

Carlie stared at her. "That doesn't make sense," she said, but her voice lacked conviction. Her mind swung back to his protection spell, which had made them invisible to everyone. She'd thought he'd meant uninterested, not *literally* invisible.

Fortunately the waitress came back with their order, and by the time they'd put honey in their tea and buttered their scones, Rhiannon had forgotten about the subject, busy talking about the stalls she'd been to while Carlie was having her session, then eagerly showing her the gorgeous dress she'd bought. "I thought I could wear it to tomorrow night's ritual," she said, eyes lit up with excitement.

Later she dragged Carlie back to the shop where she'd bought it to see if she could find a dress too, but while she tried on several pretty gowns, she couldn't decide which one she liked best, so decided not to get one. Undeterred, Rhiannon continued leading her into the next aisle, and they had so much fun checking out all the pretty clothes, incredible jewellery, various arts and crafts, and the amazing array of healing methods on offer.

When they stopped at a colourful stand offering past life readings, Carlie asked her friend if she believed in them. Rhiannon nodded.

"Well, I don't know for sure, obviously, but I love the idea. And it makes sense to me – maybe that explains why we're drawn to some people and not others as soon as we meet them. And just imagine, if you knew that your boyfriend now had been your true love in a previous life too? How romantic would that be!" she grinned.

"Wait," she said, as she saw Carlie blush. "Why do you ask? Do you believe in them?"

"I don't know, I'd never actually thought about it before. But Rowan said something about us knowing each other from a past life…" she admitted, then trailed off.

Rhiannon stared at her. "What did he say? Come on, spill!"

"Well, it's silly really – even if reincarnation is real, this isn't. It couldn't be. He said he was King Arthur and I was Morgaine, his soul mate and magical partner in Camelot, and that before that we'd been high priest and priestess in the Western Isles." She laughed, feeling foolish for even saying it out loud. "But he was just being nice, trying to make me feel better after I broke down and cried on his shoulder."

"You cried on his shoulder?" Rhiannon demanded, her voice higher pitched than usual.

Carlie shrugged. "Sure, I started crying when he was asking about my parents, and he gave me a hug."

Her friend's eyes grew wide. "I think he really likes you! He never touches people, let alone claiming that they've been lovers throughout time," she said, echoes of disbelief and admiration in her tone.

Carlie scoffed at the very idea of that. "That's ridiculous," she insisted, blushing again. But she had to admit that a tiny buried part of her was excited to hear that, and hoping it could be true. "How do you know he never does that? He might say it to every girl he meets," she replied, then was surprised to realise that she really wished her friend's assertion was true.

Rhiannon shook her head. "No way. I've read interviews with him and seen him on TV. He's always private, almost secretive."

The beeping of Rhiannon's alarm brought their conversation to a halt. "Oh, it's time for our readings in the psychic room," she said, anticipation colouring her words. She handed Carlie a small ticket.

"Yours is with Isabella, and mine is with Carmen," she added, as she grabbed her friend's hand and excitedly dragged her through the crowd to the back of the huge hall.

When they finally got there Carlie blinked, surprised by just how many psychics and mediums they'd managed to squeeze into the room, each at a tiny cafe-style table with an empty chair opposite them for the person they were reading for. She didn't know how they could concentrate with all the noise of voices and moving furniture, or the press of bodies and closeness in the room – she admired their obvious focus.

The two girls were each shown into the room, and their tables and readers were pointed out to them. They split up, Rhiannon walking over to a table near the back of the room, where a cheerful-looking woman wearing a gorgeous purple scarf over her hair and holding a deck of tarot cards sat, while Carlie's table was near the front.

Nervously she walked towards her psychic, a woman in her fifties with a friendly demeanour, who was wearing a bright yellow dress and a big smile. She stood as Carlie approached her, firmly shook her hand, then indicated she should sit in the chair opposite her.

"Hello lovey, what can I help you with today?" she asked.

Carlie shrugged her shoulders, suddenly anxious.

"Love-life, work, health, study, problems with your parents?" the woman asked her breezily.

Carlie froze, then forced herself to relax. *Not so psychic so far.* "Just a general reading would be fine," she managed to stutter.

"Okay lovey, give me a piece of jewellery."

Carlie's eyebrows shot up.

"You haven't done this before, had a reading?" Isabella asked her, and she shook her head. "It's for the psychometry reading. I hold something that you keep close to you, and get messages from it. It connects me to you energetically, and helps me to communicate with your guides," she explained gently. "It can be a ring, a necklace, or even a house key will be fine."

Tentatively unclasping the necklace her mum had given her for her seventeenth birthday, Carlie handed it over, then sat expectantly, watching as Isabella held the crystal pendant in her outstretched hand, closed her eyes, and seemed to hum a little as her face moved, several expressions flickering across it in turn – concentration, questioning, sadness, understanding. Finally she opened her eyes.

"This will be a wonderful year for you," she began, voice cheerful. "Much better than the year just gone." Carlie nodded slightly, non-committedly. That wouldn't be hard.

"I see some very close friendships, and success in an area of study that is new to you, but which will bring you great satisfaction."

Carlie smiled happily, admitting to herself that she was surprised that the reading seemed accurate, but relieved too at the message. She had decided to change her planned career, from criminal law to grief counselling, and it was reassuring to hear confirmation that it would work out well.

"And there will be a resolution with your mother," the psychic continued. Carlie gasped, and Isabella looked up and frowned, then closed her eyes again. "Mother figure," she corrected, but this time Carlie heard the hopeful note in her voice.

Sitting quietly, her shoulders slumped, she admitted to herself that while she'd doubted the possibility that the woman really had psychic powers, some part of her had actually hoped that she was genuine. Realising that something had upset her client, Isabella asked if she had any specific questions.

"My grandmother?" she asked quietly.

"Ah, your mother figure," she replied, relief in her voice. "She will have a few small challenges, but there will be an unexpected solution to the major problem, so tell her to be patient and not to worry."

Carlie nodded, but she was no longer quite as interested in what the woman was saying. "And my migraines?" she asked.

"Migraines?" Isabella asked. "Hmm, just a second. Oh yes, they're from the fish," she said.

"The fish?"

"If you stop eating fish, your migraines will disappear," she replied, voice smug.

Carlie sighed. "I've never eaten fish in my life," she muttered. The woman gazed off to the left, a thoughtful look on her face, then replied excitedly. "Oh, it's your fillings!" she announced.

When Carlie looked blank, she added: "The mercury in your fillings, that's what's causing your migraines. You need to go to the dentist and have them replaced with newer, less toxic ones."

Carlie raised her eyebrows, but she didn't say anything to contradict her this time. Yet there was a sinking feeling in her gut that was making her feel sad. Wasn't any of this real?

"I'm getting a message for you too," Isabella added, suddenly far more confident. "There is a sense of betrayal in your future."

Her voice trailed off, and Carlie felt a shiver of anxiety. The woman in green had mentioned that she had the potential to betray someone close to her, and she didn't want that to be true.

"I can't see clearly who it is that will betray you, but make sure you stay aware," she warned. Carlie relaxed a little, strangely glad that it would be her that would be betrayed. Reinforcement that she would betray Rhiannon would have undone her.

"You'll doubt yourself, and doubt a very close friendship, but remember how strong you are, and trust yourself and your intuition. You'll know the right choice to make, when the time comes."

A bell rang, and Isabella thrust her hand out to Carlie. "Well, I hope that helped," she said. "Best wishes and bright blessings!" And she was dismissed.

Shuffling back through the reading room to the entrance area, Carlie was swept along by the other people who were trying to get in or out, and it was a while before she finally caught up with her friend. Rhiannon was all happy and giggly, excited by the prospect of a tall, fair-haired and handsome guy sweeping her off her feet by Christmas. She wondered who it could be, whether she'd already met him or he was so far a stranger, whether he was a student at their school. Carlie let her chatter wash over her, happy to just smile and nod.

When they were both sitting down at the cafe again with another cup of tea though, Rhiannon grew more serious. "She said it would be a nice distraction from my pain, and that I shouldn't feel guilty about it," she sighed. "But it's such a hard balance to strike isn't it, living your life, trying to plan for the future and enjoy the good things that come along, while still honouring your grief and not wanting to forget the one you loved and lost," she said, voice filled with longing.

"I'm happy at the idea that I might find someone to love, and someone who will love me, but it also makes me feel sad and guilty. Mum should be there to help me buy a dress for the school ball, to share my happiness with me. She should be there at my wedding – not that I'm anticipating that happening any time soon!" she giggled, as Carlie's face must have expressed a little shock.

"But she'll never see her grandchildren, which breaks my heart, and I'll never have her there for advice and help. We'll both miss out on so much now..." she trailed off.

Carlie leaned over and hugged her friend, mentally reprimanding herself for judging her for seeming to be too happy about her reading. "You're right, it's so hard to swing between joy and anticipation, and then guilt for feeling those things. But you do deserve happiness," she insisted, and she meant it.

Rhiannon thanked her, then asked how her reading had gone.

"Well, I'm not entirely convinced about how good she was," Carlie admitted. "She told me that my migraines are caused by the mercury in my fillings, and that if I have them all removed and replaced by a dentist, the migraines will stop."

Rhiannon looked at her expectantly. "That's good, isn't it?"

Her face twisting into a grimace, Carlie shook her head. "Not really – I don't have any fillings."

Rhiannon tried not to laugh as she motioned for her to continue. That was a pretty direct and indisputably wrong hit.

"She did say it would be a good year for friendships, and that I've changed my career goal, which is true – but then she said I would have some resolution with my mother, and we both know that isn't ever going to happen."

Rhiannon leaned over to embrace her friend, tears in her eyes. "I'm so sorry, maybe that wasn't the best idea I've ever had. Do you want to try to book another one, or should we just indulge in a bit of retail therapy? I saw some beautiful jewellery when I was wandering around before that I haven't shown you yet."

Carlie smiled. "Thank you Rhiannon, you're so sweet," she said, making an effort to throw off her negativity for her friend's sake. "She was right when she said I have some wonderful friendships around me. And you're right when you say we need to hit the shops. Let's go!" she giggled.

Arm in arm, they walked around the stalls again, pausing whenever something pretty caught their eye. Rhiannon got excited when she saw a pair of silver butterfly earrings that matched Carlie's coven dedication ring, and bought them for her, while Carlie was ecstatic when she found some that matched her friend's dragonfly ring, and quickly returned the favour.

For the rest of the afternoon they tried to lose themselves in the festival, sampling weird sounding new drinks, listening to spiritual teachers and healthy eating experts at the speaker's cafe, having a reconnective healing session to try to understand what it was, then checking the program and realising that Rowan was running a seminar at four o'clock.

"Can we go, can we go?" Rhiannon asked Carlie, who nodded, looking forward to learning more about what he did herself.

The first thing that struck her when they walked in and took a seat was how normal he looked compared to most of the other psychics, healers and artists they'd seen that day. There wasn't a purple hue, piece of velvet or feather to be found, he was just wearing jeans and a long-sleeved black t-shirt, his long hair pulled back into a low ponytail.

Carlie had imagined that he was just going to talk, but the first thing he did was get them all to stand up, spread out around the edge of the room, join hands and take a few deep breaths. Right away they all began breathing in unison, then she felt a strange tingling up her spine, like a wave of energy, as Rowan came around the circle and blessed each of them. Part of her was dying to open her eyes and watch him, curious about what he was doing, but she also wanted to stay in the moment – she didn't want to lose the feeling of connection that was racing through her, so she made herself keep them closed.

She was very aware of Rhiannon, standing beside her and holding her left hand; she felt her presence energetically, like a protective guardian who had vowed to keep her safe. Tears welled in her eyes, and she was overwhelmed with gratitude for her friend, who was holding her together while also trying to cope with her own loss. She felt her heart warming and expanding, and tried to send appreciative thoughts to her. And maybe it worked, because Rhiannon squeezed her hand, and she felt an answering warmth spreading up her arm and into her heart.

Soon they were allowed to take their seats again, and Carlie smiled as she saw the radiance on her friend's face. She desperately hoped that Rhiannon would receive some healing energy today, because she really deserved it, and really needed it.

Rowan took them through a deep meditation, guiding them as they went deep into their own hearts and minds, and journeyed to a place deep in the forest, where a series of animal spirit guides came to aid them with their emotional and physical attributes. Carlie met a sweet little deer, who said she'd help her be ready to accept love; an energetic dolphin, who told her he would help her learn to be playful again; as well as an old grey owl, who swooped towards her and offered its wisdom and insight into people's motivations.

As everyone spent a few moments swapping stories afterwards, Rhiannon told Carlie that she'd encountered a swan, which made her think of the painting Rowan had created for her, who said she'd assist her with clarity and purpose; a condor, who wanted to help her deal with her sense of loss; and an ox, who ordered her to start sharing the burdens of her family with others, and stop insisting she could handle everything. Carlie hugged her friend, blown away by how right that had been. Rhiannon had certainly taken on a huge amount of responsibility since her mum had died, and perhaps it was time she handed some back.

Rowan asked if anyone would like to share the animals they'd met and the messages they'd received, and several people were eager to do so. He glanced at Carlie, but she shook her head, blushing. There was no way she wanted to talk in front of a bunch of strangers, especially when the messages were so personal. She'd told him about her parents, but no one else needed to know. She was content with the knowledge she'd gained during the exercise – she

didn't need anyone else to validate it. And it seemed that there were people there who really wanted to talk about their messages, or really needed to, to get feedback from him and the rest of the room on what it meant, and she was happy to let them do so.

After some lengthy discussions, Rowan talked a little more about what he did – he preferred no labels, but conceded that he was part druid, part shaman, interested in herbal lore, meditation, working with the seasons, shamanic journeying, energetic healing and art therapy. He had recently had an oracle deck published, and each card had a beautifully drawn herb or sacred tree on it, with its purpose, magically and medicinally, written underneath, and expanded upon in the guidebook. There were also instructions for different ways of working with the cards, and a link to his website, where he had recipes for herbal brews, incenses and foods that could be made with each plant too. He opened up a new pack, shuffled them well, then walked around the room, handing a card to each person in the seminar.

"This is the plant that has a message for you today, which you can take home with you," he said. "There is a basic meaning written on the card, and studying the painting of the plant will also help you understand it, as I've worked hidden symbols into each one. If you want to learn more you can check out the herbs tab on my website, or come down and read the guidebook at my stand after this session. And of course you can buy a deck too, if you like what you see." He laughed self-deprecatingly, and several people smiled and said they would definitely be getting one after the workshop.

Carlie looked at her card. It was tansy, a plant associated magically with the dead, which was used in rites of death and rebirth. She felt a chill, which Rhiannon must have picked up on, because she turned to her and gazed down at the colourful picture in her hand. "Oh, that's a great one!" she said. "Rebirth of the self is a wonderful thing – it really *is* going to be an awesome year for you."

Carlie hugged her friend. She always sensed when she was worried, and knew just what to say to reassure her and turn the situation around, into a better light. "What did you get?"

"Wood betony, a herb of grounding, of home and hearth, of responsibility. But oddly enough, even though I watched him shuffle the deck and distribute the cards, and none were turned upside down, this one was reversed. Which means the message is the opposite of what it says – which ties in with my animal guides, telling me to stop taking on so much responsibility. Not sure how Dad will take that of course, but I guess I can only try," she said, hope in her voice.

Carlie smiled reassuringly. "I'm sure he'll understand, especially as this is our last year at school, and you'll need to be able to do a lot of homework." They both rolled their eyes and sighed dramatically. "He probably doesn't even realise how much you're doing, and will be horrified when he figures it out. There's no way he expects you to be doing it all, he probably just hasn't really thought about it."

Rhiannon hugged her. "Thanks Carlie – you're wiser than you look," she giggled. "It's funny how it's always harder to see the truth about your own situation. It's easy for me to advise other people, but I can't do it for myself."

Their attention was drawn back to the front of the room when Rowan announced they would be doing a quick closing ritual before they had to wind up. They looked at the clock, surprised that two hours had passed by so quickly.

As they put the cards they'd received in their bags and shuffled towards the door, Carlie felt a hand on her shoulder and spun around. "Did I do okay?" Rowan asked her, and he sounded nervous.

"It was wonderful, thank you! I've never done anything like this before, but it was amazing," she admitted.

His eyes crinkled as he grinned at her, which she found particularly endearing. "You're a natural," he said. "So intuitive and wise." She looked at him, puzzled. How would he know that? Before she could wonder aloud, Rhiannon turned, noticing that Carlie had stopped, and made her way back over to her.

Rowan smiled at her. "Your friend here has a big future, although she won't listen to me." His kind eyes dulled the sting of his words.

Rhiannon laughed. "She won't listen to me either, but I think you're right. Maybe we'll have to gang up on her together, see if we can make her understand and accept it."

"Good plan," he replied, turning to Rhiannon and gazing at her so intently that she blushed and looked away. "Hey, I still have a few readings to do here, a few paintings to create, but do you both want to come to the after-party tonight?" he asked them. "Lots of the presenters and exhibitors will be there with their friends – it's always lots of fun."

Carlie shook her head, but Rhiannon ignored her. "We'd love to!" she said, excitement dancing in her eyes as he handed them two passes to get in. "We have an assignment to do on goddesses for school, so we can pick your brain," she grinned.

He laughed. "Sure, happy to help."

Rhiannon put her arm through Carlie's and waltzed her away. "Oh my god, this is so cool! He must really like you," she teased.

"That's crazy, he was just being polite," Carlie said, feeling unsettled by the invitation. "We should head home – if we can catch the last train I'll be able to help Gran in the shop tomorrow before we start setting up for the ritual."

But Rhiannon was adamant. "My cousin was hoping we'd stay with her, so she can take us to the markets in the morning. She's going to the theatre tonight though, so this is perfect. I'll call her now, and let her know we'll be over later tonight. I know where she leaves the spare key."

Carlie tried to argue, but her friend was determined that they should go to the party, and although she was reluctant to admit it, part of her really wanted to go too. She knew there was no way Rowan could actually like her, but he was really cute, and there was something about him that really fascinated her. He was so wise, so compassionate. Imagine what she could learn from him if they did manage to talk a bit tonight...

Suddenly the huge crowd, the flashing lights and the intense noise didn't bother Carlie quite as much. Her friend's giddy excitement was starting to rub off on her, and she practically skipped down the next aisle with her. She even let herself be talked into trying on some more dresses, and secretly enjoyed it.

"Come on, I've been saving up for this for so long, hoping I'd find something really special here," Rhiannon said. "I can't remember the last time I went shopping – I even have the birthday money Mum gave me, back before, well…" she broke off, looking so sad that Carlie hugged her and gave herself over to her ministrations.

In the end they both bought a new dress to wear that night. Rhiannon's was a deep forest green, embroidered with oak leaves in all the colours of autumn. Carlie's was midnight blue, with tiny stars sewn onto the fabric of the skirt, and the bodice emblazoned with ivy leaves, little flowers and two bees peeking out from beneath some petals. Then Rhiannon insisted they each get a matching necklace, and they found the perfect ones, Carlie's a silver bee charm on a strand of yellow obsidian crystals, her friend's a delicate silver chain with a single silver oak leaf charm.

They headed off to a nearby cafe to drink tea and fill in time before the party started, and changed into their new outfits in the bathroom there. But as they headed back to the festival venue, Carlie got cold feet. It was crazy for them to go there. Not that Rowan would even have time to talk to them, since no doubt there would be lots of far more beautiful and interesting women there, but even if he did, what would she say? She had nothing clever to offer, nothing to share, and she was shy around guys at the best of times, let alone with one she admired. Desperately she tried to talk Rhiannon out of it, but there was no changing her mind once she'd settled on something, and she was determined to go to this party.

"Come on Carlie, don't be a stick-in-the-mud," she pleaded. "Just imagine all the awesome people we'll get to talk to! And who knows, maybe the objects of our affection will be there – the ones we called forth with our love spells."

That was partly what she was afraid of, but she didn't want to disappoint her friend. She owed her so much. "Fine, but you can't leave me on my own, okay? Promise?"

Rhiannon laughed, and held out her little finger. "Pinkie swear," she said, grabbing Carlie's little finger and shaking it. "Besides, don't you want to see him? He's gorgeous, admit it."

Carlie blushed and ducked her head. "Okay, maybe he is, but it doesn't matter – I won't be able to talk to him. I'm too shy."

Rhiannon giggled. "Well, we're about to find out," she said in a loud stage whisper, turning to greet Rowan as they walked in the door. He'd obviously been waiting for them, and his face lit up when he saw Carlie.

"Hi girls," he said, and hugged them both. Then he called a friend of his over, an older man with long silver hair and a long silver beard. "Rhiannon, this is Kevin – he works with goddesses and has studied them for years. He's even published a book on them. He's happy to help you with your assignment – and he'll keep you busy while I get to know Carlie," he added. While his tone was light-hearted, almost jokey, Carlie wasn't sure how to take his comment. Was he just being polite and thoughtful, or was it a bit weird that he'd found someone to occupy her friend so he could get her alone?

But Rhiannon was smiling at Kevin and shaking his hand, letting him guide her to the drinks table then settling down next to him on a small couch and chatting animatedly. *So much for her pinkie swear.* Yet she looked really happy, and relaxed. In contrast, Carlie was terrified, feeling awkward and shy, and totally out of her depth. Rowan put her at ease straight away though, talking about some of the readings he'd done that day, and sharing a few funny anecdotes about his clients until she was more comfortable.

Once she realised how easygoing he was, and how sweetly down to earth, she was surprised to find that they had lots to talk about, and that he was an amazing listener. When he asked her if she wanted to talk more about her parents, she shook her head, insisting that she didn't want to bore him. Gently he took her hand, and turned to stare directly into her eyes.

"Oh Carlie, please don't think for a moment that you're boring, or that I, or anyone, wouldn't want to hear your stories. Sometimes it can help to share a burden, and while I know I can never erase your pain, maybe you'll feel a bit of peace by talking about them. Not the accident, if you don't want to, but tell me about your mum and dad. What were they like? What did you like doing with them?"

He smiled at her. "Talking about them, introducing them to people, is one small way to keep them alive in your heart. Believe me, I know. I lost my dad when I was twelve."

"I'm so sorry," she said, and she knew she would give anything to be able to ease even the tiniest bit of his pain for him. She froze. Where had that thought come from? But he was smiling at her, making her tummy flutter, and her suspicions quickly floated away.

"Hugs can help too," he said, eyes mischievous as he took her in his arms again. She felt a little weird at first – she'd never been a big one for touching at the best of times – but slowly she started to relax into it, and was surprised to find herself liking the contact. As soon as she thought that, he held her tighter. Her fear reappeared. Did there have to be another person who could apparently read her mind? It was unsettling.

But he soothed it away, and eventually she let herself go, allowing herself to feel the warmth and safety of being in his arms, to feel the warmth seeping into her heart, the sense of belonging. It was exactly like her dreams. Oh god, he really was the guy in her dreams. But how could that be?

Pulling away, she broke their contact, muttering that she had to go to the bathroom. As she walked away from him, she could feel his eyes watching her still, and a great wave of confusion washed over her. She had felt loved as he held her close, and that was just too weird. She didn't even know him. And it was impossible. Shaking her head, she rolled her eyes at her imagination running so fast and so far away from her. As if he could love her.

He was a healer, a teacher, famous in his world. She was just a silly school kid. He was just being nice to the poor little orphan girl he'd met. She was surprised when she felt disappointment at that thought, and realised she actually missed his arms being around her. That was strange. Maybe she needed to get out of there, because he was making her feel too many things that she just wasn't ready to feel.

When she got back out to the party room though she saw that Rhiannon was still laughing and chatting with Kevin, and it touched her that her friend was enjoying herself. She worked so hard, and so rarely had fun, that she knew she couldn't make her leave yet just because she felt intimidated. She deserved a little levity from her usual responsibilities. Certain that Rowan would be talking to someone else by now, she looked around the room. Maybe she could use this as a chance to practise talking to someone she didn't know, to let go of a little of her shyness. Before she took another step though, she felt Rowan's presence at her side.

"I figured we needed refills," he said, handing her a glass of iced tea. She was ridiculously happy that he still wanted to talk to her, relieved that he'd respected her request for a non-alcoholic drink, and felt really special. There were so many people there who were more interesting than her, more worldly, but he didn't leave her side all night. And she was surprised, and surprisingly sad, when Rhiannon came over to tell her that four hours had passed and they really had to get going. Rowan held her hand, begging her to stay longer, but she couldn't. Screwing up her courage, she leaned in and kissed him on the cheek, then turned and fled, catching up with her friend at the front door and racing up the street to the station.

As they got the train to Rhiannon's cousin's apartment, Carlie was quiet, her mind a whirl of emotions – longing, regret, hope, joy, confusion. Rhiannon didn't seem to notice though, regaling her with anecdotes from her night. Kevin had been lovely, and said so many funny things. She couldn't wait to write down the stories he'd told her about some of the Celtic deities. He'd introduced her to someone else she admired too, and she was going to get some of the books he'd recommended tomorrow morning, before they headed home.

Carlie nodded whenever she paused, trying to seem interested, but her attention was on the things Rowan had said, the way he'd made her feel – and the mystery of the dreams she had been having that involved him. He was definitely the guy she'd seen while they were casting the love spell, and she blushed as she remembered the dream she'd had about him just the night before, where she'd been lying in his arms in an amazing faerytale bed, held so close, feeling so safe and secure and loved.

In stark contrast, she spent a restless night on the cousin's lumpy couch, tossing and turning as she remembered the way Rowan had looked at her, and the beauty of the painting he'd created of her.

On the train journey home the next day she was still preoccupied, and not even the magic of Rose's enchanted Mabon ritual that night erased him entirely from her thoughts.

Chapter 8

Questioning the Gods

The next Tuesday night at their coven meeting, the girls decided to research more gods and goddesses, and they had a lot of fun together flicking through reference books, comparing the qualities and characteristics of different ones, taking note of the similarities and the differences. Inspired by Rhiannon's conversations with Kevin, they focused on Celtic deities to start with, and planned to explore other pantheons in the coming weeks.

Carlie adored all the stories they read about them, the melding of faerytale and history, gods and goddesses being reduced first to fae creatures and later to mere myth and legend, their power and influence waxing and waning in different eras. She also loved the way these deities were so much a part of the landscape here, inhabiting the sacred hills, blessed lakes and holy springs. And she was especially fascinated with how belief in them had changed over the centuries, and the resurgence of that belief in modern times.

She was still pondering it all when she got home from school the next day, and found Rose in the kitchen blending spices. Dropping her bag on the floor, she perched on a stool at the counter and started chopping the vegies Rose had out on the bench for dinner.

"Gran," she began hesitantly, as she carefully sliced into a plump home-grown pumpkin. "You know all the gods and goddesses you pray to, and who you invoke in your rituals?"

Rose nodded.

"Well, um, do you believe in them literally? I mean, are they real? Or is that a rude question? Sorry, if it is..." she trailed off, not really sure how to word what she wanted to know, or whether it was okay to ask about it at all.

Her grandma smiled. "It's okay to ask me Sweetheart, and any of the people at our group workings. But some people do take offence to anyone questioning their faith."

"Sorry Gran."

Rose smiled again, and shook her head. "It's not a bad thing to ask though, at least to me. I think it's really healthy, and really important, to ask questions. If you profess to believe in God, or many gods, you should be able to explain your beliefs, not be scared that they'll crumble to dust with a well-aimed question."

Carlie nodded gratefully, then raised an eyebrow quizzically.

"Sorry," Rose laughed. "I wasn't trying to change the subject. I do believe the Great Mother Goddess is real, that she exists on an etheric plane where we can communicate with her through ritual and dreams. She's kind and loving, and she's spoken to me many times in my life, and guides me in all that I do, in a way." She paused for a moment, choosing her words carefully before continuing.

"It's not that she tells me what to do, or takes the responsibility for my choices away from me in any way, but if I ask, and if I listen, and if I watch for signs, I can understand her messages, and I feel that she shares her wisdom with me from time to time."

Carlie looked thoughtful. "But if that's the case, if she's a wise and kind sort of mother figure, why would she let you lose your daughter, and your husband, especially so close together? How can you be okay with her doing that, taking them from you long before they should have died?"

"Sweetheart, I don't pretend to know the mind of the goddess. And believe me, I ranted and railed at her when I lost them, screamed challenges to her, threatened to turn my back on her. I think everyone of faith does at some point. But I can't accept that their deaths were her will, or her plan. Sometimes terrible things happen, things that go against the plan she has for us, and it's up to us to find the meaning in them. So eventually I stopped being angry at her, stopped turning away from her, and allowed myself to find comfort in her again."

Carlie nodded, reminded of the blue-clad woman she'd met on Winter Hill, who'd also said that sometimes bad things just happen, and there is no reason, no purpose. "But what about all the other ones, the gods and goddesses that you call on in rituals – Ceridwen and Bridie, and Persephone and Demeter?"

"Well, everyone has a different view on that, even amongst our group. To me they are all aspects of the Great Goddess, faces of her if you will. Rhiannon and Bridie are her in her aspect as the young maiden, and we can communicate with them on questions about love and friendship. Arianrhod and Modron are her in her guise as the mother, and we can work with them on issues of nurturing and fertility, be that of family, plans or dreams. And Ceridwen is her in her aspect as the crone, the wise old woman who guides us and challenges us," Rose explained.

"And because she is really without gender, she also comes to us in male form if we need that, as the sun god at Yule, or Cernunnos, the horned god, in spring. For pagan men especially it can help to have a masculine face of the divine, and for women too. The main difference between Christian and pagan religions, to me at least, is that they see the divine as male only, whereas for us it is balanced, it is both masculine and feminine."

Carlie considered this for a while. She thought about the gifts she and Rhiannon had been given, an athame and a chalice, which symbolised masculine, for the athame, and feminine, for the chalice, and the balance of the two.

Breaking in to her reverie, Rose continued. "Of course that's just my view – others believe they're all separate deities, part of a grand Celtic pantheon. Some also incorporate deities from other pantheons into their spiritual life and rituals, like the Egyptian deities Isis, Osiris and Ra, or those the Vikings worshipped, such as Thor, Loki and Freya, or Greek gods and goddesses like Zeus, Hera, Artemis, Ares and Athena, or their Roman counterparts Jupiter, Juno, Diana, Mars and Minerva. There are so many from around the world, so many you may connect with."

Carlie struggled to get her mind around it all. "But how can they all be right? I mean, doesn't each religion say that the others are wrong? And if that's the case, which one is correct?"

Rose smiled. "Ah Sweetheart, the age-old question. I guess each person has to decide for themselves, work out which is right for them, what speaks to them, discover who they can believe in."

"But how can I choose?" Carlie asked, confused by the idea that you could just decide to believe in one or the other, or both. "And what if there are none I can believe in?"

Her grandma came around the counter and hugged her. "It's wonderful that you're asking questions and challenging viewpoints, rather than just accepting what you're told, by me or anyone else. All I can suggest is that you experience as much as you can. You'll get to know lots of Celtic deities when you work with our group, and I know you and Rhiannon are doing research on your own, so maybe you could explore some of the other pantheons together, perhaps work with Isis or Freya or Artemis. And there are often workshops at the centre, everything from Buddhism and Shamanism to Druidry and Asatru, and you're welcome to take part in any of those that touch a chord with you, or just make you curious," Rose said.

"There are similarities as well as differences between all the world's religions, and I think you can choose to focus on either the things that join humanity together, or the things that tear them apart. That's where eclectic witchcraft comes in, people taking a little from each one. Even amongst Christianity there are those who just take the bits they like and believe in them, rather than having to accept every premise of the religion."

"But that's where I get confused," Carlie said, interrupting. "Don't you have to either believe in and accept it all, the good and the bad, or else reject it all? How can you just cherry pick the parts that you like and believe in those, and pretend that the rest, the crueller parts, don't exist?"

Rose paused for a moment to pour boiling water into the teapot, and the comforting scent of chamomile wafted over to Carlie.

"I can't speak for Christianity, but I know people who've been able to reconcile the fact that there are parts of it they don't believe, but other parts they do, and they are at peace with that," Rose said. "And for the pagan religions, or spiritual paths, I think that freedom to choose and experiment and create a belief system based on your actual experiences is part of the joy of it, tailoring it to your needs and wants. But maybe you'll feel more comfortable simply working with nature, with herbs and other forms of healing, without giving it a human face or attributing any form of deity to it. You could look into humanism too, if you're interested." She smiled as she poured the tea into two mugs and added a spoonful of honey, then handed one to her granddaughter. "What brought this on?"

"We were talking about deities at school today," Carlie replied. "The teacher said he's a Christian, so he believes in the 'one true god', as he put it, and then he told us that lots of people around here believe in gods and goddesses. He didn't exactly say it was wrong to do so, but he definitely didn't approve."

Her grandma sighed. "Your school is supposed to be secular, and teaching all different forms of spirituality, not just one, so I'm surprised at that. But I guess he's entitled to his beliefs, as we are to ours. Don't let him make you feel wrong in any way. Spirituality is a personal thing, and you need only follow your own heart and mind. There are many eclectic witches who take a little bit from Shamanism, a little bit from Buddhism, a little bit from Druidry, a little even from Christianity," Rose said.

Carlie was puzzled. "But don't they contradict each other? If you believe in one, don't you have to disbelieve the others?"

"Well, some forms of the Abrahamic religions definitely insist that all other forms of worship are wrong, and some have a mission to convert every unbeliever, but you'd be surprised by how many people do accept other strands of spirituality now. This is definitely a far more tolerant age, and it's a wonderful time to be able to learn about all sorts of different religions and spiritual practices.

"So all I can really suggest is to try to work out the things that bring you peace and contentment, that help you challenge yourself and your beliefs, and encourage you to grow and develop wisdom.

Seek the path that has meaning for you, even if it's an entirely new one," Rose said.

"Thanks Gran. It seems weird now that I never talked about this with Mum and Dad. I couldn't tell you what they believed, or even if they believed anything at all. But Dad did always say the Bible was the greatest work of fiction ever written."

Rose laughed. "I wish I could have met this Oliver."

"Me too," Carlie said, smiling sadly. "I went to church with my other nanna a few times when I was little, just at Christmas, but all I can remember is lots of singing, and a priest with a really droney voice. None of my friends were particularly religious either. There were a few kids at school who went to church and stuff, the Greek families mostly – I remember because their Easter sometimes fell at a different time to the western one."

Suddenly she felt embarrassed that she didn't know more about what her parents had believed. Or maybe they hadn't. "I guess Mum and Dad could have been atheists," she said hesitantly. "But they were good people, always helping our community, raising money for good causes, volunteering their time."

"Oh Sweetheart, I'm sure they were. How religious someone is has no bearing on how good or moral they are. A few of the girls in our ritual circle are atheists, and they're the kindest, sweetest and most caring people I know. I'd argue that they're actually *more* caring and 'moral' than many religious people. As long as you take responsibility for your actions, and do the best you can to live a good life, it doesn't matter whether you believe in a god, or gods, or nothing. Too many people use their religion as an excuse to *not* be the best people they can be, instead of using it to inspire themselves to be even better," Rose said.

She paused. "Now, I need to get these in the oven. Did you want to do your homework before dinner, or are you starving?"

Reluctantly Carlie picked up her bag and climbed the stairs to her room, to get her maths assignment done, before joining her grandma for dinner then having an early night. She had so much to ponder it was exhausting.

Chapter 9

Opening Her Heart

On Saturday morning Carlie woke up early. She felt restless, like there was something she had to do but she couldn't remember what it was. The tor kept popping into her mind, so she pulled on her jeans and a woollen jumper, laced up her sneakers and tiptoed downstairs. Grabbing an apple from the fruit bowl, she quietly let herself out the back door and walked through the garden, smiling at the scent of herbs in the air as the first streaks of colour lit up the dawn sky, and headed towards the hill.

Disappointment shot through her as she neared the top and saw that there was already someone sitting on the summit waiting for the sun to rise, just as she'd wanted to do. But her breath caught in her throat as he turned his head and looked straight at her. It was Rowan. A smile lit up her face, and her heart started beating really fast. Recognising her, he quickly stood up, eyes crinkling with joy, and walked towards her, pulling her close into a tight hug, then spinning her around in a circle. She tipped her head back and laughed as her feet left the ground and the sky spun around her.

"I can't believe you're here," she whispered breathlessly when he finally set her down. She felt giddy from the spinning, and giddy with joy. "I wasn't sure I'd ever see you again," she admitted.

"And it's such an amazing coincidence. I wasn't planning to come up here today – I was just going to sleep in for a while, hang out with my grandma, then make a start on my next assignment before I meet up with Rhiannon this afternoon."

He touched her cheek, and her heart flip-flopped in her chest. "You came because I called you," he said simply.

She raised her eyebrows questioningly.

"I was sitting up here, sending a message to you, my heart to yours, asking you to come up and meet me. Our hearts are obviously attuned to each other," he explained.

Blushing, she shook her head. "How can that be?" she asked him. "We barely know each other." But her voice quavered with hope.

"Surely you felt it too Carlie," he said, voice low and husky. "We have something special. I knew the first moment I saw you – it was like we were meant to be together."

She stared at him in wonder. "How could you be meant to be with me? Surely there's someone really special out there for you, someone more important than me," she said, flustered.

Shaking his head, he drew her close, into the circle of his arms, where she felt the comfort and safety she'd been craving all over again. It felt so familiar, maybe because she'd dreamed it so often. He kissed her forehead, making her knees tremble, then drew her down onto the grass next to him, his arm around her shoulders as they gazed at the spot where the sun would soon rise.

"You *are* important Carlie," he whispered, lips in her hair. "You *are* special. Can't you feel our connection?"

She turned to him, eyes shining with joy. "Yes, I feel it," she admitted. "I just can't believe that you could feel that way about me."

He stroked her hair, then stiffened as a dog bounded up to them and they saw someone climbing the hill, just as the sun burst above the horizon in all its golden finery. He stood up, then took her hand and pulled her to her feet. "Come on, why don't you show me your town?" he asked her.

Smiling, she led him down the steep side of the hill, avoiding the newcomer, and they spent the morning together wandering through the country lanes, talking easily. Carlie was surprised by just how comfortable she felt with him, but she figured that, because she'd poured out her heart to him at the festival, and he'd sensed some of her turmoil psychically, she didn't have to present a happy front or be constantly aware of keeping her barriers up.

That's what had been so exhausting at school, feeling every moment that she had to protect others from her grief, her pain, to ensure they weren't uncomfortable around her or unfairly burdened. That's why she was always monitoring her words before she spoke, conscious of how she was coming across. It was only with Rhiannon, and now it seemed with Rowan, that she felt this amazing sense of freedom. It was so wonderful to be able to say the first thing that crossed her mind, to share her fears when he asked.

"Oh Carlie, don't ever think you're a burden, to anyone," he said, and she smiled gratefully.

As the day progressed she was so touched that he shared things with her too, things he didn't share with anyone, according to Rhiannon. He said he didn't want to dwell on the sad parts of his life, but he'd already told her that his dad had died when he was twelve, and today he confided in her that his father had left him and his mother when he was little, running off to be with a much younger woman, so he hadn't had much of a relationship with him even while he was alive. There was bitterness and anger in his voice, so she didn't press for details, but she felt honoured that he'd shared that much with her.

Changing the subject, he asked her what she thought about her new life in this country, then told her that he lived in a small town just a half hour drive from her village, and that while he sometimes missed the city, he loved being so close to nature. Excitement bubbled inside her when he revealed where he lived – she'd imagined that he was based in London, which was four hours away.

Grinning, he took her hand again. "I know, it's awesome isn't it. I think it's meant to be, us meeting last week, and living so close to each other." She could barely breathe, overwhelmed that he seemed to like her as much as she liked him, and appeared to want to see her again as much as she did too.

Later they wandered back to where he'd parked his car, and he pulled out a picnic basket and blanket. They walked hand in hand along an oak-lined path to one of his favourite places, a small meadow on the edge of a stream, the bank shaded by two weeping willow trees growing close together. She laughed in delight. She'd never been here before, and it was beautiful.

The gentle sound of the running water was so peaceful and soothing to the soul, and when they sat on the bank, backs to the solid, nurturing strength of the trees, she let out a sigh of joy and relief, a breath she hadn't known she'd been holding. She turned to him, eyes soft, a smile lighting up her face.

He opened the basket and started feeding her autumn berries and wedges of cheese with freshly baked bread. Before he ate anything he crumbled up a cookie and placed it carefully on the ground, muttering what sounded like a prayer as he did so, then followed it with a splash of juice. It touched her deeply that he also left a libation to the god and goddess, and she felt like she'd known him forever, and that they would never run out of conversation.

He regaled her with stories about some of the workshops he'd run and the people he'd taught, some funny, some touching, then allowed her in to small glimmers of his past and his complicated family.

Feeling more at ease, she told him about her life back home in Sydney – not that it was her home any more – and opened up to him about her hopes and dreams, what she wanted to do with her future, a bit about school and Rhiannon, and a little of her sadness and guilt over her childhood best friend, who she felt so far away from, not just geographically, but also emotionally.

He was so kind and concerned, hanging on every word, really listening to what she said, and responding with practical advice and sweet sentiments. When she got teary as she recalled the last time she'd been with her parents, he drew her into his arms and held her close. A shiver ran through her as emotion flooded her. She'd never felt so safe, so protected, so loved, but she shook her head, knowing she shouldn't jump ahead of herself. He was a teacher, a healer, no doubt he knew how to make people feel comforted, and loved. As if he could love her!

But his empathy made her realise she was falling head over heels for him. A part of her panicked, and wanted to run. Another part insisted that she not be so naive as to think he could feel anything for her. And a third part tried to shut out her doubts and self-criticism, and simply enjoy the feeling of being so nurtured and understood, even if this was the only moment they ever had.

Focusing on the latter, she took a deep breath, and with a great effort her tears finally stopped, and she began to feel like she had her emotions under control again. But at that exact moment, he slowly lifted her chin and kissed her gently on the lips, and all her composure slipped away as she let herself dive down into the sensation.

His kiss was so soft, so sweet, that she sensed herself dissolving into him, felt her soul merging with his. She knew it sounded sappy, and her sceptical side was rolling its eyes at her, but she could feel their energies dancing together, entwining as they connected on the deepest level she could imagine. Then, after what seemed like forever – or may have been just a single heartbeat – he gently pulled away.

"I hope that was okay," he whispered. "I've been wanting to kiss you since the moment I saw you this morning."

Blushing, she tried to calm her racing heart enough to speak. "It was more than okay," she said shyly. "I, um, I loved it."

Slowly they leaned back in and melted into each other again. Time ceased to exist as she lost herself in the sensation of their lips connecting, and his arms tightening around her. They finally broke apart when they heard the sound of a dog barking and a human whistling, and she glanced down at her watch.

"Oh my god, I was supposed to be at Rhiannon's two hours ago," she said, panicked. But it fell away as soon as she gazed into his eyes again. Reluctantly she looked away, trying to steel herself for their parting. "Thank you for bringing me here," she said with a shy smile. "It's so peaceful, like we're in our own little world."

He took her hand, and kissed it gently. "I wish we could stay here always, just the two of us – away from everyone, from friends and family and school and work." Touched, she nodded her agreement, then finally plucked up the courage to ask if she'd ever see him again.

"Oh Carlie my sweet, of course!" he laughed. "Wild horses couldn't keep me away from you."

Chapter 10

Spilling Her Secret

Tentatively she knocked on Rhiannon's door, anxiety at being so late warring with the thrill of euphoria as she replayed every moment she'd shared with Rowan since their dawn meeting.

"Oh thank goddess! Are you okay?" Rhiannon asked, worry in her voice as she opened the door and ushered her inside.

Carlie nodded, still trying to get her breath back after her mad dash from the corner where she'd regretfully said goodbye to Rowan. "I'm so sorry I'm late Rhi, but the most amazing thing happened this morning. You'll never guess who I…"

She trailed off as they walked into the kitchen and Rhiannon's dad turned and said hello. After a hurried greeting while her friend made them cups of tea, the two girls raced upstairs to the privacy of Rhiannon's bedroom. Carlie curled up in the window seat, hands wrapped around her mug, eyes shining.

"So spill!" Rhiannon urged as she sprawled across her bed, tea in one hand, biscuit in the other.

"Well, I woke up really early this morning, like, insanely early, with this desperate urge to get up and climb the tor," she began, but broke off as her friend raised one eyebrow, disbelief etched across her face. "I know! I hate getting up early, especially on weekends. And the sun hadn't even risen, so you can imagine my shock that I was contemplating walking up the hill in the near-dark," she grinned.

"But I decided to follow my intuition, or whatever it was, and went – and there was already someone sitting at the top."

Pausing, she gazed at her friend, unable to stop the smile spreading across her face at the signs of her impatience, as well as the news she was holding so close to her heart but wanting so badly to share.

"It was Rowan," she finally blurted out.

"*Rowan* Rowan? Rowan from the festival? Tall, dreamy eyes, gorgeous and amazing Rowan?"

Carlie nodded.

"And you've been with him since before dawn?" she shrieked. "What–? Where–? How?"

A blush stained Carlie's cheeks as she nodded again. "It was amazing. He was amazing. I apologised for interrupting him –"

"Oh honey, you have to stop apologising for everything."

Carlie nodded impatiently. "I know, but… he said he'd summoned me, that that was why I'd felt I had to go up there so early. And we sat there for ages, just talking…" She drifted off, a faraway look in her eyes and her mind clearly elsewhere.

When Rhiannon offered her the plate of cookies she jolted back into the present, and saw that her friend's eyes were sparkling with excitement too, and curiosity. "What does that mean?" she begged.

"He said he'd been thinking about me all week, couldn't get me out of his mind, and he knew he had to see me."

"But how did he know where to find you?" Rhiannon asked, a touch of suspicion creeping into her voice.

"He didn't. He knew which village I lived in – you told him, remember? – but that was all. That's why he had to summon me. And so I went to him. And after we'd talked for a while, he put his arm around me and held me close as we watched the sun rise."

Rhiannon gasped, as excited as her friend now.

"Then someone else walked up, which kind of broke the moment, so we left and wandered around town, just talking and laughing, getting to know each other. He's lovely. And I felt so comfortable with him – I could tell him things I've only ever told you before, and he shared things about his life too. About his father, who left him and his mother when he was little. And then he pulled out a picnic basket from his car and took me to the most gorgeous place, on the bank of a stream, and we sat there and ate and talked, and talked and ate, and oh, he's so lovely!"

She pressed on, telling an enraptured Rhiannon every sight, sound, word and glance she could recall, voice full of excitement and joy and wonder, words tumbling over each other as she tried to express everything in her heart.

Finally Rhiannon held up her hand. "What aren't you telling me?" she asked, eyes narrowing with mock suspicion.

Carlie tried to look innocent. "What do you mean?"

"I know you're holding something back. Out with it!"

Carlie blushed. "Um, he kissed me."

Rhiannon squealed. "What was it like?"

"It was really lovely," Carlie said, her blush deepening. "I really did go weak at the knees, as cliched as that sounds," she offered shyly. "But shouldn't we start our assignment?"

Her friend laughed. "Okay Missy, I'll let you off for now, but when are you going to see him again?"

"I'm meeting him tomorrow morning. But would you mind if I told Gran that I'm hanging out with you if she asks me? It's just, well, I thought maybe I should wait and see if anything comes of it before I tell her about him. I mean, we still don't know each other that well, me and Rose, and..."

Rhiannon cut her off. "That's a good idea. There's no point upsetting her with the knowledge that you're dating a much older shaman guru guy, just like your mum."

Carlie paled. "Oh god, do you think..."

"I'm teasing," Rhiannon said with a grin. "Wait and see what happens before you tell anyone else – and that's good advice no matter who the guy is. So, tomorrow I'm getting the bus over to the library at Smithfield, and your grandma will never know you weren't with me. But only tell her if she asks – the less lies we tell, the easier it will be. And you'll owe me one!" she said, only half joking.

Carlie nodded, then turned to pick up her book.

"Wow, Rowan kissed you!" Rhiannon said with a grin. Carlie threw a pillow at her, then turned back to their assignment.

Chapter 11

Falling

The next few weeks passed in a blur of stolen moments. Carlie was flat out with homework, her Tuesday night meetings with Rhiannon and the full and new moon rituals at Rose's healing centre, while Rowan had to travel some of the weekend days to teach workshops, and had commitments with students several week nights. But on a few afternoons he was able to drive over and meet her after she finished school, and they went and sat by the stream at their special place, talking, catching up on their weeks, gazing at the waning moon overhead, and each time spending just a little bit longer kissing each other goodbye.

And the previous weekend Rose had asked her to catch the bus over to Smithfield, which happened to be where Rowan lived, to pick up another herb order for her, so Carlie had managed to plan a lunch date with him, and they'd loved walking around the medieval style town, huddling in a cosy tea shop after they got caught in the rain, shivering against each other as their clothes dried out, the hot tea warmed them, and the heat between them increased a little more.

She was a bit scared at just how much she missed him when they were apart, and how intensely her feelings for him kept growing, but she still didn't really know what was happening between them, so she tried not to say too much to Rhiannon, in case it came to nothing. But it was getting harder and harder not to mention him, when every time they managed to see each other she felt herself falling deeper under his spell.

Finally this Sunday they would have a whole day to spend together – Rowan had no teaching commitments, and her grandmother was running an all-day workshop and wouldn't be around. The day couldn't come fast enough for Carlie, and when it finally dawned she leaped out of bed, hurriedly showered and dressed, then raced downstairs for a quick breakfast. Rose was leaving for the shop soon to get set up, and wouldn't be home until later that evening. Carlie waited impatiently for her to go, nervous that the knock on the door would come before her grandma had left. But finally she hugged her goodbye, told her to have dinner without her as she'd probably be late, and headed out the door. Carlie sighed with relief.

Sipping a cup of tea, she stood at the back door, excitement warring with nervousness within her. She'd been sad that she hadn't been able to join Rowan at his new moon ritual last Sunday night, but they'd met up after school three times this week, Monday, Wednesday and Thursday. She couldn't get out of her Tuesday night coven meeting with Rhiannon, and even though she was desperate to see Rowan, she didn't want to let her friend down, or be one of those girls who sacrificed friendship for boys. She'd made a commitment to Rhiannon, and to herself, to dedicate time to their magical work, and she wanted to be there. Of course that didn't mean she had to be as patient as usual, or that she stopped wishing every other minute that she was with Rowan, so the night had felt much longer than usual.

And somewhat regretfully, she'd promised to spend the Friday night with Rose, grinding up herbs, packaging up little spell bags for the shop, grabbing a quick dinner at their favourite cafe to catch up on their week, then cooking a large vegie and tofu lasagne and a banana cake together for the workshop she was teaching today.

But now, finally, they had a whole day to themselves, and she couldn't wait. When she heard the knock on the door, she flew to the front of the house, heart beating wildly, and wrenched it open. She grinned as she saw him standing there, a bouquet of daisies in one hand. He scooped her up in his arms and held her tight as he kissed her, making her giggle and blush, and drag him inside before anyone saw them. "Come in," she begged, and he handed her the flowers and followed her inside.

Filled with joy, she led him through the lounge room and out to the kitchen, which was so warm and cosy even on this chilly late autumn day. Luther stared up at Rowan from his perch on the counter, eyes wary. Carlie laughed. "Come on Luther, come and say hello to Rowan." The black cat gazed at her for a moment, then jumped down to the floor and sauntered out the back door. "Sorry," she said, embarrassed, but Rowan just shrugged.

"Maybe he's jealous. He probably thought he was the only guy in your life," he grinned, his eyes crinkling in that way she loved.

She giggled, then, suddenly shy again, walked over and put on the kettle. "Tea?" she asked, to give herself something to do.

When he nodded, she pulled out the teapot, cups and saucers and a jar of herbs, while he looked out the window at Rose's garden. "Your grandmother really is a kitchen witch, isn't she," he stated. Her eyes widened, and she was about to leap to her grandma's defence, but he held up his hands in a peace-making gesture.

"Relax, it's a compliment. Her garden is beautiful," he said, and this time she heard the admiration, rather than the imagined censure, in his voice. "My dad healed with herbs too, and I've been studying them for a long time. It's a good thing to be a kitchen witch," he insisted, then grinned as he walked over towards her. "I like witches," he added, voice teasing, as he kissed her on the forehead.

He leaned across to the counter next to her and lifted up the jar of herbs. He unscrewed the lid and inhaled deeply, then his lips widened in a sexy smile. "Jasmine huh. Are you trying to make me fall in love with you Miss Carlie?" he asked.

"No, of course not!" she retorted, blushing furiously, and her voice a little shaky. "It's just Gran's newest blend, to bring a bit of summer to the cold months."

He pulled her close, hands on her shoulders as he peered down at her, holding her gaze intently. "Hey, relax, I'm just teasing you. Besides, you don't have to cast a spell on me to make me love you."

She stared at him, breath caught, frozen. Had he just said what she thought he'd said?

"Carlie, I love you," he whispered, staring into her eyes, into her very soul. He drew her even closer and leaned down, hands strong on her shoulders as he gently pressed his lips to hers. She was trembling, so relieved that his hands on her shoulders were keeping her from falling. Falling. It was literal and metaphorical. Falling over, falling under, falling for him. Her head spun as she tried to take in that he loved her. A wave of pure joy swept over her, and she felt butterflies in her tummy. He loved her. He wanted to kiss her. He was kissing her.

The whistling of the kettle drew her back from the clouds with a thump, and she blushed as she pulled away and turned the stove off, then lifted the heavy kettle and poured the steaming water onto the herbs in the teapot. She was too scared to look at him, suddenly terrified that she wasn't a good kisser, that he'd changed his mind, that he regretted telling her that he loved her, or that it was all a practical joke and he was just laughing at her.

She felt him step towards her and gently turn her to him. Softly he stroked her cheek, his eyes bright with emotion. "You're so beautiful Carlie," he whispered to her. "Come here."

And suddenly she was in his arms again, held close against his heart, his hands in her hair and his lips on her forehead, her cheeks, and finally her mouth. Time stood still as she fell into him, felt her heart open wider, and her soul leap up to meet his.

Time stopped, and she wasn't sure how long they stood there, her back against the kitchen counter, his arms holding her tight, their lips joined. Gentle. She felt so protected, as though nothing could ever hurt her, nothing could ever sadden her. As that thought registered, she froze. Sensing her pulling away, Rowan released her and stepped back, giving her space. Space she'd wanted, but the moment she had it she craved the closeness again. What was wrong with her? She couldn't even think straight. Being held by him was intoxicating, brain jumbling. She tried to focus again.

"Are you okay Carlie?" he asked, his voice soft, sweet.

She nodded, but he could see the fear in her eyes. "Hey, talk to me," he said, gently raising her chin so that he could look right at her, right into her eyes. The love on his face touched her heart, and she smiled wanly.

"I'm sorry, I just... for a minute there I..." she broke off, but he nodded for her to go on. She blushed. "I just felt so safe in your arms," she whispered. "For a moment I felt so happy that I forgot how much I've lost. I forgot my grief, my anger..."

He poured her a cup of tea and handed it to her. She shivered as his fingers brushed against hers, her tummy tightening as the butterfly sensation returned.

"Baby, it's okay to feel happiness, to feel love. You can't punish yourself for what happened to your parents. And it doesn't mean you've forgotten them, or you love them any less. They'll always be a part of you. But I can't believe that they'd want you to suffer, that they'd want you to cut yourself off from joy, or from love."

She shook her head. "I know, but it's just..." she trailed off again, back into silence.

"You have no reason to feel guilty, I promise you that. And I understand how you feel, I really do," he said gently. Then, putting down their cups, he took her hand. "How about we go for a walk, maybe climb Summer Hill, then we can come back here and you can give me the tour?"

She smiled gratefully. Part of her had been dreading having to show him her room, the intimacy of that a little too much for her right now. She picked up her keys from the kitchen bench and stuck her wallet in her pocket, and they walked out the back door and climbed the hill. Once out of the house and striding along the back lane together she felt the tension lift, and they spent the next few hours sitting in the autumn sunshine, chatting, sharing more about their lives, and their hopes and dreams for the future.

Shyly she told him more about her desire to be a grief counsellor or social worker when she left school, and he was so encouraging, leaving her feeling so touched that he had such faith in her.

Afterwards they wandered into town to grab some lunch, then made their way back to the cottage, where they drank more tea, and Luther finally came over and joined them – and allowed Rowan to pat him for a while.

"Phew," he said, laughing. "I was worried he was going to hate me forever, and try to convince you not to like me either."

Carlie grinned. "Don't be silly, no one could change my mind about how I feel about you," she admitted, blushing a little. "And cats can't talk anyway!"

A serious expression slid across his face as he gazed at her. "Are you sure about that?" he asked, and she was surprised that there was no note of teasing in his voice. Then again, she certainly had wondered a few times over the last three months if Luther was communicating with her in some way.

"I think this cat has magic, and could do anything it wanted to," Rowan continued. "And he's definitely on your side. He won't let anyone hurt you, won't even let them get close enough to you to try." She stared at him, confused. Was he communicating with Luther now? "I love that about him, don't get me wrong!" he added quickly, and leaned down and stroked Luther's head. The cat stared up at him, green eyes still slightly wary, but seemingly content for now.

"It makes me happy to know that you have an animal ally here, someone watching over you," Rowan said, as he drank the rest of his tea. He put the cup down gently, then stood up and took her hand. "So, are you going to show me around?" he asked, a cheeky smile replacing his more serious expression.

Nodding despite her nervousness, she took a deep breath, then led him through to the lounge room, pointing out the books she'd been reading, the pots of basil in the window box – "Ah, for harmony in the home," he said cheerfully – and the vividly coloured crystals hanging from the lamp shade.

"That's Gran's room through there," she said, pointing to her door, "and the main bathroom is in here. My room is upstairs," she added, shy again. Rowan pulled her in close.

"You don't have to show me, I don't want to make you anxious or scared," he said softly. His understanding touched her, and swallowing down her doubts, she took his hand again and led him upstairs.

"That was my mum's bedroom," she whispered, pointing quickly to the room at the front of the house, then turning her back on it. She couldn't think about that right now.

"And my room is in here. Sorry about the mess," she added, although she'd tidied up last night, and it looked fine. She led him inside, leaving the door open, and walked across to the window, staring out at the silhouette of the sacred hill that had so enchanted her the first night she'd come in here. So much had happened since then, it hurt her head to think too hard about it. She'd become close to her grandmother, the woman she'd feared was a monster, she'd made a dear friend who was helping her cope with her loss, and now...

Rowan's hand was gentle on her shoulder as he turned her around and pulled her into his arms. Resting his chin on the top of her head, he held her close. "And now you've met a man who loves you deeply," he whispered. Tears sparkled on her lashes, but they were happy tears, and her heart melted as she gazed up and saw the love in his eyes. She couldn't believe he could feel that for her, but she felt the truth of it as his lips lowered to hers, and hers rose up to meet them.

The world stopped turning as they kissed. She could feel the energy of the brooding tor over her shoulder, sending her strength to anchor her in the room, to keep her from floating away. They sat on her bed for a while, talking, before he leaned in and started kissing her again.

They both jumped, and sprang apart, when Luther leaped up onto the bed, then slowly relaxed back into each other as they realised it was just the cat. But when Luther placed his paw on Rowan's leg, he turned towards him, gazing deep into the feline's eyes before nodding regretfully. Then he took Carlie's hand and leaned over and kissed it, – like that first day when they'd met – his lips gentle, respectful.

He smiled up at her. "I'm sorry my love, but I have to go. Your grandmother is on her way home, and she's not ready yet to meet me, or know how deeply our feelings run."

Carlie stared at him, puzzled. How could he have any inkling about that? "What... How do you know?" she asked.

Cupping her face in his hands, he leaned in to kiss her once more, then reluctantly got to his feet.

"I'll come back on Wednesday, meet you after school?" he asked, pulling her up to stand next to him. "Tuesday is your night with Rhiannon, right?"

Vaguely she nodded, still confused. What was going on? How did he know? Had Luther somehow told him that Rose was on her way back? That was crazy, surely.

Leading her back downstairs, Rowan picked up his jacket from the kitchen table, and drew her into his arms again. Her head was spinning, and it didn't stop when they kissed again, it just spun even faster. They stood together, clinging to each other, full of yearning and regret, until he broke away from her, raced over to the sink with his cup and washed it, dried it, then put it away in the cupboard.

"I love you Carlie, so much," he whispered, as he held her tight one last time. "And I'll be dreaming of you every night until I see you again," he promised. And then he was gone, out the kitchen door and through the garden and the back gate, at the exact moment she heard the key turn in the front door. Carlie looked down at Luther in shock, but his gaze was as serene and unfathomable as ever.

Rattled, she put the kettle on and called out a greeting to her grandma. Rose breezed into the kitchen, then paused, eyes sweeping the room before she focused on Carlie. "Was someone else here today?" she asked sharply.

Carlie shook her head. "No, why?" she replied quickly, then stumbled on before she lost her nerve. "Would you like a cup of tea? I just came down to make one before finishing the rest of my homework," she said, heart racing as she told the little white lie. What had happened to her, that she could lie so easily to her grandma?

But Rose smiled. "That would be lovely, thank you Sweetheart. It was quite a day today – wonderful, but I must admit that I'm kind of glad it's over. I think it will be an early night for me tonight," she added, yawning, before she started to unpack the dishes from the lunch they'd made and refill the half empty herb jars she'd brought home with her. Carlie quickly prepared the tea, then escaped back upstairs to her room. She pulled out her school books, just in case Rose came up to check on her, but then just sat on her bed, staring out the window, eyes unseeing as her mind whirred and her heart sighed.

That had been weird. She turned as Luther jumped up on the bed and made his way into her lap.

Stroking his head, she wished again that he could talk, and smiled as she remembered his eventual friendliness to Rowan.

Rowan. Oh goddess, he'd said that he loved her. It couldn't be true though, surely. That was crazy! She was reluctantly prepared to concede that she was head over heels in love with him, but how could he love her? She wasn't special enough for him, smart enough, pretty enough – just *enough* in general. Luther put his paw on her arm, breaking her train of thought, and she gazed at him, grateful for the distraction. Then she opened her books with a sigh – she figured she really should start doing her homework, since it was due tomorrow and she hadn't done a single bit of it.

It took her twice as long as it should have though, because she kept pausing, remembering another perfect moment from their day, something he'd said, the way he'd gently stroked her cheek, the way he'd kissed her and sworn his love. And when she finally got to bed and drifted off to sleep, her dreams were full of him, and Luther's green, all-knowing eyes.

Chapter 12

Facing Her Demons

Tray balanced precariously in one hand and school books in the other, Carlie slowly made her way over to their usual cafeteria table. Rhiannon closed the notebook she'd been scribbling in and glanced up sharply.

"What's wrong? You look like you've seen a ghost," she said, then winced. They'd both love to see the ghosts of their lost parents, so it wasn't an apt analogy. "Well, you look pale and worried," she clarified.

Carlie smiled wanly as she sat down and picked listlessly at her salad. "Well, I haven't really told you how often I've seen Rowan in the last few weeks," she began shyly. "Not because I didn't want to tell you, but I just wasn't sure what was happening, and I would have been too embarrassed if it all came to nothing."

Rhiannon laughed. "Don't worry, I've managed to kind of piece it all together. The days you loitered after school, when he came to meet you – I had to stay back to get some history notes one afternoon, and when I finally left I saw you walking along the road by the tor together, hand in hand," she grinned.

"And last Saturday when you got the bus over to Smithfield for the day to run Rose's errands, I ended up finishing with Brodie early and going over there too – I was hoping I could catch up with you and we could go shopping together, or see a movie or something – until I almost walked in on you both in the tea shop."

"Why didn't you come in and say hello?" Carlie asked her friend, genuinely puzzled.

Her friend smiled. "You looked like you didn't want to be disturbed, shall we say," Rhiannon replied, wiggling her eyebrows suggestively.

Carlie blushed. "Well, I'm sorry I didn't tell you – I was dying to, you have no idea. But it doesn't matter now anyway. I just, I can't see him again," she muttered.

Rhiannon touched her hand, offering comfort and sympathy. "What do you mean?" she asked, concern making her words sharp. "I can tell how much you like him. What did he do?"

"Nothing," her friend sighed, then grimaced. "Well, he said he loves me," she finally whispered, inexplicable pain colouring her words, anguish clear.

Rhiannon was confused. "But that's good isn't it? I mean, you love him, right?" she trailed off.

Her friend nodded sadly.

"So shouldn't you be happy? That's really exciting, surely?" She chose her words carefully, but her expression revealed her confusion.

Tears started pouring down Carlie's face. "But that's just it," she sobbed. "He can't love me. How could he?"

Rhiannon stared at her friend, aghast. "I don't understand," she said, standing up and moving around the table until she was kneeling in front of her friend. "Why can't he love you?"

"Because I'm no one. He's so amazing, so brilliant, so powerful. I'm nothing next to him," she choked out.

"Oh Carlie, that's not true," Rhiannon said, heart aching at her obvious pain. "You're amazing too. You're kind and sweet and clever, and you've endured more than most people do in a lifetime, and can still smile, still love."

Carlie shook her head. "You don't understand. He can't love me, because I'm nothing. I'm a fraud. He needs someone clever, sparkling, beautiful – someone else, someone better than me. He couldn't possibly love me, not really."

"But he says that he does love you," Rhiannon insisted, voice carefully calm. "Why would he lie about that? Why can't you accept what he says?"

Carlie took a jagged breath, and her words sounded as though they were being wrenched from inside the deepest, most broken parts of her soul. "He can't love me because that would mean I was worth loving, that I was special," she said flatly. "And I'm not."

Her voice was so matter-of-fact that it broke Rhiannon's heart. She stood up, then fell down into the chair next to her friend and pulled her close into a hug. After a while she released her and took her face in her hands, holding it steady, as she stared into her eyes.

"Now you listen to me Carlie Parker," she said, voice stern but face soft. "You *are* special. And you are absolutely worthy of love. I adore you, and you mean the world to Rose. And there's no reason on earth that Rowan couldn't love you too. Where is this coming from?" she demanded.

But Carlie was sobbing too hard to respond. Rhiannon let her cry for a little while longer, patting her shoulder soothingly, then she stood up and took her hand. "Come on, let's get out of here for a while," she said, pulling her to her feet. She led her outside, then across the sports field and into the small wooded area behind the school. The cafeteria really wasn't the place for such a distressed and emotional conversation.

Finally Rhiannon paused, sat down on a fallen tree trunk and pulled Carlie down beside her. "So how did you leave it after he told you this? When are you seeing him next? Or did you already dump him?" she asked, voice surprisingly harsh.

"He wants to take me out on Wednesday night, for a proper romantic date," Carlie sighed, fingers making air quotes around proper and romantic. "He said he wants to pick me up after school, drive over to Smithfield to see a movie, then go to some special new restaurant that's just opened…"

"Ooh, I read about that one, that would be amazing!"

Carlie shrugged. "But how can I go? I'm a fraud. I'm not worthy of him. And I don't feel right about telling Rose just yet – older boyfriend, shamanic healer, has a car – and I can't just be out that late without telling her where I'll be," she said, trailing off, voice a mixture of hope and hesitance.

Rhiannon thought fast. "Okay, how's this? You can tell Rose we've changed our coven night for this week, and you'll be at my place on Wednesday night. Dad and Brodie are going up to London for an orthodontist appointment and will be staying over, so they won't know either way."

Carlie smiled hopefully, and Rhiannon realised just how much her friend was falling for the guy, which touched her deeply. She'd had such a dreadful time lately, surely she was due a little happiness.

"I hate to lie, and I'm really terrible at it, so don't make this a regular occurrence, okay?" she warned, face mock stern. "But I think the guy deserves a chance. If he tells you that he loves you, then I believe him. He wouldn't say it otherwise, I promise you. And PS, you obviously really like him, so give yourself a chance too, okay?"

Carlie nodded, overwhelmed with gratitude for her friend.

"And tomorrow night, our real Tuesday night coven time? You will be at home doing your own ritual of self-love and self-acceptance, all right? And I'll be testing you on Wednesday about it, and checking your notes, so don't think you'll get away with skipping it!" she said.

Her sternness soon dissolved into laughter, and Carlie finally managed a real smile.

"Now we really should get back," Rhiannon said, then grinned at Carlie. "You don't want to get detention after school on Wednesday!"

Carlie laughed, and shyly hugged her friend. "Thanks Rhi, for being so sweet," she said. And was surprised to find that all of a sudden she couldn't wait for her date with Rowan.

Chapter 13

Dear Diary…

In the end she never did do her homework from Rhiannon, her ritual of self-love, because when she got home from school that day there was a large parcel with lots of Australian postage stamps on it sitting at the front door, addressed in Sandy's curly writing. Excitedly she scooped it up, raced inside and up the stairs to her room, then threw herself down on the bed. Ripping open the package, she found some clothes she'd never seen before, a few books and what looked like a jewellery box, which she impatiently cast aside as she searched for a note from Sandy.

When she found it she was frustrated by its lack of information, but then she pulled out the last object in the box, a small package wrapped in layers and layers of tissue paper and surrounded with metres of ribbon tied securely with a series of knots. An unsealed envelope was slipped under the ribbons. Curiously she slid it open, and pulled the card out.

A post-it note was stuck to the front.

Dear Carlie,
I guess this is for you. I haven't opened it, so I have no idea what it is, and I pray I'm not causing you more pain by sending it. Know you can always call me if you need to talk.
Love, Sandy xx

Slowly, tentatively, she opened the card.

Dear Future Daughter,
I don't know whether you exist or ever will, but if you do, I want you to have this. I almost burned it, in a ritual of cleansing and closing of chapters, and who knows, perhaps I still might. But it is a cautionary tale of sorts for any young woman, and if you can take anything from this, it will have been worth me living through it...
Tomorrow I marry the man I love, and step from my past into my future. And so I am locking this book away, with a few other things from my former life. I am grateful that it all led me here, but I no longer need the reminders of the things that I regret...

Carlie stared at the package. She desperately wanted to open it, but she was scared. When she'd laid her hand on it she'd felt a wave of sadness wash over her, and she wasn't sure she could survive drowning in the emotions of her mother, who she already missed so much. Curiosity finally won out though, and she cut through the ribbons and tore it open. A purple journal lay amongst the lashings of wrapping. She gently traced the cover with her finger, then, heart in mouth, turned to the first page.

Dear Diary, I'm lonely, won't you send someone to hold me…

That's how I started off my last journal, but this one will begin with…

THANK YOU! I've found the person I was wishing for, and although I can't believe he wants to be with me, apparently it's true! His name is Andre, and he's a healer and a psychic and all kinds of amazing things. And he's gorgeous too, long dark wavy hair, deep brown eyes I could drown in, and such a kind and gentle face. He's so special – people kind of hero worship him, which is why it's been so hard for me to believe he could care about me, because next to him I'm nothing.

I met him in a tarot class – he's the teacher, and he is so incredible. I've been going to his class every week (along with Mike – he wouldn't let me go on my own, sigh), and the first few weeks I was too intimidated and in awe of him to say much at all, but slowly I got more comfortable, and started chatting to him a little bit.

Then last week he asked me to help him set up for the next part of the class in our break, and oh my goddess, at one point his hand brushed against mine and I got goosebumps. And when I looked up at him, he was staring right at me! I blushed of course, and he laughed, and told me I was beautiful. I could barely breathe for a minute, but then I figured he must say that to all the girls – we're all a bit in love with him, and while I desperately wanted to think he meant something by it, I knew it was just wishful thinking.

Except maybe it wasn't, because tonight… I can still barely believe it! He asked me if I could stay back to help him with something. Mike said I couldn't, because he was driving me, but Andre dismissed that right away, and said he'd take me home! Mike didn't want to leave me alone with him, I know that, but he finally did. And then we just sat there and talked – he hadn't actually wanted me to help with anything, he said he just wanted to get to know me better. So we talked and talked, kind of personal stuff, then he drove me home. I didn't want to go inside, and he didn't want to leave – and then he kissed me! And it was amazing! It really did take my breath away ☺

Mike and I have kissed before, but compared to this, that was just two fumbling teenage friends locking lips to see what it was like. This was different – full of passion and love and longing. I could have stayed with him all night, just sitting there in the car with him, kissing, leaning into each other. But then I saw the porch light go on, and our front door opening, so I had to jump out and hurry inside. Mum asked about Mike (of course, she loves him!), but I said he'd had to leave early so Andre had offered to bring me home. Then I raced upstairs before she could ask me any more questions, because I just wanted to relive our kisses.

I still can't believe he'd want to kiss me. Me! I'm not special or beautiful or amazing like him. Why would he want to spend time with me? But he must, because he asked me to meet him tomorrow.

He'll pick me up outside the church at 10am, which gives me time to go to school, be marked off the roll then leave after the first class. I can't wait! I should try to sleep though, so the morning gets here quicker, and hopefully I'll dream about him too…

Oh oh oh! I don't even know where to begin! We had the most amazing day. I guess I shouldn't go into too much detail, just in case someone reads this, but it was incredible! We drove over to Smithfield, since it wouldn't do for me to get caught skipping school, and wandered around all day, holding hands, talking. He actually cares what I have to say about things. He listened so intently to everything I said, it was just awesome. And he's so sweet and encouraging, and has so many wonderful stories of his own to share. I learn so much by listening to him, and I just admire him so much, quite apart from everything else I feel about him. Like, how much I love kissing him…

I was so sad when we had to head back – I could have stayed with him forever! But I had to get home before Mum was finished at the shop. So now I'm just counting down the minutes until the weekend, when we can spend the day together again….

The weekend was so so beautiful, but in a way it feels too precious to write about, like I'm trivialising it by breaking it down into what we did and where we went and what we said, even how much we kissed. It's like, this feeling I have for him is too big to contain, and far too magical and mystical to try to explain. I just, I feel like I'm floating on a cloud, like my heart is about to burst wide open with everything I'm feeling. Knowing what this feels like, I know it's the first time I've been in love, in proper love. I adore Mike, and I love him dearly, but oh goddess, this is just so much more. More intense, more amazing, more joyful, more exciting, more wonderfully love-filled and inspiring and huge. Sometimes I feel as though I can't breathe, because I love him so much, and other times it's like he's my oxygen, and I won't survive without him. Guess they always said love was a paradox…

I really wish I could tell Mum, because surely she'd be happy for me, but some part of me wants to keep it to myself, not let anyone's judgement or misconceptions taint its purity. How could anyone understand what we have? And I couldn't properly explain it, impress upon someone just how much I love him, so I'd rather keep it to myself, guard it like a precious gemstone, a precious moment, a precious heartfelt connection…

It was so good, yet so weird, to see him at class this week. We managed to get a moment alone before it started, when Mike went to make a cup of tea. Andre kissed me, and held me like he never wanted to let me go, then whispered that we have to keep it a secret, because it won't look professional if he's in a relationship with one of his students. YES, HE SAID HE'S IN A RELATIONSHIP! This isn't a one-sided crush, like Mike has been trying to tell me, it's real. And I think Mike must have sensed something, because when he came back he just looked at me, so sadly, then sat in silence through the class. At the end he just muttered that he had to go and Andre could take me home, and I was so grateful. Another hour together, just the two of us.

The moment everyone left we fell into each other's arms, and he said the last few days have been hell, being away from me, that it hurts him physically to be separated from me. I know just how he feels, but I can't believe he could feel that for me too! I mean, he's so amazing. He's so spiritual, so wise, so accomplished, so artistic, so everything! And I'm just a school kid.

Argh, I shouldn't be writing this, because when I think about it too hard, it really doesn't make sense to me that he could like me so much. When we're together I just feel the magic, just FEEL our connection, and revel in it, and in how amazingly he treats me, how precious he makes me feel. But when we're apart, I can't help wondering what he sees in me. I'm nothing compared to him. He could have anyone, anyone at all, so why would he choose me? But then I remember our kisses, remember how it feels to be held in his arms, and I'm just filled with love all over again… Oh, I can't wait until we're together again. The days in between seem so torturously long…

Carlie smiled. She couldn't believe that she was going through the exact same situation that her mother had experienced when she was her age. Hugging the book to her chest, she felt more connected to her mother than she ever had. And it was so comforting to know that her mum understood exactly how she was feeling – the wondering if she was worthy, the battling to understand how someone so spiritually advanced could care about *her*, just a school kid, not especially smart or beautiful or charismatic or enlightened. She still struggled to believe that Rowan could love her, but it helped so much knowing that her mum had fought the same battle.

She closed her eyes as she felt tears well. "Oh Mum, why couldn't you be here now, when I need you?" she whispered. "If only I could talk to you, you could help me understand all this, reassure me about Rowan." Suddenly her door rattled, and she snapped her eyes open, but it was just Luther, coming to comfort her again. He had an uncanny knack of knowing exactly when she needed him to sit with her, curled up in her lap with a little paw on her knee, and purr away her sadness.

Reluctantly she put the diary down. Although all she wanted to do was race through it to the end, to read every single word right now, part of her didn't want to rush it. This book was a last precious link to her mother, her final chance to be close to her, and she wanted to savour every single page. It felt so exciting, so magical, to know that she had more to read, and she vowed to ration it out, no matter how impatient she got. Standing up, she wrapped the book back up in all its layers, retied the ribbons, then buried it in the bottom of her deepest drawer. Until she'd read it all, she didn't want Rose to see it, just in case there was something in it that would cause her even more pain than she'd already suffered.

Chapter 14

A Night To Remember

The minutes crawled by like hours the next day, and Carlie wondered if her classes would ever end. When the bell finally did ring, she hugged Rhiannon goodbye then raced down the corridor to the entrance. Despite her initial hesitation and nerves over being with Rowan, and going on their first proper grown-up date, now she couldn't wait to see him and be with him. And she'd promised herself – and Rhiannon – that she'd try to accept the possibility that he really could care about her as much as he said.

Bursting with excitement, she pulled open the heavy front doors and stood for a moment, eyes darting around wildly until she saw Rowan across the car park, leaning against the big old oak tree in the far corner. She flew down the steps, and his face lit up when he saw her running towards him. He grabbed her and spun her around, laughing, kissing her and trying to speak all at once. Eventually he set her down and led her over, hand in hand, to his car.

"I've missed you so much," he said, voice thick with emotion, as he opened the passenger side door for her.

"Me too," she replied, breathless, her heart spilling over with joy as he kissed her again, then let her climb in to the car.

As they turned onto the highway leading out of town, she grabbed a long black skirt out of her bag and pulled it on under her uniform, then awkwardly peeled that off to reveal the soft purple top she'd been wearing under it. He grinned across at her. "I kind of like you in that school uniform, but I guess it could cause a few uncomfortable questions on a night out," he said. She nodded, grateful that she'd thought to bring a change of clothes, and so happy that her top was the exact same colour as his. They looked like they belonged together.

"You look beautiful," he said, taking her hand then flicking his eyes back to the road ahead. "You were wearing a dress that exact same colour in my dream last night – that's why I wore this shirt."

"No way! You were wearing a shirt that colour in my dream last night," she shrieked, mind racing at the coincidence.

He looked across at her, smiling, eyes lingering a little too long on her neckline before he gazed ahead again. "Of course. I sent that dream to you."

She stared at him, surprise clear on her face.

"Don't believe me? We met at the bottom of Summer Hill, then you took my hand and led me to the top, before pulling me down onto the grass and…"

"Okay, I believe you," she replied quickly, blushing furiously. Oh god, he could either read her mind to see what she'd been dreaming about him, or send the dreams to her, or both. She wasn't sure which was more embarrassing, and she gazed out the window for a few minutes, trying to regain her composure. But he engaged her in conversation, and she was soon feeling at ease again.

Finally they turned off onto the main street of the town, and Rowan gracefully pulled in to a parking spot right in front of the restaurant. Turning off the ignition, he reached over and pulled her across into his lap. "I sent you the dream the night before too," he whispered against her ear, and she shuddered at the urgency in his voice, the sensation of his lips on her cheek, his hands in her hair, and the memory of that particular dream. She didn't know if she'd ever stop blushing.

"Don't worry my sweet, I don't want to embarrass you – I just wanted you to know that I've been thinking of you every minute, no matter whether I was awake or asleep." She buried her face in his shoulder, too mortified – yet secretly pleased – to face him just yet. He lifted her chin so he could kiss her, then opened the car door.

"Come on, let's go watch the movie, and get it over with so that I can gaze at you again over dinner."

Carlie was glad the only movie on at that time was a comedy, because she wasn't sure she could have handled the intensity of a romantic flick. It was hard enough to sit in the darkened theatre with him, holding hands, brushing fingers as they reached into the popcorn they were sharing, shivering as jolts of electricity raced up her arm. But she really loved the closeness she felt with him, and the friendship that was developing between them. Even if nothing else ever happened, she'd be grateful for that. When she'd lost her parents and been sent away to live with a stranger on the other side of the world, she'd thought that her life was over, and she'd never have a best friend again. Instead she'd found a kind, magical, supportive grandmother, and not just one but two amazing friends, two best friends.

Already she felt so blessed, and their dinner together just reinforced her gratitude, increased her love. And she couldn't believe how much she liked talking to him. He really listened to her, and treated her as an adult, not a kid. He was genuinely interested in her and Rhiannon's plans to study counselling together, and had some wonderful advice for other skills she could learn outside of school that would help her – weekend workshops, less mainstream but still important books, and someone he knew who she could do work experience with when it was time for her class to do that.

There were moments that she became embarrassed by the intensity of his gaze, but he always seemed to realise and break away – pause to butter some bread, order another juice, bring up a funny topic to lighten the mood – until she'd managed to compose herself again.

"Thank you so much for everything," she said, getting brave and reaching out to take his hand across the table. "I've never been in love, never really been loved. It means the world to me."

"So does this mean that you do love me?" he asked softly, and she couldn't tell if his voice was shaking with nerves or something else.

Panicked, she stared at him, eyes widening in terror. Oh god, this hadn't all been a trick had it? "What do you mean?"

He squeezed her hand, and his soulful brown eyes told her that everything was okay. "Well, you haven't actually told me that you love me," he admitted. "I've said it a few times to you, but you never reply."

Horrified that she'd hurt him and made him wonder, and realising the courage it had taken him to reveal his feelings to her, she took a deep breath. "I love you Rowan," she whispered, voice small and shy but very sure. "I really love you."

His smile lit up his face. "And I love you, sweet Carlie. No one will ever love you as much as I do," he said, reaching across and gently stroking her hair.

Her heart leaped with joy. It was still hard to believe that he could love her at all – *her!* – but she was slowly starting to feel the truth of it. And his words made her feel so special.

"You *are* special," he whispered, and she blushed again at the reminder that he could read her so well.

They talked and ate, then talked and drank coffee, until the owner finally came over and politely told them that the rest of the staff had already left for the night, and he really had to close up. Suddenly realising that they were the only two people left in the deserted restaurant, they apologetically got up to leave. Carlie couldn't believe they'd been sitting there together for four hours, so wrapped up in each other, so oblivious to anyone else around them.

It was just before 11pm when Rowan pulled up a few houses down from hers and turned off the ignition. He gathered her into his arms again, gently this time, holding her close and stroking her cheek with more love than passion, and she was grateful for that. She loved kissing him, but she wasn't ready to take it any further just yet, and while she was happy that he obviously found her attractive, it meant so much more to her that she could feel he liked being with her, just talking, as much as anything else.

Kissing her gently on the forehead, he reached around her to the glove box and opened it, then pulled out an envelope and handed it to her. Quizzically she raised her eyebrows.

"Two tickets for the festival where I'm doing a workshop this weekend. I thought you and Rhiannon might like to come. It's a two-hour bus ride from here, but I can bring you both home, and it will be worth it – there are lots of different presenters, workshops, healers, bands. And I'll get to see you," he said, cupping her face gently in his hands. "That's the most important thing, but it would be nice to get to know Rhiannon a bit as well – I know how important she is to you, and to your future plans, and I want to be part of them too."

Her breath caught in joyful surprise at his last words, and he stared down at her, a brief flash of annoyance crossing his face.

"Oh Sweet One, you have to stop doubting me, doubting my feelings for you. I love you, and I want to be with you as much as I can, and for as long as I can."

Inhaling deeply, she tried to smile. "It's not you that I doubt, it's me," she whispered. "I can't believe that I'm worthy of your love."

Lifting her chin, he stared into her eyes. "Then I'll just have to spend more time convincing you," he said, and his lips found hers for the sweetest, gentlest kiss. She lost herself in the sensation, clinging to him, and his words, and the feeling of his arms holding her safe. Finally he broke away, regret in his eyes.

"Your grandma has just left her last class, so she'll be home in ten minutes," he said sadly. "But I'll see you on Saturday, right?"

She nodded, kissed him one last time, then hurried inside the cottage. Luther glared at her, then followed her upstairs to her room, leaping up onto her bed and waiting for her to climb in before he could find his favourite spot. She pulled on her pyjamas and brushed her teeth, then switched off the light and fell into bed to relive the night in her mind. Five minutes later the front door opened, and Rose quietly made her way inside. Carlie feel asleep wondering what magic Rowan had to always know what was about to happen.

Chapter 15

Autumn's End

Staggering out of bed the next morning to get ready for school, Carlie was humming happily as she recalled her date with Rowan, and the dream that had followed it. She patted Luther, then slipped on her uniform and trudged down the stairs.

"Morning Sweetheart. Did you have a good time with Rhiannon last night?" her grandma asked.

"I had a wonderful night," Carlie said. Well, that wasn't technically a lie, was it? "And she got us tickets for the Autumn's End festival on Saturday. Do you mind if we go?"

Rose smiled. "Of course not, you'll have a brilliant time. Will you bring me back some of the bath salts from the Lavender Lady stand? They're amazing."

"Of course! Now I'd better get to school, Rhi and I need to start – well, do a bit more – work on our assignment," she quickly corrected herself. Hmm, she'd have to be careful with her stories, because her grandma was very astute. She waved goodbye and raced out the door and over to Rhiannon's. Hopefully she could catch her before she left, so she could tell her dad about their plans. They'd be in trouble if Rose mentioned it to Mike and he had no idea what she was talking about, since apparently Rhiannon had bought the tickets.

Her friend was beyond excited when she told her about the festival, and Rowan's gift, and her dad was happy for them to go. They talked of little else for the next two days at school, but finally Saturday morning dawned. They met at the bus stop at 8am, chatting happily on the long ride there, and planning which bands they wanted to see and which workshops they hoped to do.

They did Rowan's, of course, and Carlie was impressed all over again. But it was the time he spent with the girls afterwards that meant the most to her. It was important to Rhiannon too, as it was the first time she'd seen them together since the day they'd all met. When he had to leave them for a short time to do a couple of readings, she turned to Carlie, eyes shining and hand clutching her arm, and squealed with excitement.

"He's so lovely! Oh Carlie, you're so lucky!" she grinned. "Well, not lucky, you totally deserve it. But you're just so sweet together, always holding hands, smiling at each other. And the way he reaches out to touch your arm, like he's worried you're not quite real, or that you'll disappear, be snatched away from him, it's so beautiful. I can tell how much he cares about you, just by the way he looks at you, and the little things he does – his arm around you so protectively, always checking whether you need anything, giving you the shirt off his back when you're cold," she said, and Carlie smiled, snuggling down into the cosy woollen warmth of his jumper. She loved wearing it because it made her feel closer to him, wrapped up in his scent, in his warmth, almost like being wrapped in his arms.

"He's conscious of you every single moment," Rhiannon continued. "Even when he's talking to someone else he knows where you are, and is aware of how you're feeling and whether you're okay. It's so touching to see you both together. I really hope I find someone who feels this way about me," she said wistfully.

Carlie hugged her. "You will, I promise."

"Maybe I should have used your list when we did our love spell," Rhiannon replied, and they both laughed.

Although Carlie sometimes wished that she and Rowan had the day to themselves, she ended up being really glad that he'd suggested she bring Rhiannon. He'd been right, again. It was important that her boyfriend and her best friend get to know each other, get to like each other, since they were both such a huge part of her life. In addition, she was pleased that she and Rhiannon would be able to talk about him in more depth now, now that she understood how serious they'd become, and could share her wonder. She hoped she didn't bore her with her love-struck ramblings though!

After the festival wound down that evening, Rowan drove them home, keeping up an easy conversation with Rhiannon, impressing her with his down-to-earth nature and his good humour. Carlie was quiet, content to let them chat as she sat in the back seat, thinking about all the things her friend had said to her today. She was right, he was incredibly attentive to her, and so sweet and protective. Maybe one day she would accept that he could really love her. Rowan and Rhiannon both turned around at the same time, as though they'd both caught her thought at the same moment, and glared at her sternly.

"Sorry," she muttered, and they all laughed.

When they reached their village Rowan dropped Rhiannon home, and Carlie got out to hug her goodbye then climbed into the front seat. "At last! I've hated not being connected to you, not being able to hold your hand," he said, reaching over to her.

They drove around to the bottom of the tor, and he pulled over and turned off the headlights, then drew her into his lap. "God, I've missed you. I'm glad I was able to spend time with Rhiannon and get to know her a bit more, but it tortured me too, being so close to you but not being able to scoop you up in my arms and kiss you, like this," he grinned, and bent over and pressed his lips to hers.

For a long time they stayed like that, enfolded in each other's arms, lips and hearts joined. But eventually the sweeping lights of a passing car brought them back to the present, and Rowan sighed and rested his chin on her head, still holding her tight.

"I'm so sorry I'll be away for the next two weeks," he whispered, voice thick with sadness. "This retreat was booked in before we met. I've never wanted to travel less in my life!"

"I know, but we'll be okay," she said, trying to sound brave. "Surely two weeks will go quickly? I'll try to stay busy, help Gran in the shop during our week off school, then there will be all the Samhain preparations and our rituals to throw myself into. And you'll be in France – surely that will be magical."

He shrugged. "I know, but I'd rather be with you."

Her heart soared with happiness, even in this moment of sadness. Happiness that they had found each other, and connected so deeply. She vowed to remember to be grateful every day, even when she was moping and whingeing about them being apart. Grateful that she had met him, and so filled with appreciation that he cared about her so deeply.

"Me too," she sighed. "And I'm sorry I promised to go with Rhiannon to her appointment on the Saturday you get back."

"And I'm sorry I promised to help Mum out on the Sunday. But I'll be there waiting for you on Monday after school, desperate to see you, and hold you, and kiss you," he said, then proceeded to do just that, until Carlie lost all sense of time, swept away in the sensation of being loved and cherished.

Another car drove past them, the headlights illuminating the dashboard clock, and Carlie gasped. "Oh god, I really need to get home! I'm so sorry," she said, as an ache of regret settled in her stomach. Sadly Rowan turned on the ignition and drove her home, and after a few all-too-brief kisses, she tore herself away and raced inside. She tiptoed up the stairs to her room, pulled on her pyjamas and brushed her teeth, then drifted off to sleep.

It was a restless night, full of dreams where they were cruelly parted – divided by time, or by other people, even by death in one short nightmare. When she woke up she felt grumpy and out of sorts, but she tried to put on a happy face for Rose. She'd promised to help her in the shop that day, and every day of the next week if she needed her. Sighing at the irony of feeling so miserable when she finally had a week of school holidays, she dragged herself out of bed, threw herself in the shower then walked as cheerfully as she could down to the kitchen for breakfast with her grandma.

Grateful that she'd remembered to grab the lavender bath salts she'd requested from the festival – well, Rhiannon had remembered, since she'd been so wrapped up in Rowan – she put on the kettle and had a pot of tea brewing by the time Rose emerged from her room, and she actually enjoyed catching up with her over their muesli, yoghurt and tea. She realised she'd been a bit distracted of late, and promised herself that she'd spend more time with her grandma this week, and be more present when they were together.

Rose looked up at her and smiled, and Carlie wondered just how well she could read her mind. It was scary, the amount of times she'd known exactly what she was thinking. She'd never really believed in psychic ability, and her experience at the Body Mind Spirit festival hadn't changed that, but if it was true, Rose surely had a big helping of it. Which could get her into trouble if she wasn't careful.

Hmm, time to be a little more focused, a little less off with the faeries, wasting away her time wishing for Rowan. He'd be back soon, and until then she was determined to make the most of the time with her grandma, and her days doing healings. This was important to her – this was part of what she wanted to do with her life – so she vowed to dedicate herself to the experience.

"Let's go then," Rose said, placing their plates in the sink and picking up her bag. So they set off for the healing centre together, and Carlie spent a long but productive Sunday doing healings for people and advising customers on the books, crystals or herbs they might find helpful.

The next morning she was grumpy again though. It was the start of her week-long school holiday, and she lay in bed for a while, bemoaning the fact that Rowan was away just when she could have seen more of him. But with a great effort, she shook it off. Regrets were pointless, and she refused to waste her time moping. She'd done enough of that after her parents died. This week she was going to make the most of every moment – catching up on a few assignments, hanging out with Rhiannon, celebrating the full moon with Rose and the wonderful witchy women she was getting to know a little better, reading the books Rowan had suggested for her counselling study plans, and doing reiki every afternoon.

And so the time rushed by, and before she knew it, it was Sunday night, and she was packing her books for school, and feeling grateful that it was only one more week until she'd see Rowan again.

Chapter 16

The Feast of the Dead

Tuesday night, their coven night, was the eve of Samhain, so Carlie and Rose were going over to Rhiannon and her dad Mike's place for a celebratory dinner that sounded more like a mourning rite than anything else. But she knew it was important to the adults that they could honour this day together, and move forward from any weirdness. Mike's wife, Rhiannon's mum Beth, had died a year ago. Carlie's mum Violet – Mike's first love – and her dad Oliver had died almost five months ago.

When Violet had run away from home at seventeen, she'd broken not only the hearts of her parents, but the heart of Mike too. They had been each other's first love, and Mike had been a wonderful support to Rose, even as he mourned her loss himself, and he'd been there for her when her husband died soon after as well. The awkwardness now, came from the fact that Mike was not only still devastated by Beth's death, but also deeply affected by Violet's recent passing, although he was trying to hide it to avoid upsetting Rhiannon and her brother Brodie. And for Carlie, it was strange that everyone in this village seemed to have known her mum – known her better than she had, she sometimes thought – and was mourning her deeply, yet no one had ever met her dad, so he seemed to have been forgotten.

But when they'd arrived that night, Mike had taken their coats and guided them into the dining room, and she'd been shocked by the incredible effort this man had gone to. The long table was beautifully set, with candles glowing in the centre, and the scent of cinnamon and nutmeg burning in an incense holder brought a richness and air of mystery to the room. Pretty name tags had been left at each place setting, and Carlie felt a chill, then a rush of warmth and gratitude, that at one end of the table three places had been set, with crockery and cutlery and a glass chalice at each one, with her mum's name written on one place setting, her dad's name in the centre and Rhiannon's mum Beth's name on the third.

Mike would be sitting at the other end of the table, opposite the three settings of their dearly departed, with Carlie sitting on one side of the table, next to her mum's place setting and with her grandma on her other side, and Rhiannon opposite her, next to her own mum's place setting, with her brother sitting between her and their dad.

Rose didn't look at all surprised, just smiled warmly at Mike as she walked over to hug him, then embraced his two children. It hit Carlie for the first time how strange it must have been for Rose to live in the same village as Mike, to have expected him to be her son-in-law, and the father of her grandchildren, then to have seen him create that family with someone else.

Rose turned to her with a sad smile, but shook her head. "No Sweetheart, not strange. There were sad moments, of course, but I am so grateful to Mike, and to Beth, for letting me share a little part of their family with them over the years, to be invited to Christmas days and school performances, to share their good news and let me offer a little back in the bad times. I've always loved Rhiannon and Brodie deeply, and it fills my heart with joy that you are such close friends."

Mike came over and hugged Carlie hello. "We've been honoured to have you join us Rose, always, and you've certainly given us far more than we could ever hope to give you. But now," he said, turning to Brodie. "Who'd like to help me bring in the drinks while Rhiannon seats our guests?"

Brodie giggled. "I guess that would be me Dad – you're so silly." Mike winked at them as he followed his son out into the kitchen, and Rhiannon guided Rose to her chair before pointing out Carlie's place, then sitting in hers. "I'm so glad to see you both. And I'm glad you wanted to come tonight Mrs Tyler, I know this is such a difficult sabbat for you."

Carlie raised her eyebrows at her friend's strange sense of formality, then turned to her grandmother, who just smiled.

"Sweet girl, call me Rose, please. You always have," she said to Rhiannon, before facing Carlie. "Samhain is the time when the spirits of those who have passed are closest to us, so I always feel so close – yet so far – from Violet and Louis at this time. But I worry about Mike too. He's still mourning his beloved wife, yet also feeling the loss of Violet all over again. I know he's so grateful to you," she said, turning back to Rhiannon.

"Not just for all your practical help, keeping the house going, cooking the meals, being there for Brodie – but for your emotional support too. He knows how much you're hurting, which makes it even more remarkable that you've been such a pillar of strength to him. And I am so grateful to you for being there for Carlie too. You are a remarkable young woman, and your mother would be so proud of you. We all are."

Rhiannon blushed, while Carlie added her thanks and appreciation to Rose's, then giggled with her at how red Rhiannon's face was. She was saved when Mike and Brodie returned with a tall jug and poured the deep red grape juice spiced with cinnamon, cloves and ginger into all the glasses, including the three at the end of the table. Rose's eyes were wet with tears, but she smiled bravely as she lifted her glass.

"Tonight we honour the ancestors who have gone before us, who watch over us and guide our lives. And especially we have joined together to pay tribute to and share our love for three special people. Beth was a beautiful soul, a devoted and loving mother, a loving wife, and a close friend to so many of us. But she lives on in the two children she adored, and I can see her in both of you – her strength and independence in you Rhiannon, and her cheekiness and sense of humour in you Brodie."

She paused as Rhiannon lifted her glass, and Carlie looked around the table at the people who had become her family. Her friend was sad yet stoical, and the tears on her eyelashes only made her seem more fierce, more protective. Brodie just seemed happy to have people around him, and she wondered how it would feel to lose your mother so young. Then she glanced at Mike, and he caught her eye, smiling at her and conveying with the merest flicker of his eye the pride he felt in his children, and his sympathy not only for them but for her too.

For a moment she felt unsettled, as she recalled the strange parallel world she seemed to have fallen into that morning in the mists, a place where her mum was still alive but Mike had been her dad, a bitter-sweet alternative world that still made her feel guilty to dwell on. Shaking off the feeling, she bowed her head, feeling so fortunate to have so many people who cared about her – people who didn't have to, but who cared anyway. It touched her deeply that these people had opened their hearts to her. She knew most people in this situation wouldn't have.

"To Mum," Rhiannon whispered, bringing Carlie back to the flame-flickering darkness of the room around her.

"The best mum ever," Brodie said.

Mike lifted his glass too. "To Beth – my wonderful wife, your beautiful mother. So sadly missed, and yet here with us always."

He took a sip, and they all did the same, then he nodded, with the deepest respect, to Rose. She held up her glass again.

"And to Violet and Oliver. My beautiful daughter, who I have missed every day since she left us more than twenty years ago, and her beloved husband Oliver, who I so deeply regret that I never had the chance to meet. I honour you both for the gift you have given us all, in Carlie, and I welcome you both – you have a special place in my heart, and on my altar, and you of course live on in your daughter, who has brought me so much joy in my old age."

Mike smothered a guffaw. "You will never be old Rose," he said, then lifted his glass, looking serious again.

"To Violet, my dear friend. I regret that I never got to see you grow up and achieve your dreams, and that you didn't get to meet my beautiful family. And to Oliver, a man I wish I could have known and called friend. I honour your memory, and I hope that somewhere, wherever it is you all are, you have met my wife and you can all feel happiness and pride at the wonderful ways you have all touched our lives. God and goddess bless you all."

Carlie was overwhelmed by the emotions the toasts so beautifully conveyed. "God and goddess bless," she echoed, feeling so inadequate in her ability to express her feelings, and so moved by the eloquence demonstrated by Rose and Mike.

Rhiannon smiled. "I feel the same – they word it all so beautifully don't they?"

She stared across at her friend. "You too?" she asked. "You can read my mind as well?"

"Not so much. But tonight all our emotions are close to the surface, and it's not that hard to gather what you're feeling."

Carlie laughed. "Fair enough."

Brodie looked over at her, face earnest. "I'm so sorry you lost your mum and your dad Carlie," he said, and she was shocked at the wisdom and sadness conveyed in his voice. "I couldn't imagine losing both – it was hard enough losing my mum."

As her eyes misted with tears, Mike reached over and grabbed his son in a hug. It was almost painful to watch their closeness, but it was touching too. Then he sat Brodie down and tickled him. "Now you've got to help me with the food. Come on buddy," he said.

Rhiannon jumped up. "Do you want me to help?" she asked, but Mike shook his head. "You talk to Carlie and Rose. I've got a helper." Brodie looked around at them all, smiling his joy and sense of self-importance, then followed his dad to the kitchen. Soon they returned with an incredible feast – golden potatoes, beetroots, turnips and carrots roasted with sage, rosemary and garlic, pumpkin and ginger pie, a delicious nut loaf with rich onion gravy, a lentil and butternut squash casserole and delicious sides. Brodie proudly served up small meals for their three absent friends, then asked Carlie to tell them about her mum and dad, so they could feel they knew them a little bit.

She was so affected by this young boy's sweetness and strength, although for a moment she didn't know where to start. "Well, Mum was a lawyer and Dad was in sales, but that doesn't say much about them, does it?" she began tentatively.

"They still always held hands when they walked down the street. Dad would make lunch for Mum to take to work, and put little notes in it, to make her smile when she was stressed. And she'd surprise Dad all the time, buying him a book he'd been waiting to read or tracking down an album he used to love. They went on a 'date' at least once a week too, encouraging me to stay over at a friend's place, or getting a babysitter when I was younger. They said it was important to have couple time even though we were a family, and it didn't mean they loved me any less.

"At least one of them would always be at my school plays or sports days or whatever. And we took holidays together once or twice a year – nothing fancy, sometimes we'd just jump in the car and drive, and see where we ended up. Some people used to say they were like kids, so spontaneous and unplanned, like that was an insult, but they were happy. They just really paid attention to each other, you know?

"They cared about each other, supported each other. When Mum wanted to do a course, Dad made it easy for her, even taking time off work so he could do everything around the house and she could really focus. And vice versa. She didn't bat an eye when he had to travel a lot for work when the boss was away, but I know she had a friend who refused to let her husband take a promotion he really wanted because it would mean he was away sometimes."

Pausing for a moment, she took a deep breath, then gazed around the room. "I'm sorry, this must be boring for you all," she said.

Rose wiped a tear from her eye, but she was smiling. "Oh Sweetheart, you can talk about them as much as you like. I'm just so glad that she found someone who loved her, and respected her, who she could love and respect in turn. Especially after, well…"

She shared a meaningful glance with Mike, and something unsaid passed between them.

"I'm really glad too," Mike said. "It seems that we both ended up with our true love."

Carlie smiled. "I'm so glad. But could you tell me about your mum?" she asked, turning to Brodie as she remembered what Rowan had told her at the festival after-party. Talking about your lost loved ones, and introducing them to people who hadn't met them, honoured them and kept their memory alive. "What do you remember best about her?"

Brodie grinned at her, a cheeky glint in his eye. "Well, I remember that she always burnt my toast, and when she cut my hair it was always a bit crooked." They all laughed, and the shadow that had been in his eyes all night lifted a little.

"But mostly I remember that she read to me every night, curled up in bed with me, and she'd read a second book if I begged hard enough." He sighed, his mouth turning down with sorrow. "I miss her so much, but I'm really scared that I'll start to forget her. That one day I might wake up and not remember what she looked like, or what she sounded like, or what she smelled like."

"Jasmine," Rhiannon said. "She smelled like jasmine."

Rose and Mike both appeared stricken, but Brodie's sister had it under control. "How about we start a project together," she suggested to him. "We'll make a scrapbook, and every night we will add one thing to it. It could be a memory, like the scent of jasmine that always clung to her, or maybe a photo, or a list of the best stories she read to us, or a song that reminds us of her. Anything at all. We'll be like detectives, building up a case file about her so we never forget a single thing, and we can keep her close to us always."

Brodie enthusiastically agreed, and said he would start by drawing a picture of tonight's feast, and where everyone had been seated in relation to his mum. Mike was trying not to let anyone know he was crying, but the look of love and pride that he directed at his daughter melted Carlie's heart.

It didn't surprise her though. Rhiannon would be an amazing grief counsellor. She'd helped Carlie navigate the worst of her pain and anger and loss, and she was certainly keeping her little brother afloat too. For what seemed like the millionth time, Carlie sent out a prayer of gratitude to the universe for the good fortune that had sent her halfway around the world to a grandmother who adored her, a new friend who was the most supportive person ever, a village and a community that had welcomed her with such open arms, her new beloved, of course, and even what appeared to be two guardian spirits, or fae folk, who seemed to be watching out for her.

Her grandma squeezed her hand. "We're lucky too Carlie, to have you here. And we're grateful that you brought us answers about

Violet's life, and the knowledge that she was happy. You have no idea how much it tortured me, never knowing what had happened to her, if she was even alive."

Rhiannon chimed in too. "It's not one-sided Carlie – I'm so grateful to you for being so understanding of my loss, and for not diminishing it by comparing it to your even greater loss. And for helping me grieve and move forward, and finally realise what I want to do with my life, and how I can make that happen."

"I'm grateful to you too," Brodie piped up. "Rhi is much happier now, so she's stopped making my life hell."

Everyone laughed, and trying to retain the lightened mood, Mike asked Rose if she'd tell them a little about the festival they were celebrating, and she gladly changed the subject for him.

As they made their way through the platters of food, then a huge bowl of blueberry cinnamon crumble with ginger-scented custard, Rose shared some of the history of Samhain, to prepare them for the ritual the following evening. Mike and Brodie listened, as rapt as Rhiannon and Carlie as the traditions and legends unfolded, even though they knew the stories backwards. And Carlie had some idea now too, since she'd been preparing with her grandma for the last few days, cooking up apple fritters, grainy breads and fresh berry jams, drying herbs and baking pies.

The evening was far more enjoyable than Carlie had imagined it could be, and far less awkward. But perhaps she shouldn't have been so surprised that Mike was kind enough to make her feel so welcome, and generous enough to include her dad in their honouring ceremony.

Much later, as everyone said their farewells, Rhiannon leaned over to Carlie. "So, we're still on for midnight, yeah?" she whispered. "For our coven Samhain?"

"Absolutely! See you out the back at half past eleven," Carlie replied, hugging her friend goodbye.

And so, after Rose had gone to bed, Carlie pulled a thick jacket on and crept downstairs and out into the garden, slipping through the back gate into the laneway behind their cottage. It was dark, and although the waning crescent moon would start to rise soon, it would be low in the sky and obscured by cloud, so both girls had a small torch to light their way. Tonight would be freezing on top of Summer Hill, so they'd decided to do their ritual in the ruins of an old church just down the road. It had been built on the foundations of a much older temple, and there was an ancient spring that ran right beside it, which would add the blessings of water to their circle.

The cold night air pierced through their clothes and made them shiver, and they both pulled their jackets more tightly around themselves as they lowered their heads against the wind and picked up their pace. Finally they slipped within the crumbling stone walls, grateful that they were partially sheltered from the wind, yet still able to see the cloudy sky above them.

Rhiannon filled her chalice with pure water from the spring, while Carlie lit the large pillar candle they'd brought, secure in its pretty glass lantern from the icy fingers of the wind. They knew the cold would defeat them soon, so they hastily carved out the boundary of their sacred circle with the power of their words and intent, then called in the elements and the directions before sitting down together on the grassy floor. They joined hands over their makeshift altar as they welcomed the god and the goddess, then they each picked up a black candle.

Her hair whipping around her in the breeze, Carlie carefully lit her candle from the central one, hands shaking a little, and took a deep breath to calm and centre her thoughts.

I call on you Ceridwen, goddess of death and rebirth and the waning moon, on this cross-quarter night that marks the end of autumn and the beginning of the coldness and darkness of winter. In your aspect of wise crone and elder, please lend us your wisdom and prophetic foresight, and help us see through the darkness of our hearts and the veils between the worlds to the spirits of our lost loved ones, and let us know they are still with us.

Then it was her friend's turn. Rhiannon's hand was much steadier than Carlie's as she lit her candle from the central pillar, and her voice was clear and strong.

I invoke you Hekate, woman of the crossroads, goddess of death, and of balance. In this midnight witching hour, in this night of the waning moon, please illuminate the darkness and guide us on our soul journey to the heart of your wisdom, in search of answers from the ones we miss so much.

A dark shape flapped across the sky above them, and the girls both jumped, momentarily jolted out of their ritual consciousness. Then, smiling at whatever creature of the night had felt moved to watch over them, they held hands again and let their voices join together, carrying softly in the cold air.

We ask you, deities of darkness and introspection, of the wisdom of the inner mysteries, to protect us as we travel to your realm in search of answers, in search of comfort, in search of some glimmer of hope that our parents are still with us in some way. So mote it be.

Their voices echoed between the stone walls, gradually growing more quiet, then stilling altogether. Finally, their hands still linked, they closed their eyes and went within.

Carlie was walking along a deserted forest path. It was dark, and she felt skittish as she crept along, feet uncertain on the uneven ground, startling in fear as the shadows shifted in front of her and small shapes loomed towards her then faded away. Her heart beat faster, but she tried to remember the breathing exercises her grandma had shown her, and the relaxation steps from her reiki course. Slowly she began to feel more in control, and as she did, the path widened and became more gentle.

Noticing a golden glow starting to filter through the trees up ahead, she picked up her pace, eager to reach the comfort and warmth it seemed to offer. For a moment she wondered if she should be cautious, if it was all a trap to reel her in, but her heart felt lighter with every step, and somehow she knew she would be safe.

When she reached the clearing, she gasped with astonishment as she gazed on the enchanted vista before her. Tiny golden balls of light zoomed between the trees around the edge, and circled the head of a woman sitting on an ancient stone throne in the centre of everything. Her face was porcelain white, her eyes a deep fiery purple, her lips a dark berry stain that gave her an air of drama and terrible power. But despite her gothic visage, she exuded the most beautiful sense of peace, and Carlie felt herself drawn towards her until she could feel the heat of the candles arranged on the lower tiers of the weathered stone seat, and had to take a step back.

The woman had a huge leather-bound book in her lap, which she was writing in with a beautiful old feather quill. But she looked up as Carlie approached her, and when their gaze locked, Carlie froze in her tracks. The woman on the throne? It was like looking into a mirror. But how could it be her sitting there, in the middle of this forest, being watched by herself? Her brain hurt as she tried to puzzle it out, but the closer she peered at her, the more she realised that the woman looked just like her – except for her deep purple, no, violet, eyes, which matched her floaty dress. Was this the spirit of her mum then, returned to her homeland and her daughter?

"Oh Carlie, always seeking answers outside of yourself. You need to look within," the woman scolded.

Carlie smiled wryly. "I don't even know the questions."

The woman on the throne glared at her, and for a moment the mist rose up around her, obscuring her body as it snaked around her. "Wait!" Carlie cried, and the mists lowered again.

"Why are you here then?" the woman finally asked, her voice a sigh, a whisper, an exasperated communication mind to mind.

"I just... I miss Mum and Dad so much," she replied, pain crackling through her words. "And I'm worried that they didn't know how much I loved them before they died, that I didn't say it often enough. I guess I was just hoping that tonight, of all nights, they could give me a sign, or something..." She trailed off, eyes downcast, misery and loneliness swamping her.

"Sweetheart, of course they knew," the woman said gently, and Carlie's gaze snapped up from the ground she'd been staring at to the figure's face, and those vivid violet eyes. She'd sounded so much like Rose just then it was uncanny, yet there was steel and fire in her expression, and the soothing voice seemed like a trick.

She smiled at Carlie, as though she enjoyed keeping her a little off balance. "The important thing is that you learn from this fear you have, learn from this mistake. Make sure you do not leave things unsaid with anyone else. You know more than most that people can die suddenly, unexpectedly. That they can disappear from your life forever in a single moment."

Fear gripped Carlie's heart at her words, and shuddered through her body. There was something sinister in her tone, almost a threat. Did she know something of the future? Was someone else she loved going to die? Or was this about losing Rhiannon, if she betrayed her the way people seemed to think she would? Was she going to bring misery to everyone in her life?

The woman laughed cruelly. "Oh Carlie, you do not have to do something just because it is expected of you, or because someone said you would. *You* are in control of your actions. Your parents can die, and you can choose to become destructive or compassionate – or anything else. Your heart can be broken, and as a result you can choose to do the same to someone else, or be even more careful with other people's hearts," she said.

Her eyes glittered, hard and serious, as they drilled into Carlie, then she broke the contact and looked down at her lap. "This is the book of your life, and you are the only one who can control the story or change its outcome. Everything you do, you do willingly – not because you are destined to do it, but because you *choose* to do it. You choose every day what you want to do, and who you want to be. You are the sum total of every choice you make, big and small. And you have to take responsibility for your choices, and your mistakes, and the consequences of all that you do," she explained, voice stern.

"If you do not want to betray Rhiannon, do not betray her! If you do not want to regret leaving things unsaid, do not leave them unsaid! Tell your loved ones how much they mean to you. People are reminded of this for a moment when someone dies, and they tell everyone close to them how they feel, but then they forget again. *Do not forget.* You have been through so much," she said, and there was sympathy in her voice now, and compassion. "Use it to be a better person. Be aware Carlie, be conscious. Remember who and what you want to be."

The mist swirled around them, seeming to push them closer together, then Carlie felt herself being drawn backwards, away from the woman. She reached out to her, but she faded away into the mists, just as she became aware of her hands in Rhiannon's, and the warmth and comfort the sensation gave her.

Opening her eyes, she saw her friend gazing at her quizzically, and felt her cheeks, wet with tears she hadn't known she'd cried, and icy cold from the wind. The fear that had gripped her previously rippled through her, then was gone. She smiled, then leaned forward and hugged Rhiannon.

"Thank you for everything you do for me, for all the things we share. For being you. Our friendship means the world to me."

"You mean so much to me too Carlie," Rhiannon said, holding her tight. "And I don't think you realise how much you give to me, and to Rose. It's not one-sided. I know you think you just take from us and give nothing back, but it's not true. You've enriched our lives too. You've given Rose new purpose, a new depth to her existence, someone to love. And you've helped me heal as well. Brodie was right, I am much happier now, much nicer, because I know you."

Carlie felt her eyes water a little, but they were happy tears this time. "Now we should probably get home and get to bed before we freeze to death," her friend said, and she nodded.

Quickly they thanked the elements, the deities and the directions for holding them safe, and closed the sacred space they'd opened between the worlds. Then hand in hand they raced back up the laneway to where they had to part, hugged each other goodbye, then sneaked back into their houses and upstairs to the welcome warmth of their beds.

Chapter 17

In Your Memory

When Carlie got home from school the next day, Rose was in the kitchen cooking up the last few treats for the Samhain celebration at the healing centre that night. Putting on the kettle, Carlie made them both tea, then perched on the bench for a chat, noticing how tired and frail her grandma looked – so different to the powerful priestess she became at the rituals, and even the confident teacher and conversationalist she'd been last night at Mike's.

"I'm okay Sweetheart, don't worry about me," Rose said, and this time Carlie wasn't even surprised that her grandmother knew what she'd been thinking. "This time of year is always hard for me – remembering the dead, feeling the chill of winter as the world gets darker, sensing the energy of the crone so strongly. But how are you feeling after last night?"

Carlie told her she'd been really moved by the whole occasion – touched by Brodie's sweetness and Rhiannon's kindness, and so grateful to Mike for including her and her parents in their honouring of those who were gone.

"Gran, how did you feel when Mum was dating Mike?" she asked, stifling a yawn.

Rose smiled. "I was happy, of course. They'd been friends for so long, and it was really beautiful to watch them growing up together and falling in love – it seemed as though it was the most natural thing in the world. And it was hard to learn later that she'd been seeing someone else, but was too scared of upsetting me or disappointing me to tell me about him, to let me meet him. I regret that so much, that she didn't know I would have supported her no matter what."

She turned sad eyes on Carlie. "Don't ever feel scared to tell me something Sweetheart, or to share your friendships, or your relationships, with me," she said, and there was a question in her eyes. Carlie gulped, suddenly nervous, but a knock on the door interrupted them, and she went to answer it, grateful that she was off the hook for now. Did Rose know about Rowan? Had she really sensed that he'd been there that day he'd come over? She did want her grandma to meet him, and she certainly didn't want to keep sneaking around, because it made her feel bad about herself. But she wasn't sure she was ready to reveal it just yet.

Sighing, she opened the door, but she smiled when she saw that it was Miri, one of Rose's closest friends and a long-time member of her sacred circle. She was holding a huge bouquet of herbs, and had a large backpack slung over her shoulder.

"Hi Carlie, how are you? How's school going?"

"It's a lot better than I thought, thank you," she replied, smiling as she took Miri's bag from her and beckoned her into the house.

"I'm so glad to hear that. And are you coming to the ritual tonight? Samhain is always a really powerful one. And it would be lovely to have you there," she said.

Carlie felt a rush of warmth at her words. She was still so touched by how welcome she'd been made to feel since she'd arrived, and it was a real welcome, she could feel it, not just something offered out of politeness or respect for her grandma.

"Thank you, I can't wait to be there, and to take part in the ceremony – although only as a general participant, not as an active part of it," Carlie added hastily, as she saw Miri's eyes light up. "I'm not ready to help run a ritual yet, or speak in public, or be responsible for a part of it, but we've been baking the last few nights, so there are lots of yummy treats for afterwards."

Together they walked out to the kitchen, where Rose was slipping another plate of mini pies into the oven. "Hello my dear," she said to

Miri, standing up and walking across the room to embrace her. "Did you want to go over the invocations for tonight one more time?"

Leaving them to it, Carlie hurried upstairs to her room so she could start getting ready for the night ahead. At all the rituals she'd been to, she'd been amazed by the beautiful clothes people had worn, and the effort they went to in order to incorporate the season being celebrated into the way they looked, from their clothes to their jewellery, even their make-up in some cases. And while at first she'd thought that people would be leaning to the theatrical side at this one, dressing up in costumes a la Halloween, the modern incarnation of Samhain, her grandma had set her straight about that.

"Personally I kind of like the fact that secular and even religious people dress up as witches and ghosts and go trick or treating on this night, celebrating the energy of the season, even unknowingly," Rose had said, smiling at the thought. "But there's also a part of me that's offended by the commercialisation of the festival, and the simplification of its meaning. The symbolism of the ghosts isn't to scare people, but to honour those that are lost to us, loved ones who have died, as well as the ancestors, those who came before us, who fought so hard for the right to follow the spiritual path of their choice, and gave us the freedom today to do just that."

Picking up a piece of thin orange ribbon, Carlie started plaiting it into her long dark hair, allowing her mind to follow her actions as she added more, seeing it as a meditation of sorts, a slipping into the sacred space of the ritual before it technically began, starting to focus on the upcoming magical state of mind. Once she was finished, she walked over to her wardrobe and reverently took out the beautiful black velvet dress she'd chosen.

When Rose had offered her another outfit from the shop for this ritual she'd felt uncomfortable – she still had the deep red one from Lughnasadh, and the dark orange one shot through with gold from Mabon – but she had to admit that it definitely helped her slip into a ritual head space much more easily when she was dressed in something selected specifically for the night. She'd decided not to wear these clothes on normal days, just on magical occasions, so they retained the atmosphere of the seasonal ceremony, and their "specialness".

Slipping the gown over her head, she turned back to her dressing table, where her jewellery was strewn across the top. As she picked up the necklace she'd bought at the festival, the bee charm on the string of yellow obsidians, she heard a knock on her door. Opening it, she smiled at Rose as she stood there, hand outstretched.

"I thought you might have use for this," her grandma said, offering an orange fabric-wrapped parcel.

Curious, Carlie untied the ribbon, then thanked her grandma profusely. It was a beautiful silver jewellery box, velvet lined, with lots of separate compartments to put different pieces in. "Oh, it's gorgeous! And you're right, I was just thinking that I need somewhere special to put all my jewellery. Thank you so much Gran!"

Rose smiled and left the room, while Carlie took the silver box over to her dressing table and placed it there reverently. She opened one of the drawers to put the silver chain strung with the aqua aura pendant from her mum and the little vial of sand her friend Emily had given her in – then flew back downstairs, throwing her arms around Rose and thanking her again. Inside the bottom drawer she'd found a necklace of black obsidian, with a beautiful heavy pendant surrounded by smaller stones of amethyst and obsidian.

"You're very welcome, and it looks perfect on you," her grandma said, hugging her back, arms warm and comforting, her heart beating strongly against her own. "And it will help keep you safe from negative influences, and protect you from anyone wishing to harm you or hurt you," she added.

Carlie looked up, startled. Why had she said that? Did her grandma know something about Rowan? Or was she simply being paranoid after their earlier discussion?

Rose just smiled, eyes totally lacking in guile. "Now, we're going to head over to the shop, to start setting up. Would you like to come with us, or do you want to stay here a while longer and make a start on your homework?"

Carlie rolled her eyes and scrunched up her face in mock distress, but grudgingly conceded that her grandmother had a good point. She flounced back up the stairs theatrically, calling out a farewell to Rose and Miri, then opened up her school bag and got to work. It was annoying, but she had to admit that she'd definitely feel much happier when she got home from the ritual and didn't have to do it then.

When she got to the hall that night, she was transported straight to a magical land, and was once again in awe of the atmosphere and sense of enchantment that her grandma and her circle of magical friends could create, both physically and emotionally. A few people waved to her and said hello, and some even came over and hugged her as she wandered inside, spellbound by the beauty of the room.

Black velvet drapes covered the walls, and strings of faery lights illuminated the faces of the guests. A deep orange cloth covered the altar, which looked much bigger than usual, and the rich, heavy scent of patchouli hung in the air, providing a strong bottom note to the lighter scents of cinnamon and pine. Pots of bright marigolds made a circle around the edges of the room, and she could also smell rosemary, wormwood and sage.

Laura – or should she call her Ms Henderson now, even out of school? – stood to one side, next to a table piled high with orange candles. She beckoned Carlie forward and handed her two, then directed her to the slowly forming circle.

Once everyone was in place and a hush had fallen over the room, Rose stood up in the middle of the circle and raised her arms to the sky. Carlie watched, fascinated and in awe, as her grandmother slowly morphed into her high priestess persona. She didn't move, yet with every slow breath she took she looked taller, more imposing, more powerful. And then Carlie stopped thinking about what was happening and let herself simply experience it.

She felt a sense of peace come over her, felt a connection to everyone in the room slip into place, and felt her heart open up wide as she listened to Rose cast the circle, welcome the directions and the elements, and invoke the god and the goddess. Her scepticism was swept away as she dove into the sense of ritual and belongingness that washed over her, and let it draw her under.

Then she felt hands brush her cheeks and stroke her hair as Rose welcomed the spirits of all those they'd lost to be with them at this magical time, this first day of winter, of cold and introspection. Last night she'd told Carlie that this was the moment when the spirits of their ancestors and their dead could come closest, when the veils between the worlds were thin and connection was so much easier. She kept her eyes closed, desperate to believe it was her mum and dad standing with their arms around her, holding her close, and safe. Her mind drifted to Rowan, and his mourning of his father, until she heard Rose's voice in her ear. "Be here Carlie, be present."

Her eyes snapped open – and she was shocked to see that Rose was on the other side of the room, not next to her; her back was to her, and she was walking slowly around the circle lighting the candles people held from the central altar candle in her own hands. As though she felt Carlie's gaze on her though, she turned her head, and nodded once to acknowledge that she'd caught her thought.

A shudder rocked through Carlie, and she looked around wildly, confused and slightly, irrationally, afraid, until she caught Rhiannon's eye. Straight away she felt calmer, more grounded, and she smiled in gratitude at her friend and magical partner.

Finally Rose reached her, and smiled sadly at her granddaughter. "For Violet," she said, as she lit the first candle. "And for Oliver."

Tears welled in Carlie's eyes as she realised the significance of what was happening in the room – people were lighting a candle for everyone they'd lost, then bringing them together in a touching ceremony of remembrance. A single tear spilled over and ran down her cheek, but she smiled bravely as she followed the person next to her to the altar, which was much bigger than usual, and slowly filling with the candles placed on it so reverently by the ritual's participants. As she set hers down in two small silver holders, and watched the individual flames flicker then grow strong, becoming a part of the growing spiral of light, she offered a prayer of gratitude to her parents. She found that she couldn't address a deity she wasn't sure was really there, but she knew, deep in her bones, that her parents were with her on this night, were with her always, and that was enough for her right now.

Looking up, she saw Rose staring at her, pain warring with joy and pride in her eyes. She smiled shyly, then turned and walked back to her spot, and the rest of the ritual passed by in a strange haze as she tried to tell her parents all that was in her heart, and listened closely, hoping she would hear them reply.

By the time the beautiful ceremony came to a close, Carlie felt emotionally drained – lighter in some ways, and glad, but heartbroken too. She waited until she could catch Rose's attention, then told her she had to go. Her grandma held her close, then kissed her forehead, which made her blush as thoughts of Rowan kissing her there swept through her body and her heart.

"Of course Sweetheart," Rose said, her high priestess persona slipping for a moment. "Do you want someone to walk you?"

Carlie shook her head. She needed some time alone, some time to process all the emotions that were so rattling her. Her grandma smiled, kissed her again, then bid her farewell.

When she got home, she threw herself into bed, still wearing her dress, and cried. She cried for her mum and dad, and for Rhiannon and the mother she'd lost. She cried for Rose, the bravest person she knew, and she cried because she missed Rowan so much and wished so desperately that he was here with her right now, holding her safe in his arms, soothing her heart, wiping away her tears. She knew that was a selfish wish, in the face of so much suffering and loss, but he always made her feel so much better. Still, she would get to see him on Monday afternoon, after the longest two weeks of her life. Finally managing to smile, she drifted off to sleep.

Chapter 18

The Winter Queen

The next morning at school, Carlie and Rhiannon met out the front and walked in together, still buzzing from their ritual. They paused when they saw a banner across the hallway, announcing the upcoming Yule Ball, which was to have a masquerade theme.

Rhiannon squealed with excitement. "Ooh, they thought they might not have it this year, but I'm so glad they are! They're always such fun, and it would have been awful to miss out on it now that we're finally seniors. We're the oldest this time, so someone from our year will be crowned the Winter Queen and the Sun King."

Carlie grinned at her enthusiasm. She'd never been one for social events, but she figured it would be fun to go to something like this with Rhiannon. "So what's it like?" she asked, and grinned as her friend's face lit up and she eagerly started to explain that it was a huge end-of-term winter ball, which students from several surrounding schools would be attending, since each one was quite small, and a lot of the kids knew each other from weekend sports games, other electives and community groups. This year it would be held in Smithfield, at the school's gymnasium. Carlie felt a stab of sadness, that it would take place in Rowan's town yet he couldn't be there with her, but Rhiannon was oblivious.

"I wonder if they've appointed the organising committee yet?" she was asking, eyes shining with joy. "I'd love to do that. How about you? It will involve some after-school meetings, a few weekend days, then probably every Saturday for the month leading up to it…"

Carlie shook her head regretfully. "Sorry, I promised Gran I'd help in the shop on weekends in the lead-up to Christmas, do some reiki if anyone asks for it, and man the tills so the other girls get time with clients. But I can't wait to hear all about it," she said.

Rhiannon pouted for a moment, then shrugged and rushed off to the principal's office to see if she could sign up. When Carlie met up with her a few classes later, she excitedly announced that she was on the committee, and pulled out a notebook where she'd already started to brainstorm ideas. "Let me know if you think of anything," she said, enthusiasm brimming over, and Carlie laughed.

"You're so cute!" she teased. "I've never seen you this excited."

Rhiannon rolled her eyes and laughed too. "I know, I'm a bit tragic. I just wanted to be on the committee so badly last year, but the timing didn't really work out. But now I finally am!" She paused, face falling. "I'm so sorry though, I'm going to have to rain check our trip on Saturday, as that's when the first meeting is. I'll call today and see if I can postpone the appointment. I hope that's okay with you?" she asked nervously.

Carlie considered teasing her by saying no, but she couldn't do it to her. "Of course!" she grinned, and meant it. Then she realised that this could be a good thing for her. Her grandma knew she was going out for the day with Rhiannon. She could still go, on her own, and spend the day with Rowan. He was returning from his trip late on Friday night, and would be home all day Saturday.

This was perfect. She'd been so desperate to see him before Monday, and now here it was, handed to her on a platter. Suddenly she felt just as happy and excited as her friend.

That afternoon Rhiannon went home with Carlie after school, so they could start planning their Yule Ball outfits. Rose was there when they arrived, and she put the kettle on to make tea while the girls leaned up against the kitchen bench and chattered excitedly.

"We could do a traditional Santa vibe, you know, red dress, fluffy white trimmings, tinkling bells on our black boots, but that seems a bit obvious," Rhiannon said, kicking off their costume planning session. "And not very magical."

"There's the Snow Queen too, from the faerytales, and from the Narnia stories as well, all icy white and frosty, glittering and diamond drenched," Carlie offered.

"And there are the winter goddesses," Rose added. "The Celtic Cailleach Bheur, who rules the dark half of the year, the Roman winter goddess Angerona, Scandinavia's Frau Holle, the Norse goddess Frigga, the Italian witchy figure La Befana, who rides around on a broom delivering lollies, the Hopi's Spider Woman. And the Yule colours of red, green and white too, as well as gold for the sun."

Rhiannon smiled ruefully. "If we had someone to go with, a date, we could go as the sun god and sun goddess."

"Or the sun god and the moon goddess," Carlie said. If only she could take Rowan – that would be perfect for them.

"Well, I guess we could go together, me as the sun goddess and you as the moon goddess," Rhiannon replied with a giggle.

Rose smiled at them as she poured out the tea. "You will both be beautiful, whatever you go as," she said wistfully. "I remember when your mum went to her Yule Ball Carlie, with your dad Rhiannon. They looked gorgeous together, and so happy. A few of the teachers told them they would have been crowned the Winter Queen and the Sun King if they were seniors – and they probably would have been the following year, but Violet left home before that, and Mike didn't end up going."

She turned away, but not before the two girls had seen the emotion on her face. Carlie suddenly felt bad. Was she just a constant and painful reminder to her grandmother of the daughter she'd lost? Was her being here actually making it worse for Rose, bringing up old memories that she'd rather forget, making the pain of her loss fresh again, over and over?

As she stared morosely into her tea she felt a hand on her shoulder, and looked up into her grandma's wet eyes.

"Oh Carlie, please don't ever think that I regret having you here. I know the circumstances of you coming to live with me were terrible for you, but I'm so happy that you're here, so happy we found each other after all this time. Of course it hurts, when I think of your mother and what we both lost, but all these memories you bring up for me are wonderful memories, and I cherish the moments I have with you, as well as the moments they bring back to me of when Violet was young. They're sad, but a kind of happy-sad."

Rose folded her into a hug, and this time Carlie didn't even mind that she'd obviously read her thoughts again.

"You know, I think some of your mum's old dresses are still in her room, and some of our old ritual clothes and robes," her grandma offered. "You should both have a look through them – there might be something you like, or something we could transform into what you'd like, for the ball."

Carlie wasn't sure what to say to that – it would be amazing to see some of her mum's old clothes, but she remembered how hard it had been for Rose when they'd entered that room not so long ago, after it had been locked up and shut away for so many years.

"Gran, had you really not been in Mum's room since she disappeared?" she asked quietly, nervously.

Rose glanced at her, surprise on her face. "Of course not. I spent hours in there, days, after she'd gone, trying to find a clue to her whereabouts, or a psychic link, or something. Anything. And when we called the police, of course they looked through it too, trying to find leads. In the end I locked the door, because I was spending too much time in there, becoming obsessive. It took Elsie to recognise it though – she came down to stay with me after Louis' funeral, and again when I started to realise that your mum was never coming back. She saw what I was doing to myself, and told me I had to stop spending all my days in there. It was her idea to put a lock on the door, and she took the key home with her, so that I wouldn't be tempted," she said.

"Not that it really helped – whether I was sitting on her bed hugging her pillow or downstairs cooking in the kitchen, or even at the shop, Violet was all I thought about."

Wiping the tears impatiently from her eyes, she beckoned the girls to follow her. Rhiannon squeezed

Carlie's hand as she stood up, and together they headed to the stairs. At the top, Rose opened the door – it was no longer locked – turned on the light and ushered them in. Then she went over to the closet and pulled open the door. The girls gasped. Inside was a riot of colour, vivid red velvets next to sparkling silver sequins and cool blue and green silks, with scarves of every shade imaginable, and a variety of styles of shoes spilling out of the bottom.

Rose smiled at them. "Your mum used to love op shopping, and we made quite a few outfits ourselves too. But I'll leave you to it. Try some on, take whatever you like – I can't wear them, and, well… they're all yours," she said softly. The unspoken words, that Violet would never need them, hung in the air between them, but Rose simply ran a hand over the fabrics then headed back downstairs.

"I'll be in the kitchen making a vegie and tofu lasagne if you need me – and Rhiannon, you're more than welcome to stay for dinner if you'd like," she called out.

Both girls shouted out a thank you, then turned back to the wardrobe. They didn't know where to start, but at an unspoken signal, both reached towards the coat hangers and pulled all the dresses out, laying them on the bed, which was now dust-free.

Then the fun began, as they started trying them on. Some seemed a little old fashioned, which they supposed made sense, and others were a bit too loose or too tight. But finally Rhiannon slid into a bright red velvet dress with deep emerald holly leaves embroidered around the hem and neckline, which flared out over her hips and wrists and fit her perfectly. The gown's vivid hue suited her colouring and her personality, and when she spun in a circle it floated out around her, then fell in gentle waves. She grinned.

"This is it! I love it!" she announced joyfully, then stopped abruptly. "Well, if you don't mind Carlie? I mean, it's yours, of course. If you want to wear this one…" she trailed off.

Carlie smiled. "It's totally you, and totally yours – it looks gorgeous on you. And besides, I think I like this one," she said, as she lifted up a long, luxurious swathe of white fabric. She held it in front of her, then slipped it over her head. Like Rhiannon's dress, it fit her like a glove, and perfectly suited her shape and colouring. It had a fitted white brocade bodice, with tiny crystals sewn onto it, then it swirled out into a ballerina-style skirt that was a froth of soft tulle. Bell-shaped white organza sleeves added movement and sophistication, without being fussy, and her long, loose dark hair was the perfect contrast. She looked like a faerytale princess.

"You look amazing!" Rhiannon cried, her eyes widening and her lips turning up. "It's like it was made just for you."

Carlie twirled around, feeling a mixture of joy and sadness. She felt close to her mum as she stared at her reflection in the mirror, seeing the resemblance now, thanks to Rose's old photos, and loving that she was wearing a dress she'd once worn. But it made her sad too. It was like Rhiannon said – their mothers should have been here to share their excitement about the ball, to help them pick out a dress, do their hair, share their secrets and their crushes.

Rhiannon smiled sadly at her, and came over and gave her a hug. "We have each other though," she said softly. "And you have Rose, and I have Dad and Brodie. It could be worse."

Carlie nodded, and made an effort to regain her cheeriness. Reluctantly they changed back into their normal clothes, and carefully hung the rest of Violet's dresses back up. When Rose called out to them that dinner was ready, they were surprised to discover that three hours had passed. Rhiannon hugged Carlie goodbye, then thanked Rose for the dress and the dinner invitation, but said she had to get home before her dad started worrying.

Over their meal, Carlie listened, rapt, as Rose reminisced about Violet as a teenager, sharing stories both happy and sad. And that night they both dreamed of her.

Chapter 19

Tainted Love

On Saturday Carlie woke up early and slipped quietly out of the house before Rose surfaced. She didn't want to lie to her grandma directly, so it was better that she just assume she was still spending the day with Rhiannon. Hurrying down to the High Street, she breathed a sigh of relief as she made the early bus with just seconds to spare. Pulling out her maths book, she tried to study for a while, but finally gave up, too excited by the thought of soon being in Rowan's arms to be able to concentrate on anything else.

Staring impatiently out the window, her headphones in, she daydreamed about spending a whole day together. The last two weeks had dragged by so slowly, but she was trying to see that as a positive, that she'd missed him so much. She certainly knew that she really loved him now, if she'd ever doubted it before.

When they finally pulled in to his village she leaped off the bus and rushed down his road, excitement pounding through her veins. It was only minutes until she'd see him, and she smiled as she anticipated the look on his face when he saw her. Quickly she raced up his stairs, then, heart in mouth, knocked on the door. She'd never been inside his apartment before, and she was so curious to see where he lived, where he spent his nights as they dreamed of each other.

Then she panicked. Oh god, what if he'd forgotten what he felt for her while he was away? What if he'd met someone else? Suddenly nervous, every second she waited stretched out into an eternity, and all her old doubts started swooping around in her head, immobilising her with the fear that she'd lost him, that he'd forgotten her, that he'd gone somewhere else or found someone else.

Desperately trying to shake off her negativity, she summoned up her courage and knocked again. After another interminable wait, she finally heard footsteps echoing down the hallway. As she stood there shaking, part of her wanted to flee, but another part wondered what on earth had gotten into her. They loved each other. They'd been eagerly awaiting the day they'd be able to see each other again. And any second now he'd open the door and she'd fly into his arms, and all would be right with the world.

Eventually she heard the key turn in the lock, then the door was cautiously opened. He stared at her, eyes bleary and momentarily unfocused, long hair messy but adorable. He was wearing a pair of old tracksuit pants and a loose tank top that really showed off his arms and shoulders. Carlie blushed, even as she moved towards him and whispered "surprise".

"Hey baby," he croaked, enfolding her in a hug then pulling her inside. "It's so good to see you. I thought you were spending the day with Rhiannon today. What time is it?"

Oh god, she hadn't even thought about what her early start would mean for him. "Um, it's 8.30," she mumbled. "Do you want me to come back later?"

He shook his head. "No, of course not, but come to bed with me for a while. My car broke down on the way back from London last night, so I didn't get to sleep until after four," he said, voice still cracked and low.

Taking her hand, he led her back to a darkened room at the far side of the apartment, closed the door behind them then crawled into bed. Terrified and deeply unsure of herself, she stood in the gloomy space, halfway between the door and the bed, and stared at him. What should she do? Did he just mean for them to sleep, or did he intend something else with his invitation to come to bed with him? He opened one eye and peered up at her. "Come on my love, I'm not going to try anything, it's just way too early for me to be awake."

Taking a deep breath, she crossed the space between them, kicked off her shoes, and gingerly lay down on the edge of the bed, her back to him, her body tense. She felt him move behind her, and stiffened as he pulled her into his arms and up against him, scooping the blankets over her so they were cuddled up close together. "I missed you baby," he whispered, his lips in her hair, and his arms wrapped tightly around her. "I'm so glad you're here."

And then she felt him relax against her, his breathing slowing and deepening, and she realised he'd fallen asleep. She sighed with relief – then was confused to discover that a tiny part of her was disappointed that he really had meant what he'd said.

Rolling her eyes at herself, she acknowledged how crazy that sounded, then she let go of the breath she'd been holding, and felt herself relax into the warmth of his body and the bliss of being held so close. She could feel his heart beating, his breath in her hair, the strength of his arms as they drew her closer and held her safe against the world. She drifted off to sleep with a smile on her face, and even as she dreamed, she felt his arms around her.

A few hours later, as the sun drifted higher and made the room a little brighter, she was awoken by his kisses on her neck, and his hands running through her hair. He turned her to face him and pulled her closer, kissing her passionately on the mouth, sending a shiver of pleasure through her as his tongue met hers. She kissed him back, wrapping her arms around him and holding him tight, moaning as she felt his hand on her tummy, softly stroking her bare skin. Her breath caught as he inched higher, pushing her t-shirt out of the way, his touch leaving a trail of fire in its wake.

Shivering with desire, she tried to silence the part of her mind that was telling her to stop. She wanted to stop thinking, to simply abandon herself to the sensation she felt in his arms, love and lust mingling powerfully, trying to drive rationality from her mind.

But as he reached around to unhook her bra she froze, suddenly unsure of herself. The fact that no one knew where she was made her feel vulnerable and exposed. Reluctantly she remembered how much it meant to her that he was prepared to wait until she was ready. And in more sober moments –

when his touch wasn't leaving her incapable of coherent thought – she knew that moment hadn't come.

He groaned as she stopped kissing him and pulled back, away from him. "My god baby, you're driving me crazy. Come on, let me hold you," he pleaded, voice still heavy with sleep. "Don't tease me like this," he added, reaching out for her, trying to crush her against him and under him.

Her breath became ragged with fear, and she shrunk in on herself, trying to make herself smaller, more still, trying not to inflame him any further.

Abruptly he opened his eyes, which widened with shock when he saw her expression. He released her immediately, and shame and regret crossed his face as he inched himself further away from her, putting enough space between them that they couldn't accidentally touch.

"I'm so sorry Carlie, I forgot myself for a moment. I've just missed you so much. And I love you so much. I'm really sorry. I promise I'll never try to make you do anything you don't want to do." He looked mortified, and she felt terrible that she'd made him feel so bad.

"It's not your fault," she whispered, suddenly wishing she hadn't stopped him. "And it's not that I don't want to do it," she added, blushing furiously as she remembered the passion between them. "I just, I'm not quite ready, and I'm so sorry about that. I know it's not fair to you."

Slowly he reached out and stroked her cheek, gently, restrained, careful not to scare her. The love and respect in his touch made her ache with longing, and with joy and gratitude. "Oh my love, you have nothing to apologise for," he said softly. "*I'm* so sorry. I was half asleep, and I'd been dreaming that we were, you know…" he paused, looking slightly uncomfortable. "And when I woke up and felt you in my arms…"

He trailed off again, and she stared at him, suddenly afraid that he'd want to break up with her now, find someone who could give him all that he wanted.

Before either of them could speak, there was a knock on his front door. She stared at him, eyebrows raised in question. He shrugged, and she saw his mind ticking over, then he sighed. "I'd better check, just in case it's Mum turning up early."

They both stood up, and Carlie pulled on her boots as he threw a long-sleeved t-shirt on over his tank top. She blushed again, as she remembered how amazing he'd looked standing in the doorway that morning, and he winked at her before leading her back out into the lounge room. "Make yourself at home," he said, kissing her demurely on the cheek then walking down the hallway and opening the door.

"Sweetheart, how was France?" she heard a woman cry, before she heard the sound of kissing. Carlie's blood ran cold, and she felt herself sinking into the couch in dismay.

"God I've missed you. When did you get back? And how were the ladies across the channel?" the woman was asking. Her voice got louder as she followed Rowan inside – and the expression on his face didn't do anything to reassure her. He looked... Guilty? Embarrassed? Was he blushing? He was uncomfortable, that was plain to see.

When the woman stepped into the lounge room, Carlie's heart sank even deeper. She was gorgeous. Grown-up and sexy gorgeous. And glamorous and confident and self-assured. She didn't bat an eye as she glanced at Carlie from top to toe, then turned back to Rowan with a dismissive smirk. "So I guess you didn't need to find romance in France," she teased. "You've already found my replacement, and you're already in bed with her too I see."

Carlie's hand reached up to her messy hair, and she realised she must look like she'd just rolled out of bed. Which she had. The woman was staring at her like she was someone Rowan had pulled in off the street last night, a stranger who meant nothing to him.

And what did she mean, about her being a replacement? She was mortified, but mostly she was angry at herself for ever thinking he could be interested in someone like her. She felt so young, so unworldly, so naive compared to this woman, and she didn't like it. She had to get out of there. Standing up, she grabbed her bag and walked towards the door.

Rowan winced, and looked over at her with apology written all over his face. "Baby, wait. Don't leave. Tell me what's wrong," he implored her. "This is just –"

"No, don't," she said. "I have to go." She could hear the ice in her voice, as well as the shakiness. He put his hands on her shoulders and tried to draw her to him, but she shook him off and paced down the hallway. He followed after her, but she kept walking, back straight, eyes on the door. "Carlie, she won't be here for long – we can go out, spend the day together."

Feeling she could drown in the sadness she was feeling, she turned to face him. He saw the anguish in her eyes, and tried to reach out to her, but she shook her head. "Goodbye Rowan," she said, a cold finality in her tone, then she stomped off down the stairs.

"I'll see you on Monday," he called out after her, but he couldn't be sure she'd heard him.

Carlie was shaking by the time she collapsed into a seat on the bus, and it took most of the journey home to get her emotions under control enough to focus on her surroundings. She still felt tears welling whenever the face of that woman slid into her mind though, so she decided to climb the tor before she faced Rose.

Her thoughts were a confused jumble – she didn't know if she felt upset that he'd pressured her about sex, disappointed that she'd said no, or angry about the mysterious woman who'd interrupted them. Who was she? Why had she made her feel so insecure, just minutes after Rowan had told her again how much he loved her? Was she just sensitive because the woman had exuded such an air of confidence and sexuality? Did that make her feel guilty about turning Rowan down? Or was she just garden variety jealous that Rowan had another woman in his life?

Oh god, now she really wished she'd stayed to hear his explanation. What if she was torturing herself over nothing? But even if it was all perfectly innocent and it was his sister or something, the woman had made her feel small and uninteresting, and totally naive and not good enough for Rowan – and that was her own issue, not the woman's. And not Rowan's either. Suddenly stumbling on a rock, she gazed around herself and realised with a shock that a thick mist had risen up around her, and she no longer knew where she was. Peering ahead, she could just make out the branches of an apple tree in front of her. She must have weaved her way around the lower slopes of the tor to the far side. A chill settled around her, and the sense of isolation she felt in the alien white landscape made her feel even worse.

Her breath caught when she saw a figure materialise out of the fog. It was the green-clad woman, the Keeper of the Hill, who she'd met the night of their coven dedication. She tried to remember her words. *You can call on me when you need to ground yourself, and connect back to the earth, or need to feel my nurturing and protection…* She smiled despite herself. She did have need of that right now.

Then she shivered as she remembered the rest of the message from that mysterious full moon night. She was going to betray the person closest to her. Yet hadn't *she* just been betrayed by the person closest to her? Had the message been wrong all along? Should she have been guarding her own heart all this time, rather than worrying about how her actions would affect someone else?

The figure glided forward, and shocked Carlie by sweeping her into a hug. She hadn't seemed the nurturing type. "I apologise for that," she whispered. "I was a little out of sorts at our last meeting."

Carlie giggled. Shouldn't these Otherworldly beings or whatever they were be above things like impatience and grumpiness? Weren't they meant to be all love and light and positivity? She felt the woman laugh as she released her. "Clearly immersing yourself in the mysteries with your high priestess grandmother and your magical friend has not lessened your cynicism," she said with a wry smile.

Carlie grinned. "I'm sorry," she replied, but her amusement faded as the face of Rowan's visitor flashed through her mind again, and she sighed. "I thought I was going to betray someone, not be betrayed. Couldn't you have warned me about that instead?"

Brianna smiled serenely. "Patience beloved. Everything is not as it seems. You are so quick to judge, without waiting for an explanation."

"Some things are pretty obvious," she retorted. "Someone claims they'll wait for you, then doesn't. Says they love you and only you, but has someone else."

Suddenly a raven cawed overhead, the mists swirled around them, and a dog barked somewhere nearby.

"I cannot stay," the figure in front of her said, then handed her a green-velvet-wrapped bundle that seemed to materialise from somewhere within the folds of her cloak. "This is for you and your friend – she will know which one is for each of you."

Then she leaned forward and cupped Carlie's chin in her hand, gazing deep into her soul. "Keep your faith. Trust your heart," she whispered, then faded back into the mists. A moment later the sun came out, the sky cleared, and a man wandered around the curving path towards her, a dog at his heels.

"Afternoon," he said politely as he swerved around where she was standing, feet anchored in the earth. She smiled, but was too surprised to respond. There was no sign that the woman in green had ever been hovering there in front of her, comforting her, offering advice she wasn't sure was worth taking. Yet in her arms was the package, wrapped in a green the exact same colour as Brianna's cloak.

She shook her head, mind a whirl of contradictions and questions. She felt unsettled, and even more confused than she'd been before, but at least she wasn't dwelling on Rowan's betrayal quite as much – she was dying to know what the woman had given them.

By the time she got back to the cottage and was making dinner with Rose, her sadness had returned with a vengeance, but she managed to keep a brave face while she was with her grandma, not wanting to have to explain her bad mood.

Later, she jumped when she heard a knock at the door. Heart racing, she went to answer it, her smile faltering when she saw it was Rhiannon, not Rowan. With a sickening thud she realised that part of her had hoped he would come over to explain, to apologise, to beg her to forgive him. To hold her close and promise he would never hurt her again. Sighing, she hugged her friend and led her inside.

"Tea?" she asked, and Rhiannon nodded gratefully.

Rose smiled as they entered the kitchen. "Hello sweet girl. You two are so adorable – spending the whole day together, then still wanting more time with each other at night."

Rhiannon looked blank for a moment, but quickly recovered her composure. "Well, we figured we should do a bit more on our assignment," she said to Rose, motioning to the messenger bag on her shoulder, before shooting daggers at Carlie.

"I'm not complaining!" Rose said with a smile. "I'm just so happy that you both have each other."

Carlie poured water into the kettle, then went to the sink to wash up their dinner dishes, careful to keep her back to Rose. She knew she was a bad liar, and she would find it hard to keep a straight face if she had to look her grandma in the eye. But Rose motioned her away. "You go upstairs and make a start girls, and I'll bring up the tea when it's ready."

The two girls climbed the stairs and collapsed on the floor in Carlie's room, backs resting against her narrow single bed.

"So I'm guessing you didn't tell Rose about my change of plan, and you went and saw Rowan instead?" Rhiannon asked her, and there was a thread of anger in her voice.

Carlie nodded sadly, oblivious to the flatness in her tone.

"Be careful with your lies Carlie, your grandmother isn't stupid," her friend snapped, but her demeanour gentled as she saw the look on her face. "What happened?"

There was a knock on the door, and Carlie jumped up to open it. Rose stood there with two mugs of tea on a tray, and a plate of cinnamon cookies that smelled divine.

"Thanks Gran," she said, forcing happiness into her voice as she took the tray. Her grandma looked searchingly at her, then smiled and left them to it.

"Did he hurt you?" Rhiannon asked impatiently as she picked up her tea and took a sip.

"No," Carlie said, then faltered. "Not really…"

Embarrassed, she told her friend how bad she'd felt for waking him up, and how nervous she'd been when he'd said to come to bed with him – then relieved when it became obvious that he actually did mean to sleep.

Rhiannon smiled. "That doesn't sound so bad, especially as he was probably beyond exhausted after his trip."

Carlie blushed. "Well, we slept for a while, then I woke up to him kissing me, and trying to... I don't know, go further."

"Oh my god! Did he force you to –"

"No!" Carlie insisted. "He tried to convince me, but he finally stopped. But it was weird, it was almost like he didn't realise it was me for a minute."

"And will he keep trying to convince you until you give in?" Rhiannon asked, and Carlie heard the outrage in her voice.

"I don't know. I do feel guilty though. I mean, isn't that what you're supposed to do when you love someone?"

Her friend looked horrified. "Of course not Carlie, you're supposed to respect your girlfriend or boyfriend's decisions, to wait until they're ready, no matter how long it takes."

"I know, and he does, he's usually really good about it..."

"Don't you dare let him pressure you into this Carlie!" Rhiannon said, voice fierce. "And don't make excuses for him. Any guy who thinks that behaviour is okay should be avoided at all costs, no matter how sweet he appears to be the rest of the time. Believe me, I know."

Carlie pasted a smile on her face, then realised how often she'd been doing that today. "I won't. And he won't." She couldn't admit how close she'd come to giving in, not because he was pressuring her, but because she wanted to. Then again, given what happened next, she was beyond relieved that she hadn't let her desire lead to a decision she would have regretted.

"But that's not the worst thing that happened," she finally said, and Rhiannon's eyes widened. "I was saved by a knock on the door. He answered it, thinking it might be his mum, but it wasn't – it was this stunningly beautiful woman, dressed all sexy and glamorous, who kissed him hello, then remarked on how quickly he'd replaced her. It's weird – I realised that I don't know any of his friends. He could have this whole other life I don't know about. He could be seeing other people for all I know."

Tears started to spill over her lashes, and Rhiannon put her arms around her. "I'm sure he's not seeing anyone else," she said, but Carlie could hear the doubt in her voice. Clearly the idea of him two-timing her wasn't a total shock to her friend.

"What did he say about her? Did he introduce you?"

Carlie shook her head. "No – but I didn't stay around to hear it, I must admit. He begged me to stay, and he wanted to talk, wanted to spend the day together, but I was too upset. I didn't want to start crying in front of her. So, I don't know, maybe that's it for us."

Rhiannon shook her head. "You can't just leave it like that!"

"He said he'd see me on Monday after school, so I guess I'll know for sure then. Oh! But I have something for you – I'm so sorry, I was so preoccupied that I forgot about it."

Reaching over to her bag, she gently pulled out the velvet-wrapped parcel. Rhiannon's eyebrows lifted in surprise, all thoughts of Rowan driven from her mind. "You saw her again? When? Where? What did she say? Which one was it?"

Carlie couldn't help laughing, that her friend would instantly assume any gift was from some Otherworldly apparition they had no idea how to explain. Yet she was right.

"I saw her this afternoon. I was in a strange mood when I got off the bus, and I was too scared to come home and face Rose straight away, so I thought I'd climb the hill, see if I could gain any sense of perspective from being at the top," she began.

"But instead I somehow wandered into the mists and found myself weaving around the lower slopes, amongst the apple trees, far from the path to the summit. And Brianna emerged out of the mists, and talked to me for a moment, saying to trust and have faith, and then she gave me this, and told me to give it to you, because you would know which one of us had need of which object."

Carefully, respectfully, she handed the package to Rhiannon, who held it reverently, then slowly untied the silver ribbon and unwrapped the velvet folds. Nestled inside was a beautiful wand made from a tree branch, with symbols engraved into it and tiny crystals embedded along its length. Beneath it sat a round wooden disc, its surface smooth, carved with a pentacle pattern on the top, and with a large rose quartz crystal set in a hollow in its centre. Both were breathtaking, and both exuded an air of magic. "Earth and air," Rhiannon said, awe in her voice.

She held them out to Carlie to show her, then placed the wand on the floor as she took the pentacle to her heart and held it there, eyes closed. Next she put it down and picked up the wand, repeating the process to connect deeply to each of the objects. Then she handed the first of the ritual tools to Carlie.

"This wooden disc was made from a piece of oak, from a tree that had fallen, rather than being chopped down," Rhiannon said, voice serious and still filled with wonder. "Oak is considered the king of the forest, and is revered for its size and great age. It represents courage, strength, stability and endurance, which will certainly be of use to you. It's also good for divination and inner reflection, for connecting you to your inner knowing and your authentic voice. And of course the rose quartz is there to amplify your feelings of self-love, self-healing, self-esteem and compassion to self," she added.

"The pentacle is used by witches as an amulet and symbol of protection, and this piece can be used to represent earth on our altar. The pattern can also be traced in the air, with an athame or wand, or even just your finger, to invoke the elements and the directions in ritual. In many traditions the lower left hand point of the star represents earth, the lower right represents fire, the upper left air, the upper right water, and the topmost point spirit," she explained, and Carlie traced over the pentacle pattern as she listened, feeling grounded and secure despite her sadness.

As she took the ritual tool and held it to her own heart, she smiled, hoping the rose quartz would imbue her with all its qualities. She felt a warmth coming from the disc, a sense of security and grounding that she desperately needed today. "Thank you," she said softly, as she placed it in her lap, then picked up a cookie and sipped her tea.

Next her friend took the wand in her hand, where it sat so beautifully, so elegantly, looking like an extension of her own body.

"It's an elder wand," Rhiannon explained in reverent tones. "It can be used to represent air on our altar, and it can also direct energy in spellcasting as well as carving out a ritual circle, the sacred space between the worlds. The elder tree is considered the queen of the forest, and it has a powerful feminine energy, holding the wisdom of the crone within it," she added, gently stroking the wood.

"It represents renewal and regeneration, and aids in emotional transformation, and it also offers protection and can help deepen visions and visualisation rituals." She traced the symbols carved along its length as she spoke, then softly touched the small amethyst crystals embedded in the branch and the moonstone at its tip.

"Now we have our four ritual tools," she said joyfully. "It seems that we have friends who want to encourage our magic."

The thought cheered Carlie up, and they spent the next few hours planning rituals they wanted to perform and areas they wanted to research on their coven nights. For a little while she was able to lock her sadness away, but when she got into bed and curled up under the covers later, the pain returned, even more sharply than before, and not even Luther's warm body snuggled up in the crook of her knees could bring her any comfort.

Chapter 20

The Betrayal Continues

Her heart raced as she ran down the corridor, the thing that was chasing her filling her with fear and panic as it gained on her. She could hear its heavy foot falls, feel the heat of its breath on her neck. Relief surged through her as she saw Rowan up ahead, and she desperately reached out for him, eager to feel the warmth of his arms around her, as being held by him was the safest place in the world to her. But when he turned around to face her she was shocked to see the chill in his eyes, and the smile he gave the thing standing menacingly behind her. Panicked, she turned around to face whatever had been chasing her – and recoiled as she realised it was the woman who'd knocked on Rowan's door the other morning. Her face was lit with triumph, and a sickly sweet smile twisted her lips upward.

"Aww, poor little Carlie," she said, leering at her. "Abandoned by her parents, and just not enough for the man she claims to love. He needs a real woman," she crowed, thrusting one hip forward and licking her lips suggestively. Horrified, she turned around to Rowan, praying that he'd argue, that he'd deny it, praying that he'd tell this awful woman that he loved *her*, that she *was* enough. But he was fading away into a swirl of fog, his voice mocking as it echoed back to her as if from a great distance. "Oh Carlie, if only you could have shown me how much you love me, if only you didn't insist on holding yourself back, denying me, denying yourself..."

A soft touch on her face made her shrink back in fear, until her eyes snapped open and she realised it was Luther, her little protector. Relief washed over her, even as she realised her pillow was wet from her tears. It had just been a dream. That woman wasn't really tormenting her, Rowan hadn't really abandoned her – it was just her feverish imagination. She patted Luther's soft head, and was grateful when he curled up on the pillow next to her, little paw on her cheek, and started purring. His presence gave her comfort, and the soothing rumbling sound from his chest seemed to lift her spirits, lift her vibration, so she finally drifted back to sleep. And this time she felt Luther with her in all her dreamscapes, a guardian against pain.

In the morning she laughed at herself for letting her paranoia about that woman invade her psyche and her dreams. She had nothing to worry about – she knew how much Rowan loved her, how close they were, how strong their bond was. And he'd be there after school today, and she'd apologise for running off without letting him explain who the woman was, and he'd tell her she was his sister or his best friend's wife or an old workmate or something, and everything would be perfect again.

Except he didn't turn up. The final bell rang that afternoon and she raced down the front steps, eager to fly into his arms, to put her stupid fears behind her. She turned in the direction of the tree he always parked beneath, but he wasn't there. For half an hour she sat on the bench out the front, excitedly standing up every time she heard a car turning off the main road, then sinking back down, deflated, dejected, heart aching with pain and regret, and increasing frustration.

She knew that if this was a normal afternoon she would have just assumed he'd been held up, or worried that he'd been in an accident, but today she had a sinking feeling that he wasn't coming, and her sadness slowly started to solidify into anger. He was in the wrong here, not her. He'd tried to push her into something she wasn't ready for, and he'd invited some pretty woman around to visit him on the day he thought she'd be with Rhiannon and unable to see him.

Her growing paranoia made her start wondering about her dreams too. He'd said in the past that he could send them to her – so had he sent the nightmares last night to let her know how he felt? To warn her away from him? With every extra minute that passed she got angrier and angrier, and by the time Rhiannon came out from her Yule Ball planning committee meeting, after she'd been waiting for an hour, Carlie was livid. She barely saw her friend approach her through her tears, but she felt her presence just before she sat down next to her and slipped an arm around her shoulder.

"I'm so sorry..."

She wiped her eyes and tried to smile. "Silly me, huh, thinking I could date him, that he could really love me, that a silly, naive schoolgirl could ever be enough for him," she hiccuped.

Rhiannon made comforting sounds, but didn't try to argue with her or convince her otherwise. Clearly a big part of her now agreed with this assessment. "I guess it's just hard, with him travelling so much, and meeting so many women, women who clearly all adore him, to know if you can trust him," she offered. "I suppose you'd never know what he got up to while he was away, who he was with. And it's weird – he's a healer and a spiritual teacher, yet he's not honourable with his word."

"What do you mean?" Carlie asked, surprised by how disapproving Rhiannon had suddenly become of the man she'd professed to be such a fan of just two weeks ago. Part of her had assumed that Rhiannon would defend Rowan, would convince her that there was a reasonable explanation, that he had just been held up. That it would all be okay. She deflated even further.

"He can't teach all that stuff, about being honest and honourable, and committing to your purpose and all that, then just stand you up, without a word of explanation. Say that he'd be here, but not turn up, especially after his behaviour on Saturday," Rhiannon said angrily.

"I did run off without letting him explain the other day," she replied quickly, bemused that she was defending him now, despite her hurt.

"Oh Carlie, don't start creating excuses for him. Don't be one of those women who allows herself to be treated badly, who condones or even blames herself for it. He tried to pressure you into doing something you didn't want to do, he invited some mysterious woman over to his place when he thought you were safely off doing something with me, and now he hasn't even bothered to turn up, to try to explain his behaviour."

"Wow, way to kick a girl when she's down," Carlie pouted.

Rhiannon had the decency to look regretful. "I'm sorry, I didn't mean that to sound so harsh, I'm just really mad at him for making you feel like this. You deserve better."

Carlie tried to smile, while Rhiannon looked thoughtful. "You know, after our Samhain dinner, Dad was talking about your mum's shaman guru guy. He was so glad that she had found real love with your dad, because this guy had apparently treated her really badly. He convinced her to give all her power to him – she stopped seeing the magic within herself, and in her connection to the earth, and decided that it would all come from him. Don't do that Carlie, don't give up on our magical workings, on what you're learning with Rose," she said, her voice urgent.

"I'm not saying Rowan's exactly like that, not at all, but there's always a problem when there's such a power imbalance – even when it's only in your head. You think Rowan is more powerful than you, more magical, more *everything* – and he's not. But in thinking that, you're diminishing yourself by being with him."

Rhiannon paused, thinking carefully about what she said next. She looked like she wanted to continue her criticism, then suddenly changed her mind. "What are you going to do?" she asked instead.

Laughing bitterly, Carlie shook her head. "What can I do? I guess he chose the other woman, *woman* being the operative word. So I should retreat gracefully I suppose," she sniffled. "What other option do I have? I can't chase after him – it wouldn't really work by bus," she said, trying to joke, but managing only the faintest of smiles. "Still, I guess it means I'll have more time to help Rose in the shop, more time to study, and more time for our magical work. I guess you're right, I have neglected that a bit. I'm sorry."

Rhiannon smiled reassuringly. "Rose will love that, and so will I. But I feel terrible – I have to go home now and look after Brodie, because Dad has a meeting tonight. Will you be okay? Do you want to come over tomorrow after my committee meeting gets out? We can do our new moon ritual, and you can sleep over – we can stay up all night chatting and eating cookies and moaning about boys – personally I reckon they all suck."

Carlie smiled. "That would be really nice."

"Now, shall I walk you home? You're not going to wait any longer are you?" she asked, disapproval clear in her voice.

Shaking her head sadly, Carlie linked her arm through her friend's and stood up. "No way, let's go," she said. Casting one last glance in the direction of the main road, she resolutely turned her back and started heading home. She managed to maintain a brave face all the way, even forcing herself to laugh at some of the outlandish ideas that had been proposed at the organising meeting for the ball. But relief flooded her as Rhiannon finally waved goodbye and headed home – she couldn't wait to get inside and let the tears that had been building up fall, and she was grateful that Rose was teaching a meditation class after work that night so she had the house to herself.

Pouring in a liberal dose of bubbles, she ran a hot bath and lay amongst the sweetly scented foam, letting her tears slide down her cheeks and join the water swirling around her. Her emotions were whirling too, sadness and guilt warring with anger and shame, a confused mess that was leaving her head ready to explode. She wanted to get out and take some painkillers for the migraine that was starting, but she didn't have the energy or the mental strength to move. And a small part of her wanted to let the migraine engulf her, wanted to feel physical pain in the hopes it would obliterate her mental anguish.

She'd been shivering for ages before she realised the water was stone cold. Grimly she forced herself to get up and get dry, then, too upset to eat, she climbed the stairs to her room, threw herself on the bed and cried herself to sleep. She was relieved that she was so exhausted, so mentally drained, that when she finally passed out into slumber she had no memory of whether she'd dreamed or not.

Chapter 21

New Moon Wishes

The next day, Carlie felt like a ghost as she floated through school, barely present in each of her classes, barely focused on anything that was said. Rhiannon was sympathetic but preoccupied, distracted by her meeting that afternoon. The committee members from the other schools were coming over for a major planning session, and Carlie thought her friend seemed uncommonly eager to spend time with these other students.

When the end of school bell finally rang, Rhiannon raced off with a quick "see you tonight," and Carlie slowly packed up her books – there was no need to hurry out ever again. Picturing a couple of hours spent moping while she waited for Rhiannon to finish, she put her headphones on, cranked up Platinum Brunette's latest album and listlessly headed for the exit. Unusually for her, she was one of the last to leave, and she kept her head down, not wanting anyone to see the tears in her eyes.

So she didn't see his car parked under the oak tree, or see Rowan walking towards her with a beautiful bunch of flowers entwined with ivy. But she felt his presence just before he reached her, and she looked up, confused. He smiled gently as he handed her the bouquet. "I'm so sorry I couldn't be here yesterday my love. Mum got really sick, and I had to take her to hospital. She was too scared for me to leave her alone, but god I missed you," he said, leaning in to kiss her.

Jerking backwards, she stared up at him, and he took a step back too, confused. He couldn't understand the anguish in her eyes. "What's wrong baby, are you okay? You look so sad." Her face crumpled, and he pulled her into his arms, holding her close and stroking her back tenderly. "What is it? Is your grandma all right?"

"Rose? She's fine I guess."

He cupped her face in his hands. "What's happened? Why are you crying?" As the doors to the school opened and a few stragglers walked down the steps towards them, he put his arms around her and guided her to the car, shielding her from sight with his body. Unlocking the passenger side, he lowered her into the seat, then crouched down beside her, still holding her hands.

"Baby, I can't help you if you don't tell me what's wrong. Are you okay? Why are you looking at me like that?"

"You're here," she whispered, and the surprise in her voice tore at his heart.

"Of course I'm here. I was devastated that I couldn't see you last night, and I've been thinking about you every second today. I couldn't wait to get here!" he said.

Some of the pain and stress left her face, and she managed a small, wobbly smile. "I thought you didn't want to see me again," she admitted, voice soft, embarrassed.

Shocked, he stared at her, clutching her hands tightly. "Why on earth would you think that?"

Cheeks flushing red from embarrassment, she looked at the ground. He lifted her chin so he could gaze into her eyes again. "My love, please, why would you think that?"

"Well, it was all a bit... weird on Saturday, and then that woman came over, the one who said I'd replaced her, and she was kissing you..." she said, words tripping over each other in her haste to get them out. "Then when you weren't here yesterday, I guess we just assumed –"

"We?" he asked.

"I was still waiting for you when Rhiannon's meeting for the ball finished, and she saw how sad I was, and, well, she knew about the woman from the other day, and when you didn't turn up it seemed obvious that you'd chosen her, and she convinced me that I couldn't ever really trust you, because you're away so much, and have so many girls throwing themselves at you, and…"

"Come here," he said, pulling her to her feet and into his arms. "I love you Carlie," he whispered fiercely, then unwrapped his arms but kept his hands on her shoulders so they were still connected, holding her still as he gazed into her eyes. "Firstly, Rhiannon has no idea how I feel about you, or whether or not women 'throw themselves at me' – which, incidentally, they don't. And even if they did, it wouldn't matter to me. I love *you*," he said, with emphasis on the 'you'. "And I'm sorry that you were upset about Jay coming over –"

Carlie blushed. "That was Jay, your manager? Your manager Jay is a woman," she repeated, feeling sillier by the minute.

He nodded. "Yeah, I thought you knew that," he replied softly, looking perplexed that it would matter either way.

"I thought you were spending the day with Rhiannon, so I said it was fine for her to drop by so we could finalise the details for our Yule retreat. Which you would have known if you'd waited just five seconds and let me explain."

The red flush on her cheeks intensified.

"She's got a strange sense of humour at the best of times, but she'll be mortified when she finds out how much she upset you with her joking around the other day," he said, tenderly tucking a stray curl behind her ear.

"Please don't tell her," she implored him. "I'm embarrassed enough over all of this, and the conclusions I jumped to. I don't think any of those things on their own would have thrown me, but after Saturday morning and that whole weirdness about me not wanting to, um… well, and then Jay turning up, and then you not being here yesterday…" Carlie's voice faltered, and she felt a tear slide down her cheek. "I'm so sorry."

"Oh baby, *I'm* sorry," he said, and she could hear that there was real pain in his voice. "I had no idea you were torturing yourself over this. I feel terrible that I hurt you, but I didn't know you were feeling any of this. Can you see that from my perspective there was nothing wrong, that I thought we were fine? So I wasn't avoiding you or trying to cause you further pain, even though you saw it that way. And me not being here last night didn't mean I didn't want to see you, I just couldn't leave Mum on her own there."

"Yeah, I can see that," she admitted sheepishly. "So I guess this is the definition of catastrophic thinking, from that book you suggested for my course?"

He nodded. "It's letting your perception – which is not based on the truth – change how you view a situation, and reframing everything that happens afterwards in that light. Taking one tiny thought, one simple misunderstanding, then running with it, allowing it to colour everything else in your world, see events through a different lens, and so judge them more harshly than you otherwise would have, and give certain actions far more weight than they deserve. Getting so paranoid that you spin one incident outwards to mean the end of the relationship, when I didn't even realise you were upset."

Her brain whirred. His words made sense. She remembered thinking yesterday that if he hadn't – in her mind – chosen someone else over her, she would have just assumed he was running late or that the car had broken down, or been worried that he might have been in an accident. God, she'd invented an entire scenario in her head, spent the last three days obsessing over his supposed betrayal and convincing herself it was all over, that he didn't love her and perhaps never had – yet none of it was based in reality. And while she'd been beating herself up and wallowing in pain, he'd been completely oblivious, through no fault of his own.

He tilted her chin up, so she was looking directly into his eyes. "I'm guessing that you felt bad about us not sleeping together the other morning, guilty even?" he asked her gently, kindly. "And that made you much more sensitive to Jay's comments, and started this whole negative train of thought?"

She nodded, squirming a little under his intense gaze, and blushing beet red.

"Carlie, I promise you, I don't mind waiting for you. And I don't feel like I'm missing out on anything," he insisted. "Being with you in a cafe, holding hands and gazing into your eyes as we share what's in our hearts, sitting on the bank of our stream, kissing you and holding you close – that's more intimate than most of the sex I've ever had."

She grimaced, hating to be reminded that there had been girls before her, *women* before her. It made her feel even more inadequate, more insecure. But that was her issue, something she had to work on. She took a deep breath, and tried to put her worries into perspective. It was the least she could do.

"Yes, I've had girlfriends before, and I've had sex before," Rowan said, voice gentle, arms holding her safe. "But what I'm trying to say is that I would much rather spend time with you, just the way we are, than have sex with anyone else."

"But Jay is so confident, so sexy, so overtly sexual, so many things that I'm not," Carlie blurted out, and he sighed.

"Baby, it's you that I want to be with, haven't you been listening? If I wanted to be with someone else, I would be."

The simplicity of that statement left her breathless, and the truth of it slammed through her. Here she'd been, inventing all manner of scenarios, when in the end it all came down to that. He was with her because he wanted to be. And if he didn't want to be, he wouldn't be. She smiled, finally accepting that truth. "I feel like an idiot," she conceded, trying for a light tone, trying not to blush.

"No, I don't mean that," he insisted. "Feeling things doesn't make you an idiot. But if you ever have doubts again, will you talk to me about them? I really wish I could have stopped you on Saturday before you ran off, let you know that Jay is just my manager, nothing more. And I would have come over on Sunday, but I knew that you were helping Rose in the healing centre, so I couldn't go there, and I had my mum arriving. Oh my love," he said sadly, pulling her back into the safety of his arms. "I'm really sorry you felt all this."

She leaned into him, feeling the warmth and security of his embrace, and the love that flowed between them as they stood together, heart to heart, wrapped up together in their own little world. The sound of an approaching car brought them back to the real world, and he hugged her tight then released her. "Shall we get out of here?" he asked her gently. "Go somewhere?"

She nodded happily and climbed back into the car. And they had a beautiful night together, holding hands as they drove back to his village, sitting in a cosy cafe drinking tea and eating scones as they talked, catching up on the two weeks they'd been apart.

Rowan told her about the retreat he'd facilitated in the French countryside, and the ancient standing stones they'd performed a powerful rite within, then showed her photos of the enchanted faerytale forest of Broceliande, the home, according to legend, of Merlin's tomb, and the Lady of the Lake's abode.

In turn Carlie told him about helping Rose in the shop, how much she'd loved doing healings for people, and about their Samhain celebrations – the beautiful dinner at Mike's place, her midnight meditation in the churchyard with Rhiannon, and the ceremony Rose facilitated the following night, that had brought her to tears with its moving candle ritual. She cried a little as she described it, and he leaned forward and tenderly wiped the tears from her eyes.

Carefully she glossed over school though – she hated being reminded that she was so much younger than him – and tried to change the subject whenever he asked about her last few nights of anguish, although judging by his sweet protectiveness and care, she had a feeling he knew anyway. She tried not to feel too embarrassed by that – live and learn, right?

Later they wandered along the High Street hand in hand, browsing through the bookshop, the florist and the witchy store, then they went back to his place, and she was so happy when she saw that he'd set up a candlelit picnic on the lounge room floor. For a moment she felt a pang of remorse that she'd stood Rhiannon up, but Rowan told her not to worry, that she would understand how important this night was to her, this resolution of their misunderstanding.

She wasn't sure that was strictly true, but she forgot all about her friend when Rowan poured out champagne glasses filled with sparkling grape juice, fed her delicate spinach and pumpkin-filled dumplings and other vegetarian delights, then brought out two little pink cupcakes decorated with red hearts and topped with a candle to help cast their new moon wish.

"New moon blessings to you my beloved," he whispered. "I hope we can put this misunderstanding behind us and let tonight's lunar energy mark a new beginning for us."

Leaning forward, she kissed him, slowly and deeply, and they sat there for ages on the red blanket on the floor, in the flickering light of several candles, holding each other close, whispering their love for each other, and feeling the magic of the new moon and their new understanding of each other and themselves.

She knew, if he asked her right now, that she would stay the night with him, that she would happily, even eagerly, give herself to him and take their relationship to the next level. But he didn't ask her. Maybe he was aware of what she was feeling, and wanted to make sure she was absolutely ready before that happened, so she wouldn't regret it later. She tried to be glad that he was proving he wouldn't take advantage of her in her romance-weakened state, but part of her wished that he would. *Poor guy, he just couldn't win with her.*

When the clock struck ten, he loosened his arms from around her, kissed her on the forehead, and whispered that it was time for him to take her home. She tried not to show her disappointment, tried to focus on feeling happy that he respected her so much and was not willing to put any pressure on her, or add any misunderstanding to what they had together, but she laughed inwardly at the irony.

He got her home just before Rose was due to arrive back from her circle, and as he kissed her goodbye she was filled with longing, to spend more time with him, to be closer to him, to make sure he knew how sorry she was – and how much she loved him. "I love you more," he whispered, then watched as she slipped inside the cottage and went upstairs to bed.

Chapter 22

Making Amends

As she got ready for school the next morning, Carlie was suddenly nervous. She knew that missing their coven night and bailing on her sleepover plans would have hurt Rhiannon, and she was pretty sure she'd disapprove of her giving Rowan a second chance too, after her speech the other night. But she couldn't just throw away what they had because of a simple misunderstanding.

Surely Rhiannon couldn't be mad about that? She appreciated that her friend was looking out for her, and that her motivation was pure, but it seemed she'd got the wrong idea from her conversation with Mike about her mum's older shaman guru guy boyfriend – Rowan was nothing like him, yet she was acting as though they were the same person.

Squaring her shoulders, she took a deep breath before walking in to class and sitting down next to her friend.

"Hi," she said shyly.

Rhiannon stared at her for a long moment, before sullenly returning the greeting.

"Please don't be mad at me," she implored. "I know you're upset that I didn't stay over, but I'll make it up to you, I promise."

"Oh my god Carlie, I'm not angry at you, I'm *worried* about you. I didn't know what had happened to you when you didn't come over last night, but I couldn't exactly pop by Rose's and ask her, since

I was probably your alibi again," she snapped, rolling her eyes when her friend blushed.

"For god's sake, I don't want to be your fall back plan, and I don't want to be part of your lies. It's not fair to me, or to Rose. I thought you were better than that, but it seems that your growing deceit doesn't bother you – it appears to be as natural to you as breathing now, which is disappointing," she sneered.

"Rhi, Gran was teaching last night, and didn't get home until after I did, so don't worry, I didn't have to lie to her," Carlie retorted. "And I don't want to deceive anyone, ever. I'm really sorry that I let you down – I didn't plan it that way, it's just that Rowan was waiting for me yesterday, after school, and I figured he deserved the chance to at least explain what had happened."

Her friend looked unimpressed. "So I take it you're back together, and everything is wonderful again – until the next time of course. What was his excuse for treating you so badly on the weekend, and for standing you up the other day?" she asked. "And, more importantly, how could you just forgive him?"

"Because I love him, and he loves me, and because he explained everything, and it was all a misunderstanding," Carlie said defensively. "His mum arrived on Sunday to stay with him for a few days, and she got really sick the next day and he had to take her to hospital. They were there all afternoon and into the night, and she was really scared, so he couldn't leave her. She got out the next day, so he came to meet me straight away – he was waiting for me yesterday when school ended, with a beautiful bunch of flowers wound around with ivy, and he was really apologetic."

Rhiannon rolled her eyes, but motioned for her to go on.

"The woman who was there on Saturday was his manager Jay, which I would have known if I'd stayed around and let him explain – she was just there to sort out some details of the Yule retreat with him, and will apparently be really embarrassed that her bad joke about her being replaced upset me so much."

"That's great Carlie, but what about how bad you felt being compared to a 'real' woman – as *you* described her – and what about that whole forcing you to have sex thing?" Rhiannon said angrily.

"That's not fair Rhi, he didn't force me to have sex – nothing actually happened. And he's mortified that I felt pressured in any way. He'd been dreaming about me, and then he half woke up, and I was lying in his arms, so..." she blushed. "He stopped the second I asked him to, and he knew straight away that I wanted him to back off. And he's finally convinced me that just being together is enough for him – it's *my* paranoia that makes me feel as though I'm not enough, that I'm not doing enough, it's not his fault," she said, and smiled happily as she realised that she actually did believe this at last. She was getting better.

"So you don't have to worry about me Rhiannon, I'm fine. We're fine. He feels terrible about that morning, and he promised it wouldn't happen again."

"That's what they all say," Rhiannon muttered, but she was saved from having to repeat herself, or hearing how Carlie would respond to her dig, when their teacher stepped into the room and class began.

The tension between them defused over the course of the day, and by the time the final bell rang they were back to normal. They went home together, back to Rose's cottage, and drank cups of tea with her before going upstairs to work on their assignment. Carlie carefully avoided the subject of Rowan, but was happy and relieved that she and her friend seemed to be over their spat from earlier that day.

The next afternoon she saw Rowan, but she didn't get a chance to mention it to Rhiannon at school on Friday, because her friend had left that morning to spend a long weekend with her grandma up north. This left Carlie free to help Rose in her centre on Saturday, doing some healings in the morning and helping out in the shop in the afternoon, then spend Sunday with Rowan, wandering around his village, seeing a movie, and just enjoying being together. Holding hands, dreaming of their future plans, sharing precious golden moments that she knew she would treasure forever.

She shivered as a thought whispered through her, to make the most of it while they still could, but Rowan leaned over at that moment and kissed her cheek, then gathered her into a hug, and she forced the sudden fear that had gripped her to melt away.

Chapter 23

Messages From the Other Side

Rhiannon had been away for the whole weekend, then was off sick from school for the next two days, but now it was Tuesday night, and Carlie couldn't wait to get to her place for their coven meeting – and to tell her about her magical weekend, full of such beautiful moments with Rowan.

Her friend smiled as she opened the door and ushered her in. "I'm fine!" she insisted as Carlie hugged her tight and asked how she was. "I stopped throwing up at lunchtime today, so I'll be back at school tomorrow. And don't worry, I'm not contagious," she teased.

"I'm so glad. And I've got so much news Rhi, I've been dying to see you," Carlie said as they settled on the bedroom floor and pulled out their Book of Shadows, notepads and pens.

"Me too," Rhiannon replied, voice sober.

"He really does love me! I've finally been able to accept it – and he wants us to go away together at Christmas!" Carlie burst out, at the exact same time that Rhiannon said: "You have to break up with him, he's bad news."

They stared at each other, shock registering in green eyes and blue.

"Why?" Carlie gasped.

"What?" her friend stuttered.

"You first," Carlie said icily, suddenly not so keen to share her romantic news with her friend.

So Rhiannon poured out her heart. She'd been to a psychic fair at her grandma's village, and had a really intense two-hour reading. The fortune teller had described her mum, and her mum's passing, and delivered beautiful messages from the spirit realm for her. Carlie's heart clutched as she saw the naked pain in her friend's eyes, and the desperate longing for these messages to be true. She knew just how she felt because she felt it too, the intense yearning for connection, for a sign, for some little thing that would make her feel her parents were still with her, even in death. She jumped as Rhiannon's voice broke her out of her reverie.

"But then she said my best friend is in danger, and I have to make sure she breaks up with her boyfriend."

Carlie gazed thoughtfully at her friend. Clearly that was ridiculous, but she couldn't just flat out say the reading was wrong or the woman was deluded, because insisting that this part of the message was unfounded would invalidate the rest of what she'd said, and she knew that Rhiannon needed to hold on to those words from her dead mother.

"Rhi, she doesn't know Rowan, or me. She's never met either of us, or come into contact with us, so she couldn't know anything about us. *You* don't even know Rowan that well, so she couldn't be picking stuff up from you about him. Besides, maybe she even meant Debbie or Sue," she suggested, naming the girls at school who her friend had been close to before her mum's death caused her to push everyone away.

"Oh Carlie, I wish it was that simple, believe me. I don't want it to be you, but she was so specific. It was my newest friend, my sister of the heart, the one who had just suffered a terrible loss. And it was definitely Rowan who was dangerous – an older man, a shaman, a mysterious weaver of dreams and lies, who can dazzle people and keep them guessing, keep his own darkness hidden. She said he'll break your heart, and cause you deep pain – he'll hurt you in a way you won't be able to recover from."

Carlie stared at her friend. She was touched that she considered her the sister of her heart, but the rest? "I think if I could go on after losing Mum and Dad, and thinking for so long that I had killed them, I can cope with any pain," she said coldly.

"But she's wrong, in that part at least. He's not dangerous, he's the kindest, gentlest person I've ever known. I trust him with my heart, with my life, and with myself, body and soul."

Defiance snapped from her eyes as she glared at her friend. "I can't believe you could just blindly accept that Rhi. You know the woman at the Body Mind Spirit festival was totally wrong during my reading, and she was world-renowned, so why not this one too?"

Her voice gentled a little as Rhiannon stared at her, mute, but she was still infuriated. "I know you want to believe it's true because of the messages she gave you from your mum, but this part of the reading being untrue doesn't take away from that. She might just be wrong about this part – it seems that I'm hard to read for after all," she said, trying to sound light-hearted and jokey, but not being totally successful.

There were tears in Rhiannon's eyes. "Maybe, but she knew stuff about him, about people he'd treated badly in the past. And she saw visions of him Carlie, and of you – she described you both physically down to a tee, like I'd shown her a photo of both of you, and then she talked about moments to come that she was being warned about.

"She told me that she saw a vision of him getting angry at you and throwing you through a glass coffee table, with blood everywhere. She saw him holding you down and forcing you to have sex with him, while you lay there in terror. She saw him berating you and belittling you, extinguishing your light, then hurting you because you no longer shone as brightly."

Carlie was horrified – not at the visions she was describing, but that the woman would say such cruel and obviously untrue, random things to her friend. No wonder she was upset.

"I just don't trust Rowan," Rhiannon continued, eyes sad but defiant. "He's so much older than us – don't you think it's weird that he wants to be with a schoolgirl?"

A wave of anger and betrayal swept over Carlie. Betrayal again. "So you don't *really* think I'm good enough for him, even though you insisted I was. I'm not spiritual or worldly enough for him?" she asked, tears welling in her eyes and pooling in her throat as she tried to stop them falling.

"No, of course not. You know I don't think that. He's lucky to be with you. But he's bad news. I know you don't want to hear this, but I can feel it in my bones about him. I just don't want him to hurt you," she insisted.

Carlie glared at her. "Don't you see Rhi? He's not the one hurting me, *you* are!" she said.

Her friend looked sad, but she didn't stop. "I don't want him to break your heart, destroy your confidence, ruin your life. Force you to do something against your will. How much do you really know about him? Do you even know how old he is?"

"I know everything I need to know," Carlie snapped, hurt. "And I know that we love each other. Are you just jealous that I've found someone who loves me?"

A knock at the door startled them into silence. Rhiannon stood up and opened it, pasting a smile on her face as she took the proffered tray of tea and cookies that her dad handed her. Carefully she placed it on the floor between them, then sat back down opposite her friend. But as soon as the door shut, her face fell.

"Oh goddess Carlie, I'm really not jealous. How could you even think that? I'm scared for you, and I just want you to be happy – I care about you, that's all," she said. "Truce?"

Glaring at her, Carlie considered for a moment, then gave a reluctant nod and picked up her mug of tea.

"So, I guess we should start tonight's coven meeting with a cleansing and space clearing ritual?" Rhiannon asked, one eyebrow raised in question.

Carlie's lips twitched, and although she wanted to stay mad at her friend – and deep in her heart she was – she nodded again, and moved to the dresser to pick out the incense blend they would need. And for the next two hours the two girls lost themselves in ritual and magic.

Chapter 24

Dear Diary...

As she walked down the front steps of her friend's place later that night, Carlie took a deep breath, drawing strength from the waxing moon as it sailed lower in the sky, and the bracing wind that made her pull her coat more tightly around herself. Feeling wound up from her disagreement with Rhiannon, which had never been far from her mind even as they wove their magic, she ran back to the cottage, the physical exertion centring and calming her.

When she got home, she climbed the stairs to her room and paced around between the bed and the dresser, restless. It really bothered her that her friend was so unsupportive of her. If the situation was reversed, she would be so happy for Rhiannon, would celebrate the way she was dealing with her fears, moving through them, learning about relationships and herself, and growing and healing through loving and being loved. Suddenly remembering that her mother would surely understand her, she knelt down by her dresser, slid out the bottom drawer and reverently unwrapped Violet's diary. Curling up on her bed with the precious book, she started reading.

I haven't written much lately because I've been so busy, trying to spend every spare second with Andre. And I'd much rather be with him than writing about being with him ☺ I'm just so happy! He makes me feel so beautiful, so smart. He hangs on my every word, really listening to me, really hearing me, and just treats me so well, like a goddess. At least once a week he picks me up after school and takes me out, to a fancy restaurant or to the theatre or something, which is amazing, but I also love the times when we just wander around the countryside holding hands, or sit by the river, just talking, sharing our dreams for the future, occasionally kissing...

Okay, maybe not so occasionally, but I feel funny writing that in here, because our relationship is so much more than the physical, it's a really deep soul connection, like we've been together forever and keep meeting and coming back together again in every lifetime. The other night he said we'd been King Arthur and Morgaine in a past life – I was his true love, his Queen of the Heart, and his equal in power and influence, although I wasn't always recognised for my contribution. (Women never are!) And more importantly, he said I'm his Queen of the Heart now too. Oh, I love him so much!

Carlie stopped, stunned. That's what Rowan had said, that they had been Arthur and Morgaine, soul mates through time. Could more than one person have been someone from the past? Maybe she and her mum had been more connected than she'd realised, part of the same soul group or something? But did that mean Rowan and Andre were linked? It seemed unlikely – and she was still sceptical about past lives – but what a fascinating thing to ponder...

Then again, it could just mean it was a good line, and that lots of spiritual guys used it. With a shudder, she realised that Rhiannon's words were still making her feel suspicious of Rowan, so she turned back to her mum's hand-written pages.

I couldn't quite believe it – why me? It's so weird, when I'm with him I feel so loved, and he makes me feel important, and worthy of love, but when I'm back home, away from him, all my doubts start surfacing again, no doubt helped by Mike's negativity. But Andre has written me some beautiful letters and cards, so whenever I start feeling that way I re-read them, and am able to regain some of my confidence and remember how I feel when I'm with him. And it's getting a little easier to believe him, the more time we spend together.

Mum knows something is going on – she commented today on how radiant I look, how happy I am, and wondered what it was from. Well, she wondered whether it was because of Mike, because she can't imagine me with anyone else. Poor Mum, I know she's always wanted me to end up with Mike, and I don't want to disappoint her, but this is just so much more! More grown up, more real, more loving.

I did come very close to telling her about Andre, because I want my parents to know him, but something stopped me. Mike suggested that I shouldn't tell Mum and Dad about him yet, because they'd probably freak out since he's so much older than me, and has been married before and stuff. I'm sure they'd love him if they met him, but since it has to be a secret anyway, so no one knows he's dating a student, I'm fine with not telling them for now. We have the rest of our lives together to wait for the right moment...

Ooohhh! We got to spend the whole weekend together, because Mum and Dad were away, staying with Elsie and Daniel for one of their three-day get-togethers. I felt a bit guilty, because Andre cancelled a workshop so he could spend the time with me – he told them his wife was sick and he had to stay with her and look after her! But we had the most amazing time. It was just us, no one else – no students wanting his time, no Mike trying to tear us apart (I'd told him I was going with my parents to see Elsie, so he didn't know I was at home). And it was so beautiful, we got on so well, and he said we should run away and live together for always!

I thought he was joking at first, but he said it again on Sunday, and we started talking about it semi-seriously. I'd always thought I would stay here after school, work with Mum in the shop, study to be a counsellor or something. But I can do that anywhere. And anyway, Andre said I could be part of his work, teach with him, and that would help so many more people than I ever could any other way. I know that Mum would be upset if I left, but she's always said I have to follow my heart, and Andre is definitely my heart... and my soul, and my love.

Sigh, I really thought that Mike and I were still best friends, deep down. And that he would have grown up a bit by now and accepted that I love Andre, and that he loves me. Yet today I told him that we're planning to live together once I finish school, and he was so mean.

But I guess I shouldn't expect anything else. Things have been awkward between us for a while, because Mike is always trying to convince me to break up with Andre, telling me that he's not good enough for me, that he'll cheat on me, that he'll hurt me.

And he seems to sense whenever I'm feeling doubt, feeling that I'm not worthy, and he tries even harder then. Although that's been backfiring a bit lately, because it actually makes me more determined to stay with Andre, and prove Mike wrong. He obviously doesn't like Andre at all, or trust him, and he spends most of the time we're together, at school or wherever, telling me to end it with him. That he can't be trusted. That he just wants me for one thing. But I know that's not true. He's never pressured me to do anything, and he tells me all the time how much he loves me.

I don't know why Mike is being like this – can't he see how happy I am? How happy Andre makes me? How much he's upsetting me? Why is he trying to ruin it? I wish he'd stop, because sadly it's just ruining our friendship, because his bitterness is getting so frustrating.

I want to find a way to stay friends with him – we've been best buddies since we were kids, before, during (and hopefully after) we were dating – but it feels like he's trying to push me away, trying to make me choose between them. But I don't want to choose, I want them both in my life. Andre says that Mike's just jealous, but surely that can't be it. We've talked about it, and Mike knows we're only ever going to be friends now, Andre or no Andre. Plus I think he's been spending time with Beth, who is so lovely. I hope something develops between them, because he deserves to be happy.

But it's the dark moon tonight, so I'm going to do a ritual to release the pain and sadness I feel about Mike, and the resentment that's building in me, because I want us to be able to be friends again, close friends, to go back to how we used to be, and for him to be happy for me. And I want to banish the negativity I feel from him, and his jealousy and misunderstanding. It's ironic really – he keeps telling me that Andre will hurt me, but it's him *that is actually causing me pain, not Andre.*

Carlie closed the book, shocked. The parallels between her mum and Mike, and herself and Rhiannon, were startling. Rhi was trying to break her and Rowan up, for no good reason – a psychic who'd never met either of them couldn't know what might or might not happen in the future, no one could. And she'd said to her friend just tonight that it wasn't Rowan who was hurting her, it was *her*. Rhiannon was causing her pain, just like it had been her mum's best friend hurting her, not the boyfriend who was meant to be so terrible.

But why? She kind of understood it with Mike – her mum had wanted them to go back to being best friends rather than boyfriend and girlfriend, but he was still in love with her and wanted to be with her. Rhiannon did sound jealous, but she wasn't sure why. She still spent time with her, they still worked magic together at least once a week, they saw each other at school, hung out afterwards. Was Rhi just feeling lonely, and didn't like that she wasn't spending every minute with her any more? Or maybe she was upset because she hadn't met a guy that she liked, so she was feeling left out?

Yet why would that make her want to break her and Rowan up? Try to twist everything and convince her he was bad for her, when he made her so very happy? Maybe she'd have to do a spell to release the pain and hurt she was feeling from Rhiannon?

She was about to turn the page and read on, when she heard the front door open. Quickly she hid the diary back in her drawer, and went downstairs to help her grandma make a late dinner. And by the time they'd eaten, and caught up on their days, she was too tired and discouraged to read any more.

Chapter 25

Meeting the Dead

Groaning, Carlie snuggled down deeper under the covers as she reluctantly opened her eyes. It was so cosy in bed, but she knew she should probably get up soon. After spending a beautiful day with Rowan yesterday, hiking through a nearby forest for a picnic by a lake and a ritual performed in a circle of stones, she'd promised herself she'd spend time with her grandmother today. Rose was teaching her Sunday afternoon herbal class later in the day, so that left the morning for them. Dragging the quilt off the bed and wrapping it around herself, she crept out of bed and peeked out the window – and blinked in surprise. Everything was blanketed in white, and looked so magical in the pale winter dawn. It all seemed so peaceful and soft, the whole world washed clean and pure and bright.

Quickly – well, as quickly as you can with all the layers necessary – she pulled on all her clothes from the night before, wound a scarf around her neck, grabbed her gloves, pulled a beanie over her messy hair, laced up her boots, grabbed a jacket and raced downstairs. She'd never seen snow, and she was as excited as a little kid as she opened the door and tentatively stepped outside. It looked so beautiful, so pure. Jumping down the steps into the tiny front garden, she pulled off one of her gloves and knelt down. Reaching out for the snow, she was surprised by how soft it was, and how clean and sparkly it looked, illuminated by the rising sun as it struggled to pierce the clouds.

Giggling, she picked up a handful of the stuff and squeezed it into a small ball. Her fingers started tingling, although they felt more hot than cold, which she'd always thought was a strange paradox. Grinning, she grabbed some more snow, adding it to the ball, and decided to try to make a snowman. She added and shaped, packed and prodded, until she had a round ball for the lower body, another for the torso, and a smaller one for the head. This last one fell apart the first time she tried to add it to the body, which made her stammer an apology to the poor little misshapen snow creature.

But she persevered, and finally got all three balls compacted and in order, and sitting reasonably neatly on top of each other. She glanced around, finding two small twigs she could use for arms, two pebbles for eyes and a broken piece of rosemary for the mouth.

Carlie stood back, admiring her little creation, then jumped, startled, when she heard Rose's amused "good morning" from the front door. She spun around. "It snowed! I've never seen snow! This is so awesome!" she squealed, hopping up and down in excitement.

Her grandma smiled at her, as though she was a child. "It's not quite so awesome when it snows every day for three weeks, and just getting to the shop to open up is such an arduous task," she explained. "But yes, it can certainly be fun."

And she came down the steps, boots on under her nightdress, and a thick coat over the top. "Bet I can make another snowman quicker than you can," she said, laughter in her voice.

Carlie stared. Seriously, her grandmother was challenging her to a snowman making competition? "You're on!" she said with bravado, and moved a little further from the path to where there was more snow. She began scooping and shaping again, but was amazed to see that Rose already had her snow creature made, complete with twig arms and herb facial features, while she was still on the torso. Shrugging her shoulders, she jumped on top of hers, squashing it into the ground. Her first snowman, imperfect but so sweet to her, would have to do for now. She pulled her gloves back on, suddenly realising how cold her hands were.

"Okay, you win," she giggled. "Guess that means I have to go in and put the kettle on."

Rose nodded. "Absolutely. Meanwhile, I'm getting in the shower before my hands freeze off." Laughing together, they walked back into the house, and Carlie felt a little of the warmth from her hands trickling into her heart. It went without saying that it totally sucked that her parents were dead, but she was grateful every day that she had such an amazing grandmother.

After spending the morning mixing herbs and making incense together, Carlie wandered into town, still smiling as she marvelled at the snow that clung to the trees and cloaked the world in such an immense and comforting silence. When she walked past the graveyard alongside the church though, her eyes misted up. It looked hauntingly beautiful all wreathed in white, yet so achingly sad. She went inside and wandered between the graves, tracing over the names of the dead, touched by the love so apparent in the brief epitaphs, horrified by the youth of some of those being commemorated, and painfully aware that she was on the other side of the world from the resting place of her mum and dad.

She could never bring flowers to their graves, sit by the side of them and talk to them, tell them how much she missed them, ask their advice. She had photos of the funeral, and she knew her mum's best friend Sandy took flowers once a week on her behalf, but it wasn't the same. She couldn't even explain the yearning she felt – she knew the people weren't still there, hanging around in their graves in case someone came to pay their respects, yet there was something comforting about having a place to visit, somewhere to make a pilgrimage of sorts to. To feel that there was somewhere that you could connect with them, even if only in your own mind.

She kept walking, only half-reading the names on the headstones, until a small bouquet of herbs caught her eye. Rosemary, mistletoe and bay laurel – herbs for remembrance, for the dead, for the beloved. Herbs for those who were left behind. Curious, she crunched through the snow to the grave, and as she read the inscription on the stone, she felt her body sinking to the ground of its own accord.

Here lies the body of Louis Tyler – beloved husband of his forever love Rose, adored father of Violet and admired friend of so many – but not his soul, which flies on angel wings to heaven.

Oh god, this was the burial place of the grandfather she'd never met. Rose's husband, who couldn't handle the grief of losing their only daughter, so drank himself to a watery grave via an accidentally-on-purpose drive off a bridge, rather than finding a way to continue on. She felt a sharp stab of regret, to have lost the chance to meet him, and see what had lived on of him in her mother, and even in her.

But more than that she felt such sadness for Rose. What a remarkable woman, to have coped with the grief of losing both her daughter and her husband within weeks of each other. Somehow she had found the strength to remain in the same village, in the same house even, just in case Violet had ever found her way back to her.

Unfortunately she hadn't though, too scared at first to even try to get in touch with her mother, and then, as the years passed, perhaps too mortified by her behaviour to reach out? But she had made provisions that in the event of her death her daughter would find Rose, and for that reason both Carlie and her grandma would be eternally grateful that she hadn't left town.

How strange to think that if her mum hadn't let her friend Sandy finally know – just a few months before she died – that her mother was actually alive and living in England, Rose would still be wondering what had happened to her daughter, and Carlie would be living with Sandy, or with Emily's family, finishing her last year of school and about to start a law degree. She'd loved her life, and would no doubt have been content to continue on the old path, living in Sydney, working for a law firm, sharing an apartment with Emily, bereft of her parents but comfortable in the life she'd planned.

But now, oddly enough, she couldn't imagine how that would have brought her joy. Since she'd moved to England she'd been learning reiki and other healing methods, taking part in rituals with her grandmother and a circle of amazing women, and planning a career change – she wanted to be a social worker or grief counsellor rather than a criminal lawyer. It was amazing to her how so much could change in such a short amount of time.

Her letters to Emily were getting shorter and shorter, and less and less frequent, as were Emily's to her. It wasn't for any particular reason though, it's just that it was hard to maintain such a close relationship from a distance, especially as the tragedy Carlie had endured had changed her so fundamentally. So she was glad that Emily had found new friends, and she was grateful to Rhiannon for taking her under her wing and becoming such a wonderful and supportive part of her life. It certainly didn't mean she could only be friends with people who'd lost someone, but at this early stage, when she felt so raw and burdened by her grief, it had been such a relief to have someone else who understood her, who didn't place any demands on her or feel neglected when she was having a sad or stressful moment.

And indirectly it was Rhiannon who'd made her think about grief counselling or social work. Not because her friend planned to do it – it had been her idea after all – but because having a person like her in her life had made surviving the first stages of her own grief and anger so much easier. Not easy by any means, but less difficult. And she was thrilled that Rhi had decided to study the same course, so they could go through it together. She'd be an amazing support to anyone who came to her for counselling, and Carlie hoped that she could be that helpful and comforting for grieving people too.

As she felt the snow melting under her and soaking into her jeans, she looked up at the gravestone again. "Hi Grandpa," she whispered. "You don't know me, and I'm so sorry about that, but I just wanted to say hello, and let you know how much Mum loved you. I know it didn't seem that way, but we found her Book of Shadows, and Mike filled in some blanks too, and it was only ever her fear of harm coming to you if she stayed that kept her away. Although, that happened anyway, didn't it..."

Sighing, she trailed off. She felt a bit silly talking into thin air, but for some strange reason it offered comfort to her to imagine that her grandfather was there beside her.

"Your wife is an incredible woman – she's so strong, and so in love with you and with Mum even now. She definitely saved my life, and

I mean that literally. She pulled me out of the pit of despair I was so self-indulgently drowning in, and helped me see some kind of possibility and purpose to life again. I'm so sorry you didn't feel you could stay and live your life with her Grandpa," she added sadly. Pausing, she reached out and traced his name on the headstone.

"Anyway, I have to get back and do my homework, but it was really nice chatting to you. And I feel close to Mum and Dad while I sit here with you, so thank you so much for that too," she finished awkwardly. "I'll come back again some time."

She saw movement out of the corner of her eye, and jumped, startled and flushed with guilt, as she saw Rose approaching her.

"I'm sorry Gran, I was just walking through the cemetery, and came across Grandpa's grave. Actually I saw the bouquet of herbs first, then I found him," she said, words tripping over themselves as she rushed to explain. "I've never been here before, never even thought to look, but I won't come back if you'd rather that I didn't," she finished.

Rose touched her arm. "Sweetheart, relax, it's okay. It's more than okay! I feel terrible that I didn't think to bring you here before, but it's lovely hearing you say 'Grandpa' – he would have loved that. I would have loved that. I'm sorry that you never got to meet him, or him you, and it breaks my heart that he didn't know that Violet was okay, that she'd found love and happiness, that she'd had you," she sighed.

"I come here every few days, just to say hello, or think about things, and you're more than welcome to come with me, or you can come on your own whenever you'd like to," she added.

"But maybe we should get out of this cold wind – I think it's going to snow again soon. How about we head down to Kylie's Cafe for a hot chocolate?" Carlie nodded, glad she hadn't upset her grandma, and suddenly wanting that hot chocolate more than anything in the world. Simple pleasures – a sweet little snowman, a hot, sweet drink, and a few kind, sweet words.

Chapter 26

When the Moon Is At Its Peak

Carlie and Rhiannon hung out together on Sunday afternoon, doing homework, trying out recipes for the upcoming winter solstice, and studiously avoiding the topic of Rowan. And things seemed to be fine between them at school on Monday, which was a huge relief. Rhiannon was preoccupied with the Yule Ball, which was less than a month away now, and Carlie was happy to let her talk endlessly about the committee's ideas for decorations, food and drink options – Rhiannon had convinced them to include a few pagan offerings – and their negotiations with a local band, so she could daydream about Rowan.

The next day was the full moon – it would become full just after 3am – so they decided to climb the tor for their coven meeting and perform their ritual under the open sky. Winter had set in though, and the nights were freezing, so when her alarm went off at 2.30am Carlie almost switched it off, rolled over and went back to sleep. But she didn't want to miss this special time, or let her friend down again – she knew her patience with her was wearing thin, and she wanted Rhiannon to know how much she valued the time they spent together. Slowly inching her way out from under the covers, she allowed herself a moment of regret for the warm cosiness of her bed, then stood up.

Keeping her warm pyjamas on, she reached for her long midnight blue velvet dress, the one embroidered with stars, bees and flowers, and pulled it on over the top. She followed it with Rowan's thick woollen jumper, and wound the scarf she'd knitted with Rhiannon at their last new moon ritual around her neck, then shrugged into her warmest coat and pulled a beanie onto her head. Picking up her heaviest boots, she tiptoed as quietly as she could down the stairs in her thickest socks, her little black ritual bag and a torch in hand. At the kitchen door she bent down and slipped on her boots, then crept out through the garden to the back gate.

She caught up with Rhiannon near the base of the hill, and they walked the rest of the way together in companionable silence. The serious atmosphere of their rituals always descended as they climbed, as though they left their normal selves behind at the stone that marked the halfway mark of the upward path, and stepped into their magical selves. Their long hair trailed out behind them, Carlie's dark tangle of curls glistening in the moonlight next to Rhiannon's blonde waves. White clouds glowed as they raced across the sky, and tiny stars twinkled, before being covered briefly then revealed again.

They made it to the top with a few minutes to spare. As Carlie ignited a white candle in a tall glass holder, then lit a lavender smudging bundle from the flame, Rhiannon lifted her moonstone-tipped wand and traced the outline of a circle by walking around her friend, wand held up to the sky to capture the energy of the moon as she focused her intent on the ritual they were about to perform.

Once she'd completed the circle, she placed the wand on the altar in the east, to symbolise air, alongside her chalice, which she placed in the west to represent water. Then Carlie took out the small silver god and goddess statues her grandmother had given her the week before, and arranged them in the centre of the altar, with her pentacle in the north to symbolise earth, and a small gold candle next to her athame in the south, to represent fire.

Carlie cleansed their ritual tools with the purifying smoke of her lavender bundle, then smudged Rhiannon, before handing the herbs to her friend so she could be smudged in turn. Once that was done, Rhiannon picked up the small bottle of essences she'd blended that morning – jasmine, sandalwood, lemon and vanilla – and anointed her friend on the forehead. Eyes glowing with joy and connection,

Carlie took the bottle and repeated the process with the richly scented full moon oils. Then, hair loose and hanging around her like a cloak, Rhiannon held her arms up to the sky.

> *Moon goddess, we welcome you to our circle tonight,*
> *And ask that you lend us your strength and your light on this beautiful night.*
> *Fill us with your energy and intuition, your wisdom and sight.*
> *Please help us know what it is that we need to know, and see what we must see.*
> *Fill us with love and patience, and honour us with your beauty and strength, and all the potential and promise you hold within you.*
> *And help show us what and who we can be.*

Carlie gazed at her friend in awe, marvelling at the beautiful words she always came out with, and at the golden moonlight that was flooding her face and illuminating her with an eerie but magical glow. As though it really was listening to them, the full moon had peeked out from behind the clouds just as they'd cast their circle, and now it was sailing across the sky unhampered, shining down on them with its gentle light.

It never ceased to amaze her when the clouds parted at the very moment that the moon became full, as if there really was magic in the world. And she loved watching her friend as she gathered the goddess energies within her and channelled them outwards.

As she basked in Rhiannon's light, she felt herself grow radiant, although she knew that her friend wouldn't see it like that – she'd insist it was her own light she was feeling. "Your turn," Rhiannon whispered, breaking into her thoughts.

Smiling, Carlie turned to the south.

> *Element of fire, we invoke your strength and passion, your power and compassion. Please fill us with your seeking spirit as we learn and grow.*

Then she turned to the west.

Element of water, of emotion and balance, we invoke you on this night of intuition, to help us develop our inner sight and learn to trust our inner knowing.

Then she turned to the north.

Element of earth, please ground us and hold us safe, and lend us your anchoring ability as we fly upward and outward on this night of magic.

Lastly she turned to the east, where the moon had risen earlier that night, and where the sun would rise again a few hours from now.

Element of air, of insight and new beginnings, please help us to see what we need to see for the month ahead, to find within us all the answers we seek outside.

She paused for a moment, as a memory flooded back to her of the Samhain ritual they'd done together in the ruins of the church, where the woman on the ancient, carved stone throne had told her the same thing. Perhaps she was learning a little after all.

"*Oh Carlie, always seeking answers outside of yourself. You need to look within,*" the woman had scolded her. "*You are in control of your actions, and you're the only one who can control the story or change its outcome. Everything you do, you do willingly – not because you're destined to do it, but because you choose to do it. You choose every day what you want to do, and who you want to be.*"

It was true, she realised. She was becoming more and more aware that it was up to her to create her future, create her destiny, create who and what she wanted to be. Flooded with new awareness, she joined hands with Rhiannon in the centre of their circle, and they threw their heads back so that their faces were turned to the sky, and to the great golden ball of light that bathed them in its magical glow.

"*When the moon is at its peak, so our hearts' desires we seek,*" they said in unison, and smiled across at each other.

Then they gracefully sank to the ground and bowed their heads to meditate on the month ahead. Usually they focused on their coven work at this time, the things they were learning individually and together, lessons they wanted to explore. But tonight Carlie felt restless. If it was the desire of their hearts they were seeking, she wanted to focus on Rowan. So she cast out a wish for him on the wind, a fervent prayer to unite them heart and soul. And she smiled as she felt the power of his need for her. It made her feel strong, powerful – almost goddess-like.

Well, Rhiannon did say they were supposed to embody the goddess at these rituals, and for the first time she really felt that within her, within every cell of her body. A connection to the earth, to the moon above, to the spirits of the land and its people, and to Rowan. He was a few hours away tonight, leading a full moon ritual for a group he worked with a few times a year. But she felt connected to him, because she knew they were gazing at the same moon, sending the same wishes to the sky. He'd said to look to the heavens when the moon became full and he would be sending his love to her, and she felt it in a great big rush of emotion that made her sway where she sat.

She felt Rhiannon's hand on her arm, saw her staring at her with concern and a flash of fear as she opened her eyes, then sensed herself coming back into her body.

"Are you okay Carlie?" her friend asked, worry in her voice.

She nodded and smiled back at her. "Just feeling it all," she whispered. "The beauty of this night, the connection we have between us, the moon." She gestured above her, around her. "I never felt this back home. Not because I couldn't feel it there – I'm sure I could have if I'd known about it. But Mum hid all this from me, and from herself it seems, and now it feels like there was always a part of me missing, a piece I didn't even know was lost. I don't know how Mum could have lived that way."

Closing her eyes again, she soaked up all the energy of the moment, then finally opened them once more. It was time to farewell the quarters, to thank the moon goddess for being part of their ritual, to close circle, then to ground themselves with elderflower spring water and the full moon cookies she'd baked the night before.

They poured a little of the drink onto the ground, then crumbled up one of the cookies. Carlie always wondered if it would be a faery, or maybe a big black raven or a small brown bunny, that would partake of their offerings. She'd like to think it was the former, but as much as she wanted to believe in the fae realm, she wasn't totally convinced it was real. Still, she was sure a raven or a bunny would appreciate their little treat too.

She giggled as they sat together on a blanket on the top of the hill, the candlelight dancing between them and fluttering in the wind as they came back to earth, and back to their bodies. It was cold, but they both felt warmed and energised from their ritual, and while they hunched down into their coats and pulled them more tightly around themselves, they didn't want to walk back down to their beds, or back down to the real world, just yet. While they remained up on the tor they still felt a part of the magic of the earth, of the universe; out of step with the normal, mundane world they usually inhabited. And they didn't want that to end.

But eventually they both started yawning, so they slowly gathered up all their ritual pieces and blew out the candles, before letting their eyes grow accustomed to the dark so they could begin their careful walk back down to the ground, and to the so-called real world.

Although the ritual was over, they still felt a shimmer of the magic as they picked their way solemnly to the base of the hill and hugged goodbye, before gliding back to their beds for another few hours of sleep before the alarm went for another school day. Carlie was careful not to wake Rose, although she supposed her grandma would be happy to know she was continuing the magical education she had begun with her.

Chapter 27

A Small Sacrifice

Cursing when the alarm went off again, for school this time, Carlie dragged herself out of bed and pulled on her uniform, grateful that she didn't have to think about what to wear at least. Her brain felt a little foggy, but she focused on the moment the moon had come out and shone down on them last night, and her spirits lifted a little. It was going to be a long day though. Grabbing an apple and a muesli bar from the kitchen, she kissed her grandma goodbye and set out for school.

Her heart leaped when she saw Rowan's car a few blocks down the street. He was sitting in the driver's seat, passenger side window rolled down, shivering as a few flecks of snow drifted in. "Hey, are you okay my love?" she asked, jumping in and winding up the window.

He pulled her into his arms in answer. "Oh god, I just needed to see you," he sighed, squeezing her so tight she could barely breathe. Holding him close, she stroked his back, trying to offer him the comfort and support he always so freely gave her.

"What is it?" she asked gently. "Can I do anything?"

He looked across at her, and the hope in his eyes touched her heart. "Mum had to go back to hospital early this morning," he whispered.

She'd never seen him look so scared, so vulnerable. "Well, surely they allow visitors? Why don't we go and see her?" she offered, and saw his face brighten with hope.

"Really?" he asked. "She's probably in surgery now, but would you really come and wait with me? What about school?"

Shrugging, she took his hand. "It's only one day, and it's important to you. I love you, you know," she told him.

He smiled. "I know. Thank you, so much."

Looking down at her uniform, she hesitated. "Um, is this going to cause problems?" she asked.

He turned and looked in the back of the car. "What about this?" he replied as he reached over the seat then handed her a soft black jumper.

Taking off her blazer, she pulled it on over the top of her school dress. It actually made a big difference – her skirt could be any navy skirt, since the top was now fully covered. She snuggled into it, loving the feel of the wool against her skin, but loving even more the knowledge that it was his, that it smelled like him, and that she felt closer to him while she was wearing it. "Perfect," she grinned.

He leaned over and kissed her, then pulled out from the curb. She felt a pang of guilt as they passed the school, and for a moment she panicked, worried about what her grandma would say if she found out, and what lessons and homework she'd miss. Then she shrugged off the thought as she recalled the look of gratitude in his eyes when she'd offered to go with him. He'd done so much for her. This was the least she could do.

Besides, part of her was really curious about meeting his mother. Rhiannon had started harping on about how little she really knew about him, and insinuating that it was a problem that she hadn't been introduced to any of his friends or family members – although when she'd mentioned it to Rowan the other day, he'd laughed and told her that she could have met Jay, if she hadn't run screaming from his apartment. She still blushed at how silly she'd been that day.

Still, Rhiannon would have to let up a little after she met his mother, surely. She wondered what she was like, and whether she'd approve of her son's girlfriend, or if she'd be on Rhiannon's side, thinking she was too young, too naive, too not-good-enough for her talented son.

"She'll love you," Rowan said softly, and she was touched, as she gazed over at him, to see the pride in his eyes, and to realise that he actually wanted her to meet his mum. Today wasn't just about supporting him while he waited and worried for the outcome of her surgery, but to take their relationship a step further, to let her know how important she was to him – that he wanted her to be a big part of his life, and not be shut off in a secret part where no one else he cared for knew about her.

"Thank you," she whispered.

As it turned out though, his mother was in surgery for much longer than he'd anticipated, and he wasn't allowed to go in and see her until later that night. So after spending most of the day at the hospital together, drinking bad coffee, talking about the upcoming winter solstice, wondering if they'd be able to spend more time together in the school holidays, and debating when they would tell Rose about their relationship, he reluctantly took her home.

Despite the sad circumstances, she was really glad they'd had the whole day together, and that she'd been able to support him in some way, keep his mind off his worrying. And she was even more touched by his confession when he pulled up a few houses down from Rose's, and drew her into his arms.

"Thank you so much for coming with me today," he said, as he leaned down to kiss her. "It meant the world to me that you would take a day off to cheer me up and keep me sane. But I have to admit, mostly I was just so desperate to spend time with you, because I can't bear the fact that I won't get to see you this weekend. Is that silly, that I miss you so much?" he asked. "That I can't face the thought of us being apart for a week?"

She shook her head, smiling joyfully as she kissed him back. "I love that you miss me, that we miss each other, when we're apart. And while I do feel a bit guilty that I took the day off school, I'm really glad I got to spend today with you. Not being able to see you this weekend fills me with dread too."

His arms tightened around her, and he rested his forehead on hers. "I love you so much baby," he whispered.

"I love you too. And I hope you get to see your mum tonight, and she's soon on the mend."

Chapter 28

I'm A Let Down

The joy of her day with Rowan quickly evaporated when she opened the front gate of the cottage to find Rhiannon camped out on her front step, face grumpy and unimpressed. "Where have you been?" she demanded, and Carlie found her happy mood trickling away in the face of her friend's obvious anger. What did it matter to her where she'd spent the day?

"We were supposed to present our goddess talk today, but I couldn't because my partner wasn't there," Rhiannon snapped, disapproval radiating from her. "So I rang, worried that you were sick, but when Rose answered and you clearly weren't there, I had to make up some crappy excuse about why I'd called, so she wouldn't know that you weren't at school."

Carlie had the grace to look sheepish. "I'm really sorry Rhi, I am. I'd forgotten about the presentation," she mumbled.

"That's not the point though, is it?" her friend retorted. "I shouldn't have to lie for you, you shouldn't be missing school, and Rose shouldn't have to be disappointed in you after all she's done to help you."

"Ouch," Carlie said. "That's a low blow."

Rhiannon rolled her eyes. "Sorry to upset you and your plans," she muttered sarcastically.

Carlie put her bag down with a sigh. "I apologise, really," she replied earnestly. "But Rowan came by early this morning, and he was really upset because his mum was in hospital having surgery. He said he just needed to see me, to hold me, before he went in there – so I offered to go with him and wait until she got out of surgery. And he was really grateful, and also happy that I would be able to meet her. He was so afraid for her Rhi, and I figured one day of school wouldn't be too bad to miss." She trailed off. "I didn't mean to miss this day though," she added, looking embarrassed.

Rhiannon stood up. "And did you?"

"Did I what?" Carlie asked.

"Did you meet his mother?"

Carlie blushed. "Well, no," she admitted reluctantly. "She was in surgery for a lot longer than they expected, and he has to go back again now and wait on his own."

"So he didn't really want you to meet his mother, he was just trying to manipulate you again, prove how much power he has over you by having you drop everything and do what he wants," Rhiannon said, and Carlie was shocked by the venom in her tone.

"He was scared Rhi. I'd do the same for you too," she said defensively, but her friend just scowled at her.

"So, can I come in?" Rhiannon demanded, then rolled her eyes again. "I'm not really all that excited to hang out with you either, but we really need to go over our presentation. I'd thought that we could have prepared for it at lunchtime today, but tomorrow we have history first thing, so we'll have to be ready to do it in the morning."

Reluctantly Carlie let her friend inside.

"And just a tip, you might want to tell Rose you came home with a bad migraine or something, because she'll find out for sure that you were absent from school – she knows all the teachers there, especially our history teacher," Rhiannon said. "That's what I told Ms Henderson anyway, so you may as well stick with that story."

Carlie nodded as she led her friend up the stairs to her room. "Thank you Rhiannon, I do appreciate it. And I am sorry you had to lie for me. It won't happen again."

Rhiannon rolled her eyes and got out her school books. "Make sure of that, *please*," she said, stressing the last word. "I'm a terrible liar, so it's more than likely that we'll both end up getting into trouble, rather than me being of any help. And," she added, voice more serious, "I don't want you to risk anything for that guy. He's not worth it. No guy is worth it. I can't believe you're still seeing him for a start, but that you would do something so stupid as skipping school for him is beyond me. Don't risk your grades and your potential future on him. And don't risk alienating Rose."

Carlie nodded, but inside she was fuming. What right did her friend have to tell her what to do? She was just jealous, she'd admitted as much when they'd first met Rowan at the Body Mind Spirit festival, how much she liked him, how amazing she thought he was.

"God Carlie, don't be so stupid!" Rhiannon burst out. "I'm not jealous, not even close, and I wouldn't date him if you paid me. He's an amazing healer, sure, and a talented teacher, but he's a mess as a person, clearly. He's manipulating you and you can't even see it."

Carlie began to retort, but her friend shook her head. "Enough for now, let's just go over our notes for tomorrow and then I can leave you in peace." Realising she'd just read her mind again, Carlie was about to complain about that, but Rhiannon shot her a look of pure anger, and she decided to let it go for now.

She didn't like it though – it felt really invasive, especially now, when they were so at odds over her continuing to see her beloved. And it seemed as though Rhiannon could – and would – use that power of hers to manipulate her, to try to influence her to break up with Rowan for no good reason.

She wanted to scream out her fury, but she realised she'd achieve nothing by doing that. There would be other ways, she mused, but for now she just needed to focus on their project so she could be alone again. They settled down and opened their school books, getting out what they'd each written and comparing notes and theories. When they both felt confident that they had it down, Rhiannon packed up her school bag, moved to the door and offered Carlie a half-hearted wave as she stepped out onto the landing. "I'll see you tomorrow, right?" she asked plaintively, threateningly.

Carlie nodded, then stayed on the floor where she'd been lying, not seeing her friend out. Luther came in and rubbed the top of his head against her hand, and she patted him until he was purring loudly and she had begun to feel calmer. Such a non-judgemental creature. She was so grateful to him. And to Rose.

Then she sighed. Could Rhiannon be right? Suddenly she heard Rowan's words in a different light – that because he'd now be away this weekend, ruining their plans to spend that time together, he'd assumed she should drop everything and skip school in order to spend the day with him, just so they wouldn't miss out on seeing each other when he was busy. Which she'd thought was really sweet at the time – that he was so desperate to see her, and wanted to make up for the time they'd miss out on this week. That didn't mean he was manipulating her though, just that he loved her and wanted them to spend time together. *Right?*

Flopping over onto her back and staring up at the ceiling, she sighed again. If she believed Rhiannon, she'd turned into a horrible person – a liar, a bad friend, a user, a let down – and an idiot too, it would seem, unable to think for herself or make a decision, handing over her will and her power to someone else, and doing only what some guy wanted, being at his beck and call regardless of her needs.

But that wasn't true. She *wanted* to be with Rowan, for a start. And today *she* had offered to go with him to the hospital, he hadn't even asked her to. Plus he'd done so much for her since they'd met, from teaching her healing methods and helping her work towards her career dream, to being so supportive throughout the grieving period that she was only just beginning to emerge out of.

So, in that light, sacrificing a single day to comfort him when he was scared wasn't a big deal. Rhiannon was just looking for the bad in him – she was overlooking all his other traits, all his wonderful traits, and everything he had done for her...

Chapter 29

Dear Diary...

Feeling sad that there was tension between her and her friend again, especially over a guy, Carlie crawled over to her drawers and pulled out her mum's diary. It always seemed to provide some insight into what she was going through, although she had no idea how that could happen. But she was just so touched to be learning about how wonderful her mum's life had been, and how deeply she'd been loved, and in love. She was still puzzled about what had made her move across the world though, leaving her friends and family forever, with no explanation or even farewell...

Dear Diary,
Oh goddess, I've done it, and I don't know how I feel. This morning I left home. It was so hard, but knowing that I'm saving Dad's life by leaving sure made it doable. And it made my last ritual with Mum last night all the more precious. It was Mabon, the festival of Demeter and Persephone, of mothers and daughters, of gratitude and harvest and love. And it was beautiful, really powerful and sweet. I sent prayers to the goddess all the way through it, begging her to keep Mum and Dad safe, to let them recover from me leaving and be happy together.

Mum did ask if I was okay when we got home, but I told her I was just tired, and needed to get to bed, and she believed me. It made me sad that she did to be honest. I think part of me really hoped that she'd somehow figure it out, and stop me going. But I kissed her goodnight, then went up to bed and lay awake all night, too nervous to sleep, too scared I'd miss the train and my plan would be ruined.

But it went off without a hitch. I got up as soon as there was some light in the sky, crept downstairs with my backpack and let myself out the back door. I left a note, saying I was fine but I had to go away for a while, that I'd be in touch. And then I caught the train into the city. Andre was waiting for me when I got there this afternoon, as planned, and he brought me back to the B&B, which is really sweet. I think I'll like it here.

He can't stay tonight because he has some things to sort out with his ex-wife, but I don't mind that at all – I'm feeling a bit sad and mopey, which I guess is to be expected. I'm just nervous, and of course I have regrets about leaving, and not being able to tell Mum and Dad why I'm going. I know they'll be worried, but I had no choice – I couldn't stay there and be the reason that Dad dies. I'd rather never see my parents again, but know that they are well and happy and alive, than selfishly stay there and basically kill my dad.

I'll miss them so much though. I'm not sure I'll be able to cope without them, but I must stay strong. And I worked out the perfect spell to cast before I left, which I've copied into my Book of Shadows, a spell to draw a daughter to me, who will grow up stronger and better than I could ever hope to be, and step in to fill the hole in their hearts. I feel terrible about leaving them, especially Mum, because we loved working together, and I know her dream was to leave her healing centre to me. But I'm not strong enough. I can't challenge the gods and ignore what the reading said, even if it's not true. I'd spend my whole life waiting for some catastrophe to happen, wondering each morning if this was the day I'd do something stupid – or not do something – and cause my father's death.

So, tonight I'm just going to run a bath and read for a little while, then set up my altar and say a few prayers for Mum and Dad. And for me and Andre. And while part of me is really sad about leaving, part of me is really excited too. Lots of people leave home when they're seventeen, to start their grown-up life, to be independent, to grow into themselves… My new life begins now, and I can't wait!

It's been a week since I left home, and being with Andre is everything I could have hoped for and more! He's so wonderful, and he treats me so well. I'm still in the B&B, while he sorts out the house, but he comes by at least once a day, and spends most of his nights here, which is amazing (blush). He's so kind and caring and thoughtful – he brings me over meals or takes me out, and the one time he couldn't be here for dinner he sent his assistant over with food so I wouldn't have to trouble myself going out. Who thinks of things like that!

He's generous too. Until we move into our house (our house!) there's no point me looking for a job, so he's given me some money so I can feel independent – enough to get the bus to the library or go across to the supermarket and get food or whatever. He thinks he might be able to get me a job with his manager too, which would be amazing, although I'd like to keep doing some healing work, like I was doing at Mum's. I'm trying not to think about how much they must miss me, or how much I miss them. Kids leave home all the time at my age, so it's not so weird, right?

When Andre came over last night he said I'd have to stay here a bit longer, as there have been delays with the house or something. Which is fine, I do like it here. It's nice to have a bit of space as I get used to being away from home, although I hope it's not for too much longer. I want to start my new life! And Andre said he'd rather that I don't go out exploring on my own, just for my own safety, which was odd. He assured me it will be different once we have our house and it's my own neighbourhood, but he said he worries about me, being on my own here.

It was a bit weird, I must admit. Yesterday was the only time I've been out on my own, and I just went to the library to see if I could borrow some books then came straight back. I'm not even sure how he knew I'd been gone to be honest, but he was being so lovely, and was so concerned, so of course I assured him I wouldn't go out without him. It's only a small concession on my

part, and he has enough to worry about right now, so I don't want to cause him any extra stress.

Today he brought a girl called Jasmine over to meet me. She's the daughter of his manager, and takes part in his local shamanic circle, and she's really sweet. He had to leave to teach a two-day workshop, and he didn't want me to be alone all weekend, so she offered to stay with me while he was gone. I said I'd be fine – I'm a big girl – so she didn't insist, but she told me to call her if I ever need anything, even if I just want to chat. She's so lovely – she's probably around thirty or something, and she's so caring, and kind of motherly almost. I hope we'll be really good friends. I must confess that I miss Mike a lot, much more than I imagined I would. So it was really nice to have Jasmine here for a while, to just have someone to talk to, to joke with, to be silly with. Andre's very much an adult, so I try to be a bit more serious – and a little less goofy – around him...

Sorry I haven't written for a while Diary! We had a few days together when he got back from the workshop, and we spent the whole time here, ordering in food, just staying in, talking, kissing, laughing. It was like playing house, and I can't wait until we can finally move in to the new place. Plus I've been really busy reading and taking notes, which is leaving me no time to write.

Andre gave me all these books to study, really heavy texts about shamanism and healing and soul mates and quantum physics and all kinds of things, and they've been fascinating. It was strange though, once I'd finished reading them all, he grilled me on the subjects, like he didn't trust me that I'd read them – but then he invited me to be part of his main teaching circle. I guess it was some kind of test, to make sure I knew enough about his work, was "enlightened" enough for him. Lucky I passed I suppose!

Words can't even begin to describe how amazing it was to sit in the circle with him, and the other people in the group, and work magic together for the first time. I'd been really missing that, since Mum and I used to do rituals all the time – new moon, full moon, dark moon. Solstice, equinox, cross-quarter day… I'm going to learn so much from Andre, grow so much, I just know it. And Jasmine is part of the circle too, which was such a relief, especially the first time, to have someone I knew there.

I've been a few times now, and Jasmine said the other night how different Andre is with me, compared to past girlfriends, and how much he must care about me and want to be with me. It made me feel all warm and gooey inside. I mean, he tells me he loves me, and I finally do believe him, but he must have been in love with a lot of people before me, so it meant so much to me to know that he's different with me, that I'm special to him in some way. Jasmine also told me that he's never let previous girlfriends or even wives be an important part of the rituals. That just meant the world to me!

Hooray! We've finally moved into our place, and it's amazing! It's sort of a townhouse or something – it's as big as a house, but there are a few other apartments on our floor. When I walked in for the first time I just burst into tears. Happy tears! This is our home, where we will make our life together.

I wish Mike could see me here, see how much I love my life. Then he'd know he didn't need to be suspicious, or doubt Andre's motives. But I've got to stop thinking about Mike – I have to put my past behind me and move forward. Because it's such an awesome life to move forward into. Of course I miss Mum and Dad, and all my old friends, but the time I spend with Andre is so beautiful, and working together with his main circle is just mind blowing. We do rituals together, and it's so much more powerful than anything I've ever experienced before, even with Mum.

Jasmine told me that since I joined the circle, and it's become clear that we're in love and together (it was a secret at first, but Andre finally told them because he said he didn't want to keep it quiet any longer), we've brought a whole new dimension to the group's work – that our relationship and the love and trust we share has pushed the magic further and higher and made it more powerful than it ever was before.

And we're achieving amazing things as a circle – we've done some healing ceremonies that have been incredible, and so many people have thanked us for making them well. So I'm doing what I always planned I'd do – helping people, doing healing work – I'm just doing it for more people, with even better results. I can't have any regrets about that!

The sound of the front door opening made Carlie hastily wrap the diary back up in its many tissue paper layers and return it to its hiding spot at the bottom of her drawer, but she was smiling, and feeling so much more peaceful than she had been when Rhiannon had left a little while ago. She knew that something bad must happen to her mum soon – something that would send her fleeing across the ocean to the other side of the world to get away from it – but it made her so happy to know that, for a while at least, she'd really loved her life, her spiritual, inspired-by-Rose life.

She'd found meaning and purpose, and great passion – she'd been loved and adored and cherished by a man she seemed to almost worship, and who others obviously admired so much. And although Violet had doubted for a while that someone so wonderful could love her, she'd finally managed to accept it, which meant that her mum had loved and been loved by three extraordinary men in her lifetime – her childhood best friend and first love Mike, the mysterious Andre, and later Oliver, the man she'd married and had a child with, and spent the rest of her life with.

And maybe it wasn't Andre that had been the problem that made her flee? Maybe it was something else? Either way, it was so lovely to feel that what she was experiencing now with Rowan had echoes in what her mum had had with her "older shaman guru guy", as Rhiannon called him. She herself had felt unworthy of being loved by someone so amazing at first too, just as her mum had, but through her relationship with Rowan she was starting to recognise her own light, acknowledge her own worthiness. His love for her and his amazing kindness and support was making her more confident, helping her see her own potential and how much she could achieve, and the many different ways she could help people.

Most of all, his love was helping her heal. Being held in the safety of his arms was allowing her shattered heart to reassemble itself, or start to at least. His compassion for her was helping to fill the gaping void that the death of her parents had left within her. The sheer happiness she felt when she was with him was a soothing balm to her soul. And the joy she felt in loving him back was giving her the space and serenity to grow, to blossom, to let go of her bitterness and the anger that had been poisoning her heart. She was a better person through loving and being loved by him, and it was even sweeter to know that her mum had felt the exact same emotions and the exact same deep healing with Andre that she was experiencing now through her own love story with Rowan.

As she skipped downstairs to help Rose make dinner, and spend some time catching up with her, Carlie felt light and almost carefree. She still had lots of sad moments, and she regretted constantly that her mum and Rose couldn't have been reunited, that her grandma never got to meet her dad, and that her grandpa Louis never knew that Violet was okay. But she was so grateful for her life here – for her friend Rhiannon, for her lovely grandmother, and especially for Rowan. It might have all turned bad in the end for her mum and her shaman guru guy, she didn't know, but Carlie had a very good feeling about her own future with *her* sweet shaman...

Chapter 30

Meet the Parent

The next couple of weeks flew by, with extra homework as Carlie and Rhiannon prepared for their term gradings and exams, and lots of research being done together on their coven nights as they prepared for the winter solstice. The girls had smoothed over their tension about Rowan somewhat – it certainly helped that Rhiannon was so preoccupied with the Yule Ball planning committee and had extra meetings with them, which gave Carlie the freedom to see lots of her boyfriend without feeling that she had to explain herself to her friend or feel guilty for wanting to be with him.

The Saturday before Yule, she got the early bus over to Rowan's so she could spend the day with him. He was facilitating a retreat over the solstice and would be away for several days, so they were trying to cram in as much time together as they could before that. They went for breakfast at their favourite cafe, then lingered over pots of tea, catching up on their lives, and dreaming about all the time they'd have to spend together over Christmas, when Rowan's retreat was finished and Carlie had two weeks of school holidays.

Finally he looked at his watch, then stood up. "Come on, let's get out of here. Did you want to try those recipes today?"

She nodded, and they wandered back to his apartment and through to the kitchen. Carlie unpacked her bag, which was full of herbs, some fresh, some dried, while Rowan got out a chopping board, some glass bowls, a mortar and pestle and his boline, the special white-handled knife for cutting herbs. He was helping her create some herbal bath oils and potions as part of her Yule present for Rose, because she wanted to let her grandmother know how much she appreciated all the lessons she'd been teaching her, and how dedicated she was to the magical path that she'd been exploring with her and with Rhiannon.

A knock made them both freeze for a moment, remembering the last time it had happened, then Carlie laughed. "Go on, answer it. I won't run away this time," she promised, kissing his cheek then turning back to the herbs she was chopping.

"It could be my mum," he warned her. "She really wants to meet you. And, um, I may have told her you'd be here today."

She pulled a face, but shrugged. "Unless you're worried that she won't approve of me?" she asked, raising one eyebrow.

"My love, she'll adore you. And she's been wanting to meet you for a while now – it's not me who's too embarrassed to introduce you to my circle," he said, then smiled to take the sting out of his words. "Just joking! But I wouldn't care if she didn't approve. I love you, and that's all that matters." He kissed her again, then went to answer the door before the person could knock for a third time.

"Hi Mum," she heard him say, loud enough for her to catch, and a shiver of nerves went through her before he came back into the kitchen with a tall red-headed woman in tow.

"Mum, this is Carlie," he said. "Carlie, my mum Louisa."

Carlie put down the knife and walked over towards her, arm outstretched to shake hands and greet her. "It's lovely to meet you Mrs Dunbar," she said warmly, and she genuinely was happy to finally meet her. Surely Rhiannon couldn't complain any more, after she'd spent the day with Rowan's mum! Clearly he wasn't trying to hide her from the people in his life, as Rhi had claimed.

So preoccupied with thinking all of this was she that it took her a moment to realise that his mother was still standing in the doorway, face frozen, expression blank, as though she'd seen a ghost, or worse.

Rowan turned to her, clearly surprised by her silence. "Mum?" She spun around to him, shock still etched into her features, but when she saw his expression she took a deep breath, made a huge effort to relax her face, smiled at her son, then turned back to his stunned girlfriend.

"Hi Carlie," she began nervously, moving over and taking her hand, then folding her into an awkward embrace. "I apologise, you must think I'm very strange. You just reminded me so much of someone I knew a long time ago." Obviously still rattled, she paused for a moment, trying to regain her composure and steady her voice.

"I'm so glad to meet you at last though. Rowan has been talking about you for weeks, and I've never heard him so enraptured by someone. You really bring out the best in him, and I thank you for that," she said, gently letting her go, and seeming much calmer.

Rowan put the kettle on, but Carlie said she'd make the tea while they caught up. She was desperate to keep busy as she tried to figure out what that had all been about. His mum's reaction to her had unsettled her, but finally she shrugged it off, and the three of them had a lovely afternoon, his mum reminiscing about what Rowan had been like as a kid – cheeky and mischievous mostly, and always wanting to heal the family pets – which embarrassed him, but had Carlie in fits of giggles.

After they finished their third pot of tea, Louisa stood up and told them that she really should go, and let them have some time together. "It was so lovely to meet you Carlie," she said, smiling, and her pleasure was clear this time. Giving her a big hug, his mum lowered her voice and whispered in her ear.

"Thanks again – you make Rowan so happy, and that's all a mother could ask for. I'm so sorry I won't ever be able to meet your mum and dad, but you're a credit to them. You're an amazing young woman, and I can't wait to spend more time with you." Then Rowan walked Louisa down to her car, while Carlie leaned up against the sink, overcome with emotion. Maybe his mum really had liked her.

"She loved you," Rowan said when he returned.

A smile lit up her face. "Really?"

"How could she not?" he grinned, then pulled her into his arms. "Come here. There hasn't been enough hugging today." Carlie melted into his embrace, then suddenly she started laughing, and he let her go, mock glaring as he asked her what was wrong.

"Nothing's wrong, I'm just remembering that incident at your primary school one long-ago autumn equinox," she giggled.

Rowan half smiled, half grimaced. "Well, I'm just glad you finally got to meet Mum. She's been asking me when she could see you for a while now. And she was really happy that she finally got the chance to. And she wasn't joking, she's told me a few times that I've been a nicer person since I met you – more caring, more considerate. And it's true. Loving you, being loved by you, it's changed me. You've changed me. I love you so much Carlie."

Leaning forward, she kissed him, feeling relieved and grateful. "You've helped me be a better person too, and helped me deal with my grief, helped me heal. And I'm really glad I got to meet your mum. Now I feel even closer to you, like I know you a bit better or something."

"Even though some of those stories were a bit on the embarrassing side?" he asked wryly.

"Especially because of that," she giggled. Then her face turned serious. "Rhiannon can't complain now, surely. You're obviously not trying to hide me away from the people in your life if you invited your mum over to meet me."

Rowan shook his head. "I'm so sorry my love, I know Rhiannon's disapproval of me is making things difficult for you. Please let me know if I can do anything to help. I hope she'll eventually realise how much I love you, and lose her distrust of me, because it's killing me to see how sad this is making you. And I'm disappointed in her, that she's hurting you so much."

Carlie smiled, so grateful for his patience. Then she saw the clock and panicked – the last bus was leaving soon, and she had to be on it. They quickly finished the potions and bottled them in pretty glass jars, then Rowan insisted on driving her home, so they could steal a few more precious moments together.

Chapter 31

A Midwinter Night's Dream

School let out early the day of the Yule Ball, so everyone could go home and get ready. Rhiannon had been at the venue all day with the rest of the committee, decorating the place, getting the food sorted and overseeing the soundcheck of the band they'd chosen, but she met Carlie back at her place afterwards, so they could get ready together and psyche themselves up for the night.

Carlie had been floored when she realised how much the approaching festive season was making her miss her parents even more. People often said holidays like Christmas made grieving harder than usual, but she hadn't believed it – it didn't make any sense to her. And yet it was proving to be true.

Rhiannon had been a great support – she'd experienced the same thing the year before, on her first Christmas without her mother, and this year wasn't much easier for her. In addition, she was feeling guilty that she'd been so excited about the Yule Ball and being part of the planning committee, but Carlie finally convinced her to see that she had no need to feel bad – and she was honouring the magic she'd shared with her mum by including their ritual foods in the catering.

Carlie had to admit that she was also feeling shy about spending the night with so many people she didn't know. Although she occasionally chatted to other people at school, she spent most of her time there with Rhiannon, or racing out the door to meet Rowan, and hadn't become close to anyone else. Plus there were a few other schools involved, and all their students would be there too.

"You won't leave me on my own for too long will you Rhi?" she implored her friend. "I know you have to do a bit of committee stuff, but we'll be able to spend most of the night together, won't we?"

Her friend nodded. "Of course, and I can't wait. It will be so nice to be able to hang out together and just have fun. Relaxing, dancing, chilling out – no homework, no coven research, no planning meetings, no boys – just us, having a good time."

Carlie smiled gratefully. It was weird, that in spite of their tensions over Rowan, she felt much closer to Rhiannon than to Emily, her best friend from her old life, and she knew that was in no small part due to their shared grief. Rhi just *got* her so much more than anyone else could, she understood her pain, her guilt, her fear. But it wasn't just that. She also felt more herself with Rhiannon than she'd ever been before – which wasn't fair to Emily, because she'd really only become her true self after her parents died and she was set adrift, emotions laid bare, and forced to grow up and really comprehend her own self, and the depths, and shallowness, of her own heart.

Rhiannon had gone through her own dark night of the soul, and her own growing up and into herself, when her mother died. And it was through her conversations with her friend, and her observation of her kindness and caring, that Carlie had understood the dream she'd had her whole life – to be a lawyer like her mum – was not in fact her dream, but her family's.

When she'd spent time alone, thinking about her life and her losses, and seen the way Rhiannon was coping with the aftermath of her mum's death while helping her dad and her brother heal too, and the wisdom she'd been able to share with her, she'd realised just how much she wanted to help others in her position, young people experiencing loss, trying to navigate their way through the pain and anger of grief and get to a place of acceptance.

Sometimes she wondered what would have happened to her if she'd still been living in Sydney with her parents – would she have gone to university and become a lawyer as she'd always planned, and have dedicated herself to that? Or would she have still somehow come to the same realisation that she had here, that it wasn't actually what she wanted to do with her life? She didn't know, and she supposed it was no use worrying over it, because her life now was here, and wishing for something else would be pointless.

Trying to shake away this train of thought, she wondered why she was getting so deep all of a sudden, when she should be getting ready for the ball. Did she feel guilty still, guilty that life was going on for her, that she was learning how to laugh again, how to enjoy herself? She would never stop missing her parents, or grieving their loss, but it wasn't all-consuming any more, like it had been six months ago, and while she supposed that was a good thing, it still kept her up at night, making her feel bad.

Wrenching her attention back to the present, she vowed to remember every moment of tonight's rite of passage, even the getting-ready-with-her-friend part. She smiled as Rhiannon twirled around the room in her bright red dress with its holly leaves, laughing joyfully at the way it fell around her, then moving over to the dressing table to start putting on her make-up. Smoky eyes and blood-red lips, with vampy nail polish to match.

They were in her mum's old bedroom, because it was so much bigger than her own. Rose had offered for her to swap rooms, but she wasn't ready for that yet. There were enough ghosts in her life. But tonight they needed the space to get dressed and to spread out Rhiannon's make-up, and room to stand by the large mirror and check out their dresses and do their hair. Forcing a less sombre mood, Carlie pulled her own dress on, then added deep purple lipstick and dark plum eyeshadow, and clipped a few long white hair pieces through her dark curls, adding an extra touch of winter to her outfit.

They both turned as they heard a gasp at the door, and saw Rose there, smiling at them through eyes misting with tears.

"Oh girls, you look so beautiful. And Sweetheart, I remember your mum trying that dress on for the ball she didn't end up going to." She stepped into the room, and handed Rhiannon a red velvet box. "Here's a little gift for you, I hope you like it," she said.

Intrigued, Rhiannon opened the lid, and tears welled in her eyes. The box held a stunning silver necklace that incorporated huge pieces of garnet in variously sized teardrop shapes, and matching earrings. It went perfectly with her dress and make-up.

"Oh Mrs Tyler, they're so beautiful! But I couldn't..."

"Nonsense sweet girl, as soon as this one came into the shop I knew it was for you," she explained. "It's just a small gift to show my appreciation for your wisdom and the friendship and support you've so effortlessly offered to Carlie. Your mum would be so proud of you – not just tonight, seeing you blossoming into a beautiful young lady, but knowing what a fine person you've become, how caring you are, how strong."

Rhiannon walked across the room and hugged the older woman. "Thank you," she whispered. "You have no idea how much I've always appreciated you, how much we all have, and how important you've been to me all my life, not just recently."

Rose was deeply moved, and took a moment to compose herself before she handed a purple velvet box to Carlie. Her granddaughter's eyes widened as she looked inside. Nestled on the fabric was a stunning deep violet amethyst crystal, set amongst several sparkling clear quartzes. "I bought it for your mother, hence the violet, to wear to her Yule Ball, but of course she never went. I thought you might like to wear it tonight, and to have it," Rose said, trying to smile.

Carlie's eyes sparkled with tears. "Oh Gran, it's beautiful. And it goes so perfectly with this dress."

Rose nodded sadly, and watched as Carlie did the necklace up and added the matching earrings. Shaking her head, she tried to clear the image of her long-lost daughter from her mind, but it was hard, seeing her granddaughter wearing the same dress, the same jewellery, having the same long dark hair, the same smile.

"Now off you go, you don't want to be late," she said, voice wavering with emotion, and walked back down to the kitchen to put the kettle on. There was so much sadness in this moment, of what she had lost, but so much joy too, and so much gained. She knew she was lucky, despite the tragedies that had defined her life...

Carlie and Rhiannon pulled their coats carefully on over their dresses, picked up their masquerade masks, and made their way down to the High Street, where the school bus was waiting to take them all to the dance. Their cheeks were flushed with excitement, and they barely felt the cold as they met up with their classmates, who were eagerly chatting about what the night had in store for them.

Despite Rhiannon being on the organising committee, she hadn't revealed any details yet, so speculation began to grow.

"There'll be a band," shouted one girl, who was dressed as a winter faery. "There's got to be a band."

Rhiannon raised her eyebrows coolly and just smiled. "Maybe," she teased. "Who can tell?"

There were catcalls from the back of the bus, and pleas for her to talk, but she refused to confirm or deny.

"Mistletoe – there'd better be mistletoe, and lots of it!" one of the boys, who was dressed as Saint Nick, yelled.

"And spicy apple and cinnamon punch," added another.

"And lots of cute guys from the other schools," said one of the girls. Everyone laughed, but Carlie noticed that Rhiannon blushed at that comment, and she made a mental note to grill her about it later. By the time they arrived at the Smithfield High gymnasium where it was being held, they were all in high spirits. They clattered down the bus steps, the girls giggling in their unfamiliar high strappy shoes, the boys trying to look as dignified as they could in their borrowed suits. There were some wonderful costumes, and when they all slipped their masks on, it added a heightened sense of reality, and a very real atmosphere of mystery and romance.

A few of the guys from their school were in Santa costumes, some were elves, and three had dressed as Zorro, to fit in with the masked ball angle, and there were a couple of Batmans too, which Carlie thought was creative, and brave.

Some of the girls were dressed as angels, with pretty gold masks like the old-style Venetian ones, there were a few Santa and Mrs Clauses, and lots of faeries and woodland sprites. Rhiannon was the only Holly Maiden though, and Carlie was the only Snow Queen, which they were very happy about.

Pausing in the entranceway, Carlie looked around and smiled. She'd seen the gymnasium earlier in the week when she'd come over with Rhiannon, before the committee had started work on it and it was still a bare, draughty room, devoid of all warmth or character. But Rhiannon and her fellow students had totally transformed it. Now it looked like a faerytale realm, with rich red and gold velvet drapes covering the bare walls, a huge golden chandelier casting light and shadows from the high ceiling, and tiny twinkling faery lights strung everywhere.

A beautifully decorated pine tree stood in one corner, giving off an intense, crisp scent, and weighed down with tinsel and red and gold streamers. Silver stars hung from the boughs, and more faery lights looped themselves around it.

Along one wall there were benches, covered in vividly coloured fabrics and groaning under the weight of so many yummy foods – platters of cupcakes topped with green icing holly leaves and red icing berries, cinnamon cookies, mince tarts and chocolate crackles, bowls of candy canes and stacks of faery bread. On a side table there were several bowls of spicy apple cider with cinnamon sticks floating in them – the boy on the bus would be pleased – and some of grape punch, and in the centre was a huge chocolate Yule log cake, which she and Rhiannon had made the night before, and which looked even better, and more festive, than she'd expected.

She turned to Rhiannon and hugged her. "You've done such an amazing job, it looks really awesome! I can't believe the transformation. You guys should go into events management!"

Rhiannon hugged her back, eyes shining with joy. "Yeah, it turned out pretty well didn't it? And now I just have to check in with the committee," she said, before blushing furiously.

Carlie stared at her. "Hey, what's going on?" she asked.

"Well, John is on the committee too, and I really like him," she said softly, suddenly looking shy and unsure of herself.

"Wait, what?" Carlie shrieked, before Rhiannon shushed her. "Who's John? Why haven't you told me about him? Is he nice? Oooh, which one is he?"

"He's the tall fair-haired one over there, dressed as the Oak King. He's from Smithfield High, and he's really sweet. We get on really well, he's so smart and funny and kind, but he doesn't like me like that," she explained, eyes downcast. "I don't think he really noticed I was a girl, to be honest."

"Oh Rhi, how could he not notice you, you're adorable!" Carlie said. "And you look so beautiful, so radiant. Plus you match – did he know you were coming as the Holly Maiden?"

"I'm not sure, but yeah, I guess we do match," she grinned. "But what about you?" her friend asked, voice suddenly hopeful.

"I'm fine, honestly. Now go and say hello to him before someone else does," Carlie insisted.

She smiled as Rhiannon floated over to a group of people she'd never seen before, then she filled a cup with punch and stood on the edge of the dance floor, watching people dance, trying to work out who they were dressed as, and daydreaming about seeing Rowan again. Suddenly she realised a guy on the other side of the room was staring at her. He was dressed as the Stag King, with antlers on his head and an intricate mask, and pale leather pants and no shirt. He was getting lots of sideways looks from the girls there for his amazing physique, and he did look incredible. When their gaze locked he started sauntering towards her, and her breath caught in her throat.

"Hey baby," he said huskily, when he reached her side. He slid his arm around her waist and pulled her in close. "You look beautiful tonight, as always."

"Rowan, what are you doing here?" she hissed. "This is just for school kids. How did you even know it was on, or where it was being held? And aren't you supposed to be at your retreat now?" she asked, looking around nervously, hoping no one had noticed him. Hoping Rhiannon hadn't noticed him.

"You mentioned it once, a few weeks back, and it's in my home town – I have a few friends who live around here. As far as anyone knows, I'm Paul from Smithfield High – he's sick, so I came in his place." He smiled that sexy smile, and Carlie could feel her happiness that he was there warring with her fear that he'd be discovered and she would end up in trouble. Or even worse, get Rhiannon in trouble.

"And yes, I should be at the retreat now, but as long as I make it by early tomorrow morning it will be fine," he whispered. "I just had to see you my love, I've missed you so much. I can't bear being away from you. When can we tell people we're together? I need you Carlie."

His grip on her tightened, and while she loved knowing he missed her as much as she did him, part of her was alarmed that he'd turned up. He'd wanted them to be a secret because of his teaching, and she'd told him they had to stay low profile too, to avoid Rhiannon's wrath for a start. God, she hoped his costume would hold up to scrutiny. Then she grinned. It – well, what little there was of it – was certainly being scrutinised by all the girls there, and she had to admit she liked it too. She'd never seen him with his shirt off, it was winter after all, but he really was gorgeous.

Noticing Rhiannon heading towards them, she grabbed Rowan's arm. "Come on, let's dance," she blurted, and dragged him out onto the floor. They danced for what seemed like hours, slow songs and fast songs, and her heart beat a little bit faster every time his hand brushed hers. She felt herself starting to drown in his eyes again, but every time she forced herself to break the intensity of their gaze, the way his mask sat meant that she found herself focused on his lips instead, and imagining how amazing it felt when he kissed her.

Oops, she was getting distracted. She had to pay attention, keep Rhiannon from seeing him. But when he pulled her closer as the music slowed again, she felt herself melting into him. His lips came down on hers, and she felt herself floating away, intoxicated by the magic of the night, the nearness of his body and the connection she felt between them. Head spinning, she kissed him back, only returning to the room when the music stopped and the principals from her school and Smithfield High stepped up to the microphone.

"We just wanted to wish you all a magical Yule and an enchanted festive season, and we're so happy to see so many of you from different schools introducing yourselves, getting to know each other, coming together and having fun," one said.

"We don't want to keep you from the festivities, but we just wanted to thank all of the organising committee – Rhiannon, Tracy, Karen and Peter from Summer Hill High, Lynn, Cameron, John and Annalie from Smithfield High, and Luke, Simone, Helen and Claire from Maryborough High," the other added.

"You've done such an amazing job, in such a short amount of time, and the hall looks magnificent. Everyone, can we give them all a big round of applause?" Enthusiastic cheers rang out around the room. "And you'll all have extra credit noted on your report cards this semester," he finished, to more cheers, especially from the organising committee.

Carlie waved over at Rhiannon, who was at the side of the stage with the rest of the group, blushing a little, but smiling widely. She was relieved to see that she was standing next to John and they seemed to be getting on well – she was happy for her friend, and hopeful that she'd gather the courage to tell the guy she liked him. And, she had to admit, she was also grateful that it was keeping her occupied and away from Rowan.

"Now, it's time to reveal the Winter Queen and the Sun King, and this year it makes us very happy to announce that they are from different schools, furthering the ties we've been hoping to forge in the wider community. These two have the most fitting costumes, being the Snow Queen and the Stag King – either great planning or a wonderful coincidence. So, Carlie Parker from Summer Hill High, and Paul Vickers from Smithfield High, please come forward, and then you can start the next dance."

Carlie stood frozen in shock as the spotlight was angled at them. Bad enough she was being singled out, but to be singled out with Rowan, who wasn't even a student? Now everyone would know, and she'd be in trouble, and Rhiannon would suffer too – or simply hate her. She wasn't sure which was worse.

Incapable of thought, let alone action, she slowly became aware that Rowan had taken her hand, kissing it as he bowed low over it, and was now dragging her forward to the stage. The Smithfield principal shook her hand then placed a diamante tiara on her head, which went beautifully with her necklace, while the principal from her school handed Rowan a gold-plated crown, which he wrapped around his upper arm then squeezed closed, so it sat like an ancient Celtic armband on his impressively muscled bicep.

Then, before "Paul"'s principal could realise it wasn't him behind the mask, Rowan swept Carlie back onto the dance floor and began the dance. They were soon joined by heaps of other couples, including Rhiannon and John, and the whole room seemed to shake as everyone joined in. Relief swept over her, and she finally felt herself relax a little.

When the song was over, Rowan weaved her gently out of the crowd to the back of the room, then towards the back stairs. "Let's go outside for a bit, so we can be alone," he urged.

She shook her head, not sure she wanted to leave the safety of the room, but his grip on her tightened and he steered her out the door and over beside a tree. He started kissing her again, harder and more forcefully than he had before, pushing her up against the rough bark of the tree trunk.

"Stop," she gasped, trying to catch her breath. "We have to go back inside."

He shook his head. "No, we need to be alone together," he said, voice ragged with longing. "I want you to know how much I miss you Carlie, how badly I want you."

Panic flickered through her as she finally realised she was in way over her head. Despite his protests that he was happy to wait, he wanted more than she was prepared to give, and it sounded like he was determined to get it tonight, whether she wanted to or not. Could the fortune teller have been right?

Rowan stepped back suddenly, as if sensing her turmoil and her desire to escape, or her awful final thought.

"Sorry baby, I just miss you so much," he said softly, regret turning his voice husky. "You look so beautiful tonight, and I've been so desperate to see you all week. I just want to hold you, just want to be with you," he pleaded, and she felt the emotion in his words, felt the truth of his feelings.

"And I wanted to give you this, so you know just how much I love you," he finished. And he pulled a small blue velvet box from his pocket and handed it to her. For the second time that night she froze. Her breath caught in her throat, and for a moment she seemed unable to move, or to think. Gently he touched his fingers to hers, helping her open it. "Don't panic, it's just a small thing to remind you of me," he said, as her eyes caught the dazzle of the moonlight on a small clear stone set on a beautifully engraved silver ring.

"It's called a herkimer diamond, but it's just a crystal," he explained softly. "I have one too, its twin," he added, pulling the small stone out of his pocket to show her.

"It binds two people together, joins their souls and makes it impossible for other people to tear them apart, no matter how hard they try. It's a great healing stone too, which is perfect, because you are a healer, but mostly it's a stone of connection, of attuning two people to each other and drawing them to the same planes of consciousness, where they can stand together, equal. You're my *equal* Carlie," he said, emphasising the last bit, voice drenched in emotion as he reassured her that her greatest fear was unfounded. "There is no 'more than' or 'less than'. I love you totally, and fully, as much as you love me, if not more."

He lifted the ring from the box and placed it on the middle finger of her right hand – no connotations of marriage or engagement, she was pleased to note. "It's a friendship ring, if you will, a token of how I feel about you," Rowan said with a wide smile. "A token of my eternal love for you."

Reverently his hand traced her cheek, catching the tear that had fallen from her eye, then moved slowly down her neck until his fingers reached the necklace she was wearing. "This even matches the ring," he smiled. "It's perfect, like you."

"It was my mother's," she whispered, heart swelling with love and making it hard to breathe, let alone speak. "A violet for Violet, Gran said. She gave it to me tonight." He froze at her words, then pulled himself back a step, away from her.

"I thought your mother's name was Fiona," he said sharply.

She shrugged. "Her mum called her Violet," she replied, not wanting to go into it now, just wanting to focus on the beautiful gift he'd given her, on the promise it held. Maybe he wasn't just after one thing, as Rhiannon had been trying to convince her. Maybe he really did love her, as hard as that was to accept. She looked up at him. "Why?"

He smiled shakily. "No reason, it's just that I want you to know that I care about you, and that I do listen, so I was surprised that I'd misheard you on something so important." He held out his hand to her. "I don't only want to have sex with you Carlie, I love just being with you. I love *you*."

Taking a step towards him, hope shone in her eyes. "Really?" she asked. "But I'm not ready to, you know... And I'm so, well, I don't know. I'm nothing special."

Cupping her face with both hands, he stared into her eyes, and she felt her heart open wide with love and joy. "Carlie, you're more special than you know. How come you can't see that? How come you won't believe me?" he pleaded.

She shrugged helplessly. "I don't know. I'm just a normal girl, like anyone else. But you're so talented, so amazing. People look up to you, they learn from you. I'm nothing next to you."

"Oh Carlie," he said, and she felt the pain in his voice at her words, felt the love he had for her as he held her close. Intellectually she still couldn't believe that he loved her, but a small part of her felt the compassion and truth in his words, and responded to that, tried to hold on to that and will it to be true.

He drew her close, and for long moments they stood together, foreheads resting on each other's, heart connected to heart, souls speaking to each other, and she felt so warm and safe there that she never wanted to leave the circle of his arms.

Regretfully she straightened and broke away from him as she sensed footsteps behind her, then spun around when she heard her name being called. Rhiannon was standing there, arms folded against the chill in the air, and an apprehensive look on her face.

"Carlie," she repeated. "I couldn't find you, and I was so worried about you. Are you okay?"

Carlie nodded, and smiled. She was more than okay.

"And you must be Paul?" Rhiannon asked, turning to her companion. "Wait a minute," she said, fury turning her voice cold as she recognised him. "It's you!"

Rowan shrugged. "Hi Rhiannon, it's really lovely to see you again. You look beautiful. And congratulations on the ball, it's been such a wonderful night." Carlie winced. She knew he wasn't being sarcastic, but she also knew that her friend would probably take it that way, and she grimaced as Rhiannon's reply spewed forth.

"I can't believe you'd come here. How dare you? And what about Paul? Does he even exist? Why wasn't the school principal suspicious when you were crowned *prom* king?" she demanded. "You haven't been to school for years."

"Paul's a family friend, and when he told me he was sick and wasn't coming tonight, he offered me his ticket. I figured it would be simpler to just say I was him – with the mask nobody noticed. I thought it would be easier on everyone."

"Easier on *you* perhaps," Rhiannon spat. "What's Paul going to say at school when he finds out that he was not only crowned Sun King, but that everyone saw him making out with Carlie?"

"That is a small complication, but I'm sure he'll live it down – he might even be happy about it. I notice you weren't upset when you thought Carlie was cheating on me with Paul though," Rowan sighed. "Anyway, it's more than two weeks until school goes back, so most people will have forgotten." His arms tightened around Carlie's waist. "But I'm not here to cause trouble. I just came to see my beloved, and tell her how much I miss her."

Rhiannon rolled her eyes. "Missed having sex with her you mean. I saw you two out here."

"Rhiannon!" Carlie was shocked out of her silence. "It's not like that. We were just talking."

Her friend laughed meanly.

"And yes, we kissed once. But Rowan came here to tell me how much he loves me."

"Love?" Rhiannon asked derisively. "He wouldn't know the meaning of the word."

"That's not true!" Carlie said, tears in her eyes.

"Rhiannon, please," Rowan said softly, calmly, beseechingly. "Carlie's right, I came here because I love her, and that's the simple truth. But I don't want to cause any problems, especially tonight, because this is your night. So I'll go now, but please believe me that I adore your friend, and please know that you can't scare me off just because some little old lady who's never met either of us warned you that I was bad news."

Shock swept across Rhiannon's face at his words, but he turned to Carlie, cupped her face in his hands once more and gave her a long, sweet kiss. "I love you baby, hand on my heart, and I will never hurt you. I'll see you soon." And he slipped away into the night, blending into the trees, antlers and all.

Rhiannon turned to her friend to berate her, but paused when she saw the tears in her eyes and the pain on her face.

"How could you do that?" Carlie whispered.

"I'm just looking out for you," Rhiannon replied, but there was a note of hesitation in her voice.

"No, you're not. If you cared about me at all you'd know how happy he makes me, and how much he cares about me."

"He doesn't care Carlie. Remember the reading I had – the woman said he was bad news, and that he would hurt you, physically and emotionally. And remember Dad's stories about your mum's shaman guy too – I just want to protect you from all of that."

"No, you don't, you're just jealous that someone loves me. You're too shy to ask John out, so you just want me to be miserable too." As soon as she said it she regretted it, and the look on Rhiannon's face made her feel awful, but she continued.

"I'm sorry Rhi, I don't want to hurt you, but you have to butt out of this one. I've seen Rowan a lot lately, while you were so busy with the ball, and he really does care about me. He's never pressured me, and he won't. He came tonight to give me a present, look."

She held out her hand, and Rhiannon gasped when she saw the ring sparkling on her finger. "It's a friendship ring, a token of his love – his words, not mine. It's a herkimer diamond, and he has one too, part of a set of two. It means that we are bound together, and it's a promise that we will always return to each other, even if something – or *someone* – tries to part us."

Rhiannon raised her eyebrows again, but this time she looked less certain, and more impressed.

"I'm sorry Carlie, I really am. It would just kill me to see you hurt, because you've been through so much."

Carlie tried to smile, but it was a struggle. "I know, and I'm grateful for that, but you have to realise that *you* are actually the one who is hurting me. You have to trust me."

"I do trust you, I swear, I just don't trust him."

"Rhi, we've been through this."

"I mean it Carlie. There's something not quite right about him, about this situation, him chasing you, and coming here. You said before that he could have anyone..."

Carlie felt tears well in her eyes again. "So now you agree with me? You think I'm not special enough for him?"

"Of course not! You know I don't mean that, and that I think you're amazing. It's just..."

She broke off as one of the teachers came out the back door and called out to them to come back inside before they froze to death. Part of Carlie was glad their conversation had been interrupted, but another part of her was angry and upset, not at what Rhiannon had said, but at how her friend's doubts fed into her own and were making her question Rowan all over again. Which made her even angrier.

When they walked inside, John was standing at the door, obviously looking for Rhiannon. She hesitated, not sure whether to talk to him or to continue her conversation with her friend. But Carlie was not in the mood to chat, so she shook her head fiercely at Rhiannon, motioned for her to go to John, then turned her back on them and walked back into the crowd. Finding a seat on the far side of the press of dancers, she sat there alone, seething with anger. Looking down at the beautiful ring as she twisted it on her finger, her heart lifted as she remembered Rowan's face as he'd given it to her, the promise he'd whispered to her as he'd slid it on her finger.

Gently she pulled it off and placed it on the ring finger of her left hand, where it fit perfectly. She imagined Rowan smiling at her as he put it there, as they stood under a trellis of white roses and promised to love each other forever.

Then she rolled her eyes at her own silly thoughts. That was certainly letting her imagination run wild. There was time enough for wedding daydreams a few years from now. But she left the ring on that finger, and replayed their time together out under the oak tree in her mind, happiness rushing through her as she recalled his words of love and promise. A guy from her school came over to ask her to dance, but she shook her head and gazed off into the distance, more than content to just sit and daydream until this crazy night ended.

Finally the last song was announced, then people started gathering their coats and filing out to the buses. Rhiannon came over and stiffly told Carlie that she had to stay behind to clean up, and she was glad. She wanted to hold on to her joy, to this feeling of loving and being loved, for as long as possible, and she knew Rhiannon would spoil it. That thought made her sad, but she pushed it away, trying to remind herself that her friend was just concerned about her, as misguided as that worry was.

When the bus delivered them back to their village, Carlie floated home to the cottage and up the stairs to her room. She lay awake for hours in her cosy little bedroom, dreaming of Rowan's kisses – the sweet ones as well as the more demanding ones – and feeling surprised when she discovered that part of her wished she hadn't stopped him as soon as she had.

Chapter 32

Solstice Eve

The next morning she woke up angry, furious with Rhiannon for trying to tell her what to do, trying to ruin her relationship, and mad that she still felt bad about what she'd said to her friend in response, when it was Rhiannon who was in the wrong. But mostly she was devastated that she wouldn't see Rowan for the next few days, because his Yule retreat started that morning. He'd wanted so badly for her to be there with him, and she really wished she was.

Replaying Rhiannon's words from the night before over and over, she got madder with each repetition, feeling the injustice of the way her friend had treated Rowan. Finally she stomped downstairs to get some breakfast, trying hard to shake off her bad mood so she didn't inflict it on her grandmother. Who was smiling warmly at her and asking her how the ball had been.

"It was fine," she said, voice short, but the look on Rose's face snapped her out of her brooding, and she made an effort to smile, and be a little less crabby. It certainly wasn't her grandma's fault that she felt like this. "Sorry Gran, I'm just really tired and not feeling so great. But it was beautiful. Rhiannon and her friends did an amazing job. I danced a lot, and I was crowned Winter Queen, which was a bit embarrassing, but kind of sweet." She smiled at the memory of Rowan's arms around her as they started the dance, of his lips on hers as they stood outside under the oak tree. Then her grandma's voice brought her crashing back to the present, and she hoped she hadn't looked too far away.

"Oh Sweetheart, I'm so happy that you had a great night. I've been worried about you, because you've been so preoccupied. But I know how hard things like Christmas can be when you've lost your loved ones. I didn't even acknowledge the festive season for the first five years after Violet and Louis left me, so just be gentle with yourself. Check in with how you're feeling, and know that you're not obliged to do anything that will make you feel even sadder, even if people think it will be good for you. If you can't face people, you don't have to, no excuses necessary."

Carlie threw her arms around her grandma. How could anyone be so sweet, so kind, so perceptive, all the time? She certainly didn't deserve it. "Thank you," she said, voice choked with emotion. Rose wiped a tear from her own eye and hugged her back.

"I'm off to the healing centre now, but hopefully it will be fairly quiet today so that I can start setting up for the Yule ritual tonight. Did you want to come down and help me decorate?"

Carlie shook her head. "I'm not really feeling very well, so I thought I'd go back to bed for a while, if that's okay? And maybe I'll just go to Rhiannon's tonight and do a ritual with her, possibly stay the night. I don't want to bring the mood down if I'm too sad to be part of it, and I don't want to infect half the town if this is catching," she said, trying to sound sick.

She felt a flash of guilt at the concern on her grandma's face, but she wasn't sure she could face everyone at the ritual, or put herself in the right head space to weave magic. No doubt she'd ruin the whole thing with her anger and negativity, and she didn't want to be responsible for that.

Rose was staring at her, torn, worry in her eyes. "I feel terrible leaving you if you're not well, but there isn't anyone else who can open today. I'm so sorry Sweetheart, I didn't realise you were coming down with something, but I guess it is a lot colder here than you're used to. What can I do? Do you need me to make a herbal remedy, or should I call the doctor? We do have a 'proper' one in town."

Feeling bad that she was lying, Carlie took her grandma's hand. "I'll be fine, honestly. It's nothing serious, so please don't worry. I know how important this ritual is for you, for everyone, and I'll be there in spirit if I can't make it in person."

Rose looked somewhat appeased, so Carlie grabbed an apple and went back upstairs. She was surprised to realise that she really didn't feel that great, and bed sounded wonderful. So she crawled back under the covers and pulled her mum's old quilt up over her. A little while later she heard a knock on the front door, then Rose welcoming Rhiannon and leading her up the stairs. Carlie was relieved that her grandma's voice sounded much less worried than it had before.

"I'm so glad you're here sweet girl. Carlie isn't feeling too good, so she said she might just do her Yule ritual with you tonight, rather than come to the big one. I'm so happy that you two have created such a wonderful magical group. It does good things to my heart watching you both grow and blossom."

Their voices grew louder as they climbed the stairs, then Rose bustled into Carlie's tiny bedroom, kissed her goodbye, wished them both a blessed Yule, then hurried back downstairs and off to prepare for the solstice ritual.

Rhiannon stood in the doorway, clearly uncomfortable, and Carlie felt a moment of pleasure at that thought. But then she relented. This was her best friend after all. "Come in silly," she said, her smile only partly forced. "I hope you didn't have to stay too late last night cleaning up?" She paused as Rhiannon blushed. "Or was it a good thing that you had to stay back, because you got to talk more to John?"

Rhiannon's cheeks went a deeper shade of red.

"And he asked you out?" Carlie pressed. Her friend squealed with excitement, ecstatic that she could talk about it.

"Yes! He invited me to a concert they're having in their village this afternoon."

Carlie forced a smile. "I'm so happy for you," she said. And she was. Her friend might have bugged her last night, but she deserved some joy in her life. "So what's he like?" she asked, and Rhiannon finally relaxed.

Moving into the room, she came over and sat on Carlie's bed, grabbing her hands in excitement. "He's so lovely, and apparently he'd been wanting to ask me out too, but he wasn't sure whether I liked him, or was just being polite when we talked."

"Yeah, being polite can be a bitch," Carlie said, and they both laughed a little, relief mixing with humour.

"It was so nice though," Rhiannon continued. "I guess we were both more relaxed, and it was certainly good to not have a teacher involved in our conversation, like they were in our planning meetings. So we talked a bit, and danced a bit – even a slow one – and during the very last dance he kissed me!" she squealed, eyes shining with joy.

"What was it like?" Carlie asked, trying to sound interested.

"Well, we were both a bit shy – I know I'd been wanting to kiss him all night, and he said later that he'd wanted to kiss me all night too. But we finally did, and it was lovely. So gentle, so sweet," she smiled, and her eyes had the faraway look of someone contentedly reminiscing on a beautiful moment.

"So you're going to see him today?" Carlie interrupted.

"Yes! I mean, if that's okay with you?" she asked hesitantly, the worry on her face revealing that she desperately wanted to go, and that while she was asking her permission, she was counting on a yes. "I thought you'd be doing the ritual at the healing centre."

"Of course it's okay," Carlie said, forcing a lightness into her tone. "And although you've kept him a secret, I've guessed for a while that you like someone, and this is a great time to go see him – discover whether you still like him in the cold light of day," Carlie teased.

"His parents will be there though, and his younger brothers, so I'm a bit nervous," Rhiannon whispered, and Carlie did all she could to reassure her.

They talked for ages, giggling about some of the outfits from the ball, working out how Rhiannon could deal with the pesky little brothers if they tried to tease her, and mentally going through her wardrobe until she decided what to wear. But eventually she broke off, that topic exhausted, and looked uncomfortable again.

"Look Carlie, I'm really sorry about what I said last night," she said, sounding sincere.

Carlie forced a smile "It's okay," she muttered.

"But it's just that I worry about you," her friend blundered on. "I know you think you love him, but you're too young to commit to anyone. He's so much older than you, and... my god, he's so... well, I mean..." she stuttered.

Carlie glared at her. "He's so what?"

"Well, he's a guy, a hot-blooded grown-up guy, as everyone noticed last night with that outfit he was wearing, or not wearing, as the case may be. So he's going to want to have sex with you. If you haven't already –" she broke off.

Carlie was angry, yet calm. "Not that it's any of your business, but no, we haven't. He hasn't pressured me at all, he's happy to wait until I'm ready, no matter how long that takes. He actually likes talking to me, as surprising as that might sound to you," she said, sarcasm making her voice bitter.

Rhiannon looked sad. "I don't mean that Carlie, I promise."

Carlie shrugged, defensive now. "He's twenty-three. That's only six years older than me. Louis was ten years older than Grandma Rose, and they were very happily married."

"But it's a lot right now," Rhiannon argued. "You're in school, and he's travelling the country teaching, meeting hundreds of women who no doubt throw themselves at him. I'd just hate for him to hurt you, especially with what your mum went through, with the older shaman guru guy who treated her so badly."

Fury stabbed in Carlie's chest, and anger flashed across her face. "How dare you talk about my mother? You don't know her, don't know what happened between them." Tears trembled on her lashes, but her voice was fierce. "He was the first man she really loved, and she never regretted any of it."

She felt a moment of triumph as a look of pain crossed her friend's face, but then she just felt bad. "I'm sorry, I shouldn't have said that, of course she loved your dad. It's just that Andre was her first grown-up relationship, and she loved him deeply."

"How do you know this?" her friend broke in suspiciously. "You can't twist it around now to try to justify being with Rowan. Dad said he'd treated her really badly, and was jealous and possessive."

"Sandy found Mum's diary in a safety deposit box, and sent it to me a couple of weeks ago."

Her friend couldn't mask her surprise. "You never told me that. Did it answer any questions, like why she ran away?"

Carlie shrugged. "I haven't finished it yet. I'm saving it, savouring it, trying to make it last so I can feel close to her for longer."

For several minutes they were both quiet as they pondered their losses, and the pain they'd experienced at the death of their parents. Rhiannon was one of the few people who would understand why Carlie wanted to string the diary out. Slowly the anger drained away from both of them, and they sighed at the same time, then looked up at each other and smiled.

"We shouldn't be fighting," Rhiannon said softly. "It's the festive season, the time for family and friends, and forgiveness. I just care about you, that's all. And I'm here if you need me."

Carlie nodded gratefully, then rubbed her hand impatiently across her face to wipe away the tears. Her ring sparkled in the pale sunshine streaming in the window, catching Rhiannon's eye, and her friend quickly reverted right back to her previous objections.

"I just don't trust him," she blurted out. "And I'm only saying this because you're my best friend, and because I care about you – otherwise it would be much easier if I didn't say anything. But the reading was so clear, and according to her visions, he's going to leave you heartbroken, and possibly physically beaten as well."

Carlie stared at Rhiannon, fresh tears in her eyes. "Just go. Go and see John, and have a great time with him," she said angrily.

"Just think about it," her friend insisted. "He's a bad influence on you, and you don't need that. You need to focus on school, not skip classes to be at his beck and call. And you said you wanted to help Rose in the shop, but instead you're lying to her, sneaking around, bringing him into her house to do god knows what behind her back."

She paused for a moment, and Carlie stared at her, speechless. "You don't turn up for our coven meetings, you take me for granted, and you expect me to back up your lies or provide an alibi for you," Rhiannon continued. "I don't think I can be around you, and watch you ruin your life. Watch you betray me, betray Rose, betray yourself

– become someone you don't want to be. Please, you have to break up with him. Otherwise I just… I don't think I can be your friend." And she turned and fled down the stairs.

Carlie stared after her, stunned by the anger in her friend's voice and the ultimatum she'd delivered. How could she expect her to give up the person she loved just because she didn't approve? Expect her to "prove" how much she valued their friendship by making such a huge sacrifice? Especially as she was off to spend the afternoon with the guy she liked, which meant skipping their Yule ritual. So it was okay for Rhiannon to have a boyfriend and stand her up, but she couldn't see Rowan? That was a bit hypocritical, surely.

She wished she'd thought to say that to her friend, but she'd been too shell-shocked in the moment to reply. Now she sat on her bed, dazed, wondering how on earth their conversation had spiralled so far out of control. When Luther leaped up onto the bed and settled down in her lap, she was grateful for the distraction, smiling as she stroked his head and let his purring calm her down.

"Oh Luther, what am I supposed to do now? I love Rowan, but I care about Rhiannon too. She's my dearest friend – she's been so good to me, and we've helped each other so much. And she's always so understanding, which is what makes this so weird. She really loved Rowan when we met him, and when we all spent that time together, the three of us. And I've only skipped school once, and only missed one of our coven meetings. She made it sound like I was never at school, and never with her doing ritual, that I'm not committed to our magical life, but I am. Surely it seems like an overly dramatic response, that I have to choose between them just for that?"

Luther lifted his head a little and gazed up at her, expression serene, aloof, forever unknowable.

"What should I do Luther? I don't want to lose Rowan, and I shouldn't have to, but I don't want to be one of those girls who chooses her boyfriend over her best friend either," she sighed. "Rhiannon and I are so close, we've shared everything, helped each other grieve – and we're planning to go to uni together, study together. I don't want to lose all that."

But the more she thought about it, the madder she got. She knew she wasn't just being defensive – Rhiannon was definitely over-reacting, and over-exaggerating any supposedly bad thing she'd ever done for Rowan, or he'd done to her. And Rhiannon had been so rude to him last night, while he'd been a perfect gentleman, polite and respectful, and leaving the ball – leaving her – just to keep Rhiannon happy. So Carlie lay there, running things round and round in her mind, until she felt her head would explode.

Finally she threw back the covers, stumbled out of bed, and opened the door of her closet. She chose a deep ruby-red velvet dress, pulled on black tights underneath it and a thick black coat over the top, and laced up her thick black boots. Then she pulled down her backpack and shoved a change of clothes, her wallet and her mum's diary inside, and raced down the stairs and out the front door before she could change her mind.

She'd told Rowan she couldn't go to his retreat, partly because she wanted to spend Yule with Rose and Rhiannon, and partly because, well, her grandma had no idea she was even dating anyone, and would no doubt be less than keen to have her going away with him for the weekend if she did know.

But Rose would be out tonight, and would think she was at Rhiannon's, and her friend would be away with John. So no one would ever know if she slipped off now and stayed away until tomorrow. She did have a pang of conscience as she remembered Rhi accusing her of using her as an alibi, but what choice did she have? She was going to go crazy if she had to stay here on her own, obsessing over the ultimatum her friend had given her. And she desperately needed to see Rowan. She couldn't wait until next week, she wanted to see him now. Wanted to continue their conversation from the previous night, and their kissing too. Smiling down at the beautiful ring he'd given her, she remembered how tightly he'd held her as he'd whispered his love to her, how close she'd felt to him as he reassured her that she was special.

There was a bus just pulling in as she raced up the road to the stop, so she took it as a sign. She was meant to be with him. Smiling, she curled up in her seat and pulled her mum's diary out of her bag.

Chapter 33

Dear Diary...

She flicked through it to find where she was up to, and discovered a bunch of loose-leaf pages that had been inserted into the diary, like a letter added much later. Horror engulfed her and her heart broke as she read the pain-drenched words, and finally began to comprehend just how bleak her mother's life had become.

My dearest daughter,
Talking to you is the only thing keeping me sane right now, and yet you don't even exist, so perhaps I'm not so sane after all. But I have fifteen precious minutes alone, and I keep hoping that if I can just confide in someone, even someone who only exists as an idea, I'll somehow see something that makes sense, find out what went wrong, and what I'm doing that makes him hate me so much – and hopefully discover why I'm in this hell, and find a way out.

I don't know though, some days I think the only way I'll escape this is through death – mine, his, at this point I don't really care which one. How can I have stopped caring? Mum would be horrified if she knew what I'd become, but even she seems so far away now. Did I ever really know her? Work magic with her? Love life and my family with her?

This did start out as the most beautiful love story ever told though, and I think it's important to remember that. He taught me so much about myself, and for a while I really blossomed in his care, I became so much more than I'd imagined I could be. I thought he would be your father, I really did. When I sent out my spell to Kali to bring you to me, I pictured his face as part of our perfect family. But I can never let that happen now. That would be a fate worse than death for both of us.

But perhaps I should start at the beginning? He was the man of my dreams – quite literally, because I dreamed about him for weeks before I met him for the first time, dreams he told me he had sent to me. And he was amazing – so powerful and magical and strong, so charming and charismatic. He swept me off my feet, and I couldn't believe he could like me, let alone love me. It took him a long time to convince me. And he swore that no one would ever love me the way he did. Which sounded so desperately romantic at the time, but now that thought fills me with bitter amusement and the deepest dread, and I pray that no one else will ever love me like he does. But I'm getting ahead of myself...

I loved him for a long time, admired him, worshipped him in a way. And when he did a tarot reading for me that said my father would die if I stayed at home, then begged me to come and live with him, I was flattered, and excited, and so desperately happy to be with him. I felt sad that I was leaving my parents, but I knew it was for the best if it would save Dad's life, and while of course I wished I could explain it to them, why I was leaving, I always assumed there would be time later to sort it all out.

And it was wonderful at first, living with him, spending all our time together, working magic with him, doing rituals at his workshops around the country, learning from him, so much, about life and healing, and about myself too. I felt so proud to be the so-called love of his life, to watch him work, to know that of all the women he could have had, he'd chosen me. I felt really special, and I loved him so much. And for a while he loved me too, purely and with both passion and compassion. He helped me be a better person, inspired me and challenged me and adored me.

The change was subtle at first. He started to criticise me for the things he used to compliment me on. He stopped welcoming me to his circles as often, letting me take part in his work. Slowly it became clear that he thought I was less than him, that all women were, and that my main job was to cook, clean and look after him, and do everything he wanted me to do whenever he wanted me to do it.

Even then I defended him, twisted it around in my head – I was lucky to be able to care for him, to serve him. He constantly told me that he could have any woman he wanted, that they would beg for the chance to be able to please him, and if I didn't submit, he might just do that. The scariest thing is that this became a new kind of normal for me, and I stopped thinking it was remotely strange. How insane is that?! When we were at his retreats we were surrounded by women who loved him, who wanted him, and who thought I was so lucky to be with him. For a while I thought I was too.

Then he started getting paranoid and suspicious. He became jealous of the guys in our group, who we'd worked with for ages and who were like part of our family. He'd claim I fancied them, and make a joke of it, but I didn't find it funny at all. I became hyper-aware of how I acted around them as a result – I barely spoke to them, too scared to even glance their way in case he caught me looking at them and decided that was proof I wanted them – and that made me sad, because we'd been friends, and here I was treating them like they wanted to be with me but were beneath me, too far beneath me even to talk to them, which wasn't the case at all.

At first I was strangely flattered, that he was so devoted to me, that he wanted me so much and loved me so deeply, but then the suspicion became nasty, and he started accusing me of awful things, things I'd never do. He'd scream at me that he knew I'd had sex with other people, that he'd seen it psychically so there was no point lying to him, but it wasn't true. It was particularly distressing because he was the only person I'd ever slept with, and I didn't want to be with anyone other than him, ever. But his insistence had me doubting my own sanity at times, questioning if I actually had cheated on him, even though I knew that I hadn't.

Even that I put up with and endured without complaint – I figured maybe it was the price to pay to be with someone so amazing? And who was I going to complain to anyway? Everyone around me thought *he was perfect, without fault, a god of sorts. And in between there were still moments where I was happy, where he treated me so well, like he had in the beginning, so I hoped that once he'd learned to trust me, and realised how crazy it was to think I'd cheat on him, it would be okay, it would go back to normal.*

I was a fool. Men who treat women that way don't ever stop, they escalate. The times he treated me well got fewer and further between, and his cruelty increased. He started hitting me, hurting me, and soon he stopped apologising for it, stopped begging me to forgive him and promising it would never happen again, because by then he didn't care. By then we both knew it would happen again. And everything became my fault. I was bringing the punishments on myself. If I only treated him better, if I wasn't such a whore, then he would be nice to me. He was doing it for my own good, apparently…

The letter ended and the diary began again, but Carlie paused, shocked. How had her brave, confident and spiritual mother become such a shell of herself? How had a man done that to her? If only she could have made her way back home to Rose, she would have recovered. But it seemed that the more he tore away her self-esteem, her sanity even, the less she felt deserving of being saved, and that thought overwhelmed Carlie with despair.

She couldn't imagine her mum like that, so scared, so paralysed. She'd been so confident, so assured, when she knew her, the powerhouse lawyer, the family breadwinner. She would never have put up with this. But somehow this man had scraped away the very essence of who she was, had beaten all the strength and self-belief out of her. She wasn't sure she wanted to keep reading – it felt so personal, like she was betraying her mother by learning all this – but she had to find out what happened. And at least she knew, as awful as everything she was describing was, that her mum had escaped. Somehow she'd found the strength to leave, to flee to the other side of the world, and she had found happiness.

Today I returned from grocery shopping to find him sitting at the kitchen table, arms folded, glaring at me. I knew that look, and I quailed inside at what was to come.

"Where have you been?" he demanded, and I told him I'd been buying food for dinner, which I had been. He didn't believe me, so I showed him the docket from the supermarket, and gave him his change. He went through every grocery bag, then grabbed my purse and rifled through that too, but there was nothing to find.

"Where else did you go? Who did you meet?" he demanded.

"I didn't meet anyone," I replied, perplexed.

"Don't lie to me. I called the grocery store, and you were there half an hour ago. Where else did you go?"

I blanched. Suddenly he had me questioning myself, but I hadn't done anything wrong, or anything other than what I'd told him. I explained that the bus had been fifteen minutes late, but even though I showed him the ticket, he didn't believe that either. He screamed "Liar!" at me, and worse, and then he hit me. As I crumpled to the floor, sobbing and clutching my jaw, he rang the bus company – and when they said the bus had been delayed due to an accident, he shrugged and told me to get up and start making dinner.

Carlie could barely breathe. Her mind reeled as she tried to comprehend what she was reading. Her bright, brave, strong mother had been a victim of domestic violence. Of brutal physical and psychological abuse. Her stomach clenched and she felt sick, furious at the man who had done this to her, angry at her friends for letting it happen. Surely someone must have been aware of what was going on? Or was he such a good manipulator that they were oblivious?

It sounded like he'd cut her mum off from her old friends and family, and isolated her from any potential new people in her life, so that she had no one to confide in, no one to help her see just how wrong all this was. She didn't want to keep reading, but she felt compelled somehow. She had to know how bad it got, and also how her mum had eventually escaped. Thank god she knew it had a happy ending, or she didn't think she could continue. She turned back to the diary. A few pages had been torn out, then the entries re-started.

Oh my god! I feel so stupid. I just found out that his ex-wife isn't so ex. That they're still married. And he has a son, who's just a little kid. He'd mentioned doing something with a nephew once before, but no, that was a lie. It was his child. Discovering this made me feel so sleazy, even though I had no idea he was still married, or had any children – he told me he'd been separated from his wife for two years, and that he was glad they'd had no kids because it made it easier to leave her, that the divorce had just been a formality.

But no. She actually thought they were still together, that he was just doing a lot of travelling at the moment for workshops and retreats. Which means that some of those nights that he's been away from me, saying he was working, he must have been staying with them. Tucking his son into bed. Sleeping next to his wife. Sleeping with his wife?

I asked him about it when he got home, and he denied it at first, then he demanded to know who'd told me. I wasn't going to give Jasmine up though, because it seems like she's my only friend now. And eventually he shrugged that off anyway and tried to turn it around on me. That it was all my fault – I was an evil whore who tempted him away from his wife and child, I was a home wrecker. When I reminded him that he'd insisted to me that he was divorced and childless, he just smirked and said that's what I'd wanted to believe. God! It's so infuriating.

And then he turned it around again, and said I was just upset because I was cheating on him. Which doesn't even make sense. He knows where I am every minute of every day, and it's usually with him, or waiting for him, or crying in a heap on the floor after another battle, either physical or psychological, unable to muster the energy to get up, let alone go anywhere. He keeps saying that he can "see" me cheating – he describes it in detail, like some kind of dirty fantasy of his, all the supposed sex I'm supposedly always having, with men I've never even met, even a woman yesterday, apparently. It really does my head in.

At first he made me wonder if I actually had been doing the things he said I did – but I know I haven't. That I wouldn't. And usually that I couldn't, because all the times he says all this is happening, I've actually been with him. It just doesn't make sense!

It's making me question his work as a healer and teacher too – if he is so wrong on this, if he can swear blind that he's "seen" me cheating, does that mean he isn't as psychic as he claims? Are none of his visions true? Or is it just me that he lies to? And if he's prepared to lie and manipulate in his work, to swear his "vision" is true when it is patently false, what does that say about his ethics towards all his students?

But I think I'm the only person he treats like this – I pray I am anyway – because every now and then he gets really upset and implies that I make him behave badly, that he doesn't do this to anyone else, that he doesn't want to treat anyone this cruelly, least of all me. And then he does it all again...

Oh goddess, please give me strength. I've been working in a bookstore for the last few months, so I can earn a bit of money and not feel so totally dependent on him, and it's been wonderful. I've been able to have normal conversations, see again what normal life looks like. But it's all over now – he just rang my boss and told him I wouldn't be coming back. And all for a lie. One of the girls was running late for her shift today, because her mum's in hospital. So I stayed at work until she got there, and she was very apologetic, and very grateful. I was a little nervous about getting home late, so when the elevator was taking ages I got a bit frantic and raced up the stairs. I pushed open our door, and he was standing there, waiting for me. I threw my arms around him in the doorway, kissing him hello, but he didn't hug me back.

"Where have you been?" he snapped, and I took a step back, surprised at the threatening tone of his voice.

"Cathy was running late for her shift because her mum's in hospital, so I said I could stay a bit longer, cover for her. But it was only half an hour, so I didn't think you'd mind," I babbled.

He glared at me, then started hurling accusations again. "You're seeing someone else, aren't you? Don't insult my intelligence by lying to me. I saw you together!" he insisted.

I stared at him, shocked. "I've been at work, call my boss and ask him. You couldn't have seen me with anyone."

"I don't need to call, I've seen you, in my meditations. All the sordid details. Are you trying to say my visions are false? I know you've been with another guy, and you've just been kissing him. Why else would you be so out of breath?"

"I ran all the way from the bus stop then up three flights of stairs," I said, alarmed that he was becoming so irrational even more quickly than usual.

"You're lying!" he choked out, his face red with anger.

I felt a very real flicker of fear. What was going on? "Baby, I'm not lying," I managed to say, but my voice trembled a little. God, would he take that to mean I was lying?

As if he'd sensed my thought, he took a step towards me. "Don't lie to me!" he shouted, arm raised, and I braced myself for the blow.

When it didn't come, I took a deep breath. "I'm not sure why you think I would lie about that. If I wanted to be with someone else, I would be. But I don't. I only want to be with you."

"I know you've been with someone else," he screamed at me. Then he started to tear my clothes off me, right there in the very public hallway, in order to "prove it" apparently, which rocked me out of my daze and made me yell back.

I just don't understand how he can accuse me of things I haven't done? I must have finally got through to him, because after a long time he calmed down a little. And I held my ground, and eventually it was him who looked away. "Okay," he conceded. "But I've been cheated on before, and I know what to look for. Don't think you can trick me. I know what women are like, what you are like."

His words hurt so much, because I'd only ever been honest with and faithful to him, but the mood seemed to be passing him by, so I bit my tongue. And eventually he sighed, and apologised, which was a shock.

"I'm sorry. I'm just getting so many strange messages from you right now, different energies. You're thinking about other men, and it's throwing me. Come inside," he said, then he dragged me in and slammed the door behind us. Okay, so it was an apology of sorts. By that point I was happy to take it.

God I wish I could call Mum and have her come and get me, take me away from this craziness, make everything all right again, like she always did when I was in trouble as a kid. He's told me several times that if I even try to speak to Mum he'll hurt her, or worse, so I can't take the risk. But I don't think I can survive this much longer.

Last night was harrowing, even more so than usual, and the scary thing was that I hadn't done anything to start it. Not that I ever do, but this one came from so far out of left field, without any warning sign so I could steel myself for the storm to come. We'd had a really nice evening – we made dinner together, then watched a movie, curled up on the couch, content. It was almost like old times. And then he turned to me, and there were tears in his eyes.

"I don't want to be with you, I don't want to love you," he whispered, his voice tortured. "I don't want you to have this power over me. I'm always so strong, I'm always the powerful one, the one who is in control. But you make me so weak. Why do you do this to me? Why do you have this power?" he asked, voice ragged, imploring. "What's so special about you?"

"I don't have any power," I replied, surprised and more than a little rattled by his words. I'd never been so powerless.

He grabbed my arm and dragged me into the bathroom, then broke open his razor and held the blade to his wrist. "This is what you make people do," he said, eyes wild. "You make them want to kill themselves."

I sunk to the floor, head against the wall to try to stay upright, and begged him not to do it.

"Why not?" he asked, voice desperate.

"My god, you can't do this. People need you. You need you. You need to be here," I stuttered.

"Do you need me?" he demanded.

I stared at him, terrified. Terrified to say the wrong thing, to set him off, to make him carry out his awful threat. "Of course I do," I replied shakily.

"Do you love me?"

I nodded, too scared to do anything else.

"Say it!" he growled, menace in his voice.

So I said it.

"Like you mean it."

"I love you," I repeated, putting as much force as I could into it, trying to sound as genuine as humanly possible, though my voice shook with the super-human effort.

He smiled, and a look of triumph lit up his face, then he laughed, a horrible, cruel laugh. "You didn't really think I'd do that did you?" he asked mockingly. "You didn't really think that you had the power to make me do it?"

I was trembling, the earlier rush of adrenaline long gone, and a strange hollow exhaustion taking its place. "Of course not," I sighed. And I was suddenly terrified, because the blade was still in his hand, but now it was pointing at me, and his smile had become sadistic.

He pulled me to my feet and dragged me into an embrace, and I tried so hard not to stiffen in his arms, not to inflame him further – tried not to wonder where the blade was.

"I was only joking," he said.

"It wasn't funny," I muttered, voice flat. This rollercoaster of emotions was tying me in knots, and I didn't know what I thought or felt any more. Everything now was simply a reaction to his mood, an attempt to pacify him, to always say the right thing. My whole life was now a delicate balance of tightrope walking and tiptoeing on egg shells. I felt broken, and I knew I couldn't go on like this much longer.

Suddenly his face changed, like another person had taken control of his brain, and he smiled at me.

"I love you so much, you know that right?" he said.

I nodded, numb.

"No one will ever love you as much as I do. They'll never love you the way I do," he continued, self-satisfaction evident.

"I know," I said, conciliatory, plastering a smile on my face. But where once that statement had made me so happy, had made me feel so special, now it just terrified me. God, I hope no one will ever love me this much, in this way, EVER.

Carlie paused as the bus came to a stop, and jumped out, a little panicked, when she realised it was time to change buses. She felt strange, as though she'd gone through all the awful things her mother was writing about. Taking a few deep breaths, she checked the timetable then walked over to the kiosk and bought a cup of tea and a chocolate bar. She had a few minutes, and she felt the need to ground herself back into her body, back into the present, because reading about the harrowing things her mum had endured was making her head spin and her heart hurt. As she sipped her tea she felt slightly calmer, and the sweetness of the chocolate soothed her jagged nerves a little.

Her bus arrived then, and she climbed aboard and found her seat, then reluctantly pulled her mum's diary back out of her backpack. Part of her wanted to throw it away, or burn it as her mum had considered doing, so she couldn't learn about any more of her suffering, but something made her open it back up and keep reading.

There were more pages missing, and a large section of the next entry had been scribbled out. She could just make out the end of it…

I know it infuriates him when I won't drink alcohol with him, but I'm scared of losing control around him, of being even more vulnerable than I already am, possibly saying something in the heat of the moment, when my inhibitions are lowered, that will set him off. So I was happily surprised when we were out last night, and he stopped insisting I drink with him, and told me he'd get me an orange juice.

Of course I should have known he would do something awful – he must have spiked my drink, because I came to twelve hours later, aching and bruised, with no recollection of what had happened to me, except that he said, with the sleaziest grin, that he had some wonderful photos of me, and that I'd better not ever upset him or displease him, or else he'd send them to a sleazy magazine to publish, then to my mother. I feel sick even wondering what he did to me, and how it came to this. The worst part of all is that this has become my normal. I'm not even shocked or outraged any more, I'm not surprised by the depths he'll go to. I'm just numb.

I don't know how much longer I can cope with this – I feel like soon I'll break into a million pieces and disappear. Just cease to exist. He "let" me come to his shamanic healing retreat this weekend, and said it was going to be a new start for the two of us. And I can't believe I actually fell for it. That I forgot there would be an ulterior motive.

I met some really nice people on the Friday afternoon, all women of course, I wasn't stupid. I was bunking in with a sweet mother-and-

daughter pair, Maria and Lenore, and I had dinner with them, but as I was heading over to the shower block after that, Andre grabbed me and started kissing me, then begged me to come to his cabin. I reminded him that we had to pretend we didn't know each other, but he was crying, pleading, saying he really needed me to be with him. So I went, and as soon as we were inside, he broke down.

"Oh my god, I'm so glad you're here," he said. "I just can't stand it, all these people demanding my attention, all with their pitiful little problems, all trying to make everything be about them. That woman with the drum, my god! Could she be more annoying?"

"Her name's Maria, and she thinks the world of you," I said, shocked at his lack of compassion.

"They're all the same, they just want someone to make them feel important, someone to tell them how special they are, and what to do with their life."

"They think you're a god," I said, giggling a little at the thought. "Be nice to them."

He stared at me, and it was like a switch had flipped in his mind. I froze, because I knew what that meant. He demanded to know why I didn't see him the way other people did. Said everyone at the retreat, and everyone else he'd ever met, thinks he's a god, and treats him that way. Except for me.

"They respect me totally, but you don't. You question me, challenge me. Why don't you treat me the way I should be treated?" he demanded. "Why don't you think I'm a god?"

My face was still throbbing from where he'd hit me the day before, for saying thank you to the bus driver, so I wasn't as careful as usual. "Perhaps it's because I know you better than they do," I replied, no longer willing or able to bite my tongue. "Or maybe it's because you treat them better than you treat me."

"What?" he shouted. "I treat you better than anyone."

"No, you don't," I said, voice expressionless, like a robot. "You're jealous and violent and cruel, and you don't trust me."

He was shocked. "Of course I trust you. And I'm not jealous, or violent or cruel," he said, genuinely surprised I would say such a thing. "You're my consort, it's because of me that people respect you."

I just stared at him. No one here knew I was with him, because he wanted it to be a secret, and I was glad of that, so there was no way they would think anything of me either way. Besides, how on earth anyone could respect me, now that I'd sunk so low, I had no idea. And how could he even begin to think he was treating me well?

And then he started his usual ranting. I don't appreciate him like everyone else does, I don't recognise his true worth. I'm an ungrateful whore who just came this weekend so I could have sex with another guy, I only wanted him for his money, blah blah blah. Then he tried to drag me into bed, and I tried to get away – his awful accusations never do put me in the mood – but he grabbed my arm so tightly that I know there will be bruises tomorrow, and ripped my jumper off.

"Why do you think I asked you to come," he asked roughly, and I froze, horrified. "I could have any woman here you know, from the youngest to the oldest. They beg me for it. So why do you think you're so special?" he shouted.

My blood ran cold, but I managed to screw up my courage and speak. I had nothing left to lose. "Then you should go and have one of those women," I said. "But be careful, because it would be easy to ruin your reputation if you tried to force someone to have sex."

"I don't have to force anyone," he retorted, anger blazing in his eyes. "They all want me."

"Then go and be with one of them," I cried. My voice shook, but I managed to maintain eye contact. And I saw the moment he deflated, then watched, shocked, as he burst into noisy sobs. He apologised, which he hadn't done for a long time, and begged me to forgive him; implored me to love him. So I tried to reassure him, to comfort him, even though it was the last thing I wanted to do. Sometimes he's like a little kid, so needy. Where was the self-possessed and self-confident "god" they all saw? I tried to explain again how important he'd said it was that I didn't stay with him here, that people thought he was above "petty human relationships" as he put it, but his body started shaking again, and I could feel sobs building up within him. I couldn't believe that I was the mature one.

He dragged me down onto the floor with him, holding me so tight I could barely breathe.

"I need you," he cried. "How can you reject me when I'm being so open with you, when I'm begging you to stay with me? I'm not sure I'll survive the night if you leave me now."

I didn't know what to do. His voice was getting louder, and his state of mind more hysterical, and if I didn't do something soon the whole camp would come rushing in, wondering what was going on, and then they'd all know anyway. Maybe it would be easier to just do what he wanted and stay. So I gave in – and it was the longest nine hours of my life. He raged between begging me to stay, threatening me with violence, then curling up in a ball, crying hysterically and threatening to kill himself if I left. I swung between reassurance and empathy to fear and anger, and a hundred emotions in between.

For a while he was convinced that I was a spy, sent to trick him into revealing his secrets, then that I was a government agent, trying to set him up, trying to destroy him. When his eyes alighted on the small black base of one of the lamps in the room, he swore blind that it held a bug, planted there by the CIA to record his conversations, and he became hysterical until I put the lamp outside.

It was all getting way too crazy for me, and I almost walked out, but as always he seemed to sense when I'd reached my breaking point, and was all of a sudden sweet and conciliatory, full of apologies and a rare moment of candour and sanity.

But then when I said I needed to go to the bathroom, he flipped out again, accusing me of planning to leave him, and sneaking out the bathroom window, off to meet some stranger in the forest to have sex with him. The more I denied this the worse and more paranoid he became – it wasn't until I showed him there was no window in there that he let me go in, and I finally had two minutes to myself.

When I emerged he'd made me a cup of tea, exactly the way I like it, and we talked rationally for half an hour. Then just as I felt lulled into a sense of security, and thought maybe we could finally get some sleep, he turned on me again, saying I was a whore, that I was using him for money, that I used sex as a weapon, then berating all the people who had come to the retreat again, complaining that they didn't understand him or value him enough, that they were selfish and self-obsessed, and that I was the worst of them all.

As I tried to stay calm, he grabbed me again, dragged me into the bedroom, and told me to get undressed, to do what I was there for. But I couldn't bring myself to do it – I felt like I'd been through a psychological war, and the thought of being intimate with him made my blood run cold.

So he ripped my clothes off me and forced himself on top of me, and held me down until he was done. I tried to shut down, to become numb to it all, to escape at least mentally from the most mortifying moment of my life. But my tears just seemed to turn him on more, and he kept going. His hands all over me made my skin crawl, but he didn't appear to notice, or care. And when it was finally over he held me close, and told me how much he loved me, and that just made the whole thing worse. I lay in his arms, frozen with shock, unable to move, to even think straight, just praying, over and over, that I would eventually be able to get out of that room.

When the sun finally rose, I felt relief wash over me. Surely it would have to end now, he would have to let me go. He'd have to pull himself together, sort himself out, and get out there and teach. I crept into the bathroom and stood at the sink staring into the mirror. Horror shot through me as I gazed at my reflection. My skin was as pale as a ghost and there were huge black circles under my lashes, but it was the expression in my eyes that scared me the most. I looked like a zombie, with not an ounce of energy or will left, drained of every bit of whatever it was that made me, me. It was like I had left my own body and gone off somewhere to hide.

Yet when I came back out he was calm, and totally himself again. And he looked amazing, like he'd slept for nine hours and didn't have a care in the world. How come I looked like I'd been tortured for the last twenty-four hours, and he could have walked off the set of a fashion shoot?

"Thanks so much for staying last night," he said, smiling at me and moving forward to hug me. "Now you'd better get back to your cabin, so no one knows you stayed over." And he winked at me, as though it had been me who had begged to stay with him.

"Oh, and here's a shirt you can wear – yours looks a little ripped," he added, with a lascivious grin that turned my stomach. Like it wasn't *him who had torn mine off so he could force himself on me. But I put it on and ran out the door, and I'd never been so grateful to see the sun, or people, in my life.*

Breakfast was beyond embarrassing. Maria had been worried about me, because I hadn't been in the cabin when she woke up this morning, and because I looked so terrible. I lied though, of course, something about a migraine, and a nightmare, and needing to clear my head, and she seemed to accept it.

And Lenore was bubbling over with excitement. "I had the best dream last night – really meaningful, and for once I actually remembered it. I've had a situation at work that I've been really torn over, but in my dream Andre was there, and basically told me what I should do – then showed me a vision of what would happen with each of the other possible choices, so I could know I was making the right decision. It was amazing! Already he's solved my problem! I told you, this guy is incredible!"

My face ached from the smile I tried to paste across it, and Maria gave me a searching look. "Are you sure you're okay honey?" she asked. I nodded. I hated lying to them, hated being forced to lie, but what could I say? The amazing Andre is a cruel and manipulative bully of a man? A violent sociopath? No one would believe me.

Just then he walked into the breakfast room – speak of the devil – and walked straight over to us. "Thanks so much for spending the night with me Violet," he said, so loud, then leaned down and kissed me, in front of everyone. I was mortified, and shocked and angry too. The hypocrisy and injustice burned in me, but he didn't notice, or care. He simply breezed off and sat at another table, and one of the young girls there jumped up to get him some porridge, while another one got him a coffee.

I looked at Maria and Lenore, and quailed inside as I tried to reassure them. "It wasn't like that, I promise. And I'm so sorry, I didn't want to lie to you, but he insisted no one could know I was there – just talking to him – in case everyone got the wrong impression. Which they have now," I stammered, blushing beet red.

I saw a strange mix of admiration and jealousy in Lenore's eyes, which worried me, but Maria gave me another searching look that made me feel really uncomfortable. It was like she could see inside my heart, and knew the truth, and I hated what she must think of me, of how weak and pathetic I had become.

But I was saved by the bell, so to speak, as right at that moment the retreat organiser stood up and started explaining how the day would work, and people scraped their chairs back as they stood up and stacked their plates, or raced back to their rooms to get pen and paper, or grabbed a last mug of coffee.

Andre began the day with a beautiful ritual, which I just couldn't reconcile with the man he'd been last night. Then we broke into small groups to work on individual issues and activities, and he moved between them all, listening carefully to each one, offering suggestions, explaining concepts clearly, making every single person he made eye contact with think they were the only person in the world.

I watched him, one part impressed by his deception, one part horrified. He'd spent a lot of time last night railing against these people, saying they were stupid and didn't deserve his time or attention, let alone his help, but here he was, making them love him. And it was all a lie.

At one point Maria came and found me, and put her arms around me. She said she was really worried about me, and wanted to know if she could help me, but Andre swooped in and separated us, and kept us apart for the rest of the weekend. And when it was finally over and we had packed up and were heading home, he was his old loving self, saying how much it had meant to him to have me there, how he really hoped I'd come to more of his retreats with him now. And then he said he had to spend the night with his mum, that she was sick and scared, so he dropped me at home then left. I don't know if that means he's staying with his wife, or with some other woman, and to be honest I don't actually care.

I need some time alone, time to think. So now here I sit, trying to make sense of what has happened. He's been violent before – I've lost track of the injuries, the blood, the bruises, the brutal hair pulling that leaves no mark but gives me a migraine that lasts days. And he's been psychologically abusive too many times to count, so much so that often I doubt my own sanity.

Certainly I doubt my worth. But this is the first time he's ever held me down and forced me to have sex with him, and I feel like that should be the line in the sand that can't be crossed. The line has moved several times in the last few months, I know, and I've endured worse and worse treatment from him without complaining – treatment I'd always thought I would end a relationship over immediately if it happened to me.

But I worry that if I can't get away somehow, I will end up accepting this too, and blaming myself. I have to save myself, I have to get away somehow, otherwise there will be nothing left of me. And yet, where can I go? He stopped me from working, so I have no money and am totally dependent on him. And he scares away anyone who wants to be friends with me, anyone who shows any concern for me, so I'm completely isolated. I just don't know what to do…

Chapter 34

A Tangled Web

Carlie was so engrossed in the diary that she nearly missed her stop, but the driver remembered her stating her destination, and called out to her. As she wandered up the road to the cafe where retreat-goers were meeting, she felt dazed, and fear and anger at what her mother had endured warred with the compassion she felt for her. Violet had only been seventeen, the age she was now, and she'd been alone, cut off from Rose and Mike, and from anyone who could have helped her make sense of the situation she'd found herself in. She couldn't imagine ever being that isolated from the people she loved – the ones who were still alive anyway.

Another pang of guilt washed over her, that she was lying to her grandmother again, and she felt nervous that she would get Rhiannon in trouble if anyone found out where she was. But she was so desperate to see Rowan again, to try to figure out what she felt for him, and what she should do about the ultimatum Rhiannon had delivered.

Over a comforting cup of chai she was introduced to an older woman, Cressida, and her daughter Vicki, who offered her a ride out to the retreat space. A wave of sadness shuddered through her as she recognised a little of her grandma in the tall grey-haired woman, and she wondered if, had things been different, it could have been Rose and her daughter Violet at a weekend retreat together – maybe even all three of them. But she made an effort to shake off the gloominess and tune back in to the conversation, and smiled as they raved about how much they were looking forward to the weekend, and how amazing Rowan was, how much he had helped them to heal from a bitter divorce and a crushing lack of self-worth in Cressida's case, and a complicated health issue in her daughter Vicki's.

On arrival they were directed into the large common room where they would have their meals and perform some of their rituals. The moment she walked inside she saw Rowan across the room, talking to a pretty woman who was clearly besotted with him, leaning in close, touching his arm as she made a point, stroking his chest. Her heart lurched, Rhiannon's accusations that he'd find someone else in her absence playing over and over in her head, along with her mum's description of her shaman boyfriend's words. "They all want me." "I could have any woman here." "They beg me for it."

Cressida touched her shoulder, and she jumped. "Are you okay?" she asked. With an effort, Carlie tore her eyes away from Rowan and nodded. "We're going to grab a cup of tea, would you like me to get you one?" her new friend said. "We have an hour to hang out here and mingle before the program starts."

Carlie smiled. "Thank you." As the other woman walked over to the kitchen area, she felt Rowan's eyes on her, and looked back over. Shock crossed his face, then something she couldn't quite place, then he smiled and walked towards her. He held out his hand.

"Hi, I'm Rowan, it's lovely to meet you," he said, then winked at her. "I can't believe you're here, but I'm so glad," he whispered, and the love she saw shining from his eyes soothed her a little. "But oh my god, I want to hold you!"

She smiled. "Me too," she whispered back.

He stared at her searchingly. "Are you okay?" he asked, voice still low. "You look sad."

She tried to smile, but her confrontation with Rhiannon and the words she'd read in her mother's diary were swirling around in her brain. "I'll be fine. It's a long story. I just needed to be with you tonight," she replied.

He stared at her appraisingly, eyebrows raised, and she blushed. "I don't mean that! I just –"

"Rowan, welcome," a tall man interrupted them. "I'm sorry I was delayed for a few moments, but let me show you to your cabin. Do you need a hand bringing your things in? My daughter can help," he said, motioning to the pretty woman Rowan had just been talking to.

"That would be great, thank you," he told the man, shaking his hand then turning back to Carlie. "It was so nice to meet you. I hope you enjoy the weekend," he murmured, then followed the man and his daughter outside.

She nodded, forced a smile, then wandered back to Cressida in a daze. As she sat down with them and drank her tea, she let their words about how great Rowan was wash over her. She knew he couldn't make it obvious that they were together, but surely it was a bit cold to pretend he'd never met her before? He knew most of the people here, had done ritual with them a few times before, so it was conceivable that he had with her too. Yet he was treating her like a total stranger. Or was she just projecting Rhiannon's prejudices on to him, creating fears where there was no need for them?

Trying to shake off her weird mood, she joined in their chat. They all adored Rowan, credited him with changing their lives, and were so excited about the weekend ahead. She concentrated on summoning a memory of how he made her feel, the warmth and sense of security she felt in his arms, and this soothed her.

She reminded herself too that it had been love in his eyes as he'd greeted her, and he'd been genuine when he told her how happy he was to see her. She shouldn't let her mother's awful experiences impose on hers. And just because Violet realised she should have listened to her friend about her relationship, it didn't mean there were parallels there. Rowan wasn't Andre. And she didn't need Rhiannon's voice in her head trying to convince her that he was too old, too untrustworthy, too ready to cheat on her, too bad for her in general. Her friend didn't know him like she did.

By the time the ritual started she was feeling much more cheerful, and she let herself be swept away in the beauty and magic of the Yule's Eve ceremony. She could feel Rowan's energy in the circle, feel the warmth of his arms around her, and she clung on to that, hoping everything was still okay between them.

When they broke for dinner, she found herself looking around for a new table, since Cressida and her daughter were at one that was already full. A woman looked up and caught her eye, motioning to the empty seat opposite her, and she smiled her thanks. But as she sat down, the woman's face paled and she saw fear in her eyes, much like the look on Rowan's mum's face.

"Hi, I'm Carlie," she said nervously. "Um, have we met?"

The woman jumped, brought abruptly back to the present by the sound of her voice. "I'm so sorry, I'm Jasmine. It's lovely to meet you. I just… well, I apologise," she said, flustered and clearly rattled. "You're just the spitting image of an old friend of mine, but it can't be… you're from where, Australia?"

Carlie nodded, but her mind was whirring too. Jasmine had been her mum's only friend in the circle. "Do you mean Violet?" she whispered, and the woman across from her nodded, shocked.

"How do you know her?" she asked. "But this means she's okay, right? I thought… well, I never knew what happened to her – she just disappeared," Jasmine stuttered, voice cracking.

"She was my mum," Carlie replied. "And she was okay, but she died in June this year." She felt tears well. It was still all so fresh – her loss, her beginning of a new life in a new country, all the new people she'd met, and all the strange discoveries she was making about her mother, and herself.

"I'm only just finding out about her life in England – she changed her name when she got to Australia, and never spoke to me or Dad, or her best friend, about her past. I didn't even know I had a grandmother until recently, because Mum had always said her parents were both dead."

Jasmine reached out a hand and grasped Carlie's, sympathy oozing from her as she tried to hide the shock and sadness she was clearly feeling, which was mixed with relief too. "I'm so glad she got away," she said. "I always worried that he'd do something bad…" she broke off.

"You mean Andre?" Carlie asked. "I've just started reading her old diary, which explains a bit of what happened – that they were totally in love, and she gave up her family to be with him, but once they were together he changed, became violent and cruel. So much so that she was scared for her life?"

Jasmine nodded, and Carlie felt herself break all over again. She'd been hoping that her mum's diary entries had been exaggerated, made more dramatic because she was young and in love, or felt guilty for leaving home in such tragic circumstances.

"It was no exaggeration, I promise," Jasmine said, breaking into her thoughts. Carlie looked at her questioningly, heart beating faster as she sensed herself getting closer to the mystery of her mother.

"I met Violet when she started coming to our circles, and it was obvious that she loved him deeply, and that he loved her even more. They had such a strong connection, which was brilliant for both of them, at first anyway. They really inspired each other, and encouraged and supported each other, and their love brought a whole new dimension to our group work – it pushed us further and higher with our spellworkings, with our goals – and some of the rituals we performed then, and the spells we cast, were so powerful.

"He seemed really proud of her, and so enamoured with her. Violet was young and beautiful, self-confident, friendly, clever, deeply spiritual and magical from the work she'd been doing with her mother before I met her, and she had a light within her that drew people to her," Jasmine remembered.

"But then Andre became insecure and paranoid, and it was so strange. He'd always been amazing, so spiritual, so wise, so compassionate. And he was – at least he was with everyone else who'd ever met him, everyone else in our circle. It was just her that he reacted to so strongly. It was like they were playing out this past life drama where one of them had betrayed the other or something – he kept accusing her of cheating on him, of breaking his trust, of trying to destroy him and his work, but there was nothing of the sort from her.

"She was devoted to him, had eyes only for him, had been swept off her feet by his charisma and charm, and of course it didn't hurt that he was so powerful, so magical. Half the women he met fell in love with him, and I know he'd had relationships with some of them before, but never like this. He became obsessed with her, and lost all rationality. She didn't even look at or speak to any of the guys in the circle or at the retreats he led, but he accused her of chatting them up, of sneaking around with them, of having sex with them. I didn't know this until much later though, I promise, not until just before she left. They both hid it so well," Jasmine said, and there was regret and remorse in her voice.

"At first she thought it was sweet that he so clearly cared about her so much, and flattering that he was a bit jealous. But when it started blurring into obsession, she got scared. Which he sensed, and which only made him worse. More controlling, more paranoid, more unbalanced. I'd never seen him like that before, and I'd seen him with a few girlfriends, and three wives. He'd always been so considerate, and so rational. But as he became more and more obsessive, the circle started to fall apart, and people stopped coming, which isolated Violet even further. It was so sad. All the things he'd loved her for – her light, her independence, her strength – he tried to destroy, maybe so no one else would love her, maybe because he just couldn't stand the reflection of her light..."

Carlie felt a rush of love and warmth for her mum. All this time she'd thought that Violet had been so cruel to leave Rose in a purgatory of not knowing if she was dead or alive, but she'd been in a hell far worse all that time, unable to reach out to her mum. She took a sip of her tea, feeling so sad for the woman who'd been so traumatised by all that she'd endured that she'd never felt able to get in touch with her own mother, to feel the comfort and immense healing power of Rose's love.

Jasmine gazed across at Carlie and broke into her thoughts. "So, is it weird doing ritual with Rowan?" she asked, and Carlie stared at her, perplexed. She shook her head. "Should it be?"

"Well, it's just strange that Violet's daughter would want to work magic with his son," she said.

Carlie's face went white, shock robbing her of her voice and her thought process. "His son?" she finally choked out.

"Yes, Rowan is Andre's son. You didn't know?" Carlie shook her head again, mouth open and head spinning. "He would have been, I don't know, two or three when Andre left his wife and child for

Violet. Not that it was her fault," Jasmine added quickly. "He'd told her he was divorced, and had mentioned Rowan once as his nephew. She was devastated when she found out."

Oh god, that could explain why Rowan's mother had looked so terrified of her. She wondered if she'd mentioned her suspicions to her son. Was that why he'd freaked out when she'd said her mum's name was Violet at the ball last night? Had that confirmed Louisa's suspicions? No wonder he'd looked at her strangely when he saw her earlier today, that expression she hadn't been able to interpret.

Feeling his eyes on her now, she looked up. He'd just walked in to the dining room, and someone had already jumped up to wait on him hand and foot. Like father like son? She shook her head, not wanting to believe he was anything like his dad, but a wave of sadness engulfed her when he looked away and went to sit with the pretty woman from earlier, who was clearly a little bit in love with him. Her stomach turned as she watched her fawn over him, touching him way more than was necessary.

Jasmine drew her back to their conversation. "Don't let him bespell you Carlie," she said gently. "I saw what his father did to Violet, saw him turn from loving her, almost worshipping her, to acting like a wife-beating husband as he tried to break her. He thought she was so beautiful, so smart, so independent and strong-willed, such a free spirit – all traits that he loved at first. But then he became paranoid, and didn't want anyone else to speak to her, even look at her, so he tried to diminish her. She did nothing to make him doubt her, nothing at all, but that didn't matter to him, he'd convinced himself that he'd psychically seen her doing all those terrible things, so it must have been true. But they were just delusions, not psychic visions. I've wondered since if he had bipolar disorder. Certainly towards the end he was self-medicating with alcohol and cocaine, which obviously didn't help his paranoia.

"Violet went from being flattered that he loved her so much, to terrified he would destroy her. Eventually I started to realise some of what was going on, and became scared he would harm her, or worse. I'd decided that I would have to convince her to leave, or help her escape, I wasn't sure which, but by the next circle she'd disappeared.

"Of course he interrogated all of us – Where had she gone? Who had helped her? – and later the police got in touch. Apparently someone, an old friend of hers from her home town, had mentioned that Andre may have been a threat to her, so the police questioned us, and him too, but he really was genuinely worried about her. He couldn't find her, not through legal channels, not through psychic means. It really was like she vanished into thin air. She sent me a postcard though, from London airport, which just said: 'I'm safe, thank you for caring.' And I never heard from her again."

"Mum mentioned a retreat like this one in her diary – I was just reading it on the way here. It seems that what he did to her there was what gave her the courage to leave when she got the chance. But what happened to Andre? Did he hurt anyone else?" Carlie asked.

"Once he accepted that she wasn't coming back, he had a bit of a meltdown. He cancelled his workshops and teaching circles, and said he was going to South America to find himself again. I think he was actually scared about what he'd turned into, how obsessive he'd become. Someone mentioned that he'd married a young Brazilian girl while he was there, but I don't know if that's true. And I heard many years later that he'd died."

Carlie nodded. "When Rowan was twelve. They weren't close though – he doesn't speak very highly of him, if he mentions him at all," she said, then stopped, embarrassed that she'd revealed that she knew Rowan so well.

Jasmine raised her eyebrows questioningly. "When I heard that Rowan was teaching, and realised who he was, I decided to keep an eye out for him, or an eye on him, just in case."

Suddenly Carlie felt as though the room was closing in around her. "And you think that Rowan –" she broke off, unable to put her question into words, but Jasmine shook her head.

"God no, I'm sorry, I didn't mean to imply that. But it's a strange kind of responsibility and, I don't know, fame of sorts, that healers and teachers like Rowan are weighed down by. It would be very easy to have your head turned, but he seems to be handling it really well. You can tell in ritual with him, he's very calm, very balanced, very inclusive. Whereas for all his claims of being spiritually enlightened,

Andre could be a misogynistic jerk. He loved your mum's free spirit, until he decided that she belonged to him and he had to break it.

"But Rowan's not like that. His mother brought him up well, and he's a credit to her. It was the best thing that ever happened to the two of them, Andre leaving them when he did. So you have no need to feel guilty about it," she said, smiling across at Carlie, who felt a rush of relief at this revelation. She had been feeling awful that Rowan's dad had left him and his mum for her mother, and had no idea how he'd feel about it if he found out, and whether she'd be able to hide the knowledge from him. Or did he already know? Was there any way he could know?

Jasmine broke into her thoughts. "I'm so glad to know that Violet was okay, that she found happiness, and that she had you."

Carlie smiled, and suddenly realised that knowing any more details about Andre was of no benefit to her. It was in the past. And trying to draw parallels to bring the spectre of his cruelty here, in the present, wasn't fair to herself or to Rowan. But in front of her was someone who had known her mum before she became Fiona, so she had a great opportunity now to learn more about her when she was younger.

"Tell me what she was like when you knew her," she begged, and Jasmine smiled. They sat there for a long time, finishing dinner, then drinking endless cups of tea and eating cinnamon cookies, reminiscing about the past, then sharing stories of more recent times. Eventually, as the fire burned low, they bid each other goodnight.

Carlie hadn't nabbed a bed earlier in the day, but she knew there were still some bunks free in cabin three. So she headed there now, backpack in hand – but as she reached the darkened doorway she felt a hand on her shoulder and jumped, barely stifling a scream before she realised who it was.

"Carlie, oh god, I've been waiting so long to see you, hold you. Come here," he whispered, pulling her into his arms. She melted into him, felt herself relax and really breathe fully for the first time all day. "Come on," he whispered, and led her through the darkness to his little cabin, candlelight spilling out of the windows and looking so welcoming, so magical.

They walked up the two steps hand in hand, then he unlocked the door and drew her inside, arms going around her, lips finding hers and kissing her hungrily. "I've missed you so much," he sighed, and she nodded, kissing him back, as he drew her down onto the couch and into his lap.

Her body responded to his touch, but her mind wasn't quite as comfortable. So many thoughts were whirling through her mind – Rhiannon's ultimatum, all that Rowan's dad had put her mum through, the memory of the woman he'd sat with at dinner, and her hands all over him. The images started to blur, to meld with Rhiannon's conviction that Rowan would cheat on her, and her mum's description of Andre leading her back to his cabin at a retreat a lot like this one and torturing her for nine hours.

"It's been torture to see you here, so close but so far away," Rowan said, and his voice brought her abruptly back into the room, his use of the word torture sending a shiver up her spine. "I wanted to grab you in the middle of the circle, announce to everyone that I love you, just so I could hold you, and kiss you," he whispered, hand gently stroking her face, his touch so warm, and his eyes sparkling in the candlelight with love and desire.

"Why didn't you?" she demanded. She kept her tone light, like maybe she was joking, but she was curious. "Or at least concede that you'd met me once or twice before, instead of treating me like a total stranger, and going out of your way to avoid me."

"What do you mean?" he asked, and the pain in his eyes at her accusation took her breath away. But she couldn't stop herself. She might sound petty, but she felt restless and confused, and was struggling not to lash out at him.

"Today, with the retreat owner, you made a point of saying it was nice to meet me."

"I'm sorry baby, I didn't mean anything by that," he said, and she could hear the regret in his voice. "I'd just rather he didn't know about us, because it can make people a little uncomfortable. It wouldn't affect us at all, because working magic with you only makes me stronger, but some people think any romantic attachment can weaken the circle or corrupt the teachings, that it's unprofessional."

"What, like your dad was?" she challenged him, eyes fierce, shield rising around her heart.

He gazed at her in confusion. "What do you mean about my dad? He's been dead for more than ten years."

"He was pretty unprofessional with the way he treated my mum," she said, tears trembling on her lashes. She didn't want to cry, didn't want to feel weak, but all the things she'd read on the bus today, everything Rhiannon had said, the sense of injustice she'd felt when Rowan hadn't acknowledged her, and had chosen to sit with the flirty woman instead, all mingled together into a fiery blend of emotion.

Carefully, deliberately, he set her down from his lap onto the couch beside him. He was still holding her hands though, which she was glad of, and she could see his mind working, see some things registering, others being discarded. Finally he shook his head.

"Carlie, my love, forgive me please, but I don't know what you mean," he pleaded. "Tell me what's wrong."

"Didn't your mum tell you why she looked so scared of me when we met the other day at your place?" she whispered, pain crackling in her voice, even as she realised that she'd felt slighted then too. Oh god, this wasn't his fault, she couldn't hold him responsible, but it was too late now. She'd opened a wound in both of them that ran much deeper than either had known, or would have admitted.

He touched her cheek, hands so gentle still, and eyes filled with his usual tenderness. "Yes," he said softly, simply, honestly. "After I took you home last week, Mum rang, and she finally revealed a lot of things about my father, things she hadn't told me because she wanted to protect me, wanted me not to hate him. But she admitted that when I was little, Dad had an affair with one of his young students, a girl who looked exactly like you. She told me her name was Violet, which is why I was surprised last night when you said that was your mum's name. It wasn't the only affair he had apparently, but he left us for this girl, and that was new."

Carlie blushed, sensing how awful it must have felt, to have been deserted for some teenager.

"That wasn't what upset Mum though – she was actually relieved when he left," he added quickly, holding her hand tighter. "But a few of her friends from his teaching circles, from when she still used to go, had told her that he was becoming irrational, and warned her to avoid conflict with him, and keep me safe. She didn't think much of it, apparently he was civil to her when they did have to talk, but then the police arrived to question her. The girl had gone missing, and a friend of hers had mentioned Dad's name. For a while there she was terrified that my father had… done something terrible to this girl."

He looked haunted, and Carlie took his hand, suddenly desperate to reassure him, to comfort him. "He was awful to her, but he didn't kill her," she said, shuddering at the word, at the idea, that this was even a possibility. "Mum escaped to Australia, and she ended up being really happy. It wasn't the life she'd envisaged, or with the man she'd imagined, but she found love, and contentment."

"And she had you," Rowan said, voice sad, regretful, but filled with love. "Mum was also worried that if you were Violet's daughter, my father could have been yours too," he conceded, and she stared at him, horror-struck. "It's okay though, he's not!" he added quickly. "You would have had to be a few years older than you are."

She wrinkled her nose. "Finally a reason to be glad I'm so much younger than you," she muttered.

He looked at her closely. "What's wrong baby? You say that like our ages matter."

"Don't they?" she sighed.

"No," he said firmly, then stood up and paced around the room. "Tea?"

She nodded, and watched as he walked over to the sink in the bench along the wall, filled the kettle then hunted for tea bags and cups. He was trying to stay busy, trying to work off his agitation, she noted, recognising one of her traits. Once that would have made her happy, to note more similarities between them, but now she wasn't so sure.

Finally he came back over and handed her the tea. "It's just normal tea, and normal milk," he said apologetically. She shrugged. Not having soy milk or earl grey tea was the least of her worries right now.

He looked up abruptly. “But wait, how could you know he was my dad?” he asked. “And why didn’t you say something before?”

“I didn’t know, not until tonight. The woman I was talking to at dinner stared at me the same way your mum did, like I was a ghost or something. Turns out she was part of your dad’s teaching circle too, and knew my mum back then.”

He nodded thoughtfully, then seemed to be gathering his courage. “Is there something else bothering you my love?” he asked hesitantly. “You seemed upset when you got here today, before you knew it was my father, but you only said that it was a long story, and you needed to be with me tonight.”

She blushed at the naked desire she saw blazing in his eyes, but the things she’d read in her mum’s diary were haunting her even more now that she knew the connection between Andre and Rowan. In her mind it was Rowan doing those awful things, Rowan holding the razor blade to his wrist, holding her mum down and forcing himself on her. Panicked, she shook herself, trying desperately to get the images out of her head.

“I was reading my mum’s diary on the bus trip over here, and what he did to her, it was so awful. She was so terrified. I didn’t know it was your dad then, but there were already parallels – he was a healer, like you, older than her, like you. I just…”

He pulled her back into his arms, but she struggled against him. “Carlie my love, that’s awful, but don’t let it come between us.” She stiffened as he reached out to stroke her cheek, then recoiled at the pain she saw in his eyes at her reaction. “I’m not him Carlie, you have to believe me. I would never hurt you. I’d slit my wrists before I ever allowed myself to hurt you.”

“I know, I just…” her face creased as she struggled with so many warring emotions. She hadn’t even known Andre was his dad when she’d read the diary, so this couldn’t be about Rowan.

“What is it my love?” he asked softly, tenderly. “Talk to me. We can figure this out.”

“Rhiannon came over this morning,” she began, and tried not to laugh at his quick attempt to smother his annoyance. “She *is* my best friend,” she said defensively.

He smiled. "I know, and I respect that. But I also know that all of a sudden she really doesn't like me, and I'm not sure why. It can't just be because of that fortune teller, surely?"

"I'm not sure either," Carlie said, shrugging helplessly. "She's so adamant that I break up with you – she claims you're too old, you're bad for me, you just want me for sex, you'll cheat on me if I don't give it to you, you'll discard me if I do. She's been drawing parallels between us and my mum and her 'older shaman guru guy' as she calls him, and she doesn't even know he was your dad yet..." She sighed.

"But you know those things aren't true," Rowan said, voice pleading, and she felt his frustration as well as his love for her and his fear of losing her. It should have reassured her, but her heart was still uneasy, and she didn't know why, or how to soothe it.

"She also said she couldn't be my friend if I stayed with you, that she couldn't watch the making of such a terrible choice, see me hurting Rose so badly, lying to people, sneaking around, and ultimately being heartbroken by you," she whispered.

He stared at her, more shocked than she'd seen him before, anger and sympathy both crossing his face too, warring for dominance. "But that's blackmail. That's not fair to you," he insisted. "And still not a single valid reason."

"Still, that's what's been torturing me. I don't want to be one of those girls who gives up her friends for a guy. I don't want to be ungrateful to her for all that she's done for me, and I don't want to hurt Rose by lying to her, going behind her back, breaking her trust. Not after all she's been through," she said, then she shivered at the look on his face. So much pain.

"And I don't think you're too old, but maybe I'm too young," she added, realising the truth of it as she said the words. "I need to help Rose in the shop and at home, and focus more on school, concentrate on getting into uni so I can study to be a counsellor."

"You could always work with me," he offered – but he knew the moment that the words had left his mouth that he'd said the wrong thing, and regret settled in his eyes.

"That's what your dad said to Mum. But I need to forge my own path, follow my own heart," Carlie replied. Tears were beginning to fall, carving out a trail down her cheeks, but despite her desperate sadness she felt right somehow. She had Rose and Rhiannon, and the magic that they wove together. And her desire to help other grieving people was becoming increasingly important to her, as a way to honour the memory of her parents. It would have to be enough for now.

Rowan's face was pale. "But you are my heart Carlie," he whispered, voice strained. "I love you so much, and I know that you love me. Isn't that enough?"

"I do Rowan, I love you more than anything, and this is killing me," she said. Taking a deep breath, she tried to hold on to the strength it had taken to make this decision, to tell him. "You have no idea how much this is hurting me, but I can't honour my parents, help Rose, study hard enough, continue my magical education, if I'm obsessed with you and wanting to spend every moment with you.

"And I can't keep lying to Rose, begging Rhiannon to cover for me, sneaking around. That's not me. I don't want to be the type of person who practises deceit, who hides her true self. I don't want to be what the woman in green said I would be, the betrayer of those closest to me," she whispered, voice haunted.

Tears formed on his lashes, and she watched them spill over and run down his face. God, she wanted to reach out and stroke his cheek, stop his tears, kiss his lips, hold him close, tell him she didn't mean it, that of course they should be together. But she couldn't. She knew she was breaking his heart as well as her own, but she also knew that it was for the best.

"I'm sorry," she said, voice cracked with pain, then picked up her bag and fled. She had no idea what she was going to do, but she couldn't stay in the room with him for another minute or she would take back her cruel words and throw her arms around him, begging his forgiveness, begging for him to keep loving her.

Through her tears she saw that the lights were still on in the dining hall, so she headed there. Maybe someone had a phone and she could call a cab. She was half happy, and half disappointed, to see Jasmine at the urn, about to make another cup of tea. But when she saw Carlie's tear-stained face she put her mug down and raced over. "Are you okay?" she asked, fear in her voice.

She nodded, though her heart was shattered, and tried to stifle her sobs as Jasmine spoke. "Tea?" she asked.

Carlie shook her head, even as she smiled at the crazy English notion that a cup of tea would solve everything.

"I need to get out of here. Do you think I could call a cab?"

"I'll drive you," Jasmine said, and she'd rinsed her cup, picked up her purse and was leading Carlie out to the car park in a matter of moments. They pulled out quickly, tyres squealing, and Carlie was shocked out of her reverie by the anger stamped across the other woman's face.

"Did he try to hurt you? Force you to do anything?" Jasmine asked, voice fierce and eyes blazing.

"It's not Rowan," Carlie said quickly. "I promise." Jasmine glanced over at her, eyes searching her face for something, and seeming to find enough to reassure her, for now at least. Carlie was touched that she was so quick to jump to her defence.

"He's the best person I've ever known, and probably no one will ever love me the way he does," she said, feeling sadness at the truth of those words, and realising as she said them the startling differences between her relationship and her mum's. Violet had been so glad that no one would ever love her the way Andre did, but Carlie was devastated at the thought that no one would ever love her as much and as well as Rowan did.

She sighed. "We're both desperately in love. It's just... too much for me. I think I'll always think of what Mum went through at his dad's hands. And I know that's not fair, but maybe my friend is right, maybe I am too young for him. Maybe I lack the courage to love him as he deserves to be loved, as he loves me. And I know it's not fair to him, to leave like this, to run away, but surely it's better that I do it now rather than later, when we fall even more deeply in love?"

She paused for breath, trying to get her tears under control, and stared out into the darkness for a while in silence.

"But don't you deserve to love, and to be loved?" Jasmine finally asked, voice gentle, hesitant.

"Oh god, please don't give me a reason to take it back!" she implored her. "Of course I want to be with him, with all my heart, but I have to be strong. Me being with him hurts the other people in my life, and I can't do that."

Jasmine held her tongue, and they drove for a long time without a word, both lost in their own private worlds, gazing out at the lonely highway.

"Um, sweetie? I don't know where you live," Jasmine finally said as they approached a large intersection, and Carlie came back to the present with a crash.

"If you could just drop me in Smithfield I should be able to get a bus from there," she said.

Jasmine leaned over and took her hand, and pain seared through her as she remembered all the times Rowan had done that. Gasping for breath, and unable to speak, she sobbed once, before she got herself under control again.

"I'll take you home Carlie," the older woman said. "You're in no fit state to be waiting for buses in the middle of the night."

Grateful, Carlie finally managed to tell her where she lived, and Jasmine eventually got a smile out of her as she recalled more memories of Violet as a teenager.

It was almost midnight when Jasmine pulled up just down the road from Rose's cottage and gave Carlie a hug and her phone number, which she insisted she could call any time she needed to talk, day or night. Overwhelmed by her kindness, Carlie hugged her back, then stole around the side of the house and in through the back door, trying not to wake Rose. She couldn't face anyone right now, no matter how well meaning and filled with love they were. As quietly as she could she tiptoed up the stairs, then she threw herself down on her narrow bed, crying into the pillow until there were no tears left.

But sleep eluded her, and her mind raced ever faster. It was even worse because she knew she'd done this to herself. She was causing so much pain to them both, and now she was torturing herself over whether she'd done the right thing or not. After tossing and turning for ages, she finally lit the candle on her bedside table and crept out of bed, over to where she'd dumped her backpack, and pulled the diary out. Maybe her mum would have some wisdom for her…

Chapter 35

Dear Diary...

It's funny, sometimes the most insignificant of chance encounters can change your life. Can save your life. I didn't even know his name for ages, just appreciated his kind hellos whenever I saw him, his offers to help me if I was carrying heavy shopping bags. Of course I could never let him help me, or let him into our apartment, or even return his greetings, because Andre would have known somehow, and I was always terrified of doing something wrong – or anything he would consider was wrong – for fear of his anger.

Oliver lived in the same building as us, and although I barely spoke to him, too afraid to, if I'm honest, somehow an unlikely rapport developed between us. It was pretty one sided – he'd ask how I was, he'd tell me about his day, and I would stare at him, mute with fear that somehow Andre would twist even this into something ugly. He'd become so jealous, so controlling, so angry. He was convinced that I was chatting up every guy I met, from the plumber who came to fix our hot water to the guys in our ritual circle who he was certain I was having sex with. So I tried to avoid Oliver – he seemed so sweet, and I didn't want him being dragged into our drama, didn't want him being hurt if Andre ever grew suspicious.

But while I never told him anything, somehow he noticed the bruises everyone else refused to see, and saw me shrink into myself when I was with Andre, in a way no one else ever did... Somehow I'd found a friend, in the most unlikely place, from the most unlikely country. He was a backpacker from Australia, living in London for a while, and he offered me friendship when I needed it. Maybe that's the Aussie way, I don't know. But I will forever be grateful that he persevered with me, no matter how many times I ignored and rebuffed him.

One afternoon Andre and I had a terrible fight, worse than usual – and that's saying something! It was only a few days after the retreat where he'd forced himself on me, and I could feel myself disappearing, losing myself, becoming just a shell of a person. He said he'd overheard me on the phone to Mike, planning to escape. Which was laughable – I knew I couldn't use the phone, I knew he had it bugged, and there was no way I could call Mike, or would call Mike, and drag him into this. I'd given up hope of ever seeing him again.

But Andre didn't believe me. He screamed at me, awful, ugly accusations, said with such conviction that I started wondering if I'd really done all those terrible things after all. But they weren't true, so for some stupid reason I continued to deny them – and he threw me into the glass coffee table, which smashed, and cut me up pretty badly. I couldn't even stand up, I was in so much pain, but he came at me again, lifting me up, hand biting into my shoulder, his other hand over my mouth to smother me as I clawed at him, desperately trying to breathe. He continued his awful abuse, shouting things so cruel that I wondered what he'd ever seen in me, how anyone could ever love me, let alone him, if I was all those terrible things.

Carlie stopped, stunned. It wasn't Rowan in that fortune teller's vision, forcing her to have sex and throwing her into a glass table, it was Andre and her mum. Andre who no doubt looked a lot like Rowan, and her mum who had looked so much like her at that age. Tears blinded her. Rhiannon had been so wrong. She had been so wrong. It was never Rowan. Heart breaking a little more, but not knowing what else to do, she kept reading.

Finally I started to black out, and part of me welcomed the thought of oblivion, of release from the pain, from the mental anguish, from the fear that now consumed every waking moment. Then someone hammered on the door, and he dropped me onto the floor and stomped off down the hallway, threatening to kill whoever had knocked. He didn't come back though, and eventually I realised that the person who'd knocked had gone, and so had he.

I lay there, crumpled on the ground, shaking, crying, sending a prayer of thanks to the goddess that I'd survived one more beating, even though part of me wondered what the point was. It was inevitable that he would go too far at some point, and I would die, so what did it matter if it was today or any other day?

Then slowly I became aware that someone was standing in the room with me, and a shiver of fear and shame rocked through me. Was it a neighbour, drawn by the crash? Or had Andre come back to finish me off? But it was Oliver, so gentle, so out of place in this shambles of a room, with this wreck of a person. He winced as I turned towards him, and I raised a hand to my face and realised there was blood still pouring out of the cut on my scalp. As ever, the wound wouldn't show though – they were always well hidden.

Panicked, I told him he had to go, quickly, that he needed to escape before Andre came back, but he shook his head and came over to me. And he lifted me up, so gently, and pulled off his long sleeved t-shirt and used it to try to stop the blood. There was still some glass in some of the smaller cuts, and he pulled them out, his face contorting with emotion each time he thought he'd hurt me, but by this stage I'd become almost oblivious to the sensation of physical pain.

He wanted to take me to hospital, or call the police, but I freaked out on him, and eventually he promised he wouldn't. I became increasingly hysterical the longer he stayed though, scared Andre would come back and kill us both. Finally I got through to him, and he agreed to go – but then he said he was leaving for Australia the next day, and had actually come to say goodbye.

I'd never felt so sad, or so desperate. I hadn't realised how much I'd come to depend on him and his sunny nature, his quiet acceptance, his occasional smiles and hellos in the corridor. Then he said: "Come with me." That we could go backpacking around Australia, and he'd teach me to surf, and I could hang out with his buddies – take a bit of time out to think clearly. I shook my head, knowing it was impossible. He'd find me, he'd stop me, and he'd make this kind stranger's life hell.

"He'll kill you if you stay," he said, as though he'd heard my thought. But there was no judgement in his voice, no drama, it was just a simple statement of fact. Which I already knew, of course, and was numb to, but there was something about the way he said it, the look on his face, the compassion in his eyes, that made me suddenly cling to a skerrick of hope that there could be an escape from the inevitability of my life.

It sounded crazy, and wildly impossible, but he said a friend of his had an old passport in her maiden name, and no plans to travel for a few years, and we looked a little alike. So I became Fiona Scott, nineteen years old. I gained two years, and even got a new birthday. But I wasn't thinking about the future at all, by then I was just thinking day to day, how to survive one more day. If I thought at all, I guess I imagined that eventually I'd go back home and pick up my old life with Mum, become Violet Tyler again, and straighten out the ID issue. But that never happened.

And so I grabbed my diary, a change of clothes and three hundred pounds from Andre's drawer, then we went down to Oliver's apartment. I cut off my hair and bleached it blonde, to look more like Fiona – to look less like myself – then we left for the airport, too scared to stay in the building, even inside behind a locked door, in case Andre somehow found us. Oliver bought me a plane ticket, and we stayed the night in the gate lounge, him watching over me like a guardian angel when I finally slept for a few short hours, then we flew out early the next morning.

It was the perfect escape – even if Andre did have all those "high up" contacts that he'd threatened me with, they wouldn't be able to track me because I didn't travel under my own name. And he'd never even known Oliver existed, wouldn't know his name even if someone described him. It probably wouldn't have worked now, with whiz bang computers and high alert security, but somehow I got away with it. It did help that Fiona's passport photo had been taken when she was fifteen, so obviously she would look a bit different by now, four years later. And who knows? Maybe the goddess granted me one last favour, even though I'd turned my back on her.

Don't misunderstand me – although I'm recounting this calmly now, I did totally freak out, somewhere over Europe, that I was flying across the world with a stranger. Had I learned nothing?

It horrified me that the first real conversation I had with this man was on a plane to Australia with him. I was actually more dependent on him than I'd been on Andre, and it's a testament to his patience and kindness that I didn't try to throw myself off the plane somehow. So yes, of course it seemed crazy to do this – but my life was crazy. I no longer knew what normal was, what safe was. I guess I'm just really lucky he didn't take advantage of me too, that he was so trustworthy and so honourable.

We spent some time in Sydney, staying with his parents for a while. I don't know what he told them about me, but they were so lovely, and said I could stay in their spare room for as long as I needed to. It took a while for me to stop jumping whenever there was a knock on the door, or flinching when the phone rang, but they were very patient with me, gave me a lot of space, and I was indebted to them until the day they died for their gentle acceptance and immense warmth. Mum would have loved them, and loved Oliver too.

Because he was so kind. So patient. So sweet. He is so kind, so patient, so sweet. And he did everything he possibly could to reassure me that he didn't expect anything from me, that I didn't owe him anything, then or ever. He introduced me to all his friends, and encouraged me to become their friends too, especially the girls, independent of him – although I was painfully shy for a long time, overly cautious and scared of giving anything of my past away, so I didn't become close to any of them until a year or two later.

But they were all so lovely, and when a few of them said they were going to travel up north and pick fruit in Queensland through the summer, I told Ollie I'd like to go too, to earn some money and start trying to live in the world. So we all went. We didn't earn enough money to stay anywhere fancy or go out every night, but it was nice – we stayed in a hostel on the beach, sat around at night having picnics on the sand and just talking, laughing, joking, just being normal young people. It amazed me how carefree they all were – yet after a while I was even more amazed to find myself joining in.

When they drifted back to Sydney to their real lives, Ollie and I got the train south and then went across the Nullarbor, and worked through vintage season, picking grapes through the night at a vineyard on the south-west coast for two months. Then we moved on, travelling north to follow the sun, spending days at the beach, camping out and just watching the stars, slowly opening up to each other. It was amazing – after the stress of that time with Andre, just drifting from place to place, with no real job and no commitment, no pressure, was perfect. It was everything that I needed.

Ollie told me later that he'd fallen in love with me the day he rescued me, when we stood in the bathroom of his tiny London apartment and he watched me chop off my hair, bleach it blonde and gather my courage to escape. But he never told me that at the time, never let me know by word or action – was always so desperately careful to never let me feel pressured in any way.

Years later he revealed to me that when he was growing up, his next door neighbour had been a victim of domestic violence, so he'd recognised the signs when he first saw me, and felt compelled to help me because their friend had been killed by her husband. He was only twelve when that happened, and it had affected him deeply. In some way I think saving me healed the guilt he'd always felt about not intervening, the powerlessness of knowing it was happening but not knowing how to help.

We picked up bar work here and there – Ollie taught me how, and since I was apparently legal now, being suddenly nineteen, I could get jobs in pubs too. I desperately wanted to be self-sufficient, and to eventually earn enough money to pay him back for the cost of the plane fare and the time I'd spent with him in Sydney before I'd got work. We always worked cash in hand, and Ollie booked the hostels, just to be on the safe side, but I opened a bank account in Fiona's name, since the only ID I had was her passport, and slowly I became her. I went for my driver's licence in her name, I introduced myself to everyone I met as Fiona, and even Ollie called me that, because he'd never actually known my name in London.

I felt sad that Violet had disappeared, like she'd never existed, but I knew this was the opportunity I needed. No one here knew Violet, knew me, so I was free to reinvent myself, to become the person I wanted to be, to hide my shameful past from myself and everyone else. So I become Fiona – stronger than Violet, tougher, more outgoing. Fiona was less trusting certainly, less generous with her time, and far more sceptical of everything. I always shied away from the new agey events Oliver's friends invited us to, and the smell of burning sage still makes me sick to my stomach.

I wrote to Mum once, to tell her I'd found happiness, but it came back return to sender, addressee unknown, so I figured that she didn't want to see me again, or she'd moved away to start over, and perhaps I should just leave it be, let her build a new family, a new life. Now it's not much to go on, but just in case you ever need to know, her name is Rose Tyler, and she lived at 32 Meadow Lane, Summer Hill...

Carlie tore her eyes from the book, aghast. Rose lived at number 23, not 32. She'd never moved away, had stayed in the same house all these years, just on the slightest chance that her daughter might get in touch one day. Grief and such a deep sense of loss and regret overwhelmed her, and for a while she just sat there, tears running down her cheeks, eyes unseeing, as she held the book to her chest and cried. Finally though she took a deep breath and wiped her eyes, and turned back to the tear-stained pages.

This, at last, was the mystery of her mother. She was a victim of domestic violence – but she was not a tragic figure, and not a victim in the end, because more than anything she was also a survivor. She refused to have her life defined by what was done to her by a cruel man, and instead defined herself and her life by what she made of it. By how she overcame her circumstances and created a life of love and joy for herself, the man she loved, and Carlie, the child of that love.

Even her name became a conscious choice and a symbol of her empowerment. Sure, at first it was borrowed simply as a means of escape, but she took ownership of it and became the woman she wanted to be, stronger, more independent, filled with love and courage. No longer diminished, no longer scared, finally herself.

She hadn't cast off her old name as a slight to the woman who had given it to her, but as a way to pull together the shattered pieces of what Violet had become, and create a symbol of her survival, a symbol of her reweaving of her life into a woman of strength.

Carlie was stunned. She'd never known a braver woman than her mum, and she was in awe at the depth of her father, who had saved a scared young girl then helped her blossom into the warrior she had become. Many men would have liked the insecurity and weakness a woman who'd been through all that might cling to, but her dad had seen the light inside her when she was a terrified teenager diminishing herself almost to nothing – a light no one else had seen – and nurtured it, helped it grow. She prayed that she would find a man who would love her like that, then felt her eyes fill with tears as she realised that she *did* have a man like that, and she had just cruelly cast him aside.

Desperate not to dwell on that right now, she turned back to the diary. There were pages torn out, and a few blank ones, then she came to what appeared to be the end, and one final block of text. The handwriting was different – neater, stronger, less girlie – and it seemed some time had passed since the previous entries.

Tomorrow I am getting married, and I will have a new name. Not the name I was born with, or the name I borrowed to escape, but the one that represents the love I've found with a truly good man, the acceptance of his wonderful parents, which I thank the goddess for every day, and the new life of love that Oliver and I will build together. And I can't quite believe it, but today we found out that I'm pregnant, and we couldn't be happier. This is why I want to finish writing this letter to you, in case you ever get to read this, and then I will put it away forever. Because this is my new beginning. My fresh start.

I am not the girl who started this diary. I feel so much for her, and I am so grateful that she was so loved, by her parents, by her friends, by Mike, the truest friend anyone could ever have. My heart breaks for the pain she went through, the pain she caused, but to be honest it feels like all that happened to someone else. A childhood friend I'm no longer in contact with, or someone from a nightmare that used to plague me. She is not me, and I will not be defined by what happened to her. It is over, it is the past. It made me who I am perhaps, but that is all. No longer will it have any power over me. People can be defined by the worst parts of their life, or by the best. I choose the best.

So tomorrow I will become Fiona Parker, wife of Oliver, mother of our beloved child, and future lawyer. I went back to school you know, and now I'm at university. A few years ago a good man saw the potential in me, when I had lost all hope, had lost even the will to live, and he continues to encourage me to follow my heart, and my dreams, to be the best person I can be.

This is not what I ever expected my life to be like – I have a different name, a different husband, a different career, a different home country – but in many ways it's so much better. Of course I miss Mum, every single day, and I deeply regret that she'll always wonder if I'm dead. But I might have been, if I'd stayed with Andre, and so I try to be glad that, although she doesn't know it, I am alive, and I am happy, and I am loved.

I guess my daughter, if you ever read this, I want you to know not only of the pain and disappointment of love, but the beauty and goodness of it. Be wary, and don't let any man diminish you – and especially don't diminish yourself for any man, or any person. But even more importantly, don't lock your heart away and refuse to feel just in case you get hurt.

If you find a good man, a true man, one who loves you for who you are, not what he wants you to be, hold on to him. Don't let other people's opinions of him colour your judgement, and don't judge him harshly for one misunderstanding or mistake. People make mistakes – you will make mistakes, no doubt your loved one will make mistakes – but there's a big difference between someone who acknowledges their error, asks for forgiveness and is determined to prove that they'll never do it again, and someone who can't even see that what they did is wrong.

Be honest, be fair, listen to his point of view and his explanation, and make sure you are not responding out of fear or misinformation, turning one small misunderstanding into a catastrophic event that colours everything you see from then on.

Don't judge him on another person's idea of him, or break up with him because they said so. Everyone has a motive, everyone has a different perspective, and no one knows the real story, your story, except you. And don't let your perception of everyone be tainted by the actions of one person. Some people are cruel, yes, but one bad man does not mean all men are bad. Some people are amazing, inspiring. They will lift you up, help you grow, help you be better, help you find what it is within you that makes your heart sing, makes you feel all the amazing possibilities of this amazing life.

Don't ever let a man bend you to his will, but equally don't let a friend make your decisions for you, issue you with ultimatums or decide what is best for you. You must trust your heart. The wisdom within your soul. The light that shines so brightly within you.

And if you find someone who loves you, flaws and all, who encourages you to shine ever brighter, well, be brave enough to give your heart to them. To dive into the great unknown and risk everything for the love you will share. Because it's worth it. It's so worth it. You are so worth it.

Chapter 36

The Choice

Carlie stared at the words on the page, at the wisdom her mum had left her with. To follow her heart. To let her light shine. To trust her own wisdom. To not cave in to a boyfriend – or to a friend. To choose what was right, what was fair, what made her heart sing. She knew some people would expect her to choose Rhiannon. Her grandma might too. Wasn't that what women were taught, that the sisterhood was more important? To never let a man come between two friends?

But the problem with that was that it wasn't Rowan who was coming between them. He'd been nothing but sweet and kind to Rhiannon, helping her with her magical studies, inviting her to the festival, including her, acknowledging her importance in Carlie's life. And he'd always encouraged her to spend time with Rhi, despite the fact that he liked her a little bit less every time she tried to encourage Carlie to break up with him. Every time she tried to convince her he was capable of the awful things that her mother had suffered.

She sighed. She knew there were also those who would say she should be with the man she loved, and sacrifice Rhiannon's friendship, especially as that was the only option she was giving her. Thinking about it like that, it seemed more logical to choose Rowan. He was the one who wanted her to be happy, who encouraged her to choose the best option for *her*. She still couldn't understand why Rhiannon was demanding she break up with him in the first place.

But was this the betrayal that the woman in green had spoken of? Did she know even then that she would be faced with a choice between Rhiannon, the girl who had helped her so much in her grief, and Rowan, the man who had taught her how to love and be loved? And did Brianna expect that she would choose the guy, and betray her friend? Know even then, before Carlie had ever met him, that it would come to this? Was that what she'd meant, that she should do what Rhi wanted rather than betraying her?

But if she accepted her friend's ultimatum and broke up with Rowan – stayed broken up with Rowan – wasn't she betraying herself? Betraying her own heart? Shouldn't she be willing to risk her heart for the man who treasured her so deeply? Be brave, like her mum, and seek out the deep and desperate all-consuming love that she now knew was possible?

And why did she even have to choose? Her mum had had the love of her life as well as her best friend Sandy. Couldn't she choose both as well? Rowan accepted the importance of Rhiannon in her life – why couldn't her friend accept him? Or at least accept that she loved him. That she wanted to be with him. Because she'd realised, as she read her mum's words, that she did want Rowan, that she loved him desperately, and she was mortified that she'd let her friend's words, and her mum's old stories, turn her against him.

How could she have looked at him and seen his father? How could she have connected herself with her mother in that tragic scenario? How could she have doubted him for one moment? She'd done just what her mother had warned her against, let the actions of another man colour her perception of him. Let the words of her friend – words that had no foundation – influence the way she thought of him. But she and Rowan were not their parents. They weren't destined to play out their lives, doomed to repeat their mistakes. They could choose their own path, their own love, forge their own way forward.

Climbing out of bed, Carlie threw back the curtains, letting the waxing moon shine in on her, feeling the presence of the nearby hill silhouetted against the dark sky connecting her to the earth, to the beating heart of the planet and all that lived on it. She tried to reach out with her mind to Rowan. So often when they were apart they'd stared up at the same moon and felt connected, and she could swear he was doing that now, reaching out to her, holding her close, stroking her cheek as he whispered words of forgiveness and love. Closing her eyes, she sent out a prayer to the moon, and a prayer to him, that it was not too late. That she could reverse this mess she'd created, and take responsibility for the cruel things she'd said – and take power over and ownership of her choice. She was choosing him. And she was choosing Rhiannon. *She was choosing them both.*

Groping around on her desk until she found the cards she'd bought the other day, she climbed back into bed, smiling as Luther jumped up and settled on her feet, purring happily, as though to tell her she'd finally made the right decision. And as she gazed at her cat friend she felt her heart lighten, and knew that she had. Rhiannon had to understand that she would not choose one over the other. She loved them both, and it was time she told them that.

Dear Rowan, my sweet beloved,
As soon as I left tonight I knew I'd done the wrong thing, made the wrong choice. Because I choose you. I love you. I want to be with you. That's the truth of it, and anything else is superfluous. How I deal with Rhiannon, when I tell Gran about us, they're just details to be worked out. They don't affect the only thing that actually matters – the fact that I love you.

I'm going to come and see you in the morning, get the first bus back so that I can tell you all this myself, but I want to write it down too, right now, in this moment that I choose you, because I'm sure you will feel it. I'm sure you will know it deep in your bones, in your heart, in your soul, and you will feel my arms around you until I can be there in person to tell you, to hold you, to love you. I can feel your arms around me too, I'm sure of it – I can feel your love, and I thank you with all my heart for your forgiveness.

I deeply regret the pain I caused you, caused both of us, tonight. I let other people's opinions cloud my judgement, and allowed someone else to make a decision for me. And I'm sorry, so sorry, for thinking for even a second that you could be anything like your father. I know you're not. I feel that in every cell of my body, every beat of my heart. And I am not my mother, though I love her dearly. You and I are not fated to walk the path of our parents, but to forge our own path, our own destiny. Lives entwined, souls in harmony, hearts as one.

I choose Rhiannon too, and I hope that one day soon you'll both see in each other what I see. She is the sister of my heart, and I value her highly and deeply – but you are the love of my life, and I will not give you up for anyone or anything.

You have opened my heart to love, after I thought it would be closed forever. I thought I was unloveable, unable to love, unworthy of being loved, but your patience and compassion have transformed me. Being loved by you has made me blossom, has given me the courage to let my light shine, has made me a better person. Your mum got it wrong – it is you who has changed me for the better, not the other way round. You have transformed me. You have healed me, in so many different ways, and I am so grateful to you.

And I will love you forever,

Your Carlie xx

Dear Rhiannon, sister of my heart,

I went to see Rowan today, and I broke up with him, because of the ultimatum you gave me. But I've been thinking about it every moment since, and I know that I made the wrong decision. I will not choose between you. I love you both. I choose you both.

I appreciate that you are concerned for me, and I'm grateful that you care so much, but please know that there is nothing to fear. Rowan loves me, and he will never hurt me. I know this in my heart, in my mind, in the very bones of my body. And there's something I learned from my mother today – Rowan is my Oliver, not my Andre. He is the man who makes me more, not the one who diminishes me. He is my beloved, and being loved by him has healed me in so many ways. I hope that when you come to know him as I do, that you will see us together and recognise how much we love each other.

And I want you to know too that he has always honoured you, and your importance in my life. Even tonight, even when I told him I had chosen you.

Another thing I learned from Mum today – if Rowan didn't want to be with me, he wouldn't be. It's that simple, and that complex. He doesn't gain anything from being with me – it would be so much easier for him if he wasn't with me, if he didn't have to sneak around, and wait for me to finish school before he can see me... if his girlfriend had a car, and was free to travel with him... if she didn't have a curfew, if she wasn't too scared to tell her grandmother about him... But he loves me despite all that. He loves ME.

I love him so much, and I love you too. I hope one day you'll be able to see in him what I see, be able to spend time together with us both like we did at the Autumn's End festival. And I hope you won't carry out your ultimatum, because I would be devastated to lose you. You are the sister of my heart, my dearest friend, and I value you and want you in my life.

Much love, Carlie xx

Hand cramping and eyes feeling tired from her furious writing, Carlie finally put the cards in their envelopes and wrote Rowan and Rhiannon's names on theirs. As she snuggled down under her mum's old quilt, she felt as though a huge weight had been lifted from her shoulders, and was filled with incredible relief that she had made this decision. Now she couldn't wait to get up in the morning and rush off to see Rowan.

A tiny flicker of fear shot through her, as she wondered whether she would be too late to make amends, but she could feel his arms around her somehow, would have sworn that he was sending the same message to her. Luther miaowed, and climbed up the bed, close to her head, so she fell asleep to the sound of his purring, with a smile on her face and an incredible lightness and sense of hope in her heart.

Chapter 37

For A Short Time

The hammering on the door woke her, and she struggled up from the depths of her beautiful dream, clinging to the memory of Rowan's arm around her, his hand stroking her face, his lips warm on hers. Smiling, she dragged on a pair of jeans from the messy pile on the floor and his cosy black jumper from the end of her narrow bed, and made her way downstairs.

Excited, she pulled the door open, expecting it to be Rowan, called there by her dream, by the message of love that she'd sent him. But her smile faltered as she gazed at the man and woman standing under the stretch of blackberry vines twisting overhead. They were police officers, the man holding a package wrapped in heart-print paper, with a card with her name on it nestled under the ribbons. She stared at them, a shiver of dread racing up her spine.

"Can I help you?" she croaked, fear already tightening her throat.

"Are you Carlie?" the woman asked, and she nodded, terror clutching at her heart as she tried to wake up, tried to kick her brain into gear, tried to understand what they were doing there.

"There was an accident this morning," the woman said, voice gentle, soothing. "Do you know the young man? Long black hair, tattoo of the moon on his wrist?"

Face ashen, heart pounding, she nodded again. "My boyfriend Rowan," she whispered. "What happened? Where is he?"

"He was just down the highway, on his way here I guess, but his car must have slid off the road in the snow," the man said. "We found your address in his wallet..."

"But is he... What has... Can I see him?" She stopped, unable to bring herself to ask what she most needed to know.

"I'm so sorry," the woman said, reaching out for her as she staggered a little, clutching the door frame, trying to stay upright. "The ambulance came, but it was too late." The space around Carlie opened up, all noise receded, and time seemed to whir around her, stretching, slowing, collapsing in on her. Slowly she slid to the ground, not even aware she was falling. Not aware of anything but the crushing pain and anger swelling inside her. This couldn't be happening, not again. She couldn't lose him too. That wasn't fair. Not now, not when she still had to tell him how much she loved him.

"Carlie, what is it?" Rose asked, hurrying towards the three people standing in her doorway, catching her distraught granddaughter as she sank to the floor. A small part of Carlie felt Rose's arms around her, holding her close, holding her safe. Not safe enough though. Never safe again. That part of her was also aware of the snow falling around them, twirling in the doorway, catching in her hair. Like diamonds, he'd said. The rest of her was just numb, so numb, and cold and dead inside.

The tiny part of her that remained there in the present was relieved when Rose took charge and invited the officers inside, but she couldn't move. Didn't want to move. Thought she could just stay there, slumped and frozen in the doorway, snow in her hair, in her face, in her heart. Stay there forever. Her shattered heart had crumbled into pieces again, and there was just a gaping wound where it used to be. An endless black hole that would never be filled again.

The male officer had come back out when she didn't follow them, and he lifted her to her feet and half carried, half dragged, her inside to the warmth of the kitchen, where Rose pressed a cup of tea into her cold hands. She shuddered as she inhaled the scent of ginkgo, valerian, juniper and cayenne, her grandma's blend for shock, honey stirred into it but unable to mask the smell or the taste. But she swallowed it dutifully, too numb to argue.

She wished she could swallow something stronger, something that would end her pain forever. The officer had steered her into a chair and settled down next to her. He was asking her questions, but she stared at him blankly. She couldn't understand them, couldn't make sense of the words floating around his head, jumbles of letters moving through the air. Then finally one landed. Parents.

"His mum is Louisa, Louisa Dunbar. From Smithfield," she whispered. "His father is dead. Like everyone else," she muttered, and broke down again.

Later, she became vaguely aware that Rose had shepherded the officers out. Heard, on the edge of her consciousness, the sudden rain as it poured from the sky, the thunder rumbling across the village, and the lightning that was splitting the heavens apart. It was perfect, she thought bitterly, and wanted to run outside into the storm and let the lightning split her apart too. Tears finally came, and she felt the sobs wracking her body.

Shaking with anguish, she ran up the stairs, threw herself through her bedroom door and slammed it closed behind her. Crawling into the far corner, she crouched there, knees pulled up to her chin, arms wrapped tightly around her legs, trying to make herself smaller, trying to diminish herself in an effort to diminish the pain. She rocked, slowly at first, then less gently, as wrenching sobs shook her body, shook her world.

Through the mist of her tears, her gaze flitted wildly around the room, coming to rest on the altar she'd so carefully constructed with Rhiannon. A huge chunk of rose quartz sat in the north, mocking her with its promise of forgiveness, compassion and unconditional love.

Fat lot of good that had done her.

Close to it was her athame, the ceremonial dagger she'd been gifted by a woman more mist than substance. Snatching it up, she held it in her hand, its weight a welcome distraction, grounding her in her body, in her pain. Holding the point of the blade to her wrist, she tried desperately to find one single reason not to draw it across the delicate skin, draw it through the blue vein, draw out a river of blood, and draw this painful existence to a close.

He'd promised her that he would slit his wrists before he ever hurt her, but that had clearly been a lie. Fury raged through her, red hot, and suddenly the thought of oblivion, of letting herself drown in this swirling crush of despair and never come up for air, seemed the most welcome idea in the world.

But in the end even that effort seemed too much for her, and she slumped on the floor and allowed her mind to shut down as the pain of her loss tore her heart into a million broken pieces.

For three days she didn't leave her room, didn't eat, didn't even seem aware of her surroundings. Someone had lifted her into her bed, but she didn't know who. Christmas morning dawned, then set, and she didn't even notice. Sometimes she sensed Rose, putting another cup of herbal tea in her hands, holding her head up and forcing her to take a few sips. She thought Rhiannon might have been there once or twice too, but she wasn't sure, couldn't be sure, because she also thought her mother had been there, sitting on her bed, holding her hand, smoothing back her hair, and she knew that couldn't be right. Everyone she loved left her. *Everyone.*

She thought she'd never stop crying, but eventually her body couldn't make any more tears, and she sobbed without them, great gulping breaths torn from the very centre of her soul, which wracked her weakened body until she slipped back into welcome oblivion again. Finally Rose came in, with Mike behind her for moral support.

"Sweetheart, you have to get up now, you have to eat. Can you do that for me?" Carlie stared at her, hollow eyed. Dead inside. She didn't want to ever move again. Moving hurt. Living hurt. Loving was a pain beyond all measure. Mike came and sat on her bed, and took her hands gently in his. She tried not to recoil, but it was hard. He smiled at her, sympathy and caring oozing from every pore.

"Carlie love, do you think you could get up, just for a little while? Just have a piece of toast? Even half?" He leaned in closer and lowered his voice. "Your grandma is really worried, and I'd ask, if not for yourself, that you do it for her," he said beseechingly.

Looking over at Rose, she saw her, really saw her, and her heart constricted. There were great black smudges under her eyes, and her face was gaunt, sadness etched in jagged lines across it. She was so frail, a million miles from the grand high priestess she usually appeared to be, just an old woman who had endured more tragedy than any one person should have to. Glancing back at Mike, she saw the suffering writ deep in his eyes too, and slowly nodded. He smiled at her, a small smile, patted her hand, then helped Rose back downstairs, leaving her door open so she couldn't descend back into the dark that had so consumed her.

Carlie lay in bed for a few more minutes, crippled with despair, then she forced herself to get up. Her body ached. She was stiff and sore, and her legs buckled under her as she tried to stand. Every step was a huge effort, but the memory of her grandma's face pushed her on. Gazing down at herself, she saw that she was still clad in her old jeans and his woollen jumper, the clothes she'd pulled on three days ago – or was it three years? – in that time when she'd been so filled with joy and optimism. When she'd been about to tell him that of course she loved him, as much as he loved her, and she desperately wanted to be with him forever.

Turning towards the door, she caught sight of her reflection in the mirror, and walked closer, shocked. She looked like a zombie, dark circles smudged under her lower lashes, hair lank and lifeless, lips pale, and her eyes bloodshot and deadened of all expression. No wonder Rose was worried about her.

Slowly she picked up a skirt from the floor, then dragged open a drawer and pulled out a clean t-shirt and underwear, and walked into the ensuite next door. She turned on the hot water, piled her hair into a knot on the top of her head – washing it would have to wait – and stepped into the shower. Then she stood under the stream of scalding water, hating the feeling of her body waking up. She didn't want to wake up. Being awake was too painful.

When the water ran cold she stayed there, liking the sensation of pain as it chilled her through, matching her frozen heart. But eventually she sighed, and turned off the shower, then stepped out and dried off. She dragged on her clothes, then pulled Rowan's jumper over her head. It still smelled of him, of lemongrass and vanilla, and precious moments spent together outside, and the sweetness of his hugs. She couldn't choke back the sobs or stop the river of tears as she felt his arms around her, felt his lips on her ear as he whispered how much he loved her.

Every fibre of her being ached to crawl back into bed, wanted to slip back into oblivion, but she knew that Rose was waiting for her. So, heart filled with dread, she made her way downstairs, Luther weaving around her ankles, helping her into the kitchen. Rose stood there, trapped between the sink and the bench, a piece of toast on a plate in one hand, looking totally lost.

"I'm so sorry Gran," Carlie croaked, as she fell into the older woman's arms, tears trickling down her face and soaking into Rose's hair. Her grandmother was all she had now, and she didn't even know how long she'd still be with her. "I'm sorry I didn't tell you about him, didn't let you meet him. I wanted to wait until I was sure, which was stupid. I was sure the minute I met him. He was sure the minute we met. I just…" she trailed off, tear-stained face filled with anguish and regret.

"Oh Sweetheart, I'm the one who's sorry. We're all so sorry."

Carlie looked up at her, puzzled. "Rhiannon told me about him," Rose said. "Not the misunderstanding – well, that too – but she told me how much he loved you, how protective he was of you, and how deeply sorry she is that she came between you."

When Carlie looked even more puzzled, Rose took her hand and gently led her over to the table, sat her down and placed the piece of buttered toast in front of her.

"She found the card you'd written her, and it really affected her. She feels terrible, and hopes you'll be able to forgive her."

Carlie shrugged. "I can't feel anything right now. Not love or forgiveness or empathy or anger or even the will to go on," she said, voice small. But she picked up the toast and took a bite, and forced herself to swallow it down.

"You need time Sweetheart, time to process it, time to feel it."

"But not time together," she whispered, tears welling again in her eyes, and pain exploding in her brain.

"I'm sorry," Rose whispered. "My dear girl, if I could change this, bear your grief for you..."

"Oh Gran, you must think I'm so silly. I only knew him for three months, from Mabon Eve to Midwinter Eve, just a quarter turn of the Wheel," she sobbed.

"No Sweetheart –"

"But I loved him. He listened to me, he believed in me. I couldn't tell Rhiannon all my doubts about wanting to be a counsellor, but I could pour everything out to him, and he never judged me, he just held me, and listened to me, and then made me feel like I really could do that, really could help people. And he helped us both with our coven work, with our research – he helped Rhiannon connect to more magic than she ever had in her life. And me too. The most connected I ever felt to magic was when I was with him, just sitting by the stream talking, listening to the bees, holding hands as we climbed the hill. Connecting to nature, to the earth, to each other." She rubbed her eyes impatiently, sick to the death of the tears, of the salt, of the pain.

"And he healed me," she whispered, voice shaky, but determined to let her grandmother know just what he had meant to her. "He gave me the strength to go on, to open my heart to love again, when I thought I never would, not after –" She broke off, the deep hurt naked and raw on her face.

"Yet it was nothing, really. What's three months? No one else even knew that I knew him, knew that he changed my life..."

"Carlie, look at me." Surprised by the force of her grandma's voice, she raised her head, and Rose took both her hands and stared straight into her eyes, into her soul. "You have to know that the length of time means nothing. You can mean more to somebody you knew for a single day, than someone you knew for a year. Fall in love more deeply, share more of yourself, with someone you only spent a short time with, than you ever could in a lifetime with someone else. The length of time has no bearing on the strength of the love, or the depth of the meaning, that two people have for each other, or on the power they wield to change each other irrevocably for the better.

"And I know you can't see this now, but to have someone touch your life so deeply, open your heart so wide, it's a blessing. It's more than most people will ever have. It will take time, but I know that you'll be able to see that some day," Rose said, holding Carlie's hands, holding her gaze, making sure she was listening to every single word.

"He has changed you forever, and will be a part of you forever. And to be changed by someone, to change them – to each become more than you were before, through your love – that's the rarest and greatest magic of all."

Carlie stared at her grandma, tears pouring down her face, listening but not listening. Eyes blank.

"And besides, I did know him," Rose added, eyes twinkling, and Carlie looked up at her in surprise.

"I met Rowan a few years ago at a healing course, and he was lovely. And a great healer and teacher. I'd seen him a few times since then – this industry is smaller than you'd think – and then he came into the shop last week," she said. Carlie's mouth fell open.

"He wanted to let me know how he felt about you, how much he loved you," Rose told her with a smile.

"But –"

"He said you weren't ready to tell me, that you were worried about what I'd think, but he wanted to let me know how much he respected you, and to assure me he was taking things slowly. That he would never hurt you. That you were the goddess to him, and you shone brighter than the moon and the stars."

"I just… Oh my god, I can't believe he did that," Carlie whispered. "And you didn't say anything to me?"

"This was your story to tell Sweetheart, and your responsibility, to work out when you were ready to share it with me," she replied, glancing pointedly at the toast with its one tiny bite out of it. Carlie dutifully picked it up and took one more mouthful, then she sighed, seeming to collapse back in on herself.

"How did you do it Grandma?" she whispered. "How did you manage to go on?"

"There is no secret to dealing with grief Sweetheart," Rose said, her own voice thick with unshed tears. "There's no easy solution, no map to guide you.

You just get out of bed every morning, and try to get through the day as best you can. Some days are more difficult than others, some less so. And you just keep doing that. Over and over again."

"I don't know if I can do it, not after I lost Mum and Dad too. It's not fair," Carlie said, voice broken and cracked with pain.

"It never is fair. But did you tell him how much you loved him?" Rose asked gently.

"Of course, every time we saw each other," she replied.

"Then there's some consolation in that," her grandma said. "Regret is a terrible thing to die with – and to live with. The last thing I said to Louis was to pull himself together, for Violet's sake, and it's hurt me every day since, that as he died he was replaying words of condemnation from me, not words of love."

A tear trickled down Carlie's cheek. "The last thing I said was that it was over. That I loved him but I had to end it, because me loving him was hurting the people closest to me."

Rose stared at her granddaughter, shocked.

"Rhiannon told me that she couldn't be my friend any more if I stayed with Rowan," Carlie said, voice barely a whisper, before she broke down in tears again.

Rose gathered her into her arms, patting her shoulder and holding her tight as she sobbed. "Yet it seems that both of you knew that it wasn't the end. You'd already decided to fix it, and he was on his way to see you, to fight for you. He knew."

"Thank you Gran," Carlie said, trying hard to smile, but not having much luck.

"Oh, but this is for you," Rose announced suddenly, and pushed the heart-print-paper wrapped package across to her. "You can open it upstairs if you'd rather."

Slowly Carlie reached out her hand to the parcel, tracing the love hearts with her finger, then gazing at her name scrawled across the card in his familiar looping script. Holding it gently, almost gingerly, in her hand, she stood up and stumbled back to her room in a daze.

Chapter 38

The Dark

Holding the package like it was the most fragile thing in the world, she sank down onto her bed. She sat for a long time, just looking at it, tracing over her name on the envelope. She wondered if he'd had any idea, as he'd scrawled her name, that it would be the last thing he'd ever write. More importantly, she wondered if he'd known that she'd changed her mind, that she was going to see him that morning and take back her cruel words, beg him to take her back, to forgive her, to keep loving her.

Finally, breath held, she slid the card out of the envelope. Tears welled in her eyes at the beauty of the painting on the front, two lovers holding each other tight, oblivious to the world around them. Smiling through her tears, she opened the card.

My Sweet Soul Mate and Beloved,
I'm coming to see you in the morning, first thing, to tell you how much I adore you, and beg you to change your mind, but I wanted to write it down too, hoping that you can feel every word I write as I write it, feel me thinking of you, feel my arms around you, feel my love. I want you to know, no matter what happens, how much I love you, how much I will always love you.

I hope it's not just wishful thinking, but I can feel you with me right now, your lips on my hair, your voice in my ear, whispering your love across these miles that separate us, telling me you've changed your mind.

I want to apologise to you my love – finding out that it was my father who treated your mother so badly shook me to my core, but please know that I am nothing like him. I barely knew him, and what I do know of him, what I've learned recently, I despise.

I know we haven't been together all that long, in some people's eyes, but it feels like forever, and it will be forever. I fell for you in the dreams we shared before we ever actually met. I was smitten the moment you walked up to my stand at the festival to have your painting done. And I fell hopelessly in love with you that first morning we spent on the tor, as I held you in my arms and we watched the sun rise, as we sat by the stream together and just talked, just held hands.

Every day I'm away from you hurts me physically – you are the missing piece I'd been searching for, and once found I couldn't bear to be apart. You make me feel whole.

Your love has made me a better, kinder person, with more depth than I ever imagined possible. My mum was right, she realised it even before I did, that I am more myself when I am with you, that you have helped me recognise my light and encouraged me to shine it. I feel like we're meant to be together, that we're destined for each other. Whether we were together or not in a past life means nothing, because we are together now, and that's all that matters.

I don't want to keep us a secret any more. I want the whole world to know how much I love you – our friends, my students, your grandma. How could anyone be upset by how much I love you? How could that hurt anyone?

Because I love you Carlie, and I will fight for that love. I know you long for me as much and as deeply as I love and long for you, and I know we can figure out a way to make this work. I will never give up on you, on our love, and I will be there with you soon, to tell you all of this in person.

Until then my precious beloved, my sweet goddess, know that I love you, and I always will.

Forever yours, Rowan xx

She sat on her bed for a long time, motionless, holding the card to her heart, tears pouring down her face. It was all so surreal. Then finally, slowly, she reached out for the package, and carefully untied the ribbons and peeled off the heart-print paper, folding it neatly so she could keep it always.

Gently she lifted the delicate froth of black lace from the paper and let it spill out over the bed. It was the most beautiful dress she'd ever seen, like a gothic bride's dress. A lump formed in her throat as she thought back to the Yule Ball, when she'd sat in the corner, moving his beautiful ring to her left hand, imagining weddings and honeymoons and a whole lifetime together. This was too cruel.

Running her fingers over the soft tulle of the skirt, she sobbed as she gazed at the bees embroidered on the bodice, and thought back to the first time they'd met, when he'd said that he saw bees around her. Clumsily she got to her feet and pulled her clothes off so she could slip the dress over her head. It felt so soft on her skin, and fit her like it had been made for her. Which, according to the note attached, it had been, her Christmas gift from her beloved.

Her gaze flickered back to her bed, and she saw a smaller package, wrapped in the same heart-print patterned paper. Sinking down onto the floor, she picked it up, then impatiently tore the paper away. Inside was a small box, and a note.

My Dear Sweet Goddess, who I love beyond measure...
I wanted to give you this the other night at the ball, wanted to slip it on the ring finger of your left hand and pledge to spend my life with you, but I sensed that you weren't ready. That I would have freaked you out. So I gave you the herkimer diamond ring instead, put it on the middle finger of your right hand, rather than where I wanted to see it.

But I want you to have this, to know that my promise then and now is a forever promise. Eternal. And whether you start wearing it now or it takes ten years until you are ready, please know that I will wait for you forever, and love you always, no matter what. I want to spend my life with you Carlie, I want to love you every single day, and I will.

And the day that you feel ready to wear this ring, and agree to marry me, to spend your life with me – loving each other, supporting each other, helping each other dream and scheme and grow stronger and more joyful because we have each other – I will be the happiest man alive.

I will love you forever my precious beloved,

Your Rowan xx

Choking back tears, she opened the small box, and gasped in astonishment. Nestled on a bed of black velvet was the most beautiful jewel she'd ever seen, a deep violet amethyst that matched her mum's necklace, the one she'd worn to the ball, which already seemed so long ago, although only a few days had actually passed since that night. The precious gemstone was set on a pretty rose gold band, engraved with swirls of ivy on the outside, while inside it eight words were etched. *Lives entwined, souls in harmony, hearts as one.* The same words she'd written to him.

Quickly she slid it on the ring finger of her left hand, the finger she'd wanted the ring to sit on at the ball, and the one he'd wanted to place it on that night. It seemed a lifetime since they'd clung to each other on the dance floor, kissed under the oak tree in the snow.

As she stared at the beautiful ring, she felt her mum there, smiling at the choice she'd made. She felt her father reaching out to hold her hand, the father whose depths she'd never guessed at. And she felt Rowan whispering in her ear. "Always and forever."

Glancing up at the mirror, she stared, transfixed. Her hair was still in need of a good wash, still piled on her head in a messy top knot, and her face was gaunt and bruised looking from the black circles under her eyes. She looked years older than she was, but not in a bad way. She looked like she'd been to hell, and was perhaps still there, but would eventually return, stronger than before, with greater purpose and passion.

She looked like someone who would find a way to survive because she knew how much she was loved. Even if that was a past tense thing...

“We’re stronger in the places
that we’ve been broken.”

Ernest Hemingway

INTO the LIGHT

"Darkness cannot drive out darkness;
Only light can do that.
Hate cannot drive out hate;
Only love can do that."

Martin Luther King Jr, American humanitarian and civil rights activist

Contents

Chapter 1

An Awakening

"Sweetheart, the funeral is this afternoon."

Carlie's eyes flickered to the door, where Rose was standing, gazing down at her with so much compassion and sympathy. For the first time in a week, she saw herself through her grandmother's eyes, and was mortified. She hadn't left her room in days, hadn't showered, hadn't even spoken to anyone in what felt like forever.

Forever. Suddenly her life felt way too long, stretching interminably out into the distance, too many days of torture ahead, too many months of agony to deal with, too many years of loneliness and pain to even contemplate.

Six months ago she'd lost both her parents in a car accident, and now she'd lost the love of her life too. It wasn't fair.

"I can't go," she whispered, body weak, eyes haunted. Rose wished there was something she could do, something to ease the pain etched deep into her granddaughter's face. But she knew from bitter experience that there was nothing she could say or do that would help, not really. Not yet. She could only let her know that she was there for her, ready to listen if she needed her to, or to hold her if she wanted comfort.

She understood the young girl's pain because she'd lost her family too – her daughter and her husband, more than twenty years ago –

and there were still nights when she woke up gasping for air and some semblance of sanity, plunged back into the nightmare of fresh pain, as though it was happening all over again. Catching herself as she sighed, she took a deep breath and steeled her heart. It was time for her to be there for Carlie, to be strong, and to show her there was a way forward through grief, a way to live with this searing pain and find some joy in life despite the scars that criss-crossed her heart.

Slowly she walked into the small room, expecting at any moment that Carlie would throw her out, but her granddaughter sat unmoving in her narrow bed, not exactly welcoming or inviting her in, but not forbidding it either.

Rose's eyes were drawn to the hulking hill she could see out the window, and she felt its pull, its strange hold over her. She'd never been able to leave this town, even though it was all she had wanted to do when she lost the only two people she'd ever loved.

Part of her had stayed in case her daughter ever came back to her, too scared to even go on holiday in case that was the day Violet returned home. But part of her had stayed because she felt as though she was physically connected to that blasted tor, anchored to it, weighed down by the ancient mound of earth. Sometimes she felt nurtured and protected by it, inspired even, but other times it was a weight around her heart, oppressive and dark, smothering her and any chance she ever had to escape.

"I feel it too," the girl on the bed whispered. "I'm not even from here and it won't let me leave. It won't let me go away from this place, and it won't let me end things either." Pain seeped from her words, and was etched deeply into her face.

"Oh love, I'm so sorry," Rose said, voice cracked and broken.

"It's not *your* fault," Carlie retorted, and the unspoken next words hung in the air.

"It's not your fault either Sweetheart," Rose added quickly, but Carlie shook her off when she tried to hold her.

"Of course it is, don't you see? If I hadn't broken up with him, if I hadn't believed Rhiannon's story, or believed Mum's book and thought he was evil like his dad, none of this would have happened. If I'd spent the night with him, you wouldn't have even known I'd left, and he'd still be alive. Why didn't I stay with him? Why didn't I trust him?" Her chest heaved and a sob escaped, but her eyes remained dry. She had no more tears.

"Oh Carlie," Rose said, heart breaking for the granddaughter she'd only recently learned existed, but had so quickly grown to love. Finally she couldn't bear it any longer, and she scooped the girl into her arms. She felt her stiffen with resistance, then finally give in, too worn down to fight. But the close contact obviously made her uncomfortable, so Rose reluctantly let her go.

"Would you like me to come with you Sweetheart, or would it be easier to go on your own?" she finally asked.

Carlie stared up at her, expression blank. "Go?"

"The funeral," Rose said softly, gently. "We'll have to leave in an hour so we can get there in time."

Her granddaughter looked so young, so innocent, and yet so aged, curled up in the corner of her narrow bed.

"I can't go," she replied, eyes deadened and vague.

Rose took a deep breath. The last thing she wanted to do was force the girl to do something so terribly sad, but she knew that she would never forgive herself if she didn't go. Screwing up her courage, she caught Carlie's eye and held her gaze.

"I know it will be hard, and horrible, and sadder than anything you should have to face. But I also know you will regret it if you don't go. You will feel guilty and you will beat yourself up for it." Pausing briefly, she considered her words carefully, then dared to speak them. "And I know that it's not your responsibility to help her through this, but it would mean the world to Rowan's mother if you could bring yourself to go today."

Carlie glared at her grandmother, a flicker of anger dancing across her face before the vacant look returned, shutters slamming down around her heart. "You spoke to her?" she asked, aghast.

"She came into the shop yesterday, to make sure you had received her letter, and to see if you were okay," Rose sighed.

For a moment it looked like Carlie would cry, but instead she slowly inhaled, visibly steeling herself for more pain. "How is she?" she asked softly. "Does she blame me too?"

Rose stared at her granddaughter, confusion in her eyes.

"Sweetheart, no one blames you, I promise. To be honest, she's worried about you. And she wants to apologise to you."

Carlie looked at her blankly, but before she could ask what on earth Rowan's mum would have to be sorry for, they heard a knock on the door, and Rose regretfully stood up. "You'll be glad that you went," she insisted, as she headed for the stairs.

"Fine," Carlie finally blurted out, no longer caring either way. Nothing could make her feel worse than she already did.

As her grandmother went to answer the door, Carlie picked up the envelope lying on her bedside table and removed the page inside, with its curly writing and ivy leaves sketched in the margins.

Dear Carlie,
I'm so very sorry for your loss. And this is one of those rare times that a person can honestly say that they know just how bad you are feeling – all the sympathy cards I've received from friends have been full of kind words, but none of them can understand just how empty our hearts are, just how pointless our lives feel right now. And it must be even harder for you, to have lost your family so recently, and now be suffering this new blow.

I just wanted to make sure you knew how much Rowan loved you, how much he wanted to be with you. Please don't think that because you hadn't known each other for a long time that it meant any less to him – he'd never talked about anyone the way he talked about you, never cared so deeply. You made him come alive in a way I hadn't seen before, and it makes my heart a little lighter to know how happy he was before he died.

Tears streamed down Carlie's face, and she sniffed noisily as she wiped them impatiently away. She felt like a fraud, that Rowan's mother thought so highly of her, when he'd actually died miserable, thinking she hated him and never wanted to see him again. He'd died because she had made a terrible mistake, hadn't been smart enough to listen to her own heart. Hadn't believed him or trusted him.

Wouldn't it be the height of rudeness for her to turn up to the funeral of the person she'd caused to die? Wasn't it disrespectful to his grieving mother who had been through so much already? Wouldn't she be doing the poor woman a favour by *not* attending?

She turned back to the note, knowing what came next, but still not quite sure how she felt about it.

It would mean so much to me if you felt able to come to the funeral service, so we could farewell him together, let his spirit soar away on a cloud of our love and best wishes. Your presence there would give me strength, help me cope with such an awful day. Not that I want to guilt you into coming, or pressure you in any way, although you might feel that from my words.

Oh Carlie, I'm so terrified of this final farewell, but I just want to honour him and his memory properly, and I can't do that without you. The details are attached, and please let me know if you need a lift – or if you need anything at all. As strange as this may sound, I feel so close to you, because you were so close to Rowan, and knew him in a way few people ever did.

So, I really hope you are able to come, for your own sense of closure, and because I know it is what Rowan would want.

You are in my thoughts and prayers.

Much love, Louisa xx

Sighing, Carlie folded the thick paper and slid it back into the envelope, then returned it to the top drawer of her bedside table. She felt sorry for the woman, if she was pinning all her hopes on *her* to make her feel better. But she was also a little uncomfortable at how intense his mum was being, and how much importance she was placing on her to help her in her grieving – not to mention the guilt trip she was laying on her to make her come.

Still, she did feel responsible for Rowan's death, so surely the least she could do was show up to his funeral if that's what his mother wanted her to do. She felt like she owed her big time. Besides, shouldn't she want to be there anyway, to say goodbye to the person she'd loved so much? Why was she resisting it so strongly?

Crawling out of bed, she walked on unsteady feet to the ensuite and turned on the shower. The hot water was so wonderfully soothing, so she abruptly switched it to cold. She wanted to suffer in some way, do some kind of penance.

Finally though, her grandmother's words floated back to her, and she reluctantly added a little hot to the water so she could stop freezing and focus on them. She knew that her grandma was right, that she would regret it if she didn't go. Didn't they say the only things you regret are the things you didn't do? Allowing her petulance to stop her from going to say goodbye would be cutting off her nose to spite her face. Surprising herself a little, she giggled. When had she become such a lover of cliches?

Turning off the water, she stepped out onto the cold floor and wrapped a towel around herself. Gazing into the mirror, she wiped the steam off in a wide arc, and was jolted back to reality. She looked terrible. Her face was gaunt and pale, with dark smudges under her eyes, and she'd lost weight, but not in a good way. That explained the constant worry she'd been seeing on her grandma's face whenever she'd let her into her bedroom to talk. Clearly the refusing to eat thing hadn't been a great move.

Shrugging at her reflection – because what did it matter what she looked like? – she pulled on some leggings and Rowan's black jumper, one of the few links she still had to him, and gingerly walked downstairs and out to the kitchen. Her heart squeezed when she saw the fear flicker across her grandma's face as she watched her enter, still shivering from the shower.

But priestess-trained Rose recovered quickly. "I've made some vegie soup, could you try a little bowl? Or a few spoons of yoghurt? I know you don't feel like eating, but you're going to make yourself ill if you don't get any nourishment at all."

Reluctantly Carlie nodded. And suddenly she couldn't believe how selfish she'd been, again. Like her grandmother needed more things to worry about on her behalf. "Either," she sighed, and concentrated hard on trying to finish the small bowl of soup that

Rose quickly slid in front of her. She inhaled the soothing qualities of the fragrant herbs in the broth, realising immediately that this was a healing soup her witchy grandma had whipped up, filled with medicinal and no doubt magical herbs amongst the finely chopped fresh vegetables.

"I'm sorry you thought I needed a healing brew," she said, trying to sound stern, but surprising both of them when a small smile crossed her face.

"I'll take that smile, no matter how small it is," Rose beamed, and the joy and the relief in her voice made Carlie's stomach clench in guilt and fear.

"I'm so sorry Gran – again – for worrying you so much. I promise I'll start eating again. And I appreciate how much you care about me, and look after me, and that it hasn't been easy having me here. I'll make more of an effort, I swear."

Rose reached out and tucked one of Carlie's long dark curls behind her ear, her touch tender and full of love. "No one blames you for being upset and having a tough time Sweetheart, and we all have different ways of coping. It's actually normal for people to stop eating when they're grieving – and it's not a bad thing, for a few days. The numbing chemicals that the brain floods the body with so a person can cope slow the digestive system, to conserve energy just to function, just to breathe. But it can't continue – now that the shock has worn off, you need to start focusing on yourself, you need to build up your strength to help you cope with going on with your life."

"But I don't want to go on with my life. What's the point?" Carlie demanded, but her grandmother could sense in her tone that the fight was going out of her, and she would start accepting the situation, and tentatively looking forward, soon enough. It never ceased to amaze her how resilient the human spirit was. How even though you could be convinced that the grief and the pain were too much to bear, that it would be best to end it all, some part of you would eventually rally, would start to see the occasional reason to stay, the rare beam of sunlight and joy piercing the blackest moments. She knew those latter moments well, had spent her fair share of time living in that pit of despair and darkness, where it seemed there was no way out, and that life would remain an unbearable trial not worth living. But she also knew the solace that could be found in the tiniest gestures, those random acts that brought joy to the heart – the kind friend there to help shoulder the pain, or the sense of meaning and purpose that could be just enough of a thread to hang on to and move forward with.

For Rose, it had been the magical community she'd forged around her that had given her a reason to live, after her daughter had disappeared forever and her husband had taken his life. Her best friend Elsie had lit up the darkest corners of those darkest moments, had rocked her while she cried and then taken her hand to lead her out into the light. Her role as a priestess had given her purpose, and her marking of the seasonal festivals through the rituals she facilitated at her healing centre had provided her life with meaning, and allowed her to find an inner strength that she hoped had helped others.

All of which made her terrified for her granddaughter. She didn't know what she could offer to make Carlie want to go on. When her parents had died six months ago she'd lost everything – her family, her home, her friends, her future career, her country even – sent to the other side of the world to live with a stranger. Despite her pain and grief though, she'd made a friend and fallen in love, until her boyfriend had been ripped cruelly from her as well.

Her friend Rhiannon seemed to be the last thread holding her to life, although that relationship seemed strained right now. As she spooned herbs into the teapot and filled it with boiling water, she wondered if she should weave a spell to heal it, or trust that the two girls could work it out for themselves.

Chapter 2

A Friendship Unravelled

"Rhiannon's been around again, wanting to see you. And she brought some flowers, and a card," Rose said, voice tentative, as she pulled a red envelope from the kitchen drawer and gestured to the pot of purple hyacinths on the windowsill, flowers that represented apology and the asking of forgiveness. Scowling, Carlie glanced at the red envelope, but she didn't pick it up.

"For what it's worth, she's really sorry. And you have every reason to be angry at her," Rose added.

Carlie looked up at her in surprise, expression wary.

"She only told me a little, either from her own embarrassment or because she doesn't want to divulge any of your secrets, but she did say that she really regrets interfering in your relationship, and trying to make you break up with Rowan," she said.

"She didn't *try* to make me break up, she succeeded," Carlie snapped, anger shooting through her body. She flashed back to all the awful things her friend had tried to convince her were true about her boyfriend. That he would cheat on her, and hurt her, physically and emotionally. That he was just using her, and was going to destroy her.

None of that was true of course, but she'd fallen for it. And being weak, she'd done what her friend demanded. Girls were supposed to stick together, right? But what kind of friend delivers such an ultimatum? Weren't best buddies supposed to be supportive of you? Encourage you? Trust you? Believe in you, and your ability to make your own decisions?

What kind of person makes someone choose between their best friend and their boyfriend? Hot tears stung her eyes as she finally found herself back at the place where this train of thought always ended. If she hadn't broken up with Rowan, as Rhiannon had demanded she do, he would still be alive.

Rose poured out the tea and walked over to the table, placing the steaming mug in front of her granddaughter and taking her hand, yanking her back to the present. "You still have responsibility for your choices," she said cautiously. "Don't hand your power over to someone else."

"But it's not fair! How could she expect me to choose between them?" Carlie cried.

"Sweetheart, that's what she's so sorry about. She genuinely thought she was doing it for you, that it was in your best interests. It was because she cares about you so much, misguided though her actions were."

Carlie glared at her grandmother, but her face softened as Rose's black cat, Luther, leaped up onto her lap.

"I agree with you, she does seem to have been lacking any justifiable reason for her actions – and I think she's learned a lot about herself through this experience, and will be so much more compassionate in her dealings with everyone in the future," Rose added, a hopeful note in her voice.

"Well, I'm so glad someone had to die just so she could learn not to trust some old psychic who didn't know either of us," her granddaughter spat, venom in her tone.

Rose spoke as gently as she could. "You can't blame Rhiannon for his death either Sweetheart, it was just a tragic accident."

"What do you mean, *either*?" Carlie demanded, her bottom lip trembling as she pouted.

"I don't mean *that*. It's absolutely not your fault," she insisted, and at those words the young girl dissolved into tears again. Her grandma pulled her into her arms, one hand stroking her hair, trying to comfort her, the other on her back, attempting to soothe her anger away.

"There there, let it all out, you'll feel better," she crooned. "It's a horrible, horrible thing to have happened, a terrible injustice, and absolutely nothing about it is fair. But blaming someone, anyone – yourself, Rhiannon, the gods or the goddess – won't help you, or make you feel any better. It won't make it easier to cope with, it will be much harder. Believe me Sweetheart, I know."

"I just can't see her yet Gran, can you understand that? I'm just… it's just… it's all too raw," she sighed. "I don't have the energy to try to make her feel better about herself, to reassure her – I don't have it in me to forgive her yet, or forgive myself. And I can't put on a brave face right now. I don't know if I'll ever be able to, but I definitely know I can't right now."

Rose's heart clenched as she gazed at her granddaughter. She'd never seen a soul so broken, and part of her was terrified that she would lose her – that the tortured young girl would drown in her grief, unable to find a way to continue living.

But every now and then she saw a glimmer of golden light within her, strands of steeliness, strength and determination, and a passion for life that she prayed she'd be able to ignite somehow, and encourage to blossom and grow. She desperately wanted to find a way to overshadow the pain and agony that was Carlie's present reality. She could never erase all the pain – and frankly she didn't want to, because she knew it would help her eventually. But that should only be a small part of her heart, not every fibre of it, every beat it made.

Nodding sadly, she tried to infuse her smile with all the love she felt for her poor tortured granddaughter. They were each the only family they had now, the last two left standing after a trail of sadness and tragedy, but the wise priestess knew they weren't unique. At times it felt like she'd had to deal with more than she knew what to do with, more than anyone else had to shoulder, and certainly Carlie was dealing with a lot more than most teenagers had to carry.

Yet each family had its own dramas, its own loss and grief to deal with, its missed opportunities and searing pain. It was part of the rich warp and weave of human experience, the depth that gave meaning and purpose to life and made the joy so much sweeter. The important thing was to hold on to all the love and happiness you could, treasure each precious moment, every bond you had, and pray it was enough to sustain you through the harrowing days.

Rose was determined that she wouldn't lose the beautiful, fragile girl in front of her – the girl who had been such an unexpected and wonderful blessing for her, when she'd been resigned to living out the rest of her lonely days on her own, with only the magic she wove with the villagers to sustain her.

Yet she had a feeling that Carlie would be one of those people who emerged from tragedy even stronger, her character forged in the fire and steel of grief, her actions tempered by loss and the immense compassion and wisdom she would soon realise she had within her.

Shuddering, she acknowledged that it could still go either way though. Carlie could grow stronger from her journey through hell, or let it defeat her and sweep her away from the world.

"Well, when you're ready you can read her card, think about her words, and how much she cares about you and is sorry. But for now we should head off, okay?" Rose suggested gently.

Sighing as though the weight of the whole world was on her shoulders, Carlie finally nodded.

"And, um, did you want to get changed before we leave?" Rose asked hesitantly, scared that the question would anger her feisty granddaughter and change her mind about going.

Carlie's eyes flashed. "What's wrong with this?" she demanded, and Rose tried to hide her smile.

"Nothing at all Sweetheart. But we really should go now," she said, shepherding her out the door and into the car for the bleak drive to the church.

Chapter 3

Happy Never After

Carlie felt like she was sleepwalking through the funeral, her body there, responding to people's looks of sympathy, but her mind and her heart trapped somewhere dank and dark. Not the welcome blackness of oblivion, which she'd retreated into several times in the past week. This was the darkness of awareness, of suffering and horror and fear and guilt, the place where each thought brought physical agony, each word spoken rubbed salt into her already gaping wounds.

But it was the naked, raw pain etched deep into the face of Rowan's mother that almost brought her undone. Her grandmother had mentioned once that losing a child was even worse than losing a parent or a partner, because kids were supposed to bury their mum and dad. Not quite as early as Carlie had had to, she'd conceded, but it was the expected and natural order of things. When that was reversed it left an ache that nothing could ever soothe.

Seeing Louisa at the church doors, welcoming people with the ghost of a smile, a pale face and trembling hands, was a dagger in her heart. She wanted to turn and flee, to try to outrun her own pain, and the haunting pain on his mother's face, but Rose placed a hand on her back at the exact moment her body prepared for its desperate flight. There were disadvantages to having a priestess for a grandmother, she thought wryly, and heard Rose stifle a giggle at that. *Damn mind-reading witch!*

"Sorry," her grandma whispered, as she pushed her into Louisa's arms. "Sorry on both counts."

"Oh Carlie, I'm so glad you came, thank you so much. I wasn't sure you would actually turn up," Rowan's mum said.

"Nor was I," Carlie muttered, then tried to pull herself together. It wasn't just about her today. She had to consider other people too. "I'm so sorry for your loss Mrs Dunbar."

"And I'm so sorry for *your* loss," the woman replied, voice cracked with pain. "And it's Louisa, please."

Carlie nodded reluctantly. It seemed a strange time to be quibbling over names, or trying to increase their intimacy – Rowan was the only thing they'd had in common, and he was gone. There was nothing to hold them together now.

"I'm sorry I haven't been over to see you either, to spend time with you, comfort you. I feel like we're bound together forever now," his mother said, but Carlie was saved from replying to such a strange sentiment when Jay walked up and took Louisa's hand.

She hurried inside, not quite ready to face Rowan's manager. A blush stained her cheeks as she remembered her only encounter with the glamorous, beautifully dressed woman. It had been at Rowan's apartment, when he'd returned from a retreat, and when Jay had knocked on the door Carlie had hastily decided that he must have been two-timing her. God, why had she never trusted him? He'd given her no reason to doubt him, but she'd acted like a jealous kid. Which she supposed she was, or she had been. *What had he ever seen in her?*

"He saw your incredible spirit and your immense strength Sweetheart," Rose said gently from where she was seated next to her on the hard wooden pew. "Your beautiful open heart."

Frowning, Carlie turned on her grandmother, eyes flashing. "I feel like I don't have a heart," she said angrily. "It's too broken. Too many times. What's the point of caring for someone when they always let you down, when they always leave you? It would be better to never love at all, surely."

"No, of course it wouldn't," her grandma replied, shocked.

"Yet you never found love again after Grandpa died, did you?" Carlie asked accusingly. A wave of horror swept over her then, as she saw her life stretching ahead of her, lonely and filled with bitterness, and no respite in sight.

She shuddered. She'd lost her parents, she'd lost the love of her life, she'd lost her home, her school, her friends, her whole past, and everything she'd ever known – god, it seemed like she'd even lost her two closest friends, one through distance, and one through... who even knew? But whichever way she looked at it, there was no rosiness in her future.

She was saved from having to hear her grandma raving about the so-called joys of life when a woman came over to talk to Rose. Finally left in peace, Carlie gazed around the church, eyes drawn upwards to the towering ceiling – and she wondered suddenly why Rowan's mum had chosen to have a Christian ceremony. Rowan was a druid, a shaman, more spiritual than religious, and he believed in past lives and reincarnation, not some rigid notion of heaven or hell.

The thought shook her. She didn't know what she believed, or whether there was anything after death. Her parents hadn't been religious, and while she'd taken part in goddess ceremonies with her grandmother and her circle, and loved doing them, she wasn't sure whether deity was real or just a beautiful metaphor. Of course she wanted desperately to believe that there was something after death, some vague notion of a spirit realm where Rowan might be now. She wanted to feel his presence in her life, to be able to communicate with him, sense him around her – but she wasn't convinced that it was anything more than wishful thinking on her part.

And could she go on, without the knowledge that he was in a better place, or that he would always be with her in some way? With his mother? Was that the comfort people sought in religion – was it just balm for the terrifying possibility that this was all there was?

Part of her wished she could believe that his death had happened for a reason. That's the consolation people offered the grieving as comfort, but she just couldn't buy it. He'd only been twenty-three, in love with his work, so alive with the sense of purpose and passion it brought him, so happy and at peace knowing that he was helping people find their own truths, become the best versions of themselves that they could.

And as hard as it was for her to believe it, he'd been in love with her. Had wanted to marry her even, when she was ready. How could anyone suggest that there was some reason for his death, some greater purpose? And did they really believe that, or was it just a lie they told themselves to try to cope with the terrible truth – that awful things happened, all the time, and that life was terribly, terribly unfair? Was it just a platitude they uttered because they were too uncomfortable with death, with grief, with the tragedy of life?

She supposed that thinking there was a reason someone had died might make the loss easier to cope with, but would it really? The person was still gone. And what possible purpose could there be for his mother to suffer? Or for her to go through this heartbreak again? Rowan had been helping her come to terms with the death of her parents, had been helping her heal. Now she felt even worse about their loss, if that was possible.

And she wasn't sure how much more she could handle. Someone had told her once that a vase that was broken became even stronger in the places where it was mended, and that it was the same with hearts – we're strongest in the places that have been broken. But she didn't buy that. Besides, what if it wasn't just a small crack in her heart that had to be fixed, but instead it had been shattered into a million little pieces, pieces far too small to ever be able to be remade? That was how she felt. She was just broken pieces on top of broken pieces. It seemed as though her heart was just one seething mess of ever-widening wounds.

And how could scars even begin to form, and she start to heal, if she just kept being torn apart?

Chapter 4

Lightning Crashes

Back home a few hours later, Rose parked the car, turned off the engine and sat quietly, nervously, in the driver's seat.

"Will you be okay if I pop down to the shop for a little while?" she asked carefully. She wasn't sure whether Carlie wanted to be alone or needed to have someone with her, but she was prepared to spend less time at her healing centre if her granddaughter needed her. "I'm happy not to go, if you want some company," she added. "But I don't want you to feel smothered if you need some time alone..."

Carlie stared at her grandma through red-rimmed, world-weary eyes, seeing her fragility as well as her strength. Her attempt to give her space yet not leave her on her own. She didn't know what the poor woman had done to deserve a messed up seventeen-year-old landing on her doorstep, but she was grateful that her mum's friend Sandy had tracked her down.

"I really appreciate you Gran, more than you know. More than I say. And it was beyond awful today, but I'm glad that you made me go, and grateful that you came with me – I'm not sure I could have handled it otherwise. But I'll be okay. You need to go to work, and I need some time on my own," she said softly.

"I'll be fine, I promise," she continued, as she saw the reluctance on Rose's face. She couldn't blame her. She hadn't exactly been acting sane of late, or displaying the best judgement. But finally her grandma nodded, gave her a quick hug, then peeled herself out of the small car and turned and walked towards the village.

As soon as she was out of sight, Carlie opened the car door and gasped for breath. She felt the blackness descending, and shivered, wondering if she should grab a warmer coat, but she couldn't be bothered. Everything was an effort now, even the thought of unlocking the front door and climbing the stairs to her room. Shrugging, she turned and headed away from the village, her steps aimless, her mind carefully blank as she tried to avoid the painful thoughts that were attempting to land and take hold.

Being at the funeral had shattered her. Hearing people she'd never met or even heard of waxing lyrical about a man it sounded like they didn't know had disconcerted her. School friends who hadn't seen him since he'd begun walking the druid path six years ago. A now-married and pregnant ex-girlfriend who'd cheated on him when they'd dated for a few weeks in college, who said she was going to name their baby after him. Carlie had felt sorry for the husband, tied to a woman glorifying a man she'd dated briefly several years ago then forgotten about until now.

At least Jay's speech was genuine. She'd worked closely with Rowan for the last few years, had booked his events and travelled with him, been the shield between him and the rest of the world so he could concentrate on his spiritual work and not worry about logistics and other mundane details.

She'd come over and given Carlie a hug at the end of the service, and told her that she knew how much Rowan had loved her – that he'd asked her to cut back on the retreats he had to travel a long way for, so they could spend more time together.

"Don't ever doubt his love for you Carlie," she'd whispered. "No one here knew him, and he would have been horrified that all these people were here, like ghouls in need of drama, feeding off the tragedy. Even I was intruding, really. All he wanted was more time to spend with you, to convince you of how much he loved you, and that there was no one else for him."

Carlie had broken down at her words, and Jay had patted her back kindly, if a little awkwardly, before her boyfriend led her out of the church, a supportive arm around her. Smiling as she recalled Jay's kindness and reassurance, even though it reminded her of how stupid she'd been to be jealous of her, she lifted her eyes to gaze around her.

Her heart started racing as she realised that she was walking down the oak-lined path to "their spot", the place Rowan had taken her to on their first date. The place where he'd first kissed her.

Filled with a deep sense of dread, she entered the small meadow on the edge of the stream, and felt her heart beat even louder as she gazed at the softly sloping bank shaded by two weeping willow trees that grew close together.

Back then, she'd laughed in delight at the beautiful space, had found the gentle sound of the running water so peaceful and soothing to the soul. Now, her eyes spilled over with tears as she stared at the two trees, stark in their winter guise, and saw the ghosts of her and Rowan as they'd sat on the bank together that morning, their backs to the solid, nurturing strength of the willows. She remembered the joy she'd felt in that moment, the smile that had lit up her face as his closeness had lit up her heart.

A bone-chilling wind tore through the trees, and her heart ached as she heard the whisper of her voice from back then, echoing across time. "Thank you for bringing me here," she'd said shyly, still so nervous in his presence, so unsure of herself. "It's so peaceful, like we're in our own little world."

He'd taken her hand then and kissed it gently. "I wish we could stay here always, just the two of us, away from everyone, away from friends and family and school and work," he'd said.

And he'd kissed her, her first real kiss. Raising her hand, she ran a finger along her lower lip, trying to imagine him with her still, imagine his lips on hers, his arms around her. Trying to imagine the warmth she'd felt when she was with him.

Angrily she shook off that thought. He wasn't here to hold her close, he wasn't ever going to kiss her again, or stroke her cheek. The icy fingers of wind tore at her clothes, pulling strands of hair from her messy bun and chilling her to the core – which made her happy.

She wanted to suffer, she wanted to feel her body as aching with cold as her heart ached with grief and loss.

Storm clouds gathered overhead as she stood there, and she smiled as rain started to fall. When lightning flashed, lighting up the darkness that was descending, she shivered, then started to laugh, a note of hysteria in her voice. Maybe she should just sit down on the cold earth and let the rain fall on her as the thunder crashed around her. Perhaps she'd even catch pneumonia if she stayed long enough, and not have to decide whether she wanted to live or to die – surely in her weakened state she would struggle to fight it off.

But then her restless thoughts flickered to Rose, and she knew she couldn't cause her any more pain. For a moment she felt a warmth at her shoulder, as though Rowan was standing behind her, hand guiding her to turn around, to get to shelter, to get home and to go on living. Sighing, she ran back up the hill, sloshing through puddles with grim satisfaction, shoes muddy and ruined, water seeping in and turning her toes ice cold.

Finally she made it back to their cottage, turned the key in the lock and dripped her way down the corridor. Luther took one look at her and miaowed sternly, his eyes jumping from her to the bathroom door and back again, his meaning clear. Leaning down to pat him, she laughed when he grumbled at all the water falling on his head, then stalked away from her to the warmth of the kitchen.

"I love you Luther," she called after him, giggling at the expression of indignation on his adorable fuzzy black face.

Knowing that the cat was right though, she walked into the bathroom, stripped off her wet clothes and stood under the scalding shower until the water started to run cold. Leaping out, she grabbed the towel and dried herself roughly, then raced upstairs to dress in her warmest clothes.

There was an apple on her bedside table, no doubt placed there by Rose as an unsubtle hint to eat, so she curled up in bed and crunched into it – her grandmother would have to be happy with that – then lay down and waited for the sweet oblivion of sleep to claim her.

Chapter 5

The Last Goodbye

The next morning dawned bleak and grey, but Carlie awoke with her eyes dry for the first time since Rowan had died nine days ago, shocked to feel the tiniest threads of her own strength tugging at her heart. She lay in bed, stiff and silent. It was New Year's Eve, and Rose was running a ritual at the healing centre that night, for people to let go of the pain of the current year and usher in a fulfilling and joyful new one. At least it was, quite literally, impossible for her to have a worse year than the one just gone, so she supposed she should be grateful for that at least.

She'd begged off attending though, and Rose had agreed, understanding that being with a group of people releasing pain that paled into insignificance next to her own wouldn't be good for Carlie. Not that anyone's pain was more or less important than someone else's, but she didn't think her granddaughter's presence would be uplifting for the other participants either.

Instead Carlie had decided to do her own ritual, so she spent the morning forcing herself to eat, and trying unsuccessfully to lose herself in a book. But finally it was time to prepare, so she gathered all the things she'd need, had a chamomile-scented bath, then opened her small wardrobe and reverently took out the gorgeous dress Rowan had given her for Christmas.

Her breath caught as she remembered the moment she'd lifted it from its wrappings and held it to her heart. It had been a few days after he'd died, when Mike had finally convinced her to get out of bed and eat something, for her grandma's sake, and she'd found the parcel the police officers had brought from the car wreck.

It was like a gothic bride's gown. A lump formed in her throat as she ran her fingers over the soft tulle of the skirt and gazed at the bees embroidered on the bodice, bees that had meant so much to them both. She slipped it over her head and smoothed it down. It was so soft on her skin, and somehow it made her feel closer to him. As she slid the amethyst rose-gold ring that had come with the dress onto her ring finger, she whispered the words engraved on it: *Lives entwined, souls in harmony, hearts as one.* She could sense his arms around her, feel his breath in her hair as he whispered: "Always and forever" in her ear.

Still drowning in memories, she pulled on a coat, picked up her black velvet ritual bag and slipped out the back door and through the garden to the laneway. She headed towards the tor, then turned off towards their special place. The wind whipping restlessly through the trees added to the wildness she felt, and she pulled her coat more tightly around herself as she wandered through the bleakness of the wintry late afternoon.

Although she'd been to their place by the river just the day before, the sadness she felt as she approached still overwhelmed her, and for a moment she worried that she wasn't ready for this, that she didn't have the strength to go on. The grief stabbed at her like a fresh knife wound in her heart, and she found herself crouched down and doubled over, gasping for breath. Eventually she managed to calm herself down though, imploring her shattered heart to be strong, for this afternoon at least.

Taking a deep breath, she shrugged off her coat and lay it on the ground, then sat down on it, dress whispering around her, and ritual bag in her lap. Reaching inside, she took out a tealight candle in a glass holder and carefully placed it at her feet, then pulled out the bouquet she'd carefully wound together from sprigs of rosemary and bay laurel, berries and leaves from the holly tree, and a tiny branch

of mistletoe that she'd woven into the centre. These were herbs for remembrance, for rebirth, for the dead, for the beloved, for those left behind. Squeezing them tightly, she winced as the sharp edges of the holly leaves pricked her skin, but she kept holding them close. She needed to feel pain, needed to feel some kind of physical sensation in the hope it could balance out the anguish in her heart.

As blood trickled down her wrist from her palm, she let it slowly sprinkle over the bare earth, watching as if from a great distance as the ruby-red drops soaked into the ground. She wanted to leave a part of herself here, in their special place, wanted to feel some connection with anything that had mattered to the two of them. If she closed her eyes she could almost see the ghosts of the two of them beside her. She'd been so innocent, so full of hope then, as she gave her heart away for the first time.

"Oh Rowan," she sighed, her heart constricting in her chest. "How could you leave me? This feels like a punishment for my bad decision, like the universe didn't give me a chance to correct it, even though I had decided I was wrong, that I had to be with you, so soon after I broke both our hearts." The sky was starting to darken with the approaching night – the light faded so early here in winter – but she liked that, liked how miserable the whole world seemed, as though all of time and space was grieving with her.

"I miss you so much Rowan, and I miss what we should have had – time to get to know each other better, time to fall even more deeply in love with each other, time to grow up and grow older together. You must have thought I was so stupid, so naive, so young. And you were right. Getting spooked by the intensity of our feelings, too scared to trust you, to let myself fall, to believe that you – *you!* – could ever care about me. Yet I could feel the truth of it in my bones. My heart knew you loved me, even if my brain refused to accept it.

"I'm so sorry I wasted the precious time we had with my insecurities, so sorry I listened to Rhiannon when I should have only listened to you. How could she – how could anyone – understand what we felt for each other? Know how deep our connection was? I didn't even know myself, not consciously, even though it had become a part of me, a part of my soul. Everything seemed so hard, yet loving you was the easiest thing I've ever done. I didn't have to think about it, I just felt it, so deeply within me."

A tear trickled down her cheek and froze there, and she wished she could break it off and keep it, because it felt like a part of them, something that only they could share. But did she really want to remember him with tears? Not that she seemed to have a choice in that, she thought wryly, and laughed mirthlessly.

Growing impatient with her sadness and the endless, bottomless grief, she made her mind go blank. Carefully she laid out a black cloth, then set down the pentacle she'd been gifted by Brianna, the mysterious woman in green, just after Samhain. Then she positioned her altar tools around it – a heart-shaped rose quartz crystal in the north for earth, a chalice of spring water in the west for water, a black feather in the east for air, and a candle in the south for fire.

After that she placed the beautiful herkimer diamond ring Rowan had given her at the Yule ball in the centre of the altar, stifling a sob as she thought of the future they should have had together, the promise held in the ring. He'd told her that herkimer diamonds meant they'd be together forever, but clearly that was a lie.

Sighing, she picked up her athame and traced a circle between the worlds. It was just a small one, since it was only her now, and she felt smaller without him, diminished in size and significance. She moved widdershins, against the sun, since she was trying to release and banish what she could of her pain with this ritual.

Within this circle, that my intent will form,
Between the worlds, a safe place born.
Ancient beings of this sacred place,
Smile on me with your endless grace.
Please hold me close throughout this rite,
And heal my heart on this year end night.

Sensing the air shimmering around her, for a moment she felt a pang of longing for Rhiannon and the magic they'd woven together. But she pushed that thought aside as she lowered the ritual knife and focused on the sacred items on her makeshift altar. Reaching out her hand, she touched each one in turn as she invoked the energy and strength of the elements, and the power and spirits of the four directions.

Spirits of the east, and element of air,
Please carry away my sadness and pain,
and share your wisdom with me tonight.

Spirits of the north, and element of earth,
Please ground me with your strength,
and watch over my sad yet sacred rite.

Spirits of the west, and element of water,
Please wash away all I can no longer bear,
and soothe my heart after this lonely fight.

Spirits of the south, and element of fire,
Please burn away my pain and grief,
and allow peace and acceptance to ignite.

Another tear trickled down her cheek, but she took a deep breath and tried to inhale the strength and solidity of the earth beneath her, the clarity and inspiration of the air around her, the nurturing power of the water beside her, and the smouldering sensation of the fire within her. Finally she lifted the small statues of the god and the goddess and cradled them in her lap.

Goddess of love and compassion, magic and moonlight,
Please hold Rowan safe throughout his eternal night.

God of strength and sunshine, love and might,
Let him know how much I love him and miss his light.

As she felt the magic of the ritual settle around her shoulders, warming her with its growing familiarity and gentle power, she suddenly felt more lost than she ever had.

"Oh Rowan, how could you leave me? Leave me here to face life without you, face your death without you? It breaks my heart, not knowing if you knew that I'd changed my mind, that I was coming to see you the next morning, coming to tell you that I loved you with all my heart and soul. That I love you.

"Those words were for you, for always. *I love you.* I thought I would never say them to anyone else, that they were my gift to you. Now here I am, at seventeen, thinking that I'll never say them again full-stop. I just... oh god, I wasn't ready for you to leave me. Why couldn't we have had one more day, one more week, one more year? One more forever."

For a long time she sat silently, liking the sharp pain of the cold as it burrowed under her clothing and chilled her skin to match her heart.

"You healed me you know," she finally whispered, despair colouring her voice. "You helped me begin to emerge from my grief at losing Mum and Dad, begin to feel whole again, complete. But now I feel more lost than ever. I've lost my purpose, and my meaning, because my love for you was what was keeping me together. It was your strength that was holding me up, keeping my head above water. And now I'm drowning again, but this time it's even worse, because I know what I could have had, and what I never will have again."

A sob choked her, but she swallowed it impatiently back down, her words tumbling out of her, voice edged with hysteria.

"When I wrote to you that night, after I left you, and ran from you, I had finally realised how much I loved you, how important you were to me, how much I was willing to give up to be with you. And I want you to know that. God how I wish you could have known that. It seemed like you felt my words – I sensed our souls reaching out to each other as I wrote them, felt you touch my heart and hold it close – but I will always wonder if I imagined that. Always worry that you died thinking I didn't want to be with you. Always regret that I wasn't able to tell you just how deeply I'd fallen for you. It would kill me if I discovered that you had no idea. And I'll never really know either way."

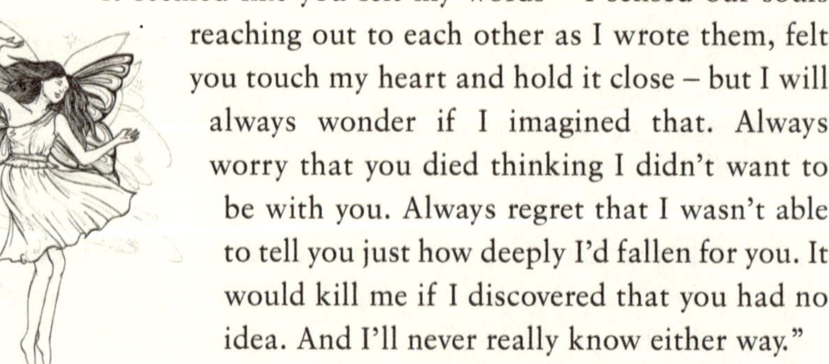

Another sob escaped, wrenched from deep within her, and she paused for a moment, trying to get her breathing under control. A viciously cold wind tore through the trees, creating tiny waves on the dark water of the stream beside her.

"Listen," a voice crooned, and she concentrated all her senses on the sound. Had it been a voice? Was it a word she'd heard?

"Listen to what?" she thought impatiently, but she closed her eyes, trying to identify the tone of the voice, or the direction it was coming from. Was it just the wind, or her feverish imagination? Or could Rowan still be with her? Did his spirit live on? In her rational mind she was sceptical of there being anything after death, but oh, she so desperately wanted to be wrong about that.

Feeling a hand in her hair, tenderly stroking it, she leaned in to the gentle touch like a kitten, almost purring. It was impossible, she knew that, but for just a moment she allowed herself to dream that he was still with her.

"Love never dies," the voice said, and she still wasn't sure if the words were in her mind or from somewhere outside, or even whether it was a male or a female speaking.

"His love will stay with you forever," it continued, a gentle sigh, but it had given itself away. It said *his* love, not *my* love. Her eyes snapped open as waves of disappointment rolled over her – and she froze when she saw there was a woman in a long red cloak sitting cross-legged before her, the tiny altar the only thing between them. She was close enough to touch – not that Carlie had any intention of touching her. Goosebumps prickled up her arms as she stared at the figure across from her.

There was something not quite right about her, something Otherworldly and strange. She had long black hair and a pale face, and her eyes were an eerie swirl of black against the stark white of her cheeks and the deep red of her lips. Her heart broke a little more to realise that it wasn't Rowan sitting with her. As cynical as she was, part of her had hoped it was him, or some spirit of him, that had been holding her so close and offering such warmth and comfort. She laughed, a bitter, slightly manic sound, and wondered if she'd lost her mind. Again.

"Oh Carlie, beloved, you have not lost your mind, you have simply lost your great love, on top of losing your parents," the strange woman breathed.

"Simply? *Simply!* This is simple to you? This has no importance to you? Because I've gotta say, there is nothing simple here. I'm a mess of contradictions – of anger and guilt and sadness and despair – and I don't know if I want to live in a world that is so cruel. How can I survive this? How can I see any value in going on when I know from bitter experience that anyone I ever meet I will lose? Love never dies, you say, but what's the point of that when the person I loved so much has died? *All* the people I've loved have died."

Her voice trembled with fury, and some part of her was distantly aware that she sounded like a petulant child, but she didn't care. And while part of her mind recognised that this strange figure must be related to the woman in blue and her green-clad friend, another part couldn't care less. What was the point of them? What had they really done? They'd given her and Rhiannon magical gifts, but those things meant nothing to her now.

All her magic had died with Rowan, so being offered a pretty wand or a silver chalice or whatever other ritual tools this apparition thought would mollify her was of no use. She wasn't even on speaking terms with Rhiannon, so she was no longer part of any enchanted circle. Besides, what good was magic? She'd created a love spell, and Rowan had appeared in answer to its casting. But then he'd been torn out of her life – torn out of his own – and killed on a lonely road in the snow, so what was the purpose of spells?

They'd only ripped her still-fragile heart out all the way. Had given her something she hadn't even known she'd wanted, then cruelly taken it away, just as she was beginning to appreciate its value. So she was done with magic, with love, with friendship. Right now she was pretty sure she was done with life.

The woman before her shifted slightly, and Carlie's eyes were drawn back to her face. There was an unearthly glow that seemed to come from within, illuminating her features in the deepening twilight.

"You still love Rose," the woman said softly. "And she loves you more than life itself. She wants to help you heal from this, to grow stronger and eventually be able to move on."

"And is that why you're here? To let me know you're taking her too?" Carlie demanded, before her body collapsed in on itself in new terror. Surely they wouldn't do that to her. That would definitely push her over the edge, way beyond recovery. Glaring across the altar at the woman, seeing her now as some kind of beautiful velvet-clad grim reaper, she shivered in the creeping cold and dawning horror that was her life.

Shaking her head, the woman handed her own cloak to her, then in the same instant had crossed the distance between them and was by her side, wrapping the soft red fabric around her trembling shoulders. Jumping in fright, heart racing, Carlie tried to shrug the cloak off, but it seemed so heavy, and made her feel so languid.

Slowly she felt herself melting into the warmth of its velvety folds, and the fight drained out of her. She turned her head to thank the strange woman, but she was suddenly back on the other side of the altar, sitting opposite her again, looking as though she'd never moved. The realisation sent a terrified shudder through her, then it too was gone, leaving her feeling empty, the fear and anger that had been consuming her somehow mellowing into acceptance. Furious, she stared across at the shadowy figure.

What spell had she cast to take away the anger that seemed to be the only strength she still possessed?

"What do you want?" she finally asked, resigned, feeling like she'd lost a battle she hadn't even known she was fighting.

"Oh Carlie, beloved, I am so very sorry for your loss. You have been through so much, and so much has been demanded of you, and I am truly sorry. You are allowed to be angry, to be hurt, to be depressed. The depth of your grief is a mark of the love that you shared, and you should never doubt how deep and powerful that love was. *Is*. Some people live their whole life without the opportunity to love like that, or to be loved like that."

Carlie scowled. "So that's it? Now I spend the rest of my life knowing what I could've had, but not allowed to feel it again?"

The woman smiled mysteriously. "Who knows? You could be blessed to experience a love like that again – it is up to you."

"What do you mean?" Carlie demanded, her voice high, panicked, verging again on desperate. "I can beg and plead and grovel, or fulfil some bizarre quest to prove myself, and you'll bring him back to me? You can do that?"

Her heart raced, and she could barely breathe. Did this woman have the ability to do that? Who was she? Was the Craft really that powerful? And what would it cost her? Didn't you have to sacrifice something really precious for such a bargain? Would she have to make a deal with the devil? She didn't mind, of course – she would give up anything to have Rowan back with her. Well, not Rose, but she'd give up anything else, even herself. What good was her shell of a life without him anyway?

A harsh slap across her face made her jump, and she crashed back into awareness of her surroundings. Riddled with anxiety and confusion, she clutched at her smarting cheek and stared across at the woman in red, her heart sinking as she saw the grim expression in her eyes. There was fire and ice there, and a steeliness underwritten with fury.

"This is what you think of the Craft?" she shrieked. "You, who have done ritual with your priestess grandmother, seriously believe that her honouring of nature and the seasons could involve ritual sacrifice, or bargains with some evil spirit?"

Blushing, Carlie reluctantly shook her head. "I'm sorry," she whispered, shoulders drooping and voice aching with desperation. "I guess that was too much to hope for. But I don't know what anything means any more, or involves. What is possible or merely dream."

The woman caressed her cheek, gently this time, cold fingers soothing where the slap had stung, and crooned to her. "Beloved, I know, and you must be out of your mind with grief. I am very sorry that I struck you, and I suppose I should be relieved that you drew the line at sacrificing Rose…"

Carlie's cheeks burned even redder, and she wanted to curl up and die of embarrassment that her thoughts had been heard, by this Otherworld being no less.

"What I *meant*," the woman continued, "was that it is your choice whether you spend the rest of your life alone, bitter and miserable, or if you can get to a point where your heart is open to the possibility of new love."

White-hot anger coursed through Carlie, but she bit her tongue before speaking, and the figure smiled approvingly.

"I know you do not want to think about that now, and nor should you. But one day you will have the choice, and I hope you will not react with such outrage and deny yourself happiness. I am not here to tell you there is a reason for his death, or some great purpose – there is not, and surely Brauna told you that – but to let you know that you can survive this. You can, if you choose, create your own meaning for this, and find something that will give your life purpose, make your life bearable. Through your suffering you will be able to help so many people, if you want to. And I know that is very little consolation for what has been taken from you, and it seems awfully unfair that you have to go through so much to benefit someone else."

Suddenly the grim-faced girl laughed. She couldn't help herself. What had happened to her? Surely she was losing her mind. Had *already* lost her mind. Here she was, sitting on the icy cold earth as night drew down around her, freezing her butt off in a beautiful but flimsy dress, talking to a figment of her imagination, and getting angry at a platitude which she'd no doubt hear plenty of times over the next few years.

A tear trickled down her cheek as she realised that she had never felt more alone in her life. She had thought things couldn't get worse than when her parents had died six months ago, but she was wrong – now she was not only mourning them, but the love of her life as well.

A flake of snow landed on her nose, and she felt hysteria build within her. Perhaps she'd catch pneumonia out here and die, and all her angst would be over, would be for nothing. Then she felt a hand on her face again, still not gentle, but not as harsh as the slap, and she jerked her head up.

"Please, do not joke about your own death. You are stronger than you know," the red-clad woman said softly, imploringly. "And surely you owe it to Rowan, and to the love you shared, and the respect he had for you, to honour his memory by making the most of your life. Becoming someone who would make him proud, who will do all the good in the world that he had planned to do."

Almost laughing in disbelief, Carlie stared across at the figure opposite, eyes mutinous. "Seriously, blackmail now?" she demanded. "You're going to guilt me into not killing myself? Does that ever work?" God, why couldn't she be spending time with Brauna, the sweet and patient woman in blue, or her green-robed friend Brianna? "Do you know them?" she asked suddenly. "Do they know you're here? Did they send you?"

But the figure of the woman was fading before her eyes, and as she left, so too did the warm red cloak she'd placed around Carlie's shoulders. Shivering in the suddenly icy air, and noticing just how dark it had become, Carlie quickly but carefully unwove her circle, farewelling the quarters and the deities, and dissolving the protective space she'd created between the worlds. Pouring the water from the chalice onto the ground, she hastily wrapped it in velvet and placed it in her bag, along with the feather and the crystal, then slid the ring back on her finger, next to the amethyst one Rowan had offered her as a wedding band.

Her heart glowed as she gazed at the rings, suffusing her with warmth, and she smiled despite her sadness. If she ever doubted that it had been real, that it had been as intense and all-consuming as she imagined, all she had to do was recall the night of the Yule Ball, when Rowan had professed his love for her outside under the oak tree.

"It's a friendship ring, if you will, a token of how I feel about you," he'd said, eyes shining with the depth of his feelings. "A symbol of my eternal love for you."

Slowly she leaned down and kissed the twinkling herkimer diamond. "This crystal binds two people together," he'd told her. "It joins their souls and makes it impossible for other people to tear them apart, no matter how hard they try. You're my equal Carlie," he'd insisted. "There is no more than or less than. I love *you*."

Her eyes filled as she remembered the feeling of his body against hers, the sensation of his lips on her mouth, and the vow of love he'd made to her that night. And the tears spilled over as she recalled the card that had been delivered by the police officers, with the dress and the amethyst ring, such a short time later.

"And the day that you feel ready to wear this ring, and agree to marry me, to spend your life with me – loving each other, supporting each other, helping each other dream and scheme and grow stronger and more joyful because we have each other – I will be the happiest man alive," he'd written.

God, she missed him with an ache that was physical as well as emotional, that tore at her heart. But as broken as she was, she didn't have it in her to wish she'd never met him. It was agony now, and probably always would be, but she was so grateful that she had been loved so deeply, even if it was only for a single moment of her life, one brief joyful heartbeat before a future of misery.

Picking up the candle, she slowly made her way home, forcing herself to only think of the good, to remember each precious moment they'd shared, and to let that be enough.

Her dreams that night were filled with ice-cold fear and red velvet robes that warmed her through, before turning into naked flames, smothering her and burning her to ash. She tossed and turned, crying out in the night in pain, in terror, in desperation.

Then a small paw touched her cheek, and Luther's sweet presence brought her back into the room, back into her body. Hugging her grandma's cat in relief, she stroked his head as she thanked him, and he stared at her with wise old eyes, purring and seeming to smile back at her. Settling back down in her bed, she finally drifted off again, feeling Luther's energy by her side as she slept until dawn.

Chapter 6

The Beginning of the Thaw

A few days later, Carlie was curled up on the couch, Luther purring on her lap and a fantasy novel in her hand as she tried to escape into other lands, other worlds, other lives. A tentative knock at the door brought her crashing back to reality, and her sadness crashing back into her heart. Expecting one of Rose's friends, who was dropping off some fabric for their herb bags, she dragged herself up and went to open the door – and froze when she saw that it was Rhiannon standing on the top step, shivering in the cold.

Clutching the door frame, she panicked as she tried to process how she felt. She wasn't ready to talk to her, was terrified to be alone with her. And yet that was stupid – they'd shared everything with each other, worked magic together, comforted one another in their grief, whispered their hopes and dreams to the moon as they stood hand in hand on the tor, confided their deepest secrets to each other.

Heart pounding, she cautiously faced her friend, who looked even more nervous than she was. They hadn't seen each other since the day after the ball, when Rhiannon had come over to tell her about her wonderful night with John, and that she was going to skip the Yule ritual they'd planned so she could spend the evening with him and his family. Oh, and to inform her that she couldn't be her friend any more unless she broke up with Rowan.

Anger shot through her, but she took a deep breath and tried to look welcoming. "I guess you should come in before you freeze to death," she said stiffly. Rhiannon's smile looked a little too bright, a little too forced, but she followed Carlie to the kitchen and hovered around her as she put the kettle on.

"I'm so sorry Carlie," she finally blurted. "I'm so sorry for your loss, so sorry for not being there for you – and truly so sorry for pressuring you in any way." Her smile slipped, and she reached out to her friend, trying to hug her, to connect with her, to bridge the strange awful distance between them. Carlie let herself be held for a moment, then wriggled away on the pretext of fussing with tea leaves and cups and soy milk and honey.

"I came by a few times…" Rhiannon began tentatively, and Carlie tried to remember that this was difficult for her too.

"I know," she said softly. "I just, I couldn't talk about it. I *can't* talk about it. And you were so great about my parents, and so kind to me, I just…"

"You just couldn't understand how I could be such a bitch?" Rhiannon asked flatly, and Carlie looked up at her, startled by her honesty and willingness to admit she was wrong.

"I've gone over this so many times, replaying each scenario, trying to work out why I reacted the way I did, what drove me to give you such a cruel ultimatum. You have no idea how sorry I am," she continued, voice dripping with sincerity.

Carlie stood frozen again, unable to respond. She'd thought her friend would gloss over what had happened between them, try to move on as though nothing had taken place. Admitting she was wrong wasn't something she'd expected to hear – it was weird. Then again, Rhiannon had apologised for her behaviour the day after the ball too – then gone right back to her "Rowan is bad" theme and demanded that Carlie choose between them, and break up with Rowan if she wanted to remain her friend.

Rhiannon winced. "I admit I could have acted better, I could have been more understanding, less selfish. I panicked. I put my own issues on you, and let my jealousy and insecurities colour how I saw Rowan. Please forgive me Carlie. I really am so sorry."

Handing her friend a mug of tea, Carlie nodded reluctantly and walked over to the table, sinking down into a seat with a heavy heart.

"I'm really sorry you had to go through all of that on your own too," Rhiannon continued. "Not that I probably would have been your first choice to grieve Rowan with," she said, trying for a flippant tone but not quite pulling it off.

"It's not like I have many options – it's basically you and Rose, whether I like it or not," Carlie replied, then blushed a little. "Sorry, that came out wrong."

Rhiannon raised one eyebrow, in that way that usually made her smile, then shrugged. "You deserve a few free shots at me," she said, but Carlie shook her head. She wasn't ready to be light-hearted, and she worried that she might accidentally blurt out too much or sound too bitter if she joked about her feelings.

"So how's Brodie, and your dad?" she asked instead, changing the subject to deflect attention away from herself. "Did you have a good Christmas? And have you seen John again?"

"Christmas was nice, just a quiet one with Brodie and Dad. I think it will always be hard for us, without Mum," she said, and Carlie nodded, understanding that. Her friend grieved too.

"I didn't know what had happened then, so I thought it was weird that I hadn't heard from you. Oh, here," she said, rifling through her bag. "I got you a little present." She handed Carlie a brightly wrapped parcel, but her friend had gone pale, eyes widening in pain as she gazed at the neatly tied ribbon, so like the one around her gift from Rowan – the one that had been delivered by two police officers informing her that he was dead.

Rhiannon stood up uncertainly, then took the gift through into the lounge room, leaving it under the pine tree that still stood in its pretty pot from Yule. "Later then," she said gently, as she sat back down and picked up her mug of tea.

Taking a sip, her face brightened. "John is still lovely. I've been over to his place a few times now, babysat his brat siblings with him one night, so we got a lot of kissing done that time, and he's come over to mine a couple of times too. Brodie has loved having something to tease me about, but it's going really well. I really like him."

Carlie tried to keep her face composed, but every word about kissing and closeness was like an arrow through her heart. Thankfully Rhiannon finally realised, and fell into silence with her, although that soon became uncomfortable too.

"So are you ready for school on Monday?" Rhiannon asked, then rolled her eyes at her own question. But Carlie was grateful for the effort she was making. She spared a thought for Emily, her best friend back home in Australia, whose head she'd snapped off after her parents died, just for not knowing what to say.

No one knew what to say to someone in the throes of grief, and she had renewed respect for Emily for trying so hard and persevering so long. What did they say? The friend who holds your hand and says the wrong thing is made of dearer stuff than the one who stays away, or something like that. She'd vowed to try harder, so she smiled at Rhiannon and did her best to reply.

"As ready as I'll ever be. On the plus side, no one even knew I was with Rowan, so no one will ask me about him or get all weird and quiet around me," she said. "But that makes me sad too, because it will seem as though he never existed." She sighed.

"Um, hon? It's a small village. Everyone knows your boyfriend died, even if they didn't know him, but they'll be respectful. And they all knew you were with someone, because they saw you lost in each other while you danced together at the ball, and being crowned Winter Queen and Sun King. Which, if it helps, means there will be lots of photos of you together."

Carlie's eyes misted with tears as she thought of Rowan kissing her on the dance floor, of melting into him and the circle of his arms, and feeling so loved. Of floating away, intoxicated by the magic of the night, the nearness of his body, and the beautiful, intense, inspiring connection she'd felt between them.

Admittedly, she'd been angry with him for a moment, because he'd surprised her by turning up, and she was worried that his presence would upset Rhiannon. But her fear had quickly passed, and she remembered every moment they'd danced together, and every precious second she'd stood outside under the oak tree with him, leaning up against it, being kissed so hard and so deeply.

"Of course they think his name is Paul, and that he went to Smithfield High," Rhiannon broke in, tone cheeky and bright with laughter. Carlie smiled too, trying to put on a brave face, but she was more relieved than she could express when Rose got home and dissolved the intensity in the room. Jumping up, she put the kettle on for another pot of tea, then busied herself in the kitchen as her grandmother and her friend made small talk.

Finally she brought the three cups over and sat down next to Rose, the tension lifting as they spoke about the next sabbat rather than the personal stuff the two girls didn't feel up to discussing. In just four weeks it would be Imbolc, the festival that marked the beginning of spring, and new light, new hope and new beginnings. Fear clutched at Carlie's heart. She didn't want a new beginning, she wanted the past to come back to life. The thought of closure and moving on filled her with dread, and she drifted off into her memories, unwilling to focus on reality and the relentless march of time and life.

Eventually Rhiannon said she had to get home, and Carlie nodded gratefully. She really needed to be alone. "So let me know if you want to do anything tomorrow or on Sunday, or I can just meet you at school on Monday?" her friend offered.

"Monday sounds good. I'm helping Rose in the shop this weekend, and getting sorted. I haven't even looked at my books since… since the last day of school," Carlie said, voice faltering.

Her friend glanced over at Rose, who stayed silent, her face devoid of expression, and Rhiannon forced a smile. Although she thought they were terrible excuses for not spending any time with her over the next two days, she didn't let on, and Rose clearly wasn't going to give away the lie.

So Carlie was finally able to escape upstairs to her room and curl up on her narrow bed with Luther. She was glad Rhiannon had come over and made the first move towards restoring their friendship, but she knew it would take a while longer before her heart fully thawed.

Chapter 7

For Whom the Bell Rings

The ringing of the bell vibrated through Carlie's body, setting her heart racing and her teeth on edge. Dread filled her, but Rhiannon took her hand, and together they climbed the steps to the front of the school. Carlie smiled at her friend gratefully as she dropped her off at her classroom, then took a deep breath, summoned up as much courage as she could and walked through the door. Avoiding eye contact as best as she was able to, she moved quickly to a desk up the back and pulled out her books. Nervously she looked up as the teacher came in. He caught her eye and smiled sadly at her, and she nodded briefly in acknowledgement then gazed down at her books, praying he wouldn't say anything.

One of the girls in her class ran in then, flustered and a minute late, and drew attention away from her. "Good morning Abby," their teacher said sternly, as the girl slid sheepishly into the seat next to Carlie. "I'm so sorry Mr Stephens," she murmured. "We were up all night with a sick cow."

He nodded, comprehension in his eyes, and Carlie marvelled at the lives of her fellow students. A lot of them lived on outlying farms, and school wasn't the only work they did. Back home in Sydney, no one would have known what to do with a sick animal, let alone how to run a working dairy, but kids here did.

"I'm so sorry for your loss," Abby whispered to her, and Carlie looked up in surprise. "Let me know if you need anything, or want to talk. Or not talk," she said simply, then turned back to the blackboard. Understanding washed over her as she remembered Rhiannon mentioning something about Abby on her first day of school, back in September. Her boyfriend had taken his own life, and Abby had struggled to cope.

"Thank you," she murmured, and Abby smiled at her sadly. "It still hurts, but it does get a bit easier," she replied quietly. "Is that what you were wondering?"

Carlie nodded, despair flooding her, but they were interrupted when their teacher started a quiz based on the homework he'd set over the Christmas holidays, and she had to concentrate to keep up. She hadn't opened her books once while they were off – Rowan had died at the beginning of their break, and she'd been in a haze of grief ever since. She'd only left the house twice, for the funeral and then her farewell ritual, and had rarely even emerged from her bedroom, so she hoped today wasn't going to rely too much on the reading she was supposed to have done. Luckily, in this class at least, she had covered the topic at hand at her old school, back home in Sydney, so she managed to fake her way through.

Back home… Was she always going to feel that way, like she was just a visitor here, and Australia was her real home? Or would she one day consider England to be home? Would she pick up an accent? Change her favourite foods and the way she dressed?

And what did home even mean? Was it where your memories lived, where your childhood roots lay, the place that felt like a physical part of you? Or was it the place you ended up, through accident or fate, or choice or chance, whether you wanted to be there or not?

Did she want to be here? She still wasn't sure, but it wasn't like she had any say in the matter. Rose was her only living family member, so that made it home, for now at least.

Her reverie was interrupted by the bell, and Mr Stephens hastily set some more homework before half the students bolted out the door. Abby smiled at her and waved as she left, and Carlie waved back. It seemed that people marked by tragedy gravitated towards each other, which made sense she supposed. Certainly she found it easier to be with Rhiannon, who'd lost her mum to cancer just over a year ago, than her old friend Emily, who hadn't experienced such loss – thank god. She hoped no one else their age had to go through that. Making a mental note to ask Rhiannon later about Abby, and whether she had close friends and some support, she pulled out her next lot of books and got ready for history.

Rhiannon hurried in just as the second bell rang and swung into the seat next to her. "You okay?" she asked, and Carlie nodded. All things considered, she supposed she was okay. Not good, not great, nowhere even *close* to happy, but she was okay.

Their teacher Laura came in – Ms Henderson, they should say, although they found it hard to slip back into student mode at school when Laura was part of Rose's magical ritual circle. Today she was followed by a tall, sporty looking guy with wavy blond hair.

Carlie blinked. He looked like half the guys she'd known back home, as though he'd just emerged from the waves after a long surf. Rhiannon elbowed her sharply in the ribs. "He's cute isn't he! He was in my biology class just then," she grinned. Carlie stared at her friend, unable to mask her shock, and a guilty look crossed her face.

"I'm sorry," Rhiannon whispered, stricken. "Way too soon for that." Carlie made her face as expressionless as she could, and turned to look at their teacher, who was trying to get the class's attention.

"I'd like you all to meet Jake," Ms Henderson said. "Jake, everyone," she added, sweeping her arm to encompass the whole class. "Jake is here from Australia for the school year, staying with his grandfather while his parents are working in Africa. So let's all make him feel welcome, shall we?"

"Hi Jake," the class replied, rote sing-song style, and he waved and flashed them a cheeky grin.

"Oh my god, he's to die for," one of the girls near Carlie said, which was followed by giggles and murmurs of agreement.

"Do you know him Carlie?" one of the guys asked from the front of the room. Rhiannon rolled her eyes. "Australia's a big country Dave," she snapped, instantly protective of Carlie and knowing she didn't want any attention on her.

"Carlie's from Sydney," their teacher said. "And Jake is from Perth, on the other side of the country. That's thousands of miles apart, right?" she asked, turning to Jake. He grinned at her and nodded, then turned and caught Carlie's eye.

His smile did strange things to her tummy, and she quickly glanced away. Rhiannon looked at her carefully, but she avoided her friend's gaze, ducking down to her bag and pretending to look for something. She was relieved when their teacher finally found Jake a seat at the front of the room and the class got underway. And she didn't give him another thought until just before the class ended, when Laura gave them their term assignments.

"You will all be examining an aspect of the British Commonwealth, formerly the British Empire, during the period from the sixteenth century until now. I want an in-depth essay that covers the history of the country you're studying before British rule, the circumstances of the colonisation from both our point of view as well as the perspective of the indigenous inhabitants, whether the place had 'belonged' to a different colonial power earlier, how the relationship has changed over the years, and what the status is now – for instance, after a century of British rule, India became an independent nation in 1947, after the struggle led by Mahatma Gandhi."

Everyone groaned – this sounded much tougher than last term's major assignment, which had actually been lots of fun.

"You'll be working in pairs for this one. Debbie and Peter, you have India. Rhiannon and Dave, Canada. Ally and Rob, Hong Kong. Karen and Mark, the colonies of North America. Jillian and Michael, the Caribbean." She went through the whole class, until Carlie started to think she'd been forgotten, but no such luck. "And Carlie, you and Jake have Australia."

There were mutters around the room, cries of "no fair" and "that's cheating", and Carlie was aware of her friend looking at her speculatively, but their teacher stared the complainers down. "I think it will be fascinating for our two Aussie friends to study the topic from the British perspective, and I'm sure it will be illuminating for all of us to gain their point of view on British settlement of their own country. At the end we'll be making copies of all the assignments, and you'll be learning about each of the colonies – and being tested on all of them. So you had better put a lot of effort into your paper, or the whole class could fail. Don't let us all down," their teacher warned.

"I want ten thousand words by March 14," she continued. Everyone started complaining at once, and there were moans all round. "That gives you ten weeks. We'll go through the topics to cover together, and you'll have some class time to work on it. We'll also cover some aspects this term, but you'll have to organise study sessions out of school as well. The major test will be a month later, so you'll need to study hard for that one."

The whole class was speechless for once, and Laura looked around with a wide, satisfied smile. "Apparently this subject was a little too easy last term, and the assignment too much fun, so I didn't want to disappoint you again," she grinned.

"Now, you'd better hurry to your next class," she added, as the bell rang and they all started noisily packing up their books.

"Carlie, do you have a moment?" Laura asked softly as people started filing out. Rhiannon stared at her, a question in her eyes, but Carlie shrugged. She had no idea what their teacher wanted. "I'll see you at lunch, yeah?" she said to Rhiannon, and her friend nodded, obviously curious, and left the room.

Standing nervously at her teacher's desk, Carlie began to panic. Surely she couldn't be in trouble already? But Laura smiled, a comforting smile, and she was reminded of the sweet and magical woman she'd taken part in seasonal rituals with. "You haven't done anything wrong love, don't look so scared," she said. "I just wanted to see how you were doing."

Carlie shifted uncomfortably. Maybe it would have been less confronting if she *had* been in trouble. "I'm okay," she said finally, voice grim, as she tried to keep her face blank.

"I just wanted to let you know that if it gets too much, you can tell me, all right? Jake's a history wiz, so that should take some of the pressure off, and I hoped that being assigned Australia would make it a bit easier for you. But if you need a hand I'm happy to help. I can give you some input, and suggest a few shortcuts, okay?" she offered.

A wave of exhaustion washed over Carlie. It was sweet that her teacher was so caring, so concerned, but for once she wished people didn't have to worry about her or make allowances for her. She just wanted to be a normal teenager, worrying about schoolwork and friends and parties and pop music. No special consideration for grief and loss, no cloying fussing over her or asking every five minutes if she was okay. Of course she wasn't okay – how could she be? – but that wasn't what they wanted to hear.

Sighing with impatience, she thanked Laura for her concern, swore she was fine, then hurried out of the room before her tears could betray her. Her next two classes were uneventful, the teachers seemingly unaware of her drama, and her fellow students too engrossed in their own lives to pay her any attention. She was infinitely grateful for the solipsism of youth.

Finally the bell rang and she went to meet Rhiannon in the cafeteria – but one look at her friend's inquisitive face and bright smile and she started wishing she'd gone home for lunch.

"So, what did Laura want?" she asked quickly.

Carlie shrugged. "Just to see if I'm okay, although how she could think she even needed to ask when I'm so obviously turning cartwheels with joy I don't know," she snapped. Then she sighed. "Sorry, I guess I'm just tired and irritable, and depressed, but what am I supposed to say to that? 'Oh yes, I was getting a bit sick of my boyfriend, it was such a relief that he died?' " she asked, sarcasm dripping from each word. "But apparently Jake is a wiz at history, so our assignment shouldn't be too much of a struggle, but if I need some help with it I'm to let her know. Which I do appreciate, but –

"Oh no Rhiannon, what are you thinking? I know that look," she finished glumly.

Her friend tried to look innocent, but failed miserably. "So, Jake huh. Quite the hot guy, no?"

Carlie rolled her eyes. "You seriously think I'm looking at any guy right now?"

"Didn't say it had to be you looking," Rhiannon grinned.

"But what about John? I thought that all was well with your solstice beloved?"

Her friend sighed dramatically. "Carlie, please, neither of us has to date him, I'm just making an observation. Namely, that he's a good-looking guy, and seems really sweet. Can't two friends gossip about the cuteness of a hot new boy at school?"

There was a cough close to them, and they both looked up quickly, Rhiannon slightly panicked that she'd been overheard – and even more so when she saw that it was Jake standing right next to their table, a tray of food in one hand, and a cheeky smile on his face. But she recovered remarkably quickly.

"Jake, hi, welcome to Summer Hill High. I'm Rhiannon, and this is Carlie," she said, as she held out her hand to him by way of introduction. "Although you probably know that since you're partners… well, study partners," she amended quickly. Carlie was amused despite herself. She'd never seen her friend so flustered, and it made her like Jake a little more as a result.

Jake shook Rhiannon's hand, smiled in Carlie's direction, then stood above them awkwardly.

"Oh god, how rude of me!" Rhiannon said at last. "Sit down Jake, if you'd like to. Sorry, where are my manners? You're more than welcome to join us, although if you'd rather hang out with the guys that's fine too, no pressure."

Carlie stared at her friend, perplexed. Why was she so nervous around this guy? Meanwhile, Jake was smiling at them both and taking a seat.

"Thanks Rhiannon, I appreciate it. It sure does suck being the new guy, although I guess you'd know all about that Carlie? Someone said you only started here halfway through last year, is that right?"

She nodded vaguely and stared down at her plate. Sensing her distress, Rhiannon jumped in, and spent the whole lunch break engaging Jake in conversation. Her friend had quickly gotten over her awkwardness with the new guy, and Carlie was content to keep her eyes on her food and let their chatter wash over her. It was kind of soothing in a way, like she was part of the world but didn't need to actually interact within it. Maybe she could just drift through the rest of her life like that.

Panic hit though when she finally noticed that Jake and her friend had gone silent, and she blushed when she looked up and saw that they were both staring at her.

"I'm sorry, did you ask me something?" she stammered.

Rhiannon smiled at her reassuringly. "Jake was just letting you know where he lives, so you can plan your study sessions. The good news is that you're only a few streets away from each other, so yours will be easy to coordinate. My project partner Dave lives a few miles out of town, so I'm not sure how that's going to work, although I'm dreading it already," she sighed.

"But there's plenty of time to worry about that next week, once we know what we have to cover. I'm guessing we'll probably split up the topics and do some research solo, before getting together with our study buddy to write it all up?"

Pausing, she gazed at them both with a wry smile. "I'm sorry, I'm Little Miss Chatterbox today. Feel free to chime in."

But it was the bell that chimed in then, so they got to their feet, stacking up their plates to take over to the kitchen window. Carlie suddenly felt guilty that she'd ignored Jake the whole time, so she tried to summon a smile.

"It was nice to meet you," she offered softly. "I guess I'll see you again in history. I've got English now, so I'd better head off."

He looked down at his schedule. "With Mr Ferguson?"

Reluctantly she nodded. "Great, I'll walk with you," he said.

Rhiannon grinned, as though this made her happy, and was all part of her plan, and Carlie shot daggers at her. "Have fun you two! I've got PE, so I'll see you later," she called out to them, waving to them over her shoulder as she raced off.

Jake fell into step beside Carlie, and her heart clenched with the effort as she tried not to betray her impatience. Although she seemed to have failed at that. "I'm sorry, I don't want to be a bother," Jake said gently. "If you'd rather be alone?"

Carlie looked up at him, stifling a sigh. Her bad mood and lack of enthusiasm was nothing to do with him, she just didn't want to talk to anyone. But then she remembered how out of her depth she'd felt during her first week at a new school in a new country, and her heart went out to him.

"It's okay," she said, forcing a smile and deciding to make an effort. "I've just got a few things on my mind right now. How are you finding it in England? Aside from the weather change obviously – what would it be, around forty degrees in Perth right now, blue skies and sticky summer heat?"

His face lit up, and she almost felt happy herself for a moment, because his joy at life was so obvious, so contagious. Pulling his jacket a little more tightly around himself, he admitted that he was struggling a lot with the cold, and missing his friends – and that it had been quite a shock to discover that school went back in the first week of January here, rather than at the end, as it did in Australia.

Despite herself, Carlie found herself agreeing with the stranger, and actually having a conversation with him, feeling comfortable enough with him to answer his questions, and even ask a few herself. When they got to class he followed her inside and sat down next to her, and she didn't find it too unnerving. Maybe it was because he was Australian, and there was an unspoken sense of camaraderie as a result, a subconscious desire to seek out their own kind, to band together against what at times seemed so strange and foreign.

Their teacher was running late, so they continued to talk, although Carlie closed down abruptly when he asked what her parents did and why they'd moved to the UK.

"My parents died in June. And it turned out that I had a grandmother I'd never heard of, my mum's mum, who lived here," she said quietly, voice distant and cold.

"Oh god Carlie, I'm so sorry, I had no idea," he stuttered, and she smiled at him ruefully.

"It's okay," she replied softly, and realised with surprise that it was. Not that they were dead, obviously, but that people felt able to ask her about them. That she felt able to talk about them. Jake still looked uncomfortable though, so they were both relieved when Mr Ferguson finally walked in and they got to work. And when the bell rang, Carlie packed up her books to leave while Jake stayed where he was for his next class, so they said goodbye and she walked out on her own, relieved to be alone again, but glad that she'd been able to open up a little bit to him. Baby steps and all that…

As she hurried up the stairs, she tried not to think about the vivid blue of his eyes, his surfer-fit body, or the cheeky grin that lit up his whole expression – it was just nice to see a friendly face, she told herself. And she felt comfortable with him because he was from Australia, and because he reminded her of home, and the time when everything in her life had been normal, had been happy.

God, six months ago her life had been just like anyone else's – her parents were alive, she was halfway through her final year of high school, and her plans with her friend Emily were all set. They were going to rent a place together in the city while they went to uni to study law, travel together, meet nice guys, eventually have their own families. She sighed.

In a single moment, her whole life had been turned upside down. Her parents had died, and she'd been forced to leave everyone and everything she knew and move to the other side of the world to live with a stranger. She hadn't known how she would cope with the devastating loss and the emotionally crippling grief, and she was so grateful to her grandmother, and to Rhiannon and Rowan, for helping her survive the deaths of her mum and dad.

But now she was grieving the loss of the love of her life too, blow on top of blow, and she wasn't sure she could survive this new agony. Shaking her head to try to shake off the train of thought, she reminded herself that she had to count her blessings. There were people far worse off than her. And surely she could survive this too. If Rose had taught her anything, it was how much strength a person could have inside. She just had to try to find hers…

Chapter 8

Convening the Coven

In their last class at school the next day, Rhiannon passed a scrap of paper to Carlie as sneakily as she could. Carlie unfolded it carefully and squinted at the words.

"Coven meeting tonight?"

A wave of fear washed over her. Was she ready for that? Gazing out the window, she pondered how she felt about restarting their magical meetings. Their last Tuesday night magic club had been three weeks ago – before the solstice ball, before her running away to spend the night with Rowan, before his tragic death.

Last Tuesday she'd been doing her own ritual, farewelling her beloved, alone until she was interrupted by the woman in red. The Tuesday night before that she'd still been huddled in her room, lying in bed and praying for oblivion from the moment the police officers had delivered their devastating news.

God, had it only been a little over two weeks since that knock on the door? It seemed like a lifetime ago, and in some ways it was. She felt as though she'd been torn apart, and the person she had been before the accident had disappeared, never to be seen again. Yet in other ways it felt as though it was just yesterday that Rowan had been holding her in his arms, whispering his love to her, and begging her to stay with him.

Was she ready to work magic again? Ready to make herself vulnerable to Rhiannon? Creating rituals and casting spells with someone was such an intimate thing, opening your heart to your magical partner, and opening your very being to the universe. Did she want to be so naked, so exposed, to the friend she still felt resentment towards? Could she let herself?

Sighing, she stared at the note again. She knew she couldn't hide in her room for the rest of her life, but did she need more time to huddle up in bed under her mother's quilt, locked away from the world and drowning in sorrow and grief and regret? More time to snuggle up to Luther and feel his body vibrating against her cheek as she held him tight and he purred his joy at all the extra attention?

Her desk rocked a little as Rhiannon kicked its leg, and she looked up guiltily. Her teacher was staring at her expectantly, and she panicked. What had he asked her? Rhiannon cleared her throat as she hissed the answer to her, and Carlie felt a wave of relief as she replied. She was rewarded with a wintry smile from their teacher as he turned to try to catch someone else out.

Realising that had been a lucky save, she vowed to pay more attention to the world around her, not just in her classes, but in everyday life as well. She glanced back down at the note in front of her, and quickly scribbled out "yes", before she could change her mind. It was possible she would live to regret this, but she had to make some attempt to rejoin the living. Furtively she passed the note back to her friend, who smiled when she read the answer, then bent over it to write another question. Trying not to roll her eyes as she unfurled it, Carlie glanced down again.

"Your place or mine?"

Shaking her head and refusing to risk their teacher's wrath by continuing the note passing any longer, she slipped the piece of paper into her pencil case, then turned to her friend and pointed at her. Rhiannon smiled. "Great," she mouthed.

"Ms Stark, is there something you feel you'd like to share with the class?" their teacher thundered.

Blushing, her friend shook her head and said no, and that she was sorry for interrupting. And they avoided catching each other's eye for the rest of the class, in case they started giggling and couldn't stop.

Darkness was closing in and snow had started falling by the time school got out, but Carlie was now immune to its magic. The first time she'd seen snow, a few weeks before Christmas, she'd squealed like a little kid and run around playing in it for hours, building a tiny snowman and laughing with Rose as their cheeks got redder and their hands went numb from the cold. But now it just reminded her of Rowan's car sliding off the road in the snow. Of death and anger and fear and loss.

Sighing, she raced home to get a warmer jacket and the things she'd need for their ritual. Tonight was the dark moon, a time of banishing, of introspection, of going within. She shuddered. To be honest, she wasn't sure she could go much further inward before she started coming out the other side.

Continuing her honesty kick, she admitted to herself that she was nervous about tonight. She hadn't worked magic with anyone else since the solstice eve ceremony at Rowan's retreat, where she'd felt the warmth of his arms around her in the ritual circle, even as he stood across from her and spoke words for all of them, looking at each participant in turn, not just her. That night she'd felt how much he loved her, deep in her bones, in the deepest parts of her heart, and the warmth of it had settled around her, so comforting, so reassuring, so magical.

And yet somehow she'd twisted everything around in her head, had thrown off his love for her, callously, thoughtlessly. Had pushed aside the love she felt for him. That was the night she'd told him how much she loved him – then broken up with him, breaking his heart as well as her own in the process. How could she have done that? It had seemed to make sense at the time – she didn't want to keep lying to Rose about her whereabouts, and she didn't want to lose Rhiannon after her terrible ultimatum.

Oh god, she was still so angry about that. She thought that she'd let it go when her friend had come over the other day and apologised. Wasn't that what you were supposed to do? Forgive, forget, move on? But what if she couldn't?

As she unlocked the door and pushed against it until it banged open, Luther miaowed sharply, and she picked him up and held him in her arms, patting his head until he purred. "Oh Luther, what should I do? Will I always be angry with Rhiannon? It's not really fair to her if I am, but suppressing it and trying to hide it won't be fair to me either," she moaned.

The black cat looked up at her, green eyes filled with love and understanding, then licked her on the cheek, his tongue like sandpaper. "Hey, stop it Mister," she giggled. "That tickles!"

It had done the trick though – she'd stopped obsessing over their friendship and was back in the moment. "Okay, fine, thank you," she said to Luther, affection in her voice, as she raced up to her room and grabbed what she needed. "But I do have to go now. Wish me luck!"

Rushing down the stairs and out the front door, she slung her bag over her shoulder and started to walk through the softly falling snow. As the cold sent its icy fingers through her coat she shivered. Was she ready for this? Did she want to do spellworkings to achieve future goals? Did she want to acknowledge the future, let alone plan for it? And could she open her heart to her friend, which she'd have to do if they were going to work magic, or would her anger make it impossible?

Taking a deep breath, she tried to calm herself down. This was Rhiannon she was thinking about – the girl who had helped her grieve the loss of her parents, who had helped her settle in to a new school, who had helped her find her inner magic, and who had always been so kind and considerate.

Could all of that good be wiped out because she hadn't been supportive on *one* issue? It didn't say much about her if all she could focus on was the bad, when there had been so much good. And who was she to think everyone had to be perfect all the time, because she certainly hadn't been. She of all people knew about getting a second chance, so she had to do the same for Rhiannon, surely. She deserved that much.

Cheeks red with cold and breath puffing out in little clouds of white, she finally got to her friend's place and knocked on the door. Carefully keeping her mind blank, she smiled as Rhiannon let her in and led her upstairs.

"Dad's at a meeting, but he sends his love. He's been really concerned about you, and about Rose," her friend said.

"Thank him for me, please. He's so kind. I can see why Mum loved him so much," she replied.

"Did she though?" Rhiannon asked, perching on her bed. Carlie stared at her, puzzled, and her friend lowered her gaze. "He's been talking about her recently, and he seems to think that she hated him, and that he failed her in some way."

Carlie looked shocked. "Not at all! Mum cared about him deeply," she insisted. She always felt weird talking to her friend about her dad's long-ago relationship with her mum – it felt disloyal to Rhiannon's own mum Beth. But she couldn't let either of them think that was true. "Mum felt that *she'd* disappointed *him*, treated him badly, and that she no longer deserved his friendship. She felt so bad for hurting him, and even though she realised later that she'd been manipulated into losing touch with him, she was still so angry with herself for letting him go."

Rhiannon stared at her, curious. "How do you know that?"

"It was in Mum's diary, the one Sandy sent me. She regretted hurting Gran and your dad more than anything – she said that he'd been so kind and supportive to her, so sweet and caring, but she had been too stupid to see it. Although she did mention that she hoped he would find much-deserved happiness with a lovely girl called Beth," Carlie said, smiling as she referred to Rhiannon's mum.

"Also, I know it myself, from what I've experienced and what I've seen," she continued. "Mike has been so wonderful to Gran all these years, and he's helped me too. It was your dad who finally convinced me to get up and eat something on Boxing Day, to stop worrying Gran, so please let him know that. And let him know how much Mum, Gran and I *all* appreciate him. And I understand that it's hard for you to hear him talking about my mum, but I think it's just because he's such a kind-hearted man, and cares about everybody."

"I know, and it doesn't bother me any more, I promise," Rhiannon said, voice soft. "I'm just sorry that Dad has lost both of his great loves, and we've both lost our mums. It's not the kind of kindred spirit thing I wanted to share with you."

Carlie smiled wistfully. "It doesn't seem fair, that's for sure." Gazing around the room, she decided it was time to change the subject. The scent of sandalwood was reassuring, and the candlelight made it feel so warm and inviting. Inhaling deeply, she tried to centre herself and her thoughts, throw off the sadness that always threatened when she thought of her parents.

"Do you want to do a ritual tonight, or would you rather we continue our study, or just talk?" Rhiannon asked. "It's the dark moon, so, I don't know, is that too intense?"

Carlie shrugged, still not sure herself. "I guess I've gotta get back on the horse some time, right?" she said, then groaned at the cliche.

Her friend nodded. "Was Yule the last working you did?" she asked cautiously, as she slipped off her shoes and sank down into one of the big purple pillows in the centre of the room.

Tears threatened as Carlie did the same, but she steeled herself against them and nodded. "Yep, the last group ritual I did was with Rowan that night. And it was so beautiful. So powerful and magical. Oh, and…" she began, then trailed off. She had a sudden memory of the woman in red facing her across her altar, during the ceremony she'd done down on the banks of the stream in her and Rowan's special place, but she wasn't ready to talk about that yet.

"That was the night I met Jasmine too," she offered instead, and was surprised when Rhiannon looked confused. "Oh, you don't know any of that yet do you? Jasmine was at Rowan's retreat. I ended up sitting with her at dinner, and she looked like she'd seen a ghost when she first looked up at me. When she told me her name, I realised why – I'd been reading Mum's journal on the way there, and she'd mentioned a woman named Jasmine who'd tried to help her get away from Andre, despite being in his circle and risking his wrath by befriending her," she explained, shuddering as she remembered all that her mum had been through.

Rhiannon looked rapt, and eager to know more, so in the end the two girls didn't perform a ritual or cast a spell, they just talked. Carlie shared everything Jasmine had told her about her mum and the once-loving shaman who'd treated her so badly. Rhiannon was shocked by the awful violence and abuse, both physical and mental, that Violet had endured in that relationship, and she cried when Carlie revealed that Andre had smashed her mum into a glass table, as Rhi's psychic had seen – that it had been a past event of what had already happened to her mum, not a future vision of something Rowan was going to do to her, as her friend had believed.

"Oh god, Dad would just die if he knew. He suspected that that man had been cruel, but I can't believe just how terrible it was," Rhiannon said, voice thick with tears.

Carlie nodded grimly. That hadn't even been the worst thing he'd done, but she couldn't bring herself to reveal that he'd also held her mother down and raped her. "She thought he was going to kill her," she said instead. "She'd given up, and begun to pray that he would just get it over with, but Dad found her one day, battered and bleeding, and helped her escape." Then she smiled. "Mum really did get her happy ever after, eventually."

The door downstairs banged closed, and Carlie jumped. "It's just Dad," Rhiannon said softly. They looked over at the clock on the bedside table, and were surprised to see that it was already 10pm.

"Oh god, I'm so sorry," Carlie said. "I've taken up the whole evening! But I do actually feel a little better for having shared it all with you, so thank you," she added. "I guess I should get home though – I still have a fair bit of homework to do for the morning, and I imagine you do too."

Rhiannon rolled her eyes. "Yeah, a little bit. But thanks for tonight, it's been really nice. I've missed you."

Carlie gave her friend a hug, ran down the stairs, then lowered her head and forced her way home through the still-falling snow. She was glad they'd ended up just talking all night, because she felt closer to Rhiannon again after sharing so much with her. Although she did wonder why she hadn't felt ready to tell her about the red-robed woman yet. Still, there was all the time in the world for that...

Chapter 9

A Faerytale Curse

The next few days at school passed quickly. Laura had them sit next to their study partners in history, so Jake ended up hanging out with Carlie and Rhiannon a lot, eating lunch with them each day, and walking with them to class when their schedules coincided. And she wasn't sure why, but for some reason Carlie didn't mind. Jake was a lovely guy, unfailingly polite and sensitive to her moods, and it was nice to hear an Aussie voice, and have him understand the obscure pop culture references and jokes she made, which often flew over other people's heads.

It surprised her though, that she was happy to talk to him so much after so recently insisting that she just wanted to be left alone. Maybe it was because he'd be going back to Australia soon, so there was no pressure for a lengthy or lasting friendship, which meant she didn't need to censor herself when she spoke.

Carlie was also beginning to suspect that her friend liked him, and that the feeling was mutual, which made her happy as well as less guarded in what she said to him. It was a relief that he wasn't interested in her, because she wanted nothing to do with relationships. She kept her suspicions to herself though. Rhiannon was still dating John, and she still wanted to avoid any conversations even remotely related to romance.

Her friendship with Rhiannon was also getting back to normal, which she was glad of. She didn't have the energy to be resentful, and she really wanted to be a better person, and be able to forgive her and move on. But that was tested when she met up with a visibly nervous Rhiannon at lunchtime on Friday.

"Do you mind if I spend the day with John tomorrow?" she asked, frowning in apprehension. "We could do something together on Sunday though," she added quickly.

Carlie shrugged. "That's fine," she replied. "Rose wanted me to help in the shop anyway, so it's all good. And you don't have to ask my permission – I don't expect you to be miserable and not see your boyfriend just because I can't," she added.

Her friend looked unconvinced. "But if you'd rather we hang out tomorrow, I can cancel my plans with John," she offered. "Honestly, I want to be there for you when you need me."

Carlie struggled to dampen her annoyance. "I know that. And it's fine, really, I'm not just being a martyr," she sighed. "But don't use me as an excuse, if you'd rather be here this weekend, seeing someone closer to home," she added. Rhiannon looked puzzled, but Jake came over to join them then, and Carlie changed the subject to include him.

The next morning, Carlie waited until she knew Rhiannon would be on the bus to Smithfield, then made her way over to her house. Nervously she climbed the front steps and knocked, and before she could change her mind and flee, Mike opened the door, smiling when he saw who it was.

"Carlie, hi. I'm so sorry, but Rhi's not here," he said gently.

She smiled. "I know, she's spending the day with John. I came to see you," she explained.

Looking puzzled, Mike ushered her inside out of the cold and through to the kitchen. "Is everything okay?" he asked, voice betraying his concern. He gestured to a stool at the kitchen bench, and turned to put the kettle on.

Carlie smiled. "Yes, everything's fine, or as fine as could be expected. It's just, well, I wanted to show you something."

She broke off, suddenly anxious, as she reached into her bag and felt for her mum's diary. Would it upset him to see it? Would it be better for both of them if she left it alone, minded her own business? She gazed at him, and almost chickened out, but then she remembered what her friend had said the other night. He didn't deserve to keep torturing himself over an imagined slight.

"Rhiannon mentioned that you thought Mum had been angry at you, or disappointed. But she wasn't," Carlie finally said, and she saw hope flare in Mike's eyes before it died away, and he reached into the cupboard for tea and mugs. Hesitating for a moment, she gathered her thoughts, then dove back in.

"The biggest regret of her life was that she'd let you and Gran down, and pushed you away. She really missed you. And she considered you one of her dearest friends, even years after she left home – she called you the truest friend anyone could ever have."

Mike turned back to her, hands on the kitchen bench to hold himself up. "Oh Carlie, that's so sweet of you to say, but you can't know that. You'd never even heard of me until you got here. I've always regretted how things ended with Violet, regretted not doing more to help her. She pushed me away, yes, and that hurt, but I should have tried harder," he sighed.

"I do know," she said firmly, and pulled the diary out of her bag. "Mum wrote about you and her, and how terrible she felt at the way she'd treated you. She admitted that she'd thrown away your friendship, and that she should have trusted you instead of him. And she paid for that decision," Carlie added, voice faltering a little. "It ended very badly with Andre, let's just say that. It was more awful than anyone could imagine. But as bad as it was for her, she was just really sad that she'd let you down."

Mike stared at her, eyes assessing, trying to work out if she was telling the truth. The whistling of the kettle halted his examination, and he turned away for a moment. Dazed, he poured boiling water into the cups then handed one to her, and she whispered her thanks, unwilling to point out that he'd forgotten the tea, milk and sugar, and waiting instead to see what he'd say next.

"You know, I went to see him once," he finally admitted. "Andre. To try to reason with him, convince him to leave her alone. But he just laughed in my face and threatened me. Said he'd already started turning her against me, so it would be very simple to ensure I never saw her again…" He trailed off, gazing with unseeing eyes into the distance, before finally noticing her pale, stricken face. "What's wrong Carlie?" he demanded.

"I dreamed that," she blurted out. "Months ago. You were at his place, and argued with him, and I heard him threatening you. Then Mum arrived, and asked what you were doing there. The mean guy said you just wanted to join his next tarot class, then she went inside, and he turned back to you and laughed."

Mike's face was as pale as Carlie's. "That's exactly what happened," he whispered, fear in his voice.

Carlie had frozen, hand clutching the bench top for support. "So that was him? That was Andre? He did look just like Rowan?"

Mike glanced up at her, seeing her distress. "Yes," he said, sighing. "But they weren't alike, not at all. I know that."

Smiling, she touched his hand. This wasn't about her. But it was freaking her out that she'd had the dream about her mother aged seventeen, Mike and the strange man who looked like Rowan long before she'd met Rowan, and had only discovered that her boyfriend was the son of the man who'd tortured her mum the night before he died. She tried to shake it off though. She had to be strong for Mike.

"And then he cursed you," she choked out.

Mike gasped, shocked, then reluctantly nodded. "He told me that if I got in his way, he'd make sure every woman I ever loved would die by her fortieth birthday," he shuddered.

"But he couldn't have that kind of power, surely," Carlie said, alarmed. "No one could. Curses are from faerytales!"

"Beth died on her fortieth birthday. I obsessed over it for weeks, and it still terrifies me – does it mean Rhiannon will die at forty too? That it will all be my fault?" Then his head snapped up. "Oh god Carlie, when did your mum die?"

She stared down at the diary on the bench, unable to meet his eyes. "The accident was the night before her fortieth birthday, and she died the next morning in the hospital. But that wasn't your fault Mike, it was on the other side of the world for a start. And if anyone should be blamed, it's me. I was driving the car," she choked out.

Mike looked aghast. "Carlie, no. It wasn't your fault!"

She smiled ruefully. "I know. A drunk driver went through a red light and hit us, so technically it wasn't my fault. Gran is very insistent about that. But Andre has been dead for more than a decade, and he didn't know where Mum was, and there's no way he knew the driver. Besides, you didn't come between them, he did that himself with the awful way he treated her."

Tears welled in her eyes, and Mike felt helpless all over again. He stared at the diary on the table as he took a sip of the hot water in his cup, not even registering that there was no tea in it. His face was conflicted – half of him wanted to read the book, and half of him wanted to burn it and all the awful things that must be in it.

"Was it really so bad?" he asked, voice pleading for it not to be true. "Did she get over it, do you think? I mean, was she happy in the end?" His hands shook as he tried to lift the mug again.

"It was beyond awful," Carlie said at last, finding no reason to lie. "I don't know how she survived it – she's the bravest person I'll ever know, and I didn't even realise until I'd lost her." She saw that Mike was about to break down again.

"But she was happy," she added quickly. "And it was because of you that she eventually remembered she didn't deserve to be treated that way, and because of Dad that she healed from it. I had no idea how amazing he was either," she sighed. "But I know Mum felt truly blessed because she'd been loved by two extraordinary men."

Mike started to protest, but she cut him off. "She always loved you, don't you see? She still thought of you as her best friend, and she was so devastated that she'd hurt you, that she hadn't trusted you. She still longed to see you."

Mike was shaking his head, but she took his hand again, trying to reinforce her point, while her other hand rested on the diary. "I don't think it will help you to read all of it, it will tear you apart, but there are some entries I know she would want you to see, and a postcard she wrote to you but never sent," she explained, pulling out the pages she'd photocopied in the school library and handing them to him.

Reverently he placed them on the bench between them, and a look of wonder crossed his face as he traced over the letters. "I always loved her handwriting," he said, but Carlie saw he was talking to himself now, not her. He'd disappeared into a fog of memories and regrets.

Smiling, she stood up, carefully placed the diary back in her bag, then took her cup to the sink and poured the water down the drain.

"I'll see you later," she whispered to Mike as she walked past him, but he barely acknowledged her presence, so wrapped up in the past had he become. Letting herself out the front door, she wandered back towards the cottage, towards home.

It was still chilly, but she must have been getting used to it, because she barely noticed. Her skin started prickling though when she stepped into an apple-scented mist that was wreathing itself around the base of the tor. Feeling something soft brush against her ankles, she reached down, an automatic reflex because Luther was usually weaving around her feet wanting a pat.

Then her breath caught, and she had a moment of panic as her focus shifted, and she was suddenly disorientated from the fog that seemed to be clouding her brain as well as her vision. A hand touched her arm just as she heard her name being called, and she screamed. Laughter echoed around her, before the red-clad woman materialised in front of her.

"God!" Carlie exclaimed, heart beating wildly from fright.

The figure smiled. "Hardly! But I suppose I could be described as an aspect of the goddess," she teased, head tilted as she gazed into Carlie's eyes, and into her very soul.

"Why do you have to sneak up on people?" she snapped. Her emotions were drowning her, the image of Mike's heartbroken then hopeful face fresh in her mind, and she had no patience for the infuriating apparition, who spoke in riddles about things she had no idea about.

The woman in red laughed. "Oh Carlie, beloved, it is not like I haunt this town, making conversation with everyone who passes me in the street. You are the only person that I communicate with in this place, although I have had some wonderful conversations with your grandmother over the years."

"So couldn't you have given her some comfort then?" Carlie demanded. "Why didn't you tell her that her daughter was okay, spare her some of the torture she's lived with her whole life?"

The red-clad woman gazed at her, expression stern again. "Oh Carlie, I do not know what you think I am –"

"I have no idea!" she shouted, frustration colouring her voice and upping the volume. "Half the time I think you're a symptom of my insanity, a delusion I'm creating to give myself comfort – not that you're especially great at that, by the way," she snarled. The laughter echoed around her again.

"Rose and Rhiannon seem to think you are all spirits of the land, figures from another dimension who can come through to our world to share your wisdom with us," she sighed.

"Really? But you have not told Rhiannon about me yet," the woman said, reproach in her tone.

Carlie stared at her, horrified that this... being... knew everything she said and who she said it to. That was totally creepy, but she'd have to think about that later. She needed all her wits about her to make it through this conversation.

"Well, she's met Brauna and Brianna, and she thinks they're real," she retorted. "To be honest, I haven't been sure of what to tell her about you. I don't even know your name."

"My name is Aideen," the woman said calmly.

"Fine, great, lovely to meet you," Carlie snapped. "If you must know, Rhi and I haven't been telling each other everything of late anyway," she finally admitted. "I haven't told her about you because I'm not ready to tell her about my ritual to farewell Rowan. I want to keep that to myself for a while longer."

Aideen's face softened. "Oh Carlie, you are allowed to keep some things close to your heart. And I understand that you are struggling to trust her, but she is remorseful about what happened, and feels terrible that she let you down. Try to cut her some slack. You are no angel yourself."

Carlie glared at the woman, then started laughing. What was the point of being angry at a sprite? A wisp? Someone who may or may not even exist.

And what she'd said was true. She wasn't perfect, but she'd been very open about that to everyone – family, friends *and* phantoms.

"Will I ever get past it?" she asked at last, voice thick with longing. "I want to forgive and forget, and usually I think I have, but then Rhiannon will say one thing the wrong way, and all my resentment will come flooding back. And although she apologises, and I do know that she's genuinely sorry, deep down she still doesn't approve of Rowan. And she thinks I should be over him already and off with some new guy," she huffed.

The woman in red smiled. "Carlie, you cannot expect her to think the way you do or change her fundamental belief system just because you want her to. Everyone is entitled to their own opinions, their own morals and acceptance of things. The only thing you can expect is for her to support you, even if she does not personally agree with what you are doing. You cannot control her actions, just your reaction to them. She will always think Rowan was too old for you, lots of people will, and that is fine – it only matters how you feel about it. But despite her feeling that way, she is still there for you now."

"I know that," Carlie sighed. "Deep down I know that, but how do I stop resenting her? I can't just turn my emotions on and off, yet she and Rose are all I have, so I need to find a way to deal with it somehow. And I do care about her, so I don't want my hurt to come between us and poison our friendship."

"Oh Carlie, I am so proud of you. You have learned so much in the last six months," Aideen said, beaming at her. Puzzled, Carlie lifted her eyebrows in question, and the woman in red continued. "You are accepting your part in this, and trying to meet her halfway. You are acknowledging that you need to do something to help defuse the situation, that it is not all up to Rhiannon."

Carlie smiled. The praise was very welcome. It was nice to be credited for once, to be considered sensible, since she always felt that Rose and Rhiannon were so much wiser than her. It was a tough act to follow, having a priestess for a grandmother.

Aideen touched her cheek, gently this time. And had the grace to blush slightly when Carlie flinched, recalling the night she'd slapped her across the face. "You have your own wisdom Carlie, and you have learned a huge amount in a short time. You may have only discovered magic in the last six months, but Rhiannon sees herself as your equal in your workings, not as your teacher. You have hard-won knowledge that few people your age, or indeed any age, possess, gained through your losses as well as from the time you have spent with both Rowan and your grandmother, in addition to your own seeking of answers."

Carlie nodded uncertainly. She would happily give back any knowledge she'd gained to have her parents back, to have Rowan back, but she knew it didn't work like that.

The figure gave her a sad smile. "I am sorry I cannot help you with that Carlie, truly I am. But I have something for you," she continued, reaching within her long robes.

"This is for Rhiannon," she said, handing her a red-velvet-wrapped parcel of what felt like metal rods. "And this cauldron is for you, because you have been dancing in the fire, and have survived the burning, and now have the strength to wield its power."

Carlie was speechless, staring at the old-fashioned wrought iron pot in her hand. It was beautiful, and she could sense deep magic in it, but she knew the woman had got it wrong. She wasn't the strong one, the one who could weave magic and change fate. That was Rose. And Rhiannon. And it had been Rowan, and her mother. Pretty much everyone she knew, just not her.

Slowly she gazed back up, needing to confront the Otherworldly figure, deny her words, but there was no one there. She was standing alone at the bottom of the tor, and the mists were starting to clear. Sighing, she headed home, heart full of memories of Mike's scared face, which turned into images of Rowan's as he'd whispered to her that he loved her and believed in her. If only she could do the same.

Chapter 10

No Place Like Home

On Monday Rhiannon seemed really happy, after spending the weekend with John, and she talked about him and every moment they'd been together non-stop. At lunchtime she was a lot less flirty with Jake, although he didn't seem to have noticed she was behaving any differently towards him, or that she'd been interested in him in the first place. And Carlie was relieved to discover that she was glad for her friend, that things were going so well for her with her boyfriend. A part of her had worried that she'd be annoyed, or jealous even, that Rhi got to spend time with the guy she was dating while she was alone, while her beloved was dead, so she felt good about herself that she was nothing but happy for her.

On Tuesday Rhiannon reluctantly told Carlie she couldn't meet her that night for their magical working. Her little brother had a school play on, and their dad would be working late, so she needed to go along and support him. "I'm so sorry Carlie, I feel terrible, especially after I was with John all weekend," she said. "I'm not trying to ditch you, I promise!"

Carlie laughed. "Don't be silly, I don't think that! I understand. And it's awesome that you can be there for Brodie. Please tell him to break a leg from me," she replied. And was surprised that she felt relief, not disappointment, that they wouldn't be convening their coven that night. For a moment she wondered if she should be worried about that, then dismissed her fears – she probably just needed a bit more time before she could fully trust Rhiannon again, and let herself open up to her magically. Or maybe this was just about her? Maybe she needed more time before she could open herself up to anyone, or any thing, without being swamped in the darkness of her loss.

Smiling at her friend, she told her, truthfully, that it was a good opportunity for her to do some individual work, to try to make sense of her muddled feelings, and consult Rose's books for inspiration on how to heal her grief and move forward.

Rhiannon touched her hand, eyes wide with compassion. "You'll get there," she promised. "Time really does help, even though we don't believe it while the pain is still fresh."

Carlie bit down her angry retort. Her friend was just trying to offer comfort, and she'd suffered a terrible loss as well. She wasn't the first person – and would hardly be the last – to grieve a tragic death.

The following Tuesday, the girls both had to organise last-minute study sessions with their research partners for history, after Laura sprang on the class that they'd be discussing where they were up to with their papers the following morning. The panic in the room was palpable, as it was revealed that no one had actually started their home study sessions yet.

So that afternoon Rhiannon got the bus home with Dave so they could work on their project, and Carlie stood on the doorstep at Jake's place, palms sweaty and butterflies in her stomach. Impatiently stamping her frozen feet, she wondered why she was nervous. It was just Jake. He was her friend, so there was nothing to be afraid of. Still, they'd never really been alone together – Rhiannon was always with them at lunch, or they were in a classroom full of fellow students.

Before she could wonder any further, Jake opened the door and invited her in. Following him through to the kitchen, she felt a little less anxious when she saw that his grandfather's house was much like Rose's cottage, small and cosy, with a warm kitchen towards the back and a small table in a similarly situated breakfast nook. While Jake put the kettle on and made them tea, Carlie sat down at the table and pulled her books out.

They worked well together – Carlie had done a lot of background research, now that she didn't have Rowan to spend her afternoons with, and Jake had too. And it actually felt nice to be hanging out – they talked a bit when they paused to make more tea, reminiscing about the long hot summers of Australia, and Carlie found herself laughing far more than she'd expected to, appreciating his Aussie humour and cheeriness.

As they finished their third cup of tea, Jake paused halfway through telling a joke and stared at her, face serious. "What's wrong?" she asked, assuming she'd done something to offend him.

He smiled, that sweet smile that made her tummy flip. "Nothing, it's all good," he replied quickly, stoically, but his voice was shaking a little. "I just, um... well, I was wondering if you'd like to go for coffee sometime, or maybe see a movie or something? Pop said I could take his car."

He looked so nervous, so earnest, that Carlie felt bad that she had to say no. But she just couldn't. She was in no fit state to be dating, and he was far too lovely for her to lead him on. Reluctantly she shook her head. "I'm sorry Jake, I can't. It's not you, you're a sweetheart, but I just... I can't," she whispered, staring at the floor, and feeling miserable for hurting him.

"What about just as friends then? You know, fellow Aussies, a long way from home, keeping each other company and reminding each other how to speak, what words to use..." he trailed off.

"I'm not going back to Australia. This *is* my home," Carlie said softly, wonderingly. And as the words came out, she felt the truth of her statement, and was as surprised as Jake at the sentiment. She thought she'd pictured herself going back to Sydney in a year or two, once she'd finished school and qualified for uni, but it sounded like that plan had gone out the window, some time between landing here six months ago, a stranger in a strange land, and today, a sad but strangely content student who had come to love her grandmother deeply. How unexpected.

"Are you okay Carlie?" he asked, voice gentle, and she looked up at him and saw the concern in his eyes, the softness of his mouth as it turned down in compassion, the kindness of his expression.

"What do you mean?" she stuttered, as she felt her body preparing to flee. But was running the way to handle anything?

"You have the saddest eyes I've ever seen," Jake blurted out, then blushed. "I'm sorry, I shouldn't have said that."

She stared across at him. "You think it's weird that I feel sad?" she responded, genuinely curious about what he thought.

"I'm not sure what's going on in your life – I know your parents died, and of course that would make you grieve deeply. But when I asked Rhiannon why you were always so sad, she said to ask you myself, that it was your story to tell."

Carlie raised her eyebrows, pondering. Did Rhiannon just mean she should tell him about Rowan herself, or was she alluding to the fact that she had hurt Carlie so deeply, and that might be what was upsetting her? Or did she just think that the more she said out loud that Rowan was dead, the more she told people, the more quickly she'd face up to it and move on?

"My boyfriend died on the morning of the winter solstice," she said finally, deathly calm. "Just before Christmas. He was coming to see me, and his car went off the road in the snow. So yes, I'm pretty sad, and I imagine I will be for quite some time."

Shock flashed across Jake's face, then he stood up, moved around the table and drew her into his arms, holding her tight.

"I'm so sorry," he whispered, voice low and gentle. "Of course you have every reason to be sad. My god, after everything you've been through, that seems like the cruellest blow."

Time seemed suspended as they stood there for several long moments, Carlie in the warm cocoon of his arms, not thinking, barely breathing, just grateful for the comfort and strength she felt pouring into her. For a split second when he'd embraced her she'd frozen, her first instinct to slap his face and run out the door, but his holding her didn't feel sleazy at all, it just felt warm and supportive and like a friend should.

Gently he let her go. "Friends?" he asked, and she nodded slowly, shy all of a sudden, but touched that he'd had the courage to ask her about it, and the understanding to not press her on anything more than friendship. He really was a great guy, she thought ruefully. It was a shame she wasn't interested – he'd make someone a wonderful boyfriend.

"I don't have much experience with loss myself, but if you ever want to talk, or if I can ever do anything for you, let me know, okay?" he implored her, and she nodded and thanked him profusely.

The sound of keys rattling in the front door broke the emotion of the moment. "I should go..." Carlie whispered, and was confused when she felt relief warring with disappointment in her mind. But before she could examine her response, Jake shook his head.

"It's just Pop, and he'd love to meet you. He's Australian too," he grinned, then turned and walked out to the front door to help his grandfather in with the grocery bags.

"Pop, this is my friend Carlie, the Aussie girl from school. Carlie, this is Richard Mattherson."

Carlie held out her hand. "Hello Mr Mattherson," she smiled.

He shook his head and pulled her in for a hug. "Richard, please. Mr Mattherson makes me feel so old, although I guess to you two I am," he said, eyes twinkling. "Now, have you got the kettle on yet Jake?" he asked, turning back to his grandson, and sighing theatrically when Jake shook his head.

"Youngsters these days, I don't know," he chuckled. "Come on, it's time for tea, and I've got some lemon cake to share – Iris insisted on baking me one because I've been fixing her gutters and clearing out her back shed."

Jake smiled at Carlie as he turned to fill the kettle. "Pop lost his wife eighteen months ago, and he's got more women looking after him than he can handle. He's always done odd jobs for the women of his church – taken them grocery shopping each week, kept their cottages in working order, sorted out their gardens – all of which he'd happily do for nothing, but they all insist on baking him dinners and leaving them on the front porch, or dropping off cakes or jams or pickles or freshly baked bread. I've never eaten so well in my life – these women can really cook!" he said, then lowered his voice conspiratorially. "I think they're trying to win him over through his stomach. There are a few widows with their eye on Pop."

"I heard that Jakey," his grandfather said, mock stern, but then he laughed. "They're all lovely women, but I don't think any of them want to be tied down, so there's no need to worry. It will still just be you and me here."

Jake clasped his grandpa on the shoulder as he walked over to the pantry to get the tea, and Carlie's heart lifted to see the obvious affection between them. He motioned for her to take a seat again, while Richard sliced up the cake and handed her a piece.

"Thank you," she said, and politely took a bite. "Oh my god, this is so good! I might need to meet this Iris, and see if I can steal the recipe."

Richard grinned. "She keeps them pretty close to her chest, but I'll see what I can do. Do you like cooking?" he asked her, as he brought the milk jug, sugar pot and some delicate cups and saucers over and sat down with her at the table.

"I never used to, but since I've been living with my grandma I've been helping her out, making dinner some nights, but also baking desserts and other treats for our rituals and things..." Her voice faltered, and she suddenly worried that this man might not approve of Rose and her seasonal ceremonies. If he was a serious churchgoer, he might frown on energy healing and crystals and honouring the goddess and the forces of nature.

But he laughed as he cut her another slice of the lemon cake. "Don't you worry, no one in this village has any problem with Rose Tyler. Marcy was a churchgoer, but she told me once that she and her sister had been to a few of Rose's full moon ceremonies when they were younger. And as far as I've heard, I don't think there'd be a single person in this village that Rose hasn't brought healing or comfort to in some way, be it with her herbal remedies or her midwifery skills, or raising money for someone in need."

Carlie was grateful. That description certainly gelled with the impression she'd formed of her grandma, and she was relieved that religion hadn't caused any issues for Rose, with Richard and Marcy at least, as she'd discovered it sometimes could.

"She's certainly had her hands full dealing with me for the last six months," she admitted, and there was admiration in her voice. "And it was hard for her, because my mum – her daughter – died just before I came here. Gran had always hoped that one day she would return home, or get in touch with her at least, but unfortunately I was the bearer of bad news." Her eyes misted with tears, but she kept talking.

"And I feel sorry for her, because I was not a nice person in those first few weeks. I was so angry, so nasty, so consumed with hate and suspicion. Rose is an amazing woman to have put up with me."

Jake smiled at her, and reached over and squeezed her hand. "I can't imagine you being anything like that," he said, and she laughed.

"I was, believe me. Rhiannon helped too. She told me I was allowed to lash out at people for the first few weeks of grieving, but then I had to get over myself and stop being so selfish."

"Sounds like a sensible girl to me," Richard said, and Carlie nodded. He'd just lost his beloved wife, but could still appreciate Rhi's blunt survival comments. Yeah, her friend was pretty smart.

The three of them talked for a while, Carlie enjoying being amongst Australian voices again, and feeling relaxed and at home. But when Jake stood up and said he had to start cooking dinner, Carlie finally looked at the clock and realised she'd better get back to her grandma's to start the food prep too.

"You're welcome to stay and eat with us," Richard said, voice threaded with hope, but Carlie thanked him as she shook her head – she had to get back to Rose. She had a new appreciation for caregiver grandparents, and wanted to do her bit.

"Thank you so much for the tea, and the cake, and for making me feel so welcome. It's really nice to hear Aussie voices – it's funny how comfortable it makes me feel. But I'll see you tomorrow Jake, and Mr – I mean Richard, thank you, and I'm sure I'll see you soon, with this crazy assignment we have!"

Jake led her out to the front door and offered to walk her home, but she said she was fine, and that he'd better get back to the kitchen and get cooking. They laughed at that, then he gave her a quick hug goodbye, and Carlie headed off, smiling in delight at the few soft snowflakes that were falling, all lit up by the golden almost-full moon. As much as she'd loved talking to those sweet

Australian guys, she felt amazingly at peace with her surprising realisation that England was now her home. She'd experienced tragedy here, but also so much love, and she felt as though she was more herself here than she'd ever been.

Maybe that was what loss did, strip away the things that weren't important and make you really look within and work out what was meaningful to you. For her, it was her grandmother, her last remaining family member, and her friends. Despite her current issues with her, that meant Rhiannon, her magical partner and ally in grief, and Emily, her childhood bestie who she was determined to stay in touch with even though they were now so far apart geographically as well as emotionally.

And maybe it would also include Jake, a kind, thoughtful boy who seemed to care about her. She smiled too as she realised how much she'd come to appreciate and value Rose, and how much she already liked Richard. There was wisdom in age, now that she had the patience and the opportunity to experience it.

Then she giggled. She couldn't forget the strange women she'd met in the mists either. She still wasn't entirely sure that they weren't just figments of her imagination, or a trick of the light, or something else equally bizarre, but whatever they were, they'd offered comfort when she was distressed, and a metaphorical kick in the butt when she'd needed to stop obsessing over her own misery and realise that other people were suffering too.

She was still puzzling over the Otherworldly beings when she walked up the garden path of their cottage, calling out to Rose that she was home as she wandered down the hallway and out to the kitchen. The whole house smelled delicious.

"Hi Sweetheart! The vegetable and tofu lasagne will be ready in about fifteen minutes, and the salad is almost done," her grandma said as she whirled around the kitchen, chopping up fresh herbs from the garden, grating cheese, dancing over to the fridge for another cucumber. "How was school? And I got your note, thank you. How did your study session go?"

At Carlie's silence she glanced up. "Is everything okay?" Rose asked, a touch of panic crossing her face.

But her granddaughter smiled. "Yes, it's all good. Jake and I got a lot of work done, then we had a cup of tea with his grandfather, who he's staying with while his parents are working in Africa. And we had the yummiest lemon cake – although I'll still eat dinner, I promise!" she added quickly.

Rose laughed. "There's nothing wrong with the occasional piece of cake, and you more than burn it off with all your tor climbs. I didn't know Jake was staying with his grandfather though. I'm trying to figure out who it could be – I thought I knew everyone here."

Smiling, Carlie raised her eyebrows and looked questioningly at Rose. "Guess you don't know all the eligible bachelors in town after all," she teased. "But he hasn't been here for that long. His name is Richard Mattherson, and he's from Perth originally, in Western Australia, and although he met and married Marcy in London, and lived there for a long time, they went back to Perth years ago to be close to their son, Jake's dad, and look after Jake when his parents had to travel for work. But when Marcy got sick they moved back here so she could be close to her sister and their other kids, and they bought a little cottage at the bottom of the tor," she explained.

"Marcy and her sister used to stay in Summer Hill when they were teenagers, and she and Richard spent their honeymoon here, so it meant a lot to both of them. And when Marcy died eighteen months ago, Richard couldn't bear to leave, because he feels like her spirit is still here – and her ashes are scattered on the tor and in his garden, so physically she's here too. And their daughter lives in London with her kids, and their other son is in Wales, so he wants to stay close to them, especially as Jake's parents are off working in Africa – there's nothing for him in Australia now, even though he was born there."

Rose stared at her. "And you relate to that somehow?" she asked, trying to interpret her granddaughter's tone.

Carlie laughed self-consciously. "Wow, you're good Gran. I hadn't even made that connection, but yes, I guess I do, because today I was actually thinking that this is my home now. That there's nothing holding me to Sydney, no reason to go back." She blushed a little, and her voice softened. "Despite everything that's happened here, it's started to feel like home."

Panic constricted her heart as she suddenly wondered if Rose would think that was a good thing or a bad thing, and whether she actually did have a long-term home here.

"Oh Sweetheart, of course it's a good thing! And of course you have a home here, for as long as you want it," her grandmother said, coming over and drawing her into a hug, and Carlie relaxed into her arms, feeling a weight lift from her shoulders, and a contentment settle in her heart. She felt so safe here, so secure, so at home – just the way she'd felt in Jake's arms that afternoon.

The thought shocked her, and she untangled herself from Rose and strode across the room, getting the plates and cutlery out for dinner, body moving as her panicked mind tried to compute that stray thought. How could two people feel like home? And how could a boy she barely knew make her feel so safe? Finally though she laughed at herself. How silly she was. Something about Jake or his grandfather must have reminded her of her dad. Maybe their Australian accents, or a phrase or expression they'd used that her dad had used too.

Quickly changing the subject, she asked Rose how the healing centre had been that day, and when they'd start preparing for Imbolc, and every time the thought of being in Jake's arms flitted into her mind, she shook it off and asked another question about what she needed to do for the ritual.

Chapter 11

Twisting the Knife

"So, how was your night with Jake?" Rhiannon asked Carlie, wiggling her eyebrows suggestively, when they finally caught up in their lunch break the next day.

A flash of annoyance swept over Carlie, and she stared at her friend in confusion. "What do you mean?" she asked. "We did some research, I had a cup of tea with his grandad, then I walked home and had dinner with Rose." She pushed the thought of being in Jake's arms out of her head. That had just been a strange mix-up of memories and wishful thinking, of missing her dad and the times they'd spent together.

"But he's nice, isn't he?" Rhiannon pressed, her tone teasing.

Carlie shrugged. "I guess so, why?"

"And he's cute, right?"

Impatience stabbed at Carlie. "Do you want me to ask him out for you?" she asked, barely containing her frustration.

"Don't be daft, I've got John," Rhiannon laughed. "I was thinking of you. Maybe the four of us could double date or something? He does seem to really like you, like, *like* like you. And you're both Aussies, so you have a lot in common."

"Seriously Rhi?" she snapped, and she was as sad as she was upset with her friend at her line of questioning. She'd thought that she and

Rhiannon were beginning to understand each other again, to move past their little bust-up and be supportive of one another like they were before.

"The love of my life just died, or have you forgotten about that? The funeral was only three weeks ago. I'm not sure if you remember him? His name was Rowan, and you used to think he was really amazing," she said, her voice dripping sarcasm. "He helped us with our assignments, and took us to festivals – and he respected you as my best friend perhaps more than he should have, if you can seriously ask me this."

Rhiannon blushed a little, but she didn't seem perturbed, or put off in any way. Nor did she seem to hear the warning tone in her friend's voice. "I know Carlie, and I get it. But you'd only been together for a few months, so you need to keep a bit of perspective," she replied, laying her hand on Carlie's arm when it looked like she was going to get up and flee.

"I don't mean you should be totally over him already and never think of him again, or try to forget how important he was to you, but life goes on. You can't put your whole life on hold and act like a widow at seventeen," she said.

"Surely I'm allowed to grieve for a few weeks though?" Carlie retorted, voice cold.

Rhiannon mustered a smile. "I'm sorry, I guess this is coming out wrong. I just don't want you to punish yourself for something that isn't your fault, or feel that you have to deny yourself happiness and friendship, or a new relationship, because he died. I don't mean to offend you hon, I promise."

Carlie stared at her friend, genuinely puzzled. Rhiannon had lost her mother, so she knew grief didn't pass quickly, or have rules or set start and end points. At the very least she should realise from her angry response that she obviously wasn't interested in Jake, and let it drop.

"I'm glad you're not *trying* to offend me," she said, as politely as she could muster. "But I don't know how to be any clearer – I don't want to date anyone right now, so there's no point going on with this. Why don't you tell me how Brodie's play went, or how it's going with John, and let this subject drop?" she insisted.

Finally her friend seemed to hear her. "Brodie was adorable – he was really confident, and did such a good job. I was so proud of him," she beamed. "And it's going really well with John, I really like him. Actually, we're going to see a band near his place on Saturday night, if you want to come. You could ask Jake too," she suggested.

Carlie rolled her eyes in exasperation, and Rhiannon sighed. "I meant as friends, so you'd have someone to talk to while I was with John, and so you could meet my boyfriend properly, okay? But Carlie, don't exaggerate the impact too much. I know you think you really loved Rowan, but there's a chance that you would have broken up with him a few months from now, and dealt with it all then, and then you would have moved on, met someone else. And later you would look back and think your time with Rowan was a nice teenage romance, one of many," she said, blundering onwards, oblivious to the increasingly angry expression on Carlie's face.

"Death can add more weight to a relationship than what was truly there," Rhiannon continued. "Like, for example, someone having a nasty ex-wife to deal with is one thing, the guy can move on and date again, and the new girlfriend doesn't feel threatened, but being a tragic widow with a sainted dead wife is a totally different story, and is so much harder for someone new to deal with."

Carlie glared at her friend. "I'm guessing you're not trying to upset me as much as it sounds like you are?" she asked, her eyes starting to water a little as the hurt lodged in her heart.

"Geez, you're so sensitive," Rhiannon griped.

Shocked at her friend's words, Carlie blinked in surprise, then took a deep breath to try to compose herself and respond calmly.

"Let me be clear. The guy I love just died in a tragic accident. He'd told his manager he wanted to travel less so he could spend more time with me. He was helping me heal my grief at the recent death of my parents, which, you know, is still pretty hard to deal with, and he loved me deeply. I can't just 'get over it', no matter how much I want to. And I really thought that you would understand this.

You've lost someone close to you, so you know how hard it is to cope, and that it's impossible to just go on like nothing happened."

"You can't compare losing my mother to losing your boyfriend," Rhiannon said indignantly.

"I'm not Rhi, god! I'm just asking that perhaps you could be a little more understanding, and try to hear me when I say that I need some time to process my grief and loss, to get over the guy I loved so much – and that finding someone else to date is really not at the top of my list of priorities." She sighed impatiently. "I can't even look at another guy, let alone want to go out with anyone. And seriously, someone being Australian – from the other side of the country no less – is not really a reason for me to want to go out with them."

"I'm sorry Carlie, I do understand that it's hard for you," Rhiannon said, tone conciliatory. "And I'm sorry about the way my words came out – I didn't mean to be insensitive, or to upset you in any way. I guess I just hope that soon you'll be able to look at your relationship slightly more big picture, and put it all in context. You hadn't been together with Rowan that long, and... well, you know, if something happened to John now, I mean it would be awful, and I'd be sad, but I'd get over it."

"Please stop," Carlie said sharply, imploringly, her voice thick with pain and unshed tears. "I really can't talk about this any more. And Rhiannon, wow, maybe you should have a think about why you *wouldn't* be a mess if your boyfriend died. What's the point of being with someone you're not totally in love with? Who you wouldn't miss if, heaven forbid, something happened to them? And how can you even talk about him like that?" she asked.

And, face showing her horror, she picked up her bag and ran from the cafeteria.

Chapter 12

Wishing On the Moon

Avoiding Rhiannon the next day was fairly easy – they had no classes together on Thursdays, and Carlie raced home for lunch instead of getting it at the cafeteria as she usually did. She hated being upset with her friend again, so soon after they'd reconnected, but she knew if they continued their conversation from the previous day she might say something she would regret, something that would hurt Rhiannon as much as she'd just hurt her, and she didn't want to do that, no matter how satisfying it might feel in the moment.

As frustrated and annoyed with her friend as she was, she was hoping they could get past this, and she figured that some time apart, for both of them to calm down a bit, might help.

Which explained why she was climbing the sacred tor alone at three in the morning, to perform a full moon ritual on her own. Remembering back to the first full moon ceremony she'd done, just a few short weeks after she'd arrived in England, she marvelled at how far she'd come in less than six months. Her wide-eyed naivety and the scepticism she'd thought was protecting her had unravelled during her time here, as she walked through the countryside, took part in Rose's beautiful sabbat celebrations, and let down her guard at coven meetings with Rhiannon. Her heart had broken open to the magic she now saw so clearly in nature, and in people.

Finally she reached the summit of the tor, with just moments to spare before she knew the moon would become perfectly full. With growing excitement, she opened her ritual bag and took out the athame, then slowly, reverently, stepped out the protective circle.

Within this circle, that my intent will form,
Between the worlds, a safe place born.
Ancient beings of this sacred hill,
I call to you with my deepest will.
Please hold me close throughout this rite,
Reveal the magic on this full moon night.

Gently, solemnly, she honoured and invoked the elements and the directions.

Guardians of the north, and element of earth,
Please ground me with your strength and nurturing,
and watch over my sacred rite.

Guardians of the east, and element of air,
Please grant me your intuition and clarity,
and share your wisdom with me this night.

Guardians of the south, and element of fire,
Please burn away my fears and doubts,
and flood me with your power and might.

Guardians of the west, and element of water,
Please wash away all I no longer need,
and allow me to soak in this magical moonlight.

Confidently, joyfully, she welcomed the god and goddess to join her.

Goddess of love and compassion, magic and moonlight,
Please bless me with your presence during my sacred rite.
God of strength and sunshine, love and might,
Please shine your blessings on me tonight.

While her brain still wasn't certain that there were literal gods and goddesses, or actual beings of light or guardians of the directions, she knew there was *something* up on this hill. A sense of magic that settled around her like a cloak as she carved out a space between the worlds. A sensation of mystery where all things seemed possible. A moment frozen in time, where she felt Rowan's arms around her, his sweet breath in her hair, his warm kiss on her cheek.

Was that all magic was? A remembrance of who you were, a glimpse into the potential of what you could become? Did she even exist? Was everything an illusion? And if so, was there a way for her to slip between dimensions again, to find a parallel world where Rowan still lived?

Sinking to the cold ground to sit cross-legged in the centre of her sacred circle, she closed her eyes and slowly inhaled, feeling herself descend into a meditative state. She was hoping the full moon would illuminate a way for her to resolve her issues with Rhiannon, and let her know how hurtful she was being with her whole "get over it already" attitude to Rowan. It was only a month since she'd lost him, and she still missed him terribly, with an ache that hurt her physically as well as emotionally. Why couldn't her friend understand that?

Sighing, she pushed that dilemma to the back of her mind and tried to focus on the coming month. What did she want to manifest into the world, into her life, in the next moon cycle? Could this high tide of lunar energy enhance her healing?

Yet as she peered into the very depths of her soul, she saw the conflict within herself. Did she even want to have her grief soothed, or would she prefer to hold on to it, wear it as a badge of honour and strength? But that was crazy, surely. What benefit was there in continuing to suffer? Yet did that mean Rhiannon was right? *Should* she be over Rowan by now?

Continuing to breathe in the moon's silvery light, she tried to centre herself within her heart. There was no joy in martyrdom, she knew that, nothing to be gained by closing her heart and walling it off forever to avoid hurt. Then again, what did she gain from opening her heart? More pain? More hurt?

Bringing her grandma's face to mind, she tried to envision what she would suggest, going deep within, into a kind of trance state. What would a wise priestess elder say about grief, about loss, about pain? Surely she would say to honour the blessings of your time with your loved one, to hold them close always but to move on, to risk everything to love again.

And yet… Rose never had. She'd stayed in the same house all these years, a space infused with the tragedy that continued to define her, a space holding her heart captive. She encouraged Carlie to appreciate life, to make herself vulnerable, yet she was still trapped, still waiting. Her heart broke at the thought of her grandmother in pain all this time, alone all this time. How had she not seen that before?

Sensing movement, she snapped open her eyes, and was relieved to see that it was just a small rabbit creeping across the grass in front of her. She smiled, the spell breaking as she came back to the world. Her time was up – it was time to go back down the hill, back to the "real" world, and try to get some sleep. Heart surprisingly light, she farewelled the directions and the deities, and closed her sacred circle.

But as she bent over to pick up her bag, a wave of emotion slammed into her and she fell to the ground, still clutching the athame she'd used. As she tried to catch her breath and refocus her blurry eyes, she stared at the knife, which seemed to be burning in her hand. It had been a gift from Brianna, the woman in green, for her coven dedication ritual with Rhiannon five moons ago.

"It's to cast a circle, to focus and direct energy within that circle, and to remind you to focus on the positive in your life when you are away from the circle, away from your friend. Keep it – and your friend – close to you," Brianna had instructed.

Reluctantly she admitted to herself that she hadn't really done that. She was here on the hill on her own, without her magical partner, and suddenly she felt furtive, sneaky. She could have invited Rhiannon to join her, to make up for the ritual they'd missed on Tuesday night, but she'd wanted to do this on her own. And what had that achieved? Now she was sitting here alone, and feeling just as miserable as she ever had, with an extra dose of guilt to top it off. God, why was everything so hard? She'd never analysed her every thought and emotion before, never obsessed over how her actions impacted on other people. Never given such weight to one bad thing a usually perfect friend had done. What was wrong with her?

"There is nothing wrong with you beloved. You have just had your heart split open by all of your losses, so everything has more weight," said a voice, and Carlie jumped in fright. She stood up, athame still in hand, and turned towards the sound. It was Aideen, the woman in red, no doubt here to gift her with some more cryptic comments.

The mist-shrouded figure laughed. "I will try to be less cryptic this time, shall I?" she asked, and Carlie blushed. She still wasn't enamoured with the mind-reading skills of the people – or beings – here.

"You keep being disappointed that Rhiannon is not perfect, but no one is. She is seventeen, give the girl a break. She is an amazing young woman, but you expect too much from her."

Sighing, Carlie interjected. "But she was so mature, and so compassionate, when we first met – she knew the perfect things to say, and was so wonderful and supportive, so understanding of my grief and anger over the death of my parents."

"Yes, and she is still that caring and compassionate, especially on the topic of losing a parent, because she has been through that too, and worked a lot of it out as she went, realising what she needed and what would have helped her to heal in the best way. And because of that you put her on a pedestal – then when she did not have the answer you wanted, and did not understand your new grief, you decided she must be a terrible friend and that she had failed you. But it is only because of your expectations that you are so disappointed. If you had not held her up to such a high standard – one that *you* set, not her – you would not be feeling let down," Aideen admonished.

"You are not being fair to her Carlie. She is not perfect, and she would be the first to admit it, to insist on it. Certainly she does not expect you to be perfect all the time, or to always know the exact right thing to say. She is forgiving of your less-than-perfect moments. She cuts you slack because you are grieving…"

"But I'm not perfect, she knows that!" Carlie cried.

"Exactly. And nor is she. But you expect her to be perfect, and act like she has committed an unforgivable crime when she is not. She cares about you Carlie. And yes, it was incredibly insensitive of her to try to set you up with someone so soon, but she just does not understand the depth of your loss, and she cannot. No one can," Aideen said, tone softening a little.

"Well, Rose can understand, because she loved Louis so much, and could never be with anyone else after he died," she continued. "But your connection with Rowan was much deeper than people know – and that was primarily because you were both keeping it a secret, so you cannot blame them for not realising."

The red-clad woman's voice became gentler as she continued. "Rhiannon just wants you to be happy, and she thinks that spending time with Jake, and having a boyfriend again, will make you happy."

Carlie stared at the mist-wreathed figure mutinously. "But what right do I have to be happy, when there's so much suffering, so much pain, in the world?" she demanded.

"Oh Carlie, what right do you have to be unhappy? Everyone deserves happiness," she replied, compassion and love in her voice.

"But I can't just replace Rowan with the first guy who comes along," Carlie argued. "Doesn't Rhiannon realise how hard it will be to find anyone even remotely interesting enough, amazing enough, compassionate enough, after him? He's the most incredible person I've ever met, and no schoolboy, however sweet, could come close to him. I can't imagine I'll ever love anyone as much as I loved him, or meet anyone who loves me as much as Rowan did, who sees so much potential in me, and inspires me so deeply to want to be a better person. How could she think just anyone would do?"

The woman in red gazed at Carlie serenely, and placed a soothing hand on her shoulder. "She does not know because you did not share that with her. I am not blaming you for that, beloved," she added quickly. "You knew that she did not approve of your relationship, so you tried to spare her feelings, tried not to upset her. But you have not even spoken to her about your decision to refuse her ultimatum and choose them both, or explained to her just how much you loved and valued Rowan, and why, and how much he loved and adored you. Perhaps you could show her the letters and cards he wrote to you, and the one you wrote for him that final night?" Aideen suggested.

"It might help her to understand just how deep and devastating this loss is for you. If you are able to really open your heart to her and allow her to see your vulnerabilities, see all of your grief and the full depth of your pain, she may be more sympathetic. Rhiannon cares about her boyfriend, but it is nothing like what you and Rowan shared, and she will not be heartbroken when it ends. That is why she does not comprehend the immensity of your grief."

"Wait, it will end?" Carlie interjected, forgetting for a moment all the other advice the red-clad woman had been trying to impart to her.

"Oh Carlie, she is only seventeen. They only get to see each other on weekends, and they have different goals, different values, different hopes for their lives. It is pleasant enough for now – he is a wonderful boy, and she is getting to experience a relationship that does not demand too much from her. But John is not her grand, all-consuming love, not like Rowan was for you," Aideen said softly.

"So help Rhiannon to understand, help her to see what a relationship can be. And start judging her the same way you judge yourself. She is human. She is kind and compassionate, but she is not all-knowing. And her choices and opinions and actions come from what she has been through and experienced, her worldview, her values, her self-worth. Give her a break Carlie, let her be her imperfect self, and be patient with her. Help her learn a new way of seeing things, a new way to approach things. You both care about each other dearly, so do not let your hurt and indignation, and your need to be right, come between you."

Carlie sighed, but she reluctantly nodded her agreement.

"Now go, dawn is not far away, and you need a little sleep before school," Aideen whispered.

"Thank you," Carlie began, but the red-robed woman had already faded into the mists. She laughed. She would never get used to these beings who were there then not there. Apparitions perhaps? Ghosts? Figments of her imagination? She'd given up on trying to figure them out, because whether they really existed or not didn't actually matter – they always gave her great advice, advice that she knew deep in her heart to be true, and gave her new ways to see the situation she was facing.

As she stumbled back down the tor in the pre-dawn dark, she wondered whether Rhiannon had met the woman in red too, and vowed to finally tell her friend about her encounters, and ask about hers. Yawning, she let herself into the cottage and tiptoed upstairs to bed. Luther miaowed impatiently, then walked up onto her pillow, snuggled up close to her head, and started purring.

Feeling content, she drifted off into a dream of Rowan. He was sitting on the bank of the stream at their special place, leaning up against the trunk of the willow tree and smiling at her, that smile that lit her up inside, and made her feel so safe, so loved. The sun beat down on them from a cloudless blue sky as he beckoned her to him, then stood up to enfold her in a warm hug. Leaning down, he gently kissed her, and her heart overflowed with love for him...

Until suddenly her eyes started to fill with tears as she realised this couldn't be real. It was the sunshine that had given it away, because they'd met in autumn and loved each other through the turning of the leaves and into the snowy chill of winter. Her dream self pushed that logic aside though, even as tears leaked out onto her pillow, disturbing Luther, who licked at her face in concern and compassion, grounding her back into her body.

But she'd take it, take these hours with him on the bank of the stream in their special place, take these kisses and this embrace that was melting her heart with joy. She'd take anything, for as long as she could hold on to it, even if it wasn't real. Sighing in her sleep, she turned onto her side and hugged Luther close, and the little black cat started purring again, glad that she was safe, and feeling okay again, for these hours at least.

As a wintry beam of pale sunlight crept in the window and softly caressed her face, Carlie's eyes slowly opened, and she smiled, relaxed and happy for the first time in ages. She snuggled down into the covers, into the warmth of Rowan's strong, supportive arms, and the love she'd seen shining in his eyes – until real life crashed over her, and she sat up abruptly as she realised it had only been a dream.

Tears threatened, but before she lost her cool, Luther climbed into her lap and batted her with his paw, and she gazed into his deep green eyes and felt the strength flowing from him, calming her, soothing her. She patted his soft, fuzzy head and smiled at him.

"Thank you buddy," she sighed. "I really am so grateful to have you in my life."

Shivering as she climbed out of bed, she grabbed her school uniform from the back of the chair where she'd thrown it the night before, and hurried into the ensuite to have a scalding hot shower. God it was cold here in winter!

Tiptoeing downstairs, she was surprised to find Rose already in the kitchen. "Tea?" she asked, and Carlie nodded gratefully. "Are you okay Sweetheart?"

Carlie shrugged. "Okay-ish. How about you? And how's work? Sorry, I've been so caught up in my own dramas I haven't been paying attention to anyone else's," she said guiltily.

Rose hugged her. "Everything is fine. How was your full moon ritual?" she asked, eyes twinkling.

"Oh no! Did I wake you up when I got home? I'm so sorry!"

"Don't worry, I never sleep the night of the full moon," Rose laughed. "I spend the night in bed, reading my Book of Shadows by candlelight and writing – dreams, spells, meditations, invocations, whatever comes to me. I can always have an afternoon nap if I need to, but somehow the moon seems to recharge me enough anyway," she said, then broke off.

"Are you and Rhiannon friends again yet?" she finally asked.

Carlie shrugged. "I think so… well, I don't really know. I mean, we were, but then she started harassing me about going out with Jake, and when I told her that it was too soon to even think about dating, she snapped at me to get over Rowan and move on, and said that I needed to get some perspective. That we weren't together long enough for me to be grieving. But it's only been a month since he died. Surely I'm allowed to be sad for a little while longer?"

"Oh Sweetheart, of course you are," Rose said, pulling her into a warm embrace. "Take as long as you need. Grief is different for everyone, and yours has been loss on top of loss, so don't feel any pressure to 'get over it'. There are stages and phases of grief – you might feel okay one day and soul crushingly sad the next, and that's fine. I'm shocked that Rhiannon would be so impatient with you though, I thought that she of all people would understand."

Carlie nodded, although oddly enough Rose's condemnation was making her feel a little defensive of her friend. "Well, I guess I never really told her just how much I loved Rowan, and how close we became," she said sheepishly, echoing Aideen's words. "I knew she didn't approve of us, so I played it down to her."

"Maybe it would help if you explained all of that to her," Rose agreed. "I know she really does care about you Sweetheart, and I'm sure she just wants you to be happy."

"I guess so," Carlie conceded. "But that reminds me, I need to show her something," she said. Grabbing an apple from the bench, she drained her mug of tea, kissed Rose goodbye, ran up the stairs to her room and pulled a package from her bottom drawer, then hurried out the door to school.

Chapter 13

A New Friend

Disappointment swept over Carlie when she got to school and remembered that Rhiannon wasn't going to be there that day – she and Brodie had left early to spend a long weekend with their grandparents. When she noticed Jake walking towards her, looking so happy to see her, she blushed and raced off in the other direction, suddenly paranoid that he knew Rhiannon had been trying to set them up. Keeping to herself all day, she managed to avoid him by sneaking off to the library and studying in the lunch break, and taking the seat next to Abby in their English class so they couldn't sit together as they usually did.

Giving Jake the cold shoulder made her feel bad – they were friends after all – but she saw him differently now, felt pressured by him because of what Rhiannon had suggested. It wasn't fair to him, but she felt irrational and out of sorts today, her emotions jumbled. One minute she thought Aideen was right, and it was her fault Rhiannon had no sympathy for her loss, then the next she'd be overcome with anger at everyone around her for not knowing how she felt and what she needed, with her deepest fury reserved for the friend who more than anyone *should* have known.

When the bell finally rang she breathed a sigh of relief and dragged herself home, feeling even sadder than usual. Walking numbly through the cottage gate and up the steps to the front door, she jumped in fright when she heard a loud, angry sound. It was Luther, looking ferocious and making a terrible racket.

"Hey buddy, what's wrong?" she asked, kneeling down and tentatively stretching out her hand, careful not to scare him. What could make him utter that kind of noise? He allowed her to pat him, then finally rubbed up against her leg, purring, so she figured he must be okay, although she still had no idea what he'd been so upset about. But when she rose to head inside, he led her over to the corner of the front porch, and miaowed insistently. Slowly she crouched down and peered into the shadows.

A pair of frightened green eyes stared back at her, and a tiny pink tongue peeked out as she heard a soft squeak. Carlie turned back to Luther, who pushed her outstretched hand towards the shivering ball of black fluff. He nudged her again, until she cautiously extended a finger to stroke the small cowering creature. Breath held, she waited, not wanting to alarm it, and terrified that she'd hurt the scrap of a thing if she touched it.

Luther miaowed at it once more, reassuring, and the tiny kitten lifted its head nervously to Carlie's finger. Gently and very carefully, she patted the soft fur between its tiny ears. It was shivering, but she wasn't sure if it was cold or scared, or both. Feeling totally out of her depth, she looked down at Luther, and after some pointed glances and a few nudges, she finally got the message that he wanted her to sit on the top step. Dropping her bag, she slowly lowered herself to the cold slate, and watched as Luther half shepherded, half pushed the little ball of fluff up onto her lap.

When Rose came home an hour later, Carlie had the kitten in her arms, snuggled up against her heart and gently purring, both of them oblivious to the cold, while Luther sat on her lap looking like a proud parent as he watched them both. Tears rushed to the older woman's eyes, but Luther gave her such a stern look that she took a deep breath, sniffed once, then straightened her back and got her emotions under control.

"So, we have a new addition to the household," she finally said, voice composed. "You must all be freezing though, and hungry. Come on inside and I'll fix us some dinner, and we can all warm up."

Together the motley crew traipsed inside, Carlie and the kitten shaking with cold, and the warmth of the kitchen suddenly more inviting than ever.

Rose slid a lasagne into the oven, then busied herself with saucers of milk and cat food. Carlie sat on the floor, looking dazed, the tiny kitten cradled in one hand against her chest while her other hand gently stroked it. The bundle of fur gazed around, curiously taking things in now as its fear began to dissipate. And Luther stood by their side, supervising still, like a royal guard.

"What are you going to call her?" Rose asked, her heart swelling with love and pride when she saw the compassion and concern in her granddaughter's eyes as she carefully held the precious little creature. It seemed that Luther had known what she needed to heal her heart better than anyone.

Carlie looked up, joy warring with caution in her eyes, still scared that the small, sweet creature could be snatched away from her at any moment. "Call her? Do you think we can keep her?" she asked, excitement and hope rich in her voice.

Rose laughed. "I don't think we have any say in the matter – Luther has decided for us. You're this little one's keeper, her warrior while she grows up. She'll need a lot of care though, because she looks really young. Are you up for it?"

Carlie's smile was the only answer Rose needed, and she felt some of the weight she'd been carrying lift from her shoulders. The morning the police officers had come around to inform Carlie that Rowan was dead, she'd feared for the sanity of her granddaughter, who was already so tragically bereaved and dealing with so much loss and upheaval in her life. She hadn't been sure the poor girl would survive this second loss, which had made her doubly concerned when Rhiannon had confessed that she'd hurt Carlie so badly with her actions. Who knew it would be an animal to look after that could provide just the thing she needed to have a reason to want to live, a reason to get up each day? Well, *she* should have known, Rose thought, but recriminations were pointless. Luther had got it sorted.

Sinking down on the floor opposite her granddaughter, Rose smiled as Luther came over and sat in her lap, looking up at her with so much love and trust. He'd been such a wonderful companion to her for so many years, and she was so very grateful to him. There had been days when she'd felt the same way Carlie did now – hell, she still had those days sometimes – and Luther had been there with her, knowing when she needed him to stay close to her, to curl up on her pillow with her and guide her through her dreams and nightmares, drawing her out at crucial moments with his little paw on her face, and also knowing when she'd needed space.

And it had been Luther who had gotten through to Carlie too, she reflected. When her granddaughter had arrived on her doorstep almost seven months ago, she'd been terrified for the child. Her grief and anger were writ so deep in her heart, pain was scored across her face, and bitterness was poisoning her soul. But Luther had gently led her back to herself, giving her something to love that was not human, since she'd been so deeply suspicious of people in general, and Rose in particular, back then. The sweet cat had sat with her in her darkest moods, kept her company when she needed it, and stood over her as a brave guardian during her night terrors.

Rose couldn't lie – she had felt hurt when her companion of so long had ditched her so quickly and easily, as though he no longer cared, but she'd known he was helping her granddaughter as much for the girl's sake as for her own. Carlie had hated her when she arrived, with a vitriol that had shocked Rose. It had taken several weeks to discover the reason – that Rose's daughter Violet had never mentioned her own mother to Carlie, had never told her that she had a grandmother in England.

The poor girl had been under the impression that Rose was a cruel and unforgiving woman who'd driven her own child away from her, so nasty and mean-spirited that Violet had fled to the other side of the world to escape her.

It was some time before Carlie began trusting her, and started to open her heart again. To lose both parents just after your seventeenth birthday was a bitter blow for anyone to deal with – and to then lose your boyfriend so soon after that, when you'd only just started to inch back out into the world, well, Carlie was far stronger than Rose was, to still be here, to still be standing.

She was damaged, of course, and hurting more than she was letting on, but after she'd opened the package Rowan had been bringing her, put on the beautiful dress and the gorgeous ring, and read the two heart-wrenching, love-filled cards, she had seemed to rise from the ashes of her soul, to make a decision to live. Yet Rose knew it was a knife-edge situation that could change at any moment, and Rhiannon's strange attempts to set her up with a new boyfriend had her teetering back on the brink of despair.

Gazing down into Luther's green eyes as they communicated their love and respect to each other, Rose didn't realise her granddaughter was staring at her just as intently. The look Luther and Rose were exchanging made a lump form in Carlie's throat, so touched was she by the obvious love and respect these two had for each other, cat and crone, witch and familiar.

"I'm so sorry Gran, that I took Luther away from you," Carlie whispered, heart catching as she watched them together, Luther curled up in Rose's lap, purring and rubbing against her as she stroked his sleek black head.

"Oh Sweetheart, not at all! Luther is his own very independent being, and he's known better than me this whole time about what we both needed, and what he could best do to help us heal and grow stronger. And now he's brought you this precious little scrap of a thing to care for, and love, and be responsible for. Are you up for the challenge? She'll need a lot of attention, a lot of love."

Carlie grinned, eyes on the tiny bundle of fuzzy black fur in her palm, well and truly in love with the cute creature already. "Oh yes," she breathed. "I'd be honoured to care for her."

Luther purred even harder at that, and looked up at Rose with a slightly condescending air. She laughed as she patted his head. "I know my sweet, you've always known better than me, had more magic than me. You truly kept me wanting to live when the despair was getting too much for me."

Carlie looked up in shock, and Rose sighed even as she smiled. "Oh Sweetheart, I know what it's like to lose your beloved, it's like your very heart has been torn from your chest, and you think there's no point going on, no point living without them in the world. Luckily for me I suppose, I had to stay strong, stay living, just in case Violet ever came home."

Carlie's breath caught. "You mean, you thought about..."

Rose nodded reluctantly, eyes sad. "Of course, but I could never do it, not when there were reasons to stay. And Luther was one of them, of that I am sure," she said, smiling again. "And of course if there was ever any chance of your mum coming home, well, there was no way I was going to let her down..."

"But now?" Carlie asked, fear clear in her voice.

Rose stared at her, puzzled. "What do you mean?"

"Well, Mum isn't ever going to come home," she whispered.

Understanding dawned in Rose. "Oh Sweetheart, I have you to live for now, and you have me. And this one too," she added. "What will you call her?"

Carlie gazed down at the fuzzy little midnight-black creature now snoring gently in her lap. "I've thought of a few possibilities, but the more I sit with her, the more I think she should be named Luna," she finally said, and at the name the kitten opened her eyes and peeked up at the girl she'd happily accepted as her guardian, and gave the tiniest mewling squeak.

"Sounds like she approves of that name," Rose said, laughter in her voice, and Luther, still sitting in the older woman's lap, lifted his head and miaowed his agreement too.

The delicious aroma of the lasagne eventually drifted over to them where they sat on the floor, and Rose carefully put Luther down beside Carlie, then creakily got to her feet to get their dinner out of the oven and serve it up.

"You happy down there?" she asked, and Carlie nodded. Rose handed her one of the bowls, then settled down next to her again, Luther returning to her lap. They spent the evening on the floor, the cats purring in their laps, and occasionally allowing them to get up to make another pot of tea.

Rose shared some of her memories of Luther, and what a wonderful support he'd been to her, in her magic, in her life, and in her grief. Carlie apologised again, for monopolising him since she'd arrived, but her grandmother brushed her off. Luther went where he was needed, where he needed to be, and now he'd brought Carlie a new companion, a precious little friend who required her to focus all her love and attention on her, invest herself and her presence into her, which seemed to be the perfect antidote to her sadness.

For a moment Carlie felt overwhelmed by the responsibility, and the fragility of the life that had been entrusted to her. Could she guarantee that she was prepared to stay alive? But just as she wondered that, Luna looked up at her with wide, trusting eyes, and her heart melted. Yes, she would stay alive for this small bundle of fur, and for her grandma, who had suffered enough for one lifetime.

Finally, as their eyes began to droop, cat and human alike, Rose announced that it was time for bed, so they all stood up and stretched.

"Where should Luna sleep?" Carlie asked. Rose glanced down at Luther and he seemed to nod, before gently nudging the kitten towards the back door and leading her outside. Rose and Carlie did the dishes together as they waited, and put saucers of fresh water out, then the two cats popped back in through the little cat door, and Luther led the way to the stairs.

Rose laughed. "Looks like Luther has it all worked out. He has always thought this was his house though, not mine," she said, voice thick with love and amusement.

Carlie kissed her grandma goodnight, then followed her feline friends up to her bedroom, trying not to laugh as Luna struggled so comically with the size of the stairs. Quickly she brushed her teeth, then slipped into her pyjamas and under the blankets, giggling at how adorably cute the critters were. When she was settled, Luther picked Luna up in his strong jaw and leaped up onto the bed, then prodded her until she was curled up on Carlie's pillow.

Then, job done, he retired to the end of the bed, standing guard over them both. Carlie's heart filled with love as she slid down under the covers. She patted Luther and thanked him again, then wished him sweet dreams and settled down on her side, eye to eye with the fluffy black kitten.

"Okay little one, I promise I'll do my very best not to squash you, and I have a feeling Luther will be watching over us anyway. I hope you can get some rest." Smiling sleepily, she scratched the kitten's soft head. "Thank you both for caring about me," she whispered as she drifted off to dreamland.

She woke up once in the night, to a soft, furry paw on her face, and realised that she'd been sliding into a nightmare again. Gazing at the kitten in wonder, she thanked her, murmured at her to go back to sleep, then passed out again herself. It was the best sleep she'd had in weeks, her dreams guarded by the ferocious protector cat and his sweet new charge.

When the pale sun drifted through the curtains the next morning, Carlie sat up and gazed around her. Both of the cats were sitting at the end of the bed, giving themselves a bath, and she laughed in delight at how cute they looked together.

"What are we going to do today guys?" she asked. Luther jumped gracefully down to the floor, and he and Carlie watched, breath held, as Luna stared at the distance between the bed and the ground, seeming to weigh up her options. Plaintively she miaowed at Carlie, who scooped her up in her arms for a quick cuddle, then gently placed her on the floor next to Luther.

He looked at her approvingly, and she felt ridiculously happy and accomplished for getting that job right at least. But it was a short-lived feeling, as Luther's gaze quickly became impatient. He stared at her, then turned to the door, then glared back at her again, until she finally got the message: *Hurry up and get dressed so we can eat.*

Quickly she did as she was told, and the three of them were soon downstairs again in the warm and cosy kitchen, having breakfast and drinking tea with Rose. Carlie grinned, her spirits lifting as she felt the pure, uncomplicated love of their two animal companions, and feeling so grateful that it was Saturday so that she could spend the day just chilling out with Luther and Luna.

Chapter 14

Moving In and Moving On

The weekend was filled with laughter and joy, as Carlie and Rose delighted in Luna's bouncy, pouncy cuteness. As they gathered in the kitchen at lunchtime on Sunday to make a pot of vegie and lentil soup, Luther suddenly turned serious, going into teacher mode. He shepherded Luna around the cottage, showing her all the rooms, miaowing a little at the bottom of the staircase as if giving the kitten instructions, then demonstrating how to best climb up the lounge chair to get to the window, where a cat could perch on the sill and look out to the garden and the tor.

The two of them also spent a long time at the cat door leading from the kitchen to the back garden, Luther patient yet insistent that the little ball of fluff work out how to push against it herself and get outside. It was probably a good lesson, Carlie thought, in case Luna wanted to go out in the middle of the night and Luther didn't feel like leaving the cosiness of the bed they all shared.

Once the kitten had mastered getting out, they spent almost as long on the other side, until the shivering pair finally burst back through into the warmth of the kitchen.

Carlie swooped down and sat on the floor, gathering them to her and holding them close, patting them until they'd stopped shivering with cold and were purring contentedly again.

"Crazy kitty," she said to Luther in a mock scolding tone, although the love in her voice was evident too. "Did you really have to go out while it was so chilly? I'm sure I saw snow!"

He gazed at her calmly, and it looked as though he was raising one eyebrow in scorn, to let her know the question was beneath him. She laughed. "Okay buddy, you know what you're doing. I'm just glad you both eventually worked it out – it's freezing out there!"

After bowls of hot soup and more cuddles, and a little saucer of milk for Luna, Rose went to the cupboard under the stairs and pulled out a thick woollen midnight blue blanket flecked through with golden stars. Bringing it back out to the kitchen, she made a little nest under the table, close to the heater, and offered it to the kitten, who stared at it blankly.

Finally Luther sighed dramatically and nudged the little kitten over to it, showing her how she could snuggle down into it and create a warm bed. The two of them curled up in there together and had an afternoon nap, and Carlie marvelled at how peaceful and relaxed they both looked, and how easy it was for them to fall asleep.

Rose busied herself making a new pot of tea, then sat down at the table above the snoozing cats. Handing her granddaughter a steaming mug of chai, she gazed nervously across at her.

"What's up Gran?" Carlie asked, sensing immediately that there was something on the older woman's mind.

"Ah Sweetheart, you're getting more intuitive by the day," she smiled. "But it's nothing bad, not at all..." Trailing off, she took a slow sip of tea, breathing in the warming, soothing scent of the cinnamon, ginger, nutmeg, cloves and cardamom, and seeming to draw strength from the familiarity of her herbs and spices. Then she put down her cup and spoke.

"I was wondering whether you'd like to move in to your mum's old bedroom?" she began tentatively. "Yours is so tiny, and the front room has a desk in it, and bookshelves, so you could do your homework in there if you wanted to, and there's lots of cupboard space, and room for Rhiannon next time she stays over. And of course, now that there are two royal creatures living with us, you might need a bigger bed. I'm just really sorry I wasn't ready to open it up and clear it out for you when you got here," she said with a sigh, then paused when she say the concern on Carlie's face.

"Don't worry, I've totally cleaned and dusted it since you were last in there. There's a new bed, and new sheets and things. And I promise there are no spiders, or webs, any more, and not a hint of mustiness. It's as good as new," Rose insisted, misconstruing Carlie's emotional concern for one of cleanliness.

Carlie's mind raced. She wasn't sure how she felt about it – did she want to spend her life in the shadow of her mum's memory? If she moved in to her old room, would she be committing to nights spent with ghosts? Days haunted by what-ifs and never-weres?

Her mind jumped from reason for to reason against and back again – until it hit her, just what it would have cost Rose to clear out all traces of her beloved daughter, and what a sacrifice she had made for her. Despite her hesitations, she was touched.

"I'd love to," she said firmly, trying to convince herself as much as her grandmother. She wasn't at all sure that she wanted to move in to Violet's bedroom, but she didn't think she could say no a second time. And it would be great to have bookshelves, and a proper desk for studying. Sealing the deal was the fact that she could already picture Luna and Luther racing around the room, and peeking out from the glass-walled balcony, which would be beautiful in summer.

"Thank you Gran," she said, and her smile was genuine this time. "I really appreciate you doing all this. But how on earth did you manage it without me knowing?"

Rose laughed. "Miri came over and helped me with the cleaning and sorting, the first few days you were back at school, and Mike helped with the bed – he ordered one online for me, and came over when it was being delivered to help them get it in and set it up, and they took the old one away."

Carlie's brow furrowed, and both of them realised at the same time what that would have cost Mike emotionally, having to dismantle his dead childhood sweetheart's bed.

"Damn it, I didn't even think of that," Rose sighed.

Carlie shook her head. "It would have been so much harder for you," she replied, feeling the weight of it, the pain it would have inflicted, for her grandma to have to go through all her lost daughter's things, things she'd locked away for the last twenty years so she didn't have to look at them, or remember, or hope.

"It was hard, harder than I imagined," Rose admitted. "But it was time. And it was wonderful too," she added, eyes glistening. "In hiding away and avoiding the bad memories, I also lost the good ones. I've been going up there some nights, after you went to bed, and sitting in the chair on the balcony, remembering. Going through her wardrobe, smiling as I recalled when we made a certain dress, being proud of how she'd saved up for a particularly elaborate ritual gown, laughing at one of the skirts that had taken us days to sew because we'd cut the pattern wrong. And sitting on the floor with her jewellery box, recalling the stories of every piece, where they'd come from, the times she'd worn them, the significance they each held."

Carlie refilled their cups as she tried to disguise her longing to have known that side of her mother, then handed one to her grandma. "I'm really sorry I didn't appreciate you when I first got here, and that I didn't understand the depth of your pain. But I know that this must have been really difficult for you, and I want you to know how much I appreciate you doing it for me, and how much I appreciate you full stop. But you didn't throw everything out, did you?" she asked carefully, not knowing what answer she hoped for.

Rose smiled and shook her head. "I couldn't quite bring myself to do that. Besides, as we know from the Yule Ball, you fit into most of Violet's clothes, so the offer still stands – it's all yours now. You should go through it all, if you'd like to, and see what you want to keep. We can take the rest to the homeless shelter, or we can just bag everything up right now, if you'd rather not look at any of it. But there's an empty wardrobe in there, as well as the one filled with Violet's clothes, so there's no hurry – you'll definitely be able to fit your meagre possessions into the second one, so just do what feels right for you."

Before Carlie could answer, there was a knock at the front door. She glanced over at Rose, quizzical, but her grandma shrugged and shook her head, so she stood up and went to see who was there, the two cats suddenly awake and weaving around her ankles, Luna following Luther's lead as closely as she could, with hilarious results. Still giggling, Carlie pulled open the front door, and froze. It was Rhiannon.

"Oh, it's you," she said, a little surprised, and suddenly anxious. They hadn't spoken since Wednesday, when she'd been so angry at her friend for trying to push her to date Jake, and telling her to get over Rowan. Should she do as red-robed Aideen suggested, and show her the letters in an effort to resolve the situation, or would it be easier to remain aloof, and let the distance grow between them?

Noticing that Rhiannon looked even more nervous than she felt, she softened a little, and smiled at her.

"Um, hello," her friend began. "I just got back from Nan and Pop's, and I was wondering if I could join you for a cup of tea or something?" she asked, her words so formal, her voice shaking a little with apprehension. Carlie finally took pity on her. Life was too short, surely, to hold a grudge.

"Come in, we were just about to make a fresh pot of tea," she said, and ushered her through into the warmth of the kitchen. Realising her friend had stopped, she turned around, and laughed as she saw her face, eyes wide as she stared at the kitten.

"Oh, this is Luna," she explained, just as the little ball of fluff tripped over her own feet again. "Luther brought her home for us to look after. You can pat her if you like, she's very friendly now."

Rhiannon slid down to the floor and cautiously held out her hand. Luna looked over at Luther, who inclined his head in what seemed to be approval, because the curious little kitten stepped closer to the new arrival and let herself be patted for a moment, before racing back to Carlie and hiding behind her legs, then peeking around them and regarding Rhiannon with mischievous bright green eyes.

"She's adorable," she said. "And she clearly loves you already."

Carlie's face lit up. "I think that's why Luther brought her here, to give me something to love, something to be responsible for, something to want to hang around for."

Rose tried to hide her tears by busying herself making the tea, and Rhiannon felt ashamed. She really hadn't been there for her friend when she'd needed her, but she could change that from now on. She looked around until she spotted Luther, and went over to pat him. "You're a very wise cat Luther," she said, sinking down onto the floor next to him. "Thank you for caring for my friend when I was too stupid to do it myself."

Rose poured out the tea and brought the steaming mugs over to the kitchen table, near the warmth of the heater. "Okay, enough of us sitting on the cold floor – my poor old bones don't appreciate it, and I think the cats will be okay without us being down on their level for a little while at least," she said, casting a hopeful look over at Luther.

"He really does run this house, doesn't he," Carlie laughed. "But I think you're right, I'm still a bit stiff from sitting on the floor for so long the last two nights – although it was worth it to help her settle in," she added, scooping Luna up for a cuddle then placing her gently on her lap, where she purred much more loudly than they would have thought possible from such a tiny body.

Luther, work done for now, curled up on the blanket at Rose's feet and had another nap.

Beckoning Rhiannon over to sit with them, Rose gave her a hug, then handed her a mug of tea, and the three of them talked happily about the upcoming ritual at the healing centre, the slow approach of spring, then about the assignment Laura had set them in history. When Carlie mentioned Jake, Rhiannon kept her face carefully expressionless, not saying a word that might annoy her friend. Instead it was Rose who asked a question.

"How's his grandfather doing? I remembered a bit more about his wife after we spoke the other night. Her sister asked me for a herbal remedy to lessen Marcy's pain in her final weeks, and Marcy sent a lovely card thanking me. I never met her husband though, I think he was a bit suspicious of us 'long-haired hippie women', as Marcy's sister told it." She smiled as she said it though – it had taken a while to develop the strength, but Rose had stopped taking offence at the way some people viewed her and her healing work long ago.

"He's good, I think," Carlie replied. "He said he's really happy that Jake is staying with him this year, that it gives him a reason to get up in the morning."

Rose smiled. "I can relate to that sentiment. Well, you're welcome to invite them over for a cup of tea if you'd like to. But now I'm afraid I'll have to love you and leave you for a while, because I must get back to the healing centre for a few hours. Will you be okay with the cats? And are you happy to just have soup again tonight Sweetheart? I'll pick up some fresh bread on the way home."

Carlie nodded and kissed her grandma goodbye, then turned to her friend. "I'm going to move in to Mum's old room, so do you want to give me a hand? Or just chat while I do it?"

"Sure, if that's okay," Rhiannon said hesitantly. "But I can go home if you'd rather do it on your own?"

Shaking her head, Carlie stood, holding Luna close to her heart, and led the way to the stairs. "You can help me go through Mum's clothes if you'd like to. Gran said we can keep what we want, and take the rest down to the homeless shelter, so maybe that would be a good first step. I'm sure there are some people in need of extra coats and jeans right now. And maybe we'll find something to wear to the Imbolc ritual next weekend."

Luther got up and followed them, and leaned gently against Carlie's ankle as she stood at the door to the upstairs front room, heart hammering in her chest. The last time she'd been in there had been the night of the Yule Ball, when she and Rhiannon had got dressed together, in her mum's clothes, and had so much fun doing each other's hair and make-up, laughing and feeling so happy and excited about the night to come.

God, that was only five weeks ago, yet her life had spiralled so badly off track since then. Her beloved boyfriend had died, and she'd thought she'd lost her best friend too – had *wanted* to lose her best friend. But Imbolc was all about new beginnings and fresh starts, so perhaps it was the perfect time to move in to a new bedroom, with Luther and their new little furry companion, and to forgive and forget with her friend.

Taking a deep breath, she opened the door and stepped across the threshold into the room.

"Wow!" Rhiannon exclaimed from behind her. "When did you do all this? It looks amazing!"

Carlie shook her head. "I didn't do anything. It was all Gran, and Miri helped her, and your dad too. I'm not sure about the painting and stuff though..." she trailed off, gazing around herself in wonder.

The walls had been transformed with the palest purple paint, with a contrasting deep violet shade around the windowsills and the door to the balcony. The thick dark curtains had been replaced with gauzy white ones, which brightened the room immensely and filtered the soft winter light in beautifully. The desk in the corner had been cleared, and there was a lamp with a purple shade on it in the corner. The bed was a new four-poster made from wrought iron, with ivy swirls worked into the frame, and black netting draped around it, making it look cosy and inviting.

Carefully she set Luna down on one of the four big pillows, and grinned as the kitten snuggled down into it and closed her eyes. Looking around for Luther, she saw him standing near the door, waiting. "Come on buddy, you're welcome too. Hop up with Luna if you feel like a snooze," she said, pointing to the bed, and Luther leaped up gracefully and cuddled up to the kitten.

"It looks so different to when we were in here getting ready for the ball, and even more so from the first time I saw it, when it was dark and dusty, like no one had been inside, or opened the windows, for decades. Which was the case I guess. There were cobwebs everywhere, and thick layers of dust," Carlie said.

"I just can't believe what an amazing job Gran did with it – she must have been planning this for weeks! And to have managed to keep it a secret is impressive too. I don't know how she did everything without me knowing."

Walking over to the larger of the two wardrobes, Carlie opened the door, and was met by a riot of colour and fabric. They both gasped, overwhelmed at just how many clothes there were.

"Gran said they made most of the clothes themselves, which amazes me – I can't even sew on a button," Carlie grinned.

"Me either," Rhiannon replied. "And I just love how colourful everything is too. Look at this gorgeous dress," she said, pulling out a peacock blue confection that was layered over vivid green tulle and shot through with golden thread.

"Try it on," Carlie urged, and the girls spent the next two hours pulling clothes out of the wardrobe, trying them on, swapping outfits, laughing as they swirled around in jewel-bright creations, sighing at the ones that were too tight or too loose, cooing in admiration when something fit like a glove, when the colours best suited them, when the style was totally them. Halfway through, Carlie paused, shocked to realise that she was actually having fun.

"I thought it would make me sad to be in here, to be wearing Mum's clothes, but it makes me feel closer to her," she admitted when they both collapsed on the floor for a mini break. "It's the strangest thing – all my memories of her seem to have been enhanced by my time here, by getting to know what she was like when she was younger. I think she's morphed into something between Rose's idea of her and what she was actually like when I knew her, as an adult – part truth, part ideal, part figment of my imagination made real. And I wonder if I'm somehow affecting Gran's memories of her too, since we apparently look so much alike, and share some character traits. It's such a strange thing, memory…" she sighed.

"And in a weird way my dad is more real to me now, because nothing has changed my idea of him. He's still exactly as he always was to me, and always will be, yet here I sit in Mum's childhood room, amongst all her clothes – none of which she would have been caught dead in when I knew her, by the way, she was always so elegantly dressed, so lawyerly professional, so black-grey-beige. It's like I have two mothers, and I'm not sure which one is the real one."

"I guess they both are," Rhiannon said softly, and her heart lurched when Carlie looked up at her with her sad green eyes, so much pain in them along with the hope. Then just as it was starting to get a little too intense for them, Luna woke up, so they crawled over to pat her, and dance around the room with her, giggling as she tried to pounce when the curtains stirred in the breeze, trying to maintain their composure when Luther jumped from the bed and went to the kitten's side to calm her down, his seriousness in contrast with her frivolity making them want to collapse on the floor and laugh forever.

Later Luther pushed open the little cat flap in the balcony door and took Luna outside to look around, to sniff out the corners and oversee their new territory, which the girls agreed was the sweetest thing ever. When the cats eventually tired themselves out, they curled up in the comfy reading chair next to the desk and napped, and the girls turned back to the wardrobe, determined to finish their job.

Carlie pulled out several pairs of jeans, woollen coats and jumpers, some hand-knit, from the shelf above the dresses. She kept a pair of jeans that fit her perfectly, a long violet-coloured coat and two thick jumpers, since her own clothes weren't really designed for the icy English winters. The rest they folded up for the shelter, since warm clothes would be far more useful for people in need than the beautiful but less substantial dresses, although they added them to the pile too, after they'd chosen three each. Carlie also kept a pair of warm and sturdy winter boots that would make walking outside far less gruelling, but put the rest of the boots and shoes aside, knowing there were plenty of people who needed them more than she did.

They both jumped when they heard the front door, and realised Rose was back home from work. Four hours had passed, and they hadn't moved a single thing into Carlie's new room. But she shook her head when her friend apologised – there was no hurry, and besides, the bed had been made up with gorgeous midnight blue sheets patterned with stars and two matching blankets, so she could easily grab her mum's old quilt and sleep there tonight regardless.

Rose knocked at the door then, and laughed when she saw all the neatly piled clothes. But she was impressed when the girls showed her the few things they wanted to keep, and told her everything else could go to the shelter. Glancing at her watch, Rose asked if they wanted to help her take some of it down now, since it looked like it was going to be another freezing night, so they leaped up and started squeezing all the clothes and shoes into bags. Rose added a few blankets from the linen press on the landing, picked up the basket of food she'd brought home to add to their contribution, asked Luther to keep an eye on Luna, then led the way back outside and into the village.

Carlie was grateful for the warm boots she'd kept – and really glad that the rest of the footwear and all the clothes could help keep someone else warm through the icy nights. As the volunteer's eyes lit up at the size of their bundles, Carlie's heart swelled, and she was glad her grandmother had suggested it – it certainly put her own problems in perspective. There were people in this country, in every country, sleeping on the streets in ridiculously cold temperatures. She may have lost her parents and her beloved, but she still had people who loved her and a warm bed to sleep in.

After they'd dropped off all their bags she hugged Rose and Rhiannon, and thanked them for looking out for her. Then they headed back to the cottage to eat hot vegie soup and fresh warm bread. Later Rose made herself scarce, sensing that the two girls still needed to talk. It was awkward for a moment, but eventually Rhiannon screwed up her courage and spoke, her face contrite and her voice a little shaky.

"I'm so sorry about the other day, I really am. Everything I said came out wrong, and I wasn't being fair to you, or honouring your grief. I of all people should know there's no timetable for healing, and simply being told to snap out of it is worse than useless. Please forgive me Carlie," she implored.

Carlie reached out and hugged her. "I'm sorry too," she said. "And I can't expect you to understand how I'm feeling because I never told you just how much I loved him, or how close we had become, because I was scared of upsetting you. I played down our feelings for each other because I knew you didn't approve –"

Rhiannon tried to interject, but Carlie shook her head. "It's not a criticism of you, I'm just explaining why I didn't share everything about Rowan with you. And I've realised that I told you about my struggles with him and the one time I thought he was cruel to me, but I never told you how easily it was resolved, and that it was my own misunderstanding, not his actions, which caused the problem in the first place. He was always so kind and sweet and protective of me, and never did anything to hurt me. I just let my insecurities run away with me, which was unfortunately the bit I confided to you," she sighed.

"So I feel awful that I misrepresented him to you, because that wasn't fair to him. And it also means I can't blame you for thinking badly of him as a result, because I never told you that I'd been wrong about him that day. And I never told you how amazing he was to me, how much I loved him, how deeply he cared about me, how kind he was." She paused for a moment, trying to keep her emotions under control enough so that she could continue.

"Plus we were keeping our relationship a secret from Gran – which was my idea, not Rowan's – so that also meant I couldn't share everything with you. And I feel awful that I left you thinking that he wasn't good for me, because that wasn't fair to Rowan, and it also meant that you didn't like him, and led you to make that awful ultimatum," she said, her voice a sigh, her face creased with bitterness.

But Carlie's angst wasn't directed at her friend, it was directed inward, at herself. If only she'd shared with Rhiannon just how much she'd loved Rowan, just how amazing he'd been to her, how good he was, perhaps none of this would have happened. They'd all be friends now, and Rowan would still be alive.

"You know what's funny?" she mused. "After all my efforts at secrecy, Gran knew about us anyway. Rowan was brave enough and grown-up enough to go into the shop and talk to her. She'd met him before and really liked him, and she liked him even more when he told her how he felt about me, how much he loved me. He wanted to reassure her of how much he respected me too, and that he would never hurt me. He told her that I was the goddess to him, and shone brighter than the moon and the stars."

Taking a deep breath, Carlie willed the tears not to fall. "Anyway, I can't change the past, I can't erase my regrets or what they wrought, but maybe I can help you understand how I felt, how I feel now, and show you why I'm so devastated still." Her voice trailed off, and she almost chickened out, but then she decided to be brave for once and take Aideen's advice.

Walking over to the corner where her school bag sat, she tentatively lifted out the pile of cards and letters that were tied together with a red velvet ribbon. "Someone suggested to me that showing you these letters and cards from Rowan, and the one I wrote to him but didn't get a chance to deliver, might help you see why it's so hard for me to just get over him."

Rhiannon watched her friend, seeing the indecision and fear on her face as she held the letters close to her heart, wanting to share them, but equally not wanting to let them out of her sight.

Tentatively, she leaned in and placed her hands around them. "I'd be honoured to read them, and don't worry, I'll guard them with my life," she whispered. Carlie stared at her, trying to determine if she was being sarcastic or poking fun at her, but there was only love and compassion in her friend's eyes, so reluctantly she surrendered the package. The red-robed woman had said that showing Rhiannon would help both of them, and she had to trust in that. She needed something to happen to bring their friendship back to the way it had been, to cut through the impasse they found themselves at.

Both girls jumped when Rose came in to put the kettle on, and Rhiannon carefully slipped the letters into her bag before hugging her friend and making her farewells. Exhausted from the moving and sorting and lugging, and all the kitten activities, Carlie soon headed upstairs to bed, cuddling up with the cats in her new room and sending a silent prayer out to Rowan, wherever he was, to let him know how much she missed him still.

Chapter 15

A Friendship Restored

When Carlie got to school the next morning, Rhiannon was waiting for her out the front. As soon as she saw her approaching she ran over and pulled her into a hug, squeezing her tight. Rhiannon's eyes filled with tears as she told her friend, over and over, just how sorry she was. Carlie smiled at her. "It's okay, you didn't know," she said gently. "I should have told you sooner."

Rhiannon shook her head as she returned the letters. "I should have had more patience. I should have asked you. Can you forgive me?"

Carlie smiled and took her hand, leading her up the school steps as the bell rang for their first subject. "Of course. Life really is too short. Now come on, we can't be late for Laura's class. We don't want her telling Gran we've been slacking off."

Feeling lighter than they had since their blow up the week before, the girls headed into their room for history, and Carlie was relieved when she noticed that a lot of her resentment towards Rhiannon had dissipated. They didn't get a chance to talk about it much, since Jake sat with them at lunch, but maybe they didn't need to. Maybe they could just move forward together, back on track, with a new understanding of each other.

The next day they headed to the healing centre after school. Rose and her inner circle were preparing for the Imbolc ritual that weekend, and the girls had offered to help. It was the night of their coven meeting, but assisting their priestess and learning how a ritual was woven together was certainly a perfect way to spend the evening they'd committed to their magical studies.

They raced up the stairs to the beautiful room above Rose's shop, but stopped abruptly in the doorway, always awed by the sense of enchantment the space held, even in between rituals. Rhiannon watched Carlie greet Rose and tell her about her day, and she smiled even while she felt a wave of sadness. Her heart had broken a little when her friend had showed her the letters and cards she and Rowan had written to each other. What they'd shared together was so precious, so surprising, so huge and all-encompassing. She'd never felt anything like it with anyone, and while it made her feel terrible, she had to admit, even if just to herself, that she was desperately jealous of her friend. To have been loved so deeply by someone – especially someone as amazing as Rowan – blew her mind.

Pangs of guilt swept through her though. Guilt for being jealous of a dead man, guilt for the unfounded suspicions she'd harboured against him, guilt for the way she'd treated her best friend, guilt for not understanding the depth of Carlie's grief. So much guilt, so much anguish, so much longing.

With regret, she remembered that first night at the party in London, when she'd been so impressed by Rowan's kindness towards Carlie – and his politeness and consideration towards her, the tag-along friend. The day they'd all been together at the autumn festival, when he'd arranged tickets for them both and spent the whole time being so careful to include Rhiannon, even though she knew how much he'd wanted to spend the time alone with Carlie. And the way he'd honoured her, and her importance to Carlie, even when she'd been an angsty teenage bitch about him. God, she'd misjudged him so badly.

Not at first – she'd encouraged her friend to be with him in the beginning, pushed her to get past her shyness and get to know him. But later she'd tried to talk her out of the relationship, worked against her, been so negative. She couldn't even remember why, which was embarrassing. Had she acted like that purely out of jealousy? What was her motive for her actions? It was true that some of her concerns were valid. Carlie *had* skipped school one day to be with him, although even that had been for a very good reason, and had never been repeated. And she'd been lying to Rose, or withholding the truth at least, which wasn't good – especially as Rose would have been supportive of her dating Rowan. Oh the irony.

The more she thought about it, the more dreadful she felt. It pained her to admit that she hadn't been a good friend to Carlie, before Rowan's accident as well as after. Yet as cruel as she'd been, Carlie had always been good to her, had encouraged her when she talked about John, even though it must have been a knife through her heart to hear about it.

Goddess, she'd been feeling so superior, because she thought she was so mature, so grown-up, so supportive, so kind, and all along it had been Carlie who was the better friend, the better person, the less judgemental and petty. She'd actually agreed to her ridiculous ultimatum, out of respect for her, because she valued their friendship above her own needs, even after that friend had demanded such a terrible choice from her. She was just glad that in the end Carlie had realised she shouldn't have to make such a decision. And even then, she hadn't ditched Rhiannon – which she wouldn't have blamed her for, frankly – but had explained to her and to Rowan that she loved and valued them both, and refused to choose between them.

Not that Rowan had demanded such a choice. God, they were both better people than she was, yet here they were, Rowan dead and Carlie so devastated, while she was happily living her life with her family and her boyfriend. Carlie was more compassionate, even in her own grief, than she was, and it hurt her to realise how much pain she'd caused her friend. If she hadn't pressured her to dump Rowan – after she'd just stood Carlie up for their Yule ritual that night to spend time with her own boyfriend no less – she wouldn't have gone to see him that night, and...

Oh god, would Rowan still be alive? Was it her fault he'd skidded off the road in the snow, because he was so desperate to convince Carlie not to do as Rhiannon had demanded and break up with him? Her blood ran cold, and her face was frozen with fear. And when she felt Carlie's hand on her shoulder, she stared at her in growing horror. Did her friend blame her for Rowan's death?

But Carlie was smiling at her. "Did you want to come to the cafe for dinner with me and Rose when we're done here, or do you need to get home?" she asked.

Rhiannon stared at her, numb, incapable of speech. Carlie looked puzzled, but they were interrupted by Miri before she could ask what was wrong. "Hey girls, would one of you be able to help me with the long trestle table?" she requested.

Carlie nodded and walked out to the storeroom at the top of the stairs to wrestle the heavy furniture inside, and Rhiannon felt even worse. The girl who'd lost everything was still the first to offer to help others. Mentally shaking herself, she took a deep breath, and decided it was time to turn over a new leaf. First, heading over to join her friend and help set up the table.

But she paused when she felt eyes on her. Turning, she saw Rose approaching her, and was suddenly nervous, but the older woman took her in her arms and enfolded her in a hug.

"Lovely Rhiannon, stop torturing yourself, please. She doesn't blame you – in fact she's only just beginning to stop blaming herself. But it's in the past now. Don't beat yourself up over past actions, past words – just be the friend for her now that you wish you had been. She's still fragile, and she needs you now more than ever. So get over yourself, okay? Snap out of it, and be the young woman I know you're capable of being."

Rhiannon hugged the wise priestess, tears of gratitude in her eyes. "I will, I promise," she whispered, and Rose felt a weight lift from her own heart. "Will you tell Carlie I had to go though? There's something I need to do."

The next day at school Rhiannon couldn't stop yawning. Carlie teased her when they sat together in class, but when her friend seemed just as exhausted when they met up for lunch, she started feeling a little concerned.

"Are you okay Rhi? Are you coming down with something, or were you up all night partying? You can't be sick for Imbolc."

Rhiannon laughed. "I feel okay, I just didn't get much sleep. But I wasn't out partying, silly! I was searching for some things I thought you might like," she explained.

Carlie stared at her, puzzled. What on earth would she like? And was this why she'd left without saying goodbye last night?

"Well, um, I hope it won't upset you, but I'm not sure what you have to remember Rowan by," Rhiannon began, voice hesitant. "So I went through all my old spiritual magazines, and the newspapers Dad keeps, and searched online as well, and looked through all my photos too," she explained, then pulled out a thick purple folder from her bag and handed it over with a sad smile. "How about I get us a drink?" she asked, and stood up at her friend's vague nod and went over to join the long cafeteria line.

Carlie gazed down at the folder, curious but apprehensive. Screwing up her courage, she slowly opened it and pulled out the contents. On the top were several large photos of her and Rowan at the Yule Ball, as they were crowned Winter Queen and Sun King, and as they danced together afterwards. The joy on her face in the photos stabbed at her, but it was the love in his eyes as he gazed at her that broke her heart and made the tears fall. She traced over his face with her finger, remembering the way she'd felt in his arms, the whole world receding, as though they were the only two people on earth.

There were also a few snaps of the three of them together at the Autumn's End festival, pictures she didn't even remember being taken. She smiled through watering eyes as she saw how happy the three of them had been, how supportive her friend looked back then, how kind Rowan had been to both of them.

Under those was a series of interviews he'd done over the last couple of years, but it was the most recent one that made her breath catch in her throat. While the others talked about his work, his healings, his retreats, his oracle deck and his upcoming book about the magical and medicinal power of herbs, which she knew she would love reading later, the one on the top was a newspaper interview he'd done just before his winter solstice retreat. It had come out on the morning of the Yule sabbat – the morning he'd skidded off the road in the snow and died.

"Young healer in love" was the headline, and she quickly scanned the article, smiling sadly at the photo of him, his deep brown eyes piercing to her very soul, and his admission that he was cutting back on his travel because he'd fallen in love a balm to her wounded heart. It was tangible proof that she hadn't imagined how he'd felt, or exaggerated what she'd meant to him.

"I've never seen a love like it," Rhiannon said softly as she came back to the table with two juices. Carlie looked up in surprise, forgetting for a moment where she was, and that her friend had been sitting with her just moments before.

Rhiannon handed her one of the cups. "Do you want me to leave you alone for a while?" she asked quietly.

"No, it's fine. Thank you for these," she said, gesturing at the photos and articles strewn around her. "It means a lot to me."

Rhiannon nodded sadly. "It's the least I could do," she sighed. "I am so sorry that I was such a bitch to him, and to you. Seeing the photos of us at the festival together reminded me how wonderful he was to me, when he really didn't have to be. Which made me feel even worse for coming between you."

Carlie smiled through her tears. "It's okay," she whispered, and Rhiannon leaned in and gave her a grateful hug.

When the bell rang for their next class, Carlie considered feigning illness and going home, but then decided to tough it out. Tonight she could read everything her friend had compiled for her, and gaze at the pictures to her heart's content, but she needed to keep up with her schoolwork if she wanted to make it to university, and be able to study in order to help others who were grieving. Although for the first time she wondered if she was really going to be any use to other people suffering the death of their loved ones, when she was still so easily brought to her knees by the pain of her loss...

Chapter 16

Her Sweet Protector

School seemed even longer than usual the next day, and Carlie was filled with a sense of dread and anxiety throughout each class that she just couldn't shake. She drifted off in history, disappointing Laura when she fudged an answer, and was impatient with Rhiannon when they sat together at lunch, unwilling to confide in her about what was stressing her out, and hoping to avoid discussing it. Because this afternoon Jake was coming over to the cottage to work on their assignment with her, and she was nervous.

The last time they'd been alone together was when they were studying at his grandad's place, and he'd asked her out on a date. He'd been lovely about her turning him down, and seemed content to just be friends, but since Rhiannon's insistence that she should go out with him she'd suddenly started feeling uncomfortable around him, as well as guilty for rejecting him. She was also a bit worried that she'd freak out having him in her home, when the only guy who'd ever been there was Rowan.

Finally though the school bell rang, and it was time for her to face her fear. Telling herself that there was no need to worry wasn't helping, but she had to find a way to calm herself down. Although she was mostly moved in to her new bedroom, and her desk and books were in there, she'd decided they should work in the kitchen, because she felt weird about the idea of inviting a guy into her personal space. She wasn't sure what that meant – she had no qualms letting Rhiannon in, and Jake was nothing more than a friend. But she could tie herself in knots trying to psychoanalyse herself, and she wasn't in the mood for it right now. Nor did she have the time.

They walked to the cottage together, not saying much, then she led him through to the kitchen and offered him a seat at the table. Turning the heater on, she looked around for Luna and Luther. They usually hung around downstairs, mostly in the kitchen, but she figured that if it had gotten too cold they might have looked for somewhere warmer to burrow.

"I just have to find the cats – we have a new kitten, so I want to make sure she's okay," she explained. "But how rude. I'm sorry, would you like a cup of tea?" she asked, and Jake nodded gratefully. She put the kettle on and got the teapot and tea leaves out, then walked through to the lounge room, peering into corners before racing up the stairs.

Standing in the doorway of her old room, she looked around in astonishment. Now that she'd been sleeping in her mum's room, this one looked so tiny in comparison. The narrow bed seemed as though it wouldn't fit a child, let alone her and two cats, and she wasn't sure how she'd crammed all her clothes into the small wardrobe.

Yet the view of the tor out the window still took her breath away, and she could feel its energy reaching out to her just as strongly as she had the very first time she'd stood in this room, staring at the hill, being so deeply affected by it yet having no clue as to what it all meant. Not that she had much more of a clue now, but she'd done some amazing rituals atop it, both alone and with Rhiannon, and met some… Women? Otherworldly beings? Figments of her imagination?

Jumping when she felt a hand on her shoulder, she spun around, scream in her throat, and came face to face with Jake.

"Sorry, I didn't mean to scare you, I just wasn't sure where you were. Are you okay?" he asked, concern on his face.

She blinked. God, had she just totally zoned out, and been standing there for ages, lost in a world between worlds?

"I'm fine, sorry," she said, trying to step around him, to go and check her room for the cats, and resigned to the fact that he'd follow her there too. But he'd stopped in the doorway to her old room and was staring out at the tor, just as drawn in as she'd been by its magic.

"Can you feel it too?" she asked softly.

He nodded, eyes still focused on the hulking hill. "I've never seen it from this angle," he whispered. "But I've dreamed about it, without really knowing what it was. Last night I was running through these tunnels that were inside the hill – which doesn't really make sense, I realise that – and it felt like I was being chased by something, and yet I didn't know what it was, or what it could mean…" he trailed off. "Sorry, now you probably think I'm completely nuts," he added, rolling his eyes at himself.

Shaking her head, Carlie turned back to him, and the hill. "You're not crazy," she offered, unsure of just how much she wanted to tell him, or how far to go to reassure him. But he looked really nervous, clearly wondering what she thought of his announcement, so she figured it couldn't hurt to put his mind at ease.

"I've had loads of dreams where I was running through those tunnels, sometimes chasing, sometimes being chased," she began, voice a little hesitant. "And sometimes they're more magical-slash-bizarre than reality based. But there really are tunnels under there, a whole network of them. Surveyors found them a long time ago. So you're not as weird as you imagined."

Jake smiled, that genuine, slightly cheeky smile that transformed his face. "Thank you for laying that worry to rest," he said, tone jokey and light-hearted, but his eyes revealing just how relieved he was. "Now where are these cats of yours?"

Reluctantly she led him across the landing and up the stairs to the front room, her room now, and opened the door. Luther looked up from the bed as she walked in, stretching his big cat stretch, and Luna woke up at his movement and tried to imitate him, which was adorably cute. She still had no idea how Luther got through closed doors into their rooms, but she'd given up thinking she'd ever discover his secret. Sitting down next to them, she patted them both, glad to see they were warm and happy, but when Jake poked his head around the door, Luther immediately jumped onto her lap, so that he was positioned between her and the stranger in the entranceway, fur standing on end, his eyes boring straight into Jake's.

"Wow, you really have a protector there!" he said, taking an involuntary step backwards.

"Sorry," she replied, as she placed a calming hand on Luther's head. "It's okay buddy, Jake's a friend, just a friend," she whispered soothingly. She felt a stab through her heart as she recalled Luther's reaction to Rowan, and how happy her boyfriend had been to meet him and know that she had a guardian watching out for her.

After a wary, suspicious beginning, Luther had ended up loving Rowan, and had somehow managed to communicate with him, which had puzzled Carlie no end. She recalled the day that Luther had jumped up on her bed – the old narrow bed – when she and Rowan were kissing, and somehow let her boyfriend know that Rose would be home in ten minutes. If only he could have warned him that awful solstice morning as well...

"Are you okay?" Jake asked, his voice seeming to come from a great distance, and she crashed painfully back into the present.

"I'm sorry, I'm just... remembering. Luther *is* a protector," she agreed. "And this is Luna, our new kitten. She's just a ball of fluff right now, but Luther is showing her the ropes."

As she tenderly picked her up, she noticed Jake looking around her bedroom, and all her feelings of discomfort returned.

"So, we should probably go downstairs and get to work," she said hastily. "And I really need to feed the cats, and finally make our tea." Jake blushed a little at being caught snooping, and quickly turned and led the way back down the stairs, Luther at his heels, and out to the kitchen.

The afternoon passed quickly, and by the time Rose arrived home they'd done a big chunk of work and felt happy with their progress. Jake leaped to his feet when she walked into the kitchen, and had his hand out to introduce himself before Carlie had even put down her pen and said hello.

"Gran, this is Jake," she said, trying to smother a grin at his eagerness. "Jake, this is Rose Tyler."

"It's so lovely to meet you Mrs Tyler," he said, his face lit up again as he turned his smile on her. "I've heard so much about you, and it's an honour, really."

"Rose, please," she said, smiling back, although she looked a little perplexed at his enthusiasm. "It makes me feel so old to be called Mrs Tyler. And sit down, please, just relax. There's no need to stand up on my account."

Nodding, he sat back down, but he continued to stare at her as though she was something wonderfully unusual, totally fascinated by her and hanging on every word she uttered.

Carlie stood up. "Tea for you Gran?" she asked. "And would you like another one Jake?"

"Oh, I don't want to impose," he replied, almost shy, as she filled the kettle with water and put it on the stove.

"Nonsense Jake, it's no imposition," Rose said. "And I was just about to put a spinach and ricotta pie in the oven, if you'd like to stay for dinner. There's plenty – I made it this morning, and Carlie and I certainly can't get through a whole one."

He turned to Carlie, eyebrows raised in question, and she shrugged, concentrating on scooping out fresh tea leaves into the pot and rinsing their mugs. "Well, that would be lovely, if it's no trouble to either of you. Can I help with anything?" he asked.

"If you two could make the salad, that would be great," Rose replied. "I just have to finish up some bookkeeping, but the pie should be ready in twenty minutes, if that suits everyone?"

Jake nodded eagerly, and Carlie piled up their books and cleared off some room for her grandmother at the table, then started pulling ingredients for the salad out of the fridge. She wasn't sure how she felt about this development.

She'd been ready to say goodbye to Jake, but she knew better than to challenge Rose when she'd made up her mind about something. So while they washed and chopped the lettuce, capsicum, carrots, radishes and tomatoes, she and Jake chatted about Australian summers and what he usually did in his school holidays. Pausing to make the tea and take her grandma a cup, she smiled as she realised she was actually enjoying talking to Jake. Who'd have thought?

Finally, as the enticing aroma from the oven was making their tummies rumble, Rose packed away her paperwork while Carlie set the table and Jake put his books, notepads and pens back in his school bag. Then she carefully took the pie from the oven and carried it over to the table, before grabbing the salad bowl and taking a seat opposite Jake.

"It smells amazing Mrs Tyler," he said, and Carlie smiled. He was very polite, she'd give him that.

"Thank you Jake, and it's lovely to have you here. Are you okay with me saying a blessing before we eat?"

His eyes widened, but he nodded quickly, and Carlie tried to smother another grin. Rose took Carlie's hand in her left, and Jake's in her right, so Carlie took Jake's other hand in hers, then bowed her head and closed her eyes.

Goddess, we thank you for the bounty we are about to eat,
And for the family and friends who make us complete.
In gratitude we share this simple meal,
Grateful for the love and support we feel.

After a moment of silence, Rose squeezed their hands, opened her eyes and served out a huge piece of pie for Jake. "How are you enjoying your new school?" she asked, as she handed him the salad. After thanking her for the pie and spooning out some lettuce and tomatoes, Jake told her that he was settling in well, but was always really grateful to hear a familiar accent whenever he had a class with Carlie. Then he talked about the aid work his parents were doing in Africa, which fascinated Rose and Carlie, and the various travelling they'd done over the years that had taken them away from him.

Later Rose brought a hot apple and cinnamon crumble over to the table, which she'd also whipped up that morning, and Carlie eyed her suspiciously. Had her grandmother known they'd be having a dinner guest tonight, long before she even knew that Jake would be there to study this afternoon?

Her attention was brought back to the present when Jake admitted that part of the reason that his parents had sent him to stay with his grandfather this year was that they were starting to worry a little about him living on his own.

"I could have stayed with my best mate and his family, but Dad was really concerned about Pop living on his own. He was devastated when Nan died, obviously, but he's had a few niggling health issues too, so my parents sat me down and asked if I'd be prepared to spend the year with him, help him out a bit. You can't mention any of this to him though," he insisted, suddenly looking panicked that he'd revealed too much.

"Your secret is safe with us Jake," Rose assured him. "And that's lovely that you were so happy to help him out."

"It's no trouble, and it was the least I could do. Nan and Pop moved to Australia for ten years just so they could live near us and look after me when my parents had to travel for work – they'd stay with me at home so my schooling wasn't disrupted, and they'd cook for me, and take me to school and to sport and to piano lessons and what-not. They were so wonderful. And I really miss Nan," he said, and his eyes glistened a little as he spoke.

"But you two must have had wonderful times together over the years too, right?" he asked, trying to deflect their attention away from him while he composed himself.

Carlie blushed and Rose looked uncomfortable, and they caught each other's eye, wondering what to say, and who should say it. Finally Carlie spoke. "I didn't know I had a grandma until last June, after my parents died," she said softly, simply. Jake looked shocked for a moment, then remembered a few comments Carlie had made in previous conversations that now made sense.

"Mum lost touch with Rose after she moved to Australia – it's a long story though," she muttered, before moving on quickly. "And to be honest, I was a horror when I first got here. I blamed Gran for everything, and had decided that she must be a total monster, so I was really awful to her. And so angry. It took a while for me to untangle my misconceptions and get to the truth of it, and I'm still mortified by what a bitch I was to her. I'm not sure I'll ever forgive myself," she sighed.

Rose shook her head sadly. "Sweetheart, you have to stop beating yourself up over this. You didn't know, neither of us knew. And you were grieving the worst kind of loss. We got there in the end," she said soothingly, then turned to Jake.

"Don't you listen to her. We had a little misunderstanding when she arrived, but we quickly got over that, and it's been wonderful ever since," she explained. "I lost my daughter and my husband more than twenty years ago, so it's been a dream come true for me to have Carlie here. And we've done some amazing things together, and shared so much. We've cooked, we've planted herbs, we've sewn, we've travelled, we've woven magic together…"

Carlie looked up at her grandmother, a warning in her eyes – Jake's grandfather was still a churchgoer, no matter what he'd said to her the other day about acceptance, and she wasn't sure what he really thought about Rose's more esoteric interests. But Jake jumped in eagerly as soon as she mentioned magic.

"Actually, Pop and I were wondering if any of your rituals were open to outsiders to participate in," he said, and Carlie nearly fell off her chair in surprise. "And whether it would be okay for men to come, or are they only designed for women?"

"A lot of them are open to the public, to friends of friends, and definitely to both men and women," Rose replied. Then she paused for a moment, considering her answer carefully. "Although I don't want to give you the wrong idea Jake. Certainly there are many more women than men who attend, but that's not because we discourage them. I've always just assumed it was because less men wanted to take part, but perhaps they're not sure that they're welcome either," she mused. "Hmm, maybe I need to make that clearer to people, to the community? Thank you for voicing that," she said.

"But there are a few men who take part regularly, and a couple more who come from time to time. The next ritual is this weekend in fact, if you and your grandfather would like to join us?"

Jake's eyes lit up with joy. "Thank you, that would be fantastic," he replied. "Pop will be really happy, and he's been wanting to see you again too Carlie. I've been hoping to get him more involved in things, to meet new people, open up a little – to get him out of the house, out of his comfort zone. He lived in London and Perth for most of his life, and when he came here with Nan, she was already sick, so he barely left her side, which means he hasn't met many people outside of the church group that Nan was involved with.

"And I'd love to come too, and be part of it. I think we can all use a little more magic in our lives," he said, smiling brightly. "Do we need to bring anything, or prepare in any way?"

Rose shook her head. "There's always a brief explanation before we start the ritual, outlining what will happen, and there are people you can ask questions of at any time during it. And you can choose which bits you want to participate in, and just watch other parts if you'd rather. It's always totally up to you."

Jake suddenly looked nervous, and Carlie took pity on him.

"I was apprehensive before my first ritual too – but it was really relaxed," she assured him, and his expression lightened a little. "I didn't have to speak at all, just listen, and the directions were really clear. It was really beautiful."

Smiling with pride as Carlie spoke, and marvelling at just how much she'd changed in the last six months, Rose stood up and walked through to the lounge room, returning with a book outlining all the sabbats, which she handed to Jake.

"You don't have to read this – there's no homework, I promise – but if you're interested you can skim through a bit about the festival we'll be celebrating. It's known as Imbolc, and it marks the end of winter and the start of spring, so it's all about new beginnings, the return of light to the land, an honouring of seeds starting to sprout, the fresh growth that sustains life, and also the germination of things in our own lives that we wish to grow and nurture. Fresh starts, optimism, seeing the world anew," Rose revealed.

Jake looked fascinated, and read the back of the book with great interest. "I'd love to borrow this for a few days, if that's okay?" he asked, and Rose nodded cheerfully.

"Most people bring along a few cans of beans or a packet of rice or a carton of soy milk or something, for the homeless shelter,"

Carlie added. "I remember being so impressed by that at my first ritual, when I realised that their honouring of the cycle of the seasons and the wheel of life was not just lip service – everyone in the circle really is grateful for all the blessings they feel they have, and they're all eager to give back, and to keep things balanced."

"Yeah, Pop mentioned that you had helped Nan, and refused any money, even for the cost of the herbs you had to buy. He thought it was a bit odd at the time – sorry," he said quickly to Rose, but she smiled and waved her hand, dismissing his concerns. "He said he was so used to the church expecting money from them, that he was a bit suspicious at first – no offence!"

Rose laughed. "None taken."

"But he was very grateful – he said your herbal concoctions eased Nan's pain a great deal towards the end, which gave them more quality time to be together. He said that was the best gift of all, the thing that meant the most to them. There's no present like time, isn't that what they say?" he asked.

Rose smiled sadly. "I'm so sorry you both lost her," she said simply, voice heavy with compassion.

"Thank you," he replied softly. "That means a lot to me."

Carlie sighed. He was so much more gracious than she'd been. Was she the only ungrateful, moody, angry person in this town?

"Sweetheart, give yourself a break," Rose implored her, and Jake looked puzzled, clearly unaware of this priestess's mind-reading skills. Carlie smiled at her grandmother, and nodded, then got back to the topic at hand.

"After the ritual we gather together for a while, and have a cup of tea or some juice and eat a bit of food, to ground ourselves back in our bodies, and just to catch up with people, talk about the evening, or about normal life," she explained.

"So you're welcome to bring a plate if you'd like to, but you really don't have to – there's always plenty of food," she continued. "But if you don't like going somewhere empty handed, a plate of cookies, or carrot sticks and dip, just something small, would always be gratefully accepted. And I think that if there's any food left over it goes to the homeless shelter too, so nothing is ever wasted," she added, looking at Rose with eyebrows raised in question.

Nodding, Rose stood up and cleared the plates, telling Jake to relax when he tried to help, then put the kettle on. "But you really don't have to bring anything," she insisted. "No pressure, no stress. It's meant to be a relaxing, reinvigorating occasion."

The three of them continued their conversation while they had another cup of tea together, then Jake said he had to get home, and thanked them for the wonderful dinner and their company.

"It wasn't as bad as you'd expected, was it?" Rose asked her granddaughter once he'd left.

"What do you mean?" Carlie asked, shocked at her grandmother's perceptiveness.

Rose smiled at her, a knowing smile. "He cares about you very much Carlie, but you don't have to feel nervous or threatened by that. He'll never push you to do anything you don't want to do, and he is genuinely happy to just be your friend if that's what you want. I think it's important for you to know that."

"Thanks Gran," she replied, for once more grateful than alarmed by her priestess powers. "And now I really should get to bed – we have a test tomorrow, which I'm a bit worried about."

They hugged good night, then Carlie headed upstairs to bed with the two cats, and slipped into a surprisingly peaceful, dreamless sleep.

Chapter 17

A Festival of Joy and Renewal

On Saturday Carlie and Rhiannon spent the whole day with Rose in the kitchen of the cottage, grinding herbs, sewing dream pillows and blending incense in the morning, then starting to bake for the following night's ritual in the afternoon.

Carlie made chocolate-orange poppyseed cupcakes, since seeds symbolise Imbolc's energy of growth and fertility, then whipped up mini lemon cheesecakes, as dairy foods are also a strong part of the seasonal theme. Rhiannon created individual pots of baked custard flavoured with ginger, cinnamon, nutmeg and other spring spices, then churned some cream into butter and buttermilk. And Rose kneaded several trays of Bridie's bread, small loaves made from buttermilk, flour and salt and sprinkled with sunflower and sesame seeds to capture the energy of new life and new beginnings inherent in this time of year, then blended and poured out little gauze bags filled with an Imbolc tea crafted from chamomile, nettle and violets.

As the evening drew in and the sky faded to black, the silver-haired priestess taught the girls how to weave Bridie Crosses, the traditional fire wheel symbols of the goddess, out of stalks of wheat, so they could hang them around the house and in the ritual room. Then they started making candles for the ceremony. Each participant would need one for the ritual itself, and Rose also wanted to gift each person with a set of Imbolc candles along with their tea, so they could continue to weave the magic of the season when they returned home. Half of the candles would be white and the other half pale blue, to embody the innocence and purity of the sabbat and represent the cleansing power of the element of fire.

Halfway through dipping one of her candles, Carlie paused and gazed around the room. The cats were purring at her feet, the flickering light of the pillar candle in the centre of the table gave a rosy glow to everything, and she suddenly realised, in this moment at least, that she was happy. Despite all that she'd lost, she could actually see something positive in her life. Not all the time, but in brief snatches coloured by friendship and family, or magical purpose. She knew it was a fleeting state of being, for now anyway, but if she could continue to experience these golden moments, perhaps her desire to flee, to disappear from the world, might eventually wield less and less power over her.

"Oh Sweetheart, I'm so glad," Rose whispered, eyes twinkling in the candlelight as she gazed across at her granddaughter.

Carlie laughed. She would probably never get used to her grandma reading her mind, but she was starting to be less disturbed by it.

"Please don't worry. I can't read your every thought, I promise, and even if I could, I wouldn't," Rose said. "I just pick up brief flashes of emotion, not specific thoughts, and it mostly happens when we're in a ritual head space, like now – I'm sure you could glean my mood right now too, if you wanted to. But I'd never invade your privacy like that, and you can rest assured that you never gave anything away about Rowan when you were with him, so don't be scared that I know what you're thinking or what you've done or not done, okay? It doesn't work like that."

Rhiannon looked over at her friend, nervous that the mention of Rowan would upset her and spoil her fragile peace, but Carlie smiled at her. "Don't worry so much Rhi, I'm not going to fall apart every time his name is mentioned. But thank you for your concern," she said, hugging her friend, then laughing when she realised she'd just done the same thing that Rose had.

At that moment Luna woke up, yawned, then jumped into Carlie's lap, and the focus of their attention shifted. Rose got up and popped a pot of soup on the stove to warm for their dinner, and Carlie cleared some space at the table so they could eat.

After Rose had gone to bed, the two girls tiptoed upstairs to Carlie's room, flopped down on her bed and opened their Book of Shadows. Their coven homework for the week was to write about Imbolc, so they could compare notes and add to their own entries, so they stayed up for a while, scribbling down information, whispering together and trying not to laugh too loudly, before finally changing into their pyjamas, brushing their teeth and climbing into bed.

The next morning, Rhiannon left for her place to spend time with her little brother and get some homework done, before returning to Carlie's so they could take all the food down to the healing centre for Rose. Once it was all set up, they headed back to the cottage to get ready, weaving together wreaths of snowdrops and primroses for their hair, then slipping into their long velvet ritual dresses and putting on the rings they'd received from their Otherworldly friends on the night of their coven dedication.

Carlie's was a delicate silver one with a butterfly on it, with the wings made up of aquamarines, crystals of truth and trust. And Rhiannon's ring had a silver dragonfly on it, with pink rose quartz, the crystal of compassion, love and healing, forming its wings.

A flash of memory from that night hit Carlie – the two of them taking their own path to the top of the tor as darkness descended, a candle in one hand and flowers representing their friendship clutched tight in the other. An image of Brianna, the green-clad woman she'd encountered, fluttered into her mind, and she smiled as she recalled their conversation, and the beautiful athame she'd given her.

And Rhiannon had met up with blue-robed Brauna, and been gifted a gorgeous silver chalice. They still used both of these magical tools in their private rituals, along with the wand and pentacle Brianna had given Carlie for the two of them a few months later.

Now her friend caught her eye and smiled back. "It's hard to believe that it's been six months since the Lughnasadh ritual we did with Rose, isn't it?" she asked, voice hushed even though there was no one around to hear them. "I feel like I've lived a lifetime since then, so I can't even begin to imagine how you feel," she said softly.

Carlie's mouth curved upward for a fleeting moment. Rhiannon was right. Well, half right. In some ways it did feel like a lifetime ago, yet in others it felt like only yesterday that she'd been at home in Australia with her parents and her best friend Emily, cheerfully planning their university studies in law, and the apartment they were going to move in to together. But Emily had started her uni degree last week, and was meeting new people and getting on with life without her. For the first time Carlie realised that the death of her parents in a car accident and her being sent across the world to live with a stranger had impacted on Emily's life too.

God, was it really only seven months since she'd landed on her grandma's door step, hating her before she'd even met her, acting like a selfish bitch for the first few weeks as she drowned in grief and loss and a tidal wave of anger? Although the memory mortified her, she acknowledged that she really had come a long way in a short time. Much of that had been the result of the patience and compassion of her grandma, another part had been Rowan's love for her, and his ability to make her see herself in new and better ways – to want to be new and better. And another part had been Rhiannon's friendship, and her empathy and support.

"Thank you for all you've given me," Carlie said quietly. She may have lost Rowan, but she didn't have to lose her friend too. Yes, she'd been angry with her, for good reason, but if she thought everyone had to be perfect all the time, she'd have no one in her life. And she was far from perfect herself. Rose had given her a second, and a third, chance, and excused all kinds of behaviour, so the least she could do was give Rhiannon a pass. As awful as she'd been, and as bad as the consequences of her actions had turned out, she had good intentions.

Rhiannon took her hand. "And thank *you* Carlie," she whispered, a catch in her voice. "You still don't realise all you've given me. And forgiving me now is the biggest gift of all. I'll always feel bad about how I acted, and wonder if it would have panned out differently if I'd done something, or not done something..."

Carlie forced a smile. She'd always wonder that too, of both her friend's actions and her own, but obsessing over that wouldn't bring Rowan back. And hating her friend so she could carry on blaming her was pointless and wrong. She remembered Aideen telling her to let go of always having to be right, and realised that was good advice. They were both at fault, in some ways, yet at the same time neither of them were. Her head spun.

Consequences. Fate. Destiny... Action and reaction...

Sometimes she thought life was just a big cosmic joke, one that wasn't even funny. When she'd met the blue-clad woman on a misty mountain top, she'd warned her there was no deeper meaning, no grand purpose or design. That sometimes really bad things happened to really good people, for no reason at all. At the time she'd thought that was a horribly fatalistic way to live, yet it absolved you of responsibility when something bad happened, while empowering you to make your own choices and create your own life too.

Back in the village as night began to fall, the two friends made their way to the healing centre. A feeling of reverence descended on them as they climbed the stairs, and when they stepped across the threshold into the ritual room, the rows of blazing candles took their breath away. They hugged Laura, who was transformed into a strong, beautiful priestess, a million miles from her school-teacher persona, and greeted several other women from Rose's inner circle, touched that they were invited to be part of their magic.

As Rhiannon straightened her floral headdress, Carlie spotted Jake and his grandfather standing in the doorway, looking a little lost, so they went to greet them. Richard shook Rhi's hand and beamed at her when they were introduced, then leaned forward to hug Carlie, and she felt the strength within him as well as his fragility. Jake's parents needn't worry too much on his behalf.

Rhiannon tried to hug Jake then, but it was made a little awkward by the platter of food in his hands, so he quickly presented Carlie with the plate of warm scones with fresh berry jam and cream.

"Pop loves to cook, but he just doesn't do it much because it's only the two of us, and all the church ladies leave him food anyway," he grinned. "But he found a recipe in an old cookbook of Nan's for Bridie scones, which from what we read seemed fitting for this ritual, and it made him feel useful. He's been lacking in purpose since she died, so this was really nice for him."

Carlie smiled as she carried the plate over to the end of the trestle table, where it joined a beautifully coloured spread of seasonal foods and cakes. She loved the effort everyone went to here. At parties back home, her parents would grab a packet of rice crackers and a container of dip, or something equally quick and easy, to take along. But here everyone made their contributions from scratch, blending together their own dips and baking savoury crackers to go with them, whipping up cookies or desserts, even roasting potato cakes sprinkled with rosemary, as someone had done tonight, and often using their own home-grown produce.

Everyone did that here, even her. Before, she had thought that she couldn't cook, but it seemed that she could, she'd just never really tried. And she'd discovered just how therapeutic it could be, almost a meditation. She especially enjoyed it when she was making something for a ritual, and she could immerse herself in the meaning of the sabbat and the energies of the season.

Today she'd spent the afternoon slicing up the halva they'd made a few days earlier, which was infused with vanilla and sesame seeds, and cooking buttermilk pancakes sprinkled with herbs and flowers. Soon she and Rose would make them with the added magic of ingredients fresh from their garden... *Their garden*... How funny that she now thought of this place as hers, as home.

There wasn't much still growing in it right now, as the harsh winter was only just beginning to loosen its grip, so she'd used Rose's stockpile of herbs instead, the ones her grandmother had dried from her garden at the end of the previous summer. Which was when she'd arrived in the village to live with her, yet she hadn't noticed her grandma doing that. Although she hadn't been paying attention to anything back then, she thought regretfully. Still, no point dwelling on that now.

Forcing a smile, she walked back over to where Jake and his grandfather were standing, looking awkward and ill-at-ease, yet interested in everything happening around them. She remembered that sensation so vividly from her first ritual, and it shocked her, just how at home she felt here now, in this room where magic was woven, and this village where people lived close to the earth. And how confident she felt as she greeted the people she'd started to become close to, people she never would have known back in her old life in Sydney.

When Rhiannon's dad Mike arrived, she beckoned him over and introduced him to everyone. He and Richard started chatting, while Carlie and Rhiannon told Jake about their weekend of cooking. And after complimenting the girls on their dresses and the flowers in their hair, and asking after Luna, Jake told them about the plans he'd been drawing up with his grandfather to replant their vegie patch, which was inspired by his stories of Rose's amazing herb garden.

Finally the lights dimmed, and a hush fell as Rose gracefully stood up from her position behind the central altar. Carlie's breath caught as she watched her grandmother take up the etheric cloak of the priestess, marvelling as the sense of power and strength settled around her shoulders. At a gasp beside her, she turned and caught the look of wonder on Jake's face, and the gaze of surprise and admiration on his grandfather's. Catching Rhiannon's eye as she turned back, the two girls smiled at each other, more used to Rose's transformation, yet no less awed by it.

Carlie would never tire of seeing her grandma lead a ritual. It was like something out of a movie, but there were no special effects in this room. Gazing around her, she focused again on the golden threads of light she could see vibrating between everyone in the circle. The one linking Jake and his grandfather was thicker than the others, and she felt a lump in her throat as she sensed the deep love between them. Her heart ached as she thought of all the special moments they'd shared – a lifetime of beautiful memories and rich experiences, from the grand adventures they'd no doubt had to the equally wonderful and equally precious ordinary moments.

Reluctantly she admitted that she was jealous of them, and of Jake, that he'd grown up with such amazing grandparents, and had such a close relationship with them, such a strong bond, and had spent so much time with them. It was the time she envied most. But she had Rose now, and Rose had her, and they were building a universe of golden moments together. There was no point pining for what she'd missed out on – what they'd both missed out on. She just had to make the most of their time now. And she couldn't have dreamed up a better grandmother if she'd tried.

Suddenly realising that Rose had started speaking, she crashed back into the room. Oops! Wasn't that the first lesson – be present now? She didn't want to daydream away such a magical night.

"Welcome to our Imbolc ritual," their priestess began, her voice rich and deep and powerful, as though coming from the very centre of the earth itself. "Imbolc is the festival of joy and renewal that marks the turning of the wheel from the end of winter to the start of spring. It celebrates the lengthening of the days and the return of the sun and its life-giving warmth – the return of the light as it illuminates the land as well as our hearts. We honour the fertility of the land and of our own selves, in this time of hope, fresh starts and new beginnings.

"Energetically it's a time of re-awakening and re-emergence, as all of nature fills with life force and begins to quiver with the energy to grow again, and we too start to emerge from the chill of winter to re-engage with the world. And it's a time of purification and cleansing after the long dark of the winter months, of stripping away the old so that the new can emerge," Rose continued.

Feeling someone watching her, Carlie turned to meet Jake's gaze. His face was lit up with curiosity as well as awe, and she smiled at him, at his openness to new experiences, and his joy at being alive. She was suddenly really grateful for his friendship, and admiring of his attitude, and she hoped that some of his positivity would inspire her to feel that way too.

Her attention returned to her grandmother as she picked up a beautiful crystal-tipped wand from the altar, and stepped outside of the circle of people. With the wand held high, she walked slowly around the perimeter in a clockwise direction. Carlie shivered as she felt the priestess pass behind her, and her skin prickled with a sense of magic and anticipation as Rose spoke.

By my will a circle formed,
Between the worlds where magic's born.
Contain the energy raised within,
As the veils between these worlds do thin.
Hold us safe throughout this rite,
As we create magic together on this night.
The circle is cast, so mote it be.

Returning to the starting point, Rose linked the hands of the two women at the portal to close the circle, then walked back to the central altar, and the four women calling the directions raised their wands and one at a time invoked the directions in sweet, strong voices.

Water: *I call forth the guardians of the west to cleanse, consecrate and protect this space during our rite, and I ask the waters of the oceans and rivers and sacred springs to wash away anything that no longer serves us. Element of water, welcome.*

Earth: *I call forth the guardians of the north to cleanse, consecrate and protect this space during our rite, and I ask the stones, the crystals and the very earth that we walk upon to ground and strengthen us. Element of earth, welcome.*

Air: *I call forth the guardians of the east to cleanse, consecrate and protect this space during our rite, and I ask the winds of the planet, both stormy gales and gentle breezes, and the very air itself, to inspire and uplift us. Element of air, welcome.*

Fire: *I call forth the guardians of the south to cleanse, consecrate and protect this space during our rite, and I ask the flames of light and heat, and fire itself, to burn away anything that no longer serves us. Element of fire, welcome.*

As each direction caller finished her invocation, there was a gentle murmur from the rest of the circle: "Hail and welcome." At her first ritual, Carlie had been too shy to add her voice, but tonight she spoke the words with everyone else, and felt a part of something that warmed her heart, something that rooted her in this time, in this place, in this community that she knew cared for her and her family, past and present. Then Rose raised the central altar candle high, and gazed upwards.

Great Mother, divine goddess of wisdom and moonlight,
Please shine your love on us tonight.
Lord of the woods, of nature and sunlight,
Shine your blessings on our sacred rite.
And Bridie, please grace us with your transformative flames,
and help us to purify and burn away our doubt and pain.

Carlie embraced the mystery of how she felt in these moments, how connected she was to everyone in the room, how engulfed in love. Catching Rhiannon's eye, she smiled, knowing her friend understood perfectly, and the sensation of sharing this magic with her made her feel close to her again. A weight lifted from her heart as she felt their connection fall back into place.

Turning back to the circle, she blushed when Rose beckoned the two girls forward to hand out the candles they'd made the previous night so that everyone in the circle had one. A flush of nerves swept over her, but she took a deep breath, willing herself to be calm, then picked up the basket at her feet and walked around her half of the circle, distributing the pretty beeswax candles, and feeling so deeply touched by the sense of camaraderie and connection as each person received their candle and whispered a blessing to her in return.

As she moved around the room she heard Rose's strong, powerful voice outlining the ritual. Their priestess would begin, by lighting her candle and making a wish or a statement of intent as the flame caught, then she would offer the candle to Laura, who would light hers from its flame as she spoke her own wish, then offer hers to the person next to her, and so on around the circle until everyone's candle was aflame and they had made a vibrant ring of fire to fuel their wishes. Then the last person would light the large pillar candle on the altar, which would absorb and hold the magic of the group, so they could light it at future rituals to reawaken and reinforce the magic they wove tonight.

Smiling at Richard and Jake, Rose added that they could speak their wish aloud or send it out as a silent prayer, whatever they felt comfortable with, because it was the intent with which they formed and focused their wish that gave it its power, not how loudly or publicly they made it.

Then she began. “Dearest Bridie, maiden goddess, at this time of new beginnings I wish for health and healing for everyone here, and inspiration to fuel their creativity,” Rose said, as she lit her own candle, then glided over to Laura and offered its flame to her.

“Blessed Bridie, I ask for your healing for my mother, who couldn’t be here tonight,” their teacher whispered as she ignited her candle. Then she offered it to Miri, who was standing next to her, and so the flame travelled around the circle, with wishes and prayers igniting with it as it journeyed.

One person asked for insight into an issue she was facing, another for inspiration with a project he was about to begin, a third for the strength to face a challenge she felt unprepared for.

When the flame got to Richard, he closed his eyes and took a deep, silent breath, then he dipped his candle to the flame of the person next to him, and held it to his heart as he gazed at Rose in the centre of the circle. Then he turned and offered his flame to ignite Jake’s candle. His grandson looked dazzled by the occasion, his eyes shining and his face lit up with purpose and passion.

“I wish for healing and comfort for a friend who is suffering and heart-sore,” he said quietly, then looked directly at Carlie, compassion softening his features as he smiled at her. She was overwhelmed by his sentiment and deeply touched by his words, and started to panic a little as the flame came ever closer to her.

What should she wish for? Could she say it aloud, or would she keep it private? Should it be a personal wish, or one for Rose or the community? Could she even keep it together long enough to make hers, as she listened to all the beautiful wishes, felt the people in the circle connected, all one heart and mind?

Finally the candle reached her, and she tipped hers to the flame and whispered her wish so quietly that only Rhiannon, standing next to her, heard it. “Sweet goddess, or the universe, or whoever is listening, please help my heart to heal, and to one day open again, without walls, without fear," she mumbled, then turned to her friend and offered the flame to her.

Rhiannon spoke just as quietly, a little embarrassed because her dad was in the room, and not quite ready to reveal herself so deeply, yet swept up in the magic of the night and the power of the group's sharing. "Dearest Bridie, thank you so much for my remaining family and my friends. I am so grateful for all of your blessings. My wish tonight is to some day find a love like Carlie and Rowan's, and to feel worthy of the depth and the joy of it."

"Oh Rhi, of course you're worthy," Carlie whispered, after her friend had passed on the flame to the person to her left, since they were working deosil, with the sun, to raise energy and manifest their dreams and wishes into reality. Rhiannon blushed, and tried to shush her friend – she didn't want to break the spell of the ritual or distract anyone from their wish. Carlie mouthed: "Sorry," and brought her attention back to the circle.

Next Rose led them in a meditation to focus on the new beginnings they sought in the coming month, which she followed with a spiral dance to wake everyone up, refocus their minds and get their energy swirling again. Then, as laughter rang out, Rose brought them back to her again, mood serious, and began a healing spell that they all contributed to and then sent outwards over the land. At one point Carlie glanced over at Jake and his grandfather, and was moved almost to tears by the wonder in their eyes and the golden energy that surrounded and linked them.

Then finally Rose stood in the centre of the circle again to thank and farewell the deities.

Great Mother, divine goddess of wisdom and moonlight,
Thank you for shining your love on us tonight.
Lord of the woods, of nature and sunlight,
We are so grateful for your blessings on our sacred rite.
And Bridie, sweet maiden and fire goddess, thank you
for inspiring us with your grace, and offering us the power
of your transformative flame. Hail and farewell.

After that, the four priestesses thanked and farewelled the elements and the directions for their assistance and support.

Fire: *Guardians of the south, and of fire, thank you for cleansing, consecrating and protecting this space during our rite, and offering to us your flames of light and heat, and fire itself, to burn away what no longer serves us. Element of fire, hail and farewell.*

Air: *Guardians of the east, and of air, thank you for cleansing, consecrating and protecting this space during our rite, and bringing to us the winds of the planet, both stormy gales and gentle breezes, and the very air itself, to inspire and uplift us. Element of air, hail and farewell.*

Earth: *Guardians of the north, and of earth, thank you for cleansing, consecrating and protecting this space during our rite, and sharing with us the strength of the stones, the crystals and the very earth that we walk upon to ground and strengthen us. Element of earth, hail and farewell.*

Water: *Guardians of the west, and of water, thank you for cleansing, consecrating and protecting this space during our rite, and giving to us the energy of the waters of the oceans and rivers and sacred springs to wash away anything that no longer serves us. Element of water, hail and farewell.*

Finally Rose walked gracefully back over to the portal where it had all begun, and the two women on either side unlinked their hands and took hers in theirs. "By my will this circle is closed. Blessed be!" their priestess announced.

Everyone raised their still-linked hands, then spoke as one. "May the circle be open but unbroken. Merry meet, merry part, and merry meet again. Blessed be!" This time Carlie was prepared for it, and spoke the words along with the rest of the participants, as everyone enthusiastically echoed the phrase. She was surprised by how confident she'd become in these rituals, and how much a part of the circle, and of this community, she felt now, especially considering how angry and confused and almost foreign she had perceived herself to be when she'd arrived. Yet it made her heart ache for her mother, who had been at the centre of this magic once, at the same age she was now, but who had, as an adult, buried it all deep within her, cutting off all of her connection to magic, and to her past.

When Jake shyly touched her arm, she came abruptly back into the room, and the present. Turning to him, she smiled and asked what he'd thought, and he couldn't get the words out fast enough to share his excitement, and let her know how much his grandfather had enjoyed it too. She glanced around, wondering where Richard was, and was happy to see that he was chatting animatedly to Rose.

After speaking to her dad, Rhiannon came back over, and she and Carlie led Jake to the table filled with luscious seasonal treats and suggested that he eat something, to ground his energy back into the real world, and his spirit back into his body. He raised his eyebrows at the girls, looking a little puzzled – until he swayed slightly, and Rhiannon grabbed his arm.

"We mean it," she said sternly, as Carlie handed him a chocolate-orange poppyseed cupcake and watched over him until he'd eaten every last crumb.

Laughing, she suggested that he tuck in to anything else he wanted to try as well, before she headed over to help Miri make cups of tea for all the guests, leaving Jake and Rhiannon alone to talk about the ritual that had left them both buzzing.

Chapter 18

Searching for Satisfaction

Jake had taken to sitting with Carlie and Rhiannon in the cafeteria every lunchtime, chatting up a storm, but the next day he was uncharacteristically quiet, eyes gazing off into the distance. The girls giggled as they tried to get his attention.

"Earth to Jake!"

"Oh, sorry!" he said, eyes focusing on them again. "I was off in another world, a magical world, still thinking about last night," he admitted shyly. "Your grandmother is amazing Carlie, it was like she became someone else, so wild and strong and powerful, yet so welcoming and nurturing too. I've never seen anything like it.

"And you'll probably think I'm crazy, but I swear I could see golden strands, like electricity almost, running between each person, connecting all of us, all different widths and different intensities of sparkle," he raved, then suddenly looked sheepish. "God, I know that really does sound insane. I'm sorry, I'll get over it soon, I promise. It's just... well, I just loved it so much."

Carlie smiled. "You're not crazy Jake, I see it too. It's like a giant web or something, all sparkling and golden, running through the room. The connection between you and your grandfather was the thickest – it was so strong, so vibrant. The love you share is so clear," she said, smiling although her heart was crushed with longing.

"Really?" he asked, voice shy but eyes shining with hope.

Nodding, Rhiannon broke in. "I don't see it so much as sense it, and my heart felt so full when I looked at you and your grandad. Your relationship is just beautiful, and he adores you. It's given him a new purpose, you being here, much like what Carlie's arrival gave to Rose."

Jake beamed at them. "You can really see and sense those things?" he gasped, as incredulous as he was excited.

"It sounds like you can too," Carlie grinned, keeping her tone light-hearted, in case it was freaking him out. She tried to remember how she'd felt that first night when she'd seen the golden threads in the room, how she'd been so cynical still, yet secretly so hopeful that there really was magic in the world. And she'd been so awestruck by the immensity of what Rose wove within her and sent out to every person there too.

"Is there a way to practise it, or to develop it?" he asked hopefully. "Is there any way to get better at it?" The two girls exchanged glances. Should they include him in their coven study group? Did they want anyone else – and a guy no less – working with them?

They were saved from having to reply when Dave came over to talk to Jake about their athletics team training, and he reluctantly stood up, grabbed his bag and said goodbye to the girls, leaving them alone at the table.

"What do you think?" Rhiannon asked, excitement in her voice. "It sounds like he's really interested in learning, and you said he's been working hard on your assignment, so he wouldn't be slack. But do we want anyone joining us? Especially a guy?"

Carlie shrugged. "I'm not sure. I mean, we shouldn't feel obligated – we can lend him some books and head him in the right direction for his own study, and just invite him to the public rituals. And maybe he'd rather find someone more experienced to teach him anyway. It's not like he asked to join our coven."

"True," Rhiannon conceded. "But I don't think he knows we have one, so how could he ask that? I'm sure he'd be more than happy if we wanted to help him out. And it would be pretty awesome to have the power of three..."

Carlie stared at her. "You like him, don't you?" she asked, eyebrows raised in surprise, and her friend squirmed a little.

"No, of course not, he's just a really sweet guy..." she began, but her blush gave her away.

"Oh my god Rhi, you do!" Carlie said, a grin splitting her face. Then she frowned. "But what about John? I thought you guys were really happy?"

"We were. We are," she muttered, but she looked a little miserable.

"What's wrong?"

"Nothing's wrong, not really. It's just really hard because we don't get to see each other very often. I mean, we talk most nights on the phone, but we're kind of running out of things to say. And we see each other on weekends, but I can't help noticing that there are times he'd rather be with his mates, and to be honest, often I'd rather be with you, staying here, than travelling to see him. And if I *really* liked him, I probably wouldn't feel like that, would I?" she asked, voice trembling with uncertainty.

Carlie shook her head. "I'm not sure – Rowan's the only boyfriend I've ever had, and we know how that ended."

"But don't you see, it's partly because of Rowan that I don't feel satisfied with John," her friend wailed. Seeing the pain on Carlie's face, she quickly backpedalled. "Sorry, I don't mean that the way it sounded. It's just that ever since you showed me the letters and cards you wrote each other, I've wanted more. I've wanted someone to love me like Rowan loved you, and to be with someone that I love as much as you loved Rowan," she said.

"I really like John, he's a lovely guy, but we just don't have any of that passion. I'm not desperate to see him when the weekend comes around – I like seeing him, don't get me wrong, but I want someone to feel the way Rowan felt about you, about me. To be that smitten, to want to be with me every minute, to hurt when we're apart. Rowan was cutting his work back because it took him away from you –"

"Jay wasn't real happy about that though," Carlie sighed, but Rhiannon ignored her and kept talking, on a roll now.

"But that's so romantic. You were prepared to make sacrifices for each other, because you loved each other so much. And I guess I've just realised that I don't feel that way about John. He's a great guy, and we really like each other, and we enjoy hanging out together, but I can't imagine he'd be especially devastated if we broke up."

Carlie remembered the words of the red-clad woman from that night by the stream, that Rhiannon wouldn't be upset when her relationship with John ended. She wondered whether she should tell her about Aideen, but her friend was still speaking.

"And maybe even more importantly, I want someone to love *me* – the real me, the magical me – to understand how important this part of my life is to me. Someone who'll inspire me on my magical path, like Rowan did for you. I want a boyfriend who will come to rituals with me and share this aspect of my life, but John has no interest in anything remotely spiritual, and I have no interest in going to his football matches, which is what's important to him, and which I should care about, surely, if I was a good girlfriend? I guess that's why the idea of Jake is so appealing – he's interested in all this too."

Carlie smiled. "So what are you going to do?"

"Goddess, I don't know. I don't think I realised until this exact moment, telling you, that this is how I actually feel about being with him. I mean, I hadn't questioned my being with John – or whether I even wanted to be. But now it kind of sounds like I should break up with him, doesn't it?" she asked, her eyes pleading for answers, for reassurance. Carlie wasn't sure whether her friend wanted her to encourage her to break up with John though, or to insist that she stay with him. She really sucked at this relationship thing.

"I'm so sorry Rhi, I don't know what to say – I'm really not the best person to ask about this kind of stuff. But is it just because you think Jake is cute and he came to a ritual that all of a sudden you're not sure about John, or is it separate to that? Like, if Jake wasn't around, would you still be happy with John?"

Rhiannon sighed. "That's no help, that's just even more questions with even less answers," she said, pouting at her friend.

"What do you need help with?" Jake asked, suddenly reappearing and sliding back into his chair opposite Carlie. She started laughing, while her friend blushed furiously, eyes begging her not to say anything. Still, Carlie figured that she'd been no help to Rhiannon – maybe Jake had more experience in these matters and would have better advice for her.

"Well, we have a friend who's been dating someone for six weeks, and they get on really well, and have a nice time together, but it's not that desperate romantic love that people dream of, you know?" Carlie began, with a wicked grin at Rhiannon.

"So, this friend is wondering whether they should stick it out, because maybe the love will grow over time and they should just be patient? Or should they break up with the person now, even though there's really nothing wrong in their relationship, so that they're both free to find someone better for them, that mystical soul mate who'll inspire them to write poetry, and make them want to become more than they are, to fulfil all their potential, be all that the person sees in them, even if they can't see it themselves yet."

Her breath caught, and she choked on a sob. *Damn it.* She'd meant to keep her voice breezy and light, but she still wasn't able to think about Rowan and how much she'd loved him without her heart being ripped apart all over again.

"Sorry," she whispered to Rhiannon, and stood up abruptly to flee. But the bell rang right at that moment, so her friend stood up with her, since they were going to the same class, and put an arm around her shoulder as they turned away.

Jake sat for a moment, puzzled over what had just happened, and his heart heavy with sadness for Carlie. He'd had to leave behind his high school sweetheart when he moved to England, but what she'd just said made him realise that they hadn't been as in love with each other as he'd thought. It hadn't broken his heart to say goodbye to her, it hadn't even really saddened him, and now that struck him as strange. Shouldn't he be missing her like crazy? Yet he'd barely spared her a thought since he'd arrived here, and had only written to her once – and that was a brief Christmas note on a postcard. He'd felt worse having to leave his dog with his high school buddy Jeff.

He daydreamed his way through his next class, unsettled to realise just how much he was thinking about Carlie, and how many times her face drifted into his mind. She had looked so beautiful at the ritual, so radiant, so full of compassion and empathy, and when he'd opened his eyes and caught her looking at him, he'd got a queer feeling in his stomach, like butterflies.

But he couldn't like her, could he? She was gorgeous, sure, and sweet, and it was nice to hear an Aussie voice, but she was all eaten up over some dead guy, so it was pointless to think about her like that. Yet he couldn't get his mind off her. And the fact that she was so magical, that just drew him to her more.

Sighing, he tried to focus on his class, and was relieved when the bell finally rang. He wasn't sure what had come over him, but he figured that when he saw Carlie again in the next class, he'd realise how silly he was being. What on earth had made him start thinking about her like that? It must have been her talk of soul mates and poetry, mixing up with his memory of her from last night, with the magic of the ritual making her seem so mysterious, so inspiring, so free.

But when he walked in to history and took his usual seat in front of Carlie and Rhiannon, he was surprised to feel flustered. Why was he suddenly obsessing over her? He took a deep breath as he smiled at them both, trying to calm his emotions – and noticed that Rhiannon was blushing. God, what was going on today? He tried to remember their conversation from lunch, and recalled the dilemma Carlie had mentioned. Maybe it was Rhiannon who wasn't sure of her feelings for… what was his name? He vaguely remembered that she was dating someone from Smithfield High. He tried to focus on her.

"So, I was thinking about what we were talking about earlier, and I think your *friend* probably should break up with the person. Which is just my opinion of course, but if you're not in love with the guy, maybe you should end it, so he can find someone who'll love him as he should be loved, and you have the space in your life for someone you could potentially love to fit into." He was looking directly at Rhiannon as he said this, and she blushed a little, but nodded.

"In fact I've been thinking about what you were saying before Carlie, and it made me ponder my own life too. My girlfriend and I decided we'd try the long distance thing, but our chat at lunch made me realise that I don't miss her as much as I probably should. And it's the same as you Rhiannon," he said, letting the pretence they were talking about someone else drop.

"I really like her, and I'm sure if I was in Perth right now we'd still be together, but I've realised today that she's not the love of my life, so it's not fair to her to make her wait for me, and to turn down the possibility of her meeting someone who really does adore her. She's a wonderful girl, don't get me wrong, but she doesn't make my heart sing like in the movies – and she certainly doesn't make me want to be more than I am, or inspire me to be all that I could be, like you said Carlie." And he looked at her with so much love that Rhiannon felt a physical pain in her chest. A longing. Why did the good ones always fall for her friend?

Sighing, she opened her books. Still, maybe he was right – whether or not there were any other potential love interests, was she wasting her time with John, and wasting his time too? And had she just become excited at the possibility of dating someone *like* Jake, not Jake himself – someone who would make magic with her? And now she knew that nothing would ever happen with Jake, should she see if John could be that person?

She had to admit that she'd never actually asked him if he'd like to come to a ritual, she'd just assumed that he wouldn't. Maybe she just had to give him a chance. The Yule Ball had been pagan-themed, and he'd enjoyed that. Terror clutched at her as she contemplated revealing her magical self to him. Could she be brave enough? Did she have the courage to allow herself to be vulnerable enough, to show him her true heart and see what he thought of it? To be rejected after that would be awful, humiliating, but what was the alternative? To hide her real self just to keep the peace? And was it fair to him to not give him the credit for being strong enough to accept her, pointy witch's hat and all?

Chapter 19

Ritual of the Dark Moon

It was Tuesday night, coven night, and the girls had planned their own Imbolc observance, a ritual of forgiveness, new beginnings and moving on. Since it was also the night of the dark moon, they'd decided that it was the perfect time to let go of the darker emotions they'd been battling, especially the resentment and bitterness they had harboured against each other through their misunderstanding, and banish it for good.

It was their first coven meeting in Carlie's new bedroom, and as she set up for their evening she was grateful for the extra space. Soft light flickered from every corner, from tall pillar candles and spirals of tealights in small coloured-glass holders, and incense burned from a wrought iron censer on her dressing table.

At the knock on her door she gazed around and, feeling satisfied with how everything was set up, walked over and welcomed her friend in. "Wow, it's beautiful," Rhiannon said, eyes shining in the candlelight. They sat down on the floor, one on either side of the altar in the centre of the room, and Rhiannon raised her eyebrows. There was an object missing from the representations of the four directions, which wasn't like Carlie.

Her friend just smiled mysteriously. "I thought tonight we should focus on fire," Carlie said. "The fire of the Imbolc flame and new beginnings, and the fire that can burn away pain and regret, and leave only what is pure and good behind."

"That sounds really great, but you don't have fire on the altar," Rhiannon replied, feeling a little embarrassed that she had to point this out to her friend.

With a grin, Carlie placed the small wrought iron cauldron that the red-robed woman had given her in the centre of the altar space, then handed the long red-velvet-wrapped parcel to Rhiannon. "A gift for you," she said simply.

Her friend raised her eyebrows again. "Really? Another one?"

"Really," she giggled. "The woman in red this time, Aideen. Do you know what that name means?"

"Fire," Rhiannon said, gazing down at the parcel in her lap.

"Of course," Carlie laughed. Brauna, the sweet blue-clad woman of the mists, had represented water, and Brianna, in her soft green robes, had symbolised the earth. It made perfect sense that the woman dressed in the long red cloak symbolised fire.

"When did you meet her?" Rhiannon demanded, curiosity burning in her voice.

Carlie paused. Would her friend be hurt that she hadn't told her before now? "Um, two weeks ago, on the full moon," she replied.

It wasn't really a lie – she had met her then too, it was just that she'd first met Aideen five weeks ago, during her New Year's Eve farewell-to-Rowan ritual, and had seen her again and received the gifts two weeks after that, on her way home from Mike's. It was her third and most recent encounter that had happened two weeks ago.

"I'm sorry I hadn't told you about her, or the gifts, before – it's just, well... We haven't had a proper Tuesday night coven meeting, what with school plays and studying and Imbolc prepping, for so long," Carlie said, realising how lame that sounded as she spoke.

But Rhiannon shook her head. "It's okay," she whispered, knowing that it was her own fault that the woman in red had gone to Carlie when she was on her own, rather than when they were together. She'd hurt her friend badly, and as a result she didn't deserve all the magic she'd had access to before.

"That's not true," Carlie said sharply, and Rhiannon stared at her in horror. Was she reading her mind now?

"I can't read your mind Rhi, don't worry," she explained, reacting to the look on her friend's face rather than any divinatory powers, and wanting to set her mind at ease. "But I can sense your sadness, and that's why Aideen gave us these gifts I think, so we can use them to burn away the memories of past hurt between us, yet not burn the bridge that links us, because that's what we want to keep. And I reckon she's right. But please hurry up and open it! She gave me the cauldron unwrapped, but said that this one is for you, and I've been dying to know what's inside. So come on, unwrap it so we can see what it is! I have an idea, but I'm not sure I'm right," she said excitedly.

Bursting with curiosity, Rhiannon untied the ribbon and opened the parcel, then smiled. On the top was a small wrought iron tealight holder, with a vanilla-scented tealight candle nestled within it. Laughing, she lit it and placed it in the south of their altar, as the missing element she'd wondered about.

Carlie grinned too. "Lucky guess huh? Otherwise you might have thought I'd forgotten the fourth element."

Rhiannon blushed a little – she *had* assumed that – then turned back to the parcel. She gasped at the beauty of the two elaborate wrought iron candle holders, both wreathed in sculpted metal ivy leaves, one with a sun on it, and one with a moon. Two tall candles, one silver and one gold, lay beneath them, and she placed the silver one in the moon holder and the gold one in the sun holder, then positioned them on the altar too, one on either side of the cauldron.

A small folded note caught her eye, and she slowly unfurled it and read it out. "My dearest Rhiannon, here is some light to illuminate your own light, when you feel that you are drowning in darkness and cannot see what others see in you. Please trust yourself, and your worth." Tears welled in her eyes. How could a woman who'd never met her know how she would feel tonight, when she'd passed on the gift two weeks ago?

Carlie smiled at her friend as she lit the candles, then settled back in the cushions to prepare herself for the head space she required for the ritual. Breathing in the peacefulness of the dark, candlelit room, the sweet scent of the incense and the quiet exhalations of Luther and Luna as they slept on her bed, she felt her shoulders relax. She'd missed their Tuesday night magical meetings, and the sense of enchantment that they created together. And suddenly she knew that she didn't want to share it with anyone else – adding another person would throw off their carefully crafted balance, and the comfort they felt when it was just the two of them.

"I agree," Rhiannon said softly, and Carlie opened her eyes and smiled at her. "Still reading my mind, huh?" she asked, but she was amused, not angry. Her friend laughed.

"No, it's just that I was thinking the same thing. I've missed this too. Jake can join us at the sabbats and moon rituals, but there's no need for him to totally cramp our magical style."

Carlie laughed too. "Cramp our style?"

"Yes, we are very stylish – just look at us," Rhiannon said with a grin, sweeping her hand in front of them to take in their bulky woollen jumpers and the thick tights they both wore under their velvet dresses. "Now, how shall we begin things tonight?"

"I thought we could write down the things we want to let go of, then burn them in our Imbolc fire," Carlie replied, waving her hand over the cauldron in the centre of the altar, which Rhiannon saw was filled with sabbat herbs.

"We can harness the spirit of the dark moon to burn away our regrets, extinguish our bitterness, and release all the stuff we want to get rid of," she added. "Then after that we can use the energy of fire and the Imbolc flame to ignite our new passion and purpose, and make our own fresh start."

"That sounds perfect," Rhiannon said, then sighed. "I really am sorry Carlie," she whispered, sorrow colouring her voice.

"I know you are. And I'm sorry too."

"Why are *you* sorry?" her friend asked.

"I've been sad and angry, and full of the injustice of it all. I'm sure I haven't been all sweetness and light to be around."

"You've been fine," Rhiannon admitted softly. "And I'm glad that you called me out on my awful behaviour. You needed a friend and instead you got a jealous harpy, someone who wanted you to get over such a heartbreaking thing in an instant, just so I didn't feel uncomfortable. I really am so sorry. I was selfish to harp on and on about how you should just 'get over it', as though you can just flick a switch and turn off all the pain."

Carlie smiled sadly. "True."

"I mean, god, it's only six weeks today since… well, since you lost Rowan," Rhiannon said. "So you be as sad as you need to be, for as long as you need to be, and please know that I am here for you now. For what it's worth, I really regret the way I treated you, and I promise I will be more considerate in the future."

Reaching over to hug her friend, Carlie was happy to realise that their ritual of forgiveness and moving forward had already begun, even before they'd stepped out the boundary of their sacred space between the worlds and welcomed the deities and the directions. Rose was right, elaborate rituals were wonderful, but intent was the most important thing. What was in your heart meant so much more than just having the right herbs or ritual tools – although she loved all of that too.

"Okay, ready?" Rhiannon asked, and Carlie nodded, then began to slow her breathing as her friend cast the sacred circle and invoked the elements and directions. Once that was done, Carlie called on the god and the goddess to join them, aiding them on this dark moon night as they went within on their own personal journeys of introspection and reflection.

Opening her eyes, she handed Rhiannon a piece of pale green paper and a gold pen, then picked up her own and began to write what was in her heart.

Dear Bridie, maiden goddess of love and healing,
Tonight I call on you to take away our pain, guilt and anger, to assist us in letting go of our resentment, and to fill us both with love and contentment.
Please guard my heart as it heals from its loss. I know that it's better to have loved and lost than never to have experienced such

pure joy, and I am grateful to have been loved so deeply by such a beautiful soul, and to have been able to share so many precious moments with him, but I still ache with missing him. So please help me let go of my resentment and anger that he was taken away so soon, and dampen my fiery sense of injustice...
Perhaps most importantly, help me forgive and forget with Rhiannon. I don't want to resent her, or dwell on my bitterness at her actions. I know that she's sorry, so guide me to ignite the forgiveness I feel in my head, on a conscious level, into my heart.
So mote it be xx

Glancing up, she saw that Rhiannon had finished writing her piece too, so she passed her hands over the cauldron, infusing the herbs with her wishes, then lit them up. "We're shaking off the negativity and burning it away," Carlie said, smiling as the scent of sandalwood, basil and bay infused the room. "Ready?"

Taking a deep breath, she gently fed her piece of paper into the flames, watching as it blackened and burned away. For a moment she saw an image of the red-clad woman, and she flinched as flames threatened to burn her where she sat. Aideen's eyes flashed with fire, with danger, and her smile had a cruel edge to it.

"You do not need to be afraid Carlie, I will not hurt you," she crooned, as she reached in and tore open her soul. "Fire can destroy, but it creates as well. It can be healing as well as harmful. Love is like a fire, as you have learned, and there is a cost for dancing within it, but also a reward. Let this fire inflame you with the courage to take chances and risk everything, harness it to scorch and burn away your pain, then let yourself be cleansed by it. Please Carlie, let it spark new passion, inspiration, decisiveness and intention, and get you to the heart of your fears," she whispered.

Rhiannon touched her hand. "Are you okay?"

Startled, Carlie looked around the room. There was no fire, no flames, no woman in red. "Yes, I'm good, your turn," she whispered, and watched as Rhiannon did the same. As the last of the smoke drifted skyward, they both felt a shift in the room, and a great weight lifting from their shoulders, and their hearts.

"So what will we fill ourselves with instead?" Carlie asked as the fire burned down. "What's your purpose and passion for the year ahead? What new beginning do you want to bring to life?"

Rhiannon took a deep breath, centring herself as she delved into the depths of her heart, and her eyes flickered in the light of the candles. "I wanted to burn away my impatience and my guilt," she said at last, breathing her words into the cauldron. "And I also asked for the fires of compassion to light me up, and to help me develop patience and caution when I deal with anyone. Especially with you, but with others too. With guys even..."

Carlie frowned. "But what about your open heart, the passion that's so much a part of you? Don't punish yourself because of what happened with us, or rein in your free spirit and your love of life. That's not what this is about, surely?" she asked.

"You have to dive in, take a risk, be brave – you taught me that. And it might not always work out, but you have to try. It's the only way to live, to grow, to discover. Otherwise you'll regret not finding out what could have happened, and always wonder. Because you only regret the things that you *don't* do, right? Imagine if I'd followed my plan, and not stayed in London for the party you made us go to, where I talked to Rowan all night," she said.

"I wouldn't feel so terrible, so distraught, so lost and alone, right now – but I wouldn't have had the time with him that I did either, the privilege of loving and being loved, and I wouldn't give that up for any amount of peace now, as hard as it is to cope with the loss." Her voice was sad, but there was a thread of steel in it.

"No regrets, that's our motto, right?" Carlie added. "That's what Rowan would have said too – live every moment to the full, because you never know how long you have." There were tears in her eyes as she spoke, but she felt strong.

Rhiannon crawled across the floor to her and hugged her tight. "Here's to living every moment," she said.

Carlie smiled too. She had a best friend again. A new magical ally. And the power and passion of fire.

Chapter 20

Pale Green Stars

A few mornings later, Carlie woke up shivering, and stretched out her legs, hoping to burrow her feet back under Luther's warm body. With him it was as though she had her own personal hot water bottle at the end of her bed, one that was far more soothing and long lasting than the rubbery kind. A stab of fear shot through her when she couldn't feel him, and she sat up abruptly. Luna squeaked as she tumbled from Carlie's pillow onto the bed next to her, and she scooped the little kitten up in her arms, smiling at her as she stroked her adorably fuzzy head and tiny ears.

"Sorry lovely Luna, I didn't mean to startle you. Or myself. I must have had a bad dream, because it scared me when I couldn't see Luther, which is just plain silly. No doubt he's downstairs with Gran, sharing the heater with her," she said, then glanced at the clock. "Oh, and probably eating too, because it's definitely time for breakfast. We should go down and join them, huh? Are you hungry little one?" she asked.

Luna miaowed back at her, still such a tiny sound, and Carlie laughed. She was such a cutie. Pulling her warmest coat on over her pyjamas and slipping her feet into thick woollen socks, she picked up the kitten and held her close to her heart, crooning to her as she walked down the stairs.

"Morning Gran," Carlie called out as she and the kitten waltzed into the blissful warmth of the kitchen.

Rose looked up from the book she was reading and smiled at them. "Hello Sweetheart, hello little Luna," she said, and the little black ball of fur miaowed at her happily. "I've put some milk out for the cats, and I just made a big pot of chai, if you'd like a cup. Is Luther with you guys?"

The alarm Carlie had managed to set aside earlier slammed back into her, taking her breath away. Frowning, she shook her head, trying to clear it, then all three of them, as one, looked outside into the frosty back garden. The sun was rising, casting a pale golden glow over the world, and the green of the grass seemed more vivid than usual, yesterday's snow melted away and leaving a particular lushness to the garden.

She froze, her heart thudding, then set Luna down on the floor by the saucer of milk and flew out the back door. Her feet were freezing on the cold grass, the dew seeping through her woollen socks, but she didn't notice. Panic washed over Rose as she followed her granddaughter, not sure what she'd seen, but her emotions so tightly woven with the young girl's that she knew *something* was desperately wrong, even if she didn't yet know what it actually was.

Carlie had sunk down onto her knees in the dirt under the old apple tree, next to the rosemary bush she'd planted in memory of Rowan. Tears spilled over and traced an icy path down each of her cheeks, as her nameless dread finally found its reason. She reached out her arms, distraught, then rocked back and forth on the ground, Luther's lifeless body clutched to her chest, eyes streaming with tears, mind elsewhere, unseeing, recoiling in horror as she tried to understand what the frozen body in her arms could mean.

Rose reached her arms around her devastated granddaughter, heart breaking for the young girl's pain, and aching for her own. As a priestess she knew the cycles of life began, ended and began again, but as a woman she was desperately sad to have lost the companion she had loved and lived with for so long, who had worked magic with her, healed and helped her through loss, and given her something to care for when she had nothing else. And as guardian to this fragile girl in her arms, she was terrified. She could barely begin to imagine how this would affect her after all her other losses.

It was a tiny paw on Carlie's leg that brought her back to the present, back to the pain. She stared down at the delicate ball of black fur perched on the grass beside her, gazing up at her with wise and patient green eyes. The kitten was shivering as deeply as she was, and for a moment she marvelled at the effort it must have taken her to push her way through the cat door on her own and cover the vast expanse of back garden to get to her and Rose.

And to Luther. Poor dead Luther. Her eyes misted as she took in his still body, felt the chill of his bones against her heart, felt the yawning pit of loss and despair opening up around her, ready to pull her down into it again. And this time she just didn't know if she'd have the strength to climb back out. The sides got steeper every time, and far more difficult, and the effort just seemed too much to face once more.

"Miaow." It was the tiniest of sounds, but Carlie looked back down at the kitten, at her trusting gaze and small body wracked by shudders of cold and sadness, and felt the cord linking her to this tiny creature, and to life. It seemed tenuous still, but it was there, the possibility of a way up the steep sides. Luna was even more delicate, even more needy, than she was. Her eyes lifted to her grandma's, and she saw the agony of loss there too.

"I'm so sorry Gran," she whispered. "I know you loved him more than anything, and that you shared so many years, so many experiences, together. And I'm so sorry he had to look after me these last months, that you didn't have as much time as you should have with him." Her voice cracked, and she stopped, unable to go on.

Rose leaned over and hugged Carlie again, Luther's body cold and stiff between them. "And you Sweetheart, I'm so sorry for your loss. Before you trusted me, he was there for you, and I'll be forever grateful to him for that. He was the dearest friend, the closest companion, for both of us."

Gently she took Luther's body from her granddaughter, holding him close to her, and gazing down at the kitten as she awkwardly tried to climb her way up into Carlie's lap. Without conscious thought the young girl reached down and scooped her up, holding her shivering body close, against her heart, as she had that first night they'd met the sweet little kitten.

Bravely smiling through her tears, Rose looked down at Luther's body. "He knew. Luther knew that he didn't have long here, so he brought you Luna. To give you a reason to stay," she whispered. She couldn't bring herself to finish that sentence – to not just stay here, in England, with Rose, but to stay alive. How much more pain could this poor child bear?

"And you," Carlie said gently.

"No Sweetheart, I didn't need another reason, because I have you." The truth of her words hit Rose as she spoke them, and warmth flooded through her. "Don't you know how much you mean to me yet? What you've brought to my life?" she asked.

"It doesn't seem enough," Carlie sighed, pain writ large across her face. "Luther was part of you, part of us. How could he leave us like this?"

Tenderly Rose tucked a fallen strand of Carlie's hair behind her ear, the way Rowan used to do it. "He didn't want to go, didn't want to leave us, it was just his time. And really, he had a far longer life than most cats – I think he made a bargain with someone, or some thing, to be able to stay here with us longer than is usual. He wouldn't want us to be sad, he'd want us to celebrate all that we were able to share with him, and be grateful for the time we had," she said, though tears still choked her voice.

"And you are more than enough Carlie," Rose added firmly, and the young girl looked up at her, surprise on her face. Her grandmother never called her by her name, and it seemed that she'd used it to add impact to her words. How strange that her own name could sound more loving and important to her than the endearment her grandma usually used. Yet none of that changed the pain she felt now.

"It's not fair though!" Carlie moaned. The ball of fluff in her arms squirmed, and she looked down just as she felt the little paw on her face, then saw Luna's tiny pink tongue flick out to mop up her tears, taking the pain into her own body, and trying to leave only strength for her new protector.

A warmth spread through Carlie, almost against her will, and she half-smiled down at the kitten and her earnest little face as she busied herself comforting her new friend. "Thank you little one," she breathed. "I guess Luther knew me even better than I realised. And clearly I need you just as much as you need me."

Rose felt some of the weight lift from her heart as she saw the change in Carlie's face, saw the flash of joy and gratitude hiding within the sadness. Still holding Luther's body, she closed her eyes and sent a prayer out into the universe, a prayer of thanksgiving for the years she'd had with her furry companion, a prayer expressing how grateful she was for his love of her granddaughter, and a prayer to send him peacefully from this world to the next.

She wondered whether she'd still feel him with her – or see him, the way Carlie had seen Luther's mother Shadow – and the sensation of a paw on her hand, and what felt like the brush of warm fur around her ankles, sent waves of relief through her. Perhaps her familiar hadn't abandoned her just yet. But it also made her aware of just how cold it was on the frozen earth, and how cramped her legs had become, kneeling as she was in the dirt, and she shook herself. Letting herself or Carlie catch a cold or worse was not going to help Luther. Steeling herself, she placed his body gently on the ground then got awkwardly to her feet.

"Come inside Sweetheart. You and Luna must be freezing to death," she said, then cringed at her choice of words. "I'm going to get Luther a blanket, then I thought maybe we could have a little ceremony this afternoon, and bury him under the apple tree. But you need to get out of those wet clothes, and those wet socks, and get warm, and Luna needs to get out of the cold too, and have some breakfast. She's still only small, so she needs us to look after her."

Carlie stood up reluctantly, stamping the foot that had gone to sleep on the icy ground, and finally noticing just how wet and cold her soggy woollen socks were. She should have waited to put some shoes on, she knew, but when she'd seen Luther's still body she hadn't been able to think of anything else, she'd just had to get out to him, see if he was okay. The weight of grief threatened to squash her again, and drag her back down to the ground, but Rose took her arm and gently led her back inside.

"A hot shower for you Missy, then warm clothes, and boots this time. Go on, upstairs. I'll heat Luna up and get her some food."

Too exhausted, both mentally and physically, to argue, Carlie headed up to her room to get some dry clothes, then entered the small ensuite, turned on the hot water and stood under the full blast of the shower. Some of her bone-deep weariness and tension began to ease as the scalding water fell on her shoulders, but she also flashed back to other times that she'd stood in here under the falling water, feeling totally numb after learning of Rowan's death, then just as devastated still as she psyched herself up to go to his funeral a week later. Hot tears splashed down into the bath tub, mixing with the water streaming down the plug hole.

An image of Luna's delicate little face popped into her mind though, and she took a deep breath. Yes, she had to focus on the positives. Her grandma was right, it was terribly sad that Luther had died, but he had lived a long and full existence, and been so cared for and adored. He had brought so much love and healing to Rose, and to Carlie, and his life should be celebrated. Losing him was not so much a tragedy – as her parents' untimely deaths had been, and as Rowan's accident had been – but a sad yet real part of life.

Suddenly she realised the real and deeper meaning of Rose's rituals, of her honouring of the wheel of the seasonal year as a metaphor for the wheel of life, and why the wise priestess could be sad that Luther had died, but not raging with the injustice of his passing. That was the truth of nature – things were born, and they died – and it wasn't good or bad, or happy or sad, it just was. She knew that her grandmother also believed that Luther had gone to another place now, and could perhaps communicate with her from there, which would be some comfort to a person who was grieving.

And Rose also held to the idea, or at least the hope, that as well as birth and death there was also rebirth, and she could see why that would be such a reassuring belief system.

Turning the water off, she quickly dried herself, pulled on her jeans with one of her mum's thick woollen jumpers, and warm socks and boots, then slowly made her way back downstairs. Rose was at the stove, cooking a pot of cinnamon porridge, while Luna lay curled up by the heater in Luther's old basket, her tiny ears twitching as though she was dreaming.

A flash of irritation slammed into Carlie, that the kitten could already have moved into Luther's bed, but then she felt the older cat's steadying presence around her, and closed her eyes for a moment, seeing his wise old eyes gazing at her, his face smiling as he let her know that he wanted Luna to be comfortable, to be loved – that he had brought her to the cottage so the three of them could all look after each other.

Smiling that her imagination already had her communicating with Luther, she accepted that his basket no longer mattered, his body no longer mattered. He had no need of those things now, and she had to let go of her attachment to him and focus forward, on life, and on love, and on Luna.

"Can I help you Gran?" she asked, carefully averting her eyes from the back garden as she turned away from Luna and walked over to lean against the kitchen bench.

"Thank you Sweetheart, that would be great. I have to go into the healing centre for a few hours, so if you could do any of this –" she began, her arm sweeping around to encompass the three recipe books lying open on the bench, and the containers of flour, jars of spices, bowls of nuts and collection of fruits and vegetables strewn next to them. "That would be wonderful."

When her granddaughter nodded, Rose gave her a quick hug, then picked up her bag and raced out the door. Which was kind of odd, Carlie mused – she'd thought that today was her grandma's day off, but maybe she'd got it wrong. Hastily she spooned out a bowl of porridge and brewed herself a pot of earl grey tea, then she leaned over and examined the recipes she was supposed to whip up.

Gulping at their complexity, she rolled up her sleeves and got to work, determined to do her best. The hours flew by as she sifted and stirred, fried and steamed, baked and even bottled – Rose had left the ingredients and some sketchy instructions for an apple and cinnamon jam that smelled heavenly, and was probably designed to be eaten on the chai spiced bread she had beaten and kneaded into submission, and which was now rising under a tea towel before she would pop it in the oven to bake. Which she could do as soon as the nutmeg custard tarts and the delicate vegetable and ricotta filo pockets and various savoury mini pies had cooked until golden brown, and the rosemary and baked vegie quiches had firmed up.

She did have one shaky moment, when she'd forgotten what she was avoiding and glanced out the window into the back garden, her eyes staring for long moments at Luther's body, wrapped in a dark blanket emblazoned with pale green stars, before her mind took in what she was seeing, and the tears started to flow again.

Pouring herself another mug of tea, she'd gone over towards the heater and sat on the floor next to Luna, who opened her eyes at her approach, stretched and yawned adorably, then clambered awkwardly into her lap, curling up again and starting to purr as Carlie stroked her soft head. Equilibrium at least partially restored, she'd gently placed Luna back in her basket, where she'd settled down and was soon snoring peacefully, and gone back to work.

Chapter 21

The Honouring of a Dear Friend

When Carlie heard the key in the front door she looked up at the clock and realised it was already 3pm, and she'd spent the last six hours cooking. No wonder she was hungry. Putting the kettle on, she filled the teapot with fresh leaves, and was pulling a tray of apricot scones out of the oven when Rose wandered into the kitchen with a bag over her shoulder.

"Cup of tea?" Carlie asked, and her grandma nodded gratefully and sat down at the table next to Luna. "I've cooked everything that you had marked, even the jam. Is there a ritual I've forgotten about or something?"

Rose shook her head. "No Sweetheart, I just figured that having something to do while I was out would help you keep your mind off things," she replied, and looked slightly sheepish. "And we'll get to have a really yummy dinner tonight."

For a moment Carlie glared at her grandmother, then she started laughing. She could have felt angry that she'd wasted her time, but her grandma was right – it had helped her to have something serious to focus on, and suddenly the surprising complexity of some of the recipes made sense.

"So would you like a warm apricot scone with freshly whipped butter and some apple and cinnamon jam then?" she asked wryly.

"I'm having some, because I was so wrapped up in getting these dishes made properly that I forgot to have lunch. But you were right, the baking did also distract me from being quite as sad as I would have been otherwise."

After pouring out some milk for Luna, Carlie took the mugs of tea, a platter of scones and the dishes of jam and butter over to the table. "And it was a nice touch, having to whip the butter myself in order to get the buttermilk for the scones," she said, tone a little accusatory, but mostly amused.

"Sorry about that," Rose said, trying not to grin. She lifted the bag onto the table and started rummaging through it.

"I thought we could have a ceremony for Luther this afternoon, so we can lay him to rest before nightfall," she added. "Do you feel up to it Sweetheart?"

Inhaling deeply, Carlie straightened her back and squared her shoulders, marshalling her courage, then she nodded. "Should I get changed?" she asked nervously, but Rose shook her head.

"Luther would just want us to be warm and comfortable, and it's getting really cold out there. The sun's still setting pretty early."

As they drank their tea and ate their scones, Rose outlined the ritual she'd constructed, but told Carlie to jump in with any ideas she had, and to feel free to change it as they went.

"Luther loved us, the ordinary-women us, more than he cared about the priestess role, and he wouldn't want us feeling pressure to do anything too elaborate. We just want to show him how much we love him, and thank him for all he gave us, and send him safely on his way to wherever he's going next," she said, voice warm with affection.

Still feeling apprehensive, but trying to relax, Carlie followed her grandmother into the lounge room, and watched as she set up an altar on the floor, laying out a beautiful silk scarf then reverently placing the representations of the elements in the four directions. There was a small golden candle in the south for fire, a silver chalice in the west for water, a pretty pink rose quartz in the north for earth, and a dish of incense in the east for air – she could smell lavender and mint, and smiled as Rose added catnip to the blend and lit the charcoal disc. In the centre of the altar the priestess added four pieces of sugilite, a crystal associated with crossing over, in a small golden dish she'd brought from the shop.

Then just as she was about to step out the circle and create the sacred world-within-a-world they would perform their ritual inside, Luna padded into the room and awkwardly hauled herself up onto Carlie's lap. Rose smiled over at the two of them, then raised her crystal-tipped wand.

Within this boundary a circle formed,
With this energy raised, sacred space is born.
Goddess, see that our love for Luther is true,
As we entrust our dear friend's soul to you.

The hairs on Carlie's neck rose as she felt the power shifting in the room, and Luna clumsily stood up in her lap, back arched for a moment as her fur stood on end. But the kitten calmed herself when Rose sat down opposite Carlie on the floor and took her hands, and the energy around them settled. Lighting the candle, the priestess began her invocation.

Power of the south, and energies of fire,
Please hold Luther safe as he journeys through you,
Let him know he'll remain as a flame in our souls,
And we'll hold him in our hearts as a friend so true.

Motioning to Carlie, Rose handed her the glass bottle of new-moon-charged spring water, and Carlie poured some into the chalice as she shakily, shyly, began her invocation.

Power of the west, and energies of water,
Please hold Luther close as he journeys through you,
Cleanse his spirit and soothe his fears,
As we hold him in our memories as a friend so true.

Rose smiled at her granddaughter, then lifted the rose quartz crystal and held it to her heart as she invoked the powers of earth.

Power of the north, and energies of earth,
Please hold Luther safe as he journeys through you,
Ground him with our love and lend him your strength,
As we hold him in our hearts as a friend so true.

Looking over at Carlie, she inclined her head in the direction of the incense and smiled gently, proudly. She was impressed with her granddaughter's strength, and the new confidence she'd developed to take part in their rituals, especially one as sad and deeply personal as this one. If she was honest, she'd expected that Carlie would have left it all to her, not wanting to say anything aloud, but she had drawn on her love for Luther to give her the courage to act and to speak.

Fanning the incense through the air and inhaling it deeply, the young girl invoked the last of the elements.

Power of the east, and energies of air,
Please hold Luther close as he journeys through you,
Let him know we are with him in spirit, as he is with us,
And we'll hold him in our hearts forever as a friend so true.

After that Rose raised her arms skyward, eyes closed, as she drew down the goddess and welcomed her into their circle, into their grief, and into their love for their animal companion. Carlie felt a shift in the air and sensed Luther with them for a moment, paw on her knee. Then she leaned over to comfort Luna, who was glancing frantically around the room, trying to understand the changing energies.

The priestess glamour came down over Rose, and she began to speak, voice quiet yet immensely powerful. "Thank you Luther, for your kind and loving companionship, for helping me through my losses, and for being part of my magical life for so long. Even as a tiny kitten you could sense when I needed you, could sense people's energies, and could sense the swirl of magic when it visited us. You gave so much of yourself, yet asked so little in return, and I hope you always knew how much you meant to me," she said, her voice raspy with unshed tears.

"You also had a wonderful sense of fun and cheekiness, and I am grateful that you added levity to my life too, with your lightness of being and your love of merriment. For all that you were my familiar, and walked other dimensions with me in ritual and spellcasting, it was our ordinary moments that I treasure the most, cuddling up on the couch with me while I read a book in winter, playing with me in the garden and helping me dig when I was planting flowers or herbs, sitting on the back step with me and basking in the sunshine as I drank my morning coffee. And I think it will be the cat and the companion that I miss the most, even more so than my familiar."

Rose paused for a moment, overcome with emotion, and Carlie smiled sadly as she watched the joy and celebration mix with the sadness and grief in her grandmother's face, and in the set of her body. Too choked up to continue talking, she finally motioned for her granddaughter to speak, if she wanted to.

"Sweet Luther, I will miss you so much, and I'm so grateful for everything you did for me, keeping me company when I first got here, when I felt so alone..." She hesitated, embarrassed, and looked at her grandmother with eyes full of apology, but Rose just smiled and waved her hand at her to go on.

"I'm so grateful that you journeyed with me into my dreams, protecting me from nightmares, drawing me out with your little paw on my face when there was evil lurking there."

Rose's eyebrows lifted in surprise, but she didn't interrupt.

"And I'm so grateful to you for seeing Rowan's pure heart, and helping me to know that it was okay to trust him – and for warning him when he had to leave."

Rose's eyebrows shot up even further, and Carlie blushed, then nervously admitted that the first day Rowan had visited her, Luther had come in and somehow told him that Rose was on her way home, so he could leave before they were discovered. But rather than being angry, the priestess surprised her granddaughter by laughing heartily at that story, then whispering her thanks to Luther for being Carlie's confidante when she'd so sorely needed one.

Pushing through her sadness, Carlie continued. "Mostly I'm just so grateful to you for being so kind, for accepting me as I am, and seeing the good in me when I couldn't, when I was so angry and bitter that I thought there was no hope left for me." Wiping a tear from her eye, she paused for a moment and tried to compose herself.

"And thank you so much for knowing what we needed and bringing Luna to us. I promise that I will love her and care for her, and make you proud of me. Blessed be sweet Luther. Hail and farewell."

Bowing her head, Carlie sat there in silence, feeling the sadness wash over her, but concentrating only on her love for the creature who had been so dear to her, and her gratitude for all that he had taught her and brought her.

Rose gazed over at her granddaughter, proud of her that she was holding it together so well, and focusing on the joy they'd shared with Luther rather than the emptiness they both felt now that he was gone. She was struggling herself, although she'd presided over more than her fair share of funerals, memorials and rituals of farewell. So easy it had been then, to talk of the journey to the next world, to convince the mourners that their loved one was going to a better place, or a good place at the very least. That the person or animal would still be with them in spirit, still be part of them and their life.

And yet for all that she tried to convince herself of that now, she felt the hole in her heart where her familiar had resided, and acknowledged that while he may still be with her in some way, on some plane of existence, it wasn't the same. She couldn't hold him close or hear him purring as she stroked his soft head. So were her reassurances to Carlie, to her community, nothing but a lie?

A soft paw on her leg brought Rose back from whichever dark place she'd been, and she opened her eyes and looked down to see Luna gazing up at her, as though she knew what she was thinking, and was offering herself as a gift of healing. Laughing, she picked the kitten up and held her close.

"Thank you Luther," she said, smiling and looking skyward. "You will be in my heart forever. And thank you for the reminder of the wheel of life," she added, as she kissed Luna's soft head then gently placed her in her lap.

Leaning forward over the altar, she picked up three of the four sugilite crystals that had sat in the golden dish in the centre throughout their ritual. Handing one to Carlie, she then placed another one under Luna's little paw, and squeezed the third one tightly in her hand. "One crystal to represent each of us – you, me, Luna and Luther," she explained to Carlie.

"I thought we'd keep the four of them together here in the lounge room, in their dish. They've been charged with our love and our loss, and our gratitude for every day we had together, so I thought it would be a nice reminder, the energies of all four of us intertwined and woven together, throughout time."

Carlie sighed. "That's really beautiful."

Luna miaowed, a contented little sound, and pushed her crystal towards Rose.

"Thank you little one," she said, smiling as she picked up the crystal and placed it back in the dish, alongside hers and Luther's. Carlie kissed her crystal and added it to the others, then Rose positioned the dish back in the centre of the altar and began to farewell the elements and the goddess. It was time.

Carlie felt the magic swirling around her, felt her skin tingle as she watched the power collect around her grandmother and touch each of the elements in turn. Luna stared around her again, wild eyed yet safe in Rose's lap, and seeming more curious than scared. Carlie wondered what the little kitten could see, what she was feeling. Could she still communicate with Luther?

And was Luther now with his mum Shadow, the sweet ghost cat she'd met in the cottage in the mists? That thought gave her comfort, and strength, and after the circle was closed she stood up, gently lifted Luna and placed her on the floor, then took her grandmother's hands and helped her up. It felt complete.

"So, a cup of tea and one of the many platters of cookies I baked this morning?" Carlie asked, but Rose shook her head. "No Sweetheart, we still have to bury our little friend, and let him settle peacefully for his long rest."

Carlie blushed. How could she have forgotten that part of the ritual? Guessing that it had been wishful thinking on her part, that they wouldn't have to face the harsh physical reality, or perhaps denial, she began to wonder how they would do it, and whether Rose had a shovel or they would have to dig the grave with a small gardening spade. Blanching at the thought, she pulled her coat more tightly around herself, and led the way out into the garden.

Catching sight of a neatly dug hole beneath the apple tree, she stopped, startled, and almost tripped when Luna barrelled into her ankles from behind her. "You did this Gran?" she asked. "When?"

"While you were in the shower this morning."

"But I could have helped you, or done it myself," Carlie argued.

"I know Sweetheart, and I appreciate that, but you've been through enough. And I wanted to do it. It seemed right somehow, to be preparing my familiar for the next life, when I had been with him when he came into the world too."

They stopped side by side at the edge of the tiny grave, shivering from the cold and the emotion of it all. A lump rose in Carlie's throat, but she swung down when Luna looked as though she was about to jump into the hole, and quickly scooped her up. "Come on little one, you stay with me."

Rose leaned down, looking suddenly frail again, and picked up Luther's blanket-wrapped body from where it rested against the trunk of the apple tree. She held it close to her heart one last time, and whispered something softly to him, then laid him reverently in the grave. Picking up a handful of the dirt piled along the edge, she gently placed it on top of his body, then turned to Carlie to let her do the same. Her granddaughter did, then sank to the ground, the sight of the grave and the small body wrapped within the star-emblazoned blanket bringing back so many sad memories that she could no longer bear the weight of them all. Luna bounced over to her side and curled up against her knees, lending her warmth and support, and Rose placed a comforting hand on her shoulder.

They stayed there together for a long time, the three of them, lost in thought, before Rose carefully filled in the rest of the grave then scattered handfuls of rose petals on the bare earth on top. When a misty rain began to fall, just as the sun was starting to set, Rose squeezed her granddaughter's shoulder and told her firmly that they had to go inside. So Carlie stood, eyes unseeing, and followed her grandmother back into the warmth of the kitchen.

The scent of freshly baked cookies and spices hit them as soon as they walked inside, swirling around them. Carlie's tummy rumbled, and she suddenly realised how hungry she was. It seemed insensitive to eat though, but Rose frowned and gestured sternly at her to sit down at the cosy little table near the heater. As Luna leaped up into her lap, Rose put the kettle on for tea then fussed around in the kitchen, filling a platter with a selection of the treats Carlie had baked that morning, and another with more substantial fare – spinach and feta triangles, sweet pepper tarts and corn and mushroom quiches, some of them still warm from the oven.

Forcing a smile, Carlie nibbled on a vegie filo pastry and made herself focus on the positives. By the time there was a knock on the door an hour later, she was giggling at her grandma's stories of Luther as a cheeky young kitten, digging up her newly planted herb garden and shredding the new altar cloths she'd painstakingly sewn from rare and expensive fabric someone had gifted her in exchange for healings.

Still smiling, she opened the door to see Rhiannon standing on the front step, looking forlorn and bedraggled. "Come in," she said, hugging her hello then dragging her quickly inside and shutting the door on the now icy wind. "Are you okay?"

Rhiannon shrugged. "I've been better, but I'm okay. I just had a really weird day with John," she explained as she entered the kitchen and greeted Rose. "Oh my god, all this food looks amazing! What's the occasion?" she asked, as Rose instructed her to take a seat and brought her over a plate, then went back and put the kettle on to brew another pot of tea.

"I'm afraid Luther passed away this morning," Rose said softly, and Rhiannon's face registered shock and sadness, before she turned to Carlie with fear in her eyes.

"Are you okay?" she whispered, and Carlie nodded.

"I've been better, but I'm okay," she replied, echoing her friend's words from moments earlier. Luna's little head popped up from Carlie's lap and peered over the table at Rhiannon, who couldn't control the grin that spread across her face.

"She's such a cutie!" she giggled. "But how are you really going Carlie? And what happened? Will you have a funeral? Sorry, perhaps I should leave you some time to reply."

"Gran said it was just old age, and there was nothing we could have done, so we're trying to focus on the fact that he had a great, and remarkably long, life, and be grateful for the time we did have with him. And he didn't suffer, so we're doing our best to convince ourselves not to be too sad, and that it's just part of the enchanted wheel of life – but it's really hard," she said with a sigh.

"Do you think he knew he was going to die? Is that why he brought Luna to you?" Rhiannon asked.

Rose spooned fresh tea leaves into the pot before she answered. "I think so. And he was very old, although he never seemed that way. But I think he was worried about making Carlie face another loss, and of leaving her without a companion, so he found a replacement for himself," she said, as she pulled another mug out of the cupboard and poured some soy milk into a jug, and took them over to the table.

"We had a ritual of farewell this afternoon, and buried him just as the sun was setting, out under his favourite tree," Rose said, voice faltering only a little. "I'm trying not to be sad, because the underpinning of my faith is the natural cycle of life, death and rebirth, of things happening in the right time, and of energy continuing to exist even as we change form, but of course I miss him terribly. Yet I can't be anything but grateful for all the time I had with him, and I'm determined to honour his memory and focus on all the precious moments we shared."

Picking up the teapot and a jar of honey, she carried them over to the table too and set them down in the middle, then refilled the platter of cakes, scones and cookies before sliding into a chair and picking up her cup of tea.

"Should we really be eating cookies for dinner Gran?" Carlie asked, although she didn't wait for an answer before she picked up a cinnamon scroll and took a big bite.

"Oh Sweetheart, if you can't eat what you want to at a wake, when can you?" Rose said, and they all laughed. It wasn't the happiest laughter in the world, but it held a tiny bit of joy.

After a while, sensing that Rhiannon had things to talk about and confide, Rose excused herself and left the girls to it. The moment the door to her room closed, Carlie turned to her friend. "Are you okay? What happened?"

"Oh Carlie, we don't have to talk about it now! How are you doing? I can't believe Luther's gone. I'm so sorry!" she exclaimed.

Carlie smiled sadly. "I'm all right. We had a beautiful ceremony, and Gran reminded me that we should be celebrating and focusing on his life, not his death, and that he had an uncannily long one for a cat. But tell me what happened with John."

Rhiannon toyed with her mug of tea, eyes on the last choc-chip cookie on the plate. Carlie pushed it towards her. "Chocolate helps you know," she said with a wicked grin.

Rhiannon took a deep breath, then managed to smile. "You know, death really puts things in perspective, doesn't it," she mused, as she reached for the cookie. "I was stressing about John, wondering what to do to fix it, trying to figure out how much I liked him, whether we're good together or not, or whether I just like having someone to be with, as opposed to really liking being with him specifically. I'd worked myself up into a real frenzy, like it was the most important thing on earth, when really, what's the big deal? I date him or I don't date him, it's as simple as that. It's hardly an earth-shattering dilemma, so why was I tying myself in knots about this?" she asked, shrugging in an effort to seem nonchalant.

Carlie smiled at her friend. "You know, a wise person once told me that being a teenager is all about drama. That whole 'I'll *die* if he doesn't love me,' or: 'I love you, best friend, no wait, I hate you and I'll never speak to you again!' That we feel everything much more intensely than adults."

Rhiannon started laughing, so hard that she ended up doubled over, clutching her stomach, tears of amusement running down her cheeks. "I can't believe you remember that!" she giggled. "That was at Brodie's party, the day after we met. My god, I really thought I knew everything, didn't I?"

"How could I forget? I was incredibly impressed by your maturity that day. Although it seems we forget our great advice when something crops up in our own lives," Carlie replied.

"Or it's: 'Do as I say, not as I do,'" Rhiannon added with a grin. "It's always so much simpler to see the answer to someone else's dilemma than your own. Of course I could see that your mum was being overly dramatic – no offence…"

"None taken," Carlie replied, and was surprised that she hadn't become anxious at the mention of her mother.

"Yet I couldn't see it in myself," her friend sighed. "I don't know, I'd pretty much decided I should end things with John when we were talking about it with Jake the other day, but when we met up this morning I remembered all the reasons I liked him."

Smiling ruefully, she rolled her eyes at herself. "We had a lot of fun – I helped him buy a present for his younger brother, then we drank coffee for hours, and he asked if I was going to be on the summer ball committee, and said he'd love it if I was because he'd already volunteered. And then he confided in me some problems he was having with his dad, which were really heavy, and I felt honoured that he could tell me, because he's been struggling with it for a while, and doesn't feel able to tell his guy friends. So now I'm even more confused, because today I really like him, and want to be with him."

Carlie smiled. "That's great then, isn't it? You really like him, he clearly likes you, and he feels close enough to you to share personal issues with. Isn't that what you want in a boyfriend?"

Sighing, her friend nodded. "You'd think so, wouldn't you? But now that I'm away from him again, back here with you and Luna, and eating magical ritual food, I feel like I want more from my relationship. Which I know sounds insane!"

Carlie laughed. "It's not insane at all, it makes perfect sense. Especially as the reason you seemed to suddenly like Jake the other day was that he came to the ritual with us. I'm guessing you didn't bring up the witch thing today with John?"

Her friend blushed. "I'm not sure if I forgot or just chickened out. But it was going so well, I guess I didn't want to ruin things. Which in itself says something, I'm sure."

"Well, maybe you're over-thinking it now," Carlie said. "What if you try not to think about it for the rest of the weekend, and on Tuesday night at our coven meeting we can do an exercise to go within, and connect with our inner wisdom. Maybe you'll be able to figure it out then."

Rhiannon smiled. "You really are smarter than you look."

"Hey!" Carlie protested, and her friend laughed.

"Just joking. But I guess I'd better get home and let you get some sleep. And I'm really sorry about Luther," Rhiannon added, leaning down to pat Luna on her tiny head.

"Thank you," Carlie said simply as she walked her friend out to the front door. "Now, no thinking, all right? We'll figure it out on Tuesday night."

They hugged goodbye, then Carlie quietly closed the door, sagging against it as she realised how exhausted she was after such a sad day. Quickly she tidied away the dishes in the kitchen, then scooped Luna up and took her upstairs to bed, where the kitten curled up on her pillow and sighed herself to sleep.

Chapter 22

Learning To Let Go

Carlie slept in on Sunday, too depressed at losing Luther to want to get up, but finally Luna's tentative little paw on her cheek drove her into action, and she sat up and scooped the sweet creature into her arms. The kitten looked at her with so much trust that Carlie sighed and stood up. That's what she'd promised Luther, that she would care for this tiny scrap of a thing, and so she would. There was no room in her life for grief between schoolwork, homework, helping in the shop and looking after and spending time with Luna – she just had to get on with it.

With a distinct lack of enthusiasm, she moped through the next two days at school, and when she headed to Rhiannon's on Tuesday night she thought it was perfectly fitting that the whole world was grey and miserable. Dragging her feet, she recounted all her losses – her parents, her friends, her childhood home, her school, her future in Sydney, her career as a lawyer, all topped off by the death of her beloved, and now Luther, the first friend she'd made here. Just as she was getting sick of her self-pity, it started raining, so, sighing melodramatically, she pulled her mum's old coat more tightly around herself, put her head down and started to run as fast as she could.

Then abruptly she stopped, and started laughing. It was only a bit of water. She lifted her face to the sky, loving the feel of the raindrops on her cheeks, and trying to appreciate the crisp coolness of the air and the cleansing power of water as it soothed her tortured thoughts. Silver linings and all that, she thought wryly, making an effort to change her mindset to a more positive one. But when it started bucketing down, she groaned, rolled her eyes and bolted up the road. There was only so much good humour she could keep up while feeling so much like a drowned rat.

By the time she knocked on her friend's front door she was wet and shivering, out of breath and somewhat out of sorts. Rhiannon laughed as she ushered her inside, hanging her dripping coat on the stand in the hallway as they passed.

"How come you never bring an umbrella?" she asked.

Carlie shrugged. "It seemed like it was only the tiniest of sprinkles when I set out. And isn't it spring already? Why is it still storming?" she protested, petulant and borderline whiny.

"It is, but it's still the very start of spring. And sometimes winter holds on longer than we'd like it to here," Rhiannon replied calmly, as she guided her out to the kitchen and put the kettle on. "Tea? And do you need some dry clothes to change into?"

Carlie stomped her feet to shake off some of the rain. "I'm sure I'll survive," she said, voice surly, then mentally kicked herself. It was time to drop the woe-is-me attitude. "And tea would be great, thank you."

Mugs in hand, they entered Rhiannon's room, and Carlie was surprised to see it devoid of the altar that was usually set up. Her friend smiled. "I thought we could just use oracle cards tonight, find the answers to our questions. Is that all right?"

"Of course," Carlie said. "You have a big decision to make."

Picking up the card deck from her desk, Rhiannon moved to the centre of the room, and waved Carlie over to one of the big purple cushions. Casting circle around them both, she then sat down opposite her. "Want me to do yours first?"

Carlie shook her head. "You're the one who desperately needs to figure out what to do, so ask your question as you shuffle the cards, then hand them over," she instructed, her grin belying the sternness of her voice.

Laughing, Rhiannon did as she was told, then gave the deck to Carlie, who was surprised to see how nervous her friend was.

"Hey, you know that *you* decide your destiny, right? The cards are just to inspire and uncover your own heart, your own truth and choices. If you don't like the answer, you don't have to take it on board – you can do the opposite. They'll still have served a purpose by crystallising what you want to do in your mind. They're just a tool to help you see what you already know."

Rhiannon nodded. "I know, but I just have no idea what I want. When I'm with John I really like him and want to be with him, but then when I'm away from him I think we should break up."

"Yet deep down you know what to do, you're just not ready to face it. Maybe you'll get some clarity tonight though," Carlie said. "Are you ready?" Her friend nodded reluctantly, still looking worried. Smiling reassuringly, Carlie laid out the cards.

Past: Be Gentle With Yourself
Present: Be True to Yourself
Future: Learn to Let Go

Rhiannon raised her eyebrows as she gazed intently at the cards, but kept her face blank. Carlie tried to read her expression, but for now her friend was holding her cards close to her chest, so to speak. She turned her own attention to them, looking at the images on them, the words and the symbols in the borders, as well as how they'd appeared in relation to each other. Then she closed her eyes, trying to open her mind and her heart to the meaning they held for Rhiannon. Inhaling slowly and deeply, she finally started interpreting them, talking fast so her logical mind couldn't get in the way and try to influence the reading or make herself doubt what she was saying.

Past: Be Gentle With Yourself

You've been beating yourself up over things you have done and choices you have made, but it's time to stop. The past can't be undone – you need to own your decisions and take responsibility for your actions, then let it all go so you can move forward. No one is perfect, so give yourself a break. And be as gentle and forgiving with yourself as you would be with anyone else.

In relation to your question, there is no blame to be cast, and you shouldn't have any regrets about the time you've spent together. Whether you stay with him or end it, you have both cared about each other, and enriched each other's lives, and nothing will change that. He has helped you learn more about yourself and what you want – and what you don't want – in a relationship. And he encouraged you to break through your shyness, to become more active with school committees, to communicate with people you normally wouldn't, and that is a valuable thing. He's helped you to grow and become stronger and more assured.

Don't regret your time together on his account either – you have helped him immensely too, been a confidante when he needed one, and shown him a new way to look at the world. Whether your relationship endures or not, the things you have given each other will stay with you both, and you'll look back on your time together with fondness and gratitude.

Present: Be True to Yourself

At the heart of your question is insecurity about your own deepest self, and a fear that he won't like you if he really knows you. Yet it's also a wider feeling, about the whole world accepting you for who you are, and the fear you have of revealing yourself. We show a different side of ourselves to everyone we meet – we play up some aspects of ourselves with one person, play down or even hide others, and that's fine. It's not important that everyone knows everything about you. Fellow students, workmates, potential bosses, none of them *need* to know your religious, spiritual or philosophical beliefs if you don't want them to.

But for real trust and real love to grow within a relationship, you can't pretend away the things that have the most meaning to you. You can't dim your light for acceptance, deny the beliefs that are so central to your very being, or hide what's in your heart. Magic and ritual is vital to you, and any relationship where you feel you have to hide that will

remain superficial in many ways. For a true heart connection, you have to be able to share that, not laugh it off or lock it away.

So don't deny him the chance to see you, all of you, and make up his own mind. Share your spirituality and what is important to you. Be brave enough to tell him you're a witch. If he has a problem with it, then it's not meant to be, and it would be better to find out now. But imagine how beautiful it will be if he does embrace it, and embrace you in all your complexities and depths. If he can share this precious thing with you, and come to rituals with you, it will make them even more magical.

Future: Learn to Let Go

Some people come into our lives for a long time, and that's wonderful. But others only come into our lives for a short time, and that's okay too. It doesn't mean the short-term people are less important – sometimes you can learn and grow more from someone you only spend a few precious hours or days with, than someone you've known your whole life. So look for the good in your relationship, for the things you've learned and the things you've shared, and celebrate that, without feeling that you have to remain stuck there just because it was once good, or because it isn't bad. You deserve to be with someone who makes your soul sing, who loves all of you, not just the parts you choose to show, and who inspires you to be *more* yourself, rather than diminishing what's most important to you.

Cherish the people who are in your life for the long haul, but also express your gratitude for those who only come into your life for a short time, then say goodbye with a clear heart. If John isn't the person who will share your magical life with you, that's okay. Don't be scared of letting him go so you can find someone who *will* embrace your spiritual side. It's better for John too, if that's the case, that you let him go and allow him to be with someone who shares the things that are most important to him.

Carlie looked at Rhiannon, suddenly nervous. "Thoughts?"

Her friend laughed. "When you put the cards down, and I saw what they were, all I felt was relief. Relief that I should end it. And that last one made me really happy – I love that you said you can touch someone's life and heart, and be glad of that, but you don't necessarily need to stay with them. Because John is a lovely guy, and there's no real reason I can think of to break up with him. He hasn't been mean to me, he treats me well, it's just not… well, it's not what you and Rowan had," she admitted.

"I'd rather hold out for that than settle for something that's nice, but not amazing and magical and heart-opening. I want to love and adore someone, and feel inspired and passionate about them, about us, and I want to be loved and adored too. And I want that for John as well," she added.

Carlie hugged her. "Oh Rhi, you'll find that for sure, I know it. And you deserve that. You both do."

"It feels strange though," Rhiannon said haltingly. "I mean, what do I tell him? Shouldn't I have a good, clear reason? And I'm not sure that 'You're not Rowan' will cut it."

"You don't need any other reason than that you want more for both of you. You care about him, but it can take more than friendship for a relationship to work, especially if you can't – or won't – share the thing that's most important to you with him."

"But what if he argues with me, and I can't explain why we should break up?" Rhiannon asked.

Carlie stared at her, brow furrowed. "You don't actually need a reason to break up, and you don't even really owe him an explanation, if it comes to that. If it doesn't feel right to you, then you should end it. You don't need to convince him or win him over with your reason, and you don't need an excuse. It's not a topic open to discussion, it's not a debate where the person who has the most convincing argument 'wins'. If you don't want to be in the relationship, then you shouldn't be, no matter what he says to convince you otherwise. I mean, would you want him to stay with you even if he wanted to break up?"

"Of course not."

"Exactly," Carlie said. "And it doesn't mean that he's a bad boyfriend, or that you're a bad girlfriend. He'll be someone else's perfect boyfriend, he's just not yours, and that's okay. It totally depends on the chemistry of the two people involved. You and Rowan probably wouldn't have worked out either, but not because of any failing on either of your parts," she smiled.

"Hell, I'm sure psycho shaman guy was a great partner to someone else, but for some reason he and Mum brought out the worst in each other, not the best. There's someone out there who will love and support you in ways that will make you want to be the best *you* that you can be, who will recognise the deepest parts of your heart, and see you as the embodiment of the goddess. And you'll bring out their best too, and support them in following their heart and manifesting their dreams into reality."

Rhiannon reached over and hugged her friend. "Thank you for your wisdom, and your truth telling. If I'm brutally honest with myself, I would say that John really likes me, really likes spending time with me, but it's not like he couldn't imagine his life without me. So that makes perfect sense. He'll be an awesome boyfriend to someone else, and no doubt someone else will be the perfect girlfriend for him, but we just aren't that for each other.

"Thank you for this Carlie, really," she continued. "I know it can't be easy for you to talk about. But I really appreciate your analogy about me and Rowan, because he was perfect for you, but wouldn't have been for me, and vice versa. And I have to remember that it's not the worst thing in the world to be single, especially as it means I'll get to spend more time with you. Now, do we need more tea before I do your reading?"

"I don't need a reading, I'm fine," Carlie insisted, as they wandered downstairs to put the kettle on. She was quite happy for now to dwell in the present moment, to wallow in memories of Luther and the loved ones she'd lost. Not in a morbid way, but because she was finally beginning to see how blessed she had been to have them in her life at all. Of course she wished they were still with her, but she was going to focus on her gratitude that she'd known them at all, and appreciate every single moment they'd shared. She knew that some people lived their whole life without ever experiencing the love she'd had with her parents, or with Rowan.

Perhaps that last card meaning had also been for her – to embrace the time they'd had together and appreciate it, and let go of the anger that she couldn't have more. Appreciate that her life was half full from them being in it, not half empty now that they were gone. No one could take away the love they'd shared, or their presence and influence in her life.

"Earth to Carlie. What kind of tea would you like?" Rhiannon asked, breaking into her thoughts.

Carlie smiled. "Do you still have that grounding tea? The one with dandelion root, blackberry leaves, sage, and what was the other thing? Red clover? I'm feeling a little spaced out."

Her friend found the pretty jar of herbs that they'd blended with Rose during one of their practical coven-evening lessons with their priestess, and spooned the leaves out into the teapot.

"I've got some choc-chip cookies too, if you need more grounding. But you're not going to get out of having your reading hon, it has to be an equal energy exchange."

Carlie smiled, and tried not to feel too annoyed, but she suspected that Rhiannon wanted to somehow include a little "Jake's so sweet" message in any oracle reading she did for her. With that in mind, she was relieved when Mike arrived home early and sat down with them in the kitchen to catch up on their lives and their magical adventures. It reminded her, with a pang of guilt, that she still hadn't figured out anything more about the curse he believed in, and she was filled with a sudden fear for her friend.

"Oh my, is that the time? I should get home," Carlie said, standing up abruptly. "I need to finish that assignment for class tomorrow. It was lovely to see you Mike, and I'll catch up with you at school Rhi," she added, then picked up her bag and rushed down the hallway and out into the cool night air.

Chapter 23

Tea and Sympathy

As she wandered slowly home, Carlie started thinking about the curse Rhiannon's dad Mike believed had been laid on him by Andre the shaman all those years ago – to try to keep him away from her mum Violet – and his fear for his own daughter and how it would affect her. She'd meant to check some of Rose's books to see if she could find any answers there, but she'd been distracted by Aideen right after her conversation with Mike, and by her ongoing saga with Rhiannon ever since. But now she vowed to continue her search for answers, and wondered desperately if she'd be able to break the curse somehow, or at least figure out a way to protect her friend.

Part of her was amused by this new obsession. She didn't even know if curses were real, and not that long ago she would have laughed her head off at the very idea that someone could believe they had magical powers. But that was before she'd arrived in Summer Hill and discovered that her priestess grandmother could change the energy of a room with a flick of her hand. Before she'd patted the ghost of a cat, and spoken with beings of mist who took the shape of women and gave her real gifts before dispersing back into thin air. Before she'd wandered into a cottage in the mists and read a book there, one that she later found at home, just after she'd learned the cottage had burned down twenty years ago and didn't actually exist any more.

So she had to concede that although a curse seemed crazily far-fetched to her, she wouldn't be totally knock-me-over-with-a-feather shocked to be shown that they did exist. It wouldn't be the first time she'd had to open her mind to concede that something mysterious and highly unlikely was actually real, after seeing it with her own eyes or experiencing it with her own body. This village was weirder than anything she could have ever imagined, so who knew what was actually possible?

As she walked down the deserted High Street she shivered suddenly, feeling the cold mist curling around her neck. Seeing the lights of her favourite cafe on, she decided to go in, drawn by the cheeriness of the open fire and the twinkling candles on the few tables scattered around the room. She wanted to write down what she remembered of tonight's reading into the divination section of her Book of Shadows, while it was still vivid in her mind. And who knew, maybe as she wrote about the words she'd channelled for Rhi, her mind would lead her down possible avenues of how she could learn more about curses.

Ordering a pot of chai tea, she wandered over and collapsed down into one of the comfy armchairs by the roaring fire. She stared into the flames, losing herself in their dance, mesmerised by the swirling patterns that rose and fell then rose again, and trying to decipher the images she saw. What had Aideen said, harness the power of fire to scorch and burn away your pain?

The waitress brought her tea over and she smiled her thanks, still lost in thought. The cinnamon-drenched steam from the teapot brought her back into the room though, into the present, its warm earthy scent making her feel safe and soothed. She pulled out her Book of Shadows and opened it to a blank page, then selected one of her favourite purple pens to write with.

"Excuse me?"

Carlie jumped in surprise, dropping her pen as she looked up in confusion at the stranger standing over her.

"I'm sorry," she said automatically, as she picked up her pen and set it down on the table, before turning her eyes back to the tall woman before her. She was dressed in a long green velvet skirt with a long black velvet coat over the top, and looked vaguely familiar.

Maybe she'd come to one of Rose's rituals? She couldn't remember her name though, if that was the case, or place her. And she was pretty sure she knew all the women of Rose's inner circle at least, and would recognise the other ritual participants.

"Didn't your friend tell you to stop apologising?" the woman asked with a smile. Ignoring Carlie's confusion at that – since Rhiannon had certainly said that to her once or twice – she pressed on. "Do you mind if I sit with you?" she asked, and Carlie, embarrassed that she couldn't recall her name, nodded.

"Of course," she said, closing her book and stuffing it into her bag before the stranger asked about it, and mentally running through the list of all the names of the people she'd met recently. *Damn, she'd have to pay more attention.*

Then she paused. Why was this making her so anxious? Surely the woman wouldn't be too offended that she couldn't remember her name, since she was still relatively new in town and had met so many people. Yet she seemed to know things about her that someone she'd only met once or twice should have no way of knowing.

Elegantly the woman folded herself into the armchair next to Carlie, hands wrapped tightly around her mug of hot chocolate. She inhaled the sweet aroma and let out a deep, contented sigh.

"They really do make the best hot chocolate here," she smiled, eyes lit up with the joy of simple pleasures.

"I'll have to try it one day," Carlie replied, as she poured out a cup of chai, buying time as she tried to puzzle out who the woman was. She looked so familiar, it was driving her crazy.

"We haven't met before Carlie, so you can stop struggling, and thinking you're rude to have forgotten me."

Staring at the woman in confusion, Carlie was now worried in a different way. What did a stranger want with her? And how did she know so much about her?

"You could say that I'm a friend of Rhiannon's," the woman said, her voice cracked and aching with pain. "I can sense that you're worried about her. And I'm so glad that you've both reconnected. That you've been able to forgive her, and are such a good friend to her. She's true to you too, and she'd never knowingly hurt you."

Carlie nodded cautiously. "I know," she whispered.

"And I can sense how much you're worrying about Mike too. You have a beautiful heart Carlie. Your grandmother must be so proud of you," she continued.

Blushing a little, Carlie tilted her head in acknowledgement of the compliment, without actually agreeing with it, and took a sip of tea. She felt like she was dreaming, one of those dreams that doesn't make any sense. Perhaps she would wake up soon, safe at home in bed, with Luna cuddled up in the crook of her arm, warming her up, and anchoring her to safety, and sanity.

The stranger laughed, a high, tinkling laugh. "Well, maybe it is some kind of dream," she said. "But you're awake now. And the thing is Carlie, you really need to wake up. Not from sleep, but from the fog in your brain, from the fog of your memories. You already know why the curse isn't real, why Rhiannon is safe, but you're too scared to linger on how you know that."

"That's not true! I'd do anything to put Mike and Rhiannon's minds at ease," she protested.

"I know," the woman replied. "You're kind like your mother."

Carlie gasped. "You knew her?" she asked, voice full of pain.

"I did. Everyone here loved her, and felt her loss when she left the village. I know Mike never stopped loving her."

Brow crinkling, Carlie stared hard at the woman. "Who are you? How do you know this stuff?" she begged. "And how could you know about Mike loving my mum? Because that's not true. He was married to an amazing woman who he adored, who he adores still, and whose children miss her terribly."

Tears pricked the woman's eyes, and she smiled sadly. "I'm sure she misses them more than anything too," she whispered. "But this is too long a story for tonight, and all you need to know for now is that you already have the answer to Mike's fear of a curse, you just have to dive within and rediscover it. I have faith in you Carlie," she said, then stood up abruptly and walked out of the cafe.

The door banged shut behind her, making the candles on the tables flicker, and Carlie shivered in the cold draft that had rushed in. Trying to ground herself, she finished her tea and poured out another cup, noticing as she did so that the woman hadn't had a single sip of the hot chocolate she'd professed to love so much.

Who was she? How could she know so much about so many people? And who could know so much about *her*? She'd only just moved to the village. And most importantly, if the woman knew so much about the curse, why didn't she just tell her? Why was she being sent on a quest for find answers?

And what if she couldn't work the puzzle out? God, was the woman related to Brianna, Brauna and Aideen somehow? They happily handed out cryptic clues that made them seem helpful too, yet really weren't. But that was crazy, surely. Those three had materialised out of the mists, and this woman was flesh and blood, walking into the cafe, talking with her, ordering a drink and sitting opposite her.

She was jolted out of her thoughts by the waitress coming over to tell her they were closing up, so Carlie quickly drank down the rest of her chai, steeling herself for the chill outside, then wandered home in a daze. Rose had already gone to bed, so she tiptoed upstairs, brushing her teeth quickly then crawling under the covers.

Her heart lifted when Luna walked up from her warm nest at the end of the bed and cuddled in against Carlie's chest, her gentle purring sending her off to a sleep filled with dreams of her mother as a young woman, walking and talking with the woman she'd met in the cafe. Had they been friends?

She cried out for them to slow down, to stop and talk to her, to explain things, but when she spoke they faded into the mists and she was left alone. Sighing, she rolled over, and felt a little paw on her cheek, guiding her back to a wonderful dream of when Rowan was alive. She threw herself into his arms and let her mind drift away into a deep, comforting sleep.

Chapter 24

The Lure of the Dark Side

Carlie spent the rest of the week trying to nut out what the woman she'd met in the cafe had meant. How could she know something but at the same time not know it? Why hadn't the stranger just given her the answer, instead of making her feel like a failure for not being able to figure it out? And who was she anyway, and how did she know so much about her?

She'd tried to explain what she looked like to Rhiannon, hoping she might know who it was, but her description of a beautiful woman with long blonde hair, wearing a long velvet skirt and coat, didn't really narrow it down in this town.

Most frustrating of all, the harder she tried to concentrate on these problems, the further she felt she was getting from an answer. It was also making her a little unfocused at school, and Rhiannon had twice asked her what was going on and where her head was at. Fortunately she'd managed to convince her, for now at least, that she was just feeling anxious about her history assignment, but she didn't like lying to her.

Nor did she like having to keep Rose and Rhiannon in the dark. They were the two people who would be most able to assist her in figuring out the curse, but she didn't want to upset her grandmother by bringing it up, scare her friend at the thought of it, or break Mike's confidence. If only Rowan was still alive, he'd know what to do. He always knew what to do.

If only she could communicate with him in some way. Was there a magical way she could do that? She skimmed through Rose's magical books whenever her grandma was out, but she never found anything that looked especially useful. There were veiled references to seances and ouija boards, but only in reference to dark magics and mysterious ancient sects.

On Friday at lunchtime she asked Rhiannon if she'd ever performed a seance, but her friend shook her head vehemently.

"Don't even joke about it," she said, which Carlie thought was odd, since she'd meant it as a serious question. "I know how tempting the idea can be, but it's not real, and it can mess with your head. I do know how much you miss Rowan, believe me – I still miss my mum every day – but at some point we have to accept that they're gone. And while we can trust that they are still with us in some way, it's not in a tangible way that allows us to have a conversation with them."

Carlie nodded. "I know. And I do accept that he's gone. But isn't there some –"

"No, there isn't. Now promise me that you won't mess around with this kind of stuff," Rhiannon demanded.

"I promise, but geez, why are you so against them?" Carlie asked.

Rhiannon lowered her voice. "You know how Abby lost her boyfriend? He took his own life, and she was crushed. She felt really guilty – which was not helped by a few idiots at school who kept insisting that if she'd really cared about him she would have known what he was planning and stopped him, or that maybe he did it to get away from her."

"No!" Carlie cried. "That's dreadful!"

"I know, it was really awful. She was devastated, but Laura sorted them out. But my point is, Abby ordered a ouija board online, and used it to try to contact her boyfriend – but she ended up freaking herself out so badly, thinking she was communicating with demons, that she started going to some weird revivalist church, and now she's sworn off anything even remotely spiritual or magical or so-called new age. So don't be offended if she avoids you by the way, because she was warned to stay away from Rose and her 'demonic' crystals and things."

Carlie started to defend Abby, to tell her friend that she'd always been really nice to her, but then she realised that after that first day back at school, when Abby had offered some words of sympathy and comfort, she *had* avoided her. She hadn't chosen to sit next to her in a single class since. The only time they had been together was when Carlie sat next to her to avoid Jake that day, and now that she thought about it, Abby *had* basically ignored her, she just hadn't noticed because she was too busy being paranoid about Jake. Still, if it was helping her to heal to stay out of her way, well, that was fine. She knew exactly how devastating losing your boyfriend was.

Rhiannon smiled sadly. "She has been avoiding you, hasn't she?" she asked, and Carlie nodded reluctantly.

"It's nothing personal, don't worry. But Rose would warn you off seances and ouija boards too, if you asked her," Rhiannon added. "But *don't* ask her, she'd be really upset to know you were even entertaining the idea."

Carlie stared at her friend, puzzled by the secrecy. Surely she could give her a straight answer. She was even more intrigued when she figured out that Rhiannon hadn't actually said they didn't work, just that she shouldn't try them. But the bell rang before she could grill her any further, and they hugged goodbye. Tonight Rhiannon was looking after her brother, then tomorrow she was going to see John, to let him see her magical heart.

"Good luck and best wishes with it all," Carlie said softly, kindly. "I really hope he's open to your witchyness, but don't worry too much if he's not – there will be guys who are, and you deserve to be loved for your true self, your whole self."

Rhiannon smiled. "Thank you, for making me finally realise that, and giving me the confidence to reveal myself to him. I'll let you know what happens," she yelled, as she ran off to class.

Chapter 25

Right Here, Right Now

The next morning dawned grey and cold, and Carlie spent her morning doing chores and hanging out with Luna. Her thoughts were with Rhiannon though, and she hoped it was going well with her and John. After lunch with Rose, she went in to the healing centre with her and did some reiki for a few regulars.

The skies cleared in the afternoon, just as the last person left the shop, so she wandered up to the top of the tor, grateful for the time and space to process all she'd experienced in the last two weeks, from the Imbolc ceremony with Rose that they'd shared with Jake and his grandfather, to her lunchtime chat with Rhiannon and Jake about relationships, her dark moon ritual with her friend, and that strange late-night meeting with the mystery woman in the cafe. And she was still obsessing over Mike's worries about the supposed curse, and how that might affect her friend in the future. Life was certainly more magical here than it had been in Sydney, and in some strange ways more real and deep, but it was also more challenging, with the potential for more heartbreak. As what she loved grew – friends, magic, her bond with her grandmother – so did the fear of losing it all.

Breathing deeply, she tried to let her mind go blank, to let her fears wash over her, and see them being blown away by the cold breeze at the summit of the sacred hill. It was a struggle though – the more she tried not to think of something, the more her focus homed in on it, and she sighed in frustration. But the wide open sky and the energy pouring up from the earth and into her heart calmed her, and she stopped suddenly as an idea formed.

They were faced with a magical curse, so maybe that meant they could break it magically. For the millionth time she wished that Rowan was still with her, because she was sure he'd know what to do. But he was gone forever. And Rose might know something about curses, but she wasn't ready to share that part of her mum's past with her – she didn't want to upset her needlessly, or get her involved in Mike's issue without his permission. An image of some older books Rose had stored in the cupboard under the stairs leaped into her mind though, so she stood up and headed back towards home, intent on restarting the search.

As she meandered down the tor, she let her mind drift. The mists were rising up around her ankles, and she watched it form then dance apart, then reform, delicate wisps reaching out to her, beckoning her forward. Sometimes it made her smile, this magical-looking fog that cloaked the world in softness and mystery, but today the mists made her feel sad, and filled her with longing. She daydreamed about Rowan, picturing him walking by her side, holding her hand, talking as he used to, telling her that he loved her, that she was amazing, and that she could do anything with her life.

Her ankle twisted as she stepped into a depression in the earth, probably part of an old rabbit hole, and panic clutched her heart as she crouched down, clutching her foot in her hands. *Please goddess, don't let it be a break, I couldn't bear it!*

Bleakly she looked around, and realised that somehow she'd come down the slope much further along the laneway than she should have. Sighing that she'd have to backtrack even further to get home, and cursing her sore ankle, she started hobbling along the lane.

Then abruptly she stopped, staring in disbelief. Intellectually she knew that the cottage wasn't there, yet there it stood, as solid as any other house as it peeked out of the mists that wreathed it, defying her not to acknowledge it. The candle in the window flickered, and overhead, clouds that hadn't been there earlier rushed together, darkening ominously then opening up and pouring a deluge of rain down on her, soaking her to the skin and chilling her to the bone.

Shivering, she raced up the steps to the back verandah, and was only mildly surprised when Shadow, or the ghost of Shadow, rubbed against her wet legs. Desperately she looked around for Luther, praying she could hold him one last time, but she couldn't see him, and perhaps it was better that he wasn't there, or she might have started crying and never been able to stop.

Nervously she opened the creaky door and walked slowly inside – then she sank to her knees in shock and pain, the breath smashed out of her. Rowan was standing against the far wall, leaning up against the kitchen bench, the scent of the rosemary in the pot on the windowsill drifting through the dusty air between them, bringing her back to her senses.

Rosemary for remembrance. She closed her eyes, trying to block out the sweet agony of seeing the spectre before her. Rowan was dead, so she couldn't be looking at him. She'd been to his funeral, grieved with his mother, planted rosemary under the apple tree in her backyard in his memory. This was a cruel joke, it had to be. Or she was finally going crazy, her mind as cracked and broken as her heart.

Stiffening as she heard footsteps moving towards her, her breath caught, heart thumping like a wild thing in her chest. A hand came down on her shoulder, the warmth of its touch infusing her wet and shaking body with heat, drying her in an instant. Now it was fear, anticipation and the smallest and most reluctant sense of hope that was making her shiver.

She sensed someone sinking down on his knees in front of her, and felt a gentle hand lifting her chin to face him.

"Baby, I'm here." It was his voice, and suddenly the how and why of what was happening meant nothing. Opening her eyes, she gasped in surprise and joy and threw her arms around him as he lifted her to her feet, tears falling as she burrowed her face into his shoulder. She didn't care that she was making him wet as she cried. Or that there was no logical way he could actually be standing in the cottage with her.

The sweet agony as he gently stroked her hair nearly brought her to her knees again, but she stood firm. No force on earth could separate her from her beloved one second sooner than the inevitable end. Finally he broke the circle of his arms, but his hands were on her shoulders as he gazed at her, eyes sparkling with love. "Oh Carlie, my beloved, I've missed you so much," he said, a catch in his voice, which was even huskier than she remembered.

She smiled through her tears. "Me too," she whispered, voice a little shaky, but joy warming her through. Until all of a sudden she remembered. Her regret. Her guilt. Her fear. The emotions seared through her, alive and warring for dominance, her heart clenching with pain.

Swallowing down a sob, she tried to compose herself. "Oh Rowan, I'm so sorry that I left you thinking that I didn't want to be with you, or that I believed any of those terrible things Rhiannon said about you. It broke my heart all over again when they told me you were –" She stopped, horrified. *No, don't think about that right now. Don't break whatever spell this was.*

"Well, to imagine that you would think for even a moment that I didn't love you." Her voice faded away, and Rowan smiled at her, that heart-swelling, mood-lifting, love-filled smile that had always been just for her.

"Baby, don't worry about that," he whispered. "Of course I know how you felt, how you feel, how much you love me still. Even when you ran from me at the Yule retreat I knew it wasn't over between us. And I felt it, the moment that you changed your mind, the moment that you decided to be with me no matter what. And I loved you even more that you refused to choose between me and Rhiannon, that you chose us both – you're wiser than your years Carlie, and stronger than you know."

Breathlessly she stared at him, taking in every word, every expression, every crease and crinkle of his eyes as he gazed back at her, trying to capture it all and commit it to memory, to bury it deep within her heart where nothing could ever find it, and no power on earth would let it fade away. She reached her hand up to his face, wondering,

awestruck that he was standing there in front of her, solid as flesh and blood, his cheek warm under her fingers, seemingly so alive.

"It's not fair," she finally said, some of the anger returning even in this perfect moment, and her voice breaking, swollen with unshed tears. "Why did it happen?" she demanded fiercely.

Gently Rowan lifted a strand of her hair and tucked it back behind her ear as he used to, his touch electric. "Shhh, it doesn't matter now," he replied softly, soothingly.

"But it should have been me!" she cried. "You had so much to give the world still, so much to share."

"So do you Carlie," he insisted. "That's why I'm here. To remind you just how much you are loved, and valued. And to let you know that you'll be able to help so many people."

Shaking her head again, she buried her face in his shoulder, unable to trust her sight, but willing to believe the sensation of his arms around her, the strength that flowed from his body to hers. Eventually though he lifted her chin and dragged her down to the dusty floor, kneeling before her, eye to eye, and holding her hands still.

"You wanted to talk to me," he said, voice urgent, as he gazed into her eyes. "You had a question."

Her gaze drilled back into his, brain not wanting to think of anything except this single second in time, this precious, golden moment. "No, it doesn't matter. I just want to stay here with you and ignore the rest of the world, like that day at our special place by the stream," she said, desperation in her tone, in her expression, and her eyes and heart focused only on him. "I want to capture this, right here, right now, and hold on to it. Can't we just stay here, in this cottage in the mists? Together, forever, like we promised."

"My love, I don't have long," Rowan said, voice sad, and his eyes dark pools of despair. "But the answer you're seeking is in that book of your mother's, the one you were reading on the way to meet me on solstice eve."

She stared at him blankly.

"The curse, it's not real. It only has power because Mike believes it. But you know why it can't be true – and you need to remember, and let him know. He's suffered enough."

"I don't understand," she whispered, but she wasn't really paying attention to his words, she was just drinking him in, drifting between the real world and whichever magical dimension she was in now, some realm where he was still alive. She looked down at their joined hands resting on her knee, saw his beautiful tattoo of the phases of the moon, and traced over the outline with her finger. "Why can't you stay with me?" she begged.

A sudden clap of thunder exploded overhead, and Carlie jumped as the walls of the cottage shook, then screwed her eyes closed when a flash of lightning illuminated the dusty old cottage and made it seem, for just a moment, that the whole world was exploding around her. When the thunder had shaken the whole cottage, and the indistinct gloom of early evening had returned, she looked around wildly, but Rowan was gone.

The weight of the pain crushed her, and she collapsed onto the floor, tears spilling from her eyes. For a long time she sobbed, in great gasping and shuddering breaths, then for a while she seemed to sleep, suspended in some strange no man's land where things were hazy and mist-drenched, and she didn't have to think.

But finally she felt a paw on her face, and she woke up calling Luther's name. It wasn't him though, and this realisation felt like just another cruel blow in a series of devastatingly painful ones. As darkness closed in around her, she scrubbed at the tears stinging her cheeks, then slowly, unsteadily, dragged herself to her feet.

She couldn't give up yet, couldn't give in. More than anything she wanted to help Mike find peace, in honour of her mother who had cared for him so deeply, and in honour of him, for the love he had always shown to Violet and Rose. And she wanted to do it for Rhiannon's sake too, for the friend who had helped her so much. Slowly, sadly, she hobbled back home.

Chapter 26

Revealing Her Inner Heart

Dragging herself up the stairs to her room, Carlie pulled her mum's diary out of the bottom drawer where she'd hidden it and threw herself down on the bed. Before she could even open it though there was a knock on the front door. Sighing, she shoved it back under her pillow and limped downstairs, but when she saw that it was Rhiannon, she hugged her and welcomed her in.

"How did it go? Are you okay? Want a cup of tea?" she asked.

Her friend smiled. "It was fine, I'm okay, and I'd *kill* for a cup of tea," she replied, following her friend out to the kitchen.

As Carlie put on the kettle and grabbed tea leaves and the teapot from the cupboard, Rhiannon leaned against the bench, looking a little shaken as she watched her.

"So, we broke up," she finally revealed.

"I'm sorry," Carlie said automatically, and Rhiannon raised her eyebrows. "Well, even when it's for the best, I'm sure it's still difficult, and I know that you really liked him," she clarified.

Her friend nodded thoughtfully. "You're right, thank you. The whole way back I've been feeling really strange, wondering if I did the right thing, to-ing and fro-ing with my decision..."

Carlie handed her a mug of tea and led her to the table to sit down, then put some cookies on a plate and took them over.

"God, what a day," Rhiannon muttered. "I didn't sleep much last night, because I was still trying to figure it all out, so then of course I overslept and missed the first bus, which made me late as well as stressed, and that made me even *more* impatient with the whole thing. But I finally got there, and walked around to his place, and his mum was there, so we all had a cup of tea together, and she's so sweet. I'll miss her the most I think," she said, then rolled her eyes at herself. "Not exactly the best reason to stay with a guy, huh, liking hanging out with his mother?"

Carlie handed her another cookie. "It's understandable though, that you'd enjoy spending time with her, since, well…"

Rhiannon paled. "Oh god! I didn't even think of that. How predictable! The girl who lost her mother, dating someone because she likes having tea with his mum. Seems like I really did make the right decision," she said bleakly.

"Hey, don't be so hard on yourself. Just because you got on with his mum, it doesn't mean you thought she was going to replace yours or anything. I think it's nice that you liked talking to her. Rowan's mum was really lovely too," Carlie said, and although it hurt her heart to mention him so soon after seeing him, she didn't dissolve into tears as she'd expected. Rhiannon gazed at her closely, obviously a little concerned that she might break down and cry too, and pleasantly surprised when she didn't.

"Anyway, John and I went to this coffee shop we like, and chatted about our week – you know, school, annoying little brothers, the usual, then we sat in silence for a while. And it wasn't the comfortable kind either, I guess because I was still obsessing over what to do. So I was trying to remember how you'd put it the other night, you know, revealing my true self and being brave enough to risk my heart, but finally I just blurted it out – I asked him what he thought about witches and the goddess, and rituals to honour the cycle of the seasons."

"What did he say?" Carlie asked.

"He said it was superstitious nonsense that ancient peasants believed in because they didn't understand what made the sun rise and the earth turn, and that anyone who was interested in it was seriously lacking in intelligence."

"No!" Carlie cried. "He didn't!"

"He did."

"What did you say?"

"So, I guess you don't want to come to the Beltane fertility rite with me and leap over the fire hand in hand?" she recalled.

Carlie stared at her friend, not sure if she was being serious or sarcastic. "Really?"

"Really," she replied, brow furrowed. "And he stared at me like I'd grown an extra head, then finally he laughed, and decided that I must have been joking, and asked what I really meant."

"No way!"

Rhiannon laughed bitterly. "Way. My first instinct was to tell him where to go, but before I could, the waiter came over with our drinks, and John got up to get me some honey, which was sweet, so I took a deep breath and tried to figure out how I felt about it. Maybe he'd been caught off guard, and hadn't meant to be as rude as he was. Maybe he didn't understand what I was asking. And maybe it wouldn't really matter if he never came to a ritual with me – I mean, I'd rather do them with you anyway, so nothing would actually change. Anyway, I figured that I owed him the benefit of the doubt, so when he sat back down I asked if that was really how he felt about pagan spirituality."

Pausing for a moment, she took a sip of her tea while Carlie waited impatiently, then continued with her retelling. "He asked me what I meant by the term, because there are a couple of girls at his school who recently started dressing all gothic and wandering around holding crystals and muttering under their breath about putting curses on people, and he thought that anyone who could believe that curses had any power needed their head read," she said.

Carlie flinched. Admittedly she was on John's side there, although hers was as much wishful thinking that they had no power as believing that was true. Certainly she knew that Mike believed in them, and he was not a stupid or ignorant man.

"What did you say?" she asked her friend.

"I told him that no, I don't believe in curses, or casting spells on people without their knowledge, or even that gothic clothing makes a witch – that we have loads of beautiful, colourful velvet dresses for our rituals. And I tried to explain to him what I do believe, and how it feels to do a ritual with Rose, and the amazing energy that we raise together, but his face showed just what he thought of that – he looked disappointed, slightly disgusted and really horrified all at once."

Carlie's heart went out to her friend, who was trying to put on a brave face, but was obviously hurt by John's reaction to her courageous revelation of what she held so dear.

Rhiannon sighed, then she took a deep breath and bit into another cookie. "He did concede that he supposed we could get around my ill-informed views, and that we didn't have to agree on everything, but even the way he said that was really offensive. So then I suggested that maybe there was no point in us being together, if he was so dismissive of something that was so important to me, and he just kind of shrugged, and said fine, if that was what I wanted."

"Is it what you wanted?" Carlie asked.

"I don't know, but I wanted him to care! To be sad at the prospect of us breaking up," she replied, pouting.

"Rhi, that's not fair to him. You can't break up with him just to make a point. Or to blackmail him into changing his behaviour or subscribing to your view."

"I know," her friend sighed. "But, well, that made me kind of mad, so I stood up, said that it had been lovely spending time with him, and to give his mum my love, then I walked out and caught the bus home. Of course halfway back I realised that I hadn't given him any money for my coffee and cake, so I've written him a note, apologising for my oversight and enclosing a five pound note, and I'll post it on Monday."

The girls stared at each other in horrified silence for a moment, then burst out laughing.

"And are you sure this is what you want?" Carlie asked, when they'd finally managed to calm their giggles. "Does it really matter to you if he won't come to a ritual with you?"

Rhiannon smiled. "I am sure, which was a good realisation. I mean yes, we could have differences of opinion, no sweat. And if he'd not wanted to come to a sabbat festival or moon ritual with me but respected that I was going, that would have been fine too. But for him to be so scathing and judgemental, to say that anyone who enjoyed such a ceremony was stupid... well, why would I want to be with someone like that?" she asked.

"Rose is the cleverest person I know, as well as the kindest and most compassionate, and he was insulting her as well as me," she continued. "Plus it showed how closed-minded he is. I mean, we got together at the Yule Ball! We were part of the planning committee that made it solstice-themed. Surely he knew what I believed and how I felt about these things from the day we met, so he was either being deliberately cruel, or wilfully ignorant and uncaring, and none of those are desirable traits in a boyfriend."

Carlie smiled sadly. "I guess not."

"But the best thing?" Rhiannon ventured. "I'm actually relieved. I did think for a moment: 'Oh god, did I act too hastily? Should I have given him a chance to explain?' But I'm really not filled with regret, and I'm not wishing I hadn't said anything, or thinking I should go back tomorrow and tell him I've changed my mind."

She gazed into her empty cup, and Carlie jumped up to put the kettle on and make more tea.

"I'm glad Carlie, really I am," her friend continued. "Ever since you showed me Rowan's letters to you, I knew I wanted a love like that – a grand and beautiful romance, and a guy who loves me for who I really am. Someone who's passionate and caring, not indifferent, who knows what's in my heart, and shares the things that are important to me. He doesn't have to be a witch, or even have to come to rituals with me, but he can't think I'm stupid because *I* want to go. And of course it would be nice to have someone who shared that, and who was part of my magical life. Imagine going out with someone like Jake, who could be a part of it with you."

Carlie smiled. "Like Rowan was with me," she said, glossing over the Jake remark. "It's definitely a wonderful thing."

"Exactly! I'd rather be single than be ridiculed for what I hold dear, just to say that I have a boyfriend. I mean, I figured John wasn't pagan, but I was shocked that he would be so disparaging of those who are. And I guess we could have continued on for a while, but how could I be with someone like that for the long term? And how could he? And since I see no future with him, isn't it better to cut my losses now and free us both?" she asked.

The question hung in the air as Carlie made more tea, then brought the teapot over and settled back in her chair.

"I guess the answer to that is how do you feel now?" she replied. "Are you really relieved that it's over, or do you think you'll be regretting your decision in the morning? And be honest. Be brave enough to look within and discover what you're really feeling. It's no point of pride to say that you're over it if you're not, and not all relationships are the same."

Rhiannon stared at her friend. "When did you grow up and get all mature and kick-arse-advice-y?" she asked.

Carlie shrugged. "I guess I've just had more time to ponder the alternative. And someone has to play devil's advocate," she grinned. "I just remember how much you liked him at the Yule Ball, how happy you were when he kissed you, how ecstatic you were when you went to his place and decided you were dating. But I'm not trying to convince you to take him back, I promise," she added, as she saw Rhiannon's confused expression.

Her friend sat there for a moment, brow furrowed, thinking hard. Then she smiled. "He is really sweet, and we got on really well – but for me, I need to be with someone who I can express all of myself with. I don't want to diminish or hide what I hold dear, and I won't apologise for being who I am. You've taught me that. And surely if he was so totally unfazed by the prospect of it ending, he couldn't have been that into it anyway. But most importantly, if I really cared about him, if I *really* wanted to be with him, I wouldn't be feeling so relieved right now."

"And that's your answer then," Carlie said softly, and reached over to give her friend a hug. "You'll meet someone lovely, I'm sure of it. And it would be cool if they lived a bit closer too."

Rhiannon nodded. "It sure would. And hey, this means that we have more time together now – more time to study our magic and plan our future, and more time just to hang out and have fun, and there's nothing wrong with that!"

When Rose came in soon afterwards, the girls were sitting out the back, laughing hysterically as Rhiannon tried to pinpoint what traits would define her ideal boyfriend. Magical. Smart. Independent. Creative. Mature. Tattooed. Slightly wild. Witch.

Rose asked Rhiannon if she wanted to stay for dinner with them, but she reluctantly shook her head. She had to head home and pack, as they were going on a family holiday to Scotland for their week off from school, and her dad wanted to leave before dawn tomorrow to beat the traffic.

Carlie walked her out to the front door, hugged her goodbye, then headed back in for a simple meal with Rose. Then she conjured up an excuse about making a start on her homework and went up to her room. She wasn't ready to confide to her grandma that she'd seen Rowan that day, just as she hadn't been able to bring herself to share it with Rhiannon. For now she wanted to hold it close to her heart and keep it to herself, a treasured moment just for her.

Lighting the lemon-scented candle on her bedside table, she turned off the light and climbed into bed, then opened her Book of Shadows and started writing about her afternoon in the cottage. She wanted to capture every single detail, every word Rowan had said to her, every touch and caress. To commit it all to memory, and to paper, so it could sustain her through her saddest moments.

By the time she got to his cryptic comments about the curse she was yawning, so she scribbled them onto a scrap of paper that she placed under her pillow, in the hope that she would dream the answer into being, as well as into her book, which she slid under her bed. Then she blew out the candle and curled up under the covers, smiling as Luna leaped up onto the quilt next to her and snuggled her warm body into hers.

Chapter 27

Unlocking the Past

After passing the previous school holidays in a haze of oblivion following Rowan's death, Carlie was determined to make this one count. She got up early every day and climbed the tor, focusing on breathing in the energy of the spring mornings, and feeling happy as it gradually got easier to tackle the steep hill.

When she returned each morning she had a leisurely breakfast with her grandmother, rather than her usual grabbing-a-bite-on-the-run, on-her-way-to-school style, and learned more about the history of the healing centre, and how important it had become for Rose over the years. She'd been a nurse when she married Louis, then she'd taken time off when their daughter Violet was born, and her career had changed tack a little. Her best friend Elsie, who she'd been at college with, had started investigating alternative therapies, and the two women became intrigued.

Together they studied herbalism, naturopathy, nutrition, reiki, crystal healing and art therapy, and in an era where such things were far from mainstream, they worked to find a happy medium between their traditional medical training and the new information they were absorbing. Living in Summer Hill had no doubt helped – people in this village had always been a little more open to the metaphysical, and being many miles from the nearest major hospital, they were prepared to consult with Rose and Elsie, appreciating their nursing qualifications as well as the extra knowledge they added to them, and loving the passion with which they worked, growing their own herbs, constantly studying, and able to come to someone's aid at all hours of the day or night. Not to mention that their fees were barely enough to cover their costs, and if someone was struggling financially they would waive the charges altogether.

Later, when Rose embraced the goddess, apprenticed to become a priestess and began holding public rituals, the villagers simply saw it as an extension of what she was already doing for the community, and supported that too.

Carlie was glad the town accepted her grandmother and all that she stood for, and was touched that they also included her in their affections. There were more people wanting her to do reiki on them than she could fit in, and Rose was trusting her with more and more of the herbal remedy recipes every week.

So on her week off from school, she spent her mornings at home in the cottage studying herbalism texts, making potions and reading the books about grief counselling Rowan had ordered for her, then she went in to the shop in the afternoons to help out where she could – doing some energy healing work, answering queries, putting stock out, and relieving the staff when they needed breaks.

Rose even got her to accept some payment for her hours, after explaining that she'd have needed to employ someone else if Carlie wasn't there, and giving her a long lecture about valuing her own time and understanding her own worth.

The next step was to go in and open an account at the local bank, and organise for them to transfer the money from her Australian account into it. It was a strange feeling, to hold that deposit book in her hands and see her name and address typed out so clearly and officially. More and more roots were taking hold here, anchoring her to this village, and to Rose.

On Thursday Jake came in, and they went for coffee, catching up on their news and promising they'd get back to their assignment when school started the following week. He told her how much he was enjoying spending time with his grandfather, working with him in his huge vegie garden, and that he had finally managed to speak to his parents, who were loving their aid work in Africa, and relieved that he was content to be staying with Richard.

Most nights Carlie and Rose cooked together, sharing more stories from their lives, discussing plans for the garden, brainstorming upcoming courses – and spending more time than they probably should have crawling around on the floor with Luna, whose sweet nature and adorable antics were helping both their hearts to heal from Luther's loss.

And after Rose went to bed, Carlie lay awake in her big room, little Luna snuggled in her lap, and read through her mother's Book of Shadows, then her diary, feverishly searching for the answer Rowan had promised was there. The answer that the woman she'd met in the cafe insisted she already knew. But she didn't know what she was looking for, and there were times she almost cried in frustration as she went over and over her mother's distinctive curly writing.

On the Friday morning she woke up before dawn, just as the full moon was beginning to set, after a restless night of tossing and turning. She felt like the answer was on the tip of her tongue, or whatever the brain equivalent of that was, so close she could almost touch it. Picking up her own Book of Shadows, she flicked to the entry she'd written after she saw Rowan in the cottage, and went back over what he'd told her. The solution was in her mother's book, the one she'd been reading on her way to meet him at Yule. Clumsily she clattered out of bed and went to the chest of drawers to pull out her mum's diary, the one she'd tied up with metres of ribbon knotted to keep it closed, with a note to Carlie, written before she was born...

Dear Future Daughter,
I don't know whether you exist or ever will, but if you do, I want you to have this. I almost burned it, in a ritual of cleansing and closing of chapters, and who knows, perhaps I still might. But it is a cautionary tale of sorts for any young woman, and if you can take anything from this, it will have been worth me living through it... Tomorrow I marry the man I love, and step from my past into my future. And so I am locking this book away, with a few other things

from my former life. I am grateful that it all led me here, but I no longer need the reminders of the things that I regret...

It hurt her every time she read this journal, to bear witness to the pain her mother had endured, the abuse that had led her to flee to the other side of the world with Oliver, the man who would one day become her husband and Carlie's dad.

There was beauty in it too. If she could get through the horror of her mum's relationship with the crazy shaman guy, and the awful things he'd said and done to her, things that had left her half-hoping he would kill her just so her pain would end, the final section of it read like a love letter to her dad, a prayer of gratitude that he had saved her, emotionally as well as physically and literally.

Wait. He'd managed to help her escape from Andre by borrowing a friend's identity for her – that's why she had become Fiona instead of Violet. It had never been about erasing her link to her beloved parents, it was only ever about finding a means to disappear from her violent boyfriend.

Quickly she skimmed through the pages, and then there it was, written out in faded blue pen, the reason the curse was not a curse, but just the empty threats of a vindictive and cruel man.

It sounded crazy, and wildly impossible, but he said a friend of his had an old passport in her maiden name, and no plans to travel for a few years, and we looked a little alike. So I became Fiona Scott, nineteen years old. I gained two years, and even got a new birthday. But I wasn't thinking about the future at all, by then I was just thinking day to day, how to survive one more day. If I thought about it at all, I guess I imagined that eventually I'd go back home and pick up my old life with Mum, become Violet Tyler again, and straighten out the ID issue. But that never happened.

Carlie read it over and over again, the words blurring before her eyes. Her mum had become Fiona Scott. She'd opened a bank account in that name, because the passport was the only ID she had. She'd gone back to school and graduated using that name, and studied at university and become a lawyer with that name too.

Eventually she'd married Oliver, her best friend and saviour, and had taken his last name, because Scott meant nothing to her. Well, it meant survival and strength, and escape from a situation that could really only have ended with her death, but it had no family connection for her. In the absence of her mother from her life, Oliver was all the family she had.

But that wasn't what was important right now. The crucial factor was that her mum had not died on the morning of her fortieth birthday, as she and Mike had believed. She'd gained two years with her ID switch, so she would have only been thirty-eight when the car crashed. And suddenly she remembered something from her mum's Book of Shadows as well – hadn't she left the morning after one of the sabbat rituals she'd performed with Rose?

Desperately she flicked through the heavy pages of her mum's Book of Shadows, smiling as she saw the words of magic her mother had written. Her heart broke for her as she realised how much she had given up to get away – she'd loved celebrating the festivals of the wheel of the year and performing rituals with Rose as much as, if not more than, Carlie did now.

There it was. Violet had run away from home a month after her seventeenth birthday, on the morning after the Mabon ritual at the healing centre, so her real birthday must have been in mid to late August. So she hadn't even turned thirty-eight when she died. How strange, that her mum had celebrated a fake birthday, on a fake day, with a fake age. And that the real Fiona had been born on June 21, the summer solstice in England, and the winter solstice in Australia – so her mum's pretend birthday fell on one of the sabbats she would have previously celebrated with Rose and their magical community.

Carlie's head was spinning. How had Rose not realised that something was amiss? Surely she would remember her own daughter's birthday? Then again, she wasn't sure her grandmother knew that the accident had happened on the eve of her mum's assumed birthday, or which birthday that allegedly was. And when Sandy had managed to track Rose down to tell her that Violet had died, she wouldn't have mentioned that it had happened on her birthday either. Should Mike not have realised? Possibly, but he probably wouldn't have known when she'd died either, just that she had, so when he'd asked her if Violet had died on the curse date, and she'd said yes, he'd believed her. After all, why would she lie about her mum's birthday?

Suddenly she couldn't wait to tell Mike, but he was in Scotland with Rhiannon and Brodie, and wouldn't be back until Sunday night. Three long days until she could tell him, and set his mind at ease.

"You look much cheerier today," Rose said, when Carlie finally ventured downstairs for breakfast, with Luna in her arms.

"A friend was really worried about something, but I just figured out why there was no need to be, and I can't wait to tell them!" she replied with a relieved grin.

Rose looked puzzled. "Rhiannon? But no, she's still away with her family isn't she? Jake?"

"It was Mike actually," Carlie blurted out, then grimaced.

"Is he okay?" Rose asked, voice panicked.

Damn, she'd decided that she wasn't going to tell Rose any of this, or get her involved. But how did she avoid it now? "He's fine," she said cautiously.

"Can I help?" her grandma asked.

Sighing, Carlie put Luna on the floor and sat down at the table, thinking fast. She didn't want to upset Rose by bringing up Violet's death, but if she didn't reveal what had happened, her gran was going to worry incessantly about Mike. "It's a long story," she began, voice hesitant. "And I don't even understand it all myself."

Then she smiled. Gazing up at her grandmother, at her wise face and compassion-filled eyes, she knew that if anyone would believe this crazy story, it was Rose. And if anyone would have words of wisdom and useful advice, it was this priestess of the goddess.

"Okay, where do I start? A few weeks ago Rhiannon mentioned to me that her dad had been thinking all these years that Mum hated him, and that he'd let her down, so I photocopied a few pages from her Book of Shadows and her diary –"

"You have her diary?" Rose breathed, as she handed her a mug of tea and sat down opposite her.

"Um, yeah, but... well, anyway," she stuttered, then quickly got back to the topic at hand. There was no way Rose should read all the awful things that had happened to her daughter – she wouldn't be able to endure it, tough though she was.

"I wanted Mike to know that Mum had always really cared about him, and that one of her biggest regrets in life was that she had hurt you and Mike, so he had to stop beating himself up. But he told me that he'd been to see Andre before Mum went away, to try to get him to leave her alone, because he didn't trust the guy, and he didn't think he was good for Mum – which he was right about, obviously," she said, sighing as she took a sip of tea.

"He confronted him, but the shaman guy didn't care. He just laughed, and threatened Mike, insisting that he'd turn Mum against him if he tried to break them up, and he would never see her again. And then he said that he would curse him, so that every woman he ever loved would die on her fortieth birthday."

"But there's no such thing as curses Sweetheart, and Mike knows that," Rose replied calmly. "The only way a so-called curse could have any power is if the person believed it did."

"And yet Beth died on her fortieth birthday," Carlie said quietly. "And so did Mum, or so I thought, and when I acknowledged that to Mike, he freaked out. He's been terrified that Rhiannon will die young ever since."

Rose looked confused. "But Violet was only thirty-seven."

"I know!" Carlie replied. "Well, I know now. That's what I finally discovered this morning."

"That makes no sense," her grandmother said. "You knew when her birthday was."

"Actually, it turns out that I didn't know," she admitted. "Mum always celebrated her birthday on June 21 – the winter solstice, as I've come to realise. And the accident happened on solstice eve, after we'd been out for dinner for her fortieth birthday, and she died the next morning."

"But..."

Carlie smiled sadly. "There was a good reason for why I thought that, and why she did that. When my dad helped her escape from the crazy shaman, she used the passport of a friend of his, Fiona, who was two years older than her. And since that was the only ID she had when she fled, she became Fiona Scott, and got a new date of birth too. That's why she changed her name Gran, it was nothing to do with rejecting you, or her life here."

Tears were sliding down Rose's cheeks, but she smiled through them. "That means a lot to me, to know that," she whispered, voice raw and cracked with pain. "Thank you Sweetheart."

Carlie stood up and went around the table to hug her, and she had a flash of memory, of the day she and Rose had been at this same table, her leaning in and holding her grandma while she'd sat frozen, staring at Violet's Book of Shadows and learning how much her daughter had adored her, and how desperately sad she had been to be leaving home, but that she was doing it because she thought her father would die if she stayed. Perhaps there were some parts of the diary that her grandma could read.

As if hearing the thought, Rose looked up at Carlie and asked if she would share it with her. She was torn. It would break her grandmother's heart to learn of the abuse her daughter had suffered, but there were also parts in there that would soothe it – from Violet's indecision and sadness about leaving home in the first place, to her constant missing of her parents and her beautiful relationship with the man she would later marry.

Finally she nodded, then went back upstairs and flicked quickly through the diary, tearing out the worst entries, the catalogue of her suffering, the awful violence, the pages that showed just how much the shaman guy had broken her brave mother, destroyed her to the point where she had prayed for death so her suffering would end.

Hiding the pain-filled pages in her bottom drawer, she took the censored diary downstairs and handed it to Rose, fear clutching at her heart. Was this the right thing to do? Should she be showing any of this to her? She didn't know, but if it could help soothe her heart to know that her daughter had missed her every day of her life, surely that could only be a good thing?

Rose smiled, her face calm and her hand steady as she reached out for the book. "It's not your responsibility Sweetheart, so please don't feel that way. I *want* to read it, and besides, I'm sure you took out the worst bits," she added, eyes twinkling.

Carlie blushed, but her grandmother just laughed. "I'll be fine, I promise. Now, would you mind going down and opening the healing centre for me? I'm going to stay here for a while, sit with this, sit with Violet. Do you feel able to do that for me? I promise I will be okay."

Reluctantly Carlie nodded, then she grabbed a banana from the fruit bowl and the keys from the bench, and walked into the village to open the shop and welcome the first customers. She was happy that she was capable of doing it, and proud that she could help her grandma in this way. Perhaps she could offer to open up on the weekends from now on, so Rose could have a bit more free time, and let go of a little bit of responsibility.

One of the massage therapists came in at midday and saw a few clients, but for the most part it was a fairly quiet day, and Carlie was able to accept a delivery of new books, and work out how to price them all, then put them out on the floor. She loved lifting each book out of its box, smelling that awesome new-book smell, then working out which shelf to position them on.

There were a few gems there, and she chose one that she'd buy when Rose came in. It was a thick text about healing grief, and she figured it would be good preparation to have read it before her uni course started. And who knew, it might even bring her some relief from her own sadness and regret.

Chapter 28

Return of the Curse

The sun shone all weekend and the sky remained blue, but Carlie struggled to enjoy it. She was anxious to tell Mike what she'd discovered, and to add Rose's assertion that curses had no power, just in case he still harboured any self-blame or doubt on the matter. And she was hoping that Rhiannon would now stop asking her what was wrong all the time, since her own preoccupation with the curse had come to an end.

But although the two friends had planned to catch up on Sunday night if Rhiannon and her family got back in time, Carlie didn't end up seeing her friend until school on Monday, and the poor girl couldn't stop yawning. A flat tyre on a dark and lonely road meant they didn't make it home from their Scottish adventure until the early hours of the morning, and Rhiannon and her little brother had collapsed into their beds, still fully clothed, the minute they got upstairs to their rooms.

Feeling increasingly apprehensive, and desperate to put Mike's mind at ease, Carlie decided she'd think up some excuse and go over and tell him that night – but she was thwarted in her plan when she got lumbered with revision for a surprise test the next morning. Rhiannon revealing that her dad would be at a work function that evening anyway didn't totally ease her frustration.

So it wasn't until their coven meeting on Tuesday night that she finally got the chance to tell Mike what she'd learned. Rhiannon hadn't finished setting up for their ritual, so Carlie offered to go downstairs and make them cups of tea.

Mike was washing the dishes when she walked into the kitchen, and they made small talk about his holiday in Scotland and her working in the shop for Rose while the kettle boiled, then she finally gathered her courage.

"Um, Mike, I wanted to let you know that, well, firstly Rose says there's no such thing as curses, and also, I was reading through Mum's diary again, and I realised that I was wrong – she didn't die on her fortieth birthday. So there is no curse, and there's nothing for you to blame yourself for."

He stared at her, bewildered by her words, and sank down onto one of the bar stools at the kitchen bench. "I don't understand," he whispered, voice faint, expression cautious, yet a spark of hope lighting up his eyes.

"Well, it's a long story, but for Mum to travel to Australia to get away from the violent shaman guy, she had to use someone else's passport, a friend of my dad's called Fiona, and she was two years older than Mum. So that means Mum was only thirty-seven when she died, not forty, and it wasn't on her real birthday anyway, it was two months earlier."

A range of emotions Carlie couldn't identify flitted across Mike's face, too fast for her to focus on any one of them. Then, unexpectedly, he laughed.

"You know, you'd think I would have realised there was something off about that. Violet and I were the same age after all. We were in the same classes all through school, went to each other's birthday parties every year. Why didn't I think of that?" he asked, frustration in his voice, but also relief.

"Well, you would expect that her daughter would know how old she was, and when her birthday was, so I guess you took my reply on faith. It's funny, I thought it was kind of cool, when I started learning about her life here, and how much she loved magic and ritual, that her birthday was on the winter solstice – well, the winter solstice in

Australia anyway, because up here it's the summer solstice in June. But that wasn't her birthday, that was just the day she died."

Suddenly her face went white, and she collapsed back against the kitchen bench. Mike rushed around to her, holding her up while she felt the whole world spin around her and collapse from under her.

"Carlie, what's wrong?" he asked urgently, worriedly. She stared at him, but couldn't focus on his face, couldn't focus on anything. She felt herself sinking down to the floor, and sensed Mike crouched next to her, trying to work out what was wrong, and what he could do to help her.

She stared up at him, eyes wild, haunted. "It's me that's cursed," she whispered with dawning horror. "Mum and Dad both died on the winter solstice. And Rowan died then too. Don't you see? It's me that's the link here, not you."

"No Carlie, that's not true. You know it's not true. It's like you told me, they were just tragic accidents," he insisted. "There are no curses – they have no power, remember? Rose promised us that." Quickly he grabbed a glass and filled it with water, then pushed it into her hands. "Drink a little bit, please, even if it's just a sip. You've had a bit of a shock. Now take a few deep breaths. Come on, in and out," he pressed. "In and out."

She did as she was told, closing her eyes and carefully inhaling and exhaling, and eventually the room stopped spinning, just as the kettle started to screech. Mike rushed over to turn it off, and Carlie slowly got to her feet, still feeling a little wobbly, but aware that the worst of the shock had subsided.

They were pouring boiling water into mugs when Rhiannon came into the room to announce that she was ready. Carlie shot Mike a pointed glance, begging him not to say anything to her friend about her strange moment. Smiling at her reassuringly, he shook his head almost imperceptibly, to let her know that he wouldn't tell, and her secret was safe with him, while not making Rhiannon suspicious that something was going on.

"Sorry, I overfilled the kettle and it took a while to boil. But the tea is coming right up," he assured his daughter. Yawning again as she shrugged her shoulders, Rhiannon didn't seem at all perturbed by the delay, but Mike saw his chance. "Darling, you look exhausted, and Carlie, you do too. How much homework are they giving you at school?" he asked.

"Too much," Rhiannon mumbled, yawning again.

"Girls, I hate to come over all parental on you, but it's already getting late, so I think you'd be very wise to skip tonight's magical working, and both try to get some sleep. What's the point of you getting a holiday if they just work you to the bone the moment you're back at school?" he continued.

Carlie looked over at Rhiannon, worried she would still want to do some magic, but her friend looked truly exhausted.

"I won't argue with you Dad, if that's okay with you Carlie?" she asked, trying to smother another yawn.

Smiling with relief, Carlie said that of course it was fine, and slowly made her way back to the cottage. She hadn't felt tired before, but now it was coming in waves, and all she wanted to do was crawl under the covers and close her eyes.

Rose was still awake when she came in though, and looked up in surprise when Carlie walked into the kitchen, where she'd just brewed a pot of her sweet-dreams, sleep-ease tea.

"Are you okay Sweetheart? How did it go with Mike?" she asked, as she poured out another cup and handed it to Carlie.

"Yeah, he was fine," she replied, then sighed. "As soon as I told him, he realised that of course Mum had been younger, because they were the same age. He was kind of mortified that he'd overlooked that fact. But sadly it seems that I'm the person who was cursed," she added, voice heavy with sorrow.

Settling into the chair opposite her, Rose stared at her granddaughter, trying to make sense of her words. "Sweetheart, there is no curse, I told you that. It's just a fictional construct, something to scare faerytale-reading kids into behaving," she said sternly.

Carlie shivered at her tone, at her words, but she smiled when Luna jumped up into her lap, and patted the kitten absentmindedly as she tried to collect her thoughts.

"My parents died on the winter solstice, long before I knew anything about the sabbats," she explained. "And Rowan died on the winter solstice too. I'm the only link there, so it's got to be my fault, something *I* did," she muttered.

Rose got up and hugged her, and told her to drink her tea. "Sweetheart, the only thing that links those two tragic events is that they were car accidents that occurred at midwinter, when the roads were slippery with ice and snow and rain. Of course there are more car accidents in the middle of winter, especially around here. Driving when it's snowing can be very dangerous, that's why there are warning signs everywhere, especially on that bend where Rowan went off the road," she said.

"And I have no doubt that once that drunk driver hit your car, it was going to be much harder to control the steering and come out of it in once piece because of the slipperiness of the cold, wet road."

Carlie gazed up at Rose, wanting so badly for that to be true, but scared that it was just a shoddy excuse to explain away her pain. But her grandmother reached across the table and took her hand. "It's the truth Sweetheart. I promise you there is no such thing as a curse, and that you had absolutely nothing to do with either of those tragic accidents."

Carlie smiled, a tiny, relieved smile, and Rose nodded. "Now, Luna looks exhausted, even though she appeared to have been napping all day, and so do you. So finish up that tea, because it will help you sleep, and then off to bed with you, okay? Things will look much rosier in the morning."

Obeying her grandmother, Carlie swigged back the rest of the herbal brew, lifted Luna into her arms, and made her way upstairs. Without even getting changed, she lay down on the bed and slept for ten hours straight, a dreamless, uninterrupted and healing sleep that was exactly what she needed.

Chapter 29

A New Love

Carlie and Rhiannon were sitting in the cafeteria on Friday, Rhiannon lamenting that she was single and Carlie trying to counsel patience – it had only been two weeks since she broke up with John after all – when Jake bounced over to them with his tray and slid in next to Carlie.

"Do you think we could get away with not working on our assignment this weekend?" he asked her hopefully. "It's just that my cousin is coming down from London to stay for a few days, and I haven't seen him for a couple of years. So I'd feel bad ditching him and leaving him all alone with Pop to go off and study."

"Of course, we'll be fine. And we can catch up Monday after school, yeah? Besides, we've got two more weeks and we're pretty much done, so no worries," Carlie said.

"Is he Australian too?" Rhiannon asked Jake.

"No, sadly he's English," he replied, face straight, then he laughed. "Just joking! He was born in London, and has spent most of his life there, although he did live with us for a year in Perth when I was, I don't know, ten maybe, and he was thirteen."

"And is he cute too?" Rhiannon pressed.

Carlie and Jake both stared at her, and she blushed a little. "What? Can't a girl ask these things? People need to know!"

Jake laughed. "I'm sorry, of course you can ask. But I'm not actually sure – I haven't seen him since he was sixteen, and that was only briefly, when I came to London with my parents for a family reunion. He seemed kinda gangly and goofy, but I probably wasn't the best judge. And he might have grown into himself now. I think he's been apprenticing at a tattoo studio the last couple of years, so for all I know he could be a long-haired biker with a huge beard and full sleeve art by now," he grinned. Then he looked thoughtful.

"Actually, would you guys want to have lunch with us tomorrow, or do something together? I'm not sure I'm going to be interesting enough for him, so I'm worried he'll be totally bored being stuck with just me and Pop all weekend."

Carlie was about to say no – the last thing she wanted to do was go on some weird kind of double date with a stranger, and a possible bikie no less. But Rhiannon was already making suggestions for what they could do and where they could go. Jake caught her eye and smiled at her, conveying in that single glance that he understood how she felt and was grateful to her for going along with Rhiannon's plan and helping him. She shrugged, then finally smiled too. She knew she wasn't going to be able to change Rhiannon's mind now that she'd decided to do this, so she may as well make the best of it.

In the end they'd decided to just meet for lunch then see what they all felt like doing after that, and Jake kept reminding them that they could both leave at any point if they weren't having a good time. But the moment Rhiannon laid eyes on Tom in the cafe she was transfixed, and all thoughts of their prearranged departure plan in case they got bored were instantly forgotten.

"This is Tom, although apparently he prefers to be called Raven now," Jake said, as he nervously introduced the girls to his cousin.

"Hi Carlie," he said, shaking her hand. "And you must be Rhiannon. Jake's been filling me in, but he didn't tell me how gorgeous you are."

Rhiannon giggled, a touch of shyness in her expression, but when Tom took her hand and held it to his lips, she shrugged off any hesitation and hugged him. "It's lovely to meet you. Any friend of

Jake's is a friend of ours!" she said, sliding into the booth so she was sitting next to him. Carlie and Jake smiled in amusement and sat opposite them, and were more than happy to let the outgoing pair carry the weight of the conversation.

"I hope this is okay for you Carlie," Jake whispered at one point. "I really appreciate you helping me out. I know you're not feeling particularly social at the moment."

Touched that he'd picked up on that, she smiled back at him. "You're very welcome. Although it looks like we won't need to make much effort – they seem to have it all under control."

A waitress came and took their orders, amused that they were all vegetarian in a place renowned for its beef burgers. Jake raised an eyebrow at his cousin. "I thought you only ate meat, the original paleo champion," he said. "I'm sorry if you're not any more, but that's why I chose this place."

Tom shrugged. "No problem. I guess it's been a while since we hung out – what were you, thirteen or something, last time you visited?" he asked, and Jake blushed, which made Carlie feel protective of him. "I've been plant-based for the last three years, ever since I got into paganism," Tom continued.

Rhiannon's ears pricked up. "Are you in a coven, or is it less structured for you? Have you been studying? Do you have a particular focus – witch, druid, shaman – or are you more eclectic?" she asked, then paused. "Sorry for the twenty questions, but I'm always excited to meet other magical folk."

He smiled at her, a flirty smile that she responded to in kind. "I've been attending public rituals with a group near where I live, and studying with a priest and priestess I met last Mabon. They were initiated into Wicca years ago, but are more broadly pagan now, so I guess I'd just say I'm a witch. I love the discipline of learning from them though, and I've been doing a lot of self-study too. Why, do you know much about magic?"

Rhiannon's eyes lit up. "I've been celebrating the wheel of the year and the phases of the moon since I was a kid. Carlie's grandma Rose is a priestess, and one of our teachers at school is part of her circle. So was my mum – it's all quite open here, attending rituals is just part of life," she said proudly, and only Carlie noticed that her voice had thickened with sorrow as she mentioned her mother.

"I consider myself a witch too," she continued. "We celebrate the sabbats and the new and full moons with Rose – and Jake and his grandad even came to the last one, at Imbolc. And Carlie and I formed a coven six months ago, and have been studying together and doing our own private rituals ever since."

Jake gazed at Carlie, curiosity burning in his eyes, while Tom was looking at Rhiannon with new respect, and even more interest. "Perhaps we could work some magic together," he said, tone suggestive.

Rhiannon batted her eyelashes at him. "I'd love to."

The waitress came over with their meals then, and they all paused for a moment as they sorted out sauces and dressings and ordered more juices. Carlie was lost in her own little world, wondering what she would call herself if she was asked. Rose considered herself a priestess of the goddess, a pagan and a witch. Rhiannon called herself a witch too, and Rowan had been described as both a shaman and a druid. Did she need a name? A descriptor?

As if reading her mind, Tom turned to Carlie and asked her how she saw herself. Blushing a little at the intensity of his gaze – he made her feel uneasy for some reason – she stammered out that she supposed she was a witch, although she didn't take the goddess as literally as Rhiannon or her grandmother did, so she wasn't sure if she could actually claim that word for herself.

"And her boyfriend was a druidic shaman, or a shamanic druid, and they worked a lot of magic together," Rhiannon added quickly. Tom stared at Carlie, then at Jake. "Where is he today?" he asked, and the judgement in his voice made Carlie feel uncomfortable again, as though he thought she was two-timing with Jake or something, while the mention of Rowan in Tom's sarcastic tone left her feeling as though she'd been punched in the stomach.

Regret crossed Rhiannon's face at bringing it up, and Jake put a comforting hand on her arm. "He died," he told Tom, simply, gently, but with no room for further questions. And there was a note of warning and challenge in his eyes as he glared at his cousin.

Rhiannon picked up on it and changed the subject, engaging Tom in a robust discussion about the pros and cons of working skyclad, especially at this time of year, when it was still a little chilly outside. And Carlie slowly composed herself, although she remained quiet and withdrawn while they ordered coffees and the conversation swirled, fuelled by Tom and Rhiannon, who were already as thick as thieves and planning activities independent of the group.

Finally the waitress came over and told them they were closing up to prep for dinner, and the four of them slouched out into the cold afternoon air, huddling in the doorway as they pondered what to do next. Rhiannon was telling Tom about another cafe they *had* to visit because they had the best chai lattes in town, but Carlie couldn't wait to escape. Surely she'd done her duty by now?

"I'm sorry, but I've got to get home, I promised Rose that I'd help her with the herbal blends this afternoon. But it was lovely to meet you Tom," she said, holding out her hand.

He smiled at her. "It was wonderful to meet you too, and I'm so sorry about –"

She shook her head, cutting him off. "It's fine, you didn't know," she replied stiffly. Hugging Rhiannon, she told her that she'd see her the next day, then turned to Jake to say goodbye.

"I'll walk you home," he offered, and held up his hands when she started to protest. "I have to see Rose about some herbs Pop needs, so we're going the same way." He turned to his cousin and their friend. "Are you guys okay if I leave you to it? Pop asked if I could bring the remedy home this afternoon, so..."

Looking delighted to be left on their own, Tom and Rhiannon both nodded. "I've got a key to get back in, so don't worry if I'm late home," Tom said to Jake with a wink, then turned and strode off down the street with an ecstatically happy Rhiannon, neither of them sparing the others a second glance.

Jake smiled ruefully at Carlie. "I'm so sorry about Tom, he's really full on," he began, but Carlie shook her head.

"Oh Jake, please, it's not your fault, and it's not his either. I guess it will eventually get easier for me to deal with, you know? It's just so raw still, and I was unprepared for the question, so I just froze. Thank you for answering for me though, and for not over-explaining or making it into a big deal."

"I just wish I could do something to help you," he said, voice raw with longing.

"You do help me Jake, I promise, just by being so sweet, and so considerate. It means so much to me. And I really appreciate your friendship, and your understanding. I know it's not really fair to you, because I'm still so messed up, and I can't be what you want me to be. I wish I could," she said regretfully, looking away so he wouldn't see the pain on her face or the tears in her eyes.

But he could sense it, and although it broke his heart, he was determined to at least be her friend, and a real friend at that. He could pressure her – he knew that she liked him, and that he could have used the guilt she felt about his feelings for her to force something between them, but he didn't want to do that, he didn't want it to happen that way.

He wanted her to *choose* him, not to go out with him out of obligation or from feeling worn down by refusing him. Of course he hoped that wouldn't take too long, since he'd be going back to Perth at the end of the year, but he had resigned himself to trying to be patient. He really wished that she and Rowan had just broken up though, rather than him dying while they were still in love. It was so hard to compete with a dead guy, and one who seemed like some kind of magical hero no less.

"So how do you feel about your cousin?" Carlie asked him, bringing him abruptly back to the present. "Is he much like how you remembered him to be?"

"Was it that obvious?" he asked, laughing. "He is a lot more full on now, but I guess the difference between seeing him as a sixteen-year-old and meeting him again as a twenty-year-old was always going to be huge. He's a lot more outgoing than when I last saw him, a lot more confident. And he seems pretty wild. He is apprenticing with a tattooist – he did a year at a design school after he graduated, and I think he's still going, but he's also getting on-the-job training at the tattoo studio. He actually did the one of the raven on his wrist himself, which is amazing. I couldn't inflict pain on myself."

Carlie thought of Rhi's list. Tattooed. Check! Wild. Check! Witch. Check! She smiled at Jake. "Do you have any tattoos?"

He shook his head. "You?"

For a moment she pondered letting him believe that she did, but she couldn't say it with a straight face. "I was planning to get one," she finally said. "But I'm a bit cautious, because I don't know anyone here to get a recommendation from."

"What would you get?"

A dreamy expression crossed her face, and she looked up at the sky. "I'd like to get the symbol of the triple goddess, which represents the phases of the moon, and the phases of life, and would honour the magical workings I've been doing with Rose and the rituals I've been part of at her healing centre," she explained.

"How about you, have you ever thought of getting one?"

"I have considered it, although I'm not sure what I want to get," Jake replied. "Possibly a wave, to remind me of home and my connection to the ocean and my surfboard," he grinned. "Although after the Imbolc ritual, I feel as though I'd like to get something that honours my step into the magical realms too, and the impact Rose's amazing ceremony had on me and my grandfather, and the connection between the two of us. Maybe a candle flame, or even four symbols within a circle, to represent the four elements she drew on, sitting within the sacred circle I was part of."

"That sounds really beautiful," Carlie said. "So, do you think we should get one?" she asked, and she was only half joking. But they'd reached the cottage by then, so she quickly changed the subject as she led him inside and through to the kitchen.

Rose sat down with them for a cup of tea and a chat, then she bottled up the herbal remedy she'd made for Jake's grandfather, and he bade them both farewell, thanking Carlie again for helping him entertain his cousin. She shrugged and told him it was nothing – Rhiannon had done all the work after all, but she was always happy to help out a friend…

The next morning, Carlie was having an early breakfast with Rose, Luna curled up in her lap, when there was an impatient knock on the front door. Laughing, she stood up and put the kettle on, then turned to walk out of the kitchen.

"You expecting someone Sweetheart?" Rose asked, surprise in her voice at having a visitor so early on a Sunday.

"Just Rhiannon. I'm guessing she has some big news to share about a new guy," she replied, as she headed towards the front of the house. She missed the look of disappointment that crossed her grandmother's face as she went to greet her friend. It had been more than two months since Rowan had died, and Rose was hoping that her granddaughter would start finding some joy in life again soon. Jake obviously cared deeply for her, and she could tell Carlie liked him too, yet she seemed oblivious to him.

The impatient knocking came again, just as Carlie hauled open the door. Rhiannon stood on the front step, bouncing up and down with excitement. She threw her arms around Carlie, almost sending them both sprawling onto the hallway floor.

"Oh, sorry! I've just got so much to tell you!" she cried, cheeks flushed red with joy and anticipation as she followed Carlie back out to the kitchen.

"Hello sweet girl, it's lovely to see you," Rose said, amused and cheered by her high spirits. "Would you like a cup of tea?"

"I'd love one, thank you," she grinned. "Oh, isn't it a gorgeous day! I feel so alive!"

Rose smiled at her. "The joy of youth," she said, the faintest tinge of regret in her voice. "And love, if I had to guess," she continued, with a twinkle in her eye.

Rhiannon glanced at her friend. "I didn't say anything, I swear. I don't *know* anything," Carlie protested quickly.

"But you do look all excited and filled with the thrill of new love," she said, and busied herself making the tea so her friend couldn't see her sadness. It wasn't fair to bring her down, when she was so filled with happiness, but it did hurt her a bit to see her so lit up with passion and connection. Yet she was genuinely glad for her, she reminded herself. And Rhiannon finding love didn't make any difference to her or change her circumstances in any way – it didn't make her loss worse or narrow her chances of finding love one day. And her friend deserved happiness, and a guy who adored her.

And her support, she thought with a sigh, and made a conscious effort to adjust her attitude.

"Oh, he's just so lovely," Rhiannon blurted out, unable to keep it to herself. "And so magical, how awesome is that! He's been working in a coven, like us, and studying too, really experiencing it all, and he wants to share that with me," she said, then blushed. Carlie tried to hide her smile, and noticed that Rose was also trying not to reveal her mirth. So, it seemed Tom had been flirting with Rhiannon with suggestions that they do some kind of sex magic together.

Carlie took the mugs of tea over to the table and sat down opposite her friend as she tried to compose herself.

"After you and Jake left yesterday we went down to Kylie's Cafe and drank chai, and Tom was grilling me about the area, and the tor and its secrets, so I offered to take him up there. But he seemed to know it better than I do – he led me around the base of it, through the apple orchards, and each time we got to a stile, he told me it was a kissing gate, and I had to kiss him in order to get past."

Carlie's heart ached as she remembered Rowan doing the same thing, but she motioned for her friend to go on.

"Anyway, we finally got to the top, through this spiralling labyrinth path, like a maze, which was just, wow! There was so much energy coming up from the earth, I was vibrating from it! Although it might have been coming from him too – he's so powerful, and so spiritual. He talked about the ravens that were wheeling overhead, and about his raven tattoo, which is just gorgeous, and the shamanic journey he'd been on that had inspired it. And then the sun began to set, and it was just so magical," she enthused.

"And then he kissed me, properly kissed me! The world around us turned dark, but we kept kissing, and it was like we were the only two people on earth. Oh Carlie, if it was anything like this with Rowan then I totally understand now, how crushing it was for you to lose him. I feel alive in a way I never have before. It's like absolutely everything has changed – yet it's actually only me that has!"

Rhiannon beamed, her joy infectious, and Carlie willed her eyes to stay dry even as she felt the knife stab of pain in her heart.

"So, I'm meeting him at ten o'clock this morning for a chai, and hopefully lunch after that, and I wondered if you wanted to come with us? Jake will be there, so you won't feel left out if we, you know..." She looked so hopeful, so eager for acceptance and the sharing of her new adventure, but it felt like torture to Carlie, and as much as she wanted to be supportive, she just couldn't put herself through it for another day.

"I'm so sorry, but I promised Gran I'd help in the shop today," she said, looking over at her grandmother with a desperate plea in her eyes. But Rose refused to go along with it – she knew that it was time Carlie started living again, started opening her heart to new people, new experiences, new possibilities, and hiding away at home was not going to help her. Although it hurt her heart to do it, she knew her granddaughter needed a little push. And Jake was a good friend, a lovely boy with a sensitive nature, who would protect her from the worst of the pain.

"It's okay Sweetheart, Laurel is coming in today, so we'll be fine. You go and hang out with your friends."

"Awesome!" Rhiannon shrieked, as Carlie tried to mask her disappointment, and her annoyance with her grandmother. "Can you help me work out what to wear? I brought a few options," she grinned, holding up a huge bag.

Carlie felt as though she was dying inside, but she knew she had to be supportive of her friend, and she really wanted to be. It wasn't her fault that the thought of romance made her so sad. Giving her grandmother a withering stare that only made her shrug her shoulders in amusement, she finally led Rhiannon upstairs to her room, Luna bouncing around at their feet. They still had two hours before they had to meet the guys, and she was already feeling apprehensive.

"Oh Carlie, he's so wonderful," her friend said, flopping down on her bed with a melodramatic sigh. "And isn't he gorgeous? Just take-your-breath-away stunning! Oh my god, I totally know what you mean now, about the difference between Rowan and John. John was just a friend, almost a brother, compared to how I feel about Tom.

He's just so *amazing*. My tummy feels all fluttery when I think about him, and when he stares into my eyes, oh my god! It's so intense!"

Schooling her expression as carefully as possible, Carlie tried hard to ensure that only happy-for-you vibes flickered across her face. "So, you really hit it off, huh?" she commented, then smiled to herself. If nothing else, she was grateful that Rhiannon wanted to talk non-stop about her new obsession, and wouldn't even notice that she was remaining quiet.

"I know, wasn't it amazing!" her friend asked, voice full of excitement. "From the second he took my hand when Jake introduced us, I could feel it, this incredible energy between us, like fire. Like our Imbolc fire ritual. Maybe Aideen sent him to me!" she squealed, excitement colouring her voice.

"It was like we were connected, heart to heart. And just everything about him is perfect. He's magical, he's smart, he's independent, he loves music, he plays guitar, he has tattoos, he's wild – everything on my list! He's just so *cool*," she sighed, drifting off into a daydream for several moments. Carlie lifted Luna into her lap and stroked her soft head as she waited patiently for her friend to continue.

"Oh god, sorry, where was I?" Rhiannon finally asked, and Carlie laughed good-naturedly. "He's just so dreamy. And he wants to do a ritual with me, can you believe it? He's going to come down for the new moon next weekend, so we can do one up on the tor together. You'll cover for me, won't you?" she asked, glaring at Carlie as if she'd already refused. "You do owe me one you know," she insisted.

Carlie shrugged. "Okay."

"We were talking a lot about sex magic too," Rhiannon continued, enthusiasm bubbling over as she spoke. "But I'm sure he wouldn't mean to do that then, up on the tor, right? Not that I'd probably mind – every time he brushed against me I got all shivery inside, and we kissed for ages up there, and oh my god, it was so intense. Like I could have just melted into him, dissolved into him, merged into one being with him. Is that what it was like with Rowan?" she asked, but didn't wait for an answer. "My god, it was just mind-blowing."

Carlie stiffened, remembering the lectures she'd copped from Rhiannon about Rowan, the warnings that he only wanted one thing from her, that she'd better not have sex with him, because once she did he'd dump her for someone else. It seemed it was a different matter all together when it was herself getting all passionately involved with a guy.

But her friend had finally paused for breath, and she moved over closer to her and took her hand.

"I'm so sorry Carlie," she said, voice heartfelt and full of regret. "I realise I sound like the worst kind of hypocrite, and that I was out of line with you and Rowan, in so many ways. I just had no idea it could feel like this. And I know I just met Tom, and I hardly know him – and again, I can only apologise for not understanding that it could be so instant and so total – but already I feel the most amazing connection to him.

"It's like, this could be real love, you know what I mean?" Rhiannon continued. "What I had with John was just a childish friendship in comparison. There weren't any swept-off-my-feet, desperate-to-spend-every-second-with-him feelings there. But Tom makes me feel so alive, he lights me up inside in a way I've never felt before," she said, voice sober now.

"And I remember you trying to explain all of this to me when you were with Rowan, but I couldn't even begin to comprehend it then. So I'm just so deeply grateful to you for sharing your letters with me, and making me realise that being with John was nice, but would never be enough to bring me to life like this does. Because otherwise I would have been with John yesterday, and I never would have met Tom. And who knows, maybe *you* would be dating him instead of me, if you'd gone alone to lunch to help Jake."

Carlie seriously doubted that – Tom had seemed arrogant to her, too sure of himself by far, but clearly Rhiannon didn't share her view.

"And the weird thing is, even if I never see him again after this weekend, I'll feel blessed to have known him, to know this feeling, to know that this depth and passion is possible," she said. She took a deep breath, and squeezed Carlie's hand even tighter.

"I know this must be so hard for you to watch, and to listen to even, and I apologise. I just want you to know how much I appreciate your patience, and your support. I know the last thing you want to do is spend the day with us and watch us falling in love, and that you were annoyed with Rose for not giving you an excuse to avoid it."

Carlie blushed at being caught out, but Rhiannon just grinned and kept on talking. "It's okay, I understand that, I do, and it means the world to me that I know you have my back."

"I'm happy for you, I promise," Carlie said, and she smiled although the effort cost her. "It *is* hard for me, but this is not about me, or me and Rowan – it's about you, and I'll just have to work out a way to separate it so it doesn't hurt. Now, we should get you dressed. What did you bring? And what are we doing today? Just how glamorous versus practical do you have to be?"

Finally Rhiannon was happy with her outfit. Her indecision and panic had amused Carlie, since they'd both been wearing old jeans and plain t-shirts when they'd met Tom yesterday, and he'd seemed more than impressed with Rhiannon then.

Jake and Tom were at the cafe when they arrived, and both of their faces lit up when the girls came towards them and sat down, Rhiannon next to Tom on the two-seater couch, Carlie next to Jake in single armchairs opposite them. They both rolled their eyes when Tom and Rhiannon started kissing, but they were happy for them, and the new couple did draw apart for a moment when the waiter came to take their order.

"So, I was talking to Jake about the upcoming spring equinox," Tom began. "And we thought it would be awesome if you guys came up to London and joined us for our Ostara ritual. The Body Mind Spirit Festival is on during the day, then we'll be having a small gathering in the park that night..."

Rhiannon's face was transformed with joy, and she turned to Carlie, eyes sparkling. "Can we? Will you come with me? We can stay with my cousin again, like we did last time. Oh, please say yes!" she begged.

Carlie nodded, trying hard to mask her reluctance and dread. How could she not agree when it meant so much to her friend? But oh god, to go back to the place where she'd met Rowan? That would require some strength.

"Are you going too Jake?" she asked, turning to him in appeal.

"Do you want me to?" he replied softly.

"Please!" she said, and it was a heartfelt plea. Rhiannon and Tom were already kissing again. "You can't leave me with them, I beg of you!" she added, only half joking.

"Well, you did come along today *and* yesterday, for which I am eternally grateful," Jake said with a grin. "So yes, of course, I'll share your pain at the ritual too."

They both laughed, and spent the rest of the morning chatting together, since the other two were so caught up in each other.

"Do you miss Sydney?" Jake asked her, and she shrugged.

"Not as much any more," she said, voice slightly wistful. "When I got here I was determined that the minute I finished school I'd go straight back. But I feel a connection here that's hard to describe – to this village, to this land. And although I wanted to hate Gran when I arrived, thinking that she'd been a monster to my mum, once I realised that wasn't the case and gave myself a chance to get to know her, I realised how much I love her, and how much she loves me, and I don't think I could leave her. We both need each other – we're the only family each of us has now, which probably sounds a little melodramatic and sad, but it really isn't," she admitted.

"And there's Rhiannon. We've had some wild ups and downs, but she's my dearest friend, and we've decided to do the same uni course together, so I guess, as strange as it seems, I'm really settled here," she said, and surprised herself as she put her vague thoughts into words and comprehended the truth of them.

"Then there's the magic. I didn't know anything about it when I was in Sydney – Mum had closed down that side of herself, I guess because it made her too sad to remember what she'd lost. She'd denied its existence, and hidden all that she knew about it," she sighed, and Jake heard the pain in her voice.

"Sometimes I feel like I didn't even know her. So it's been such an incredible journey within, learning so much about myself, getting closer to Gran, seeing the world in a new way, becoming aware of all the potential that exists, within us, within nature, within and of the earth. Which of course would still be with me wherever I was, but for me it was all born of being in this place, working magic with the people I met here."

Her voice faltered as she thought of Rowan and all the things he'd taught her. "How about you?" she asked quickly, trying to deflect attention away from herself for a while.

Jake smiled, picking up on her not-so-subtle shift of topic, and going along with it. "I totally understand what you mean. It's been really lovely getting to know my grandfather so much better, now that I'm old enough to appreciate him, and it feels like he's opening up a little bit to me now too, after being so devastated, and shutting down, and shutting everyone out, after Nan died.

"And I know what you mean about the landscape here, I sense it as well," he added. "I feel so strangely comfortable in this place, like I've come home – which is weird, because I was born in Perth and have lived there my whole life," he mused.

"And thanks to you and your grandmother, I now feel my own magical self awakening too – I'm becoming more aware of things I had no idea of before. I'm really grateful to you for that, and to Rose for cheering my grandfather up."

Carlie stared at him, eyebrows raised in question.

"She's been so sweet to him, coming over to visit him a few afternoons every week, letting him really talk about Nan, and how he's feeling, how he's coping with his grief, in a way I'm not able to help him," Jake said. "She's an amazing woman. Just being around her is so calming, so healing."

A smile lit up Carlie's face. She hadn't known that Rose was visiting Richard, but she was glad. She knew what missing a loved one was like, and how much her grandmother had helped her cope, first with the loss of her parents, and more recently with her grief over Rowan. Not that she was over any of them by any means, but she really hoped that one day she would grow into half the woman Rose Tyler was. She really was the centre of the community here, the one who helped everyone, no matter what.

She didn't know what she – or indeed the whole village – would do when Rose was no longer with them, but she hoped that day was a long way off. Her grandma certainly looked as fit, and was as healthy, as a woman decades younger, and had such an incredible zest for life, that she was sure she'd be with them for many years to come.

Seeing Jake lift his cup to his mouth, Carlie snapped abruptly back to the present. "So what do you think you'll do after your year is up and you can meet your parents back home in Australia?" she asked, and was surprised to discover how curious she was about his answer. How strange. Yet now she saw that over the past few months she'd slowly become closer to Jake. So gradually that she hadn't even noticed, they'd developed a sweet friendship that she hadn't acknowledged to herself until today. Hadn't even recognised.

Jake had been sitting with her and Rhiannon at lunch for a while now, and they'd been working long hours on their assignment, which was going incredibly smoothly. She'd thought it was just the Aussie kids sticking together, but now it was dawning on her that she didn't really want him to leave at the end of the school year.

Right at that moment he smiled at her, and she blushed. *Please god don't let him be able to read my mind too!*

"I'm not sure any more," he finally said, and there was the hint of a question in his voice. "Like you, I assumed I'd go home as soon as school was done, go to uni in Perth, get a flat with a mate. But I'm really enjoying living here with Pop, and being in this village. I know it sounds odd, since I've spent half my life at the beach with a surfboard, but I really loved the snow of winter here, it was such a nice change from the sweltering heat back on the west coast. And, well, I hope this doesn't make you feel uncomfortable, but I really value your friendship, and I'll miss you and Rhiannon when I go home."

Carlie's cheeks reddened again in embarrassment, but she was surprised to realise that his words hadn't freaked her out, or made her want to flee, as they once would have. Instead she felt safe, and supported... and *happy*?

"I'll miss you too," she said shyly, and his face lit up with joy. Before she could panic about her admission, the waiter came over to ask if they wanted more drinks, and she was relieved when Rhiannon and Tom stopped kissing for a minute and they finally started talking as a group. She needed to ponder these new feelings when she was back in her room, away from Jake, and see what they could mean.

For now, she was relieved to discover that she liked Tom much better today – he seemed far less arrogant, and far more genuine, than he had yesterday. They discussed the upcoming spring equinox ritual they'd be doing together, and Carlie asked if they needed to bring anything – "just their good selves" – while Rhiannon was more concerned about what they should wear.

"I want to say skyclad, but I don't want to share you with anyone, gorgeous," Tom said to her with a wink. The intimacy of their shared look left Carlie feeling wistful and full of longing, which was at least an improvement on the bitterness she'd been feeling until now when she saw a happy couple. Maybe there was hope for her yet.

They all drank more tea then ordered lunch, talking all the while, then Tom announced that he had to leave to get home for work – he had a late shift at the tattoo studio that night.

"Walk me out?" he asked Rhiannon, who nodded happily and stood up as he dropped several twenty pound notes on the table and said farewell to Carlie and Jake, then walked outside to his motorbike. The two of them left inside tried not to watch, but their eyes kept being drawn back to the couple outside as they talked and kissed, talked and hugged, talked and kissed.

"He's okay isn't he?" Carlie asked suddenly, turning to Jake.

"What do you mean?"

"He's not just playing her is he? You know, string of women in London that he invites to skyclad rituals and to perform sex magic with him? Rhi just being one of many?"

Jake smiled. "He's really smitten with her," he said, voice reassuring. "He's not dating anyone else, and I think he genuinely likes her and wants to spend time with her. When he finally got home last night he talked about her non-stop, and he couldn't wait to get up this morning and come and meet her – apparently him getting up before midday for any reason is unheard of."

"Yeah, Rhiannon was the same," Carlie admitted, relief in her voice. "I'd just hate to see her get hurt, or feel used by some older city guy who was preying on her innocence, and her fascination with him because he's a witch too." Then she stopped short, suddenly paling.

"What's wrong?" Jake asked, instantly worried and protective.

She laughed, a short, mirthless laugh. "I was so angry at her, when she asked the same things about Rowan. I guess she really was just worried about me, but I thought she was just being jealous, trying to make me break up with him."

Jake touched her hand, the contact soothing. "Hey, it's great that you're worried – you should be. It's sweet, what friends should do. And he is older than us, so it's natural to wonder."

Carlie groaned. "Not as much older than her as Rowan was than me. I owe her an apology."

"Maybe now's not the best time," Jake said, and they both giggled as they watched Tom and Rhiannon locked in a passionate and very public display on the High Street.

"Or maybe it is," she interjected, as their embrace became raunchier. "I'm not sure she's going to want her dad to find out she's seeing a new guy – with long hair and tattoos no less – before she gets to tell him herself."

But as they stood up to pay so they could go and warn her, they saw Rhiannon pull the spare helmet onto her head, throw one leg over the back of the bike and wrap her arms around Tom's waist, before they roared off down the road.

Carlie sank back down in the armchair. "Okay, you win. I won't tell her now," she said with a grin. "Think you can handle another chai?" she asked, before they started reminiscing about their favourite Aussie surf breaks, artists and bands.

Half an hour later, Tom dropped Rhiannon back off in front of the cafe, kissed her briefly but passionately then sped off, and she floated back inside and flopped down on the couch, hair windswept and cheeks flushed, and a wide, joyous smile lighting up her face.

"Oh Jake, he's so lovely, thank you so much for introducing me to him. And Carlie, my god, now I get it!" she said, sighing loudly and dramatically.

"Get what?" Jake asked. Carlie looked uncomfortable, and tried desperately to send her friend "shut up" vibes, but Rhiannon was in love and oblivious to anyone else.

"Well, what she and Rowan had was amazing – it was totally real, true love, the whole let's-get-married-right-now-and-be-together-forever trip. He just adored her, and was cutting back on his work so that he could spend more time with her. And he put up with me being a total bitch to him because he loved her so much, and she loved him just as desperately," she raved.

"It was the most beautiful romance ever, cut tragically short. I didn't understand at the time though, I guess because I'd never felt anything like that. I was dating John, and he was nice, but there was no passion, not like they had. But now I get it!" she said, drifting off again with a dreamy smile on her face.

Jake was suddenly quiet, his posture rigid and cold, and Carlie was mortified. He really hadn't needed to hear that. She wished Rhiannon hadn't said anything, but it was too late – Jake was looking at her differently now, was withdrawn again, hurt, and the closeness she'd been feeling with him evaporated.

Rhiannon was blissfully unaware of the effect of her words though. "Oh, how will I survive the days until I see him?" she moaned. "I can't wait to be with him again. You'll both come to London with me for the equinox won't you? Dad will let me go if he knows I'm going with you Carlie. God, how will I get through the next week?" she wailed.

"I thought the equinox wasn't for another three weeks," Jake said stiffly, and Carlie smiled that he'd remembered the date.

"He's coming down next weekend so we can do our own ceremony on the tor, and go to Rose's new moon ritual at the healing centre together as well. You and your grandad should come too, they're really lovely evenings," she enthused.

"We probably will," Jake replied, his aloofness cooling as he remembered how magical Imbolc had been. "Pop said he really wanted to go to that one, and he'll be happy to see Tom again – not that he ended up seeing him much this weekend," he said, then laughed as Rhiannon blushed. "Just joking," he grinned, and Carlie was relieved that his good humour was returning.

Chapter 30

Big Doubts, Bad Excuses

Carlie's patience was severely tested on Monday at school though, when all Rhiannon could talk about was Tom. She tried to be good-humoured about it, and supportive and interested, and she mostly succeeded, but she had to admit that she was kind of relieved that she'd promised to catch up with Jake after school to work on their assignment, which was due in two short weeks.

It was only somewhat of a reprieve though, because Jake wanted to know what she thought of his cousin, and was having a dilemma himself, wondering if he was too boring or too bookish, not fun enough or outgoing enough, in comparison to Tom.

"Jake, of course you're not boring, and you *are* fun," she said with a touch of impatience. "What's gotten into you? And what has Tom unleashed? I'd much prefer to spend time with you than with him, you're way more interesting. And I'm glad you're not as outgoing and, well, full of yourself as he is. You're kind and considerate and sweet, and the three of us have awesome conversations at lunchtime, about all kinds of things, and do ritual together and weave magic. Why would you think you were boring?" she asked.

Cheeks turning pink with embarrassment, Jake shrugged and tried to look calm and unconcerned, but he seemed relieved by her words. "I don't know. It's just, well, Rhiannon was going on and on about how amazing Tom is, and how cool he is, and how adventurous and wild and rebellious and fascinating and magical and…"

"I know, I heard nothing else all day," she laughed. "But it's apples and oranges. You can't beat yourself up about it, and you shouldn't try to be more like him. There's no point. It wouldn't work, and it wouldn't be authentic, and worst of all, you wouldn't be happy. Please don't try to be something you're not, because what you are is really awesome. Just be yourself – I'd much rather hang out with you than Tom. Now come on, we need to get back to work, this assignment isn't going to write itself," she insisted, and Jake thanked her, a shy smile on his face, then opened his book again and got serious.

Rhiannon was still on the Tom bandwagon the next day at school, so when her friend knocked on the door that evening for their coven gathering, she realised she was feeling quite uncharitable, and hoped that they could speak of other things for a little while at least. But as it turned out, Rhiannon's next topic was just as bad.

"Jake really likes you," she blurted out, and Carlie looked up from the herbs she was blending and shook her head.

"Yes he does, I can see it in the way he looks at you. Plus Tom told me. And I hate to admit this, but I was really jealous when I realised this a few weeks ago, because it seemed like all the cool guys wanted you," she continued, a blush staining her cheeks.

"Oh Rhi, that's not true –"

"It's okay," Rhiannon interrupted. "I'm glad now that he didn't like me, because Tom is even *more* amazing – tattoos, a motorbike, a career, an artist, a witch! He's even better than I could have dreamed up with a love spell. And I know he's three years older than me, so I'm not sure when to break it to Dad, but I really appreciate you having my back on this, especially after what I did to you."

"About that…" Carlie began, and her friend looked up at her, worried that she wasn't going to keep her secret after all.

"Oh Rhi, of course I will," she insisted. "No, it's just, well, I think maybe I was a little unfair to you with the whole Rowan thing."

Rhiannon looked confused. "What do you mean? I was the one who was out of line."

"I was angry that you kept pointing out the age difference, and trying to convince me that he only wanted me for sex, and would cheat on me and all that," Carlie said.

Rhiannon grimaced. "I know, and you have every right to be angry. I'm really sorry about that."

"No, *I'm* sorry," Carlie continued. "I know now that you were just worried about me, and looking out for me, in your own unique way. I realised when you rode off on Tom's bike with him the other day – suddenly I was asking Jake all the same questions you challenged me with. 'Is he just playing her?' 'Is the making-magic-together, sky-clad-ritual promise a line he uses on lots of women?' 'Is he taking advantage of her innocence?' " she admitted reluctantly.

"All of which Jake rejected by the way – he told me that Tom is totally smitten with you. And I was only asking because I care about you and I was worried for you, but it made me realise that when you were asking me those questions, which made me so angry, it was coming from a place of love too."

Rhiannon smiled. "Well, thank you for caring about me – and for finding out the answers to those questions from Jake, because I've got to be honest, I've been wondering about them too. That's why I can't wait to see Tom again, to work out whether our feelings are real, or if I've just imagined it all."

"Oh Rhi, you didn't imagine it!" Carlie said, and finally she didn't mind talking about a relationship, since this was about how her friend was feeling, what she was worried about, not just endless babbling about how hot some guy was.

"Jake said Tom never gets up early, especially on a Sunday, yet he got up early just for you, and was so eager to see you that he beat us to the cafe. And he raved about you non-stop on Saturday night, after he finally got home to spend a few moments with his grandfather."

Rhiannon's face lit up, and she hugged Carlie tight. "Thank you for telling me that, it's a real relief. I wouldn't have blamed you if you'd wanted to smother me with a pillow rather than listen to one more thing about Tom, and I will try to talk about other things too, I promise!" she said.

And for a while they did. They finished blending their herbs while discussing the different properties and uses of them, then flicked through their own Book of Shadows and some of Rose's books to find a good recipe for new moon cookies. They'd be baking up several batches with Rose on Thursday night, for Friday evening's new moon ritual, and Carlie was also working on a healing ritual she wanted to do with Laura that night, for the community – if she managed to find the courage to put herself forward in that way.

Finally they took a break to go downstairs and make a fresh pot of tea, and Rhiannon returned to her second favourite subject. "I know you don't like Jake like that, and I'm not suggesting you date him – I've learned my lesson there – but he does really like you," she said. "What are you going to do about that?"

Carlie shrugged. "I don't know. I mean, there's not really anything I can do. What are you proposing that I should do? He asked me out during one of our study sessions, but –"

"You didn't tell me that!" Rhiannon exclaimed, looking a little hurt to have been left out.

"I just didn't want to make a big deal about it, or cause you to look at him any differently, because he's your friend too," Carlie explained gently.

"Fair enough. But what did you tell him?"

"I said that I couldn't, as nicely as possible. And that's when I told him about Rowan, and him dying so recently, so he knew it was nothing personal. I assured him that I had no plans to date anyone, that it wasn't just him."

"You *had* no plans?" Rhiannon asked cheekily.

"I had no plans and I still *have* no plans," Carlie retorted. "And I was very clear, I promise. I didn't want to lead him on, like some girls do, I wanted to be honest with him. And he took it really well, and said he was happy to be my friend, and I'm grateful for that. So we're all good," she insisted.

"But are you sure you don't want to date him? He's so lovely, and you both get on so well."

Carlie glared at her friend. "What happened to 'I'm not suggesting you date him'?" she asked, and Rhiannon had the decency to look a little sheepish. "I can't go out with someone just because he wants to, or because I feel guilty about saying no – that wouldn't last long anyway, because it would be for all the wrong reasons, and is surely not a sentiment anyone would support. And I value his friendship too much to do that to him anyway," she added.

Before the tension between them escalated any further, Rose arrived home, and Rhiannon mouthed "Sorry!" to Carlie before asking Rose how she was and getting the conversation back to more neutral ground. The three of them sat around the table drinking tea and chatting about lunar rites and recipes, and the spring equinox festival that was in less than three weeks. They discussed what kind of treats they would bake for that, and the herbs they could blend together for a sabbat incense, then Carlie broached the subject of going to London with Rhiannon to do a ritual with her cousin the night before their own, and the girls held their breath until Rose finally gave her permission.

The topic of Jake didn't come up again, and the two girls parted on good terms. But when Carlie curled up in bed later that night, with Luna nuzzling into her shoulder and purring gently, she pondered Rhiannon's words. Was Rowan the only reason she'd turned Jake down? When he'd asked her out six weeks ago, it had only been a month since Rowan had died, which was way too soon to even consider dating anyone.

She didn't feel any readier now, but a tiny voice in the back of her mind was asking whether she saw Jake as a potential future boyfriend, or if she didn't see him that way at all, and her dead boyfriend was just a good excuse to avoid hurting his feelings? As she patted the kitten's head, she thought about what she'd told him the night before as they'd studied together. It wasn't a lie, when she'd said that she would rather spend time with him than Tom, or when she'd admitted that he was fun and interesting and kind and considerate and sweet. But that didn't necessarily mean she wanted to be with him. He was more like a little brother to her. Wasn't he?

Chapter 31

Lilies For Love

Turning the key in the lock on Thursday afternoon, Carlie giggled when she heard Luna crying her squeaky little miaows from the other side of the door. As it creaked open, she crouched down and scooped the kitten up in her arms for a hug. Carrying her in one hand, she reached down and grabbed her school bag with the other and walked through to the kitchen.

"Hi Gran, I'm home," she called out, but there was no reply, and although she searched carefully, there was no note either. Which was strange, since Rose had said she wasn't working that afternoon and would be at home so they could start making the new moon cookies. Luna miaowed again, so she gently placed her on the ground and went to fill her bowl. She wondered if Rose would want her to start on dinner, or the baking, but she figured she may as well get some homework out of the way first.

By the time she finally heard the front door open, Carlie had finished everything that was due the next day and made a vegie chickpea curry, and night had long since fallen.

"Sorry I'm late Sweetheart," Rose said as she rustled into the kitchen with her arms filled with flowers and plant cuttings.

"Where were you?" Carlie asked, more sharply than she'd intended. "I was getting worried."

"I'm so sorry, I was just over at Richard's, and didn't realise how late it had become. He needed some help to plant out his herb garden, so I offered him a hand, and then he asked my advice about a recipe his wife used to make, so I showed him how to get it right, then we had a cup of tea, and all of a sudden it was dark. I'm sorry you were worried though."

Carlie smiled. "That's okay, it sounds like he really needed you today. And Jake will be glad he had a friend over to talk to."

"Well, it wasn't all one sided," Rose admitted, voice suddenly shy. "His garden is really amazing, and he gave me some great cuttings so I can grow them too, as well as these gorgeous lilies," she added, placing them on the bench then going to the pantry to find a vase. Her cheeks were pinker than usual when she started arranging the blooms, and Carlie stared at her, slightly suspicious thanks to her uncharacteristic behaviour. "Anyway, dinner smells really delicious, thank you so much for getting it sorted," Rose continued, voice striving for an innocent tone but not quite getting there.

Carlie looked more closely at her grandmother. "Are you blushing?" she asked her.

Rose laughed, although it sounded a little higher pitched than usual. "No Sweetheart, why would I be blushing?" she replied, although she ducked her head behind the flowers she was carefully placing in the vase. "Now, I'll just go and get washed up – do you need a hand first though?"

Carlie assured her that everything was under control and dinner would be ready to serve in five minutes, then started clearing up her books. By the time Rose returned she was composed again, and they spent dinnertime chatting about the new crystal therapist who'd started at the healing centre and Carlie's history assignment, which was due at the end of the following week. Rose had just put the kettle on when Rhiannon knocked on the door, and she joined them in the warmth of the kitchen, Luna snoozing under the table as they baked cookies and chatted about their new moon wishes.

"I'm hoping that Tom will make it down in time to join us, if that's okay with you," Rhiannon asked, turning to Rose.

"Of course sweet girl," their priestess replied, eyes twinkling with joy and excitement. "So it sounds as though things are going well with this young man?" she added cheekily.

Carlie almost laughed as she watched Rhiannon blush and become tongue-tied. "Um, I hope so," she said shyly. "But I suppose I won't know until I see him tomorrow night. That's why I haven't told Dad about him yet – I wanted to wait until I knew a bit more before I mentioned it. Because who knows, Tom may just not turn up, or he might see me and change his mind, or… I don't know," she sighed.

"I'm just not confident enough that anything will come of it right now – part of me thinks that last weekend was just a wonderful dream, and he doesn't really exist. So if it's not putting you in too awkward of a position, could you not mention Tom to Dad just yet? I promise I'll tell him this weekend, if there's anything to tell," she begged. "And if there isn't, he will have been saved the trouble of needing to react."

Rose smiled at the nervous young woman in front of her. "Yes, I can keep your secret for a few days, until you've decided whether or not it's worth sharing. But don't leave it too long until you tell Mike. And I think you'll be surprised. He knows that you're growing up, and that there will be boys. All he wants from you is honesty, for you to earn the trust you already have. This goes for you too Carlie. We would rather know that you're dating someone, and have the chance to meet them, and know that you're safe," she insisted.

"I'm still really sorry that you felt you couldn't tell me about Rowan, Sweetheart, and Mike is the same. We just want you both to be happy, and not to feel that you have to keep any secrets from us in order to protect us. Because it really didn't end well when Violet tried to protect me by shutting me out," she said with a sigh, then trailed off into her own little world.

Rhiannon took that as her cue to leave, hugging both of them goodbye and walking out to the front door with Carlie.

"Oh god, I'm so nervous about tomorrow night," she confided to her friend. "What if Tom has forgotten, or he met someone more interesting than me this week, or he finally realises that I'm just a boring school student, and decides to avoid the village altogether – that would upset Jake and his grandfather no end!"

Carlie took her friend's hands and stared into her eyes. "Rhi, come on," she said firmly. "You know how much he likes you – hell, Jake and I know how much he likes you, going off your very public displays of affection all of last weekend," she said, unable to hide a giggle. "Now go home, get a good night of sleep, and you'll be hanging out with him in no time."

The next day at school, Jake asked Carlie to thank Rose for cheering his grandfather up, and she narrowed her eyes. "Is something going on with them?" she asked. "She was late home last night, because apparently 'time just got away from them'," she said.

"I've been wondering the same thing," Jake replied. "They seem to have been hanging out quite a lot, and Pop is always so much happier after she's been over. All they do is drink tea, but I think Rose has become really important to him. Is that okay?" he asked, suddenly panicked, and peering at her closely.

Grinning, she nodded enthusiastically. "It's more than okay. I'm so glad they both have someone great to talk to – I'm sure your grandfather has far more wisdom than I do to share."

Rhiannon bounced over to them then, so talk turned back to Tom. The new couple planned to attend Rose's new moon ceremony with everyone else, then head up the tor to celebrate alone together. How Carlie missed having someone to be alone together with, but she smiled at her friend. "Take something warm," she warned good-naturedly. "It's going to be cold up there tonight, so I'll be snuggled up at home in bed with Luna."

When Carlie arrived at the healing centre that night with Rose, and as many containers of the moon cookies they'd baked as they could carry, she was swept up in the magic of the occasion. She helped Rose and Laura set up, gathering all the colourful cushions from the storeroom and placing them in a large circle around the room. Then as the first people started to arrive, she skipped over to the doorway to welcome them, handing each one a green pen and a few small white cards, along with a beeswax candle. Richard gave her a hug as he walked in, while Jake smiled at her and thanked her, and Rhiannon, holding hands with Tom, beamed at her with such joy that it made even her feel happy just to see it, and bask in the reflected good vibes. Rose came over to shake Tom's hand and hug Richard and Jake, and Jake and Carlie exchanged knowing glances that they quickly tried to hide from their priestess.

Finally Rose instructed everyone to gather in a circle and make themselves comfortable on a cushion, then she stepped up to the altar in the centre to begin. She smiled as everyone linked hands. "Welcome everyone. Tonight you have created the sacred circle yourselves, and have imbued it with just as much magic and protection as I ever could," she announced with a smile.

"It's wonderful to see a few new faces. Thank you for bringing your energy and intent to our gathering," she said, smiling over at Tom, then letting her eyes linger on Richard for a long moment. "I just want to outline tonight's ritual for those unfamiliar with how we work, and if anyone has any questions, please feel free to ask, at any point. There's no standing on ceremony here," she said.

Glancing around the room, Carlie saw that every person had all their attention focused on Rose, their eyes lit up already with the power of her presence and the magic of the night.

"In a moment Miri, Laura, Paulette and Belinda will call the directions and invoke the elements, then I'll welcome the god and the goddess to be with us during our rite," Rose continued. "Since it's the new moon, it's the perfect time to set our intentions for the month to come, which is why Carlie greeted you all with pen and paper. I'll facilitate a meditation, where we can each ponder on the weeks just gone, and the ones to come, and decide what intention we want to set, which area requires a new beginning, what we hope to manifest into our life. It can be a physical thing, a new commitment to an old resolution, a character trait you wish to develop, a wish for healing for yourself or another – whatever your heart yearns for, we will sow the seeds tonight, fuelled by our combined energy and woven with the power of this beautiful moon phase," she said.

"Once it has become strong and clear for you, write it out. It can be a single word, or as many sentences as you require – all it requires is that it be meaningful to you. Then you can burn the paper in the cauldron fire on the altar, and watch your intention being carried up and out into the universe with the smoke, or you can take it home with you and sleep with it under your pillow."

Turning to her left, Carlie smiled as she watched Richard's face, concentrating so hard on Rose's words, and lit up with a fierce intelligence mixed with wonder at his surroundings.

"After that, Carlie and Laura will send some reiki healing energy around the circle, then help us all do some distance healing. And then we'll farewell the deities and directions and close the circle, and ground ourselves with tea and lunar cookies," Rose continued.

"And the candle is for you to take home, to light each evening for the next month, as you focus on the intention you set tonight, staring into the flame as you concentrate on what you want. Then you can blow it out, sending the energy of your wish out into the universe. Making a wish as you blow out the candles on your birthday cake is a piece of candle magic that has survived from pagan times, and is a potent way to manifest your dreams, whatever day it is. So, are we ready to begin?" Rose asked, and an excited murmur reached her from the circle she stood within.

Later, as they drank tea and ate cookies, Richard thanked Carlie for inviting him and Jake into the magical fold, and told her how much he appreciated Rose's wisdom. "She's a wonderful woman, and I'm so grateful to her for spending some of her precious time with me, comforting me and helping me heal."

"She sees it as an honour, not an imposition," she replied. "Don't ever feel that helping you is a burden to her, or that she doesn't appreciate the gift that your presence gives her."

He smiled at her and took her hand. "I hope you realise that goes double for you," he said cheekily, and she winced, remembering how often she'd thought that exact thing, that she was nothing but a

hardship to Rose, an encumbrance she would rather not have had to suffer. "And I hope she's been able to help you heal too Carlie. I know how much you have lost, and how hard it can be to find meaning in life after a loved one has left us."

Before she was reduced to a sobbing mess, Rhiannon and Tom came over, hands full of cookies, and joined the conversation. "These are the yummiest ones we've ever made," Rhiannon grinned, and Richard laughed as he agreed, while Tom planted a kiss on her forehead before turning serious.

"It was lovely to do a ritual with you Pop," Tom said, as he leaned in and hugged his grandfather. "I'm looking forward to spending more time with you, and doing more of them together."

Jake walked over and joined them at that moment, and rolled his eyes as he heard what his cousin was saying. "And I suppose that would have nothing to do with wanting to spend time with Rhiannon?" he asked, but his tone was friendly.

"Hey, there's nothing wrong with having two reasons to get out of the city now is there?" Tom grinned. "Or three I suppose, if I was to count hanging out with you, Cuz," he teased.

By the time Rose joined them they were all laughing, and as Carlie took in the circle of friends and family around her, she felt a rush of gratitude for what she did have. When her parents had died last year, she'd thought that she would never feel happy again. And while she still missed them terribly, every day – and despaired so deeply at having lost Rowan too – she was starting to become more aware of the blessings in her life as well as the tragedies.

As she said farewell to Rhiannon and Tom and watched them set off for their tor adventure hand in hand, hugged Jake and Richard goodbye, and helped Rose lock up before walking home with her through the cool night air, she sent her wish out to the universe. For the people she had grown to care about to be happy and healthy, and for loss to leave them alone for a long while.

Chapter 32

Tattoos and Memories

The next two weeks passed by in a blur – their history assignments were due on the first Friday, so Jake and Carlie had a few late-night study sessions to get it all done, and Rhiannon reluctantly trekked out to Dave's place with him after school to finish theirs, cursing the fact that she had to tell Tom not to visit her that week. And there was no respite once they'd handed them in – the whole class now had print-outs of all the papers, on all the different British colonies, so they spent their lunchtimes and after school grilling each other on the facts they were learning. Carlie and Jake were doing a little better than Rhiannon at committing all the information to memory, because she was still preoccupied by the thrill of new love.

But finally the weekend of Ostara, the spring equinox, rolled around, and Carlie, Rhiannon and Jake were lounging around on the Saturday morning train to London, finally relaxing, for a day at least. They'd caught the earliest train possible so they could spend the day at the Body Mind Spirit Festival with Tom, before they would go out for dinner – a double date of sorts, Rhi had said gleefully – then meet up with Tom's coven for their sabbat ritual.

As they stood at the entrance, Carlie felt just as overwhelmed as she had the first time she'd attended this festival, by the noise and the colour and the crush of the crowd, and tears pricked her eyes.

It was six months to the day since she'd met Rowan here, and fallen in love for the first time in her life.

"You okay?" Rhiannon asked her softly, as she put an arm around her shoulder and held her close as they walked in. "Thank you so much for coming with me. I know this isn't easy for you, but I really appreciate it."

"I'm okay," Carlie responded, trying to reassure herself as much as her friend. It helped that Rhiannon had acknowledged what this was costing her. Besides, if she wanted to move forward with her life, she had to face these things…

Rhiannon's arm slipped from her shoulder though when she saw Tom walking towards them. They both ran to each other, and he scooped her up and swung her around before kissing her long and hard and passionately. Carlie averted her eyes. She was happy for them, but she didn't need to see their joy in being reunited.

Anticipating her reaction, Jake took her elbow and steered her into the next aisle. "Could you help me find a present for Rose today?" he asked. "Pop wanted me to buy something for him to give to her, as a thank-you gesture for her kindness."

Carlie almost threw her arms around him, so grateful was she for his consideration and empathy, for always knowing what she was feeling and how to fix it. But she managed to restrain herself, not wanting to lead him on. "Thank you," she said instead. "You really are the best friend a girl could have."

An expression she couldn't identify flitted across his face, then was gone before she could work it out. Anger, frustration, disappointment? But he smiled at her, and she tried to let her worry go. "Happy to help," he finally conceded, and they started their lap of the hall so they could check everything out.

They spent the morning going from stall to stall together, chatting and looking at all the products, some so weird they couldn't even work out what they were, others beautiful or powerful or potentially healing enough to go on their list of gift possibilities. Carlie was surprised when she had to admit that she was actually having fun. It definitely helped that Jake was just as curious-slash-sceptical-slash-amused-slash-impressed as her by the event.

When they reached the stand that Rowan had been at during the previous festival, being manned today by another shamanic healer, she froze for a moment, before quickly leading Jake to the stall opposite, where they looked at incense and herbal blends as well as cloaks in a myriad of colours and styles, Carlie carefully keeping her back to the shaman guy.

They stopped for a cup of tea, to rest their feet and unclutter their brains for a moment, then continued on with their mission, amazed at just how many different stands there were, and the wide variety of wares. When they turned into the last aisle, Carlie was overjoyed to see Jasmine in one of the booths. Her stand was called Blessed Bee, and the table was filled with gorgeously scented beeswax candles and honey-infused lotions, bath crystals, shampoos and conditioners, as well as jars of honey in different herb and flower flavours. "Oh, Gran would love these," Carlie told Jake as she approached the stand.

"Carlie, my love, I'm so glad to see you," Jasmine cried. "And I'm so sorry for your loss," she continued, ignoring the man who was browsing her products and coming out into the aisle to hug Carlie. "You poor thing, I was so desperately sad for you when I heard. How are you coping?

"It's been rough, but I'm... I'm okay," she said, and realised she was. "Rose has been amazing, and I have two dear friends who have helped me through it. This is one of them – Jake, this is Jasmine, a friend of my mum's from a long time ago. Jasmine, Jake. Another Aussie," she giggled. "But how have you been? And congratulations on the stall, it's gorgeous," she babbled.

Jasmine took her hands and smiled at her. "I'm doing really well. I got in touch with Rowan's mother when I heard the news, and we've been spending time together, which has been very healing for both of us. She's doing okay too."

Guilt washed over Carlie. She hadn't seen Rowan's mum since the funeral, and she felt bad. "Louisa is not your responsibility – and she doesn't expect you to visit her. She knows how painful that would be for you," Jasmine said, and Carlie smiled with gratitude. "Now, did you say Rose would like some of these? I can make her up a gift basket, my treat," she suggested.

"That's really kind of you, but I need to buy something for her, as a gift from my grandfather, and he would want to pay you. But maybe Carlie would appreciate something – I'm sure the relaxing bath salt mix would do her the world of good," said Jake, who'd been studiously examining the products while they talked, trying not to look like he was listening.

Jasmine smiled at him. "You're a wise young man, knowing the importance of an energy exchange," she said. "How about you have a look, see what you'd like to get, and I'll give you a discount. So you're still paying, just getting a better deal. And Carlie, if you come back here, you can decide what you'd like," she said, leading her behind the counter.

Reaching under the table, Jasmine pulled out a tray of body lotions, and leaned forward to hug her again. "He's lovely Carlie," she whispered. "And he really cares about you."

"He's just a friend," Carlie insisted, horrified that someone who knew Rowan's mum would think she'd moved on so quickly.

"I know, I can tell, but you should really think about opening your heart to this one. He has a beautiful soul, and he cares about you even more than you realise," Jasmine advised.

Carlie smiled sadly. "I know," she said, voice raw. "But I can't."

"You should think about it," Jasmine pressed. "He knows what you've lost, and won't seek to replace Rowan or make you forget him. Don't push him away just because you feel guilty."

Feeling Jake's eyes on her, Carlie blushed and looked away. Jasmine laughed, and turned her attention back to the young man she already liked, who was thoughtfully reading the labels on the jars of herb-infused honey. "Rose would love all of these, I'm sure," he said. "And the honey body lotion too."

Pulling out his wallet, he pointed at several items, and Jasmine reached under the table for a pretty straw basket. After filling it up with a sweet-scented collection of jars and bottles, she wrapped it carefully in vivid green silk and tied it with ribbons in several shades of the same hue. Then she handed it to Jake, asking for only a fraction of the value in return. As he gave her the money and she looked for change, Rhiannon swooped down and grabbed Carlie then dragged her down the aisle, calling out to Jake that she just needed to show her friend something.

Jasmine smiled at Jake. "Thank you for caring so much about Carlie," she said. "She's been through so much, and not many people are strong enough to be able to support someone through that, to put their own needs second."

"We're just friends," Jake replied quickly. "Please don't get the wrong idea. I'm not trying to take advantage of her grief or anything," he blurted out, looking incredibly uncomfortable.

"Oh Sweetie, no one thinks that. I'm just grateful that Carlie has someone to talk to, someone who cares about her. Thank you."

Relaxing a little, Jake finally managed to smile. "I just hope she'll be able to find some joy again," he said softly.

"She'll be ready to open her heart soon Jake, and I can tell she already cares about you deeply. Don't be too shy, when the time comes, to tell her how you feel."

"But I don't want to scare her," he replied. "It would break my heart to push her too soon or hurt her in any way."

Jasmine took his hand. "You don't have a scary bone in your body," she said, trying not to laugh. Then she sobered. "Jake, right now being her friend is the best thing you can do for her, the thing she needs most in the world. She needs to know she can trust you, and she needs to get to the point where she won't feel guilty taking things further. But she'll get there, and I can't imagine a sweeter person to be there for her when she does."

The girls came back then, giggling together, Carlie holding a bag and Rhiannon holding Tom's hand. When Jasmine and Tom saw each other, they both started laughing.

"These are the friends that you're bringing to the ritual tonight?" Jasmine asked, eyes dancing with humour, and Tom raised his eyebrows, clearly confused.

"You know Rhiannon?" he asked her.

"Actually no – hi Rhiannon," she smiled. "Carlie has told me so much about you. I'm Jasmine."

"Right, from the Yule retreat," Rhiannon said, then winced that she'd brought it up. "Carlie's mum's friend," she finished softly, as they leaned over the table and hugged.

Jasmine turned back to Tom. "I knew Carlie's mum years ago, and I spent some time with Carlie at winter solstice. And I've just been getting to know Jake," she explained. Carlie wondered why he was blushing, but decided she could ask about that later.

"Small world," Tom grinned. "Jake is my cousin, that's how I met Rhiannon and Carlie, they're all school friends."

"So you'll be at the ritual tonight too?" Carlie asked Jasmine, and was relieved when the older woman nodded. "Is it okay if we all come? We don't want to intrude if it's a closed sabbat."

"Of course you're welcome, the more the merrier. I was actually planning to ask you if you and your friends could come, but I guess I don't need to now," Jasmine replied.

Tom dragged Jake off to show him something, leaving the girls to catch up on their afternoon. Rhiannon could barely speak straight for her excitement, bubbling over with so much joy and enthusiasm about her boyfriend and how wonderful he was.

"He's so beautiful Carlie, isn't he!" she exclaimed, not stopping for an answer. "I'm trying not to rave about him endlessly, because I imagine you're not quite as excited about him as I am, but I can't even think about anything else," she grinned. "How could you hide how you felt about Rowan the way you did? I want to shout from the rooftops that I love Tom."

Carlie tried to keep her tone light. "Well, I wasn't ready to share it with Gran, and my best friend wasn't his biggest fan, so I kept it inside. Although poor Luther had to put up with my stories," she added. She still felt so sad about Luther's loss – but she was happily surprised to realise that she didn't feel any resentment towards Rhiannon any more. She really had let that go.

Her friend still felt guilty though. "I'm really sorry," she said again, but Carlie shook her head.

"I know you're sorry, and I appreciate it, but it's in the past now, and there's no point dwelling on it. Besides, I remember a wise person once told me to stop saying sorry all the time. That woman I met in the cafe recently reminded me of that. I'm not sure who she was, or how she knew about our conversation, but she reminded me of you. Anyway, I honestly don't feel any bitterness now, so let's put it behind us as we vowed to do at our Imbolc ritual."

Nodding gratefully, Rhiannon hugged her friend, then led her over to a table of beautiful jewellery. "Aren't these gorgeous," she said, pointing at the beautiful coloured crystals designed into intricate silverwork settings. "Which one's your favourite?"

Carlie smiled as she took them all in, then finally pointed to a large round moonstone with a silver crescent moon on either side of it, representing the triple goddess and the lunar phases. "It's just like Rowan's tattoo, and the crystal is so beautiful – it feels really strong yet also gentle, if that makes sense."

Rhiannon called the stall holder over, picking up the necklace and opening her wallet to pull some money out.

"What are you doing?" Carlie asked, panic in her voice.

Her friend smiled at her as she handed over the pound notes. "I'm buying you a present – an Ostara gift of love and new beginnings. And no, you don't have any say in it," she insisted, as Carlie tried to protest. "You honour the giver by receiving it graciously. Now put it on and show me, because it's so totally you."

Blushing with embarrassment at the unexpected gift, Carlie thanked her friend, then placed the necklace around her neck and lifted up her long dark hair so Rhiannon could do up the clasp. The pendant rested against her heart, and she felt a warm, soothing energy radiating from it into her body. She smiled. It was the first time she'd felt the joy of beautiful memories when she thought of Rowan, rather than the usual crushing sadness.

Today was the spring equinox, three months to the day since he'd died, and while she wasn't over him, she finally felt the possibility of her heart healing. Maybe it was the energy of spring, or the healing power of time, or the love and support she felt from Rose and Rhiannon, and the women of their ritual circle. She supposed it didn't really matter what it was, the important thing was the sensation of hope she was feeling. Rowan would always be a part of her, but she had to make the most of her life, for him as much as for herself. *Was this what acceptance felt like?*

"Are you okay?" Rhiannon asked, bringing her back to earth.

Carlie smiled. "You know, I think I will be," she replied, and felt her heart lift a little as she spoke the words. Well, words did have power. Words were spells, after all. Yes, she was going to be okay.

They were engulfed in a wave of energy as Tom returned and scooped Rhiannon up to kiss her. "Jake's just grabbing us coffee, but I missed you too much gorgeous girl," he said. He smiled when he saw Carlie's necklace. "I did a tattoo like that a while ago, with the yin and yang symbol within the orb of the full moon, and crescent moons either side. It was really beautiful."

Carlie stared at him. "That's the tattoo I want to get. Would you be able to do it for me?" she asked quickly, before she chickened out.

"Sure. We can do it now if you want to, I live close by. I was going to suggest that we go out for dinner before the ritual, but we can hang out at my place and order pizza while I tattoo you."

Joy lit up Carlie's face. "That would be amazing, thank you!"

He laughed. "The pleasure's all mine. I love tattooing people, especially when it means something to them. The tattoo I told you about was for a druid guy, what was his name? Hawthorn? Willow? No, different tree. I think it was Rowan," he finally said.

Rhiannon stared at Carlie. "No way!" she exclaimed.

Carlie smiled. "Even more perfect. Maybe destiny and fate do exist," she mused, then she quickly sobered. No. If that was the case, she wouldn't need Rowan's tattoo, she'd have him instead because he'd still be here. But Tom's voice broke into her thoughts before they became too melancholy.

"Is that cool babe?" he was asking Rhiannon. "Going back to my place instead of going out?" She nodded happily, although if she was honest with herself, she'd have to admit that she would have been content to follow him anywhere. Wow, she really did like him.

When Jake returned, they said goodbye to Jasmine before heading off through a park and down into the underground rail system. Tom's flat was only three stops away then a short walk, and they were soon climbing the stairs and walking through his door.

Suddenly Carlie felt nervous. Was she really going to do this? Get her first tattoo? Was it going to hurt? Would Rose be angry? What would it look like on her skin? Which wrist should she get it on? How had one off-the-cuff comment led to her agreeing to this? Ah, who was she kidding – she'd sought it out. But did she really want a tattoo? It was a forever kind of commitment, and her history with forever wasn't exactly stellar.

Tom led them into the small apartment and out to a sunroom furnished with a fold-out table, two chairs and a compact set of drawers on wheels, which appeared to hold all his tattooing equipment. He threw the phone to Jake and asked him to order the pizza, then let the girls thumb through his design folio as he set up.

His work was stunning, and there were so many beautiful designs, but Carlie had been wanting to get the triple moon tattoo even before Rowan had died, and finding the man who had created his seemed to be some kind of fate, sceptical though she was of that concept.

When Tom told Rhiannon and Jake to head out to the lounge room and read or watch TV, leaving them alone, Carlie was relieved. She needed to psyche herself up for this, and she didn't want to be their entertainment, especially if she wimped out. Nervously she watched as Tom traced the pattern she wanted onto greaseproof paper, consulting with her on size and shape, then transferring it onto her skin. Then he turned to her, tattoo gun in hand, and she smiled bravely and pulled up her sleeve to expose her inner wrist.

"Try to relax," he said. "I know that's easier said than done, but it will help. It stings a bit, but the bursts are really short, and you can breathe in between."

Carlie shrugged, trying to remain cool and calm. She didn't think a bit of pain would upset her – she felt as though she'd become immune to it over the past year. It was the memories it would unleash, and whether she could keep it together in front of her friends, that worried her more. Curiously she watched as Tom drew the ink into the tattoo machine, then her heart rate rose as he held her wrist with one hand and directed the needle onto her skin.

When it broke through she felt a burst of euphoria. It didn't really hurt, it was just a little uncomfortable, but it made her feel close to

Rowan somehow. Closing her eyes, she let her mind wander back to the night she'd met him – six months ago today – and how she'd felt as he spoke to her. So strong and grown-up, so whole, so *seen*. He'd recognised parts of her she hadn't even been aware of, seen her potential and somehow helped her to see it too. She'd always be grateful to him for that. It had truly been a gift.

As the tattoo gun kept sweeping its lines into her skin, Carlie felt one part of her mind following the drilling sound, while another part flew free. She heard Rowan's voice, whispering in her ear, words of love, of encouragement, of strength. Idly she wondered if he would always appear to her when her body was anchored in pain and her mind was soaring above her, but he shook his head at that.

"My love, I'll always be with you, but it's time for you to let me go," he said softly. "You are still alive with potential and possibility, so don't cut yourself off from the world, or from those who love you. You're surrounded by love, and the potential for love, so don't take it for granted. It's right in front of you Carlie. Don't wait so long that you lose your chance."

Suddenly the buzzing sound of the machine stopped, and she opened her eyes. Tom smiled at her. "You looked like you were a million miles away, in a happy place. That's how I feel when I'm getting inked too," he said quietly.

Shy again with this man she barely knew, she nodded, then glanced down at her wrist. The black outline was flawless, the yin and yang perfectly balanced, the crescent moons gently rounded.

"I've finished the outline, but if there's anything else you'd like to incorporate, now is the time to tell me," he offered.

Curiously she looked at him. "How did you know?"

Smiling broadly, he tapped his chest, over his heart. "I could see it in your face, and you went into the same kind of trance state that I do while I work, so I could feel some of it."

Carlie gasped and blushed ruby red, but he shook his head.

"Don't be alarmed, please, I don't eavesdrop, and I didn't get any of the specifics, but my tattooing is part of my spirituality, it's the way I express my witchyness, so I seem to be able to tune in when people are getting one as a way to express their inner heart. I'm sensing that this is the past," he said, indicating the lunar symbol on her wrist. "And while it will be an anchor for you always, you're at a threshold – poised between where you were and moving forward to where you're scared to go. So I'm guessing ivy leaves, for this sabbat, and for this feeling," he said.

"I don't know how you did that, but yes, I was thinking about ivy leaves," she replied, voice incredulous.

"I'd suggest one here and one here," he said, voice almost shy, and very respectful. She'd underestimated him. As he caught that thought, he grinned, back to cheeky, and told her that most people felt the same way when they first met him – it took a little while for his charm to slip through his outward confidence, the aloof facade he presented on first meeting to protect himself from those he found annoying and not worthy of his time.

She giggled at that, then nodded yes to the placement of the leaves, still shocked that he'd known what was in her heart. Picking up the gun, he tattooed the ivy pattern directly onto her skin, without bothering about the stencilling, and they were beautiful, ornate and delicately drawn, and perfectly balanced with each other and with the full and crescent moon symbols.

"What colours were you thinking?" he asked.

She laughed. "I'm guessing you know that too."

He was already pulling out coloured inks. "I thought yellow and red for the full moon, with the opposite colour for the dots within the yin and yang symbol, blues and purples for the crescent moons, and green for the ivy."

Carlie nodded happily and watched him as he began colouring it in, wanting to stay present with it now, breathing through the heat in her skin as though it was a ritual.

"It is, I think," Tom said to her as he worked. "A ritual, I mean. Most ancient cultures have used tattooing as part of their rituals, to denote graduation from one stage of life to another, or the achievement of a new rank or role. And although some people today get them as a fashion statement, for most it's still a form of ritual, and represents something important to them – surviving something, in your case, or celebrating an accomplishment or a new state of awareness. For many their tattoos are a diary of their life, symbols of transformation, and reminders of the beautiful moments of their life."

Carlie thought suddenly that she'd misjudged him, that first time they'd met, had missed his depth and the layers of his soul. But he shook his head.

"Nah, you were spot on that day," he said, and she couldn't help but laugh at his honesty, although she was dying of embarrassment on the inside. "I was feeling all superior, and a bit resentful that I had to hang out with my young cousin and his young friends. So I was being silly, trying to impress Rhiannon as a game, just to amuse myself and fill in time – until I realised how much I actually liked her. And how grown up Jake had become. Don't tell them that though, please," he implored her, and Carlie smiled. "Cross my heart."

"Thank you," he said, switching colours. It was almost finished, and it was so much more beautiful than she'd imagined. "I misjudged you too, and I'm sorry for that," he continued.

"Well, we're even then," she said, then changed the subject quickly, not wanting to know what he'd thought of her. "I was suspicious of your motives with Rhiannon, and I apologise for that."

He put the tattoo gun down for a moment and took her hand, gazing into her eyes. "No, you were right, and I can't tell you how grateful I am that Rhiannon has such a protective and caring friend. That first day, when I met her, I had no intention of ever seeing her again. But then after we said goodbye that night she was all I could think about, and by the next morning I knew that I liked her far more than I'd imagined. So from that moment on my intentions have been honourable, I promise."

Carlie smiled. "I can see that now," she said. "And thank you for being honest with me."

"She values your friendship more than anything Carlie, and I will always respect that," Tom said, picking up the gun to complete the work of art on her wrist. He worked in silence for several minutes, until he finally spread the completed tattoo with bepanthen cream and plastic wrap and taped it on.

"How does it feel?" he asked, just as the buzzer rang for the pizza.

Carlie's face lit up. "I love it, thank you! Now how much do I owe you?" she asked, reaching for her bag.

Tom shook his head. "No charge, I'm just really happy that I could do your first tattoo for you, and honoured that it means so much to you," he said, glancing up at Rhiannon as she walked into the room to let them know the pizza had arrived. She blushed.

"I don't mind that you told him," Carlie said to her friend, realising that she must have filled Tom in on her reasons for wanting Rowan's tattoo. Then she turned back to Tom. "But surely I can give you something for your time, or for the inks and equipment at least?"

Shaking his head again, he took her hand – the non-tattooed one – and stared into her eyes, serious for a moment. "I feel like we didn't get off on the right foot," he said softly, and it was her turn to blush. "You're very important to Rhi, so I hope we will become friends. Besides, you honour the giver by receiving with grace," he added, echoing Rhiannon's words from the festival. "And I'm honoured that I could help you," he said firmly.

"Thank you," she replied, simply yet heartfelt, and he smiled at her. "It means the world to me, really. I love it so much."

"I'm glad," he replied. "Now, we'd better get in there and eat some pizza before it's all gone, and then get ready to go."

They all sat down on the floor of the lounge room, laughing and joking as they ate pizza from the boxes, Jake entertaining their English friends with Aussie slang and traditions. Then Carlie grabbed her backpack and headed into the bathroom to change into her ritual dress, while Tom led Rhi into his bedroom.

"There's no time for that guys," Jake called out, joking, as he sat on the couch and flicked through a magazine. Carlie soon joined him, and he smiled as she sat down next to him.

"You look beautiful," he said, and she felt her cheeks grow hot. "So how's your tattoo feeling?" he asked, steering the conversation back to neutral territory. "Did it hurt?"

Grateful that he'd changed the subject, she gazed down at her wrist and wrinkled her nose. It looked weird under the plastic.

"Not really. It felt like a hot, sharp lead pencil being scraped across my skin, but every time it felt like it was about to be too much to bear, it would stop for a second, then start up somewhere else. It was kind of meditative," she said, then laughed. "Okay, it's a bit uncomfortable, but it's worth it. Are you going to get one?"

Before he could reply, Rhiannon burst out of Tom's room, long dress rustling around her legs, face transformed by joy and excitement, and her low-cut top highlighting a stunning piece of jewellery. "Look Carlie, isn't it beautiful!" she cried, pointing at the elaborate crystal setting nestled around her neck. "Tom gave it to me, an Ostara gift," she said, smiling widely.

"It's gorgeous," Carlie said. It was huge too, very different to her friend's usual taste in delicate jewellery, but the large rose quartz heart at the centre of the explosion of multi-coloured crystals definitely reinforced that his intentions were honourable, which made Carlie happy. This was certainly not the kind of gift you gave a girl you didn't care about.

When Tom emerged a few minutes later he had a deep green velvet cloak on, an intricate silver headpiece woven through his long hair, and a bag containing his ritual tools.

"You look so magical," Rhiannon breathed as she gazed at him admiringly. "I'm so excited that we can share this ritual."

"It's a shame it's not Beltane," he replied, winking at Rhiannon and wiggling his eyebrows suggestively.

She grinned back. "Don't worry my love, it's not far off."

Carlie and Jake rolled their eyes at each other, but before they could get too concerned, Tom ushered them out of the apartment and led them to a nearby park, where several people in pagan finery had already gathered. Carlie was surprised – in a good way – that there were just as many men as women there, since she was so used to working in a predominantly female circle. Glancing at Jake, she saw that he'd also noticed this, and his face was alight with possibility.

"Have you asked Tom about his coven?" she asked him. "Maybe you could study with them. You'd probably only have to be physically present for their eight sabbats."

He nodded, excitement on his face and in his stance. "Yes, we were talking about it earlier, and he said I could come up for all their celebrations, and for his monthly study circle too if I wanted to, or

I could do that part online if it was too difficult to attend in person. And he said he'll be in our neck of the woods quite a bit – although I'm guessing he'll want to spend most of that time with Rhiannon," he grinned, as they watched their friend kiss Tom, then walk back over to their side, her face aflame with happiness, while Tom joined Jasmine and a few other witches for the final preparations.

"Thank you so much for coming with me, both of you," Rhiannon said, her eyes shining. "It's going to be such a magical night, and I'm so glad that the three of us are sharing it with each other."

Soon Jasmine called for everyone's attention, and they all gathered in a large circle around the central altar. Tom was one of the direction callers, and while he didn't skip a beat or miss a single word of the invocation, he and Rhiannon couldn't keep their eyes off each other, both totally focused on the other to the exclusion of everything else, and both glowing from within as they responded to one another.

"It's beautiful isn't it," Jake whispered to Carlie, indicating the couple, and she nodded. And suddenly became aware that it had stopped hurting her to see her friend loving and being loved the way she had been with Rowan. Relief coursed through her, before she turned her attention back to Jasmine as she invoked the god and the goddess, and began to feel the magic of the ritual take hold as she dropped into the light trance state she'd come to love so much.

Happiness surged through her. She'd been apprehensive about being at someone else's ritual, at revealing her ignorance if they did things she was unfamiliar with, but it was not so dissimilar to one of Rose's sabbats. The wording was a little different, a bit more traditional, but a wave of relief swept over her, that she wasn't out of her depth as she'd feared. And finally she relaxed and let Jasmine's voice, and the magic of the night, wash over her. Healing, revealing, inspiring.

Rebirth and renewal were the themes of the spring equinox, and the words of the ritual affected Carlie deeply, making her realise that she was a million miles from the person she'd been a year ago. She'd had no idea then about the magic of ritual, the power of words, this connection she now had with nature and the earth.

It saddened her that her mother had left all this behind when she'd fled to Australia, but perhaps it hurt her too much to have been cut off from Rose and her circle, and maybe trying to recreate it in a new country, with new people, would have just exacerbated the pain.

Letting her mind drift, she tried to reimagine her business-suit-wearing mother in a long velvet gown with flowers in her hair. And a flash of memory emerged, of her mum in a pretty floral dress, bare feet in the earth as she planted herbs in their back garden in Sydney. Another, of waking up one night when they'd been camping on a beach up north, the full moon shining into her tent, and peeking out of the opening to see her parents dancing on the sand, the lunar glow shining down on them and casting their shadows out into the water.

And one more, from a rainy middle-of-winter night, when the house smelled of cinnamon and cloves, and her mother had followed their dinner of herb-sprinkled roasted vegies and spicy nut loaf with a fancy dessert she'd created which she called a Yule log.

Maybe the magic and the sense of connection had still been there in her mum, just hidden from public view. Maybe at her core she had still been her mother's daughter. That thought made Carlie happy, and she made a mental note to tell Rose when she got home the next day.

After the formal part of the ritual was completed, and Jasmine had farewelled the god and the goddess and closed the circle, they all wandered over to a nearby cafe, which had an upstairs room reserved for them. Rhiannon and Tom huddled together in a tiny corner booth, only coming up for air to order pots of tea that they didn't end up drinking, so absorbed in each other had they become. Carlie and Jake looked around nervously, feeling a little lost, but Jasmine called them over to her small candlelit table, introduced them to her girlfriend Samantha, and gestured for them to take a seat.

"Carlie, I thought you might like to speak with Sam, because she's a pantheist," Jasmine said. Carlie stared at the two women quizzically, puzzled by the unfamiliar word, but was intrigued as soon as Jasmine elaborated. The priestess said that while she was a goddess-worshipping witch who believed in the deities as literal beings, the way that Rose did, her partner was an environmental activist and scientist who held nature and the natural world as sacred, like all witches, but didn't believe in supernatural beings or powers.

It was the first time Carlie had heard the term, or the explanation, or felt such a zing of connection. Chills ran up her spine, her breath caught, and her heart felt suddenly lighter, and so much freer. It had been bothering her, she had to admit, that she couldn't make herself believe literally in gods and goddesses, as Rose and Rhiannon did. She'd wondered if it made her a fraud, to attend all the rituals and feel the magic, but accept it on a far more symbolic level than everyone else seemed to do. But as Samantha discussed her beliefs, or the lack there-of, Carlie felt more and more at peace.

She'd always admired and respected Rose's love of the goddess, and her belief in her, but she hadn't been able to make herself feel the same way, no matter how hard she tried. But perhaps there was a place for her after all, a philosophy she could embrace, people she could talk with and learn from and be inspired by. So while Jasmine continued her conversation with Jake, Carlie listened wide-eyed and rapt as Samantha shared her take on spirituality with her.

"Pantheism is a philosophy and a way of life, and a valid form of spirituality – it's just not a literal form," she explained, smiling at Carlie as she saw relief flow across her face. "There are similarities in outlook with witches and druids and other earth-based spiritualities, because we all care about the planet and our connection with the earth, but we see the goddess as a personification of nature, not as a woman or a being existing in some other realm or dimension who we can pray to or communicate with," Samantha explained.

"We have great reverence for the universe – it inspires awe in us, and an almost religious-seeming appreciation, but when we are moved by the incredible beauty of a sunset or the power of a thunder storm, it inspires a search for a deeper understanding of nature within us, rather than assuming that the goddess of the dawn had painted it for us to enjoy, or that the thunder god was angry at his brother and hurling lightning bolts at him."

Carlie laughed, but her head was spinning. It was everything she'd been thinking and feeling since she'd arrived in Summer Hill and started doing ritual with Rose, but she hadn't had the words to express it with. As Samantha spoke, it was like a weight lifted from her heart – and then she remembered Rose telling her that a few of the women in her ritual circle were atheists, and were the kindest, sweetest and most caring people she knew, more caring and "moral" than many of the religious people she'd met.

When a waiter brought them fresh pots of tea, along with platters of scones, bite-sized cupcakes and luscious fresh fruit, Carlie took a deep breath and tried to still her spinning mind, but once their mugs were full again, she turned her attention back to Samantha.

"For me, my spirituality is expressed through my work to protect the earth and its creatures, and to oppose businesses that threaten endangered animals or negatively impact on nature," Sam told her.

"I have a friend with a similar outlook who works with herbs and healing, who calls herself an atheist witch, and another who describes himself as a humanist," she continued. "But the labels don't really matter, other than to help you find like-minded people and realise that you're not alone, and that what is deep within your heart is shared and experienced by others."

"Yes!" Carlie said breathlessly. "Thank you so much for sharing all of this with me. It's such a relief to me that you've given voice to what I've been feeling so deeply within me, but haven't been able to articulate, even to myself. The beauty of nature in the village where I live now fills me with such awe, and climbing the sacred hill to watch the sun set or the full moon rise feels so magical, so mysterious and awe-inspiring, in a way I can't really explain. But it being the work of a supernatural being never rang true to me," she admitted, still finding it difficult to express what she was feeling.

Samantha smiled at her. "It's funny, people assume that not believing in a literal god or goddess means we miss out on all the wonder and beauty of the world, but I think it's the opposite. We hold nature itself as sacred and worthy of reverence, almost of worship, and we definitely feel that magic exists, it's just that rather than needing to be explained away as a supernatural being, or a supernatural force, we see it as simply unexplained science. And we hope that one day we might be able to comprehend its vast scope."

As Samantha poured more tea, Jake and Jasmine drew them back into their conversation, along with a few of the other ritual participants, and Carlie became quiet and slightly awestruck, thrilled to listen to everyone and just soak it all in. She marvelled at the gracious way people spoke to each other, and also their ability and willingness to really pay attention to what others said. It was like talking to Rose – people here believed many different things, but they all respected each other's views, and had wonderful discussions, fiery at times, but always polite, and she had the sense that they were all open to expanding or even changing their beliefs if they experienced something that made more sense to them.

When the last pot of tea had been drunk and the final platter of food had been emptied, and the owner had come upstairs to tell them they were closing, Carlie was surprised to realise how much she'd enjoyed the night. She had only come as a favour to Rhiannon, yet she'd had an unexpectedly wonderful time. Jake grinned at her, his eyes sparkling with just as much fire and intent as hers.

"Thank you for letting me be part of all this," he said, glancing around the room as they stood up and prepared to leave. "I feel so at home here because of you, and so inspired."

"Thank *you*," she smiled. "And it's *our* thing, not just mine, and you're always welcome to be part of it. Besides, if I hadn't known Jasmine, I would have felt like I was *your* guest."

"Or we're just Rhiannon and Tom's tag-alongs," Jake added, but he was laughing. "Do you think we'll be able to pry them apart?"

Carlie was dubious, and dreaded having to tell her friend it was time for them to go back to her cousin's place and get some sleep. They'd promised they would be home by midnight – how faery godmother of them – and they didn't have much time left.

"Guess we need to try," she sighed, but when they headed over to the corner booth, Rhiannon stood up without them having to ask, took Tom's hand and followed them downstairs.

As they all stood together out on the deserted street, stars twinkling and the almost-full moon sailing overhead, Carlie hugged Jasmine and Samantha, and thanked them for the wonderful night and all the intriguing, inspiring conversations.

Then she turned to Tom to express her gratitude and appreciation for the beautiful tattoo he'd done for her.

"It was my pleasure," he replied, taking her hands and staring deep into her eyes. Images flooded her mind, of Tom holding Rhiannon close, protecting her from hurt and treating her with love and respect. A weight lifted from Carlie's shoulders as she understood the message he was sending her, and she nodded in acknowledgement.

Smiling, Tom dropped her hands and took Rhiannon's. "Now let me hail a cab, and we'll drop you girls off on our way home," he said.

Jake and Carlie raised their eyebrows at each other in surprise, having expected a real battle to separate the love birds, but they were too tired and relieved to question it. They'd both started yawning, and were just happy to know that they'd soon be in bed.

There was one awkward moment when Carlie got out of the cab, then had to wait while Rhiannon and Tom kissed goodbye, a seemingly never-ending and increasingly passionate kiss. But finally her friend emerged, eyes shining, and they crept into her cousin's apartment and tiptoed down the hall to the spare room.

It was still dark when Rhiannon's alarm went off what felt like just a few hours later, and Carlie groggily rolled over, groaned, and asked what time it was.

"Sorry," Rhiannon whispered. "It's only half past five, but Tom's taking me out for breakfast before we have to go home. You're welcome to come with us though," she added, somewhat reluctantly, but Carlie mumbled "no" and pulled the pillow over her head.

"I'll be back by eleven, I promise, so we'll have plenty of time to get to the station. Is that okay? Will you be all right here on your own?" Rhiannon asked nervously.

Carlie let out a muffled: "Fine," then drifted back off to sleep, while Rhiannon pulled on her clothes in the dark then tiptoed down the hall and outside into the chilly morning air, breathing in the beauty of the about-to-rise sun and the joy of her first real love.

Chapter 33

Heart of Darkness

When the girls met up with Jake at the station later, he proudly showed off his new tattoo, which Tom had done for him in the early hours of the morning, after they got home from the ritual and before he met Rhiannon for breakfast. It was gorgeous, a delicate circle of ivy, with four quarters marked out within it, each one holding a symbol for fire, earth, air or water – a golden candle flame, a purple crystal, a black feather and a blue ocean wave.

"It's perfect," Carlie said, deeply impressed. "It's really beautiful, and it symbolises everything, even your surfing," she added, and was surprised that she felt sad at the thought of him leaving England to go home to his Aussie beach life. She would miss him.

"Thanks," Jake said proudly. "It also reminds me of you, and our friendship, and the magic that you've shared with me. The candle flame was to represent my first ritual, at Imbolc, and the crystal was from our wander through the festival yesterday and all the amazing things we saw. And the feather is to remind me of a little black bird I encountered at the base of the tor when I walked home after our first study session at your place," he said shyly.

"He was like you, so fragile, yet strong too, and wanting to fly, but too scared to spread his wings and try. I've seen him since, or one like him, flitting around the lower slopes, daring to go higher, and singing with joyful abandon. He's really come into his own, just like you have," he said softly, then blushed. "I'm sorry, I hope that doesn't offend you, he was just such a sweet little thing, and it's been amazing to see him slowly become stronger and more confident over the last few months, which you have too."

Panic clutched at Carlie's heart for a moment, at the strangely intimate way Jake was speaking, but she was saved from answering when the train pulled into the station. Rhiannon kissed Tom one last time, then the three of them climbed on board and found some seats together. But while they'd promised themselves they would study on the way home, they didn't even pull their books out and pretend to try, instead talking excitedly about their ritual the night before, how different tonight's ceremony at the healing centre would be, and tattoo designs that Rhiannon might like to get.

Carlie and Jake groaned when Rhi kept bring the conversation back to Tom, but soon they all started dozing off. Rhiannon curled up across one long bench seat and fell asleep, and although Carlie tried to stay awake, she eventually succumbed to slumber too, her head falling onto Jake's shoulder. The last thing she remembered thinking before her eyes closed was how comfortable she now felt being close to him.

Feeling somewhat refreshed when the train finally let them off in their village, they went their separate ways, to unpack and then get ready to celebrate the spring equinox all over again.

It was an evening filled with magic and power, heightened even further by the full moon, and Carlie felt it filling her up, energising her and reminding her how precious life was, no matter what you had lost. Gazing across the circle at Rhiannon made her smile, as she thought of their plans to go to uni together to study grief counselling, and continue their magical explorations as well. They'd be just like Rose and Elsie, mixing modern medical methods with traditional healing, alternative therapies and the power of ritual, and the thought of growing into a woman like her grandmother made her smile.

A few nights later, Carlie and Rose were grinding herbs together, when her grandmother brought up the topic of Jake again.

"Sweetheart, I know how much you loved Rowan, and how much you want to be faithful to his memory, but there can be room in a lifetime for more than one great love. Look at your mum, she had three. She adored Mike with all her heart, and was adored by him in turn, and for better or worse it seems she loved Andre, which he reciprocated, for a while at least, and she definitely loved your dad. You deserve to love and be loved again too, and I really hope you won't close off your heart forever out of some misguided attempt at remaining true to Rowan. He'll always be part of you, but –"

"I know, but I don't want to be like that woman at his funeral, who dated him briefly then forgot all about him, until she turned up at the church – married and pregnant no less – pretending he had always been so important to her. I don't want to minimise how much he meant to me by dating the next person I meet."

"Carlie, you are nothing like her," Rose said sternly. "Of course he was important to you, and you to him. He will always have a place within your heart, and he'll live on in the way he helped you heal your grief over your parents and develop along your magical path. A lot of people remember their first love with great fondness, but go on to have other great loves throughout their life too."

Carlie tried to interject, but her grandmother held up her hand to stop her. "I know it's different, and that if he was still here you would be with him now. But loving someone else, either now or in the future, doesn't mean you didn't love Rowan. It doesn't diminish your feelings for him, or his for you, in any way. But you honour that love by living a full life, not by shutting out the world."

"It's still so soon though," she whispered. "I'm not ready to give my heart away again, to risk all that pain."

Her grandma smiled at her, eyes filled with so much love and compassion. "Darling girl, the risk is always worth it. Love is the driving force of the universe – it can bring so much joy, and transform any pain, and truly make life worth living."

"I'm sure it can, but isn't your advice a little hypocritical?" Carlie asked her, her voice cautious but firm.

Rose stared at her, aghast. "What do you mean?" she stuttered.

"After Grandpa died, did you open your heart to anyone else? Did you let yourself love and be loved again, or did you close yourself off and deny yourself the chance to meet someone else – for more than twenty years no less?"

"That's different Sweetheart, I had to stay here in case your mum came back," she said, although her voice sounded a little uncertain.

"But you could have dated someone, right?" Carlie pressed. "Yet as far as I can tell, you've been alone ever since Grandpa died. Is that right? Did you even try? Did you go out with *anyone* after him? Or did you just give up on yourself, and think you had to punish yourself for the rest of your life?"

"Well, I suppose I didn't try very hard…" Rose reluctantly admitted, then trailed off.

Carlie's eyes flashed. "Very?"

"Okay, I didn't try at all. But I was just so busy trying to keep the shop going, trying to keep up with the healing circles and rituals, trying to help as many people as I could."

"Now you're blaming the *community*?" Carlie asked, tone pitched somewhere between outrage and disbelief. "How do you think they'd feel about that?" Rose winced, but Carlie continued her tirade.

"And there were chances, weren't there?" she insisted. "Men who showed interest, who wanted to get to know you, who wanted to love you – until you sent them packing."

Rose blushed and looked increasingly uncomfortable. "Sweetheart, it wasn't like that, I just didn't have time, and I –" She broke off, then her shoulders slumped, and she sighed. "Okay, maybe I discouraged them," she finally conceded. "But not on purpose!"

"And what about Richard?" Carlie demanded.

Cheeks flushing even redder, Rose tried but failed to look innocent. "What do you mean?" she stuttered. It was the first time Carlie had seen her lost for words in a long time.

She rolled her eyes. "You obviously enjoy each other's company. He's always asking about you, and popping over with silly excuses in an attempt to see you, and spend time with you. And apparently you spend a lot of time over there too."

"What would you have me do?" Rose challenged, trying to shift the focus off herself and avoid admitting to anything.

Shrugging, Carlie turned the tables back on her grandmother. "What do you want to do? And more importantly, what are you scared of? What's stopping you this time? It can't be Grandpa, all these years later, and sadly it can no longer be Mum, because she's not coming home to either of us."

The deep truth and the raw pain of her words echoed around the kitchen, and Rose busied herself pulling pretty glass jars out of the cupboard for them to put their concoctions in. When she finally spoke, she'd managed to compose herself – and to seize on some of Carlie's words in an attempt to change the subject.

"I want to be here for you Carlie, in a way I couldn't be for your mum. It's your final year of school, and you're still getting over the death of your parents, and of your boyfriend. You're in a new country, at a new school. I'm not going to go gallivanting around the countryside on wild nights out with someone just for my pleasure. I have a responsibility to you."

Carlie stared at Rose, shock and surprise battling for supremacy in her expression, before she finally laughed. "Seriously? That's insane. You can't blame me for this, or use me as the reason to lock away your heart and turn down the chance for love – especially when you're telling me to be brave and let someone in!" she exclaimed.

"You can do whatever it is you feel you have to do for me, which you're more than doing by the way, and still have time for yourself," she continued. "Please don't use me as an excuse to deny yourself happiness – that's not fair to me or to you. You've been amazing, and you *are* helping me through my grief, and helping me to forge a new life, but it's not a twenty-four/seven occupation. You can go out and enjoy yourself too."

Rose filled the kettle and put it on to boil, then gazed at her granddaughter with narrowed eyes. "When did you become so mature?" she asked.

Carlie smiled. "I have a good teacher," she said. "You, in case you missed that. But I always spend Tuesday nights with Rhiannon, either at her place or up in my room, and any other night I'm fine to be on my own too. There are plenty of nights you stay out late teaching and I survive, so why would it be any different to stay out late for fun? That's just a terrible excuse for avoiding taking any kind of risk, and giving yourself any kind of chance for happiness," she huffed.

Reaching up to pull down a teapot and a jar of tea leaves, Rose looked thoughtful. "Even if I could do that, what do you propose should happen afterwards? We're too old for dating, or weddings and honeymoons. And what about you and Jake?" she asked, voice veering between hope and terror.

"I'm just suggesting you go out for dinner with the guy, you don't have to get married next week," Carlie retorted. "Although I do find it interesting that you used the word propose."

She giggled as Rose looked at her sternly. "Joking! But seriously, if it did go that far, you'd just figure things out then. He'd move in here, or you'd move in there, whatever you'd prefer. Rhiannon and I are going to university later this year, so we could get a place together, and Jake will be going home to Perth. There's always a way to find a solution Gran – *if you want one*," she said.

Carefully Rose poured out two mugs of tea and took them over to the table, sitting down and waiting until her granddaughter had taken the seat opposite her. "How did this even become about me?" she asked defensively.

Carlie took a sip of her tea and gazed levelly at her grandmother. "Because you're telling me to open my heart, yet you've spent more than twenty years locked away from the world, guarding yourself from real joy, with a fortress up around your own heart. For all your priestess wisdom and the love and admiration so many people have for you, somehow you don't feel that you deserve to love or be loved."

Suddenly worried that she'd gone too far, Carlie watched in astonishment as her grandmother's face crumpled in on itself and tears fell from her eyes. Eyes that usually held joy and compassion now looked scared and defeated.

Shock radiated from Carlie, before a crashing sense of acknowledgement washed over her. "Oh my god," she exclaimed, as understanding dawned on her. She walked around to Rose and hugged her tight. "That's it, isn't it? You've blamed yourself for Mum running away, and Grandpa taking his life, so you don't think you deserve to have love, to be loved. You've been torturing yourself all these years, thinking that you have to pay some kind of penance by being alone for the rest of your life."

Rose's body shook as she cried harder, and Carlie held her tight, fragile bones echoing the fragility of her emotions, and her very soul. She cried until the tea had gone cold, her granddaughter patting her shoulder as soothingly as she could. But finally she began to mentally gather herself, her sobs growing quieter and further apart, and her body slowly becoming still.

"I'm sorry," Carlie whispered.

"Whatever for, darling girl?" her grandma asked, wiping her eyes and taking a few deep breaths, her priestess cloak of composure settling around her as she became herself again.

"I didn't mean to upset you."

Rose smiled. "You've just given me the key to transform my life Sweetheart. I was crying because it's true. All these years I've thought I was happy, that I was so spiritually aware and emotionally secure. People came to me for advice, for wisdom, for truth. And I couldn't see the biggest fault of my own life."

"It's not a *fault*..." Carlie offered, but Rose interrupted her.

"Yes it is, and continuing in this way now that I'm aware of it would be compounding it many times over. The time for denial of my past and my actions is done," she said, squaring her shoulders and smiling at her granddaughter.

"Are you okay?" Carlie asked. "Can I get you anything?"

"Maybe a new pot of tea?" her grandmother suggested. "I'm sorry, I've let this one go cold."

So Carlie busied herself with the kettle and new tea leaves, and Rose started to think about Richard in a brand new way.

Chapter 34

Blessings of Solitude

The next two weeks passed in a blur for Carlie. She worked hard on her assignments and cramming for the pre-holiday exams that were looming, and still managed to fit in some reiki at the healing centre on the weekends. For a few nights she helped Rose blend herbal potions for the shop, and she dedicated an afternoon to writing letters to Sandy and her friend Emily back in Australia. She barely saw Rhiannon outside of school though, because Tom was visiting a few times a week and monopolising all her free time.

Ostensibly he was coming down from London to stay with Jake and their grandfather, but Jake revealed that he'd barely seen him, as Tom slipped in long after midnight, and was still asleep when he got up and headed off to school the next day. But he did spend the mornings with Richard before heading back home, and Jake said their grandfather really appreciated these visits, so neither of them could begrudge the lovebirds the time they were spending together.

Rhiannon also missed both of their coven meetings, since Tuesdays were good nights for Tom to travel to their village. But despite a flash of annoyance at her hypocrisy, since Rhiannon had been so angry at her when she'd missed a single coven night to be with Rowan, Carlie didn't mind too much. She studied on her own, adding new research to her Book of Shadows, and was genuinely happy for her friend.

She was also glad when Rhiannon confessed between classes that she'd organised a dinner the previous night with her dad, Jake and Richard, both of whom Mike liked, so she could introduce him to Tom and let him know they were dating. Richard vouched for his grandson's character, but Tom had charmed her father so much that she could have done it without the extra back-up. Either way, she was relieved that she no longer had to sneak around or hide her relationship from her dad, and Carlie understood that, while feeling a little hurt that she hadn't been invited too.

Then, after the stress of their exams came and went, and the relief that they'd all done well subsided, they had two weeks of freedom from school. Rhiannon went to Brittany for the duration though, for a family holiday they'd booked the previous year. She sent postcards to Carlie almost every day, and promised she was taking lots of photos, and writing lots of notes, at all the sacred sites they visited.

She also wrote her a long letter, revealing that Tom had managed to get a few days off work to drive over to France and stay nearby, which had made it the "best holiday ever!". He'd taken her to the standing stones of Carnac and the magical Broceliande Forest, which was home to many Arthurian legends – the tomb of Merlin the Magician, where ribbons, flowers and baby booties were left in the hope he would grant people's wishes, Vivianne's Fountain of Eternal Youth, said to bestow immortality on those who drank from it, and the dramatic Valley of No Return, bewitched by the priestess Morgaine to imprison any knights who came by, in revenge for her broken heart.

A pang of longing shot through Carlie. It all sounded so beautiful, and so romantic, and she was overwhelmed by the desire to be able to share the things that meant so much to her with someone else again too, though she fought hard to conquer her jealousy.

It wasn't just Rhiannon who was falling in love either. Rose had finally summoned up the courage to invite Richard out for dinner, so they'd enjoyed several evenings together, watching movies, cooking for each other, and one night driving over to Smithfield to see a theatre production. And Jake was spending a lot of time studying with Tom in London, falling in love with magic, and with the ancient city, so she barely saw him either.

But while she'd thought she might feel lonely, Carlie was enjoying the solitude and space, and realising how desperately her heart and soul needed it. Each morning she got up before the sun to walk through the countryside, which was so beautiful as spring flourished and tiny hints of the approaching summer emerged, the wild hedgerows ablaze with pretty blossoms, ripening blackberries and the sound of bees. Now the sun was rising earlier, she loved being outside, soaking up the fresh air and sunshine, drinking in the scent of flowers and cool breezes, and feeling her body attuning itself to the energy of the land.

It suited her mood to be on her own too, to not have to talk to anyone, or explain herself, to try to come to terms with her pain and her loss and her sense of injustice in her own time and in her own way. When she was home, Luna barely left her side, and she loved the kitten's uncomplicated company, the sweet sound of her purring as she curled up in her lap while she read or slept on her pillow right next to her at night, soothing the ache inside her.

And while she wasn't ready to admit it to anyone, she'd stopped sensing Rowan around her all the time, which was making her sad. Although she'd tried many times to find the cottage again, to find him again, she hadn't been able to. The last time she'd heard him speak to her had been when she was getting tattooed, and he'd told her she had to let him go. So, slowly, reluctantly, she was starting to accept that it was almost time to look forward. There was guilt in that thought, and regret for what might have been, but also gratitude for the time they'd had together.

Looking down at her wrist, she marvelled again at the intricate tattoo design. She really loved it, and Rose had too, which had been a relief. And while the triple goddess moon symbol made her smile and remember Rowan, the ivy leaves made her think of their spring equinox ritual, and Tom and Rhiannon, and Jake. When she thought of him she thought of summer sunshine, sparkling waves, his sweet smile and his gentle nature. He was so kind to her, so patient, so respectful. It was such a shame she couldn't picture him as anything more than a friend.

Chapter 35

Ghosts of the Heart

By the time school resumed and life had returned almost to normal, Carlie was feeling much stronger. So when Rhiannon and Jake expressed their guilt at having abandoned her over the holidays, she shrugged it off and insisted it had been a good thing. She'd needed the time alone to come to her own conclusions about moving forward – if Rhiannon had been pressuring her again to get over Rowan, she probably would have dug in her heels and stayed where she was. Stuck. Stubborn. Her journey to acceptance was one she'd had to take on her own, and on her own terms.

Now there were less than two weeks until Beltane, so both girls were relieved that they could resume their Tuesday night coven meetings, after missing the last four. "I'm so sorry I put seeing Tom before our rituals, especially as I was so mean to you when you missed one," Rhiannon said, tone conciliatory, as she ushered her friend inside and led the way upstairs to her bedroom. "It was especially bad timing coming just before our France trip," she admitted. "But oh, it was so magical."

Carlie smiled as she slipped off her shoes and gazed around the room. Rhiannon had done a declutter when she got home, and there were new photos on her corkboard. "It's fine, life happens," she replied, as she walked over to look at the pictures.

"That's me and Brodie at Merlin's tomb," Rhiannon said. "And me and Tom at Carnac..."

Carlie froze when she saw the bottom image.

"And that's Mum, from when we went to Brittany four years ago. This trip was kind of a remembrance, one we did in her honour, retracing the steps of the holiday we took with her. I don't know, it probably sounds silly –"

"That's your mum?" Carlie broke in.

"Yes, haven't I shown you pictures of her before?" Rhiannon asked, surprised.

"I've only seen the ones from that dress-up party, when she was wearing a masquerade mask, and a few from towards the end of... well, from when she was really sick and had lost a lot of weight," Carlie replied.

"And lost her hair," Rhiannon acknowledged. "But this is what she looked like before she got sick. She was really so beautiful." Sighing, she walked over to look at the photo with her friend, before realising that something was upsetting her.

"What's wrong?" she asked, puzzled by her response.

"That's the woman I was talking to in the cafe that night, the one who reminded me a little of you," Carlie whispered.

Rhiannon stared at her blankly. "What woman?"

"Remember when I told you I'd met a woman who I didn't know, but who seemed to know me, and I tried to describe her, but she sounded like she could have been any of the women in Rose's circle? Well, it was her," she said, pointing to the photo.

"But she's –"

"I know," Carlie replied, wonder in her voice. "But she was wearing that exact same outfit too. And looked just as beautiful."

Rhiannon had sunk to the floor in a heap, her face frozen with fear and longing, and her eyes lit up with hope. "What did she say?" she implored.

Part of Carlie's mind registered the fact that her friend didn't doubt for a second that she had seen the ghost of her dead mother, and didn't find it at all strange – she just wanted to know everything she had said, any tiny clue as to how she was. And the rest of her mind was desperately working to try to remember every word the woman had said to her, so she could offer this small gift to her friend.

"The first thing she said was how much she loved the hot chocolate in that cafe," she recalled. "She was holding a mug of it, inhaling the scent, but I realised after she left that she didn't drink even a sip of it, which did seem weird."

Rhiannon smiled. "That was her favourite treat. When we'd ask for pizza or chips or whatever, all she wanted was a mug of hot chocolate from Kylie's Cafe," she said, eyes misting over with memories. "Even when she was too sick to leave the house, she'd send me or Brodie out to get her a takeaway cup of it. But what else did she say?" she begged.

"I asked her how she knew so much about me, and she said we hadn't met before, so I could stop thinking I was rude to have forgotten her. 'You could say I'm a friend of Rhiannon's,' she added, then told me that she knew I was worried about you, and she was glad we'd reconnected, and were such good friends, and that you would never knowingly hurt me," Carlie said, then stopped, slightly panicked. She'd never mentioned the curse to Rhi, or that she was worried about her, but her friend hadn't noticed her slip of the tongue. Instead she was staring at her, spellbound. "What else?"

"She said she could sense I was worried about Mike – it was after you'd told me he thought my mum hated him, and he'd let her down, so I'd copied some pages from her diary for him, to reassure him that she'd always considered him a dear friend, and her only regret had been hurting him and Gran," Carlie replied.

"Wow, I didn't know you'd done that. Thank you so much for sharing that with him," Rhiannon said softly.

Carlie smiled at her. "It was the least I could do."

Rhiannon was holding the photo, tracing the outline of her mother's face. Then she glanced up at her friend, eyes begging for anything more she could offer her, but Carlie was hesitant.

"What aren't you telling me?" she asked.

"Um, well, she said that I was kind like my mother, so of course I wanted to know if she'd known Mum, and she told me that she had, and that everyone in the village had loved her, and felt her loss when she left. Then she said she knew that Mike had never stopped loving her. Which made me mad, so I told her that wasn't true – that he had married an amazing woman who he adored, who he adores still, and whose children miss her terribly."

Tears pricked Rhiannon's eyes, just as they'd seemed to prick Beth's that night in the cafe. "Then what?" she asked, voice a desperate whisper. "And thank you for telling her that."

"She said: 'I'm sure she misses them more than anything too,'" Carlie replied, then threw her arms around her friend.

Rhiannon smiled at her through her tears. "Thank you."

"What for?" she asked, mystified. "I feel even worse now that it was your mum who said Mike always loved mine."

"Oh Carlie, of course he did, and that's okay. It didn't diminish his love for Mum in any way, and it just made her like him even more, to know that he would always care about someone even when they were gone," Rhiannon explained.

"It sounds like she got confirmation from you that he still loves her, and I'm so grateful to you for that. I remember just before she died, when it was getting really difficult and she was so sick, I heard her telling Dad that she wanted him to find love again after she was gone. He told her that there was no way, but she insisted – she said she knew it wouldn't ever lessen the love he had for her, he would just find some more room in his heart for a new person."

She sniffed a little, and wiped her eyes, trying to compose herself, so Carlie headed downstairs to make tea and give her friend a minute alone. When she returned soon after with two mugs, she handed one to Rhiannon, who was still holding the photo of her mother, but looking far happier now than she had before. "What's wrong," she asked as she sipped the tea. "You look a little worried."

Carlie smiled. "Am I really that obvious?" she replied. "I'm just… well, I don't know… Do you think I'm going crazy, to be seeing things that aren't really there, to be having conversations with… um, what would you call them? Ghosts?" she asked.

"I don't know. I've never seen one, but obviously I very much want to believe that you *did* speak to my mother," Rhiannon said with a half smile. "Has it ever happened to you before?"

Carlie hesitated. What if this really did mean that she was crazy, like lock-you-up crazy? "Your mum was the first one, but a few days after that I found the cottage again, the one in the mists, and Rowan was there," she admitted, voice soft, and bruised sounding.

Her friend gasped. "You never said anything about that!"

"To be honest, I thought you'd think I was going mad," Carlie admitted. "And it was the day you'd gone to see John, to break up with him. I knew you were hurt by his reaction, after you'd finally gathered the courage to reveal yourself to him, so I didn't want to start rambling on about ghosts and mists and things that were there but not there, if that makes sense. I didn't want to twist the conversation around to being all about me – I wanted to be there for you."

Rhiannon smiled. "I appreciate that. But what did he say?"

"Just that he loved me, and he knew that I loved him too, and that he'd felt it, that moment when I changed my mind and decided that I was going to choose both of you," she whispered.

"And he wanted me to stop wishing it had been me that died instead of him – I'd said it wasn't fair because he had so much still to do, so much to give, so many people to help, but he insisted that I was going to do amazing things too, and he wanted me to know how much I am loved, and valued, and that I will help lots of people."

"That's beautiful," Rhiannon said.

"I guess," Carlie replied sadly, and her friend raised her eyebrows at her. "I mean, yes, it was beautiful, but I'd pretty much convinced myself I was just dreaming it, or imagining it, that it was some kind of wishful thinking, confirming to myself that he died knowing I loved him, because that's what I've been torturing myself over. Now that I know I saw your mum though, it makes it seem more real, in a weird way. But then I wonder why I haven't seen him again? Why has he left me?" she asked, voice anxious, imploring.

"He'll never leave you," Rhiannon said emphatically.

Sighing, Carlie shook her head. "But I can't find him any more, and I no longer hear his voice either. The last time he spoke to me was a month ago, at Ostara, when Tom was tattooing me. But he hasn't spoken to me since then."

Rhiannon's eyes were wide. "But that's amazing that he did speak to you. What else did he say?" she pressed.

Carlie blushed, then reluctantly pulled out her Book of Shadows and flicked through it to a section up the back. "My love, I'll always be with you, but it's time for you to let me go," she read out, voice soft. "You are still alive with potential and possibility, so don't cut yourself off from the world, or from those who love you..."

Then abruptly she stopped. She couldn't tell Rhiannon that he'd also insisted that she was surrounded by love, and the potential for love – that it was right in front of her and she should grab it with both hands before it was too late. She knew her friend would agree with him, would push her towards Jake, and she wasn't ready to argue about that again.

"I don't want to let him go," she said instead, and it was Rhiannon's turn to lean across and hug her friend.

"Maybe my mum's words are for you too – that you can eventually love someone else, and it won't mean that you love Rowan any less, just that you've made room in your heart for another person too. Like your mum did, and my dad did – they still loved each other, even when they married someone else. And I know that if Dad does meet someone, even remarry, it won't diminish his love for Mum, or for Violet, or for the new person. His heart will just grow even bigger."

Suddenly they heard the front door open then bang shut, and Rhiannon looked over at the clock by her bed. "Oh my god, how did it get to ten o'clock?" she asked, slightly panicked. "We haven't organised a single thing for Beltane!"

Carlie tried to smother a yawn. "We'll have to do it next week, but we'll be fine, I'm sure. Maybe we can coordinate with Gran and share some of her wisdom while we help her prepare for the ritual? Not that she's been home much lately – she and Jake's grandfather have been seeing each other, so to speak, and I think it's getting serious," she revealed, and there was joy in her voice.

"Really? When did this start?" Rhiannon asked excitedly.

"Oh yeah, I guess we've barely seen each other in the last month, what with exams and boyfriends and holidays," Carlie teased, and Rhiannon rolled her eyes, pretending to be hurt.

"They'd been spending a bit of time together, gardening and stuff, and I know at first Gran was just helping him with his grief, helping him move forward. But after Ostara we were grinding herbs one night, and she brought up Jake, and suggested that there could be room in my life for more than one great love. And for some reason I called her on it – I said it was a bit hypocritical of her to tell me to move on and open my heart, when she'd denied herself love for more than twenty years."

"You didn't!" Rhiannon gasped.

"I'm afraid I did," Carlie said. "It was a long conversation, and I was as gentle as I could be, although there were definitely some tears. But in the end she thanked me – because when she really opened up and looked within, she was shocked to realise that she had denied herself love, had walled up her heart, ever since Grandpa died. And despite healing so many other people, helping them become brave enough to risk everything for love, she'd never done it herself. She didn't think she deserved it."

"Wow," Rhiannon breathed.

A knock on the door brought their conversation to a halt, and Mike opened it and poked his head in.

"Sorry Dad, we didn't realise how late it was, we were just finishing up," Rhiannon said. "I'll be in bed soon."

Mike laughed. "I'm pretty sure you're both old enough to work out what time you need to get to sleep. I just wanted to say hi, and wish you a good night, because I know *I* have to get to bed."

Carlie smiled hello to Mike, said goodbye to Rhiannon, then made her way home through the crisp darkness. It was time for her to snuggle up with Luna and get some sleep too.

Chapter 36

Another Sad Farewell

As the days grew a little longer and got a little warmer, Carlie continued to get up before dawn and go walking. It was so peaceful, so gentle, so soul soothing, to watch the world wake up and see the sky slowly colour pink-gold-lavender-blue. It calmed her, being out in nature, wandering down winding country laneways, marvelling at the simple beauty of honeysuckle blossoms, smiling at the birds she saw and wondering if one of them was Jake's friend. Sometimes she'd climb the tor, when her legs were willing, and one Saturday morning she found herself down by the stream at the place she still thought of as hers and Rowan's.

Sitting with her back against the willow tree, now so much more green and lush than when she'd been there last, in the harsh chill of winter, she laughed as she watched the ducklings dipping down into the water, little bottoms wiggling as they tried to right themselves. Then sadness engulfed her as she realised that Rowan was no longer with her, not even here, in their special place.

Yet she also felt a sense of peace and acceptance as she realised that he was in her heart, not outside of her. As long as she remembered him he would live on, and be part of her. Casting one last look around her, she slowly got to her feet, took a deep breath, then released the bunch of wildflowers she'd picked into the water.

She stood watching them until they disappeared around a bend in the stream, then began the lonely wander back home.

As she walked, she started thinking about Rowan's mother, and feeling guilty that she hadn't gone to visit her as she'd vowed that she would. But when she turned in at her gate, she was shocked to find his mum sitting on the front steps of the cottage, as though she'd conjured her into being with the power of her imagining.

"Mrs Dunbar! Hello. I was just thinking about you," she stammered. "Are you okay?"

The elegantly dressed woman stood up and hugged Carlie. "Please, it's Louisa," she said. "And I've been thinking of you too. How are you going?"

As she sat back down on the step, Carlie sank down next to her and smiled bravely, conscious of how much harder Rowan's loss must be for his mum. "I'm all right," she said softly. "I miss him constantly, but Rose has been wonderful, and so patient, and I'm getting through the days." She wondered that she'd listed patience as a major virtue, but dismissed the thought and focused on Rowan's mum.

"I'm doing okay too," Louisa said with a sad smile. "One day at a time, right?"

Carlie nodded, her heart breaking for the grieving mum.

"I wanted to come over and see you though, because I'm moving up to Scotland next week to live with my sister for a while – her daughter has just moved out, so she's feeling lonely too. So I wanted to say goodbye to you, and thank you for loving Rowan so much, and making him so happy. And, well, I was packing up his apartment, and I thought you might like a few of his things," she said, indicating a wonderful old wooden trunk she must have hauled onto the verandah earlier, which Luna was pacing around suspiciously.

"Oh my gosh, thank you!" Carlie replied, truly touched. "But are you sure? Maybe you should keep them?"

Louisa smiled, sadness and defeat warring with strength in her expression, and her posture. "No, I have lots of things to remember him by. And these might be useful to you – there are lots of his magical books, and some of his ritual tools too."

Carlie hugged her tight, tears welling in her eyes. "Thank you so much. I really appreciate it, and I would be honoured to be their keeper," she replied.

His mother smiled a little. There wasn't much joy in it though, it was like the echo of a smile from long ago, a ghost of something that no longer existed. "I know this sounds kind of weird, but Rowan mentioned to me not long before he died that if anything happened to him, he wanted you to have these," Louisa said, her voice a sigh.

Carlie recoiled in horror at her words. "You mean he knew that he was going to die?" she asked.

"I don't know," his mum admitted. "I'm not sure if it was a premonition, or if he just loved you so deeply, and was telling me this to make sure that I knew how much. But… oh, and this will sound strange, but I saw him a few times, after he died," she said.

"Once when I was walking through the park near his place, another time in a small bookstore in Smithfield that he liked, and then in his apartment, a few weeks ago, while I was sorting through his things. And you'll probably think I'm crazy when I tell you this, but the last time I saw him he spoke to me, and it was like he was there with me, talking to me, holding me while I cried. It was he who suggested that I move back to Scotland to spend some time with my sister. And he reassured me that he would still be with me no matter where I lived, but that I had to start picking up the pieces and moving forward with my life."

Taking a deep breath, she tried to hold her emotions in check before continuing. "But that was the last time I saw him, or heard him, and I hate that he's gone. It probably sounds selfish, because I'm sure he has somewhere better to be now, and I have to learn to go on without him, but I miss that, even if it wasn't real."

Carlie smiled sadly. "I saw him too," she whispered. "In a cottage that doesn't really exist. And he held me as I cried, and told me I had to be strong because I would help a lot of people. I'd already decided that I want to be a grief counsellor, but now I'm even more driven.

"And he was with me when I was getting my tattoo," she added, glancing down at her wrist. "Speaking to me, telling me he still loved me. But I don't sense him around me any more either – I haven't seen him or heard him for a few weeks, which makes me really sad. He said I had to let him go and start moving forward too," she admitted. "But I don't want to. How can it be selfish for us to want him to stick around?"

Louisa leaned across and hugged her, and for a moment they sat like that, tears mingling, sharing their grief and finding some solace in being able to talk about the man they'd both loved so much. "Maybe he feels that it's selfish of him to stick around, and keep us from living our lives," she said gently. "Especially you Carlie, you have your whole life ahead of you, and I hope it will be a life filled with love and joy."

Carlie shook her head, not wanting to think of that. "I'll never forget him," she said fiercely. "He changed me, in so many positive ways. I'm a better person now for having known him."

His mother smiled through her tears. "Thank you for telling me that. It helps me, to know that he did so much good while he was here. That he may not have been with us for a long time, but that he made a difference, however small."

They sat in silence for a long time, lost in their memories, bound by their grief yet both feeling terribly alone. Finally Louisa said she should go, just as Carlie asked her if she'd like a cup of tea. Rowan's mum smiled at her, so like her son, but shook her head.

"Thank you, but I should be getting back, I've still got lots of packing to do. I'd like to give you my new address though, if that's okay, in case you ever want to talk to me?" Her voice trailed off anxiously, and Carlie's heart broke all over again as she saw the pain etched deep into every line of her face, in the way she sat and even the way she held herself.

"I'd like that, thank you," she whispered, and reached out to take the piece of paper with the black ink scrawled across it.

Awkwardly the grieving mother clambered to her feet, and started to walk down the front path to the street. But just before she reached it, she turned back to the young girl, who'd sunk down onto the top step again, weighed down by her own pain. "And Carlie, please, don't put your life on hold," Louisa said. "You're young, and you deserve to find love again. Please don't feel guilty to live your life."

Carlie shrugged, and gazed down at her hands, clasped so tightly together in her lap to stop her reaching out for his mother. As she heard the gate open though, she called out. "Wait."

Louisa turned back to her. "I've been meaning to tell you..." Carlie began, then paused. Would this be a good thing to share with her, or would it just compound her pain?

"Please don't feel bad about my mum," she finally said, voice cracked with pain. "Rowan told me you were worried his dad had hurt her, or worse. And he did, but she survived. She got away, and found her beloved, and had a wonderful life. She wouldn't have met Dad if she didn't go through everything she did. So please, don't feel responsible in any way, or bad for her. You did nothing wrong."

Louisa's face collapsed in on itself, and as tears spilled down her face, she stumbled back along the pathway and pulled Carlie close to her, squeezing her until she could barely breathe.

"Oh Carlie, thank you," she whispered, her voice croaky, and seemingly ripped from somewhere deep and broken within her. "You can't imagine how heavily that has weighed on me."

Taking a deep breath, she slowly let go of her, and a fleeting sense of peace flickered across Louisa's face before the sadness returned. "You have no idea what a gift you have given me. Two gifts now, because I'll always be so grateful that Rowan met you."

Wiping her eyes, she backed slowly away down the path to the street. "Be well Carlie," she called out. "And let yourself be loved, please." Then she hurried into her car and drove away.

When Rose came home later that day, Carlie was still sitting on the front step, frozen there, Luna curled up in her lap. Her grandmother sank down next to her and put an arm around her shoulder. "Are you okay Sweetheart?" she asked tentatively.

"I will be," Carlie finally said. Rose nodded, then her gaze alighted on the trunk, and she stared at it, a question in her eyes.

A small smile flitted across Carlie's face. "Rowan's mum came over to say goodbye, because she's moving up to Scotland to live with her sister, and she wanted to leave me some of Rowan's books." Suddenly determined, she stood up and dragged the chest inside, then slowly and clumsily lugged it up the stairs to her room.

Chapter 37

Hanging On, Letting Go

Carlie spent the rest of the day sitting cross-legged on the floor, Luna nestled against her, slowly looking through the old trunk at all its treasures. There were beautiful books on spirituality and magic – some shamanic, some druidic, some from a witchcraft perspective – and others on different forms of divination and healing, including an amazing herbal encyclopaedia. Some seemed almost new, while others had been thumbed through many times, and it was these ones that she sat with for the longest time, flipping through the pages and reading random passages, tracing over Rowan's handwritten notes in the margins, running her hand over the precious pages that had meant so much to him. She could picture him sitting in his old apartment, poring over these books, reading by candlelight, dreaming up magic and rituals, and absorbing the information and adding it to his own personal experiences and hard-won knowledge. The world had lost a remarkable wisdom keeper when he died.

Excited by this amazing beginning to her magical library, Carlie finally hauled all of the books over to her mother's old bookshelf and arranged them by subject, spending a lot of time holding each book and considering where to put it, wanting to keep these gems that had been Rowan's physically close to her heart before she placed them in their new position.

Hearing Luna miaow as she balanced on the side of the trunk, Carlie walked back over and peered inside. Underneath where the books had been stored was a smaller chest, which she gently lifted out. Inside were several velvet-wrapped packages, which she carefully opened to reveal a host of beautiful ritual tools. There was an elaborate silver chalice, a shallow scrying bowl, a wand made from willow and tipped with a moonstone, and an athame that brought tears to her eyes as she lifted it, because it flooded her with memories of the new moon ritual she'd done with Rowan.

There was also a white-handled boline for inscribing candles and cutting herbs, gorgeous silver and gold statues of gods and goddesses, a pretty brass incense censer, and two smaller wands. And when she finally lifted the last of the tools out, she found the most precious and intimate thing of all – Rowan's personal Book of Shadows. It was even thicker than the herbal encyclopaedia, the cover crafted from weathered timber carved with Celtic knotwork and intricate spirals, and bound together with silver metalwork. The pages within were parchment-thick and covered in his beautiful handwriting, interspersed with his delicate illustrations of herbs and flowers, some of which he'd included in his herbal oracle deck.

A shiver ran down her spine when she saw the tansy plant, which was on the card she'd received in his seminar at the Body Mind Spirit Festival. Magically tansy was associated with the dead, and used in rites of death and rebirth, and she felt the same chill now that she'd felt that day. Rhiannon had told her that the plant symbolised rebirth of the self, but she shuddered as she gazed at the image. She didn't want any more rebirth, any more change, any more loss, any more grieving. Surely enough was enough.

She smiled though as she remembered that day when she'd first met Rowan. Rhiannon had insisted she get a spirit guide painting done by him, and she'd somehow ended up spilling out her story of losing her parents to him while he painted. And he'd held her as she cried, then told her to be patient with herself and allow as much time as she needed to heal and start to move forward. To not feel any pressure to stop grieving, or to keep grieving either.

Clutching his Book of Shadows to her chest, she closed her eyes and allowed herself to wallow in her memories, and to recall every moment of that magical day. The protection charm Rowan had cast so that no one at the festival even saw them as he painted her, the comfort she'd felt when he held her as she cried, when normally she would have been terrified that a stranger was touching her. His sweet insistence that they'd shared many past lives together, including one as King Arthur and the priestess Morgaine, lovers throughout time – which admittedly she'd rolled her eyes at, and was still unconvinced by, lovely though the thought was.

And then the party that night, which Rhiannon had insisted they go to no matter how hard she'd tried to say no, where Rowan had stayed by her side all evening, talking to her, making her laugh, and ignoring all the other people there who she'd been sure were far more interesting than her.

At seven o'clock Rose knocked on her bedroom door to tell her that dinner was ready, and they ate chilli bean tacos together and caught up on their days. Carlie's mind was upstairs for much of it though, floating around in the old trunk, reliving the memories held in Rowan's drawings and his words. But she snapped back to the present when her grandmother nervously told her that she'd spent the afternoon with Richard, and she finally noticed her shining eyes and the smile that was lighting up her face.

"I just wanted to thank you Sweetheart, for forcing me to face my fears and finally realise that I'd been sabotaging my chances for love. All those wasted years," Rose sighed. Then she brightened. "I can't quite believe how happy I've been since Richard and I started… well, spending time together," she said, then laughed.

"The concept of dating just sounds too bizarre at our age. And I wouldn't know how to do it anyway – the last time I went out on a date was more than forty years ago. Your grandfather was the first man I ever went out with, and I was married to him for more than two decades. And since then… well, I've barely spoken to a man, besides Mike," she admitted. "How strange that I didn't even notice."

Carlie beamed at her. "I'm so glad," she said, and she meant it. Mostly for her grandma's sake, since she absolutely deserved to love and be loved, but also because it had terrified her when she'd realised that after Rose's husband had died, she'd pushed any chance of a relationship away, had denied herself any possibility of love. It was what she'd felt like doing when Rowan died too, but when she'd pictured her life playing out like her grandmother's, it had seemed too lonely and bleak to contemplate.

"Thank you Sweetheart. It means so much to both of us to have your blessing, and Jake's too," Rose replied, face filled with love and joy. "Richard is telling him tonight as well."

Carlie peered at her, puzzled. "Telling him what?"

Her grandmother blushed. "Well, we're both too old for the dating scene, and for the casual entanglements people seem to have these days. So we've decided that we want to make it official in some way, and we thought we'd let people know next weekend at Beltane. Tom will be down from London for the ritual…"

"And Beltane is the time for making commitments, and leaping the fires with your beloved!" Carlie finished for her, excitement in her voice. "What are you going to do?"

"Well, we thought maybe Elsie could come down and do a little handfasting ceremony as part of the ritual," Rose said, her voice trembling with nerves. "But we wanted to tell you and Jake first, and see if you were okay with it before we asked her."

Jumping up, Carlie went around the table to hug her grandmother. "Of course we're okay with it! We've been wondering for a little while now, when you were going to tell us. Jake will be as overjoyed as I am. We couldn't think of two better people to find each other, or who deserve happiness more. Ooh, I'm so thrilled for you Gran!"

"You already knew?" Rose asked, half relieved, half anxious.

"Well, not for sure, but we've had our suspicions for a while," she replied, giggling. "Shall we have tea to toast the good news?"

"Actually, I baked a honey cake this afternoon, and picked up some sparkling apple juice, just in case we wanted to celebrate a bit," Rose said, sounding uncharacteristically shy again.

Hurrying over to the kitchen bench, Carlie found the freshly-baked cake sitting there ready, still warm from the oven, so she grabbed some plates and a knife and took it over to the table, then found two pretty wine glasses at the back of the cupboard and grabbed the pitcher of juice from the fridge.

Pouring out two glasses as Rose cut the cake, Carlie handed one to her grandmother then raised hers in the air. "To you Gran," she said, eyes alight with joy. "I'm so happy that you've found love, and I wish you both many years of precious moments together."

"Thank you Sweetheart. It wouldn't have happened without you," she responded, handing her a piece of the warm honey cake. "And it was the same for Richard, with Jake. He was feeling guilty about spending time with me, but Jake let him know that he deserved a chance to be happy, and even pushed him a little in my direction. He's a wonderful boy," Rose said.

"Yeah, he is," Carlie agreed, then turned the subject back to Richard and what he was like, and what the happy couple was hoping for the future. Hours later, when Rose had gone to bed and she figured she probably should too, Carlie was running her hand over Rowan's ritual tools, which she'd placed back in the small leather chest. Suddenly she had a memory of another box, another time.

Carefully she lifted Luna from her lap and lay her on the bed, where the kitten squeaked out a tiny miaow then drifted back to sleep, then she opened her bedroom door and tiptoed down the stairs to the little room she used to sleep in. Switching on the light, she walked the few steps to the wardrobe and reached carefully inside, to the back of the top shelf. When her fingers hit something, wedged right in the corner, she clumsily drew it towards her.

It was the package her mum's friend Sandy had sent her last year, which had contained the diary that had taught Carlie so much about both of her parents, and about herself as well. At the time she had been so distracted by the journal that she'd forgotten to look at the other items.

Creeping quietly back up to her room, she sat cross-legged on her bed and opened the parcel. There was a bundle of what looked like clothes, which she unfolded carefully – then she smiled when she saw the small, faded white teddy bear in the middle, with a blue ribbon around his neck. Cuddling him for a moment, she tried to imagine her mother holding him. Had it been Violet's, or was it her own, from when she was a kid? She couldn't recollect a teddy bear though, and she remembered other stuffed toys – a sweet giraffe, a fuzzy lion, an adorable elephant, a cute little monkey. The bear must have been her mother's, which made it all the more precious to her. Gently she placed it on her pillow, next to Luna, and the little kitten snuggled up against it, without even opening her eyes.

Lifting up a bright red dress next, she held it against herself, amazed at the style. She couldn't recall her mum ever wearing it, but it was beautiful, soft and warm and brightly coloured, so unlike the rest of Violet's Sydney wardrobe of lawyerly suits in neutral tones.

Next she ran her hands over a deep purple velvet gown, like something her grandmother would sell in her shop, and wear at a ritual. She couldn't remember her mum wearing that one either, but maybe she'd bought it to remind herself of the beauty of her life with her parents, and the magic she'd woven with Rose.

As she unfolded the dress to better see its pretty jagged hem and lacy edges, a small box fell out of a pocket, and she picked it up and opened it. Inside were four rings. The first two were her mum's wedding and engagement rings, two pretty, delicate, rose-gold rings, the wedding band studded with tiny diamonds and etched with swirls, while the other featured three coloured stones – a ruby in the centre, flanked on each side by teardrop sapphires, one green and one blue.

Her dad's rose gold wedding band was there too, engraved with ivy leaves on the outside, and with the words *Lives entwined, souls in harmony, hearts as one* inscribed on the inside. Just like on the ring Rowan had given her. She couldn't quite get her head around that coincidence, so she picked up the fourth ring instead, deeply curious.

It was beautiful, with a large heart-shaped rose quartz set in a raised strip of silver entwined with ivy leaves, hearts and butterflies. Carlie had never seen her mum wear it, and there was no note to say whose it was or why she'd had it. But it looked like the wedding ring you'd choose if you were being handfasted in a Beltane rite. It would be so perfect for Rose, and she wondered if she should offer it to Richard for the ceremony.

Then she gasped, as she picked up a pretty pale green dress, the skirt full with layers of tulle, lace and satin, and embroidered with ivy leaves. It was her mum's wedding dress, but she'd only ever seen it in black and white photos, so she'd assumed it was white, and somehow the ivy leaves hadn't been captured on film. It was really beautiful. And so magical. So witchy. So her-mum's-life-in-Summer-Hill-not-Sydney. So Beltane. Again she felt sad, as though she hadn't known her mother at all, or she'd only known one small side of her, while the rest had been totally hidden. As she turned the dress over, a little note unfurled from within it and landed on the bed.

Dear Mum,
I don't know if I'll ever see you again, and that thought breaks my heart. But you were with me in spirit as I sewed together my wedding dress (oh how I wish I'd had your help with it – you were always so much better than me at this!). And you were with me too while I dreamed it up, adding ivy leaves to represent our rituals, and making it green for Beltane, which is when I married my beloved.
You are with me always, and I hope you know that I have always loved you, and always will.
Your loving daughter, Violet xx

A Beltane dress for a Beltane bride. And a week from today, Rose would have her handfasting and be a Beltane bride too. The wheel of the year turning, the wheel of life turning. Sadness and joy. Love and grief. Hope and despair. The many shades of a life. The thought inspired Carlie as much as it depressed her, and she finally switched out the light and climbed into bed beside Luna and the teddy bear, drifting off into a dream where the scent of flowers drenched everything, and all she could recall of it the next day was jasmine blooms and ivy leaves.

Chapter 38

Blossoming Into Love

On Monday morning, Jake came running up to the girls as soon as they climbed the front steps at school, eyes sparkling with excitement. "Oh my god, can you believe it? Isn't it amazing!" he cried, then stared at Rhiannon in panic. "Oh, um, can we talk about it yet?" he asked quietly, turning to Carlie.

Relief washed over him as Carlie giggled, then nodded. "It's okay, Gran said we can share the news with Rhi. I was just waiting for you so we could be together when we spilled the beans," she said with a grin. "I think Gran knew it would torture us to have to try to keep it a secret from her."

"Guys, I'm right here! What is it?" Rhiannon begged, impatience and curiosity burning in her.

Jake smiled at Carlie. "Do you want to –"

"Oh god, someone tell me," Rhiannon shrieked.

Carlie laughed. "Sorry, it's just… well, you know how Beltane is all about –"

"Carlie, get to the point! Jake, what is it?" Rhiannon demanded.

"Rose and Pop are having a handfasting ceremony next weekend, at the Beltane ritual," he blurted out.

Rhiannon squealed and grabbed Carlie's hands. "Oh my god, that's so beautiful! How long have you known?"

"They told us both on Saturday night, but you were off with Tom yesterday and we couldn't find you to share the news," Jake replied. "Carlie wanted to tell you straight away, don't worry. But isn't it sweet? They're so cute together."

The bell for class rang, interrupting their excited recounting of the news, and Jake rushed off to his with a cheerful wave.

"And they want us to help during the ritual, if you want to," Carlie said, as the two girls walked down the hall together. "And Tom too, obviously. It's like we'll all be related in some way!"

"Oh Carlie, I'd be honoured," Rhiannon grinned. "How beautiful, after so much sadness. And Rose has given so much to everyone here, since way before I was born, so the whole village will be really thrilled that she's found some happiness."

"I hope so," Carlie said. "She is definitely due some joy."

The following night Rhiannon skipped over to Carlie's for dinner and their magical meeting. Their coven time was spent learning more about Beltane, the sabbat that marks the beginning of summer, from their wise priestess. Then they excitedly helped Rose plan her handfasting ritual, everything from the flowers they'd use in the ceremony to the food they'd prepare for the feast afterwards.

On Saturday morning, Beltane Eve, Carlie and Rhiannon got up early to gather pretty white blossoms from the sacred hawthorn tree, which was associated with the sabbat and used for love spells and in marriage rituals, as well as for protection and healing. And that evening they wove them together with jasmine flowers, white rose buds, violets and meadowsweet, making a handfasting wreath for Rose's hair. They spoke the words of a spell as they worked, infusing it with love and blessings.

Quickly they wove their own smaller floral wreaths too, then started on the food. A beautiful passionfruit cake in the shape of a heart, topped with cream cheese icing and crystallised violets. Rose petal biscuits, strawberry and dandelion salad, stuffed zucchini flowers, honey joys, scones with lavender jam, and mead infused with woodruff and other summery herbs.

Chapter 39

A New Beginning

Just before dawn on Beltane morning, Carlie woke to the sound of Luna's contented purring as the kitten snuggled up against her on her pillow. This afternoon she'd be helping Rose get ready for her handfasting ceremony with Richard, and her heart flooded with joy at the thought. If anyone deserved happiness after a life of tragedy interspersed with unconditional and constant giving, it was her grandmother. While most people only saw the strong and capable priestess, Carlie knew how fragile Rose could be – although she hid it well, even from herself – and how deeply sad and lonely she'd been for much of the last two decades. Her life had had purpose and meaning, and she'd created a circle of dear goddess-loving friends, but she'd walled up her heart and denied herself any chance of love.

Patting Luna, Carlie smiled at the adorable kitten. She still missed Luther dreadfully, but she was so grateful that he'd brought Luna to her and Rose. Slowly she sat up, took a few deep breaths, then dragged herself out of bed. Getting up in the dark hadn't become any easier, but the pay-off was always worth it. Slipping into her long green velvet dress, she laced up her mother's warm boots, because dawn up on the tor was still chilly, even on the first day of summer.

Tiptoeing downstairs, she grabbed an apple and slipped out the back door, stifling a laugh as Luna sat indignantly on the kitchen step and watched her creep out the back gate. Unlike Luther, the fuzzy little kitten was no fan of wet grass or early morning wanderings.

The tiniest wash of light was starting to fan out along the horizon as she began to climb the hill. It was still a while before the sun would rise, but the world was slowly awakening. Mist danced around the summit as well as the lower slopes, and Carlie felt it reaching out cool fingers, like ice-cold kisses, to touch her face, and swirling around her legs. Then, as she reached the top, her breath caught.

Someone, or some thing, was emerging from the mists. Clad in a gold robe, she seemed more real, more flesh and blood, than the other beings she'd encountered, her whole demeanour sweet and light in comparison to Aideen's strength and power, Brianna's occasional surliness and Brauna's heavy comfort.

Staring at her, mesmerised, Carlie wondered how to react. What were you supposed to do with these Otherworldly beings? Should she wait for the woman to address her, or greet her first?

The gold-clad figure smiled at her. "There are no rules beloved, and no need to stand on ceremony with me."

Relief flooded her, even as one part of her brain noticed that the woman was speaking to her without moving her lips. "It's just that Aideen and Brianna were a bit annoyed with me at times," she admitted. "I'd hate to unknowingly offend you."

Suddenly she was wrapped in the being's arms, warmth and comfort coursing through her. It was unnerving though, like a vampire standing at a distance, then in a split second enfolding you in a loving yet lethal embrace. The woman laughed, a sweet, tinkling laugh, and Carlie blushed. *Another freakin' mind reader.*

"Have no fear, you have not offended any of us. We are all so very proud of you, and impressed with how you have handled all the loss you have had to endure, and how much you have grown. As a granddaughter, as a friend, as a student. As a witch."

Shock left Carlie speechless for a moment. A witch? Was she? And more importantly, did she even want to be?

The woman of mist smiled at her. "It is nothing to be scared of Carlie. You have worked hard, you have read widely, you have practised. You have spent time in nature, and attuned yourself to the energy of the moon and sun and seasons, to the magic of the earth. You have suffered much, yet you chose to become more compassionate, where others choose the path of bitterness and revenge."

Carlie gazed into her eyes, shy all of a sudden, and feeling inadequate. A fraud. "But I'm not like Gran. I'm not sure I believe in the goddess the way she does," she whispered.

"But you are on a journey to discover what is true to *you* Carlie. You are on a quest both within and without, seeking knowledge and understanding, learning rituals and forging the confidence to change them to suit you. And you have opened your heart and your mind to experiences that would have made some people unravel, applying logic as well as intuition, and managing to marry the two without conflict," she explained.

"Most importantly, you hold nature as sacred and want to work in the healing arts, to aid people physically and emotionally. You spoke to Samantha – what could be more magical, more witchy, than protecting the earth and helping people to heal?"

Carlie smiled. Wasn't that what everyone wanted to do? Were there actually people who actively *didn't* want to protect the environment or help others?

"You would be surprised," her companion said sadly, then flinched as from somewhere far away a dog barked, and the sky lightened imperceptibly in the east. The gold-clad woman pulled her robes more tightly around herself. "I have something for you for Rose," she said, and handed over a gold-velvet-wrapped parcel. "But my gift for you is less tangible. Do you know who I am?" she asked.

"I'm guessing that you're the woman in yellow, or maybe gold. And friend to Brauna, Brianna and Aideen, which would make you the symbol of air?" she replied softly, nervously, questioningly.

"Very good," the figure of mist said, and although her words could have sounded patronising coming from someone else, somehow they didn't when they were delivered in her sweet and gentle manner. "My name is Liana. And what does air bring?"

Carlie smiled wryly. "Is this a test?"

Shrugging delicately, the woman in gold returned her smile. "There is no pass or fail, if that is what you are alluding to."

As she laughed, Carlie felt the first rays of the sun spilling over the horizon, illuminating her face and piercing through the mantle of mist of the being before her. Slowly she sank down onto the wet grass, overwhelmed, and Liana sank with her.

"Air represents thought, intellect, communication, clarity and truth," Carlie offered, voice barely a whisper as she rattled off the traits she'd learned through her studies. "It's about the dawning of a new day – moving forward, letting go of regrets and starting again, free of preconceptions and limitations. It heralds fresh starts and new beginnings, and the world and your life born anew."

The woman smiled proudly as she nodded. "Now listen carefully," she said, her voice urgent now. "Your gift is a new beginning, the opportunity for new love, but you have to open your heart and allow it in – it is not something we can hand to you in a gift-wrapped box. You have to decide whether you will take the risk or not. You have to choose to dive in, or not, and sink or swim from there."

Tears welled in Carlie's eyes, but didn't fall. "You mean Jake?"

"I mean anyone who will make you happy," Liana replied softly. "Jake cares about you, and he is patient and kind and compassionate. But you will have to let him know if you want to be more than friends, because he vowed to give you space, and he will honour that. He respects you too much to push you, which could work against him. However, if you are not ready now, if you lack the courage, I am sure there will be other opportunities for love in your future."

Surprising herself, Carlie realised that the thought of waiting into the undetermined future was making her feel a little panicky. She didn't want to wait, like her grandmother had, and end up resentful and lonely. She didn't want to miss the chance that she had.

"It is up to you now," the mist-shrouded being continued softly. "You can use Rowan as an excuse to cut yourself off from everyone, or not. Today you stand on the precipice of a new beginning, but *you* have to decide whether to grasp it yourself, or end up like your grandmother and spend a lifetime denying yourself joy. You have already recognised the futility of her sacrifice – and helped her to see it too, as evidenced by her happy occasion today – so I am hoping that you will not turn your back on the chance of happiness that stands before *you*," she said with a warm smile.

"Your life is yours, and it will be the sum total of all the choices you make, or do not make. Never think that avoiding something delays your decision. Not choosing one path because you are scared means you have chosen the other path by default. Inaction is an action, it is a choice, it is simply a lazy one."

"I just don't want to hurt Jake, I care about him too much," Carlie whispered, voice tortured. "And what if I say yes, then change my mind? Or he realises that he doesn't actually like me like that after all? I couldn't bear to disappoint him."

"Then you will deal with it then. You are not responsible for Jake's happiness, or anyone else's. But not giving him the chance – not giving yourself the chance – just in case it does not work, is not fair to him or to you. Refusing to open your heart in case you hurt someone just ensures pain. Did that work out for Rose?" Liana demanded.

"No," Carlie reluctantly conceded.

"Do you wish that you had never met Rowan, so that you could have avoided experiencing the agony of his loss?"

"Of course not!" she snapped.

"Well then," the woman in gold said with a triumphant smile, and Carlie almost laughed at the expression on her face. "Besides, it is not up to you to decide for Jake. He has free will, and he has the right to choose for himself. He is stronger than you give him credit for."

"I know," Carlie mused. She thought of all the time they'd spent together. How kind he was, how patient with her, how selfless he'd been to lock away his feelings for her so she wouldn't feel pressured. And slowly it dawned on her, that it was joy she was feeling as she thought of him, and a warmth and comfort she really liked.

And was that an undercurrent of *excitement* she felt as she opened her mind to the idea of being with Jake? Her friend Jake. Her strong Aussie mate, who let her cry on his shoulder, and who understood her sense of humour, her culture and her past. Who let her talk about Rowan even when it hurt him, and was there for her while Rhiannon was neglecting her as she fell in love with Tom.

Sweet, dependable Jake, who she obviously cared for far more than she'd admitted to herself. It wasn't the wild and dramatic passion she'd experienced with Rowan, but she was starting to realise that she didn't want that right now. She wanted slow and sweet. Companionship and sensitivity. Compassion rather than drama. Simple, uncomplicated joy. And just being, rather than becoming.

As the sun rose above the horizon, she closed her eyes against the glare, and when she opened them again she felt as though she was seeing everything in a totally new way, the whole world washed clean and born anew. Her heart born anew.

Eyes dazzled by the rising sun, she turned to tell all of this to Liana, but wasn't especially surprised to discover that the gold-clad woman had slipped away as the swirling mists dispersed. She was alone on the hill now, alone with her thoughts, and her decision.

Her decision of whether or not to take this precious opportunity for love. To treasure it, and to be brave enough to put her heart on the line for the chance. Of course Jake might have gotten over her by now, might have found someone else – Rhiannon had mentioned recently that he'd been spending a bit of time with Abby, who was in the school play with him. But she owed it to herself, and to him, to let him know how she felt.

As she wandered dreamily back down the hill, she started to laugh. She was realising that her liking Jake wasn't new, wasn't really a shock, and she wondered when her feelings for him had changed from school friend to something more. When he'd smiled across the room at her at the Imbolc ritual, his aura all lit up and golden? When he'd spent so much time helping her prepare for their presentation, because the thought of speaking in front of the class terrified her? Or was it when he'd been so kind and attentive to her at the London festival, as she'd battled the ghosts? Or at the ritual that night, after Rhiannon had ditched her for Tom?

Her pace increased, and within minutes she was knocking furiously on Rhiannon's door. Her friend ushered her inside, listening impatiently as she tried to explain what she was suddenly feeling, as she tried herself to understand what had happened to her, and when.

Smiling her knowing smile, Rhiannon led her upstairs to her bedroom. "It's about time," she grinned. "I'm not sure how much longer he would have waited."

Carlie felt suddenly panicked. "Am I too late?"

Rhiannon shook her head. "I don't think so, he doesn't seem the fickle type, but I wouldn't risk leaving it too much longer."

"But do I really like him? And can I do this? And should I? I mean, what if I hurt him? I'd never forgive myself," she sighed.

"Oh Carlie, you're hurting him by not giving him a chance. No one knows what will happen – hell, Tom and I could break up next week – but you can't live like that, you can't tiptoe through life in the shadows, too afraid to try anything just in case it won't work out, just in case it will hurt. You taught me that," Rhiannon insisted.

"Life is pain, yet it's also incredible joy. But you need to move out of your comfort zone, you need to take a risk sometimes, stop protecting your heart out of fear, in order to feel the joy."

Carlie laughed. That's what she'd told Rose too. "But is it too soon?" she asked. "What will people think? Does this make *me* fickle?"

"Oh hon, it's not too soon, I promise. You've been holding on to Rowan for a long time, longer even than you were with him. And besides, letting Jake in doesn't mean that you're turning your back on Rowan. He'll always be part of you. He'll always be your first relationship, your first love, that will never change. And he helped you grow and blossom and become who you are today – someone who can open her heart to love," Rhiannon said gently.

"But he's not here any more, and you can't spend the rest of your life wishing that he was. You deserve to be happy, more than anyone I know you deserve to be happy. And so does Jake."

Carlie smiled, a genuine, joy-filled smile. "Thank you Rhi. I'm sorry I'm such hard work."

Her friend hugged her. "You're not hard work at all, silly. But what made you finally realise how you felt about Jake?" she asked. Then she laughed. "No, don't tell me – you met the yellow-clad woman. There's gotta be four of them, am I right? Is that from her?"

she grinned, looking down at the gold-velvet-wrapped parcel Carlie still clutched in her hand.

Smiling, Carlie nodded. "Yes, I met Liana, the woman in gold, the being of light and air and new beginnings," she admitted. "But this is for Rose, not me. My gift, she said, was the gift of new beginnings, but she told me that I have to go out and make it happen myself, I have to take the risk... I'm not sure that I can though," she added, suddenly terrified all over again.

Rhiannon took her hands. "This is Jake we're talking about, your friend Jake, your study buddy, your thank-god-you're-here-too, I'll-throw-up-if-I-have-to-watch-Rhiannon-and-Tom-kiss-each-other-again partner-in-crime. There's no reason to feel nervous about talking to him," she assured her.

"I guess you're right," Carlie sighed. "But that reminds me, has Tom arrived yet? And do you think he brought his equipment?"

Rhiannon gazed at her quizzically. "Yep, he got here this morning, although he's been round at Jake's, seeing his grandad. And I imagine he brought his stuff – he never goes anywhere without it. But you can ask him yourself, he'll be here any minute."

The sound of knocking interrupted them, and they rushed downstairs to open the door. Tom stood there, a bag over his shoulder, a bemused expression on his face. "What's going on?" he asked, as he embraced his girlfriend then peered curiously at Carlie.

"Come in, come in," Rhiannon said, dragging him inside. "I think Carlie wants another tattoo. And to kiss your cousin," she added cheekily, then raced up the stairs, the other two in hot pursuit.

Chapter 40

Into the Light

Two hours later, after a brief stop at Richard's, Carlie was back at home and pulling her mum's pale green wedding dress over her head. It seemed fitting that she'd wear it to her grandmother's handfasting, so that Violet could be there, in spirit at least. "Oh Mum, I really wish you were here," she sighed. "Today would be even more magical if you and Dad could take part too."

Hearing a sound at the door, she spun around guiltily, and blushed when she saw that it was Rose.

"You look beautiful Sweetheart," said her grandma, who was smiling even as a tear trickled down her cheek.

"So do you Gran. You're glowing, and the dress is divine." It was soft and floaty, with layers of fine lace and tulle, and crafted from the palest gold material, which made Carlie think of Liana. "You look like an angel, or a sunshine faery," she said, wonder in her voice.

Spinning in a circle, the hem held up in one hand, Rose laughed, enjoying the feel of the fabric swirling around her. "I kind of feel like a faery," she grinned. "Now I'll just grab some flowers from the garden for my hair and I'll be ready," she said, turning to walk back down the stairs.

"Wait!" Carlie called out, and Rose halted.

"What is it?" she asked, concern in her voice.

"Nothing's wrong, but Rhi and I already did the flowers – we made you a wreath of hawthorn blossoms, jasmine, violets and roses for your hair, and did your bouquet too, and ours to match. They're all in the kitchen. But I have something for you," she added, and handed over the gold-velvet-wrapped parcel.

The priestess's eyes widened. "You met Liana," she breathed.

"You know her?" Carlie asked, surprised.

Rose nodded. "I met her on the eve of my wedding to Louis," she explained. "It was my first experience of magic, so it took me a while to understand how special the encounter was." She sank onto Carlie's bed, holding the package carefully.

"I'd gone for a walk around the base of the tor, the night before the ceremony. I needed to escape my house, and escape my family. My parents were deeply religious, and my mother had been lecturing me all day on the duties of a bride and a wife, and I needed a moment to myself, a moment of peace, to be sure that this marriage was what *I* wanted, and not just *her* plan."

Laughing as she saw the shock on Carlie's face, she quickly continued. "It *was* what I wanted, don't worry, but it took me finding that moment of stillness to really appreciate Louis, and what our life could be. After walking for a while, I sat down under a tree and closed my eyes to look within – and when I opened them she was perched right next to me, this mist-shrouded figure, so still, so mysterious. I panicked, of course, but she took my hand, and I felt this incredible peace and comfort, and I forgot to be scared of her," Rose revealed.

"And as she gazed into my eyes she showed me how beautiful our life would be. I saw Violet, and an image of me and Louis, older but still so happy, and the absence of the stress of my parents. And she was right, thank goddess. My father was offered an overseas post the next day, and they moved to America soon after, which was wonderful. My mother was cruel, a real monster, which made it even harder for me, that you thought *I* was a monster."

"I'm so sorry," Carlie said, voice dripping with pain and regret.

"Oh Sweetheart, you didn't know. And we got through it. But Liana gave me a necklace to wear at the wedding, to keep me calm and remind me how much I was loved. It was beautiful – a huge, gorgeous rose quartz heart perched in a delicate silver setting, with ivy leaves, hearts and butterflies surrounding the crystal."

Carlie stared at her. "Was there a ring too?"

"Well, I bought one for Violet for her seventeenth birthday that perfectly matched it. Why?" Rose questioned her, but Carlie's mind was whirring with relief. She had done the right thing, offering the ring to Richard – it would be like Rose's daughter was at the ceremony, in spirit at least, and would prove that Violet had still loved her mother, and treasured the things she had given her, even though they'd been parted for so long.

"Do you still have the necklace?" Carlie asked her grandma.

"You're right, I should definitely wear it today! Thank you Sweetheart," she grinned, then bustled out of the room. Carlie called out to her to come back again, because she'd forgotten Liana's parcel. Smiling apologetically, the soon-to-be bride walked over to pick it up, but froze when they heard a loud knock on the door.

"It's okay Gran, it's just Rhiannon," Carlie reassured her. "We still have a bit of time. Go find your necklace and open your gift, and we'll grab the flowers. Then we can walk over together when you're ready. All the food we made last night is already at the healing centre, and Laura and Miri have been there all morning, getting the ritual room ready, so everything is under control."

Rose hugged her granddaughter, then headed downstairs to finish preparing. As she flung open the door, Carlie was already babbling to her friend, their floral wreaths in her hand. But she stopped mid-sentence when she saw it was Mike in the doorway, not Rhiannon.

"Hi Carlie," he said, bemused by her confusion. "I was wondering if you'd mind if I accompany Rose today? Since our lives have been so intertwined all these years and all? And you and Rhi can follow us, carrying her bouquet, checking the dress is okay and all that?"

Carlie stared at him, surprised by the question, but was distracted by the sight of her friend racing up the steps, flustered and out of breath, and full of stammered apologies for being late.

"It's fine," she shrugged, then turned back to Mike. "Of course you can," she replied. "And Gran's almost ready, so we can be off in a moment. Come in."

She handed Rhiannon one of the smaller flower bands they'd woven for themselves, then pulled the hair clip out of her messy bun, letting her long dark curls tumble down her back, and placing the other wreath on her head. The scent of jasmine, roses and violets surrounded her, and she breathed it in. They were all flowers of love, and their heady aroma filled her with joy.

As Rose came out of her room to join them, Carlie glanced at Mike, about to say something, and was shocked to see his eyes fill with pain. Confused, she turned to her grandmother, and saw its echo in her own expression.

"Oh Sweetheart, you look so beautiful, and so much like your mum," she whispered. But while there were sad tears in Rose's eyes, she looked ecstatically happy as well. "Thank you so much for coming here Carlie, for being part of my life. You have no idea just how deeply you've changed me, how much better you've made me, and my life. Not just because you encouraged me to find love again, but because *you* have loved me, and healed me."

Carlie leaned in and hugged her, the words a healing balm for her own pain, her own soul. "Thank you Gran," she said, voice thick with emotion. "I love you so much, and Mum did too, every day of her life, in ways I'm only just coming to realise."

She felt a gentle hand on her back, and turned to see Mike, face more composed now. "I want to thank you too," he told her. "For helping Rhiannon to heal, and for bringing me peace. You're very much loved and appreciated here."

"Don't make me cry," Carlie warned, voice stern, but she was smiling. "Now we really should get our act together and go. We have a ritual to create, and some love and magic to weave."

Mike took Rose's arm, while Carlie picked up their pretty bouquets and Rhiannon lifted the hem of Rose's dress and the gold velvet cloak she wore over it, her gift from Liana. Today she looked even more like a priestess, like a goddess even, radiant with love and joy, exuding strength and power in her regal bearing, while also revealing a hint of her fragility and vulnerability, which softened her in a beautiful way.

As the four of them approached the meadow at the base of the tor, Carlie smiled at the hum of conversation and the sight of so many colourfully dressed people, all friends of Rose's, and all so happy that she was finally allowing love into her own heart, after giving so much to all of them for so long.

Richard was there, with Jake and Tom on either side of him, looking excited yet calm. Carlie's heart lifted as she saw the look he gave Rose, so filled with love and respect. Tom winked at her when she caught his eye, then motioned to Jake with a tilt of his head. Blushing a little, she glanced over at her school friend, and breathed a sigh of relief when she saw the expression in his eyes as he gazed back at her. Hopefully she wasn't too late.

"Welcome," cried a tall, imposing stranger wreathed in mist and sunshine, and wearing a long purple gown that looked as though it had been woven from a summer sunset sky. Carlie's head turned sharply towards the unfamiliar voice, confused. Rose's best friend Elsie was officiating the handfasting, wasn't she?

Her jaw dropped when she saw Liana standing behind the purple-clad woman, at the easterly point of the circle, and her head spun as she noticed Aideen in the south, representing fire, Brianna in the north, for earth, and Brauna in the west, for water. Yet no one else seemed perturbed by their presence, or even curious. Not even Rhiannon, who'd met two of them before.

Liana stared back at her, one eyebrow raised in amusement, then in an instant she was at her side, that weird vampire trick they all seemed to share. "You look beautiful Carlie, and so much more at peace than you did this morning. Nice tattoo, by the way," she grinned. "I see that you are ready to leap off the edge and test your wings, or your heart at least."

"Yes, but what… I don't understand… Where's Elsie? Why isn't anyone here freaking out at seeing four people who aren't really people? Wait, five. Who is that?" she asked, words spilling out all over each other, tripping her up as she tried to frame a coherent thought, and work out which question was most pressing.

Liana reached up her hand and cupped Carlie's cheek, and she felt the familiar sense of peace and contentment flow into her. "Beloved, calm down. Elsie is not well, so I told her that I would officiate in her place. Well, Ailia will," she said, turning to look at the purple-robed woman in the centre of the circle.

"Ailia?" Carlie asked. "I thought there were only four elements, four directions? Who is she?"

"Ailia means light, and she is here because it is time for you and your grandmother to finally walk out of the darkness and into the light," Liana replied softly. Carlie felt the truth of the sentiment viscerally, felt herself open up to the possibility of some joy diluting the sorrow that seemed to be her life.

"Do not worry, for as far as anyone here knows, Elsie is officiating. That is who they are seeing, and we are just her friends, helping so Rose's circle can relax and enjoy the ritual."

"And what do they see when they look at me?" Carlie demanded. "Am I the mad woman talking to herself, holding up her grandmother's handfasting with her delusions?"

Liana laughed, a sweet, tinkling laugh that held no malice. "Beloved, you have never been mad. But no, this moment is a pause, a breath between breaths. Time has not really stopped, we have just stepped outside of it for a beat."

Gazing at the woman in purple, who was watching them carefully, a stern expression on her face, Liana smiled at Carlie, then spoke one last time. "Afterwards, at the party tonight, tell your grandmother that Elsie is fine, that there is no need to worry. And thank her for all of us, for being such a light in the world."

Rose had turned to look at them too, and her eyes were widening in recognition. "Tell her yourself," Carlie said, slightly grumpy, as she handed the bouquet of flowers to her grandma.

Liana's laugh washed over her, and time seemed to slow down even further, leaving her in a bubble of silence. Then suddenly the gold-clad woman was back in her place, winking at Carlie, Rose was standing stoically at her side, but with a twinkle in her eye, and Ailia was calling for everyone's attention. Sound rushed back at Carlie, and she heard the gentle hum of the bees, the call of a small black bird overhead, and Laura's voice as she formally welcomed Elsie, or the purple-robed woman, to their ritual.

Focusing on the circle again, Carlie looked over at Jake and Tom, standing on either side of their grandfather, arms linked with his as he walked slowly towards Rose, who was holding Carlie's hand on one side of her, and Mike's on the other, as she moved forward to meet Richard in the middle. When they reached the central altar, the four attendants released their charges and melted back into the circle of friends and family surrounding them.

Tom found his place next to Rhiannon, and Carlie felt their joy ripple over her physically as they linked hands. Mike headed back to where Brodie stood, holding on to Laura, and she saw peace on his face, and the lifting of a weight that he'd carried for far too long.

Suddenly she realised just how much she'd come to care for everyone here, and marvelled at their acceptance of her, a virtual stranger. Then, slowly becoming aware that Jake was waiting for her, she turned towards him and offered her hand. When he saw the new tattoo on her wrist, with its circle of ivy leaves holding within it a candle flame, a rose quartz, a feather and a wave, he stared up at her, a question in his eyes.

A rush of emotion washed over her as she sensed the cautious hope rising within him, and she felt a pang of regret that she'd made him wait so long. But there was no point dwelling in the past – it was time to move forward, into the now, into the light.

"Yes," she whispered, and felt his energy expand outwards to hold her close, even as they turned to the centre of the circle and concentrated on the ceremony.

No one but Rose and Carlie knew that the women conducting the ritual were figments of light and mist, although she sensed that Laura and Miri could feel their magic, and were responding to it on some level. For a moment she thought Tom was aware of it too, as he gazed over at her quizzically, but when he saw her holding hands with Jake he just smiled and turned back to the purple-clad priestess in their midst and held the energy for her.

The handfasting was beautiful, although Carlie was so conscious of her hand in Jake's, even when the rest of the circle let go, that the details flowed over her, leaving her with a sensation of love and magic but no grasp of the specifics. But she knew Rhiannon would fill her in later. All that mattered now was that Rose and Richard were happy, and the golden shimmer around them as they spoke their vows let her know that they were.

Her focus snapped back to the ceremony when Richard offered Rose the rose quartz ring she'd entrusted to him earlier that day. The same one that Rose had given to her daughter all those years ago, and which Violet had kept, close to her heart, all that time, wrapping it up with her most precious belongings. Rose gasped, then turned and gazed at Carlie with such love and gratitude, and in that moment she knew her grandmother understood its significance, and that another piece of her heart was healing because of it.

Later, as Ailia closed the circle and people started meandering down to the healing centre to continue the celebrations, her hand was still in Jake's. He turned to her, smiling, but there was fear in his eyes too, and something else she couldn't quite figure out. She felt a shiver of apprehension, and almost chickened out, but she knew that she had to make the first move. "Are you okay?" she asked gently.

He gazed down at their hands, still entwined, and seemed to gain strength from their matching tattoos. "Does this mean…" he began, then paused. "I just… I don't want to push you… Or jump to any conclusions either, just because you're holding my hand?"

Her heart clenched at the pain and fear in his voice. "Oh Jake, I'm so sorry I took so long to be ready. You've been more patient than I deserve," she whispered. "But I, well, I really like you. I want to… well, you know." Her eyes drifted ahead of them, to where Rhiannon and Tom were kissing while they waited to cross the road, oblivious to the fact that there were no more cars in either direction.

"Really?" Jake asked, and the uncertainty that was still in his voice stabbed at Carlie, even while the hope in his eyes cheered her.

"Really," she replied, smiling up at him. He blushed, and his eyes broke contact with hers. "What's wrong?" she asked, and panicked all over again. Had she waited too long?

But finally he gathered his courage and stared back into her eyes. He was braver than she was.

"I'm not a shaman or a druid Carlie, I'm not very spiritual. I haven't studied plant medicine or crystal healing or psychic divination, or any of that stuff. I love taking part in the rituals with you and Rose, and I want to learn more, but I just… well, I'm not magical enough for you, or old enough, or special enough," he finally blurted out. "You deserve someone better, someone more… well, someone more like Rowan."

His words stung her, and she felt tears well in her eyes, but this wasn't about her hurt, it was about his, so she buried hers away to dwell on later. "I'm sorry I've made you feel like that," she said softly, and reached up her hand to cup his cheek, the way Liana had done with her to offer comfort and security. He closed his eyes and leaned in to her touch, and a little of the tightness in his expression relaxed.

Steeling herself, she took a deep breath. "I don't know what will happen with us, but I know that I want to try. And I know that I care about you deeply, in a way I never have before," she added, and was relieved when he opened his eyes and looked back into hers, hope alive again. "I know that I want to risk my heart with you Jake, and that I'm *ready* to risk my heart with you. For you."

Finally he smiled, and her lips curved up in response. "If you think I'm enough…" he said, but it was a question.

"I *know* that you are," she whispered, voice sure and strong. And she felt it, the moment his heart opened to her.

"I don't expect you to never talk about him, or what you learned from him, or to throw out all the books and ritual tools he gave you," he said then, voice low and cautious. "He's part of your magical journey, and I know that he and Rose were your teachers, the same way that Tom is for me. So he'll always be part of you, and I'm okay with that, because it's *you* that I've been falling for since that moment in Pop's kitchen all those months ago. The you that grew from being with him, and losing him. I'm not going to try to compete with someone who is no longer here, and I promise I won't be angry if you want to talk about him. I know I'm not him, and I'll never try to be."

Tears shimmered on her lashes as she circled her arms around him and held him close. "Oh Jake, I don't want you to be him. I don't want you to be anyone else, just you. Because it's you that I've been falling for, without even being aware of it," she said, marvelling at the truth of those words as she spoke them.

For a moment she wondered how long she'd been feeling this way, but she supposed it really didn't matter. She knew now.

As people started to catch up to them, Carlie let Jake go, but she took his hand again as they walked towards the village. Then as they climbed the stairs to the ritual room, Rhiannon linked her arm through Carlie's free one. "I'm so happy for you," she beamed, voice low. "And so is Tom." Carlie blushed, but didn't shush her. She was too happy to worry about her friend teasing her, or the reaction of anyone else to their new and constant need to hold hands.

They jostled inside, and Laura welcomed everyone to the celebration. Then a hush fell over the candlelit room as Rose and Richard walked in. Carlie rushed over and hugged her grandma, while Jake approached Richard and embraced him too. Then they stepped back and gave their guardians some space so everyone else in the village could congratulate them too.

Throughout the afternoon there were speeches, some funny, and some moving everyone to tears. Mike's was especially heartfelt, summing up the immense love the community had for Rose, and their joy at welcoming Richard to their ranks. Then Laura brought out the largest ritual cauldron and lit the sweetly scented apple wood within it, so the happy couple could leap over the Beltane fire hand in hand, to wild cheers, closely followed by Tom and Rhiannon.

As the excitement died down, Miri and Laura served the Beltane feast, then as night fell and moonlight shone in the window, people took to the makeshift dancefloor and the celebrations began in earnest.

When Jake asked her to dance, Carlie let him lead her to the centre of the room. As he put his hand on her shoulder and drew her close, she felt calm, and safe, and filled with warmth. She looked into his kind blue eyes and felt herself diving into his sweetness, his patience, his heart. He wasn't Rowan, no one ever would be, but that was perfectly okay. This was Jake, the guy who was prepared to be her friend if that was all she could handle, who was willing to wait for her to finally realise her feelings, and who showed her every day that consideration existed, and love was kindness.

If Rowan had been her Oliver, then maybe Jake was her Mike – the kind and considerate boy-next-door, the best friend who might, in a parallel universe, have made her mother as happy as Ollie had. Or maybe he was just himself – Jake, enough just the way he was, with no need to be anyone else, no need to sweep her off her feet with grand gestures and wild magics.

Slowly, heart in her throat, she rested her head on his shoulder. He froze for a moment, and she could picture him trying to figure out if what she'd said on the walk into the village was real. But it was only for a second, and then his hand rested on her head, and stroked her hair, and she let go of a breath she felt she'd been holding forever and relaxed into his arms. She didn't know what would happen between them, or even whether he would stay here in England or go home to Perth. But that wasn't important right now. It was only this moment that mattered.

Glancing over Jake's shoulder, she saw Rose smile at her from the circle of Richard's arms, and watched the joy on Rhiannon and Tom's faces as they danced together, and the love in Mike's eyes as he stood with Brodie. As Jake took her hand and spun her around, she tipped back her head and looked up into the twinkling faery lights on the ceiling. She felt her mother there with her as the layers of the pale green wedding dress swirled around her, and her dad's presence too as his wedding ring nestled against her heart on a delicate golden chain. She was where she belonged.

"Are you okay Carlie?" Jake asked her softly, tenderly, and her soul exhaled as she heard the love in his voice.

"I am," she whispered. "I finally am." And she smiled up at him, a smile that reached her eyes this time, and transformed her face with joy. Then she slowly leaned in to kiss him.

"Don't you know yet?
It is your light that lights the world."

Rumi, Persian poet and mystic

Thank You!

Thank you so much for reading this book,
and sharing the magic of Carlie, Rose and Violet's stories.
As an indie author, I rely on word of mouth and reader reviews to get the word out. If you enjoyed The Into the Mists Trilogy, I would be so grateful if you could take a moment to leave a review on any book site. Reviews help improve sales and ranking, and are of immense help to all indie writers.

If you'd like to stay in touch and receive free exclusive content, be the first to hear about book news and events info, giveaways and more, you can sign up for my newsletter at

www.sereneconneeley.com/subscribe.

(And don't worry, you can unsubscribe at any time...)

With love and gratitude,
Serene xx

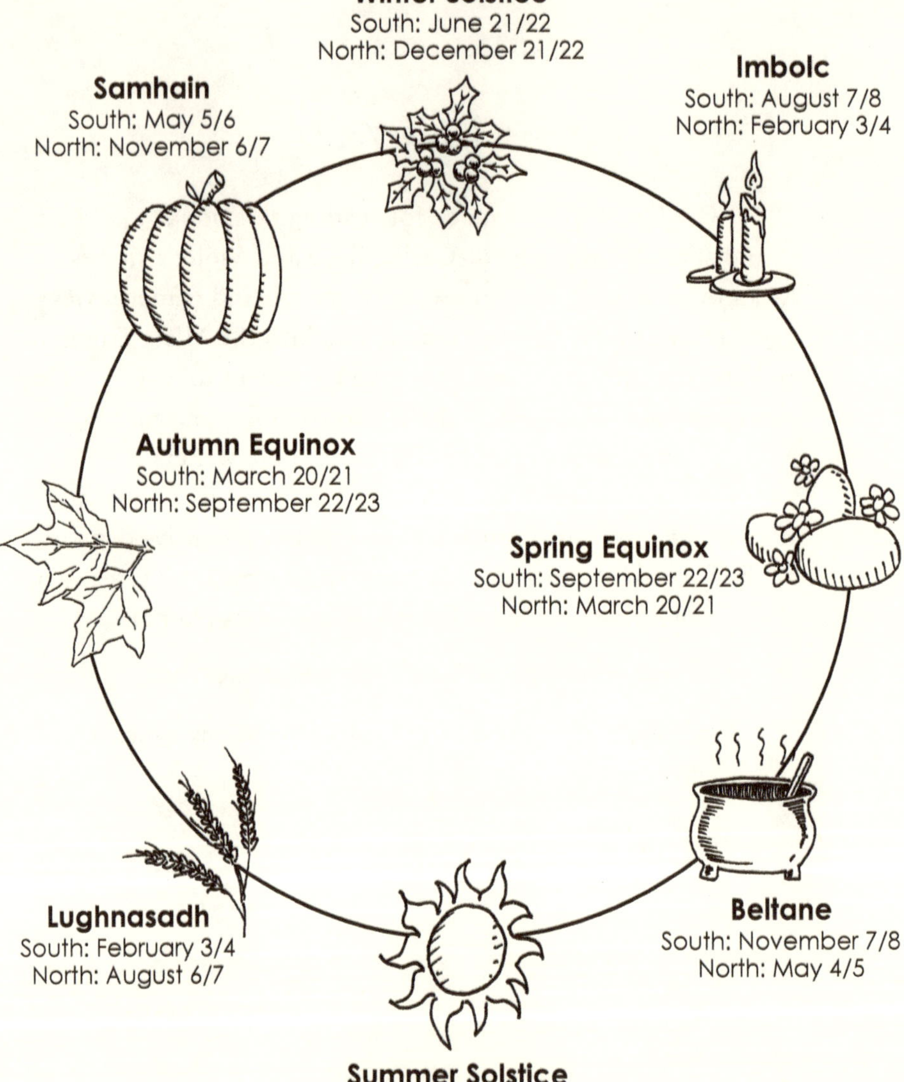
Winter Solstice
South: June 21/22
North: December 21/22
Imbolc
South: August 7/8
North: February 3/4
Samhain
South: May 5/6
North: November 6/7
Autumn Equinox
South: March 20/21
North: September 22/23
Spring Equinox
South: September 22/23
North: March 20/21
Lughnasadh
South: February 3/4
North: August 6/7
Beltane
South: November 7/8
North: May 4/5
Summer Solstice
South: December 21/22
North: June 20/21

The Wheel of the Year

Carlie's grandmother Rose and her witchy friends celebrate the eight sacred sabbats, or festivals, of the Wheel of the Year, as the ancient priestesses did, and modern pagans still do. In *Into the Mists*, Carlie took part in her first ritual, the harvest festival of Lughnasadh, where she met Rose's circle of magical, supportive women friends and saw her grandmother as a powerful, loving priestess for the first time.

In *Into the Dark*, she celebrated Mabon, the autumn equinox, with Rhiannon at London's Body Mind Spirit festival, where she met Rowan, then with Rose's circle back in Summer Hill the next night. She honoured her lost loved ones at the Samhain feast of the dead at Mike's house, then did a deeper ritual with Rhiannon in the ruins of an old temple. And tragedy visited her again at the winter solstice.

And in *Into the Light*, Rose invited Jake and his grandfather Richard to her circle's Imbolc celebration, then Carlie, Rhiannon and Jake travelled to London to share the spring equinox Ostara festival with Tom and Jasmine. And at the cross-quarter day of Beltane, which marks the beginning of summer and embodies love and commitment, Rose was part of a very special ritual...

> "The festivals of the Wheel of the Year are defined by the cycle of nature, by the dance of the weather gods and spirits of place. They require us to look not to the heavens but to the earth. They are set within our soul, watching the leaves on the trees, feeling the shifting temperature and the changing light, within and around."
>
> *Emma Restall Orr, British druid priestess, ritualist and author*

A powerful way to become more aware of your inner world is to harness the natural magic of the cycles of the seasons. The shifting energies of the earth's turning have been celebrated and utilised for thousands of years, and even today, when we are so far removed from nature, you can still tangibly feel the introspection of winter, the crisp change of autumn, the potent energy of summer and the vibrant power of spring.

Attuning yourself to the vibrations of the eight sacred festivals that make up the enchanted Wheel of the Year will fill you with strength, magic and a sense of grand possibility and potential. You'll become more in sync with your inner self and your intuition, and start to connect with your own emotional tides as you connect with the earth's.

These special days, determined by the position of the earth in relation to the sun, mark the beginning, midpoint and end of each season, and are measured today by astronomers and scientists. In the past they were calculated by druids, the philosophers and scientists of their age, and recorded in stone circles and cairns. They have been honoured for thousands of years in cultures throughout the world, so the imprint of their energy can be tapped in to and absorbed.

Long ago, when life revolved around agriculture, and the sun and moon were considered deities to be worshipped, the Celtic peoples of Europe, and many others around the globe, were in tune with nature. They had to know when each season began and how long it would last so they could plant and harvest crops, hunt migratory prey and prepare for the harsh winters. They divided their year by seasons, not months, and honoured each change, celebrating eight festivals that marked the turning of these seasons and the cycles of the earth.

There are four astronomical and four agricultural festivals. The astronomical celebrations are determined by the position of the earth in relation to the sun. These include the spring and autumn equinoxes (Latin for "equal night"), which occur when the sun is directly above the equator and the length of day and night is equal, and the summer and winter solstices (Latin for "sun stand still"), which occur when the sun is at its northern or southernmost extreme, the furthest it ever gets from the equator. These four events are the midpoint of each season – thus the summer solstice being referred to as Midsummer's Day and the winter solstice as Midwinter.

The agricultural celebrations are known as cross-quarter days, because they fall midway between the astronomical festivals. Traditionally they were tied to agricultural events such as the sowing and harvesting of crops, and they mark the beginning of each season.

Even today, when we no longer live in harmony with the earth's rhythms or agricultural cycles, people celebrate the Wheel of the Year as an honouring of nature and an acknowledgement of the continuing cycle of life, death and rebirth, both literally and symbolically.

Literally this refers to the changing seasons – the fertility and vibrant life force of summer, the harvest energy of autumn, the introspection and endings (death) of winter, and the rebirth of spring. Mythologically it was tied to the story of the god and goddess. At the spring equinox they meet and court, before consummating their love during the rites of Beltane. At the summer solstice the goddess blooms into the mother, pregnant with new life, and the sun god reaches his energetic peak. From then he weakens through the harvest time of Lughnasadh and the autumn equinox, before going to the underworld at Samhain to learn new wisdom, then being reborn at the winter solstice when the goddess gives birth to the infant sun god and the Wheel turns again, playing out the cycle on and on through time.

Once this creation story was accepted as fact. Today some still think of it as a literal retelling of a historical truth, while others feel it's simply a parable that humanises nature. Either way, it's now the symbolic meaning that's most relevant to our lives – planting the seeds of our dreams in the metaphorical spring, watching them grow and manifest in the world before we give thanks for our literal harvest, allow the things that no longer serve us to die off or be released, then start all over again with new dreams as we celebrate our own rebirth.

Becoming aware of the seasonal shifts and the patterns of nature wherever you live, and celebrating these ancient but still relevant festivals, is a simple way to tap in to the magic of the earth and start to connect with nature and your inner self.

Channelling this energy and creating meaningful rituals in your life doesn't conflict with any religion or require a belief system, as it's a celebration of the science of nature and the cycles of the planet. Many pagans, like Rose and her friends, do call on gods and goddesses, and have a personal concept of the divine as a universal creative force, but others don't believe in any form of deity, simply revering nature as sacred and as the source of life, and believing that divinity is an inner not an outer power, an energy within themselves and every other person alive.

Lughnasadh : First Day of Autumn : Gratitude

Lughnasadh, also known as Lammas, is celebrated in the first week of August in the northern hemisphere and the first week of February in the southern hemisphere, and marks the end of summer and the beginning of autumn. It's the first harvest festival, traditionally a time of feasting and of thanksgiving for the life-giving properties of the grain and nature's bounty, as well as a recognition of the cycle of sowing and reaping of the crops.

It is also the time to honour the things you have grown and created in your life, a day to harvest the fruits of your labours and acknowledge your successes and what you've achieved in the past year. Celebrate the goals you've reached and have your own festival of gratitude, in whatever form that takes. Toast your success, throw a party or do something special to mark the occasion – maybe reward yourself for your hard work with a gift you've long wanted, or some precious time off to rest and chill out. Make a list of all the things you've gained over the past year – the gifts you've been given, the new talents you've developed, the friends you've made, the experiences you've had, the healings you've received – and give thanks for it all.

Then, out of gratitude and in the spirit of the ancestors who shared the bounty of their harvest with those less well off, pay your good fortune forward. Donate to a local charity or collect food for the homeless, as Rose and her friends do, lend to a business in the developing world, or give your time to help someone, ensuring the energy of abundance continues and is strengthened. Give joyfully, with no expectation of receiving anything in return. And work out small ways in which you can make a difference to the people around you all year long as well.

As the energy begins to subtly slow, this is also a time to be patient and to trust that everything is as it should be, because there are still harvests to come. Not everything has to be achieved right now – some things take longer to manifest. The lesson of the Wheel of the Year is that everything continues, everything happens when it should, and everything is eternal.

Mabon : Autumn Equinox : Harvest

The autumn equinox, known as Mabon and celebrated on September 22/23 in the northern hemisphere and March 20/21 in the southern, is characterised by the length of day and night being equal as the sun travels back across the equator to the other hemisphere. From this point on, the days will become shorter and cooler, but this is a moment of balance in nature and within – a point of harmony and calm.

Vibrationally Mabon is a season of withdrawal, of being alone to meditate, recharge, reassess and ponder where you're at in life. The energy of the earth retreats and goes within, as does your personal power, but from this cycle you will emerge with immense strength and wisdom. It's a time to honour your achievements, experiences and growth, and to ensure balance by integrating all parts of your self. Acknowledge and celebrate what you've reaped in your own life. Feel fulfilment from each goal reached, releasing what no longer serves you in order to move forward. In the wild, old growth is cleared. In your life, cut out anything that's holding you back or preventing new life and love from flourishing, whether it's work, people, a belief system, regret or the past.

On this day, when all is balanced, witches traditionally renewed their magical commitments, and you can renew any vows you've made or pledge a new one, be it to do with magic, love, friendship, career or anything else. As the shadows lengthen, it's also a good time to scry for insight into your future. If you can, light a fire and stare into the flames, allowing your mind to go blank and your vision to blur a little, or go outside and watch the clouds scuttling across the sky, analysing the shapes and symbols you see within flame and cloud. Without over-thinking it, write down what they mean to you.

Pyromancy (fire reading) and nephomancy (cloud reading) are forms of divination that have been used for millennia. You should develop your own dictionary of symbols, as you know better than anyone what any shape or image means to you, but you can begin with standard readings, such as a heart indicating romance, a cat referring to a need to trust your intuition, a tree meaning you will make new friends and a plane foreshadowing travel.

Samhain : First Day of Winter : Death

Samhain, which is celebrated in early November in the northern hemisphere and early May in the southern, is a cross-quarter day marking the end of autumn and the beginning of the cold and dark of winter. Symbolically it is about rest and renewal, of preparing for what's ahead and withdrawing a little to conserve your energy, and releasing the things you've been holding on to in order to ready yourself for new challenges and experiences. It's also the night when the veil between the worlds is said to be at its thinnest, when people honour their ancestors and try to commune with the dead. Some set a place at the dinner table for any loved ones passed over, as Rhiannon's dad Mike did at their Feast of the Dead ritual, while others cast spells to bring their spirit back, or perform mediumship rituals to converse. This magical time and its purpose has been conserved in modern-day Halloween, which celebrates ghosts, witches and restless spirits.

The beginning of winter is a period of reflection, so spend time in contemplation. If you've lost someone close to you, light a candle and remember them. Look at photos or letters and feel their presence with you. This shouldn't be morbid – you're celebrating their life and all they meant to you. Also honour those who are here now. Call your mum and dad, visit your grandparents, or write to someone who meant a lot to you when you were growing up and thank them.

Long ago, Samhain was the end of one year and the start of the next, so it's also a powerful time to let go of the energy of the old year and old memories so you can move forward with lightness and strength. Light another candle, and by its flickering illumination, write out all the worries, frustrations, regrets and seeming failures you've held on to over the previous twelve months. See the candle flame burning them away and leaving you purified and refreshed, and breathe in this positive new energy. Then burn the list in the flame, releasing your attachment to those emotions and their power over you.

This is the time to prepare yourself for the rebirth you'll experience at Yule, but for that to happen there must be death – the death of fears and doubts, and anything holding you back.

Yule : Winter Solstice : Rebirth

The winter solstice, known to pagans as Yule and Midwinter, falls around December 21/22 in the northern hemisphere and June 21/22 in the southern, and marks the middle of winter. It's the shortest day and the longest night of the year, and marks the transition between dark and light, both emotionally and physically. It's the lowest point of the Wheel in terms of daylight and energy, with the sun rising later and night falling earlier. The land is barren and cold, there is less light, and energetically people feel tired and unmotivated.

Winter is a time to rest and reflect, to acknowledge sadness and loss – of dreams, of friendships, of parts of your self – and conserve your energy. But the solstice is the turning point in this time of darkness, introspection and dreaming. Considered the dark night of the soul, it also marks the period when the dark half of the year relinquishes its hold to the light half. From this time forward, the days will start to lengthen, the sun will become stronger, and the energy within and without will start to increase and build.

In pagan times an evergreen tree was brought inside as a symbol of the hope of spring's return, and Yule was a time of feasting, celebration and gift-giving in honour of the birth of the sun god – traditions that live on today in the Christmas tree we decorate, the presents we put under it, the huge family meal we cook, and the celebration of the birth of the son of God.

To attune yourself to this festival of rebirth, light a candle on solstice eve to symbolise the sun and its activating energy, and list your dreams for the coming year. Traditionally people stayed up all night to await the return of the light, but if you can't do that, get up for the sunrise to toast the dawn and give thanks for this energetic reawakening. Open yourself to the promise of new growth and achievement, and the rebirth of your own self and your creativity, as the sun is also reborn. Symbolically and energetically it's a time to honour your inner wisdom, consider the lessons you learned during winter's introspection, and integrate them into your life so you can start to initiate change and prepare for the rush of growth of the coming springtime.

Imbolc : First Day of Spring : Purification

Imbolc, which is celebrated in the first week of February in the northern hemisphere and the first week of August in the southern, is a cross-quarter day marking the end of winter and the start of spring. It celebrates the return of light to the land, and to our own hearts, and is a time of hope, renewal and fresh starts after winter's sluggishness.

Energetically it's a time of awakening, rebirth and re-emergence. Nature fills with life force and begins to quiver with the energy to grow again, and we start to emerge from the chill of winter, shaking off our lack of motivation and re-engaging with the world, making it a great day to sow the seeds of what you want to achieve in the coming year.

Imbolc is dedicated to Bridie, the goddess of inspiration, creativity and fire, who was later supplanted by Saint Bridget, whose festival is also celebrated at this time. Talk to Bridie – or Bridget, or the higher-self aspect of yourself – or write her a letter, and tell her what you want to create in the next twelve months. Meditate on your goals and what you hope to achieve. Don't worry about how to do it, as that will be revealed later in flashes of inspiration, guidance or outside help.

Physically it's a time of purification and cleansing after the long dark of winter, so clean your house and clear your space, sweeping out old energy and thoughts so the new can thrive. It's a good time to write about your beliefs and examine how you feel about your spiritual path too, exploring the reasons you think the way you do and perhaps questioning if there are other viewpoints you might also embrace. It's also about new beginnings, and in some magical traditions it is the day chosen for initiations and rededications, so if you want to make a pledge to a new path or a new goal, or a personal vow of any kind, you will be supported by the energy of the season.

You may like to ignite a candle to represent the coming back of the light and do some candle magic. Stare into the flame as you concentrate on what you want, then blow it out, sending your desire out to the universe. Making a wish as you blow out the candles on your birthday cake is a magic that has survived from pagan times, and is a potent way to manifest your wishes into reality, whatever day it is.

Ostara : Spring Equinox : Blossoming

The spring or vernal equinox, known to pagans as Ostara, is celebrated around March 20/21 in the northern hemisphere and September 22/23 in the southern. It's one of only two times in the year when the length of day and night is equal, as the sun sits directly above the equator on its journey north or south, creating equal light and dark in both hemispheres.

This equinox is about growth, passion and the unfurling and release of the immense potential you have within you. On both a universal and a personal level, it's a time of balance and harmony, of union between the physical and the spiritual, and the integration of your heart and soul. This can be harnessed to anchor your dreams in reality and enhance your own inner harmony as the balance of universal outer energies is reflected within. Relationships are harmonious now too, making it a good time for weddings and for healing rifts.

It's a time of growth and fertility, when new crops are sown, new shoots break through the earth, buds on the trees open, birds build nests and lay eggs, and new life is celebrated. Thanks was traditionally given to the fertility goddess Ostara, whose symbols were an egg and a hare, and who is still honoured around the world today, albeit unknowingly, in the form of chocolate eggs and the Easter bunny.

Energetically it's also a very fertile time, as the seeds you sowed of your goals at Imbolc begin to sprout and gain momentum. Paint some hard-boiled eggs with symbols that represent your desires, or buy or make the chocolate version, meditating on your own metaphorical fertility and your ability to manifest dreams into reality. Choose an affirmation relating to your desired outcome, write it down and pin it up where you'll be able to see it every day.

Go outside during the day and breathe in the fresh spring air, filling your heart with new inspiration as you fill your lungs with oxygen. In many ancient cultures, including the Roman one whose calendar we have based ours upon, the spring equinox was the first day of the year, and the sense of new hope and optimism reflected in this time remains today. It's a celebration of new life, hope, passion, growth and energy.

Beltane : First Day of Summer : Growth

Beltane, celebrated in early May in the northern hemisphere and early November in the southern, is a cross-quarter day marking the end of spring and the start of the heat and energy of summer. Evidence of new life is everywhere, in abundant blossoms, the hatching of birds and bees pollinating flowers, showing that time is moving forward and life is progressing. Women bathed their faces in the dew gathered from their garden on Beltane morning to harness the energy of youth, and flowers were brought inside to symbolise fresh beginnings and the power of nature.

Beltane was the major fertility festival. Handfasting rituals were conducted, and lovers leaped over bonfires then came together in sacred union in the fields to bless the crops with fertility. Maypole dancing, representing the union of the god (the pole) and the goddess (the ribbons), was performed to join the forces of masculine and feminine, and May Day remains a popular day to wed in the northern hemisphere.

It's a time of lovers and spells to attract love, and celebrating the fertility of life, not just physically, but also of your dreams and ambitions. Symbolically this day marks the igniting of the fires of creativity and passion, of the fertility of your dreams being made manifest, and is the time to take steps to achieve what you want. Check in on the projects you started at Ostara, and write about their progress and the ways in which they've sprouted into reality. If you need to fine tune anything, learn a new skill or let go of one aspect so it can germinate further on its own, the energy of this day will support you. Make a commitment to yourself – start a new project, apply for a new job or take up a new hobby, knowing the universe is bursting with raw energy and power that you can tap in to.

It's also a powerful time to repledge your love to your partner. You don't have to build a bonfire and leap over it, although you can! Simply lighting a red or gold candle as you stare into each other's eyes and speak your love and commitment will invoke the power and passion of the element of fire. If you're single, make a commitment of some kind to yourself, nurture a friendship, or if you seek love, sing your intention and wanting of a romantic partner to the universe.

Litha : Summer Solstice : Fruition

The summer solstice, known to pagans as Litha, is celebrated around June 20/21 in the northern hemisphere and December 21/22 in the southern. It's the longest day and the shortest night of the year, and marks the peak of energy and solar power for the year. On this day the sun reaches its northern or southernmost latitude before it turns and heads back towards the equator, so near the poles daylight lasts for twenty-four hours – the sun just doesn't set for weeks at a time. In nature, everything is ripe and abundant, and life is blooming.

It's a time of high, hot and active energy. Creativity and expression is at a peak, so stand in your power and express your needs, saying what you want rather than assuming that people know. Whereas the winter solstice is slow and introspective, its opposite is fast and effective. Make use of the active energy – this is a time to do, to get out there and harness the energising earth power and make things happen.

Follow your passion, take a chance, say yes to new opportunities and express your creativity and your inner self. This is not the time to be withdrawn or shy, it's for getting out amongst it and making your dreams come true. It's also a time when relationships – and you – will mature, and you'll apply new wisdom and forethought to your passion, so give thanks for the lessons you've learned, and allow the person you are maturing into to unfold.

It's a time of celebration too, of acknowledging how far you've come and what you've achieved. Enjoy the happiness and abundance of this season and soak up the sunshine and festive atmosphere. Traditionally people stayed up all night on solstice eve, partying around bonfires or within sacred circles of stone, then watched the sun rise the next morning, feeling it bathe them in warmth and light.

At dawn, stand with your arms outstretched and breathe in the sun's life-giving power. Let it wash over you with its healing energy and burn away anything you no longer need. Take note of how your dreams and goals are manifesting into the world, and meditate on anything that could be blocking your progress. Be open to letting go of whatever isn't working so you can move forward in a new direction.

The Magic of the Moon

Rose works with the phases of the moon in her spellcasting and her healings, and performs rituals at the new moon, dark moon and the full. Carlie and Rhiannon planned their coven dedication for a full moon, to take advantage of the energy of this phase, and witches, druids and shamans have long harnessed its power too.

The moon is a thing of mystery, enchantment and wonder, linked to intuition, inner power and imagination. To the Celts, its phases reflected the phases of a human life – birth, adolescence, adulthood, death and rebirth – and were associated with the Triple Goddess who included the aspects of maiden, mother and crone, represented by Rhiannon, maiden goddess of inspiration and the waxing moon, Arianrhod, mother goddess of fertility and the full moon, and Ceridwen, crone goddess of death, rebirth and the waning moon. In countless other cultures the moon was also seen as a goddess, who not only marked the passing of time, but increased fertility, deepened psychic powers and improved wellbeing.

Harnessing the energy of the phases of the moon can help bring a goal to fruition. These phases are determined by the moon's position in relation to the earth and the sun, as it orbits our planet every 29.5 days. The moon has no light of its own – it's illuminated by the light of the sun reflecting off its surface, and its phases are created by the amount of the illuminated side we can see from earth.

You can picture these phases by imagining a clock. The earth sits in the centre of the clock face, with the sun above twelve o'clock. The moon is at the end of the minute hand, circling around the clock face, and the earth, in an anticlockwise direction. It begins its cycle at twelve, directly between the sun and the earth, which makes the moon invisible to us because the side that's reflecting the light of the sun is facing away from the earth, towards the sun. This is the dark moon.

A day later, as the moon moves towards eleven o'clock, a tiny sliver of the illuminated side can be seen, which appears as a thin crescent. This is the new moon. In the southern hemisphere it looks like a C, while in the northern hemisphere it's reversed, appearing as a backward C, and at the equator it's horizontal rather than vertical.

The crescent continues to grow as the moon moves from between the earth and the sun, and the angle between them allows us to see more of the moon's reflected light. By the time it gets to nine o'clock, which takes about a week, it's at right angles to the earth in relation to the sun, and we see a half circle. This is the first quarter moon.

When the moon gets to six o'clock, it's on the other side of the earth from the sun, with the earth in between. The whole of the side that is visible to us is reflecting back sunlight, so we see a round moon in all its shining, golden full moon glory. The size of the moon hasn't changed, it's just that we're seeing the fully illuminated side.

After that it appears to decrease again it progresses back to the dark moon. When it gets to three o'clock we again see a half moon, but this time it's facing in the other direction. This is the third or last quarter moon. From there it continues back to twelve, with the crescent getting smaller each night, until it returns to the beginning, where it's invisible again, and the cycle starts over.

Lunar phases are printed in newspapers, moon diaries and websites like www.sunrisesunset.com, and you can also determine the phase of the moon by its shape, as well as by the time it rises, which occurs about fifty minutes later each day. It can be remembered by the old adage: "The new moon rises at sunrise, and the first quarter at noon. The full moon rises at sunset, and the last quarter at midnight."

As the moon progresses from dark to full it's the waxing or growing period, a time of new beginnings and increasing energy. As it goes from full back to dark it's the waning period, a time of lowering energy and introspection. Magical practitioners use the cycles of the moon to increase the power of spellworking, harnessing the energies inherent in each phase. So do fishermen, who understand the incredible pull the moon has on the tides of the ocean and its creatures.

Gardening also operates to the rhythms of the moon, as the lunar phase can enhance or hinder plant growth. To boost it, sow crops that produce above the ground between new moon and full, as the light and energy increases, and crops that produce below ground, such as root vegetables and bulbs, between full moon and dark.

Surfers understand its power too. The full moon magnifies weather patterns, so a winter full moon will bring stormier swells and bigger waves. The tides are more extreme at both the full moon and the dark moon – high tides are higher, and low tides lower. These two phases have an intense influence on the ocean, heightening conditions and drawing huge swells – or, if the ocean is flat, making it even flatter. Surfers going to Indonesia for a wave-riding safari book around a full moon, so they'll have optimum conditions and even bigger waves.

Hair growth is also influenced by the moon. If you want your hair to grow faster, trim the ends between the new moon and the first quarter. If you want it to grow thicker and fuller, trim it during the full moon phase. And if you really like the style and want to maintain it, have it cut around the third quarter, so it grows out more slowly.

The moon affects tides, plants, animals and the behaviour of people. Some can't sleep during the full moon, others feel more emotional or have strange dreams. It's common to feel more energetic during the waxing phase, and more tired when it's waning. There are also many tales of accidents and psychic breakdown increasing at the full moon. Today the moon's journey across the sky is obscured by buildings, and even women's cycles, which used to be connected to the moon, are often controlled by chemicals. But it still impacts our energy and emotions, and can be used to influence the outcome and power of rituals, and empower any project you want to complete.

Phases of the Moon

One lunar cycle runs for 29.5 days, beginning with the tiny crescent of the new moon, building in energy through the waxing phase to the full moon, then decreasing and withdrawing through the waning period to the dark moon, before starting a new cycle. Here are some ways to take advantage of the phases of the moon to set your goal or intention, then watch it grow to beautiful, abundant completion.

New Moon: Day 1

The new moon rises just after dawn and is up all day, often unnoticed in contrast to the sun and the bright sky, and sets just after sunset. From the moment the tiny new crescent moon is first sighted, and for a day or two afterwards, is a time of heightened energy and new beginnings. It's a good time to start new projects, make resolutions and vows you want to stick to, go in a new direction, invite something new into your life or look for a different job. Chinese New Year always falls on a new moon, as it brings energy and vitality to the coming year.

This is the time to plant seeds, both literally and metaphorically, be it in the garden or in your life, sowing the seeds of new ideas, dreams and hopes. Magical workings are most powerful during the day, when the moon is visible; during this phase there is no moon at night.

A simple yet powerful new moon ritual is to sit outside as dawn breaks, watching the sun rise and feeling the energy of the new moon as it peeks above the horizon, and write down your wish for the coming month. Work out an affirmation to support it, and keep it somewhere you'll see it often. You can also invoke maiden lunar goddesses such as Rhiannon, Bridie and Persephone to add sweet, innocent yet powerful energy to your intent.

Waxing Moon: Days 1 to 14

During the two weeks from new moon to full, the energy is strong and positive, so concentrate on attracting and drawing things to you. It's the optimal time for magical workings to manifest love, abundance and new career opportunities, and for learning new things, expanding your outlook, increasing spirituality and boosting fertility. In the waxing period the lunar energy continues to build, so whatever seeds you planted at the new moon will sprout rapidly. It's an energy of gathering, growing, strengthening and increase, so if you need to release something while the moon is waxing, reverse the intent of the spell so it fits with the energies. Rather than giving up smoking by releasing your addiction, create a ceremony to attract willpower.

If you're doing healings, draw good health to you when it's waxing, and release illness when it's waning. Maiden goddesses can also be invoked, such as Bridie, Artemis, Athena, Aphrodite and Aine.

Waxing crescent moon: Days 1 to 6

In the week following the new moon, it rises a little later each day, through the morning, and sets after sunset. This is the sprouting phase, when you nurture the seeds you planted at the new moon. It's the time to set things in motion, and brings energy and new growth to projects, helping you manifest them into reality and flooding you with strength and the energy of growth. The sliver of light represents your growing consciousness and the dawning of your potential.

Waxing half moon – the first quarter: Days 7 to 8

At the end of the first week is the first quarter moon, which rises at noon and sets at midnight (this is why you can see it in the evening but not in the morning, as it's appearing to the other side of the world then). It's halfway between new and full, and looks like a half moon. This is the growth phase, where you build upon what you've already begun, although the energy can be challenging at times, pushing you towards achieving your goals and urging you to work hard to get the projects you've planned completed. Issues can come to a head, which can be uncomfortable, but it's all part of the process of growth.

Waxing gibbous moon: Days 9 to 14

In the second week of the lunar cycle, as the moon moves towards full, it rises in the afternoon and sets in the early hours of the morning. This phase is conducive to expressing yourself, getting in touch with your feelings and taking action. It requires some patience, as things are almost, but not quite, at the peak of their potential and energy.

Full Moon: Days 14 to 16

The full moon rises as the sun sets, which is why it's so obvious and clearly seen, because it sails across the sky all night, contrasting with the velvety blackness, before setting around dawn, just as the sun is rising. The three days of the full moon – the day of, day before and day after – can be used to boost any intention or project. It represents achievement, culmination and abundance. The world is filled with energy and potential, so it's a great time for healing and manifestation.

Midnight is the most powerful time for magical work, as the moon is directly overhead. Stand beneath the golden orb and give thanks for what you've achieved so far, and breathe in the energy and power so you can harness it for self-expression and strength. Perform a Drawing Down the Moon ritual, bringing the energy of the moon, and the moon goddess, into your heart and soul. This is also a great time to charge crystals and amulets with the moon's energy, and cleanse your own physical and etheric bodies. And psychic abilities are thought to be at their strongest, so practise any divination methods you are drawn to, looking within to find answers to your questions and clues to your future.

The full moon is the high tide of power in a lunar cycle, so cast spells for completion, things you want to achieve, and anything requiring a boost of intensity, such as healing work, job hunting or love. You can also invoke mother goddesses Arianrhod, Isis, Selene, Diana, Lakshmi, Quan Yin, Demeter, Ishtar and Mama Quilla, who embody the full moon, motherhood, fertility, the earth and creation.

Waning Moon: Days 16 to 29

During the two weeks from full moon to dark, the energy is slowing, so it's a time for banishing and release work. Do a ritual to let go of anything that no longer serves you, such as a past relationship, a bad habit, a trait like procrastination, or any material objects or issues weighing you down and blocking your progress. If you need to attract something while the moon is waning, reverse the intent. Rather than doing a spell to draw love to you, which works against the energy of this phase, cast one to banish loneliness. This is a time of retreat and withdrawal, when you can invoke darker crone energy goddesses such as Ceridwen, the Morrigan and Grandmother Spiderwoman, who hold the wisdom and power of transformation, endings and rebirth.

Waning gibbous moon: Days 16 to 21

In the week following the full moon, it rises a little later each day, between dusk and midnight, and sets in the morning. This is a phase of introspection and self-assessment. In the garden this energy promotes root development; in life it's a time to stand strong and find your inner power, delving within for the answers imparted by the full moon. Magical workings are most effective from midnight to dawn, particularly releasement rituals to banish things, people or situations from your life.

Waning half moon – third quarter: Days 22 to 23

At the end of the third week is the third quarter moon, which rises around midnight and sets at midday, so if you see a half moon in the morning it's this waning one, but if you see it in the afternoon it's the waxing first quarter moon. It brings a reflective energy, and is a great time to assimilate what you've learned and achieved, and determine what you still need to do. If an issue requires resolution, work your magic and put your intent out to the universe. The energy is waning, but you can draw it inside for later use. Work on banishing illness, addictions, negativity and bad habits, releasing anything that will slow the fruition of your earlier spellworking.

Waning crescent moon: Days 24 to 29

In the fourth week, as the moon moves towards dark, it rises in the early hours of the morning and sets in the afternoon. This is the letting go phase, a time to release and banish anything you don't need so you can prepare again for the fresh beginnings of the new moon. It's the closing of the cycle, the time to reap what you sowed at the start of the month and integrate the lessons you've learned. You've done the inner work, and now you must release the outcome to the universe.

Dark Moon: Day 29

The dark moon rises at dawn, with the sun, and sets at sunset. It is between the earth and the sun the whole time, making it invisible to us. While some people take the dark moon as a day off from magic, others use it to go within, using the introspective energies to examine their feelings and thoughts and delve deep within their psyche.

While the moon is hidden it's also a powerful time to scry and perform any kind of divination that will uncover your hidden truths, and for getting in touch with your inner wisdom and approaching the Mysteries. This energy helps you explore the darkest recesses of your mind and your heart, and acknowledge your passions, your fears and your anger so you can release them to the approaching light.

This is a time to rest and renew your strength, and also to evaluate your life and your progress. The powerful, deep and transforming energy of the dark moon is an internalised vibration, so be aware of your thoughts, avoiding focusing on negativity or self-loathing in case you manifest the fears you're supposed to banish. The dark moon celebrates the crone, so invoke the energies of Ceridwen, Kali, the Cailleach, Hekate, Baba Yaga or Nephthys to help you descend to your metaphorical underworld and examine the layers of your subconscious.

Eclipses of the Moon and Sun

Lunar and solar eclipses, while fairly rare, also affect the energies of the universe, and our emotions. An eclipse occurs when one celestial body obscures another, either partially or fully. Because of the angle of their orbits, the sun, moon and earth rarely align precisely, which is the condition required for an eclipse. But when the moon is directly between the other two, which can only happen at the dark moon, it blocks the sun's light from reaching the earth, creating a solar eclipse that makes the sun seem either totally or partially invisible. And when the earth is directly between the sun and the moon, which can only happen at the full moon, the earth blocks the sun's light from reaching the moon, producing a lunar eclipse that dims or even totally obscures the moon for a brief time.

Energetically, eclipses create opportunities for change. They can sometimes push you a bit further than you wanted to go, forcing you to move forward and continue along your path. To some they are a wake-up call, nudging you on and making sure you don't lose sight of your dream. A solar eclipse, when the moon blocks the sun, is considered a peak of feminine power, and gets you in touch with your intuition. It is the perfect time to take stock of where you're at and examine your inner self. The energy of a lunar eclipse, when the earth blocks the sun and plunges the moon into darkness, gives you the strength to be honest, to yourself and others, about who you are, and to move forward without fear of judgement.

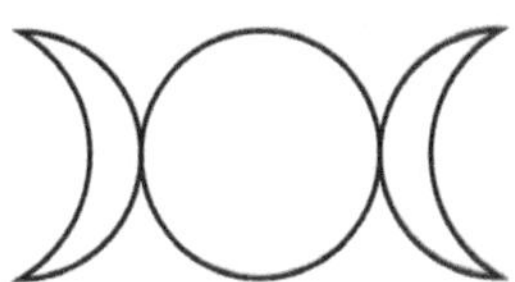

About the Author

Serene Conneeley is an Australian writer with a fascination for history, travel, ritual and the myth and magic of ancient places and cultures. She's written for magazines about news, travel, health, spirituality, entertainment and social and environmental issues, been editor of several preschool magazines, and contributed to international books on history, witchcraft, psychic development and personal transformation.

She's the author of the Into the Mists Trilogy – *Into the Mists, Into the Dark* and *Into the Light* – the Into the Storm Trilogy – *Into the Storm, Into the Fire* and *Into the Air* – and the non-fiction books *Faery Magic, Mermaid Magic, Witchy Magic, Seven Sacred Sites* and *A Magical Journey*, and creator of the meditation CD *Sacred Journey*.

Serene is a reconnective healing practitioner, and has studied magical and medicinal herbalism, bereavement counselling, reiki and many other healing modalities, plus politics and journalism. She loves reading, drinking tea with her friends, working out and celebrating the energy of the moon and the magic of the earth. Her pagan heart blossomed as she climbed mountains, sat in stone circles, climbed into ancient burial mounds and stood in the shadow of the pyramids on her travels, and she's also learned the magic of finding true happiness and peace at home.

www.SereneConneeley.com

With Thanks...

I am so grateful to my sweet husband, for his love, encouragement, support, inspiration and belief in me. For making me countless cups of tea as I wrote. For being patient when I hated the story, and hated writing, and wanted to quit. For not complaining when I'd banish myself to my little purple office and write for days. And for being the first person to read each of these books, and loving them so much...

I'm indebted to amazingly talented, kind and generous artist (and magical writer too!) Selina Fenech, for the stunning cover images for the Into the Mists Trilogy – it would not be as beautiful and as inviting without them – and to my sweet hubby and my faery friend Daniella Spinetti for the illustrations throughout.

Love and gratitude to book editor, writer and lovely friend Kylie Matthews, for sitting with Rose and Carlie in their cosy kitchen and drinking endless cups of tea with them, and reassuring me that their stories are filled with magic and worthy of being told.

Love and blessings to my wonderful writer friends, including Felicity Pulman, Lucy Cavendish, Selina Fenech, Cheralyn Darcey, Elisabeth Knowles and Nigel Bartlett, for sharing the book launches and festivals, the discussions of characters and plot, the trials and triumphs, challenges and successes, and all the craziness and wonder of our writing adventures.

Love and thanks to my inspiring workout buddies Claire, Janine and our fun fit group friends – I love sharing our progress, our challenges and our No Excuses motto for life. Working out every day keeps me sane amongst the book deadlines and work stress, and there's nothing like punching my way through a Combat session or upping my weights in Pump to gain a new perspective on a plot dilemma.

And I'm proud of, and grateful to, my NaNoWriMo buddies – Ally, Ani, Annalie, Belinda, Brooke, Carla, Cynthia, Hannah, Jasmin, Jennifer, Johoanna, Karen K, Karen P, Katie, Kelly, Kylie, Laneth, Laura, Miri, Nathan, Paulette, Penny, Robyn, Sharne and Stephanie.

With much love, Serene xx

NaNoWriMo...

Into the Mists began as a fun challenge with a few friends – to write 50,000 words in thirty days for the 2012 National Novel Writing Month (nanowrimo.org). I'd planned to spend all of October plotting out my story, but I finished work on my previous book, *Witchy Magic*, on October 31, so on November 1st I had to just dive in and start writing. And somehow I managed to flesh out my one paragraph idea – about a girl who loses her parents, gets sent to a relative in England she didn't know she had, and finds a cottage in the mists that may or may not exist – into a novel. While I spent several months afterwards rewriting and revising, Carlie's story was born in that single NaNoWriMo month, and the first draft wasn't dramatically different to the final one.

I decided to do it again in 2013 – and figured that travelling through Scotland with my hubby for the whole of November was no reason to back out. So I spent my days dancing in stone circles, crawling into ancient burial chambers, climbing snow-capped mountains and sailing across the ocean to Orkney and the Outer Hebrides, and my nights scribbling in a notebook or tapping away on a crappy little laptop. I did pass 50,000 words before November 30, but this time only half of them ended up in the finished book, *Into the Dark*, and I spent several months afterwards writing new chapters, changing a major plot line, introducing a new character, and generally messing with poor Carlie's head...

And in 2014 I signed up for NaNoWriMo again, determined to finish the trilogy. It was tough – my day job at the magazines gets even busier in November, and day one was spent with three sweet friends working out with Jillian Michaels, going to her show then meeting her – luckily she's so inspiring that I got home at midnight and started writing! Like the previous two NaNos, I'd thought I would spend October planning out the story, but also like them, I ended up starting on November 1st with a blank page... Turns out that I'm a pantser not a plotter ☺

I won't lie, it's not easy to write 1667 words a day, every day. Many days I've wanted to throw my notebook across the room and give up. Sometimes I'd rather collapse on the couch and watch Star Wars with my hubby than banish myself to my little purple office and painstakingly write another few pages. There are nights I get home from twelve hours at the magazines and would much prefer to crawl into bed than force myself to stay awake and type in the words I hastily scrawled on the bus to work, then write some new ones as well. *Most* days I'd much rather curl up and read a book than torture myself trying to write one.

I also spend most of the NaNoWriMo month thinking that my story is boring, there's no point, it's too much effort, no one cares anyway, and why am I bothering... According to my hubby though, I wrestle with these particular demons with every book, and my doubts seem to increase, rather than diminish, the more books I write.

But, I do it anyway. I tell the "it's boring" and "you're useless" voices in my head to shut up, and force myself to get at least 1200 words a day done – while aiming for 2000 to average out the less productive days. If at the end of the month I decide it's all terrible, I can delete the file and move on, or rewrite it until I'm happy with it.

Because it's only thirty days. Thirty days is nothing. It's one moon cycle. Half of one of my workout programs. Four episodes of *Arrow*. You can do anything for thirty days. And at the end of each November I have 50,000 words of a novel written, and no matter how boring or bad or whatever I think this first draft is, it's *way* easier to work with and improve than a blank page is.

Life is short. I want to live it with no regrets, and no excuses. Five years from now will I wish I'd spent more time on the couch watching superhero shows in November, or getting to bed a bit earlier, or will I be happy that I knuckled down and hit my word count targets and got the first draft of my next book finished? Like most things that are worth doing, it's not easy, but it is possible, and it *is* worth it...

My point in sharing this is that there is no secret to writing a book – you just have to sit down and write it. It's that easy, and that hard. And I've discovered that the more I write, the more I want to write, and the more the story unfolds. So don't wait for an idea to find you or inspiration to grab you – if you want to write a book (or do anything really), sit down and do it now. And don't worry, no one ever has time – you just have to *make* time...

Will I do it again? Absolutely! For NaNoWriMo 2015, I started writing about Rose and her magical life. In 2016 and 2017 I worked on Rhiannon's story – and discovered that her mother Beth also had a tale to tell, so a new series emerged. And in 2018 I'll be wrapping up Rose's epic journey – then hopefully starting a whole new world!

Also by Serene Conneeley

THE INTO THE MISTS SERIES

Into the Mists is healing, empowering, inspiring and magical. I loved every single page. I haven't enjoyed a book this much since I read *Heart's Blood* by Juliet Marillier. Can't wait for a sequel!

Julia Burdock, healer

Into the Dark is darker than the first book, but it also portrays the sweetness of love, and the power of the magical. *Into the Dark* is a compelling novel, which haunted my dreams while I was reading it, and lingered in my mind long after I'd finished it.

Felicity Pulman, author of The Janna Chronicles

Into the Light is a wonderful story and a stunning conclusion. I'm absolutely blown away by this series. It is truly beautiful from start to finish – magical, realistic, gentle, harsh, sad and joyful... I feel totally bereft that these people will no longer be a part of my life.

Kylie Matthews, book reviewer

Into the Mists: A Journal is *divine*! The lovely quotes are inspiring, and the feel of it is heart-warming and comforting. It sits on my bedside table for writing in during quiet times of reflection. It's just beautiful.

Cheralyn Darcey, eco-artist and author of Flowerpaedia

The Into the Mists Trilogy: Audiobooks will sweep you away with the melodic voice and magical story. It's written and read beautifully.

Rebecca Bosevski, author of Enchanting the Fey

Into the Storm takes you on such an emotional journey, and makes you believe in real magic. I loved it.

Selina Fenech, author of The Memory's Wake Trilogy

Into the Fire is powerful, heartbreaking and intense. So beautiful.

Beta reader

COMING SOON...

Into the Air: Into the Storm Trilogy Book Three.

THE MAGIC SERIES

Faery Magic is the ultimate guide to all things faery; entertaining, informative and enthralling. A charming book with much to offer, from history and legends, magical gifts and sacred sites and the unique beings found around the globe, to recipes and crafts to keep you busy while you explore this magical world.

Larissa Chapman, book blogger

Mermaid Magic is a wonderfully inspiring read. It really made me want to shed my twenty-first century shackles and dive into the ocean to embrace its wonderful healing powers. Mixing magic, myth and history with nature and environmentalism, it is clear, practical, well researched and written with real passion.

Sabina Collins, book reviewer

Witchy Magic is a definitive reference for the would-be witch, and entertaining and enlightening for the witch-curious. This beautiful book is for everyone, from the history buff, ritualist and nature lover to the magician, pagan and spiritualist.

Kylie Matthews, book reviewer

THE SACRED SERIES

Seven Sacred Sites is a rich and lovely, very wise and tender friend, with good advice and insights to inspire you in your travels, be they physical or imaginary. I wish I'd had it years ago.

Lucy Cavendish, author of Spellbound and White Magic

A Magical Journey is a gem for the adventurers among us. What distinguishes it is Serene's emphasis on enchanting the writing process. A fascinating concept, and gorgeous to the touch.

Joanne Lock, Spheres magazine

Sacred Journey is a treasure. Serene is a gentle, loving, wise teacher of great wisdoms, and this meditation CD takes us on a sacred journey not only into the earthly and heavenly elements and realms, but into history, spirituality and self-love.

Lucy Cavendish, creator of As Above, So Below CD

www.ingramcontent.com/pod-product-compliance
Lightning Source LLC
Chambersburg PA
CBHW030345310726
48979CB00001B/187

* 9 7 8 0 9 9 2 5 3 1 6 8 3 *